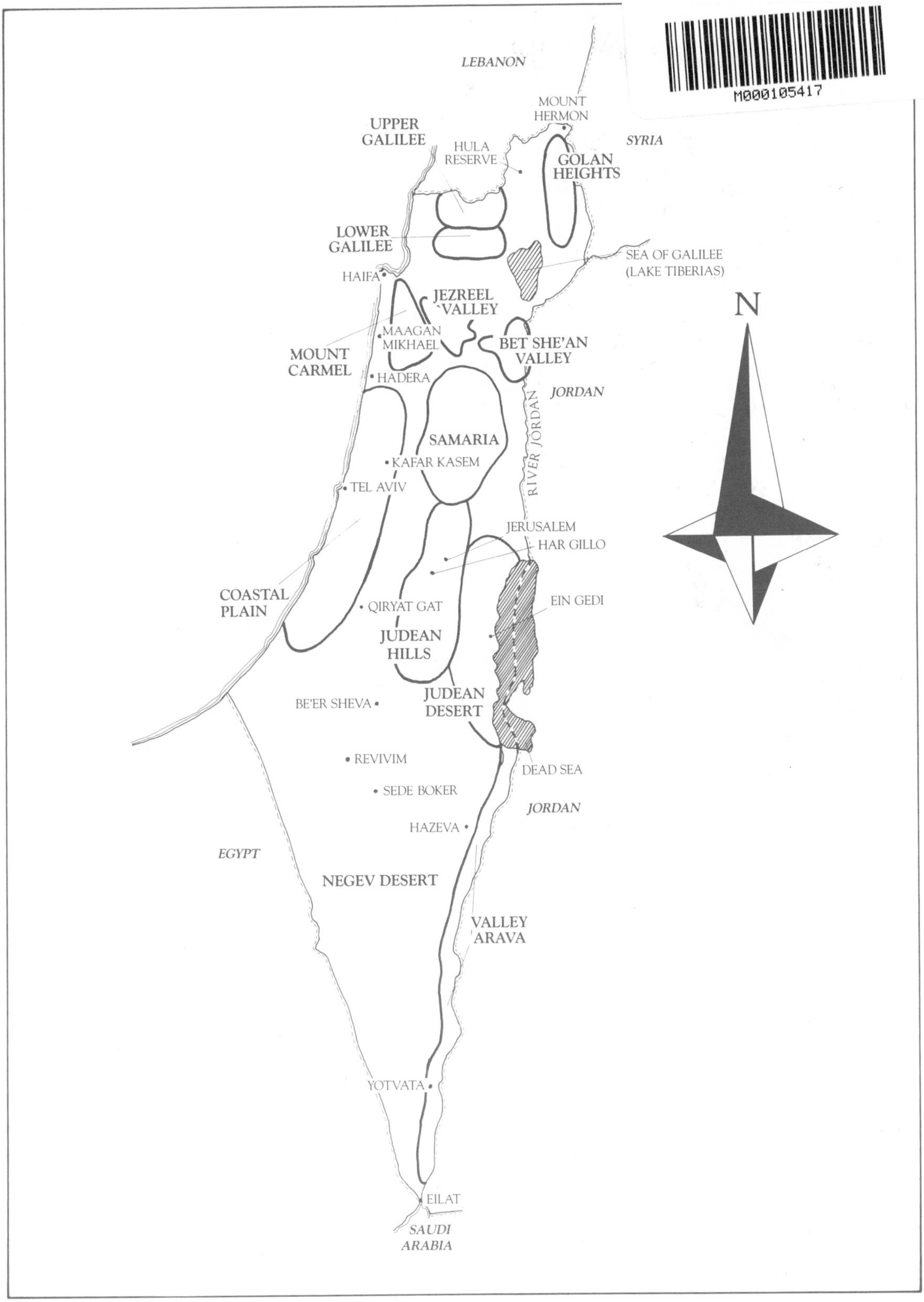
LEBANON
MOUNT HERMON
SYRIA
UPPER GALILEE
HULA RESERVE
GOLAN HEIGHTS
LOWER GALILEE
SEA OF GALILEE (LAKE TIBERIAS)
HAIFA
JEZREEL VALLEY
N
MAAGAN MIKHAEL
BET SHE'AN VALLEY
MOUNT CARMEL
HADERA
JORDAN
SAMARIA
RIVER JORDAN
KAFAR KASEM
TEL AVIV
JERUSALEM
HAR GILLO
COASTAL PLAIN
EIN GEDI
QIRYAT GAT
JUDEAN HILLS
JUDEAN DESERT
BE'ER SHEVA
REVIVIM
DEAD SEA
SEDE BOKER
JORDAN
HAZEVA
EGYPT
NEGEV DESERT
VALLEY ARAVA
YOTVATA
EILAT
SAUDI ARABIA

Jan. 25 - 93

Dear Philippe & Cindy

We hope that you will enjoy
this book and will give you the
desire to come and see it &
experience for yourself

love dad & Mom

THE
BIRDS
OF
ISRAEL

Uzi Paz

Photographs by Yossi Eshbol

THE STEPHEN GREENE PRESS
Lexington, Massachusetts

Initiated and sponsored by Mr and Mrs Alexander Abrahams, London

All royalties accrued from the sale of this book will be divided equally between the RSPB and the Wildfowl Trust

First published in Great Britain in 1987 by Christopher Helm (Publishers) Ltd.
First published in the United States of America in 1987 by The Stephen Greene Press, Inc.
Distributed by Viking Penguin Inc., 40 West 23rd Street, New York, NY 10010.

CIP DATA AVAILABLE

ISBN 0-8289-0621-1

Printed in Great Britain
by Billing and Sons Ltd, Worcester
Set by Leaper & Gard Ltd, Bristol, England
in Goudy Old Style

Contents

Hoopoe Lark

List of Colour Plates

List of Line Drawings

Preface

In recent years extensive ornithological activity has been pursued in Israel. Since Meinertzhagen's *Birds of Arabia* (1954), the only comprehensive source in the English language concerning the birds of the area and a work which summarised most of the information available up to that period, a vast amount of data has been collected on the birds in Israel. In 1960, Merom published a checklist in Hebrew of the birds of the Land of Israel, which included 357 species. In the present book about 470 species are described, and the list is still growing. This increase in the number of species recorded is the result of field surveys and in-depth research carried out by scientific institutes in the country, such as the Israel Raptor Information Center and the Israel Ornithological Center, both at the Society for the Protection of Nature in Israel, and at the Nature Reserves Authority; it stems mainly, however, from the constant and consistent activity of enthusiastic birdwatchers who are out and about in the storms of winter and in the heat of summer, at the fish-ponds and throughout the Negev, on the heights of Mount Hermon and on the shores of the Gulf of Eilat. Thanks to the efforts of some of these birdwatchers, many new species have been discovered in Israel, among them species which were previously unknown in the Western Palaearctic region. Special mention should be made of Hadoram Shirihai, who has found 17 species appearing in this book, Ehud Dovrat, who has found some ten new species, and Walter Fergesson, who has discovered a similar number; among others, Ben Dov Amir, Bazar Yaron, Gal Bruria, Golan Yoav, Horin Oz, Hovel Haim, Su-Aretz Shalom and Zeterman Afraim should also be mentioned.

Ornithological activity in Israel does not, however, consist merely of locating and identifying new species, but also of acquiring a deeper knowledge of the country's avifauna in general. More than 30 bird species have been very thoroughly studied in Israel within the context of university and other research projects. The results of many of these studies, despite their interesting conclusions which have sometimes differed from existing data in the literature, have been published in Hebrew only. Needless to say, however, they have been of great help to me. The species concerned and the researchers, whom I gratefully thank, are given below.

Night Heron (Ashkenasi, S.), Little Egret (Ashkenasi, S.), Lappet-faced Vulture (Naor, A.), Short-toed Eagle (Meir, B.), Golden Eagle (Leshem, I., Shirihai, H.), Bonelli's Eagle (Leshem, I.), Sooty Falcon (Frumkin, R.), Osprey (Ben-Hur, I.), Houbara Bustard (Lavi, D.), Black-winged Stilt (Shirihai, H., Zahavi, A.), Spur-winged Plover (Su-Aretz, S.), Ring-necked Parakeet (Dvir, E.), Barn Owl (Buchshtab, A., Brown, N.), Little Swift (Peled, N.), Bee-eater (Peuntkvitzl, Y.), Syrian Woodpecker (Barnea, A.), Pied Wagtail (Zahavi, A.), Yellow-vented Bulbul (Hason, O.), Mourning Wheatear (Zackay, G.), Blackbird (Hochberg, O.), Graceful Warbler (Paz, U.), Arabian Warbler (Afik, D.), Brown Babbler (Zahavi, A.), Great Tit (Yavin, S.), Orange-tufted Sunbird (Nahari, N.), Jay (Man, S., Hochberg, O.), Hooded Crow (Yom-Tov, Y., Eskar, G.), Tristram's Grackle (Hofshi, H.), House Sparrow (Singer, R.), Dead Sea Sparrow (Mendelssohn, H., Yom-Tov, Y.).

In addition to the above, there are surveys and censuses which take place in Israel on waterfowl and migratory birds, as well as comprehensive surveys on breeding raptors and various colonial-nesting species. Some of these were started as early as the mid 1960s and have been carried on continuously since. They supply highly reliable and accurate quantitative data, and enable us to acquire an objective specific picture of the situation with regard to each species and an authentic insight into and follow-up to the fluctuations which occur in their populations.

I naturally took into account all the above sources

when writing *The Birds of Israel*, and also scrutinised the relevant literature as detailed in the Bibliography. Besides this, I examined various bird collections in the country, mainly at the Museum of the Zoology Department of the University of Tel Aviv, which houses the largest, best arranged and best organised collection of most of the species of birds which occur in Israel. Whenever feasible, data on measurements and weight were taken from this museum; only in cases where the museum lists did not provide sufficient information or where certain species were not available have I taken them from the literature.

This book was originally written in Hebrew, for the naturalist in Israel, as a volume of the series 'Plants and Animals of the Land of Israel: An Illustrated Encyclopedia'. It was therefore written in accordance with the rules and directives of the encyclopedia editors, and consequently literature references are generally not given in the text itself. The book was translated into English thanks to the initiative of Alexander Abrahams, without whose enthusiasm and sponsorship this work would not have been published in the English language; I wish to offer him my most sincere thanks for his help and for making this publication possible. To suit this new framework many abridgments have had to be made to the original text, and I am grateful to the English editors, Chris Harbard and David A. Christie, for

their work in this respect. I am also extremely grateful to Philip Simpson for the many long hours he spent in producing such an excellent English translation of my original Hebrew script. I wish also to take this opportunity to thank the publishers, Christopher Helm Limited and in particular Jo Hemmings, for taking this whole task upon them, in spite of the numerous difficulties which arose following the translation and the distance between Israel and England.

Three persons read the manuscript and each made remarks and shed light on important points. I owe my most sincere thanks to them all: Professor Amotz Zahavi, Professor Yoram Yom-Tov and Ehud Dovrat. My special thanks also go to Haim Hovel, who placed at my disposal the draft manuscript of the Checklist of the Birds of Israel, which will be published in the near future; and to Yaacov Langer, who gathered for me the ringing data up to 1982. I also thank Y. Leshem, Y. Eshbol, A. Zeterman, E. Golani, Y. Geterman, L. Darom, D. Simon, O. Hochberg, S. Man, Y. Ivry, G. Katzir, H. Sagy and M. Adar, each of whom has gone over certain entries with which he was particularly familiar.

My thanks also go to Zilla Shariv, Curator of the Zoology Museum at the University of Tel Aviv, to Avichai Mukhtar and to Amir Ben Dov for their considerable assistance during the writing.

Introduction

The number of bird species found in Israel today amounts to about 470. This is a very large and varied number compared with other countries, and especially so in view of the limited total land area of Israel. There are three main reasons for the high number of bird species: a) Israel is located on the main migration route to and from Africa of the birds of Europe and western Asia; b) Israel has an abundant variety of environments, providing a range of habitats; c) Israel stands at the crossroads of three continents and various climatic zones, and is the scene of interaction between three biogeographical regions.

The birds of Israel are classified in 206 genera, belonging to 67 families and grouped in 21 orders. The orders containing the largest numbers of species are: Passeriformes (songbirds) with 192 species, Charadriiformes (waders, plovers, gulls) with 88 species, Falconiformes (diurnal birds of prey) with 44 species, and Anseriformes (swans, geese, ducks) with 33 species. The largest families in the country are: Sylviidae (warblers) with 43 species, Turdidae (thrushes, chats) and Anatidae (swans, geese, ducks), both with 33 species, and Accipitridae (eagles, vultures, hawks) with 32 species. The most populous genera are: *Sylvia* (warblers) with 15 species, *Emberiza* (buntings) with 14, and *Larus* (gulls) with 13, while *Oenanthe* (wheatears), *Sterna* (terns) and *Falco* (falcons) each comprise 11 species.

The number of species seen in this country has grown considerably over recent years, and it is reasonable to suppose that it will continue to do so as the number of active ornithologists increases. Despite the extensive knowledge already accumulated, much research remains to be done on the birds of Israel. In this volume, 466 species are described. Five additional species have been identified since compilation was completed.

It is customary to classify Israel's birds in five groups according to the time of year of their occurrence, although the distinction between them is not always clear. These groups are: resident (non-migratory) birds; summer residents or breeders; winter residents; passage migrants; and accidentals. Some species are represented in two and even three of these groups: the Pied Wagtail for example is known primarily as a winter visitor, but individuals also pass through the country on migration and the species is also a rare breeder. The White Stork is primarily a passage migrant, but also quite a common winterer and a very rare breeder. The Wheatear is a familiar migrant in all parts of the country and also breeds regularly on Mount Hermon.

Resident Birds

The group of resident birds comprises 91 species. These are birds that do not migrate, but spend the entire year within the confines of Israel.

This group includes large birds such as the Griffon Vulture and the Golden Eagle and small birds such as the Orange-tufted Sunbird and the Wren; common and widely distributed birds such as the Blackbird and the Yellow-vented Bulbul; and rare species such as the Bearded Vulture and the Lappet-faced Vulture. Most birds of the Negev and the Judean Desert are resident, birds such as Sand Partridge, various species of sandgrouse, Brown-necked Raven, six species of lark, five species of wheatear and others.

The Eagle Owl, Graceful Warbler and Great Grey Shrike are some of the birds which remain within their territories all year. The Chukar, Houbara Bustard, Goldfinch, Linnet, House Sparrow and Corn Bunting gather in flocks during the autumn and roam extensively. Residents also include colonial species, which roost and breed in communal sites; among these are the Cattle Egret, Griffon Vulture, Rock Dove and Jackdaw.

1

Summer Residents and Breeders

Seventy-two species of birds return to Israel during the spring and breed in the country, but only 33 have been included in this group, since the remaining 39 are mainly migrants with only small numbers breeding here. This is the case, for example, with the Little Bittern, Quail, Kentish Plover and Isabelline Wheatear.

The summer residents breed in the country, but at the approach of autumn they migrate south to Africa. The Black-headed Bunting is an exception in this respect, migrating east to winter in India.

The first of the summer residents return as early as February. The European Cuckoo is heard on the mountain slopes in mid-February, when the first Egyptian Vultures also arrive. The Swift returns in the last week of February. Then come the first of the Short-toed Eagles, Lesser Kestrels, Great Spotted Cuckoos, Alpine Swifts and Whitethroats. Most of the birds summering in this country arrive during March, including the Black-eared Wheatear, Reed Warbler, and Cretzschmar's Bunting. Some, such as the Hobby, Common Tern, Turtle Dove, Roller and Black-headed Bunting, delay their arrival until April, which is also the time that the White-throated Robin and Rock Thrush return to the slopes of Mount Hermon.

The Quails breeding in Israel disappear as early as the end of May. The Swift migrates south in June, and in July the Lesser Kestrel, Collared Pratincole, Alpine Swift, House Martin and Whitethroat migrate from their nesting areas. Most of the summer residents, however, migrate south in September, although others, such as the Hobby, Red-rumped Swallow and Cretzschmar's Bunting, linger in the country until October, while the Sooty Falcon can still be seen in Israel in November.

Breeding and Nesting

Both resident and summering birds breed in this country — a total of 163 breeding species. The nesting season in Israel is limited to the spring. A few species, such as the Barn Owl, Great Tit, Brown Babbler and Orange-tufted Sunbird, sometimes breed in the autumn too. The Laughing Dove is capable of breeding through most of the months of the year.

The diurnal birds of prey are the first to breed. The Golden Eagle may start to build a new nest as early as November, and laying usually takes place between late December and early January. Griffon Vultures lay at the end of December or in early January; the Eagle Owl lays in February, as does the Barn Owl in years when rodents are plentiful. Bonelli's Eagle lays in the Judean Desert as early as the first week of January, but not until February in the Golan. Some larks and wheatears lay earlier in the desert, provided that conditions of rainfall are normal; in years of drought they may not breed at all, and when the rains come late nesting is correspondingly delayed.

The main period of breeding in Israel begins around mid-March, when the Mallard, Moorhen, Pin-tailed Sandgrouse, Rock Dove, Little Owl, Little Swift, Great Tit, Blackbird and many others build nests. In April they are joined by many summer residents, such as the Hoopoe, Bee-eater, Rufous Bush Robin and Black-eared Wheatear. A few species, such as the Common Tern, Roller and Black-headed Bunting, do not begin nesting until May. A few species delay nesting until the end of the summer and even into the autumn: the Sooty Falcon, for example, breeds in July, August or September, as sometimes do Crowned and Black-bellied Sandgrouse.

The nesting season usually continues until the end of June, and most species have only one brood per year. Some, such as the Spur-winged Plover, Moorhen, various finches, Blackbird and many other songbirds, however, have two and sometimes three broods in a year, and active nests can be found during July and even in August.

Winter Residents

The most conspicuous group of birds in Israel is the wintering birds. Ninety-four species winter in this country, some of them in scores, or even hundreds of thousands of individuals. Most of these breed in Europe, a few in Asia. They arrive in the country during autumn and early winter, and stay until the end of winter and the beginning of spring. In those species where there is both a wintering and a migratory population, it is often hard to distinguish between them, although it is logical to suppose that the first individuals that are seen in the autumn are the passage migrants.

The Grey Heron is one of the first winterers to arrive, and it may be seen in fish-ponds from early August. The vanguard of the Herring Gulls wintering in the country also arrives at about this time, at the fish-ponds and along the sea-coast. Other wintering species, such as the Little Grebe, Teal and

Pied Wagtail, start to arrive in September, but most, including the Great White Egret, various species of duck, Black Kite, Coot, Crane, plovers and Black-headed Gull, arrive in October. Songbirds, such as the Skylark, Robin, Bluethroat, Stonechat, Starling and various finches, arrive in the last week of October and the first week of November. A few species, including the Cormorant, Mallard, Woodpigeon, Meadow Pipit and Black Redstart, delay their arrival until later in November. Rare winterers, like the White-fronted Goose, are liable to arrive as late as December and this species is also one of the first to leave, staying in the country only until the end of January.

The return migration north begins as early as February, when wintering ducks such as the Mallard, Wigeon, Pochard and Tufted Duck and other species such as the Great White Egret leave Israel. The numbers of wintering Starlings and Jackdaws also become appreciably fewer at this time. The males of most finches depart before the females, which stay until March. March is the month when most of the wintering species leave the country: Cormorant, Grey Heron, Teal, Coot, Crane, Lapwing, Skylark, Robin, Stonechat, Finsch's Wheatear and others. A few species, including the Little Grebe, Great Crested Grebe, Shoveler, Black Kite, Herring Gull and Pied Wagtail, may still be seen in April and even in May, but many of these individuals may belong to a passage and not to a wintering population.

A few species of wintering birds are territorial in their winter quarters. Robins and Black Redstarts have individual territories, while the Stonechat and most of the Pied Wagtails live in pairs in territories, although the pair bond between individuals is apparently limited to the winter period, and in the nesting areas they mate with other partners. Ringing shows that many territorial birds return winter after winter to the same territory.

Many wintering birds congregate into massive flocks. These species include aquatic birds, especially ducks, Coots and gulls. The movement of gulls between their roosting places on the sea or lakes and their feeding sites is conspicuous in most parts of the country. Mixed flocks of Chaffinches, Linnets, Goldfinches and Greenfinches gather in fields where there is an abundant supply of cruciferous plants. Starlings, whose total population in Israel is estimated at several millions, are especially noticeable in the late afternoon when they head for their roosting sites in dense flocks. Wagtails and other birds which spend most of the day in territories also gather in the evening at communal roosts, usually in settlements and towns.

The populations of wintering birds often fluctuate widely. In some years Lapwings are abundant, while in others they are quite rare. There are fluctuations in the populations of various ducks, and the White-fronted Goose, a rare winterer in many years, is present in hundreds in others. The Brambling, Penduline Tit and Hawfinch, as well as the Siskin, common in some winters, are very rare or absent in others and might be better classed as accidentals or rare winterers.

Passage Migrants

The group of birds which regularly migrates through Israel includes 121 species. In autumn they fly from their nesting sites to their winter quarters, and in spring they return to nest. In the course of this journey they pass through Israel, where they stop only for a short time. Other species belonging to this group are also found in Israel in winter, birds such as the Black Kite, Osprey, Avocet and various sandpipers. The number of these present in winter is, however, negligible compared with that of the migrants. This also applies to a few species that actually breed in Israel, but are principally migrants — the Squacco Heron, Glossy Ibis, House Martin, Whitethroat and Red-backed Shrike.

Most of the passage migrants breed in eastern and central Europe, with a small number also in western Europe. Only a few breed in Asia: these include the Greater Sandplover, the Sociable Plover and the Curlew Sandpiper, although the latter two are quite rare migrants. All of the species passing through the country winter in various parts of Africa, except the Rose-coloured Starling, which is an occasional migrant and winters in northwestern India.

Passage migrants in autumn usually precede the winter residents, and in spring they pass through after the last of the winterers have disappeared. The first signs of the autumn migration are perceptible as early as the end of June, when Little Grebes and Green Sandpipers begin to appear. In July they are joined by Garganeys, various species of sandpiper, and Swifts which have bred in Europe. In August, the rate of migration intensifies: most White Storks pass at this time, and Ringed Plovers, various swallows, Wheatears, Woodchat Shrikes and Ortolan Buntings begin to migrate through. The peak of migration occurs during September, when most migrants, including the majority of the Honey Buzzards, Lesser Spotted Eagles and Levant Sparrowhawks, pass. The most renowned of all migrations is that of the Quail, which arrives at about this time on the coasts of northern Sinai. Migration continues into October, with Tawny Eagles, Turtle Doves and Wrynecks, and is concluded in November with the passage of the pelicans, the last of the Tawny Eagles and insect-eating songbirds such as Spotted Fly-catchers, Whinchats, Redstarts and Chiffchaffs.

The spring migration starts as early as the end of January, when Tawny Eagles begin to migrate. In February, White Storks, Pintails, Egyptian Vultures, Wrynecks and House Martins are on the move. Most species migrate in March, but there are some that continue into April or migrate only then, such as Turtle Doves, Rollers, Pied Flycatchers, Masked Shrikes and Black-headed Buntings. The migration of Levant Sparrowhawks reaches its peak in the third week of April, while that of Honey Buzzards begins only in mid-April and reaches its peak in May. Still migrating in May are the pelicans, White Storks, Garganeys, Shovelers, White-winged Black Terns, swallows of various species, Golden Orioles and various warblers, notably Blackcaps and Barred Warblers. In the spring migration, males often pre-cede females, sometimes by ten days or even two weeks. This is noticeable with Bluethroats, Redstarts, Black-eared Wheatears and Blackcaps. Often adults precede juveniles, and this is typical of Egyptian Vultures, Honey Buzzards and Great Spotted Cuckoos.

Migration Routes through Israel

Songbirds, as well as various plovers and other small birds, migrate on a broad front. In the course of their journey between Europe and Africa they cross the Mediterranean, although many species prefer to cross it where there are narrow straits. Only a minority of their numbers pass over Israel, and of these most tend to migrate by night, when their con-tact calls are clearly heard; especially noticeable are the voices of buntings and bee-eaters. Birds which migrate at night rest by day and then devote much of their time to feeding. In the Mediterranean area, many find shelter among vegetation and mingle with the local birds. The most conspicuous species in this area are those which perch on electricity and tele-phone cables, for example the Turtle Dove, Roller and various swallows, or those which feed on insects in flight, such as species of swifts and bee-eaters. Migrating songbirds are more conspicuous in the desert, where they seek shade and shelter under any tree, bush or prominent rock outcrop; particularly noticeable are the Yellow Wagtail, Cretzschmar's Bunting, Lesser Whitethroat and Tawny Pipit.

Most species, although they travel between the same two regions, do not use the same route in autumn and spring. This means that some species are more common in the country in autumn, others in spring. Birds such as the Avocet, Grey Plover, Sanderling and Red-footed Falcon are more con-spicuous in the autumn, while the Pintail, Corn-crake, Roller and Pied Flycatcher are more prominent in the spring. In autumn, Quails cross the eastern basin of the Mediterranean in a single night-flight and most land on the shores of southern Israel or northern Sinai; in spring, they proceed northwards across the whole width of Israel and are heard in fields in most parts of the country.

Many of the aquatic birds migrate in autumn on a course parallel with the Mediterranean shore. This movement becomes increasingly conspicuous as they travel farther south along the coast, and it reaches a climax on the shores of the Bardawil Lagoon in northern Sinai. The true significance of this route has become clear only as a result of long-range sur-veys conducted in 1973 and 1978. In these two years, some 160,000 and 300,000 migrants respect-ively were counted, belonging to about 80 species. Particularly remarkable were the large numbers of Garganeys (196,000 in 1978), Little Stints (15,000), White-winged Black Terns (9,000) and Grey Herons (6,200). This route is entirely deserted in the spring, when different routes are used. Grey Heron, Lesser Black-backed Gull and Collared Pratincole migrate along the Gulf of Eilat and the Arava in spring.

Large birds migrate mainly in gliding flight, for which they need the warm air currents rising from dry land. For this reason they migrate overland, and by day. All the birds of prey from eastern and central Europe, as well as some from western and central Asia, pass over Israel in at least one of the migration seasons in order to by-pass the Mediterranean or the Arabian Sea. This behaviour is also characteristic of storks and pelicans.

Pelicans have a relatively fixed migration route, and most flocks follow the same course in autumn and in spring. This route passes through the Hula Valley, the Valley of Tiberias, the Harod Valley, the Jezreel Valley and along the coastal plain as far as northern Sinai. The Tawny Eagle also has an almost identical route in autumn and spring, and most of the individuals passing through Israeli territory migrate near the head of the Gulf of Eilat. The same does not apply to the storks, which follow different migration routes in the two seasons. In autumn they pass over the Jordan Valley and mainly east of the river, and only a minority of them migrate over the eastern watershed of Israel; in this season they are hardly seen at all in the west of the country. In spring the situation is quite different, with about two-thirds of the storks passing over the Bet She'an Valley and the remaining third migrating over the coastal plain.

Most of the birds of prey also use different migration routes in autumn and spring. In autumn, many of them migrate at high altitude above the western slopes of the central mountain range, a route which was discovered only in 1977. In autumn 1983, 320,000 migrating birds of prey were counted there, including some 142,000 Lesser Spotted Eagles, a much higher figure than had previously been estimated for the entire world population of this species. In the same year, 134,000 Honey Buzzards, 25,000

Levant Sparrowhawks and 7,700 Short-toed Eagles were counted there. In autumn 1984, about 380,000 Honey Buzzards were counted on this route. The peak of migration along these routes occurs in September.

In spring, most birds of prey pass by the head of the Gulf of Eilat and continue northwards along the Jordan Valley. Eilat is one of the best places in the world for observing migrating raptors. In spring 1977, some 750,000 belonging to 12 different species were counted there; these included 226,000 Honey Buzzards and 19,000 Tawny Eagles, as well as 316,000 Buzzards and 27,000 Black Kites, two species which are hardly seen at all in the country during the autumn migration.

Accidentals

The number of accidental species recorded in Israel has risen to a considerable degree in recent years, thanks to the intensified activity of a growing body of enthusiasts. The current total stands at 127 species. Among the accidentals there are birds which are seen only rarely and unexpectedly, such as the Black (Verreaux's) Eagle, which sometimes even nests, or the Painted Snipe. Others are seen very rarely, but at fairly predictable times, and include the Velvet Scoter, Goldeneye and Goosander in winter, and the Grey Phalarope and Rose-coloured Starling, which occur at migration times and could in fact be classed as rare migrants. Species of storm-petrel, and some rare species of gull such as the Mediterranean Gull, occur in the aftermath of severe coastal storms, although it is quite conceivable that some of these species are actually more common than the numbers of recorded sightings suggest. Other accidentals are not so rare, and there are some, such as the Flamingo and the Crossbill, that are seen quite often,

but at unpredictable times and places.

Many accidentals occur singly; these include the Purple Gallinule and Great Bustard. Others, such as the Red-breasted Goose, Bearded Tit and Chough, tend to occur in flocks.

Some of the accidental species have been seen only once in this country: for example the Waxwing, Black-headed Bush Shrike, Yellow-throated Sparrow Dark Chanting Goshawk, Bateleur, Shy Albatross and Rufous Turtle Dove. A few were recorded many years ago and have not been sighted since, for example the Shag (in 1934), African Skimmer (in 1935) and the Egyptian Plover (a specimen was caught in the Jordan Valley in the last century and is preserved in the British Museum). Similar cases are those of the Lesser White-fronted Goose, not seen in Israel from 1927 to 1983, and the Whooper Swan; an individual of the latter was caught in the Pools of Solomon in 1863, and the species was not seen in the country again until 1985.

Habitats

The variety of natural habitats in Israel is one of the reasons for the abundance of bird species found in the country. Israel contains desert and forest, cliffs and plains, marshlands and coastline, rocky slopes and cultivated fields, snow-capped peaks in the Hermon range and a tropical oasis at Ein Gedi. Each of these habitats has a variety of characteristic birds, and in spite of their mobility many birds remain faithful to a particular habitat and seldom stray from it.

About 70 species inhabit forests, maquis, groves and plantations; these include resident and summering birds, winterers and passage migrants. To these

some 20 accidentals should be added. Conspicuous among woodland birds are the Blackbird, Jay and Syrian Woodpecker. In the past these were confined to natural forests, but since the 1930s they have continually extended their range, penetrating orchards and even settlements. Similarly, although independently, the Wren, which was formerly confined to the maquis of Upper Galilee, has extended its range since the early 1970s to Carmel and Tabor. On the other hand, the Red-backed Shrike has remained consistent in breeding only in the maquis of Upper Galilee and Hermon.

Among wintering birds, the Woodcock does not

stray from wooded areas, while the Goldcrest and Crossbill reside almost exclusively in the upper branches of pine trees. The Sparrowhawk, Stock Dove, Long-eared Owl and Dunnock also inhabit woodland, although they are to be seen as well in artificial plantations and public parks.

About 60 regular species plus a further 15 rare species are birds of fields, pasture meadows and plains. Such places are the regular breeding habitats of the Collared Pratincole, Quail, Stone-curlew, Crested Lark, Chaffinch and Corn Bunting. They are in addition the winter habitats of the Pallid Harrier, Crane, Lapwing, Short-eared Owl, Skylark, Meadow Pipit and Rook; roaming flocks of finches of various species are also a frequent sight. Flocks of gulls, although these are birds of aquatic and coastal habitat, are often seen in fields, and especially on refuse-dumps.

There are few areas of true marshland in Israel, but for numerous aquatic birds fish-ponds and reservoirs provide a substitute. Herons, grebes, ducks, plovers and gulls of various species, and Coots and Marsh Harriers gather here. Some wintering birds form flocks which number thousands and tens of thousands of individuals. Among the species remaining in these habitats to breed, or returning to them from winter quarters, some of them in small numbers, are: Little Grebe, Moorhen, Mallard, Marbled Teal, Black-winged Stilt, Pied Kingfisher, Reed Warbler and Great Reed Warbler. Birds — resident, breeding, wintering and migrant — of aquatic environments number about 90 species, plus a further 30 accidentals.

The Mediterranean coasts are relatively poor in breeding species. Common Terns breed in a few colonies on three offshore islands, where a few pairs of Herring Gulls are also present. On the coastline itself a number of pairs of Little Ringed Plovers and Kentish Plovers bred, until most of them were exterminated as a result of pollution. The sea-coast is richer in birds in winter and during the autumn migration, when the Oystercatcher, Turnstone, Greater Sandplover, Grey Plover and Whimbrel are among the species seen there. Accidentals such as Sooty Shearwater, Cory's Shearwater and various species of storm-petrel may also appear. In the winter, the Northern Gannet, Sabine's Gull and Kittiwake are occasional visitors to the Mediterranean coast.

The number of species occurring at the head of the Gulf of Eilat is more remarkable and diverse. Various tropical species such as Pale-footed Shearwater, Brown Booby, White-eyed Gull, Sooty Gull, White-cheeked Tern and Sooty Tern appear there. Southern species such as Schlegel's Petrel, Wilson's Storm-petrel and Shy Albatross and more northerly species including the Black-throated Diver, Long-tailed Duck and Arctic Tern have also been seen.

About 30 species are observed regularly on the Mediterranean and Red Seas and their shores, while no fewer than 40 species are rare accidentals there.

More than 20 species are linked to one extent or another to cliff environments. For many of the birds of prey, a cliff-face is essential for nesting. Griffon Vulture, Bearded Vulture, Egyptian Vulture and Lanner Falcon always use cliffs, while Long-legged Buzzard and Bonelli's Eagle usually prefer to nest in such places, as does the Raven. The Rock Nuthatch and the Wallcreeper inhabit vertical cliffs, and to a great extent the Alpine Accentor and Blue Rock Thrush also do. The Alpine Swift, Pallid Swift, Little Swift and Red-rumped Swallow are also attached to cliffs for breeding, although in recent years some of them have taken to using buildings, like the Kestrel, which tends to an ever-increasing extent to breed on high-rise 'cliffs'. Also breeding on and inside buildings within settlements are the Laughing Dove, Great Tit and Hoopoe, while the Orange-tufted Sunbird is often known to build its nest in flower-pots or climbing plants on balconies.

Some 30 species breed or winter on rocky slopes or in wasteland. This is the primary habitat of the Chukar, and the breeding area of birds such as the Long-billed Pipit, Spectacled Warbler, Black-eared Wheatear, Rock Sparrow and Cretzschmar's Bunting. It is also the habitat of wintering and passage migrant species such as the Fieldfare, Wheatear and Cinereous Bunting. The Rock Sparrow prefers chalk slopes, as does the Tawny Pipit.

Even though they appear arid and lifeless, the Negev and the Judean Deserts have some 65 breeding species. About 20 of these, including the Griffon Vulture, Chukar, Rock Dove, Crested Lark and Yellow-vented Bulbul, also frequent the Mediterranean area; the remainder are confined to the desert.

Even within the desert there are different types of habitat to be distinguished. Cliffs and canyons are inhabited by the Sooty Falcon, Pale Crag Martin, Hooded Wheatear and Fan-tailed Raven, while stony slopes are preferred by the Sand Partridge, Mourning Wheatear, Trumpeter Finch and House Bunting. Broad expanses of sand are the habitat of the Cream-coloured Courser, Lesser Short-toed Lark and Desert Wheatear. Areas of sparse scrub are the preferred habitat of the Houbara Bustard, Spotted Sandgrouse and Pin-tailed Sandgrouse, while the Hoopoe Lark and the Bar-tailed Desert Lark tend to frequent sand-dunes. Ravines and wadis with trees and large bushes are the home of the Great Grey Shrike, Brown Babbler and Blackstart, while the Scrub Warbler inhabits smaller bushes. The Little Green Bee-eater, Orange-tufted Sunbird and Tristram's Grackle are found mainly in oases. About ten species are rare accidentals in the desert, including the Black-crowned Finch-lark, Thick-billed Lark, Red-tailed Wheatear and Desert Warbler.

The Hermon range is a unique habitat, surviving from the last Ice Age. Fourteen species breed there which are not known to breed anywhere else in Israel, although some, such as Woodlark, Wheatear, Rock Thrush and Rock Bunting, occur in winter or on passage in other parts of the country. The species breeding on Hermon which are not found elsewhere in Israel include the Shore Lark, Sombre Tit, Pale Rock Sparrow, Tristram's Serin and Crimson-winged Finch. The Hermon range is also the exclusive wintering site in this country of the Alpine Chough, as well as the only place where the Chough occurs.

Geographical Distribution of the Birds of Israel

Israel is located within the Palaearctic zoogeographical region, which includes the whole of Europe, most of Asia except for the southeastern tropical zone, and North Africa. Predictably, the majority of Israel's birds, 286 species, are of Palaearctic origin.

Many of the Palaearctic birds appearing in this country, whether resident, summer or wintering species, passage migrants or accidentals, have a range extending over the whole of this region or over appreciable portions of it. There are 140 such species, including the White Stork, Garganey, Short-toed Eagle, Hobby, Lapwing, Swift, Crested Lark, House Martin, Blackbird, Chiffchaff, House Sparrow and Jay. Some other Palaearctic birds, for example the Dalmatian Pelican, Griffon Vulture, Lesser Short-toed Lark, Blue Rock Thrush and Alpine Chough, are restricted to the southern parts of the region. The winterers and passage migrants come from the far north, from the arctic region, and these include the Ringed Plover, Bar-tailed Godwit, Spotted Redshank, Little Stint and Red-throated Pipit.

One-hundred-and-twenty-three species have a range limited to the Western Palaearctic region. Among these it is possible to distinguish between birds found in most parts of this area, for example the Rock Dove, Roller, Woodlark, Meadow Pipit, Robin, Blackcap, Starling and Corn Bunting (a total of 26 species), and those whose range is confined to the zones defined by botanists as Mediterranean, Irano-Turanian and Saharo-Sindian. Most of the 15 species restricted to the Mediterranean zone are birds of woodland and rocky slopes; they include Eleonora's Falcon, Syrian Woodpecker, Sardinian Warbler, Masked Shrike, Black-eared Wheatear and Cretzschmar's Bunting. A further 32 species are shared by the Mediterranean and Irano-Turanian zones, the latter being a belt of steppe extending over the high land of western Asia and penetrating into the central areas of the continent; among these species are Levant Sparrowhawk, Lesser Kestrel, European Bee-eater, Calandra Lark, Sombre Tit and Black-headed Bunting.

Thirty-two species have a range corresponding to the Irano-Turanian zone and they include the Ruddy Shelduck, Greater Sandplover, White-tailed Plover, Bimaculated Lark, White-throated Robin, Isabelline Wheatear and Desert Finch. Five species are common to the Irano-Turanian steppe zone and the desertic Saharo-Sindian zone, which extends across the whole width of the south of the Western Palaearctic, and they include the Houbara Bustard, Black-bellied Sandgrouse and Desert Wheatear. All of the 23 species confined to the Saharo-Sindian zone alone are, predictably, restricted in this country to the Negev and the Judean Desert; these include the Sooty Falcon, Spotted Sandgrouse, Hume's Tawny Owl, Desert Lark, Pale Crag Martin, White-crowned Black Wheatear, Brown-necked Raven and House Bunting.

The 23 remaining species out of the total number of Palaearctic birds are of Eastern Palaearctic origin, coming from central Asia and the steppes of Siberia. Most are rare accidentals in this country, including Red-breasted Goose, Pallas's Fish Eagle, Citrine Wagtail, Dusky Thrush and Pine Bunting.

Fifty-seven of Israel's bird species have a Holarctic distribution. The Holarctic zoogeographical region combines the Palaearctic and Nearctic regions, thereby including North America and Greenland. Examples of birds with this wide range are the Black-necked Grebe, Teal, Golden Eagle, Dunlin, Common Tern, Shore Lark, Swallow, Wren and Raven.

Other species have a range extending beyond the Palaearctic or Holarctic into Africa south of the Sahara (Ethiopian region) or across tropical Asia (Oriental region). There are 72 such species, including the Great Crested Grebe, Little Egret, Egyptian Vulture, Black Kite, Moorhen, Collared Pratincole, Alpine Swift, Hoopoe, Stonechat and Fan-tailed Warbler. A further 13 species have a cosmopolitan range and are represented in all continents of the world; examples are the Peregrine, Black-winged Stilt, Caspian Tern and Barn Owl.

The zoogeographical uniqueness of Israel is illustrated by the fact that its bird population includes species whose origin is in no part of the Holarctic region. Thirty-one species are of Ethiopian origin and some of these, for example the Squacco Heron, Spur-winged Plover, Great Spotted Cuckoo and Orange-tufted Sunbird, are common in many parts of the country. Others, such as the Blackstart, Fantailed Raven and Tristram's Grackle, are limited largely to desert environments and oases. Most of the Ethiopian species are rare accidentals in Israel, birds such as the Pink-backed Pelican, Goliath Heron, Marabou Stork, Cape Teal, Black-shouldered Kite, Bateleur, Kittlitz's Sandplover and Black Bush Robin. To complete the zoogeographical picture, six species of Oriental origin are to be added which include the Black Francolin, White-breasted Kingfisher and Indian House Crow; two species of

Nearctic origin, the Pacific Golden Plover and Pectoral Sandpiper; and a single Australasian/Neotropical species, the Shy Albatross.

The sharp contrast between a humid and relatively cool climate in the north of the country and a hot and very dry climate in the south has led to the development of different subspecies among a few of the species breeding in the Mediterranean belt on the one hand and in the Saharo-Sindian belt on the other. This applies to the Chukar, Barn Owl, Eagle Owl and Great Grey Shrike: the desert subspecies are smaller and paler.

There are no species confined exclusively to Israel. Tristram's Serin has the most limited range, being restricted to the Lebanon and Anti-Lebanon mountain ranges and reaching its most southerly point on Hermon. The nominate subspecies of the Orange-tufted Sunbird *N.o. osea* has a range restricted to Israel, southern Syria and northern Arabia.

Influence of Man on the Birds of Israel

In addition to biological, geographical and climatic influences, the distribution of birds in Israel today has been determined to a great extent by changes caused by mankind. A large proportion of these changes have had a negative effect. Thus, for example, the Middle Eastern desert race of the Ostrich *S.c. syriacus*, a unique and endemic subspecies which still existed in the Negev at the beginning of the twentieth century, has been hunted to extinction. The African Darter, of which a small breeding population used to exist in the marshes of Antakya in southern Turkey and which was a rare winterer and passage migrant in Israel, disappeared after the draining of these marshes. The same factor probably caused the Pygmy Cormorant, which was a common winterer until the mid-1950s, to disappear from this country for a period of many years. The draining of the Hula swamps removed from the list of Israel's breeding birds the Great Crested Grebe, Grey Heron, Marsh Harrier and Black Tern, for which these swamps were the only breeding site in the country. For the same reason, the Ferruginous Duck has become a very rare breeder.

Pollution of coastal waters has led to a reduction in and possibly to the extermination of breeding populations of Kentish Plovers and Little Ringed Plovers, while pollution of rivers has all but destroyed the breeding population of the Little Bittern. The widespread use of agricultural pesticides has caused severe damage to birds of prey. The White-tailed Eagle, Spotted Eagle and Peregrine have been

eliminated as breeders, while breeding populations of the Griffon Vulture, Egyptian Vulture, Black Kite and Bonelli's Eagle have been drastically reduced. Populations of the Lappet-faced Vulture and Bearded Vulture have been brought to the verge of extinction. Similarly, during the 1950s there was serious damage to the wintering populations of raptors such as the Sparrowhawk, Buzzard, Imperial Eagle, Saker and Peregrine, although some breeding and wintering raptor populations have since recovered. The use of pesticides also destroyed or greatly reduced the breeding populations of the Blue-cheeked Bee-eater and Roller and the wintering populations of the Jackdaw and Rook, although in these cases too there are signs of recovery. The conversion of wasteland into cultivated fields and changes in agricultural methods have had a severe effect on the breeding populations of the Egyptian Nightjar, which has been virtually eliminated from this country, and of the Collared Pratincole.

On the other hand, some changes have had positive effects. Several species have been added to the list of breeders: the Cattle Egret (since the early 1950s), Night Heron (1954), Mallard (1954), Squacco Heron and Little Egret (1959), Glossy Ibis (1969), Golden Eagle (first nest identified in 1972), Serin (1977) and Golden Oriole (1983). Similarly, many species have extended and broadened their range. The Spur-winged Plover, which used to be confined to northern valleys, is now common in fields in northern and central parts of the country, while the Hoopoe has not only widened its range but also has changed from a summer visitor to a resident bird. Woodland birds such as the Blackbird, Jay and Syrian Woodpecker, which were restricted to the few forests in the northern parts of Israel, are today common in all parts of the country. The Orange-tufted Sunbird, originally a bird of oases, has proliferated as a result of the fashion for landscape gardening, while the Little Green Bee-eater has thrived with the agricultural development of the Arava and the Red-backed Shrike is now regularly nesting in artificial plantations. A few species are gradually penetrating into cities and adapting to nesting on urban buildings: these include the Kestrel, Little Swift, Hoopoe and Red-rumped Swallow. Even escapees from captivity such as the Laughing Dove and Ring-necked Parakeet are in the process of expansion, and the same applies, in all probability, to the Indian House Crow.

Birds as Pests

Birds of some species cause damage to agriculture. The House Sparrow, which is found in scores of thousands around settlements, causes damage to grain stocks and crops, and flocks of Starlings sometimes consume the foodstuffs intended for livestock. In autumn, some species of lark peck at the budding crops in fields, Yellow-vented Bulbuls attack ripening fruit, while Carrion Crows devour nuts. Bee-eaters take bees and damage hives, and woodpeckers damage irrigation equipment, causing loss of water, and sometimes even sabotage telephone cables.

Cattle Egrets, which tend to breed in groves inside settlements, cause a nuisance with noise and smell, and the Rock Doves which have proliferated in the region of Eilat cause damage in the port and nuisance to the houses of the town. Black-headed Gulls congregating on refuse-dumps near Ben-Gurion Airport constitute a hazard to aircraft, and some migratory birds, especially birds of prey, storks and pelicans, also endanger air traffic.

The Nature Reserves Authority is seeking solutions to these problems, with the object of reducing or eliminating the worst examples of damage and nuisance committed by birds without causing irreparable damage to the environment.

With the exception of a few species, all birds in Israel are protected by laws for the preservation of wildlife. Between 1 September and 21 January, the shooting of certain species, by permit-holders, is allowed: Coot, Chukar, Rock Dove, Turtle Dove and Quail, and certain species of duck including Mallard, Teal, Shoveler, Garganey and Tufted Duck; the 'bag' for ducks is restricted by law to ten birds per day. The House Sparrow, Yellow-vented Bulbul, Skylark and Crested Lark are classed as pests and given no protection under the law. Special permission is required to shoot Carrion Crows.

Ornithological Research

The first ornithologist to take an active interest in this region was an English clergyman, Canon H.B. Tristram. In his book *Fauna and Flora of Palestine* (1888), many of the species known to us today are mentioned. The first Jewish zoologist, with a special interest in the birds of Palestine, was Y. Aharoni (1882-1946). Another Englishman, Colonel R. Meinertzhagen, summarised the state of knowledge in his time in *Birds of Arabia* (1954). A. Smoli compiled numerous lists of birds which were later summarised in book form (1957), and H. Merom compiled and published a checklist of the birds of Israel in 1960. R. Enbar published several books on the birds of this country (1971-82), and in 1983 H. Hovel prepared for publication an up-to-date checklist of the birds of Israel.

The largest and most important collections of preserved bird specimens in this country are in the University of Tel Aviv, in the Hebrew University of Jerusalem, in Beit Ossishkin in Kibbutz Dan, and in Beit Gordon in Degania A.

Ornithological activity in Israel today is concentrated at the Raptor Information Center and the Ornithological Center run by the Society for the Protection of Nature, which publishes a number of special bulletins, and by the Nature Reserves Authority. The most striking activity, however, is that carried out by amateur enthusiasts, whose contribution to ornithological knowledge in recent years has been immense. Yet, in spite of all this, there is still much that is unknown regarding the birds of Israel and much that awaits discovery and analysis.

Systematic List

This list covers all species reliably recorded in Israel up to the end of 1984, with a number of more recently reported ones where details are available.

The scientific and vernacular nomenclature is based on Voous (1977, *List of Recent Holarctic Bird Species*), with a small number of minor amendments where a more widely used name is given to a species.

The sequence also follows that of Voous (1977), but with important changes: within each higher taxon where several genera/species are involved, the sequence is begun with those which are commonest in Israel; in some cases this has necessitated further divergences from Voous's list.

All measurements are given in metric units. For readers more familiar with the imperial system, the accompanying tables are designed to facilitate quick conversion to imperial units. Bold figures in the central columns can be read as either metric or imperial: eg., 1 mm = .039 in or 1 in = 25.4 mm.

kg		lb	km		miles
0.45	1	2.20	1.61	1	0.62
0.91	2	4.41	3.22	2	1.24
1.36	3	6.61	4.83	3	1.86
1.81	4	8.82	6.44	4	2.48
2.27	5	11.02	8.05	5	3.11
2.72	6	13.23	9.65	6	3.73
3.18	7	15.43	11.26	7	4.35
3.63	8	17.64	12.87	8	4.97
4.08	9	19.84	14.48	9	5.59

mm		in	cm		in	ha		acres
25.4	1	.039	2.54	1	0.39	0.40	1	2.47
50.8	2	.079	5.08	2	0.79	0.81	2	4.94
76.2	3	.118	7.62	3	1.18	1.21	3	7.41
101.6	4	.157	10.16	4	1.57	1.62	4	9.88
127.0	5	.197	12.70	5	1.97	2.02	5	12.36
152.4	6	.236	15.24	6	2.36	2.43	6	14.83
177.8	7	.276	17.78	7	2.76	2.83	7	17.30
203.2	8	.315	20.32	8	3.15	3.24	8	19.77
228.6	9	.354	22.86	9	3.54	3.64	9	22.24

m		yds	g		oz
0.91	1	1.09	28.35	1	.04
1.83	2	2.19	56.70	2	.07
2.74	3	3.28	85.05	3	.11
3.66	4	4.37	113.40	4	.14
4.57	5	5.47	141.75	5	.18
5.49	6	6.56	170.10	6	.21
6.40	7	7.66	198.45	7	.25
7.32	8	8.75	226.80	8	.28
8.23	9	9.84	255.15	9	.32

Metric to imperial conversion formulae

	multiply by
cm to inches	0.3937
m to feet	3.281
m to yards	1.094
km to miles	0.6214
km^2 to square miles	0.3861
ha to acres	2.471
g to ounces	0.03527
kg to pounds	2.205

Order: Struthioniformes (Ostriches)

Family: Struthionidae

This order comprises a single family and a single species: the Ostrich. It belongs to the sub-class Ratitae — birds which are flightless and whose movement is restricted to running. In many respects, this order is one of the most primitive groups of birds in existence today.

Ostrich
Struthio camelus

The Ostrich is the largest bird in existence today: height approximately 2.5 m, weight up to 150 kg and more. Its wings are small and incapable of bearing the weight of its body, but they assist it when it changes direction or makes sudden stops when running. The wing feathers (16 primaries and 20-23 secondaries) and the tail feathers (50-60) are mainly decorative. The male has black feathers, except for the white wings and tail. The female is grey-brown.

The head and most of the neck are covered with sparse and degenerate feathers, resembling hair, and for this reason they appear naked. The skin colour revealed between the 'hairs' varies between subspecies. The legs of the Ostrich are long and remarkably strong, and the stride of a running Ostrich reaches 3.5 m and its speed up to 70 kph.

Today five subspecies of Ostrich are known. They inhabit plains and grasslands across the whole width of Africa, from the Spanish Sahara to the Horn of Africa, and also East Africa and southwestern Africa. In the recent past an additional subspecies, *S.c. syriacus*, lived in the deserts of the Middle East. This was the only subspecies found outside the limits of Africa, and it was smaller than the African races. It formerly inhabited the area between the Syrian desert and the Arabian peninsula, and its range also extended over the Negev and Sinai. In the more distant past, these Ostriches were also present in the coastal plain of Israel, a fact confirmed by the Ostrich eggs which are occasionally found in this area. In 1977 a nest was discovered near Tel Michael, to the south of Herzliyya, containing 12-15 eggs, of which five were completely intact; radioactive-carbon testing assessed their age at $5,810\pm220$ years.

There is no precise information available on when Ostriches disappeared from the Negev. In 1908, J.A. Jaussen saw a young Ostrich which had been caught near Asloj (the present-day Revivim). At the first 'Oriental Fair', which took place in 1929, one of the exhibits was a live Ostrich which had been caught at a distance of two hours' walk from Be'er Sheva. At about the same time, in 1927, Israel Aharoni saw numerous flocks of Ostriches in the Syrian desert. The firearms which proliferated in the region following the First World War, and hunting with motor vehicles, had a devastating effect. Legislation for the protection of nature came 40 years too late to save the Middle Eastern Ostrich. Since the 1930s, the Syrian Ostrich has been effectively extinct, the few remaining individuals having little prospect of survival. In 1948, two Ostriches were caught near the conjunction of the frontiers of Jordan, Iraq and Saudi Arabia; in 1966, a female Ostrich was washed up by a flood from the region of Maan in Jordan to the Arava. Since then no sighting of this subspecies has been recorded, and, apart from a few skins in museums, no relic of it remains.

In spring 1973, 18 Ostrich chicks were brought to the Hai Bar Nature Reserve in the Arava, for breeding and releasing into the Negev. These Ostriches, originally from the deserts of Ethiopia, are members of the subspecies *S.c. camelus*, closest to those which once inhabited Israel.

The Ostrich feeds primarily on grass, but also eats blossoms and the leaves of shrubs and trees (according to habitat and season). The Ostriches at Hai Bar particularly like the fruit of the acacia. Water-retaining plants are beneficial to the Ostrich in the dry season, but it also needs to drink water. When it can, the Ostrich will also catch various invertebrates, injured birds and young mammals.

Order: Gaviiformes (Divers)

Family: Gaviidae

An order of one family, with one genus comprising four species, all of them northern. Divers are the ecological equivalents of the grebes in the arctic regions, but are larger (body length 53-91 cm), and have an elongated body and medium-length neck. They are good swimmers and can dive to a depth of 9 m. Like grebes, they have difficulty walking on land, but take to flight more readily. In flight the head and neck are stretched forward, below the line of the body, giving a hunched appearance. Divers feed primarily on fish.

Divers are migratory birds which winter along the shores of seas and oceans. In Israel, two species are extremely rare accidentals.

Red-throated Diver
Gavia stellata

A small diver: body length 60 cm, wing length 29 cm, wingspan 110 cm and weight approx. 1.8 kg. In winter plumage, its back is light brown-grey speckled with white, its head grey and its belly white, and its bill has an upward-tilted appearance. It breeds to the north of latitude 60°N, and winters along the shores of the Atlantic Ocean, the western Mediter- ranean, the Adriatic, the Black Sea and the Caspian Sea.

A single individual was discovered, exhausted, in the Dead Sea on 18 December 1982.

Black-throated Diver
Gavia arctica

Larger than the Red-throated Diver: body length 65 cm, wing length 32 cm, wingspan 120 cm and weight capable of reaching 3 kg. In winter, its back is a uniform dark brown-grey and its underparts are white. It breeds to the north of latitude 55°N, and winters along the coasts of Europe, including in the Mediterranean, and along the shores of the Black and the Caspian Seas.

This is a very rare visitor to Israel. The first evi- dence of its existence in this country was a head washed up on the shore of the Gulf of Eilat on 7 March 1970. Since then, a few sightings have been recorded in Eilat (27 February 1977, 1 March 1979, 26 January 1983 and 17-25 February 1983), on Lake Tiberias (28 February 1980), and on the shores of the Mediterranean near the port of Jaffa (December 1984).

Order: Podicipediformes (Grebes)

Family: Podicipedidae

In this order there is a single family comprising five genera and 20 species, most of them confined to the American continent. The body structure of grebes is well adapted to their aquatic way of life. The legs are set at the rear of the body, helping them to swim and dive. Grebes seldom emerge from the water, being clumsy on land. The tarsus is flattened and laterally compressed, thus reducing water resistance when swimming. Each of the four toes has separate lobes. Grebes have thick, dense and very soft feathering, giving the skin good protection against moisture. To make this protection more effective, they spend many hours of the day lubricating their feathers.

In winter, the season in which grebes are most often seen in Israel, their plumage is white, brown and grey. The sexes are similar and difficult to distinguish, although the males are usually larger. The neck is long, and the bill short, straight and sharp, ideal for catching small animals. Grebes feed on crabs and fish, and also on aquatic vegetation. Their capacity for swallowing is limited, and they can eat only small creatures. They also swallow feathers, a peculiar habit the significance of which is unclear.

By expelling air from the lungs and air pockets, grebes are capable of sinking in the water so that only their head is visible.

When swimming, the grebe keeps its legs under its body; when diving, it splays its legs and sinks into the water, or jumps and then dives head-first. The dive can last for some 30-50 seconds, and the grebe is capable of descending to 6-7 m. The grebe moves faster when diving than when swimming, and the point where it emerges is unpredictable.

In the nesting season grebes inhabit only freshwater sites. On migration they pause on estuaries and sea-shores. Although they have difficulty rising from the water and have short and narrow wings, they are capable of migrating over considerable distances. Grebes are distinctive in flight, with their necks stretched forward, slightly above the level of the body, and their legs drooping at the rear.

Some species of grebe are territorial when nesting, others sometimes nest in colonies. Both members of the pair build the floating nest, which is constructed from vegetation and is anchored among plants.

In Israel two genera are represented containing five species, of which three are common and two are accidentals.

Little Grebe or Dabchick
Tachybaptus ruficollis

The commonest of the grebes seen in Israel and, as its name implies, the smallest: body length 25-29 cm, wing length 9.5-9.8 cm, wingspan approx. 43 cm and weight 125-200 g. Apart from a slight difference in size, male and female are identical. In winter they are grey, brown and white, producing an overall appearance of grey. At the approach of spring, they assume breeding plumage: the cheeks and neck change to a chestnut colour and the grey areas turn black.

The Little Grebe breeds across Europe and Asia, on the islands of the Pacific Ocean, and in tropical Africa. Within this range ten subspecies have been identified. The race *T.r. ruficollis* ranges from Britain and southern Sweden in the north to the western Sahara and northern Algeria in the south, and through the Mediterranean countries to Turkey and western Israel. Little Grebes from central and eastern Europe migrate in winter especially to Turkey, and also southwards to the eastern shore of the Mediterranean (a few travel as far as Egypt) and eastwards to the estuary of the Euphrates and the Tigris. In Israel, the Little Grebe is a common wintering and a quite rare nesting bird.

The first migrants arrive in Israel in the second half of June. The winterers begin to arrive in September, and by the end of October the full population is assembled. In the 1960s, an average of 515

Little Grebes was counted every winter. Since then there has been an increase in numbers, and the average in the late 1970s and early 1980s had risen to 920. Grebes tend to congregate on the lakes and fish-ponds; at the sewage-ponds in the Tel Aviv region for example, 425 individuals were counted on 25 October 1980. They tend to stay in small and sparse flocks, a few metres apart from one another (unlike the Black-necked Grebe, which forms denser, more regimented flocks). The wintering grebes remain in the country until the second half of April.

Little Grebes dive frequently, either to feed or to escape danger. They eat fish, tadpoles, molluscs, aquatic insects and shrimps, which they usually swallow immediately, although larger items are brought to the surface.

The Little Grebes which nest in Israel are apparently resident, although they wander outside the nesting season. The number of nesting pairs since the early 1970s has been estimated at 60-120.

The courtship of the Little Grebe takes place in February and March. The male swims around his mate, and both partners emit a shrill and delicate whistle which is heard repeatedly, especially in early morning and at twilight; the partners offer clumps of grass to one another, especially the male to the female. The nest is built in a site offering all-round visibility. Egg-laying usually starts at the beginning of April and sometimes as early as March. The clutch is usually 4-6 eggs, occasionally as many as 7. Incubation is by both parents; it begins with the laying of the first egg, and lasts 19-22 days. The parents tend and feed the young until they are capable of supporting themselves. At 44-48 days of age, the chicks are already able to fly.

In places where food is abundant, grebes rear a second brood in the course of the summer, and cases are known of young hatching as late as the beginning of August.

Great Crested Grebe
Podiceps cristatus

The largest of the grebes seen in Israel: body length 46-53 cm, wing length of male 19-20 cm and of female 17.5-18.5 cm, wingspan 85-90 cm and weight 500-950 g. In winter, it is grey, brown and white. At the approach of spring its head is adorned with two black tufts, broadening to resemble horns, and around its cheeks a rusty-gold frill develops. The male and the female are identical. The Great Crested Grebe is distinguished by its low profile and its long neck, usually held erect.

The Great Crested Grebe is distributed throughout Eurasia, tropical Africa and Australia. Small and isolated populations also nest in North Africa, especially in the Nile Delta. Within this broad range three subspecies have been identified. The one most common in the Palaearctic region is *P.c. cristatus*. The Great Crested Grebe is a resident in western Europe and the Mediterranean countries. The migratory populations of the northern and eastern parts of the Western Palaearctic winter in western Europe, the Mediterranean basin and the Middle East.

The Great Crested Grebe is quite a common winter visitor to Israel. Migrating individuals are seen on the shores of northern Sinai as early as the beginning of September, and the main wintering population arrives during October and, especially, in November. The numbers vary between 400 and 2,000, with an annual winter average of 930. The grebes congregate especially on and around Lake Tiberias, and in 1978 1,200 Great Crested Grebes were counted there out of a total of 1,400 which wintered in Israel that year. They can also be seen on Lake Kishon, the reservoir of Netofa and on the fish-ponds of the coastal plain. They stay in small and sparse groups, very rarely gathering in flocks. Return migration begins in February, and the last have left for their nesting areas by mid-March. A few individuals are seen in April, although in some years scores of pairs remain on Lake Tiberias throughout that month.

When fleeing from danger, the Great Crested Grebe dives, and is capable of staying underwater for approximately a minute. It feeds especially on fish, but also on crabs and molluscs and vegetable food. Large quantities of feathers are also commonly found in its stomach.

In the past, some 30 pairs nested at the northern end of the Hula Valley. A few pairs also nested in southern parts of Lake Tiberias, in the marshes of Cabara (in the region of Nahal Hataninim) and in other marshes in the coastal plains. With the draining of the swamps, the nesting grebes have steadily disappeared. In summer 1964, there were still four pairs in the Hula Reserve; in 1969, a family of Great Crested Grebes with two chicks was observed there for the last time. In 1969-72, further nesting attempts were made at Lake Kishon and at the reservoirs of Eshkol in the valley of Beit Netofa, but since 1973 no breeding attempts have been recorded in Israel.

Red-necked Grebe
Podiceps grisegena

Slightly smaller than the Great Crested Grebe: body length approx. 43 cm, wing length 17 cm, wingspan 80 cm and weight approx. 600 g. In winter it resembles the Great Crested Grebe, but has a greyer neck and a yellow base to its bill.

This grebe is a very rare winter visitor to this country. The population closest to Israel nests and winters on the shores of the Black Sea and in Turkey. The only observations in Israel are of two individuals in December 1974 in the fish-ponds of Maagan Mikhael and of another on 19 December 1981 on the coast of Naharia.

Black-necked Grebe
Podiceps nigricollis

Slightly larger than the Little Grebe: body length 28-34 cm, wing length 12.5-14 cm, wingspan 56-60 cm and weight 195-400 g. In winter it is clearly recognisable by its white cheeks and apparent upward tilt of the bill. In breeding plumage it has golden-chestnut ear-tufts and a black neck.

This grebe's range is Holarctic, and small populations also nest in tropical Africa. Three subspecies have been identified. *P.n. nigricollis* is distributed throughout southern and central Europe to central Asia. It winters on the shores of western Europe, and in the Mediterranean countries and the Middle East.

In Israel this is a common passage migrant and winter resident. The first individuals arrive in the second half of August, with most arriving in the second half of September. The last to depart stay in the country until the beginning of April, sometimes until the end of that month. The Black-necked Grebe prefers to congregate on large lakes, in groups composed of scores of individuals. The wintering population in Israel numbers hundreds.

Slavonian Grebe
Podiceps auritus

Similar in winter to the Black-necked Grebe: body length approx. 35 cm, wing length 14 cm and weight some 400 g.

This is a northern species, which winters in western Europe, the eastern Adriatic, the northern Black Sea and the Caspian Sea. It tends to inhabit sea-shores to a greater extent than do other grebes.

In Israel this is a very rare accidental. There is mention of this species being captured in 1909 on the shore of Lake Tiberias. In recent years only one positive sighting has been recorded, of an isolated individual which stayed in the sewage-ponds of Tel Aviv region from 6 May to 22 July 1981.

Order: Procellariiformes
(Albatrosses, Petrels and Shearwaters)

In this order there are four families: albatrosses (Diomedeidae), petrels and shearwaters (Procellariidae), storm-petrels (Hydrobatidae) and diving-petrels (Pelecanoididae). The first three are represented in Israel, while the fourth family is distributed in particular along the coasts of South America. These together comprise 23 genera and 103 species. Most of the species in this order inhabit the Southern Hemisphere; only ten breed in the Northern Hemisphere, and a few others are vagrants to the area.

These seabirds are truly pelagic. Apart from when breeding, they spend their entire lives at sea. The smallest members of the order are the storm-petrels, which flutter above the surface of the sea with dangling feet; they appear to walk on the water (hence the name 'petrel', after Saint Peter, the closest disciple of Jesus, who according to tradition walked on the water of Lake Tiberias). The larger petrels and shearwaters are gliding birds which fly with stiff wings. They fly low over the water, 'shearing' the waves and banking steeply; they can spend many hours gliding above the sea, but find flight difficult when there is no wind. The albatrosses are the largest members of the order, with extremely long wings. The Procellariiformes are also good swimmers.

Peculiar to the order is the bill, which on its upper surface has protuberant tubes to which the nostrils are linked, giving these birds a highly developed sense of smell. This assists them in finding their nests at night, and also in locating food. Fish form their staple diet, but they feed as well on other forms of surface marine life; they also consume scraps of food discarded at sea, and frequently follow ships.

All members of this order rest and sleep on the surface of the water, and rise from it easily. On land, however, they have difficulty becoming airborne.

At the end of the nesting season most members wander over considerable distances, some, such as the Sooty Shearwater, travelling fixed routes in a form of migration.

In Israel 13 species are represented, members of six genera belonging to three families. With one exception, all these species are rare or extremely rare.

Family: Procellariidae (Shearwaters, Petrels)

Cory's Shearwater
Calonectris diomedea

A large shearwater: body length 46 cm, wing length approx. 36 cm, wingspan 112 cm and weight 900 g, recognisable by its brown-grey head, back and upperwings, its white belly and its yellow bill. It is much prone to gliding and soaring.

This shearwater breeds on islands in the east Atlantic and in the Mediterranean. In the late 1970s, it was observed as a regular visitor between July and November to the Gulf of Eilat, with as many as 20 individuals occurring there together. Apparently, this is a small section of the population known to winter in South Africa which travels northward along the coasts of East Africa.

An individual was killed in the port of Jaffa on 23 September 1911. In the early 1980s, this shearwater was also discovered as a vagrant or migrant on the northern shores of Israel at the end of summer and in autumn: on 26 August 1982, 52 individuals were counted passing by the coastline south of Haifa, and on 3 September 1982 66 individuals were counted there.

Manx Shearwater
Puffinus puffinus

A shearwater of medium size: body length 34-37 cm, wing length 21.2-24.5 cm, wingspan 82 cm; the weight of individuals occurring in this country varies between 150 and 300 g, with an average of 190 g

(Tel Aviv University records). It is recognisable by the contrasting dark back and upperwings and white belly.

This species is widely distributed across the world, including on various islands throughout the Mediterranean, the Adriatic and the Aegean. Eight subspecies have been identified, the one occurring in Israel being *P.p. yelkouan*.

The Manx Shearwater is seen in Israel along the Mediterranean coast especially in the months of August and September, and again in January. Individuals, sometimes small groups, are the usual sighting, although flocks of 20 and more have been seen, especially at the end of winter. On rare occasions, it is recorded in spring. Corpses of Manx Shearwaters have been washed up on the coast after severe storms.

Pale-footed Shearwater
Puffinus carneipes

A large shearwater: body length 51 cm and wingspan 109 cm. It has chocolate-brown body and wings, pale yellow-brown bill and rosy-pink feet, and a short, rounded tail.

A tropical species and an extremely rare visitor to the Gulf of Eilat: an individual was identified at Eilat on 15 August 1980.

Sooty Shearwater
Puffinus griseus

A medium-sized shearwater: body length approx. 45 cm, wing length 30 cm, wingspan 109 cm and weight approx. 720 g. Its body colour is dark brown-grey and the underwings are silver.

This species breeds in the Southern Hemisphere and is a migrant, travelling to the North Atlantic each summer. On rare occasions, it visits the Israeli shore of the Mediterranean. All sightings have occurred between August and mid-February, and usually only single individuals are seen (though four were observed in the port of Jaffa on 16 February 1982). In the Gulf of Eilat, isolated individuals of this species can be seen throughout the year, especially from mid-March to the end of May, apparently driven to the Gulf by southern storms; up to 15 individuals may occur in a single day.

Great Shearwater
Puffinus gravis

A large shearwater: body length 48 cm, wing length approx. 32 cm, wingspan 111 cm and weight 800 g. It has dark upperparts, white underparts, a black cap with white cheeks, and a white base to the tail.

It breeds in the South Atlantic and winters in the North Atlantic, often occurring in the western Mediterranean.

A single individual was found dead on the beach at Mayan Zevi on 10 February 1976.

Soft-plumaged Petrel
Pterodroma mollis

Similar in size to the Manx Shearwater: body length 38 cm, wing length 26 cm, wingspan 88 cm and weight 250 g. Its upperparts are grey, its belly white, underwings and tail grey, and there is a grey patch on the neck.

This species inhabits the southern Atlantic Ocean, West Africa and the southern Indian Ocean. A solitary individual was found dead near Ein Gedi on the Dead Sea shore on 8 November 1963.

Schlegel's Petrel
Pterodroma incerta

An average-sized petrel: body length 45 cm. It is an overall brown, with a contrasting white belly.

Its range extends from the southern Atlantic Ocean to the mid-Indian Ocean. An individual was seen in May 1982 at the head of the Gulf of Eilat.

Family: Hydrobatidae (Storm-petrels)

Members of this family, which is found in all oceans except the Arctic, are small. There are eight genera and about 20 species. They are an overall slate-black or dark brown, and the rump is usually white. They spend much of their time fluttering above the waves of the ocean.

Leach's Storm-petrel
Oceanodroma leucorhoa

Body length 19 cm, wing length 15.8 cm, wingspan 48 cm and weight approx. 40 g. A long-winged storm-petrel with a forked tail and a bounding flight.

This species is widely distributed in the Atlantic and Pacific Oceans. A few individuals enter the Mediterranean Sea and, very rarely, visit the coasts of Israel, usually following a severe storm. Dead individuals were found on the Mediterranean coast on 10 March 1963 and on 26 March 1970, and at Ofira on 8 August 1978. A single bird was observed at Jaffa between 1 January and 24 January 1983, seven were seen there on 6 February 1985, and approximately 20 on 16 February 1985.

Swinhoe's Storm-petrel
Oceanodroma monorhis

Similar to Leach's Storm-petrel: body length 19 cm, wing length 15 cm, wingspan 45 cm and weight 40 g. It has no white rump.

This species breeds in the South China Sea, and migrates westward across the Indian Ocean between January and August. A single bird was found at Eilat during a severe southerly storm on 13 January 1958.

Madeiran Storm-petrel
Oceanodroma castro

Similar to Leach's Storm-petrel: body length 20 cm, wing length 15 cm, wingspan 46 cm and weight approx. 42 g.

It breeds in the Pacific Ocean and on islands off the West African coast. A single bird was seen on 6 July 1983 on the northern shore of the Gulf of Eilat.

British Storm-petrel
Hydrobates pelagicus

A very small storm-petrel: body length 16 cm, wing length 12 cm, wingspan 37 cm and weight 23-29 g. It has a square tail and short, rounded wings.

It breeds on islands in the northeast Atlantic and in the western Mediterranean. In winter it migrates to the western coast of South Africa and to the Adriatic. Single birds were seen on 27 September 1982 on the coast at Maagan Mikhael, and on 27 January 1984 and 6 February 1985 at Jaffa.

Wilson's Storm-petrel
Oceanites oceanicus

A typical storm-petrel: body length 18 cm, wing length 14.5 cm, wingspan 40 cm and weight (in nesting areas) 35-50 g. Its legs project appreciably beyond the tail in flight, and the feet have yellow webs.

This species breeds between November and March on antarctic and sub-antarctic islands. Outside the breeding season it migrates northward, reaching the coasts of Arabia, and occasionally the southern Red Sea. A single bird was sighted on 1 June 1983 on the northern shore of the Gulf of Eilat.

Family: Diomedeidae (Albatrosses)

Shy Albatross
Diomedea cauta

The third largest of the albatrosses: body length 95 cm and wingspan 240 cm. Its crown is white, its back and upperwings dark grey and its underparts white; the underwings are white, with a black margin. Where the wing joins the body there is a dark patch. The bill is greyish with a yellow tip.

It breeds in Australia and New Zealand and ranges over the oceans south of the Tropic of Capricorn. A single bird occurred in Eilat in the winter of 1981 and at the head of the Gulf, between Coral Island and the salt-pools, from 20 February to 7 March 1981, before being found dead and taken to the Tel Aviv University Museum.

Order: Pelecaniformes (Pelicans, Tropicbirds, Gannets, Cormorants and Frigatebirds)

This order comprises six families: tropicbirds (Phaethontidae), pelicans (Pelecanidae), gannets and boobies (Sulidae), cormorants (Phalacrocoracidae), darters (Anhingidae) and frigatebirds (Fregatidae). These contain six genera and 61 species, about half of them belonging to the cormorant family. Most members of the order inhabit the Southern Hemisphere, and only a few of them breed in the Holarctic region.

These are typical aquatic birds, inhabiting both the sea and freshwater environments, and are very rarely seen on dry land. Members of this order differ from one another in size, form and behaviour, but all are totipalmate, having webs which join together all four toes. Like many swimming and diving birds, their legs are placed towards the rear of the body, making walking difficult. They have long wings and are good fliers, and a few are also capable of soaring. Most species have an average-sized bill, while in the case of the pelicans it is long. A few species have an elastic throat membrane, which can be expanded into a large sac. They all feed almost entirely on fish.

Most Pelecaniformes nest in colonies near the water, laying a single egg, although pelicans lay 1-4, and only the cormorants may lay as many as 6. All species abandon the colony when nesting is over and migrate or roam.

Ten species belonging to five families have been recorded in Israel. The Great Frigatebird *Fregata minor* has been sighted a few times along the coasts of southern Sinai.

Family: Pelecanidae (Pelicans)

The largest members of the order, with one genus and eight species, distributed in all continents with the exception of Antarctica.

White Pelican
Pelecanus onocrotalus

The White Pelican is slightly smaller than the Dalmatian Pelican: body length 140-175 cm, wing length 59-70 cm, wingspan 270-310 cm and weight, in this country, 4.5-8.4 kg. The adult is mostly whitish-pink, with black flight feathers. The length of the bill can distinguish the sexes, being greater in the male. The immature has feathers of a brown-grey colour which grow gradually lighter, over three or four years, until full adult plumage is gained.

The White Pelican is monotypic. Its breeding range extends from Greece, through the shores of the Black Sea and the Caspian Sea as far as the Aral Sea and Lake Balkhash. It also breeds in Pakistan, Indo-China and Africa.

The pelican is a good swimmer. When swimming, its body does not sink into the water, as is the case with most aquatic birds, but is held high above the surface by means of the air-pockets dispersed beneath the skin. In addition, the bones are hollow and full of air — unlike those of the cormorant, which are solid and heavy. In order to prevent wetting of the wings in the absence of wing-coverts, the wings are held high above the water-level. This posture is particularly striking when the pelican bends its long neck to the water. In suitable conditions it is adept at gliding, for which its low specific gravity is an asset. It rises on thermals without moving its wings, and then glides towards its target.

In the natural state the pelican feeds only on fish, requiring a daily consumption of more than 1 kg. It is capable of swallowing its entire daily intake all at once: pelicans have been seen to swallow fishes 1.25 kg in weight.

The White Pelican is a widely seen passage migrant in Israel, probably originating from the colonies on the Danube Delta, in Turkey and in Greece. A pelican ringed as a chick in the Danube Delta was found five months later on the sands of

Caesarea. The populations breeding farther to the east probably winter at the head of the Persian Gulf and in northern India, with a minority continuing to Africa (an individual ringed in Iran was found at Ras Muhammad).

The best place to see pelicans in Israel is the Hula Reserve. They were conspicuous here before the lake was drained. After the draining and the establishment of the reserve, the pelicans at first ignored its existence and continued to land on the former site of the lake, which had been converted into fields. They also preferred the fish-ponds to the reserve, causing considerable damage to stocks. Only since autumn 1969 have all the migrating pelicans present in the country, both in autumn and spring, begun to land in the reserve.

The first pelicans reach the country at the beginning of September, and by the second week of October they are arriving at the reserve almost daily. The first flocks comprise hundreds of individuals, but in early November the flocks grow to a thousand and more, the largest having numbered 3,000 individuals. Towards the end of November the autumn migration is usually completed. In autumn 1971, 30,000 pelicans were counted passing through the reserve.

The pelicans arrive at the reserve from the north. Most come in in the early hours of the afternoon and roost on the banks of one of the lakes in the reserve. The following morning they fish, and when feeding is completed, at about 09.00 hours, they start to rise up, group after group, and continue on their way via the Jordan Valley and Jezreel Valley to the coastal plain, south of Carmel, and from here to the Bardawil Lagoon in northern Sinai and the Bitter Lakes along the Suez Canal.

Since 1966, some hundreds of pelicans have made annual attempts to winter in Israel. Initially these were confined to the Acre Valley and Lake Kishon but, since 1976, they have also attempted to winter on the Carmel coast and, since the early 1980s, in the Hula Valley too. The fish-farmers drive them away from the fish-ponds on the Carmel coast, and between October and December they can be seen in a raft out to sea. The degree of damage caused by pelicans has grown in recent years. In the Hula Valley an attempt has been made to limit damage to fish-ponds by stretching cables over the length and breadth of the pools and posting guards.

In the spring the pelicans return northward by the same route, between March and May, especially at the end of March and in April, and sometimes as early as the second half of February. Occasionally they cross the Sinai peninsula from Suez to Eilat and, on 26 March 1981, 3,500 individuals were seen above the Valley of the Moon, making their way along the northern Arava.

Occasional flocks of pelicans are seen at other times, usually in various places throughout the Negev. An isolated attempt at nesting in Israel was recorded in the Hula in spring 1962.

Dalmatian Pelican
Pelecanus crispus

This species is larger than the White Pelican: body length 160-180 cm, wing length 66.5-77 cm, wingspan 310-345 cm and weight 9-13 kg. It is distinguished from the White Pelican by its greyer (never pink) plumage, grey legs, yellow eyes, and in flight by its mainly white underwings.

The breeding range of the Dalmatian Pelican extends from Greece in southern Europe to central Asia. It is monotypic. It is less migratory than the White Pelican, and winters in Turkey, the Nile Delta, the head of the Persian Gulf and on the estuaries of the Indus and the Ganges.

In Israel this is a rare accidental or passage migrant. In the winter of 1982/83 one individual was present at the salt-pools of Eilat, and another spent several weeks in the Hula Reserve in winter 1983/84.

Pink-backed Pelican
Pelecanus rufescens

Slightly smaller than the White Pelican: body length approx. 130 cm, wing length 53 cm, wingspan 270 cm and weight 3 kg. Recognisable by its grey plumage and dark lores.

This pelican breeds in tropical Africa and also along the coasts of southern Arabia and the south-western shores of the Red Sea, as far north as 20°N. In Israel five immatures have been sighted, all of them along the rift valley beween Eilat and the Hula Valley: in 1935, on 15 May 1939, in 1951, on 25 May 1962 and on 31 March 1974.

Family: Phaethontidae (Tropicbirds)

This family comprises one genus with three species, which inhabit the tropical oceans. They are white birds with black markings on the head, back and wings, and the adults have very long central tail feathers.

Red-billed Tropicbird
Phaethon aethereus

The Red-billed Tropicbird is the only member of the family recorded from Israel. Adult body length approx. 100 cm, about half of this being the long tail

feathers, and wingspan approx. 105 cm. It is mostly white, except for a black eye-stripe, outer primaries and primary coverts, and dark barring on the upperparts.

Its nearest breeding areas are in the Red Sea, Persian Gulf and Arabian Sea. Visitors to Israel are mostly young birds, which range more widely than adults; they lack the elongated tail feathers.

In Eilat, two were seen on 14 May 1967 and a single bird on 14 May 1978. An adult was at the Dead Sea on 2 April 1981, and a dead bird was found in Beer Menukha in the Arava Valley on 16 March 1962. An adult was recorded at Eilat on 8 June 1984.

Family: Sulidae (Gannets, Boobies)

This family comprises one genus, although some authorities recognise a separate genus, *Morus*. There are nine species in the family, distributed in all the oceans; two are occasional visitors to Israel.

These are average to large seabirds with a long body, large and powerful bill and narrow, pointed wings. They are not birds of the open sea, and usually do not venture beyond the continental shelf. Their flight is characteristic: at uniform height, with strong and rapid wingbeats and occasional glides.

Northern Gannet
Sula bassana

Body length 95 cm, wing length approx. 49 cm, wingspan 175 cm and weight 3 kg. The adult is white, with black wingtips.

This is the only representative of its family that regularly breeds and roams in the Northern Hemisphere. It is a monotypic species, breeding in large, dense colonies on both sides of the North Atlantic. Dispersal from eastern Atlantic colonies occurs along the continental shelf of western Europe and the coasts of West Africa, penetrating also into the western Mediterranean in autumn and winter. Between the end of November and the end of April,

a few Northern Gannets make their way to the eastern Mediterranean and the shores of Israel.

In March 1971, a Northern Gannet, ringed as a chick 4½ years earlier in Scotland, was found on the beach at Ashdod. On 1 January 1983, six gannets were seen in the area of Jaffa.

Brown Booby
Sula leucogaster

Smaller than the Northern Gannet: body length 70 cm, wing length 39 cm, wingspan 140 cm; weight of the male 950 g, and of the female 1,200 g. Adults are dark brown with white belly and underwing-coverts.

The Brown Booby breeds on islands in the tropical Atlantic, Indian and Pacific Oceans. It has also bred in the southern Red Sea and on the Jubal at the mouth of the Gulf of Suez, but its present status there is unknown. Three to five subspecies are recognised; *S.l. plotus* occurs in the Indian and Pacific Oceans.

This is an occasional visitor to the northern shore of the Gulf of Eilat in spring and summer, with sometimes two or three individuals occurring together.

Family: Phalacrocoracidae (Cormorants)

The family Phalacrocoracidae is now regarded as comprising a single genus with about 30 species.

Cormorant
Phalacrocorax carbo

A large cormorant: body length 80-100 cm, wing length 32-36 cm, wingspan 130-160 cm; the male, weighing 2.3 kg, is larger and heavier than the female (1.95 kg). A black bird, with the head, nape and breast having a tint of metallic green, and the wings and back tinged with brown. The throat is bare and there is a yellow patch at the base of the bill; the cheeks and upper part of the neck are white. In mid-February, the head and neck of the adult turn white and a white patch appears on the thigh. Juveniles are brown, with whitish throat and underparts. The Cormorant has short legs placed towards the rear of the body, making walking difficult. It stands upright, and perches easily on branches, rocks, pillars, buoys, etc.

The range of the Cormorant is sporadic and extends over Europe, central and southern Asia, Africa, Australia and Canada. Seven subspecies have been identified. *P.c. sinensis* winters in Israel and breeds in Europe and Asia. Most of its European population migrate in autumn, to winter in the Mediterranean basin and along the Nile. In Israel this is a fairly rare wintering bird. A Russian-ringed individual was found at Lake Tiberias.

The Cormorant flies low over the sea, but flies high over the land and during migration. Its wing movements are slow and strong, especially in high-level flight. The Cormorant also swims well, with a low profile — head stretched forward and bill upturned. Sometimes only the head is not submerged. Cormorants dive for their prey, feeding exclusively on fish. Relatively large fish of 250-400 g are eaten.

The Cormorants arrive in Israel during November, their numbers increasing up to the end of December or early January. During this time, some acquire breeding plumage. They normally leave the country in early March; by the second half of March the last have gone, and only passage migrants are seen in April. Until the early 1950s, the Cormorant frequently wintered at Hula Lake, at Lake Tiberias, on river estuaries and on fish-ponds. Hunting by fishermen almost exterminated them.

Censuses of wintering waterbirds from 1965 to 1975 revealed that 21-63 Cormorants wintered in Israel, three to eight of them in the Hula Reserve. Hydrological restoration work in the reserve caused a change. In 1976, of 59 Cormorants counted in Israel, 52 were in the reserve; in 1978, 84 out of 110 were found there and, in 1982, the majority of the 200 birds in Israel wintered in the Hula Reserve. In winter 1985, there were 400 Cormorants in the reserve and a further 50 elsewhere.

Shag
Phalacrocorax aristotelis

Smaller than the Cormorant: body length approx. 72 cm, wing length 25 cm, wingspan 97 cm and weight approx. 1.8 kg. The Shag is similar to the Cormorant, but there is no white on the cheeks of adults. It also has a shorter neck and bill, and faster wingbeats.

The Shag breeds along the Atlantic coast from Iceland and Norway south to Morocco, and in the Mediterranean as far east as Cyprus. In this range three subspecies have been identified; *P.a. desmarestii* breeds in the Mediterranean.

This cormorant is essentially non-migratory and does not move far from the coast. In Israel it is a very rare accidental: there is only one definite sighting, of three individuals in Atlit in May 1934 (other reports may have been erroneous).

Pygmy Cormorant
Phalacrocorax pygmeus

The smallest Palaearctic cormorant: body length 45-55 cm, wing length 20.5 cm, wingspan 80-90 cm and weight 650 g. Its plumage is brown-grey in winter, and the female is slightly smaller than the

male. Juveniles have light grey underparts.

The Pygmy Cormorant breeds from Albania to southern Greece, in Turkey, on the Black and Caspian Seas and east to the Aral Sea. A monotypic species, it is resident in some colonies and migrates short distances from others in autumn.

Before the draining of the Hula swamps, hundreds of Pygmy Cormorants wintered there. Isolated individuals were also seen during the summer, and in 1940 a single nest was found. The draining of the Hula almost eliminated it from Israel. It moved to the fish-ponds, where it was ruthlessly hunted by the fish-farmers; the last individual there was recorded on 9 December 1960. The next Pygmy Cormorant in Israel was not until 10 December 1974, followed by a few more sightings until January 1982, when ten individuals were seen in three different regions. In December 1982 the species wintered in the Acre Valley and the Bet She'an Valley, and in January 1983 18 Pygmy Cormorants were counted. Since then, this has been a rare winter visitor in various parts of the country.

Family: Anhingidae (Darters)

In the family Anhingidae there is one genus and two species. These are distributed in Africa, southern Asia, Australasia and in the central parts of the New World. Some authorities, however, recognise four species, splitting the Old World darter into three separate species.

Darter or Snake-bird
Anhinga melanogaster

Body length 93 cm, wing length 35 cm, wingspan 122 cm and weight 1.4 kg. The Darter resembles a large cormorant, but has a distinctive long beak (about 8 cm) which is sharp and serrated, and a long, thin and supple neck.

The Darter breeds in Africa, India, southeast Asia, and Australasia. There are four subspecies, *A.M. rufa* occurring in Africa. In the Palaearctic region only two breeding colonies (of the race *rufa*) have been known, one in southern Iraq and the other in southern Turkey. At the beginning of the twentieth century the latter was a large colony, and African Darters were seen every winter in the Hula, in Kishon and on the Yarkon River. In the early 1950s, 10-15 African Darters still wintered in the Hula, between September and March and sometimes until April. With the draining of the marshes in Turkey, this population, most of which wintered in Israel, was exterminated. There have been no records in Israel since.

Order: Ciconiiformes (Herons, Bitterns, Storks, Ibises, Spoonbills)

This order comprises five families: Ardeidae (herons, bitterns), with 17 genera and 61 species; Ciconiidae (storks), 6 genera and 17 species; Threskiornithidae (ibises, spoonbills), 20 genera and 33 species; Scopidae (Hammerhead), 1 genus and species; Balaenicipitidae (Whale-headed Stork), 1 genus and species. The five families are cosmopolitan in range, but the two monotypic families are confined to Africa.

Members of this order are medium to large in size. In most species the sexes are identical. Juveniles are drabber than adults. Most species are marsh or river-bank birds. Their legs are long and well suited to walking and wading in mud, but not designed for fast running. Ciconiiformes are also characterised by their long neck and long bill; the latter is usually straight and pointed, notable exceptions being the crude bill of the Whale-headed Stork, the broad bill of the spoonbills and the curved bill of the ibises.

The toes are long. Their diet consists of fish, frogs, rodents, lizards, insects and other small creatures.

The Ciconiiformes are social birds. Most gather in flocks, and often have traditional roosting sites. Most nest in colonies, frequently containing members of different species. The nest is simple and constructed of coarse twigs, usually in reedbeds, willows and tamarisks. Both parents share the task of nest-building, usually with a division of labour in which the male brings the nesting material and the female arranges it. Most species are single-brooded.

Most members of this order migrate. They occur in Israel as residents, summer visitors, winter visitors and vagrants.

The order is represented in Israel by three families, 15 genera and 19 species. There is also an unconfirmed report of a Whale-headed Stork *Balaeniceps rex* caught near Ekron, not far from Rehovot, in 1930.

Family: Ardeidae (Herons, Bitterns)

This family comprises 10-15 genera, with about 61 species, of cosmopolitan range, primarily of tropical habitat and absent only from the tundra and Antarctica.

The Ardeidae are distinguished from other birds by the neck, which is curved into an 'S' shape when at rest and in flight. Its structure enables the bird to thrust the neck, together with the head and long pointed bill, towards its prey with a rapid movement. The oil gland is degenerate. The heron family has special downy breast feathers, which crumble at the edges into a powdery dust. These feathers grow constantly and are not moulted with the rest of the plumage. The heron collects the powder with its bill and transfers it to the claw of the middle toe. The base of this claw has serrations which comb the feathers, powdering them with dust and making

them waterproof. Their wings are long and broad. The length of leg depends on the feeding habits of each species of heron. The Grey Heron, which hunts in deep water, has long legs and neck; the Little Bittern has shorter legs, but has a long neck so that it can reach down to the surface of the water from its perch; the Cattle Egret, which hunts insects in the fields, has shorter legs and neck.

Feeding techniques differ between species. Some have a stealthy approach, and others stand and wait at length, watching for their prey. Others chase their prey beating their wings. Herons feed primarily on fish, but also on amphibians, insects, rodents, lizards and songbirds. They swallow their prey whole, and their capacity for swallowing is considerable; it is especially developed in the Purple Heron, which is capable of swallowing a fish some 200 g in weight, while the Little Bittern has difficulty coping with fish of 30-40 g. They do not usually spend much of their time feeding, and outside the nesting season can often be seen perched motionless for hours on end.

Herons fly with slow and regular wingbeats, and do not glide like their close relatives the storks. The legs are thrust backward in flight and protrude beyond the tail.

Two subfamilies are distinguished. The Botaurinae (bitterns) are represented in Israel by two species: the Little Bittern and the Eurasian Bittern. Both are mostly solitary in habits throughout the year. They are well camouflaged, blending into the background of reeds. At times of danger they stretch their necks upwards, merging into the vertical lines of the reeds and rushes. Members of the subfamily Ardeinae (herons) are represented in Israel by ten species. They live in more open habitats and are more distinctively coloured. At the approach of the nesting season, some of them develop long display feathers on the head, breast and back. They are social birds, living in dense or sparse flocks throughout the year. They usually nest in dense colonies, generally near water, on trees, bushes, reeds or papyrus, sometimes also on the ground. Often these are combined colonies, including not only herons of different species but also spoonbills, ibises and others.

Members of the heron family usually lay 3-5 relatively small eggs. Both parents share the incubation and care of the young. Incubation lasts only 22-30 days. Most species are single-brooded.

Since the establishment of the State of Israel, species such as the Grey Heron, the Purple Heron and especially the Little Bittern have been hard hit by the draining of swamp areas, the pollution of water, the spraying of lakeside vegetation and the effects of pesticides, which have caused a reduction in their breeding populations. During the same period, the Cattle Egret, the Night Heron, the Little Egret and the Squacco Heron, which were previously only winter visitors, have begun to breed in the country.

Twelve species of heron are known in Israel: the Green-backed Heron, the Western Reef Heron and the Goliath Heron are rare accidentals; the Eurasian Bittern is a rare winter visitor; and the Great White Egret and the Grey Heron are regular wintering birds. The remaining six species breed in Israel: Night Heron, Squacco Heron, Cattle Egret, Little Egret and Purple Heron breed in colonies, while the Little Bittern breeds solitarily. The oldest established heron colony is in the Hula Reserve, and this includes all the colonial species. Other colonies of this kind, found along the Jordan in the Bet She'an

Valley, at Mishmar Hayam in the Acre Valley and in the region of Hadera, are no less interesting and they are among the most impressive birdwatching sites in the country. Some of them are of international importance according to the criteria applied by the International Union for the Conservation of Nature and Natural Resources.

Little Bittern
Ixobrychus minutus

The smallest member of the order of Ciconiiformes: body length 32-37.5 cm, wing length 14-15.5 cm, wingspan 52-58 cm and weight 70-130 g. The Little Bittern is small and compact. It is the only species of heron in which there is a distinct difference between the sexes: the male has a black cap, nape, back and tail, white-brown neck and belly, and brown-streaked breast; the female is brown in appearance, with a greyish-black crown and nape. The flight is rapid and vigorous.

The Little Bittern breeds in Europe and western Asia, in the northern Oriental region, most of Africa, and also along the coasts of Australia. Five subspecies have been identified. The race *I.m. minutus* breeds in Europe and western Asia; it is the only subspecies which migrates, wintering in tropical Africa. In Israel this is both a breeding and a passage bird.

The Little Bittern is most active in the hours of twilight. It feeds on tadpoles, amphibians and fish, hunting from vegetation at the edge of the water.

It was always thought that this bittern migrated alone and at night, but observations in autumn on the shores of the Bardawil Lagoon in northern Sinai revealed that Little Bitterns migrate there in flocks during the hours of daylight. The usual size of flock was 35 individuals, but there were also flocks numbering 80 and as many as 100 individuals. The peak of migration occurs there in mid-September, and on 17 September 1978 some 2,700 Little Bitterns were counted. Spring migration takes place in April, when the breeding bitterns also return.

The Little Bittern was a fairly common summer resident until the early 1960s, when drainage and habitat pollution caused it to become quite rare. In the late 1970s, an estimated ten pairs bred throughout the country, half of them in the Hula Reserve. In 1985, about ten pairs bred at the northeastern end of Lake Tiberias.

Nest-building begins a few days after the return from the winter quarters. The male proclaims his territory with a sound resembling the croaking of a frog. The nest is usually built in a clump of reeds, and 4-7 whitish eggs are laid. Incubation lasts 17-19 days. At the age of five or six days the young are already able to climb, and at about a month old they can fly.

Eurasian Bittern
Botaurus stellaris

A heron of average size: body length 70-80 cm, wing length 31-35 cm, wingspan approx. 130 cm and weight 1,110 g. It is a brown-gold colour, heavily mottled and variegated with black and contrasting shades of brown.

This species breeds across Europe and central Asia to the shores of the Pacific Ocean and in southern Africa. There are two subspecies. *B.s. stellaris* breeds in the Palaearctic, and some individuals winter in the eastern Mediterranean and parts of Africa. In Israel, the Eurasian Bittern is a common passage migrant and a rare winter visitor.

This bittern is especially active at twilight, feeding on rodents, fish and amphibians, small birds and invertebrates. During the day it stands upright and well camouflaged in a characteristic posture, although it is also sometimes seen in a bowed and hunched stance with feathers fluffed and the sharp bill thrust forward in a menacing fashion.

The autumn passage takes place between the end of October and the end of December. In spring it occurs in the second half of March, less often in April and May. Because of its solitary nature and camouflage, this species may be overlooked; it is probably more common than recorded sightings suggest.

Night Heron
Nycticorax nycticorax

A heron of moderate size: body length 52.5 cm, wing length 26-30 cm, wingspan 105-110 cm and weight 375-625 g. The Night Heron is easily recognised: its crown and back are black, its wings and tail grey, its forehead, cheeks and underparts are white. Its neck is short, and its head large with a thick, black bill. Its short legs are yellow. Immatures are dark brown with whitish-buff speckles.

This heron breeds in all continents with the exception of Australia and Antarctica. Four sub-species have been identified. *N.n. nycticorax* breeds in southern Eurasia and Africa, and most winter in tropical Africa. The Night Heron is mainly a passage visitor to Israel, but some winter and nest in valleys to the north of Nahal Hadera.

Outside the breeding season the Night Heron's activity is restricted to the hours of twilight and of darkness, while it spends the daylight hours perched among the branches of trees on the banks of fish-ponds, canals or reservoirs — close to its hunting grounds. Scores or even hundreds may congregate on the same tree or in the same group of trees. During the breeding season it is also active by day, both when gathering nesting material and when hunting. Night Herons generally become active immediately after sunset. They gather on irrigated fields and pools, preferring fish-ponds: 400-600 may be observed at a single pond. They feed at the edge of a pool and wait for their prey, but will also stand in shallow water. Sometimes they fly above the water and dive for fish. They generally do not eat fish exceeding 55 g in weight. They also take mole-crickets, crabs, dragonflies, aquatic insects, rodents, fledglings, and even marsh-turtles and insectivorous bats.

Passage birds are seen from mid-March to early May, and in September and early October on the return journey. In autumn 1978, some 2,500 individuals were counted along the coasts of northern Sinai. Breeding birds arrive in mid-March. Since 1954, Night Herons have been observed among the passage, breeding and wintering heron populations. Since 1969, wintering Night Herons have been recorded in the Hula Reserve. In early autumn only a few hundred Night Herons, probably non-migratory, remain in the country; at the end of autumn they are joined by the wintering population.

The first breeding colony recorded in Israel was discovered in the Bet She'an Valley in June 1954. There were some 20 nests in this colony. A second colony, containing 30-40 pairs, was also discovered on the fringes of Nahal Hadera. The population has expanded from these two nuclei. In 1963, the first Night Herons reached the Hula Valley and eight nests were located in the reserve. In 1964, the number of Night Herons in the reserve rose to 40; in 1972 there were 300 pairs, and by 1980 the number had risen to 1,000. In 1967, they also appeared in the Jordan Valley and the Acre Valley. In 1980, the number of breeding pairs in the country was upwards of 2,000.

Nesting begins from early April to early May, and usually lasts until the end of July, but young chicks have been found in nests as late as early September, possibly from a second brood. The nest is built in tamarisk, willow or eucalyptus, and 1-5 eggs are laid, normally 3. Incubation lasts 21-22 days. From the age of eight to ten days the chicks tend to leave the nest and hide in the undergrowth. They are flying by the age of six weeks.

Chicks ringed in the Hula Reserve have been found in the Nile Delta, in Ethiopia, Ghana and Cameroon, testifying to the patterns of migration and the wintering areas.

Cattle Egret
Bubulcus ibis

A small heron: body length 45-53 cm, wing length 23.5-26 cm, wingspan 92 cm and weight 300-450 g. A white heron, with short neck and legs. Except in the nesting season, its legs and bill are yellow. At the approach of breeding, the bill and legs turn red and rust-coloured display plumes develop on the crown, breast and mantle.

Cattle Egrets breed in southern Europe, Africa, southern Asia, North and South America and Australasia. There are two subspecies. *B.i. ibis* is found in Europe, Africa and the Americas. The Cattle Egret used to be a fairly common winter visitor throughout Israel, and is now established as a resident.

This species feeds mainly on insects, especially grasshoppers and locusts, but also beetles, butterflies, flies and dragonflies. It feeds in pasture and cultivated fields, often following herds of cattle which disturb the insects from their hiding places.

The first nesting colony was established at Beit Yehoshua in the Sharon in the early 1950s. By 1955, this colony already numbered some 300 pairs. The number of colonies in the Sharon gradually increased, and a few were also founded on the southern coastal rift. Since 1965 they have bred in the Bet She'an Valley, and in 1968 pairs arrived in the Acre Valley. In 1973 they colonised the Jordan Valley, and they reached the Hula Reserve in 1975. By the late 1970s there were 650-800 pairs in the reserve. In 1975 a colony was established in the Ramat Gan Safari Park and in 1976 more than 2,000 nests were counted there, together with roosting flocks numbering some 5,600 individuals. Most of the colonies to the north of Nahal Hadera contain mixed heron species, while all those to the south of this point are composed almost exclusively of Cattle Egrets.

Nesting colonies often develop from roosting colonies. The site of the colony is usually retained from year to year, although there are always minor changes taking place, especially as a result of the 'burning' of trees by the nitrates contained in the droppings. Colonies have been found in groves of eucalyptus, pine, fir, casuarina, tamarisk, blue acacia and fig trees, and there have even been attempts at nesting in orchards.

In Israel nesting usually begins in February and is concluded in July-August, but nest-building has been recorded as early as November and chicks have been known to leave the nest as late as September and October. Usually 2-4 eggs, on rare occasions as many as 5, are laid. Incubation lasts 22 days. Many of the chicks die during the nesting process, and usually only two from each brood survive to leave the nest. From 20 days of age they roam about the neighbourhood, and are flying at the age of 30 days. They attain sexual maturity at two years, and may disperse over some distance while immature.

Many colonies of Cattle Egrets have been established within agricultural settlements; the noise and the smell cause great annoyance to the residents, but attempts to be rid of these birds have so far met with little success.

Squacco Heron
Ardeola ralloides

A small heron: body length 47-51 cm, wing length approx. 20.5 cm, wingspan 85 cm and weight 170-260 g. At rest it appears yellowish-brown, but in flight its white wings, tail and rump are very prominent.

This heron breeds as a non-migratory resident in many places throughout Africa, and as a summer visitor in southern Europe and the Near East from Turkey and Israel to Iraq and Iran. This migratory population winters in tropical Africa. It is a monotypic species.

The Squacco Heron feeds mainly on insects, also on frogs and fish, which it catches on the banks of pools, in canals and among swamp vegetation. It normally hunts in the morning and evening twilight, and hides away during the day. It is less sociable than other herons, and outside the breeding season it usually leads a solitary existence.

The Squacco Heron is a common migrant in Israel, appearing in flocks in autumn and spring, especially in the first half of September and during March and April. In 1973, the entire European population of the species was estimated at 7,000 individuals; in the same year some 2,800 migrating Squacco Herons were counted on the coasts of northern Sinai, and in autumn 1978 some 4,500 were counted there.

In 1959, this species was first recorded breeding in Israel. Nests were found in the coastal rift and in the Jordan Valley. The Squacco Heron breeds in colonies with other species of heron. It lays 3-5 eggs, and incubation lasts for 23 days. The chicks remain in the nest for about 30 days, and roam in the vicinity for a further two weeks. Its population in Israel in the late 1970s was estimated at 100 pairs, but it may be greater than this since, owing to their camouflaged plumage and shy disposition, Squacco Herons may be overlooked.

Green-backed Heron
Butorides striatus

A small heron: body length 42 cm, wing length

17.5 cm, wingspan 55 cm and weight 150 g. The upperparts are glossy green, the wing feathers are edged with brown and the crown is dark; the underparts are greyish.

This heron breeds in North and South America, Africa, Asia, Australia and on Indian and Pacific Ocean islands. There are about 30 subspecies. *B.s. brevipes* breeds on the Red Sea coast; some 25 pairs of this race breed in the mangrove thickets in the region of Nabq in southern Sinai. In Israel, this is a very rare accidental on the coast at Eilat.

Little Egret
Egretta garzetta

A small white heron: body length 52-67 cm, wing length 26-28 cm, wingspan 92 cm and weight 380-600 g. The Little Egret has a black bill, a long neck and long black legs with yellow feet which are especially noticeable in flight. There is also a very rare darker form in which all or most of the feathers are grey-black. This form is especially common in Madagascar, and individuals of this variety were seen in Israel during the 1970s and early 1980s. At the approach of the nesting season, the adult develops long, delicate display plumes on the head and scapulars.

The Little Egret breeds in southern Europe, Africa, Asia and Australia. Within this range four subspecies are known. *E.g. garzetta* breeds from southern Europe and North Africa through the Middle East and tropical Asia to China and Japan, and is also found throughout tropical Africa. The Western Palaearctic population migrates in autumn, to winter in the Mediterranean basin and in tropical Africa. In Israel the Little Egret is a breeding bird, some of the population being resident. It also occurs as a passage migrant and a winter visitor.

Little Egrets usually feed in shallow water, consuming small fish (less than 20 g), tadpoles, various insects, crabs, molluscs and other small creatures. They stalk their prey with cautious steps, or agitate the mud with their feet to disturb prey before swooping on it at a run.

Passage migrants are seen between mid-August and early October; in autumn 1978 about 3,500 individuals were counted on the coasts of northern Sinai. The return migration in spring is from late March to mid-May. A considerable proportion of the Little Egrets breeding in Israel migrates in autumn to Africa. Little Egrets ringed as chicks in the Hula Reserve have been found in Sudan, Kenya and Uganda, and a chick ringed at Tel Aviv University has been found in Egypt. Some of the breeding population are apparently non-migratory, although they wander during the winter months. The popu-

lation wintering in Israel has, like the breeding population, been increasing, with migratory birds joining the resident ones; the number of wintering egrets, however, is still smaller than the number of breeding birds. In the years 1965-71, between 300 and 750 Little Egrets wintered in Israel each year; since 1972 and up to 1982, the number has increased to between 1,220 and 2,660 birds.

In the middle of the last century, Tristram noted the Little Egret as breeding in the swamps of the Hula. Breeding was not recorded again in Israel until 1959, when the Little Egret began to nest on the banks of Nahal Alexander in the coastal plains north of Netanya. Its appearance here may have been linked to the draining, at about that time, of Lake Antakya in southern Turkey. In the following year, a nest site was found along the Jordan in the Bet She'an Valley. Since then it has extended into many areas in Israel, arriving in the Hula in 1967, in the Acre Valley in 1969 and in the Ramat Gan Safari Park in 1975. Today the Little Egret nests in all mixed heron colonies. Its population has grown in the Hula Reserve, from ten pairs in 1971 to 1,000 pairs in 1980, when a total of 2,000 pairs were breeding in the country.

The breeding birds return to their nesting colonies about April. They lay 4-5 eggs and incubation lasts 20-22 days. The chicks are able to leave the nest at times of danger from the age of eight to ten days but normally do so at 21 days old. When 35 days old they abandon the nest, and about ten days later they become independent.

Great White Egret
Egretta alba

The largest of the white herons: body length 98 cm (including some 12 cm for the bill), wing length 44 cm, wingspan 160 cm and weight 1,100 g. Similar to a large Little Egret, except for its yellow bill and its legs, which are blackish-green including the toes. At the approach of spring, the bill grows darker while the tibia turns reddish or yellow.

This egret's distribution is almost worldwide. There are four subspecies. *E.a. alba* occurs in Israel and breeds in eastern Europe and southern Asia, from Turkey to eastern China. It is a frequent migrant and winter visitor in the aquatic environments of Israel, especially in fish-ponds.

The Great White Egret hunts mostly in shallow water, but sometimes also in fields where there is a rich supply of rodents. It eats mainly fish and crabs, but also small mammals. Towards evening these egrets congregate at mass roosting sites, not necessarily near water. The traditional roosting place for those wintering on the Carmel coast and in the northern Sharon, for example, is the eucalyptus grove on the sands to the east of the crossroads of Caesarea; they arrive there after sunset, in almost total darkness. The egrets of the Hula Valley congregate to roost in the Hula Reserve.

The species arrives usually at the end of October. Most stay until the end of February or early March, although isolated individuals and small flocks may be seen as late as May. In December 1964, some 280 Great White Egrets were counted at wetland sites throughout the country. Their number has risen since then, reaching a peak of 1,700 individuals in 1978 and averaging 1,200.

Reef Heron
Egretta gularis

Very similar to the Little Egret, but slightly larger: body length 69 cm (including 9.7 cm for the bill), wing length 26.5 cm, wingspan 95 cm and weight 390 g. The clearest distinction between the two is the thicker, paler (yellow) bill of the Reef Heron. Among populations of Reef Herons, as among those of Little Egrets, there are individuals of dark colour, almost black, and there are intermediate stages with varying degrees of white and black. The dark form of the Reef Heron is distinguished from that of the Little Egret by its white chin and throat.

There are two subspecies: *E.g. schistacea* breeds along the shores of the Red Sea, the coasts of the Arabian peninsula and east to the coasts of India and Sri Lanka. Another subspecies breeds along the shores of western tropical Africa.

The Reef Heron feeds primarily on fish, which it hunts by wading in shallow water or while standing on coral reefs.

Some 40 pairs of this species have bred among the mangroves of southern Sinai. Two to three pairs have also bred in the saltmarshes of the island of Tiran. In this population the ratio is ten white birds to every dark one. It is also an occasional visitor to the head of the Gulf of Eilat, where a few individuals, four together at the most, can be seen in July-September and February-March. On rarer occasions it has visited the central coastal plain.

Grey Heron
Ardea cinerea

A large heron: body length 97-104 cm (including 12.2-13.5 cm for the bill), wing length approx. 46 cm, wingspan 185 cm and weight 1,250-2,000 g. It has a long neck and legs. The nape, sides of the neck, back and wing-coverts are grey; the head is white, with black feathers from above the eye forming a crest at the hindcrown, and the foreneck is

streaked black; the underparts are white, with black flanks. Juveniles are more uniformly grey.

The Grey Heron is the commonest and most widespread of all the herons of the Palaearctic region. It breeds from Britain and the shores of Scandinavia, east to China and Japan. In the Oriental region it is found in India, Burma and Malaysia. It is also distributed more sporadically in the Ethiopian region. There are four subspecies. *A.c. cinerea* occurs across Eurasia. The population in western Europe is non-migratory, but northern and eastern European birds migrate in autumn to winter in the Mediterranean basin and in tropical Africa. In Israel the Grey Heron is a common migrant and winter resident.

The Grey Heron feeds especially on fish, but also on amphibians, young mammals, lizards and insects. Usually it hunts by standing motionless and waiting for long periods at a considerable distance from any other heron, although sometimes it wades slowly in the water in its quest for prey. Normally only a short time is spent feeding, and the heron passes most of the day standing motionless in a particular spot. Often scores of herons congregate on the bed of a drained fish-pond or on a bank among reedbeds, sometimes in company with Great White Egrets, Little Egrets, Spoonbills and storks. Towards evening they fly to their roosting sites. The eucalyptus grove to the east of the crossroads of Caesarea is a traditional roost shared by Grey Herons and Great White Egrets wintering on the Carmel coast. The fringes of the 'Little Lake' in the Hula Reserve is another roost.

In autumn Grey Herons are seen passing over the coastal plain. The peak of migration on the coasts of northern Sinai occurs in the second week of September, and migration can continue into October. In autumn 1978 more than 6,000 migrant Grey Herons were counted there. They migrate in flocks containing scores of individuals, often together with herons of other species. The spring migration route is different, being along the shores of the Gulf of Eilat and the Arava. This migration continues from the end of February to mid-May, the peak occurring at the end of March. Wintering Grey Herons begin to arrive at the end of July or in early August, with many immature birds among them. Their number grows in particular towards the end of October. Most stay until March, but a few remain for the summer.

The number of Grey Herons wintering in the country is increasing. In 1965 800 were counted; in 1971 the number rose to 2,300, in 1972 there were some 4,850 wintering individuals, and in 1980 the number increased to 6,170. Among the wintering birds an individual has been found that had been ringed in the Volga Delta.

In 1951, three nests of this species were found in the Purple Heron colony in the papyrus thickets of the Hula swamps. The number of breeding pairs rose rapidly, and in 1953 and 1954 scores of pairs were breeding there. After the draining of the swamps, only five or six pairs continued to nest. This population was exterminated in 1964, apparently as a result of the birds eating poisoned rodents. In 1976, there was an unsuccessful attempt at nesting in the Ramat Gan Safari Park.

Purple Heron
Ardea purpurea

Slightly smaller than the Grey Heron: body length 84-97 cm (including 12.6 cm for the bill), wing length 34-37 cm, wingspan 120-150 cm and weight 740-1,175 g. The head and neck are rusty-brown, the breast is chestnut-coloured, and from a distance it appears an all-dark bird. The crown, nape and belly are black, and there is also black striping on the neck; the tail, rump and wing-coverts are bluish-grey; the chin and cheeks are white. The juvenile appears golden-brown.

The range of the Purple Heron extends over the southern Palaearctic region, the Oriental region and the Ethiopian region. In this range four subspecies have been identified. *A.p. purpurea* is found from Europe to the Middle East and southern USSR, and in eastern and southern Africa. The Western Palaearctic population winters in tropical Africa. In Israel, this is a passage migrant and a breeding species, and a few individuals winter in the country.

The Purple Heron seldom wades in mud, and normally hunts in open stretches of water among reedbeds, perching on reeds to await its prey. When fishing from the bank, it stands in vegetation and not on the exposed shore. During the day it is usually solitary. It feeds mostly on fish and aquatic insects, but also on frogs, crabs and other small creatures. When hunting, it stands and waits for prey.

The autumn migration through Israel begins in August, with a peak in the second week of September, and continues into early October. In autumn 1978, some 5,350 migrating Purple Herons were counted on the northern shores of Sinai. In spring the Purple Heron migrates north by a different route, through Eilat and northward to the Arava. In Eilat it can be seen almost every day from the second half of March to mid-May, the peak of migration occurring at the end of March. The breeding population arrives in Israel towards the end of March. They begin the return to Africa in August, only a few individuals overwintering in the country.

A large colony of Purple Herons in the Hula marshes suffered from egg-collecting until 1948. This colony grew to several hundred pairs in the years following the establishment of the State of Israel, but then the draining of the Hula reduced the colony to only a few scores of breeding pairs. It is possible that birds displaced from their former haunts in the Hula began to breed in other areas. By the end of the 1950s, hundreds of pairs of Purple Herons were breeding in the marshes of Nahal Poleg near Netanya, in the neighbourhood of Nahal Dalia on the Carmel coastal plain, in the marshes of Afek in the Acre Valley, and to the south of Lake Tiberias. Since then there has been a steep decline in the population, with many of the colonies being abandoned, and only about 45 pairs remained in the early 1970s. This decline was caused by drainage, by the destruction of vegetation around fish-ponds, and possibly by poison. Even in the Hula, there was a decline from 50 pairs in 1961 to only four in 1963. Since then the Purple Herons in the reserve have increased, and the number of pairs breeding there varies between 20 and 45. Other, smaller, colonies are active in the Jordan Valley, the Bet She'an Valley and on the Carmel coast. In the late 1970s and early 1980s, some 55 pairs of Purple Herons have bred every year in Israel.

Nesting begins in early April. The nests are usually in eucalyptus trees and olives, possibly as a result of the destruction of marsh vegetation in most parts of the country. Only in the Hula Reserve does the Purple Heron nest in traditional sites in marsh vegetation, breeding in colonies with other species of heron. In other places the colonies consist exclusively of Purple Herons. The clutch is of 2-5 eggs, usually 3, and incubation lasts approximately 26 days. The chicks can leave the nest at eight to ten days old, begin to fly at 45-50 days, and become independent at the age of about 60 days.

Goliath Heron
Ardea goliath

The Goliath Heron is the largest of the herons: body length approx. 150 cm (including 19 cm for the bill), wing length 59 cm, wingspan 220 cm. In plumage it resembles the Purple Heron, except that the crown and the belly are chestnut-coloured rather than black.

The Goliath Heron frequents marshes, lakes and also to some extent coastal waters in tropical Africa. In the past it bred in the marshes of southern Iraq, but it is not clear whether this population has survived.

In Israel this is a very rare accidental. Individuals have been seen in the Hula on 22 October 1937 and 29 September 1958, and at a few other places. The most recent sighting was on 30 March 1979 in the fish-ponds of Maagan Mikhael.

Family: Ciconiidae (Storks)

The family Ciconiidae comprises six genera and 17 species. This is a cosmopolitan family, most members of which inhabit the tropical regions of Africa and Asia. It is represented in Israel by four species, belonging to three genera.

Storks have a long and solid body, and a relatively large head and neck partially bare of feathers. The bill is long, thick, usually straight and pointed. The legs of all species are long. The wings are long and broad. The plumage is white, grey, brown and black, sometimes with a metallic gloss. The sexes are similar, although the male is slightly larger than the female. Storks fly with the head stretched forward (save for one exception) and with the legs stretched out behind. They fly and glide well over land, but avoid flying over the sea.

The members of this family are the most land-based of their order, and are less attached to water than members of the heron family (Ardeidae). They often feed in fields, on insects, amphibians, fish, lizards, young mammals and small birds.

Some species breed in colonies and others in isolation. The nests are large, built of twigs and branches and sited in high places: on trees, cliffs and even on buildings. Storks often use the same nest year after year, adding to it repeatedly so that the nest grows constantly larger. The eggs are white and 3-5 in number. Both parents incubate for 33-36 days. After the hatch both parents tend their offspring, regurgitating food for them. The young reach sexual maturity at the age of three to five years.

White Stork
Ciconia ciconia

The White Stork is a large bird: body length 99-112 cm (including 15-20 cm for the bill), wing length 53-60 cm, wingspan 180 cm and weight varying between 2.3 and 3.7 kg. All of its feathers are white, with the exception of the primaries, secondaries and the greater wing-coverts which are black. Sexes are similar, although the male is larger. The bill and legs are bright red. The juvenile is similar to the adult, but with brown rather than black on the wings and a browner bill and legs; at about 3½ months it closely resembles the adult.

The White Stork breeds in Europe, the Middle East, North Africa and central and eastern Asia. It has three subspecies. Nominate *C.c. ciconia* breeds in the Western Palaearctic and winters in Africa. On rare occasions individuals of the race *C.c. asiatica*, which breeds in Turkestan, are seen in Israel; this subspecies is larger and has a longer bill. The White Stork is traditionally a passage migrant in Israel, but it now also winters and occasionally breeds.

This stork feeds mainly on insects such as locusts, grasshoppers and crickets. It also consumes fish, young birds, amphibians and snakes.

The White Storks of Europe are divided into two populations: the western population, which is fewer in number, migrates via Spain and Gibraltar to tropical West Africa; the eastern population migrates via the straits of the Bosporus and Israel to winter in central and southern Africa. The River Elbe or the River Weser in West Germany is accepted as the dividing line between the two populations. Out of 200 ringed storks found in this country, however, the majority originated from Germany, Czechoslovakia, Poland, Yugoslavia, Hungary, Russia and Denmark; twelve had been ringed as chicks west of the Elbe and seven west of the Weser, but not a single one west of the Rhine.

Migration begins with the end of the nesting season, in late July and especially during August. The young storks, hatched the same year, migrate before the adults. Storks congregate at these times in flocks of hundreds, sometimes thousands of individuals. Most of their journey is made in gliding flight, and, according to conditions, they 'climb' on thermals of hot air.

When migrating, storks prefer to glide over land, and only when there is no choice do they cross the sea. All the storks from western Europe make their way to Gibraltar, and all the storks from eastern Europe to the straits of the Bosporus. In autumn 1972 some 30,000 storks were counted above Gibraltar, while on the Bosporus in the same year, between 5 August and 4 October, some 340,000 individuals were counted. From the Bosporus the storks continue along the Taurus Mountains, the River Orontes (El Asi) and the Beqaa Valley in southern Lebanon. During the autumn migration they are hardly seen at all in western parts of Israel; most pass to the east of the Jordan, also along the Syro-African rift, and they are to be seen especially in the Bet She'an Valley, along the shores of the Dead Sea, in various parts of the Arava and in the region of Eilat. On 13 September 1981, 6,100 White Storks were counted in the Valley of the Moon near

Eilat. The autumn passage through Israel begins in the fourth week of July and reaches a peak at the end of August and in early September, continuing into the second half of October. On 2 September 1980 a flock of about 12,000 birds was seen. The storks continue southward from Eilat along the shores of the Gulf of Eilat, traversing the southern Sinai peninsula in a westerly direction and crossing the Gulf of Suez at the strait of Jubal, which is about 30 km (19 miles) wide. In the absence of suitable gliding conditions, storks come to land close to the shoreline and wait for a favourable change of wind, and at such times many thousands may be seen congregating on the shores. They continue westward through the eastern Egyptian desert to the bend of the Nile near Qena, and then south along the river. A few storks winter in Sudan, but the majority continue southward, arriving in Zambia in mid-October, and in South Africa, some 12,000 km (7,500 miles) from their point of origin, in December. In January they begin the return journey northward, but most of the young storks remain in their winter quarters until they reach sexual maturity, at four years old.

From the end of February migrating storks are seen again in Israel, travelling north. Migration continues until mid-May and even into early June, with the peak in mid-March. The main migration route by-passes the Gulf of Suez to the north, spreading over northern Sinai and the western Negev, and proceeds towards the Jordan Valley by way of the valley of Be'er Sheva, and the Bet She'an Valley. The easterly winds, prevalent in the migration season, drive many storks westward to the coastal plain. In April 1935, after a severe and prolonged period of easterlies, the Sinai peninsula was littered with hundreds of dead and dying birds. In spring 1984, some 310,000 migrating White Storks were counted in Israel, more than half of them passing over the Bet She'an Valley.

Storks did not winter in Israel until the late 1950s. Since then the number of wintering birds has gradually increased: in 1965, 305 storks were counted; in 1970, 1,545; in 1974, 2,800; and in 1977 a high of 4,700 storks was recorded. The average number of wintering storks at the end of the 1960s was about 520, rising to 3,000 in the following decade. This increase has apparently come about as a result of the development of irrigated land and fish-ponds where the fish are easily caught.

References in the *Psalms* indicate that the stork was known as a breeding bird in Biblical times (e.g. *Psalm* civ, 17: 'The stork makes its home in cypresses'), and there is evidence that storks nested in the mid-nineteenth century in the oaks of Tabor and the carobs of Gilead. There was no further known nesting attempt in Israel until 1951, despite scores, and in some years hundreds, of storks summering in the country. In 1951, a pair of storks began building a nest on the roof of a glass factory in Kibbutz Nahsholim; five eggs were laid, but the nest was abandoned. A few more unsuccessful attempts were recorded until 1973, when the first known successful nesting took place in Be'er Toviyya: a pair of storks nested in a cypress near the edge of the settlement and two chicks were hatched, one of which survived. The same pair reared three chicks in 1974, and continued to use the same nest in successive years until 1979. Other nesting attempts were made in various parts of the country. Seven pairs began building nests in the Ramat Gan Safari Park at the end of April 1975; the nests were not completed, but one pair returned to nest there a year later, and since 1978 it has raised several broods. Additional, unsuccessful, attempts have been recorded at Tirat Zevi, at Kefar Masrik near Palmahim, and at the settlement of Keshet in the Golan. At Ramat Magshimim in the Golan Heights, two to four chicks have been raised by one pair every year since 1980. Two other pairs have attempted to breed there, one of which has so far raised two broods.

The White Stork traditionally builds its nest on trees, sometimes on rock-piles. Today the nest is frequently placed on towers, silos, chimneys, electricity pylons and other man-made structures. Pairs tend to return to the same nest year after year. The clutch is usually of 3-5 eggs, and incubation lasts 33-34 days. The parents feed the chicks with semi-digested food regurgitated onto the floor of the nest; in Israel they feed their young mostly on frogs, mice and snakes. The young leave the nest when about 60 days old, and a few days later they quit the area and migrate.

The White Stork is single-brooded, but occasionally replacement clutches are laid.

Black Stork
Ciconia nigra

The Black Stork is slightly smaller than the White Stork: body length 95-100 cm (including 18.5 cm for the bill), wing length 55 cm, wingspan 155 cm and weight 3 kg. It also differs from the White Stork in that all parts of its body are black, except for the white lower breast to undertail. In flight, the wings and neck are totally black.

The breeding range of the Black Stork extends from Spain and eastern Europe through Siberia to Japan and Korea, and there is a small breeding population in Zimbabwe and South Africa. This is a monotypic species. The European population migrates southward in autumn and winters especially in tropical Africa. Like the White Stork, the Black

Stork mainly glides, but it is able to fly straight across the Mediterranean. This species is a passage migrant in Israel, and a few also winter.

The Black Stork feeds primarily on fish. It also takes some insects, amphibians, lizards and young mammals.

Migrant Black Storks first appear in Israel at the end of August, with the main movement during September and in mid-October, while the rearguard passes by at the end of October. The spring migration begins in March, reaching a peak during April, and sometimes continuing until mid-May. Most flocks number only a few, or a few score individuals, but parties of some 500 individuals have been observed: above the Golan on 28 September 1976 and above Nahal Amud on 22 April 1982. On 26 March 1981, some 3,500 Black Storks were counted above the Valley of the Moon near Eilat.

In the 1960s this was a rare winterer in Israel, but in winter 1971 16 Black Storks were counted, and since then there has been a gradual but constant increase: 63 in 1974, 170 in 1979, and 290 in 1983. Most are seen in the Hula Valley and the Bet She'an Valley, among the fish-ponds in mixed groups with White Storks, Spoonbills, Grey Herons, Great White Egrets, and others.

Yellow-billed Stork or Wood Ibis
Mycteria ibis

Slightly smaller than the White Stork: body length 100 cm, wing length 48 cm and wingspan 160 cm. It resembles the White Stork, from which it is distinguished by its yellow and decurved bill, its black tail, and its red, unfeathered face. In the breeding season the wing-coverts and back feathers become pink. The juvenile has a greyish-brown head, neck and underparts.

This African bird is a rare visitor to the fish-ponds of Israel, occurring in various months of the year. It is usually seen singly, with occasionally two together.

Twelve sightings have been recorded since 1944, the most recent on 6 June 1982 in the Hula Valley.

Marabou Stork
Leptoptilos crumeniferus

A very large stork: body length 140 cm, wing length 67.5 cm, wingspan 250 cm and weight up to 6.5 kg. Its bill is thick and coarse at the base, and some 31 cm in length. The upperparts, sides of the neck and belly are white; the rest of the plumage is dark grey with a green tint, while the wing and tail feathers are black. A bare red sac is suspended from the neck.

The Marabou Stork is distributed throughout sub-Saharan Africa. In Israel it is a very rare accidental, with only three sightings recorded: one or two individuals in the Hula in May 1951; one in the Jordan Valley on 31 March 1957; and another in the Jordan Valley in May 1957.

Family: Threskiornithidae (Ibises, Spoonbills)

This is a cosmopolitan family, distributed in tropical, subtropical and temperate climates. There are 20 genera and 33 species in the family, of which three are represented in Israel. The Western Palaearctic species are all migratory.

These are average to large birds, with long legs and long necks. Their bills are distinctive: down-curved in the case of the ibises, and straight and spoon-shaped in the case of the spoonbills.

Members of this family are social birds. They flock together when feeding, and they nest in mixed colonies. Their diet consists mostly of invertebrates.

Glossy Ibis
Plegadis falcinellus

A bird of average size: body length 52-58 cm, wing length 28 cm, wingspan 90 cm and weight 520-600 g. From a distance the Glossy Ibis appears as a black bird with a long downcurved bill (approx. 11 cm). The body feathers are actually chestnut-brown in colour, while the wing and tail feathers are tinted metallic green.

The Glossy Ibis breeds in southern Europe, central Asia, Africa, Australia and southeastern North America. There are two subspecies. *P.f.*

falcinellus occurs as a passage migrant and rare breeding and wintering bird in Israel.

The Glossy Ibis inhabits areas of extensive marshland along the shores of lakes, in river estuaries and coastal lagoons. The drainage of wetlands has contributed to the decline in its numbers. It feeds in damp fields, in pools, on refuse-tips and in irrigation channels, but most of all in fish-ponds and sewage-farms. The diet consists of insects, mulluscs, crabs and mud-worms, also tadpoles and small fish.

The Glossy Ibis is a frequent passage migrant in this country: in September-October and March-April. Flocks, usually of 20-40 individuals, pass through and the largest flock yet seen, on 1 April 1967, numbered 214 individuals.

The Western Palaearctic birds winter especially in sub-Saharan Africa, although occasionally they are known to winter in Israel. In the early 1980s some 150 Glossy Ibises were counted wintering each year. An individual ringed as a chick on an island in the Caspian Sea has been found in Israel in the fields of Jezreel Valley. Glossy Ibises roost colonially, and those wintering in the late 1970s and early 1980s on the coastal plain tended to roost in mixed colonies, together with Little and Great White Egrets, in the eucalyptus grove bordering the reserve of Nahal Hateninim.

In 1969 a nesting site of the Glossy Ibis was found for the first time in this country, in a grove in the Acre Valley, within a mixed colony. In 1972 at least 12 pairs nested, and in 1976 approximately 30. Since 1975 some six pairs have also nested every year in the Hula Reserve, also in a heron colony. A proportion of this breeding population is in all probability non-migratory.

In the Acre Valley the ibises nest on blue acacia and eucalyptus trees, in the Hula Reserve among papyrus groves. They lay 3-5 (normally 4) eggs. The chicks hatch after 21 days of incubation and leave the nest at the age of about two weeks.

Bald Ibis or Waldrapp
Geronticus eremita

Larger than the Glossy Ibis: body length 66-72 cm (including some 14 cm for the bill), wing length 38 cm, wingspan 130 cm and weight 850-1,050 g. A mainly black bird, its feathers tinted with metallic green and the wing-coverts chestnut-brown. The head is bald, and the skin of the face red; a tuft of long and shaggy feathers extends from the nape.

The Bald Ibis formerly bred in Switzerland, Austria and Hungary, but was exterminated there as early as the sixteenth and seventeenth centuries. At the beginning of the twentieth century it was still breeding on remote cliff-side ledges in five sites in the Syrian Desert. Today the Bald Ibis survives only in Turkey and Morocco. In 1954, 600-800 pairs were breeding on high cliffs above the Euphrates; in 1981, two populations remained there numbering only 80 breeding pairs. In Morocco 12 colonies are known, most of them small, with a total of about 150 pairs. A report in 1983 estimated that only 400 of these birds survive in the wild. The Turkish population migrates to winter in northeast Africa and is a rare visitor to Israel.

A number of Bald Ibises have been taken from Moroccan colonies and sent to zoos, where they have bred successfully. In 1983 there were about 400 individuals in 33 zoos worldwide. In 1954 a few pairs were sent to the Wildlife Research Center of the University of Tel Aviv; in spring 1984 several Bald Ibises were released from there in the hope that they would adjust to life in the wild, but so far this experiment has not been successful.

After 1948, no wild Bald Ibises were seen in the country until 1970 when a few flocks of migrating birds were observed in spring in the fields of Kibbutz Eilot. One of these flocks, seen in mid-May, numbered 16 individuals. In September 1975, a solitary individual was seen near Arad; another was seen on 7 April 1980 south of Jericho, and another on 12 March 1983 north of Jericho. In March 1984, three individuals were seen in the western Negev.

Spoonbill
Platalea leucorodia

A large white bird: body length 77-89 cm, wing length 37-41 cm, wingspan 120 cm and weight 1.2-1.6 kg. The Spoonbill is distinguished from other white birds, including the various species of heron, by its bill, which is black, long (approx. 21 cm) and flat, broadening at the tip into a spoon shape. Juveniles are distinguished from adults by their black wingtips, and their pinkish-brown rather than black bill.

The breeding range of the Spoonbill extends from Europe across the Palaearctic to China, and also to India, Mauretania and the shores of the Red Sea. There are three subspecies. *P.l. leucorodia* breeds in the Palaearctic and India, the European population being migratory. *P.l. archeri* breeds on islands at the southern end of the Red Sea. The Spoonbill is a passage migrant and scarce winter visitor in Israel.

The Spoonbill inhabits marsh environments and feeds on crabs, molluscs, worms, aquatic insects and small fish, also on the seeds of aquatic plants. It feeds mainly in shallow water, and spends much of the day standing motionless.

The European population leaves its nesting areas in August-September and migrates to winter in

Morocco, the Mediterranean countries and also in Sudan and Somalia. Some of these Spoonbills pass through Israel on their way south and on their return journey northward. On 14 August 1959 some 150 individuals were observed in the Hula Reserve, but the peak of their migration through Israel occurs in September-October, and passage can continue into November. The northward migration begins as early as the end of February, and is usually completed by the beginning of April.

The number of Spoonbills wintering in Israel has increased. In the 1960s and early 1970s, their average number was approximately 115; since then this number has risen to an average of 325, with a high of 530 in 1980. Most winter at pools on the Carmel coast and in the Harod Valley. Two Spoonbills ringed as chicks in Turkey were found in Israel as long ago as in the 1950s.

In 1967 it was discovered that five or six pairs of the race *P.l. archeri* had strayed north to the island of Tiran and were breeding there, while one or two additional pairs were breeding in the mangroves near Nabq on the southern coast of Sinai. This small population is now established in southern Sinai and is non-migratory, although the birds wander extensively. It is possible that the migratory race *P.l. leucorodia* formerly bred in the swamps of Hula.

Order: Phoenicopteriformes (Flamingoes)

Family: Phoenicopteridae

The order Phoenicopteriformes contains only one family with, according to some ornithologists, one genus; others divide the five species into three genera. These inhabit most areas of the world, with the exception of Australasia and Antarctica. In Israel one species is represented.

Flamingoes have a long neck and legs; and a thick bill bent downwards in the centre at an angle of 120°, with the upper mandible smaller than the lower and both serrated for purposes of filtration. The plumage colours are pink, red, black and white.

Flamingoes are social birds, sometimes congregating in flocks numbering hundreds of thousands and even millions of individuals. They also nest in colonies, sometimes large and very dense. They choose isolated breeding sites, inaccessible to predators. The nesting place consists of a heap of mud in shallow water. The larger species lay 1 egg, the smaller species sometimes 2 eggs. Both parents incubate for a period of 21-26 days. The chick leaves the nest as early as four to ten days after hatching, and begins to fly at the age of 65-75 days, before it attains its final size. The initial plumage of the juvenile is grey-brown, and full adult plumage is gained only at two to four years of age; sexual maturity is reached at two to five years.

Greater Flamingo
Phoenicopterus ruber

A large bird: body length 125-145 cm, wing length of male 41-46 cm and of female 36-40 cm, wingspan 140-165 cm, weight of male 3.5 kg and of female 2.5 kg. Its legs and neck are remarkably long and its plumage is pink-white. In flight the red-pink wing-coverts and the black primaries and secondaries are striking.

The Greater Flamingo is found in all continents except Australasia and Antarctica, although its distribution is very fragmented. There are two subspecies. *P.r. roseus* nests in Spain, southern France, Turkey, Iran, southern Russia, northwest India and Africa. Most of the populations of Europe and Asia wander and migrate outside the breeding season; migration does not follow a regular route and wintering sites are not fixed, but are apparently determined by the climatic conditions prevailing in a particular year. *P.r. ruber* breeds in the West Indies and the Galapagos Islands. In Israel the race *P.r. roseus* occurs as a scarce passage migrant and winter visitor.

The Greater Flamingo usually inhabits saline lakes, lagoons or saltmarshes and feeds especially on small crustaceans, in particular the brine shrimp *Artemia salina*, which can survive in water of up to 20% salinity. It also consumes molluscs, insect larvae, algae and various single-cell organisms.

The Greater Flamingo used to be a rare passage migrant and winter visitor in Israel. Until 1970 a single or a few individuals were seen from time to time in various places (although in 1964 12 individuals wintered on the Carmel coast). Most of the birds were juveniles. In 1971, 12 sightings were recorded, including flocks of 20 and 21 individuals and a group of 200 migrating in early January above the northeast corner of Lake Tiberias. In 1974, 20 separate sightings were made, among them a flock numbering 50-55 individuals which lingered throughout November-December around the sewage-ponds of Tel Aviv. In 1976 some 120 Greater Flamingoes wintered in Israel, and since then until 1984 20-60 individuals have wintered every year, most of them in the salt-pools of Eilat.

Four rings found on dead flamingoes in this country showed that the birds had come from Lake Urmia in northwestern Iran. Between 1971 and 1979 large numbers of Greater Flamingo chicks were ringed there. In 1972 there were an estimated 15,000-20,000 pairs on the lake, in addition to 5,000-10,000 non-breeders. In August 1973, some 58,500 adults and 20,000 chicks were counted by aerial photography.

In 1967 a population of about 1,500 Greater Flamingoes was found to be apparently resident in the Bardawil Lagoon in northern Sinai. In April 1970 some 500 active flamingo nests were discovered at the salt-lake of E-Tina, not far from Port Said. In January 1973 the flamingo population of northern Sinai had increased considerably: some 8,000 were counted in the Bardawil Lagoon and 11,600 at E-Tina. In 1975, nesting mounds were found at the eastern end of the Bardawil, but this was, apparently, an unsuccessful attempt.

Order: Anseriformes (Swans, Geese, Ducks)

There are two families in this order. The Anhimidae (screamers) is restricted to South America. The Anatidae (ducks, geese and swans) is a cosmopolitan family, members of which are distributed in all continents with the exception of Antarctica. In this family there are three subfamilies, ten tribes, 41 genera and 145 species. In this country 33 species are represented, belonging to 14 genera, six tribes and two subfamilies. They include some of the rarest birds seen in the area, among them northern species which reach Israel at their southernmost limit, such as the Bewick's Swan and the Long-tailed Duck, and African species for which Israel is their northernmost point, such as the Egyptian Goose and the Cape Teal.

Members of the order have a broad body covered with dense plumage and large quantities of down feathers. They have narrow, pointed wings, a short tail, and most are good fliers. Most members of the order shed their flight feathers simultaneously once a year, and are unable to fly for a period of a few weeks.

The legs are short, and the three front toes are long and linked by a web (except in one species). The fourth toe is absent or degenerate, and set higher than the others; only in diving ducks and members of the Mergini tribe is it equipped with a short web, an aid in swimming and especially in diving. The bill is flat, usually broad at the tip, and ending in a curved hook. The internal edges of the bill, especially towards the front, are serrated for filtration feeding. Geese have a strong bill for grazing on grass; mergansers have a long, hooked bill with sharp 'teeth' for catching fish; sea-ducks have a strong bill for devouring molluscs and crabs; the Shoveler has a broad bill, especially suitable for filtration.

Most species nest on dry land near water, but a few nest in hollow trees or in thickets of vegetation some distance from water. The female chooses a suitable site, digging a small hollow and lining it with grass and leaves. She also plucks down from her own breast and belly and mixes it with the lining. Eggs of Anseriformes are uniform in colour, usually white or cream, sometimes light brown or grey-brown. The period of incubation, usually performed only by the female, is 21-36 days. The young are born with eyes open from the first day and covered in a thick down. They remain in the nest only a few hours, drying themselves before following their mother to water. The chicks feed independently from their first day, eating various insects located by sight. The faculty of filtration develops at the age of about a week. In their early life the mother continues to brood them. The chicks grow rapidly: members of the smaller species fly by the age of 35-40 days, geese at the age of 50-60 days and large swans at 120-150 days. Most species attain sexual maturity early, at the age of one year; swans and geese only at the age of three to four years.

Outside the nesting season the Anseriformes gather in flocks, often of several species. Most species of the Palaearctic region migrate to some extent, migrating in flocks, usually in arrowhead formation.

Family: Anatidae

Tribe: Anserini (Swans, Geese)

Members of the tribe Anserini are the largest birds of their order. Three genera, *Cygnus*, *Anser* and *Branta* occur in Israel.

The sexes are similar both in appearance and in voice. They prefer cold or cool climates, and their range is essentially Holarctic. They are winter visitors to this country.

Genus: *Cygnus* (swans)

The genus *Cygnus* contains the largest members of the family. There is no plumage difference between male and female, although the males are larger. Juveniles have grey plumage.

Swans resemble geese, but have longer necks. The neck is longer than the body, and the combination of long neck and short legs is unique among birds. On account of the position and size of the legs, the gait of swans is heavy and slow. The bill has a shape between that of geese and that of ducks, and its colour pattern is one of the features that distinguishes between the different species of swan.

Swans are good swimmers, but have difficulty rising from the water; in order to gain momentum they run on the surface, into the wind. They fly well, with the neck outstretched, and normally alight only on water. Swans feed primarily on aquatic vegetation — on leaves, buds and seeds; small animals, worms and molluscs form a small part of their diet. Their long neck is well suited to obtaining food from the bottom of water while swimming. Swans maintain a long-term bond between the partners of a pair.

Mute Swan
Cygnus olor

The largest swan: body length 150 cm, wing length 58 cm, wingspan 225 cm and weight usually 8-14 kg (sometimes up to 22 kg). Unlike other swans, its voice is seldom heard — hence its name. It is all-white with a long curving neck. It has an orange-red bill with a black knob at the base, which is larger on the male.

This swan is semi-domesticated in most of western Europe, where it is commonly seen in urban parks and public gardens. It exists in the wild state in southern Sweden, Denmark, Germany and Poland. In Russia it inhabits the shores of the Black Sea and the Caspian, and occurs east to Tibet and Mongolia. The Mute Swan has also been introduced into South America, South Africa, Australia and New Zealand. Most populations, especially those in western Europe, are non-migratory, but will travel some distance to escape from severe frost in winter. Young birds wander further than adults, and winter in flocks in shallow coastal waters, including on the shores of the Black Sea, the Caspian and in western Turkey. It was formerly a rare winter visitor to Israel.

The first sighting of a Mute Swan in Israel was recorded in winter 1948/49, beside the Jordan; another individual was found, dead, on 25 December 1961 near Acre. Two immatures were found exhausted in January 1979. In the same winter, which was particularly severe in Europe, 22-23 individuals were seen in various parts of the country. In 1980, and also in the winter of 1982/83, a few were observed in various parts of the country. At the end of December 1983 about 30 Mute Swans were counted in Israel, ten of them in one flock at the southern end of Lake Tiberias. In winter 1984/85 about 300 individuals wintered, including flocks of 15-25 individuals, most of them young, and some were seen as late as March.

Bewick's Swan
Cygnus columbianus

Smaller than the other two species seen in Israel: body length 120 cm, wing length 51 cm, wingspan 200 cm and weight 6 kg. It has a straight neck, and its bill is yellow at the base and black at the tip.

The breeding range of the Bewick's Swan of the subspecies *C.c. bewickii* is restricted to regions of tundra in northeast Europe and Siberia. It breeds on islands and peninsulas in the Arctic Circle and migrates to winter in large flocks in western Europe. In especially severe winters it is liable to wander to the southern Caspian Sea and the lakes of Iran. It is a very rare accidental to Israel in winter. Another race, known as the Tundra or Whistling Swan *C.c. columbianus*, breeds on the Canadian tundra.

The first recorded sighting of the Bewick's Swan in this country occurred on 7 December 1959, when three individuals were seen in the Hula Reserve; a few days later their number rose to eight. In December 1982, ten were seen near Kfar Menahem on the southern coastal plain. A few individuals were seen in winter 1983/84.

Whooper Swan
Cygnus cygnus

A large swan: body length 150 cm, wing length 61 cm, wingspan 230 cm and weight 8-14 kg. Its bill is black with a long yellow wedge extending from the base, its forehead is flat and its neck is held erect.

This swan breeds in the far north, in Iceland, Scandinavia and across northern Russia, and winters in northern, western and central Europe, the Balkans, western and southern Turkey, and on the shores of the Black and Caspian Seas.

Tristram acquired a specimen that had been caught in the Pools of Solomon on 5 December 1863. There were no further records until spring 1985: on 17 March 1985 three were seen at Eilat, and on 30 March a single individual was observed in pools in the Bet She'an Valley.

Genus: *Anser* (grey geese)
One of the four genera in the tribe Anserini. Members of the genus are large and thickset. The majority of grey geese have brown-grey plumage, and in most

cases stripes of a darker shade extend across the belly. The rump and undertail are white. Their legs are better located for walking, and geese are in fact more land-based than ducks. They also swim well. Their wings are long, strong and pointed; in flight, the sound of the wingbeats is clearly audible. The flight of geese is swift and straight, with necks stretched forward. They fly well and cover large distances without difficulty.

The bill is short and conical, with a projecting 'nail' at the tip and serrated sides. Geese feed mainly in fields, on grass and other vegetation. They also feed on the seeds and pods of aquatic plants, while the chicks also consume insects and worms.

Geese are distributed mainly in northern areas and migrate southward. They migrate in flocks in a 'terraced' line or in arrowhead formation, usually at night and at a considerable height.

The female chooses the nest site, builds the nest, and incubates while the male stands guard. The nest is usually on the ground, sometimes in a concealed and protected place, sometimes on piles of vegetation in water. Normally 6-9 eggs are laid, and incubation takes 25-28 days. The chicks leave the nest as early as their first day, but usually return to it at night when the mother continues to brood them. They can fly at the age of two months.

Greylag Goose
Anser anser

The largest member of the genus: body length 75-89 cm, wing length 46 cm, wingspan 150-175 cm and weight 2.4-4.0 kg. Its overall colour is grey, with dark grey flight feathers and pink legs.

The Greylag Goose breeds sporadically throughout the Palaearctic region: from Iceland, Scotland and Sweden, through central Europe and eastward to China. In this range two subspecies are known. The Western Palaearctic population winters close to its nesting zones, and also in the Mediterranean countries, Turkey and Iraq. *A.a. rubrirostris* breeds from southern and eastern Europe eastwards, and occurs in Israel as a rare winter visitor between November and February.

The first recorded individual was found on 4 December 1954 in the Hula Valley. In January 1968 ten individuals wintered on Lake Kishon, in 1969 eight wintered there, and in January 1973 six birds were found poisoned there. In the winters of 1972/73 and 1973/74, Greylag Geese were seen in various parts of the country. Since then isolated individuals have been sighted almost every winter, especially in the Hula and Jezreel Valleys and also in Eilat.

White-fronted Goose
Anser albifrons

Smaller than the Greylag: body length 64-73 cm, wing length 39-43.5 cm, wingspan 135-160 cm and weight 1.8-2.4 kg. It is distinguished by a broad white band on the forehead and by numerous thick black bars on the belly, though these features are lacking on young birds.

The White-fronted Goose breeds on arctic tundras of Europe, Asia, Greenland and Canada. In this range there are five subspecies. The Western Palaearctic population *A.a. albifrons*, which has a pink bill and orange legs, migrates to the rivers, estuaries and marshes of western and southern Europe, Turkey and Iraq. It also winters in Israel.

This is the commonest of the geese wintering in this country, usually between December and January, occasionally between November and March. Flocks numbering scores, sometimes hundreds of individuals winter in Israel, and some migrants pass through on their way south. Until recently this was a rare winter resident. In January 1973, however, at a time of severe cold weather in the Balkans and Turkey, some 150 individuals were seen in various parts of the country, from the reservoirs of the Golan to Lake Zohar in the southern coastal plain, with 66 around Lake Kishon in the Jezreel Valley. In January 1974 about 750 individuals wintered, including some 360 in the Golan and the Hula Valley and 300 in the Jezreel Valley. In 1976 about 190 wintered, half of them on one lake in the southern Golan. From then until 1982 only isolated groups of three to 17 were seen, but in winter 1982/83 at least 350 wintered. Most of the birds that winter here are immatures.

Bean Goose
Anser fabalis

A large goose, darker than the Greylag and with longer bill. The legs and bill are orange. It breeds in the Old World in areas of taiga and tundra and winters in western Europe and the Far East.

Tristram (1880) claims that this bird was offered for sale in the markets of the coastal towns of Palestine. There are more recent unconfirmed reports of three in 1973 and one in 1980.

Lesser White-fronted Goose
Anser erythropus

The smallest of the grey geese: body length 60 cm, wing length 37.5 cm and wingspan 130 cm. It is distinguished by its yellow eye-ring. It breeds in a narrow range, from northern Sweden to the Bering Strait, and winters in the Western Palaearctic region, in the Balkans, and on the shores of the Black and Caspian Seas, in Iran and in China.

An individual was apparently caught on 7 December 1927, and on 19 May 1983 one was seen in the salt-pools of Eilat.

Red-breasted Goose
Branta ruficollis

The smallest and most colourful of the geese: body length approx. 55 cm, wing length 35 cm, wingspan 120 cm and weight 1.2 kg. It has a short neck and bill and a deep chestnut belly, breast and face patch. The rest of the plumage is black, with white markings, a narrow white band separating the belly from the wing.

The Red-breasted Goose breeds on the Siberian tundra. It is a rare winter visitor on the shores of the Black Sea, in the eastern Balkans, and also in the marshes of the Euphrates and the Tigris, in Iran and in the region of the Caspian Sea. It migrates in dense flocks, not in organised formations like the grey geese. In typical goose fashion, it grazes in fields.

In Israel this is a very rare winter accidental. A few individuals and some small groups numbering a maximum of four have been recorded in the years 1958, 1973, 1976 and 1983, most of them in January.

Tribe: Tadornini (Sheldgeese and Shellducks)
Large goose-like birds, semi-terrestrial. Their bodies are large, with long necks. The bill is relatively short and thick. The sexes are similar, although usually not identical.

Breeding biology is similar to that of geese. The female builds the nest, often in a burrow or a hole in the ground, a hollow tree or dense vegetation. The Egyptian Goose and the Ruddy Shelduck may use abandoned nests, even those of hawks, in tall trees. There are 3-12 eggs, and the female incubates for 28-30 days.

The distribution of this tribe is cosmopolitan, covering all continents except North America, but most species inhabit the subtropical and the southern temperate zones. There are five genera containing 14 species. Two species inhabit the Palaearctic region, both of which winter in Israel. A third species, from Africa, is a rare accidental.

Shelduck
Tadorna tadorna

A large, mainly white duck: body length 58-67 cm, wing length 29-34 cm, wingspan 110-130 cm and weight 850-1,250 g. The head is dark green, and there is a broad band of rust-brown across the breast; in flight the black flight feathers are conspicuous. The bill is a striking shade of red. The sexes are similar, although the male's breast band is broader

and more conspicuous, and he has a distinctive red knob at the base of the bill which swells at the approach of the breeding season.

The Shelduck is found along sandy and marshy coasts and also on the shores of salt-lakes. It breeds discontinuously in the Palaearctic, from the coasts of Ireland, Britain and Norway, via the shores of the Black Sea and the Caspian to Mongolia. It is non-migratory in western and parts of southern Europe, but the rest of the Western Palaearctic population winters in the countries around the Mediterranean, the Nile Delta being its southernmost point. This is a monotypic species. In Israel it is a winter visitor and passage migrant.

This species feeds mostly on invertebrates, especially molluscs, insects and crabs. Most of the West European population congregates to moult on one small island in the German Waddenzee.

In Israel the Shelduck has become quite common in recent years. It may be seen from late October to the second half of April; odd birds are also seen in July-August. The number of Shelducks wintering in the country varies from year to year: from 15 in 1965 and 1968 to 2,650 in 1983. Usually between 100 and 250 Shelducks winter on the lakes, fish-ponds and reservoirs of Israel. In January 1973, 2,650 individuals were counted at Sabkhat E-Tina in northwest Sinai near Port Said.

Ruddy Shelduck
Tadorna ferruginea

A large duck: body length 65 cm, wing length 32-38 cm, wingspan 135 cm and weight 1.3 kg. Its body is chestnut-brown, its head lighter; the tail and primary feathers are black with a green tint, while the wing-coverts are white and produce a conspicuously white forewing in flight. The speculum on the rear wing is green. The male has a narrow black collar, lacking in the female which also has a paler head.

The Ruddy Shelduck breeds in Morocco, Greece, Turkey, the shores of the Black Sea and the Caspian, Iraq, Iran, southern USSR, Afghanistan and as far east as Mongolia and China. This is a monotypic species. At the approach of winter it roams, and also migrates. Most of the migrating birds winter in the ricefields of India and southeast Asia, also in Turkey (some 12,000 individuals every year), in Iran (on Lake Urmia in northwestern Iran some 40,000 individuals have been counted), in Iraq, in Egypt and in northern Sudan. In Israel it is a rare winter visitor and passage migrant.

The Ruddy Shelduck lives near lakes, marshes and ponds and usually (unlike its relative the Shelduck) some distance inland. It prefers vegetable food such as seeds and grass, but also consumes snails and shrimps and sometimes even feeds at refuse-tips and on carrion.

Isolated individuals, sometimes pairs, are seen at fish-ponds and reservoirs between the end of November and February, sometimes as late as March. They can occur in other months. In 1968, 44 individuals wintered in the country, 40 of them in the Bet She'an Valley. In January 1983, 48 Ruddy Shelducks were counted near the reservoir of Kefar Ruppin in the Bet She'an Valley and a further ten birds were recorded in other parts of the country.

Egyptian Goose
Alopochen aegyptiacus

A large duck: body length 67 cm, wing length 38 cm, wingspan 145 cm and weight 1.5 kg. It has a dark brown back and light brown underparts; the bill and legs are reddish-pink. The sexes are similar.

The Egyptian Goose is distributed throughout tropical Africa. In the past it was present in large numbers along the Nile Valley, hence its name, but today it is found only in Upper Egypt.

The Egyptian Goose was seen in the nineteenth century in southern Lebanon. Recently it has been recorded only twice in Israel: on 24 October 1972 in Ein Fesha, a small oasis on the Dead Sea shore; and on 5 June 1977 in Nir Dawid in the Bet She'an Valley. As the Egyptian Goose is commonly found in zoos, it is possible that these sightings were of individuals that had escaped from captivity.

Tribe: Anatini (Dabbling Ducks)

This tribe contains 40 species, which inhabit all continents of the world. All but four species belong to the genus *Anas*. In Israel ten species are represented, belonging to two genera.

In many species, the male has a colourful breeding plumage while the female is mottled brown. In this country, only the Marbled Teal has sexes similar in plumage coloration. While the females are incubating, the males begin to moult. First they moult the body feathers, to assume an 'eclipse' plumage similar to the plumage of the females. They then shed all their flight feathers at once, and for four to six weeks are flightless. During this time they hide among thick vegetation, coming out to feed only at night. After the re-growth of their flight feathers the males moult into breeding plumage. Females moult when the chicks are old enough to fly, but the change is less conspicuous. Ducks are the only birds to change their feathers twice in the year, and they wear breeding plumage as early as autumn.

These are all good swimmers. The wings are quite long and pointed, and the birds rise straight from the water without difficulty. The bill is flat and broad, with a hard and sensitive hook at the tip and serrations along the sides. The birds feed by sifting from the surface of the water, or by immersing the upper part of the body and raising the rear. Seeds, vegetation, worms and other small animals are eaten.

Dabbling ducks live almost entirely in fresh or salt water, usually shallow and/or stagnant. On migration they can also be seen on the sea — even the Dead Sea. In winter some species feed in fields, especially at night.

Apart from feeding, a great deal of time is spent roosting with the head buried among the feathers of the back. Dabbling ducks sometimes sleep on water, but more often crowd together to roost on a bank. They also spend much time preening and lubricating their feathers with oil from their preen gland. This prevents waterlogging of the feathers.

Most of the species breeding in Europe and northern Asia migrate southward in autumn, and in the course of this migration they are seen in Israel. The first migrants arrive as early as late August. The wintering ducks start to congregate at the beginning of November. Their numbers rise steadily, reaching a peak in January, but by February they are already decreasing. During March-April and in early May only a few ducks are seen, most of them passage migrants.

Pair formation takes place in the winter, when displays of various kinds take place. Ultimately it is the female who chooses her mate, and from this point on the male always follows his partner. The nest site is chosen by the female, who also builds the nest. The clutch numbers 4-16 eggs, and the incubation period is 21-28 days. The chicks of all species are similar: the down on the back is brown, that on the underparts and face is yellow, the latter with a dark eye-stripe. At the age of 1½-2 months, they are already flying and their plumage at this stage resembles that of the female adult.

Until the mid-1950s hundreds of thousands of ducks wintered in Israel. Then a steep decline in their numbers began, as a result of draining of wetlands and hunting. In 1964 the Nature Reserves Authority, a body set up with the object of protecting wildlife, began to count the wild ducks wintering in Israel every year in mid-January. Hunting was also prohibited in a few fish-pond areas. Between 1964 and 1970 the total number of ducks, including diving ducks, varied from 18,500 to 28,500, with an average of 22,300. Their number rose to an average of 57,000 (51,700-62,240) for the years 1977-82. Estimates in the period between these two sets of years assessed the number at more than 80,000.

In the early years of the census, the Teal constituted some 75% of the total population. With the prohibition of hunting an increase occurred in the larger species, in particular Mallards and Shovelers. In 1970 Teals constituted 50% of the total, and in the years 1980-82 their share fell to 30%. In 1982 the Teal was no longer the commonest duck seen in Israel; it lost this distinction to the Shoveler, and in 1983 even the Mallard was more common.

Mallard
Anas platyrhynchos

The largest of the dabbling ducks: body length 54-59 cm, wing length 26-27.5 cm, wingspan 88 cm and weight 900-1,000 g. The male has a green head, a white collar, and a chestnut-brown breast. The female is speckled brown.

The Mallard breeds in Europe, Asia, North America, Greenland and the islands of the Pacific Ocean. In this range seven subspecies have been identified. *A.p. platyrhynchos* breeds in the Western Palaearctic. In western Europe the Mallards are non-migratory. Populations in northern, central and eastern Europe migrate to western Europe, the Mediterranean basin, the shores of the Black Sea, Turkey and the estuary of the Euphrates and the Tigris. Large numbers winter in the Nile Delta, and Mallards ringed as chicks in the estuary of the Volga have been found there, as well as on the Jordan and in the Hula. Most of the Mallards seen in Israel are winter visitors, some are passage migrants and a few breed.

The Mallard feeds mainly on vegetable food — seeds, buds and leaves — but also on small creatures such as molluscs, worms, crabs, frogs and small fish.

The wintering Mallards arrive in the country in late October and early November, and stay on the fish-ponds and reservoirs until February or March. In the 1960s only a few hundred wintered in the country, the average being 550. After the ban on hunting in certain areas, a considerable increase in the number of wintering Mallards occurred. Their average number for the years 1977-82 was 11,500, rising to a peak of 21,000 in 1983. About 60% of the wintering Mallards are found in the Hula Valley, and their numbers there give the site a status of international ornithological importance.

The first Mallard's nest in this country was found in 1954 in Lake Hula. Since the draining of the marshes the number of breeding pairs has increased. In 1966 11 nests were found in the Hula Reserve, and in 1972 there were an estimated 20 families in the reserve. In 1967, a family of Mallards was found breeding on the coastal plain in the fish-ponds of Nahsholim. At the end of the 1960s and in the early 1970s the number of breeding pairs throughout the country rose to 20-40, and since then there has been a gradual increase. Breeding is concentrated especially in the Hula Valley, where in the reserve and the nearby pools some 40 pairs were breeding in 1982, and also in the Jezreel Valley around Lake Kishon and on the coastal plain. Interbreeding with domestic ducks occurs and young Mallards with unexpected colours are found.

In Israel nesting begins in March, and by April it is already possible to see families with chicks. Replacement clutches can occur in mid-June, with chicks hatching as late as the second half of July. In this country the nest is usually built on the ground, among thick vegetation close to the water. The female excavates a shallow depression and lines it with grass and leaves. She usually lays 9-13 eggs, and incubation lasts about 28 days. After hatching, the chicks spend several hours in the nest before following their mother to the water. They begin to fly at about two months old, when their plumage resembles that of the adult female. At the end of the nesting season it is possible to observe flocks numbering scores in the nesting area, increasing to hundreds in August.

Wigeon
Anas penelope

A duck of average size: body length 48 cm, wing length 24-28 cm, wingspan 80 cm and weight 550 g. The male has a chestnut-coloured head, yellow forehead and crown, grey back and flanks, white belly and black rear parts. The female is speckled brown.

The Wigeon breeds in the taiga and tundra of northern Europe and northern Asia. It is a monotypic species whose Western Palaearctic population winters in western Europe, around the Mediterranean, and along the Nile as far south as the Sudd in Sudan. It is a fairly common winterer and passage migrant in Israel.

The Wigeon arrives in late November and December, staying to the end of February or early March, a few remaining into May. Its wintering population has varied between 70 in 1965 to 1,400 in 1974, with an average of 500. Most occur on reservoirs in the south of the country, such as the reservoir of Zohar in the Lachis region.

Gadwall
Anas strepera

A duck of average size: body length 51 cm, wing length 25-28 cm, wingspan 90 cm and weight 800 g. A mostly grey duck, the male having black tail-coverts. In flight, both sexes are distinguished by the white speculum.

The Gadwall breeds in central and northern Europe, in central Asia and in North America. In this range two subspecies are known. The Western Palaearctic population, which belongs to the subspecies *A.s. strepera*, winters in western Europe, in the Mediterranean basin and along the Nile Valley, almost reaching the Equator.

The Gadwall is the least common of the wintering and migrant ducks seen in this country. Censuses have counted a maximum of 270, with a yearly average of 120.

Teal
Anas crecca

The smallest duck occurring in Israel: body length 34-38 cm, wing length 17.5-19 cm, wingspan 58-64 cm and weight 260-380 g. The male has a chestnut head, with a broad green eye-stripe; its back and flanks are silver-grey and its rear parts are yellow.

The range of the Teal is Holarctic, extending over large areas of Asia, Europe, North America and islands in the Bering Sea. In this range three subspecies have been identified. *A.c. crecca* breeds in the Palaearctic and migrates southward in autumn, wintering in western Europe, the Mediterranean basin, the Middle East, and Africa as far south as the Equator.

Teals are found in fish-ponds, temporary winter pools, cesspools, drainage channels and other fresh water. They eat most available food, preferring seeds. They winter in large flocks, but smaller flocks or individuals may be seen.

The Teal arrives in mid-September, leaving around mid-March, but some stay until mid-April. Its numbers have varied from 6,700 in 1965 to 43,000 in 1975, with a yearly average since 1971 of 28,000.

Twenty-four Teals ringed in the fish-ponds of Maagan Mikhael have been found considerable distances away: several in eastern Russia, most of them in Soviet Asia, east of the Urals. A few have also been caught during migration: six between the Black Sea and the Caspian, two in Turkey and one in Egypt.

Cape Teal
Anas capensis

An average-sized duck: body length 46 cm, wing length 19.5 cm, wingspan 80 cm and weight 420 g. A brown and grey duck with a red eye and bright pink bill.

Its range is in central and southern Africa, from southern Ethiopia to Botswana. An individual was identified on 26 June 1978 in the cesspools of Ashdod, where it remained for about two months; another accidental was recorded in May 1982.

Red-billed Pintail
Anas erythrorhyncha

Slightly larger than a Teal: body length 38 cm. Overall brown-grey with a darker crown, whitish face and cream speculum. Its red bill is distinctive.

Its range is in eastern Africa, between Ethiopia and the Cape region. A single individual was sighted several times in June-July 1968 in the fish-ponds of Maagan Mikhael.

Pintail
Anas acuta

A large duck: body length 51-66 cm (including about 10 cm for the tail in the male), wing length 26-27.5 cm, wingspan 80-92 cm and weight 800-1,000 g. A slim duck with a long neck and tail. The male has a chocolate-brown head and throat, and white breast. The female is speckled brown.

The Pintail breeds in North America, Asia and Europe. There are three subspecies. *A.a. acuta* inhabits the Palaearctic and America, where it breeds in taiga and tundra. It winters in the Mediterranean basin and in sub-Saharan Africa as far south as the Equator. In Israel this is a winter resident and passage migrant.

The Pintail winters in estuaries and along sea-coasts, preferring deeper water. On migration flocks can number scores of individuals. It appears at the end of September and sometimes stays until April. Occasional individuals summer. Its wintering numbers have varied between 37 individuals in 1965 to 1,860 in 1972, with an average during the 1970s of about 1,100. It is more common as a passage bird, migrating through Eilat in spring, from the end of February and during March. Two individuals ringed in the region of Astrakhan in Soviet Asia have been found in the Hula.

Garganey
Anas querquedula

A small duck: body length 39 cm, wing length 19-21 cm, wingspan 62 cm and weight 400 g. The male has a distinctive white eyebrow and blue-grey forewings; the speculum is light green. The female is mottled brown and has a dark eye-stripe. The male has a diagnostic crackling call.

The Garganey breeds from western Europe to Mongolia and China. It is a monotypic species. The Western Palaearctic birds winter in northern tropical Africa. In Israel this is a very common passage migrant, and has also bred.

The first birds appear as early as the end of July. Migration continues until the beginning of October, reaching its peak around mid-September. In 1973 in northern Sinai, some 96,000 migrant Garganeys were counted over 49 days, including 18,000 in a single day. In 1978 some 200,000 migrating birds were counted there. A few Garganeys stay behind to winter in the country. The spring migration continues from March to May, and is especially conspicuous during March in the Gulf of Eilat.

In 1977 a Garganey chick was found in the cesspools of Ashdod, the first evidence of breeding in this country. On 18 May 1978 a female was seen there with 11 chicks, 10 of which flew away on 11 June.

Shoveler
Anas clypeata

A duck of average size: body length 44-52 cm, wing length 23-25 cm, wingspan 70-84 cm, weight of the male 650 g and of the female 500 g. The Shoveler has a long bill which is broad and flat at the tip. The male has a dark green head, white breast, chestnut-brown flanks and a pale blue forewing. The female is speckled brown.

The Shoveler has a Holarctic range, covering North America, most of Europe and northern Asia. It is a monotypic species. Its European range extends as far south as the shores of the Black Sea, continuing sporadically to a few Mediterranean countries. Most European breeders migrate south in the autumn, some reaching the lakes of East Africa. In Israel the Shoveler is a common winterer and passage migrant.

The Shoveler arrives towards the end of October and remains until mid-May. Two individuals ringed in the region of Astrakhan in Soviet Asia have been found in this country. In recent years the number wintering has increased. In 1966, 1,000 Shovelers were counted, in 1972 their number rose to 13,000, and in 1982 it climbed to 19,500, becoming Israel's most common duck.

There is a report of a female Shoveler with four chicks observed in the Hula Reserve on 25 May 1961.

Marbled Teal
Marmaronetta angustirostris

A small duck: body length 37-44 cm, wing length 19.5 cm, wingspan 65 cm and weight 290-420 g. The back feathers and wing-coverts are creamy-white with broad brown fringes. In the field it appears light grey-brown with a dark eye-stripe. Sexes are similar.

The Marbled Teal is a monotypic species which breeds in limited and widely separated areas in the southern Palaearctic region. At the approach of winter it roams, and some migrate: the western

populations winter south of the Sahara, the eastern ones in northwestern India.

The Marbled Teal was once a fairly common breeder in the marshes of the Hula and the fish-ponds of the area. In the 1950s, an estimated 100-200 pairs were breeding there. With the draining of the Hula this duck remained on the fish-ponds but was not tempted into the reserve. In 1972 some 20 pairs were breeding in the Hula Valley, and after restoration work in the reserve it began to breed there. The number of breeding pairs has risen gradually, and since 1979 it has been estimated that some 15 pairs breed in the reserve and a further 20 elsewhere in the Hula Valley.

The Marbled Teal usually breeds later than the Mallard, and there have been no sightings of nests or chicks before mid-May. The nest is hidden among vegetation near water and the clutch size is 6-14 eggs.

Tribe: Aythyini (Diving Ducks)
Diving ducks have shorter bodies than dabbling ducks. Their legs are short and better adapted to swimming. They do not rise straight from the water but run along the surface to gain momentum. Once airborne, they fly well. The males have colourful and conspicuous plumage, while the females are a more or less uniform brown grey, without the speckling typical of dabbling ducks.

Diving ducks will feed on the surface but also dive to a depth of 2-4 m, sometimes up to 10 m. They feed mainly on snails, fish and insects. They prefer deep water and are thus likely to be found on large reservoirs and large lakes such as Lake Tiberias.

The tribe Aythyini is cosmopolitan in range, comprising six genera and 16 species, although most species are Holarctic. In Israel two genera and five species are represented.

Ferruginous Duck
Aythya nyroca

A small diving duck: body length 40 cm, wing length 19 cm, wingspan 65 cm and weight 550 g. The male is a deep chestnut colour, with conspicuous white undertail-coverts. The female is brown-black, also with white undertail-coverts. In flight, the wing has a white rear edge.

The Ferruginous Duck is a monotypic species which breeds in a few isolated sites in southern Spain and southern France, through central Europe and the Balkans to central Asia. In recent years its population has contracted in western and central Europe. It migrates southward, especially during October, to winter in north India, in the Mediterranean basin and in a few areas south of the Sahara. In Israel this is a winter visitor and occasional breeder.

This duck spends a lot of its time hidden among marsh vegetation, thus differing from the other diving ducks which prefer open stretches of water. Unlike other diving ducks, its diet consists primarily of vegetable matter.

Ferruginous Ducks remain until March in their winter quarters, which include fish-ponds and reservoirs in this country. The number wintering in Israel has varied between 24 in 1969 and 830 in 1974, with an average of about 300. They are usually seen in groups of two to five individuals among other species of duck.

Scores of pairs used to breed in the Hula marshes, but when the marshes were drained Ferruginous Ducks ceased to breed in the country for some years. In summer 1972 breeding was resumed in the cesspools of Gush Dan not far from Tel Aviv, and in summer 1974 seven families with chicks were identified there. A few years later breeding pairs were also found in the cesspools of Ashdod, and one family has been observed in the fish-ponds to the eastern side of the Hula Valley. Courtship begins from the end of January onwards. There are usually 8-10 eggs in the clutch, which is incubated for 25-27 days.

Pochard
Aythya ferina

Larger than the Ferruginous Duck: body length 46 cm, wing length 21 cm, wingspan 77 cm and weight 750 g. The male has a rusty-red head, grey back and flanks, and black breast and rear parts. The female is duller, with a brown-grey back and dark brown head and breast.

The Pochard breeds throughout Europe and central Asia. It is a monotypic species. The Western Palaearctic birds winter in western Europe, in the Mediterranean basin and in tropical Africa north of the Equator. It is a passage migrant and winter visitor in Israel.

The Pochard occurs from mid-October to the end of February, although a few sightings have been made in May and in June, occasionally large flocks. The population wintering in Israel grew from hundreds (315-1,050) in the 1960s to thousands in the 1970s (3,670-15,000, with an average of about 8,000). In the late 1970s and early 1980s, this population has declined to an average of 2,700.

Tufted Duck
Aythya fuligula

Body length 43 cm, wing length 20 cm, wingspan 70 cm and weight 700 g. The male has a striking pattern of black upperparts and white sides to the body, with a drooping crest. The female is brown, with a smaller crest. In flight, a white wingbar is conspicuous.

The range of the Tufted Duck is Palaearctic and extends from western Europe over northern Europe and northern Asia. It is a monotypic species. The Western Palaearctic population winters in western Europe, in the Mediterranean basin, on the shores of the Black Sea and the Caspian, in the Middle East and also in the Nile Delta and the marshes of Sudan. In Israel this is a familiar winterer and also a passage migrant.

The first Tufted Ducks arrive in September and stay until February, although isolated individuals are still seen in April. They winter on large lakes such as Lake Tiberias and on reservoirs. The size of the wintering population is fairly stable at around 3,500 individuals, and has varied from 1,510 in 1966 to 8,660 in 1975.

Scaup
Aythya marila

Similar to the Tufted Duck but larger: body length 48 cm, wing length 22 cm, wingspan 78 cm and weight 1,050 g. The male has a grey back and lacks a crest.

Its range is Holarctic, extending to the far north of Europe, Asia and America. The Western Palaearctic population winters on estuaries and on sea-coasts in western Europe, northern Italy and the shores of the Black Sea, the Caspian and the Persian Gulf.

In Israel this is a very rare autumn and winter

accidental between the end of October and the end of February.

Red-crested Pochard
Netta rufina

Body length 55 cm, wing length 26 cm, wingspan 86 cm and weight 1.1 kg. It is distinguished from members of the genus *Aythya* by its narrow-tipped bill. The male has a rusty-red head and black neck, brown upperparts and whitish flanks, and is also distinguished by the red bill and legs. The female is dark brown in colour with greyish-white chin and cheeks.

This is a monotypic species which breeds in the central Palaearctic region. It feeds exclusively on plant-life.

Until 1972 the Red-crested Pochard was a rare accidental in Israel. Since then it has become an occasional winter resident from the end of October to April, and there has been a perceptible increase in the number of individuals. On 16 December 1970 a flock of 46 was seen in the Hula Reserve, and on 16 January 1982 a flock of 26 on the reservoir of Revadim. In 1983, 97 Red-crested Pochards were counted throughout the country, most of them in the southern coastal plain.

Tribe: Mergini (Diving Sea-ducks)
The Mergini are average-sized to fairly large ducks, experts at hunting prey, especially fish, under the water. They are superior divers, capable of staying underwater for up to a minute and a half. They are social birds, usually hunting in company. Outside the nesting season they are mostly found along sea-coasts.

Most species of this tribe are Holarctic in origin and northerly in range. In Israel four genera and six species are represented, all of them very rare.

Smew
Mergus albellus

Slightly larger than the Teal: body length 40 cm, wing length 18.5-20 cm, wingspan 61 cm and weight 550 g.

This duck breeds in the north of eastern Europe and northern Asia, and winters in western and southern Europe. In Israel it is a very rare accidental between October and February, sometimes occurring in small flocks.

Red-breasted Merganser
Mergus serrator

Similar in size to the Mallard: body length 55 cm, wing length 22-25 cm, wingspan 78 cm and weight about 1 kg. The male has a dark green head with a conspicuous crest, a chestnut-coloured breast and grey flanks. The overall colour of the female and immature is grey, except for the brown head.

This monotypic species breeds in northern Europe, Asia and North America. The Western Palaearctic population winters in western and southern Europe, especially along sea-coasts, and on the shores of the Mediterranean.

In Israel this is a rare winter visitor between the end of November and the end of February, mostly in fish-ponds rather than on the sea-shore, sometimes wintering in small flocks of two to six individuals. One sighting at sea has also been recorded: 17 individuals among the coastal reefs near Hadera in November 1979. Most winter visitors are immatures.

Goosander
Mergus merganser

A very rare accidental in Israel. The only certain record is of one caught in the port of Jaffa on 8 January 1925.

Long-tailed Duck
Clangula hyemalis

A small sea-duck: body length up to 47 cm (including approx. 13 cm for the long tail), wing length 21-24 cm, wingspan 75 cm and weight 730 g. In winter plumage the male is mainly white, with the cheeks and flanks grey, the breast and a patch on the upper neck brown and the wings dark.

This species breeds in northern Europe, Asia and North America, occurring as an accidental in southern Europe.

One was observed on the salt-pools of Eilat in winter 1979/80, and another was seen in the same place in December 1982. In January 1983 a pair was observed swimming in the waters of the Gulf of Eilat.

Velvet Scoter
Melanitta fusca

A large sea-duck: body length 55 cm, wing length 25.5-28 cm, wingspan 95 cm and weight 1.6 kg. The male is all-black, except for white patches below and behind the eye and white secondaries. The female is dark brown with white areas similar to those of the male.

The Velvet Scoter breeds in northern Europe, Asia and North America. The Western Palaearctic population winters in northern and western Europe, along the shores of the Atlantic, in the Black Sea and in the Gulf of Iskenderun in southern Turkey.

An individual was caught in the Hula swamps on 19 November 1936. Sightings were recorded on 16 January 1942 in Ashkelon, in September 1973 in the fish-ponds of the coastal plain near Netanya, and on 9 November 1983 in the fish-ponds of Maagan Mikhael.

Goldeneye
Bucephala clangula

Body length 46 cm, wing length 20-23 cm, wingspan 72 cm and weight 800 g. A diving duck recognisable by its triangular head and by its incessant diving. The male has a bright green-black head with a white patch between the eye and the bill; the rest of its plumage is a striking black and white. The female has a chocolate-brown head, grey upperparts and white belly. In flight, the white wing patches are conspicuous.

The Goldeneye breeds in the north of Europe, Asia and America, in taiga and tundra. The Western Palaearctic population winters in western and central Europe and also in the northern Levant.

This is a very rare accidental in Israel. One was caught on 13 December 1942. Two sightings were recorded in 1969: in a temporary winter pool not far from Hadera, and on the reservoir of Kishon. There was one sighting in 1973, at the pools of Maagan Mikhael; and two reports in December 1982, from the Acre Valley and the Jordan Valley. Another spent several weeks in the fish-ponds of Maagan Mikhael in winter 1984/85, and one was recorded in the Jezreel Valley on 25 February 1985.

Tribe: Oxyurini: (Stifftails)

White-headed Duck
Oxyura leucocephala

Body length 45 cm, wing length 16 cm, wingspan 66 cm and weight 750 g. It is distinguished by its large head and swollen bill, and especially by the tail which is often uptilted at a right angle to the body. The white head of the male is distinctive even in winter. In both sexes the body is brown.

This species' range is Mediterranean and Irano-Turanian, and extends discontinuously along the coasts of the Mediterranean and of central Asia, from Spain through Tunisia and Turkey to Lake Balkhash.

The White-headed Duck is omnivorous, but feeds especially on plant-life which it obtains by diving. In the middle of the last century it was reputedly common on Lake Tiberias and in the Hula throughout the year. Today it is a quite rare winter visitor, between the end of October and the end of March, sometimes also in May and June. In some years it is not seen at all, in others there is a relatively large number of sightings. On 22 November 1972, six were observed in the coastal plain not far from Netanya. In the winter of 1976 12 were seen, and in 1978 26. In winter 1983, a total of 43 individuals was seen throughout the country. Most sightings are of females or juveniles.

Order: Falconiformes (Diurnal Birds of Prey)

According to the classification of Howard and Moore (1980), this order comprises five families, 80 genera and 287 species, distributed worldwide. Of these, three families, 19 genera and 43 species are represented in Israel. The two families not found in Israel are the Sagittariidae (Secretary Bird) and Cathartidae (New World vultures).

Members of the order are birds of average to large size, ranging from the smaller falcons to the larger vultures. They have strong and compact bodies, short necks and round heads. The bill is short, laterally compressed and with a hooked tip to the upper mandible. The base of the upper mandible is covered with a strip of exposed skin known as the 'cere' in which the nostrils are located. The legs are short and strong; the toes are relatively long, with long and sharp claws.

All members of the order feed on animal food: insects, fish, amphibians, reptiles, birds and mammals. Some feed on anything that comes their way, while others specialise in hunting a particular type of prey. A few members of the order feed occasionally, or regularly, on carrion. Birds of prey catch their prey with their feet, not with their bills as do most other birds.

The Western Palaearctic's most important autumn and spring migration routes of birds of prey pass through Israel. In autumn the raptors fly southward, mainly on the western side of the mountain ridge and especially above the area where the coastal plain meets the foothills. In autumn 1982 30 different species of raptor were identified along this route, with an estimated total of half a million individual birds, including some 320,000 Honey Buzzards, 89,000 Lesser Spotted Eagles and 16,000 Levant Sparrowhawks. In spring a different route is adopted, passing by the head of the Gulf of Eilat. In 1977 some 760,000 raptors belonging to 25 different species were counted there; about half of them were Buzzards and a third Honey Buzzards.

Raptors prefer to take weak, sick and old animals, thereby ensuring the survival of young and healthy populations of their prey. They feed on prey which are agricultural pests. It has been estimated that the birds of prey which wintered in Israel in the 1930s and 1940s used to destroy every month about 2,400 rodents in an area of 10 km^2 in the Jezreel Valley.

Nevertheless, no other group of birds has been persecuted more than the birds of prey. They are hunted as predators on agricultural livestock or because of the competition that they present in the hunting of other animals. They are also hunted for sport, stuffed specimens being highly prized as decorative trophies. High-tension electricity cables also exact a heavy toll on them. Since the early 1950s they have been threatened by the most serious hazard of all, secondary poisoning by agricultural pesticides. These pesticides were designed primarily to destroy insects, as well as rodents and other small mammals. Many were based on organochlorines; these are persistent poisons which, after destroying the pest, are liable also to kill the predator that eats its carcase. Of 31 raptor species which used to nest or to be winter residents in this country, 23 have declined in numbers and some have been exterminated altogether. Among the species no longer breeding in this country are the Spotted Eagle, the White-tailed Eagle and the Peregrine, while the Black Kite, Bonelli's Eagle, Egyptian Vulture and Lesser Kestrel have become extremely rare. Among the many wintering raptors which have grown scarce and even disappeared are Black Kite, Levant Sparrowhawk, Sparrowhawk, Buzzard, Imperial Eagle, Hen Harrier, Pallid Harrier, Saker and Merlin. Since the 1970s there has been a revival in many of the populations of birds of prey, mainly those of the Kestrel which have returned to their former numbers before the pesticide poisonings.

Birds of prey have been declared protected species in Israel since 1955. Feeding-stations have been in operation since the early 1970s near Sede Boker in the central Negev and in the estuary of Nahal Hever

50

on the Dead Sea shore, and since the late 1970s in the southern valley of the Arava not far from Eilat. Captive breeding projects have been set up for

indigenous Griffon Vultures and Lappet-faced Vultures, and also for White-tailed Eagles and Bearded Vultures imported from abroad.

Family: Accipitridae

The largest family of diurnal birds of prey, comprising over 60 genera containing 218 species and including most of the familiar predators: kites, vultures, harriers, hawks, buzzards and eagles.

They are distinguished from the Falconidae by their large heads and normally broad and long wings. Their backs and napes are usually dull brown, dull grey or black, with lighter bellies. Bright plumage coloration is exceptional. Only in harriers and a few of the hawks is there a colour difference between the sexes. In most species the female is larger than the male.

Like most members of their order, the Accipitridae normally catch their prey with their feet. The claws of the rear toe and the central of the three front toes are the basic killing instrument, working together like a vice. The lateral toes assist in holding the prey and in steadying the bird when standing or walking. The length of the toes and claws is determined by the size of the prey rather than that of the predator itself. Hawks which catch birds in flight have long and slender toes, with growths resembling calluses on the underside, to give added grip when holding prey. Hawks also have long legs, suitable for snatching birds out of thickets. The White-tailed Eagle, which feeds on fish, has barbs on its toes. Eagles, which hunt various mammals including small predators, have feathers covering the leg as far as the toes, apparently to protect the leg from being bitten by their prey. The Short-toed Eagle, which feeds on reptiles, especially snakes, has short toes and claws for a more effective grip on its prey. The Honey Buzzard, which digs in the ground with its feet to expose the nests of bees and wasps, has long claws which are blunt and not curved. Vultures and other carrion-eaters, which have no need to kill their prey, have relatively weak toes and short, blunt claws.

The bill is also adapted to the particular feeding habits: hawks, which prey on birds with soft skin, have a short bill; the eagles prey on mammals with thick skin and have a larger bill. Carrion-eaters have a strong bill for punching holes in the skin, although the Egyptian Vulture has a thin and relatively delicate bill for picking the bones of the carcase.

Wing structure is also connected with lifestyle and hunting habits: the wings are short and rounded in hawks, which inhabit forests and need to manoeuvre adroitly among the foliage; they are long and broad

for gliding in carrion-eaters. The tail is long in the hawks, in Bonelli's Eagle, in the Bearded Vulture and in harriers — which have considerable powers of manoeuvring in the air. It is short in the gliding species such as Griffon and Lappet-faced Vultures.

Most birds of prey are territorial, and the larger the prey the larger the territory. Only carrion-eaters, such as the Griffon Vulture, and insect-eaters, such as the Lesser Kestrel, are colonial. Only a few of the predators take their prey in rapid flight. Many species tend to use dynamic or gliding flight in turns, depending on the terrain. A few of them are apt to hover, a behaviour typical of the Short-toed Eagle, the White-tailed Eagle and to some extent also the Buzzard. Harriers also hover from time to time. Buzzards, kites and a few species of eagle, which find their food on the ground, stand on a branch or the edge of a cliff watching for prey and then swoop on it at great speed. The food is first partially digested in the crop, from where it passes into the stomach, which dissolves all the undigested elements. Feathers, hairs and fragments of bone are accumulated and regurgitated in pellet form 8-12 hours after eating. The pellets contain bones and fragments of bones.

Many of the birds of prey inhabit the northern Palaearctic region and migrate in autumn. In spring, when they return to their territories, courtship begins, usually executed in display flight. The female usually flies beneath the male or watches his antics from a perch. Sometimes both members of the pair join in aerobatic displays. Vultures, which do not have such aerobatic skills, glide side by side with wingtips touching.

Many of the Accipitridae, for example, Bearded and Griffon Vultures, Golden and Bonelli's Eagles, nest on inaccessible cliff-faces. Others, including kites, the Lappet-faced Vulture and the Short-toed Eagle, nest in trees. Harriers build their nests on the ground. It is mostly the female who chooses the nesting site and does most of the building, but with kites the male is the principal nest-builder. The Sparrowhawk builds a new nest every year. Most other members of the family renew the old nest, adding only twigs and lining; such nests may be used year after year, and some are known to have been in use for 60 and even 80 years.

The Griffon Vulture, the Lappet-faced Vulture and the Short-toed Eagle lay a single egg. Most eagles and buzzards lay 2-3 eggs. The harriers lay 8 and even 10, perhaps owing to the fact that they nest on the ground. An egg is laid every two or three days. Incubation begins with the laying of the first egg. Among carrion-eaters both partners incubate; in all other species, the female incubates while the male supplies her with food and usually relieves her only when she is feeding. Incubation is prolonged, about 30 days in harriers and hawks and 50 days and more in vultures. Hatching is in accordance with the order of laying. The youngest chicks are also the weakest, and when food is short they cannot compete with their older siblings and die of hunger. Sometimes, especially among eagles, the older chick kills the younger one. The mother feeds the chicks bill-to-bill with scraps of meat supplied by the male. When the chicks grow older the parents leave prey in the nest, where they tear it up for themselves. Vultures regurgitate semi-digested food for the chicks. The development of the chicks is slow. At two to three weeks old they grow a second covering of down, which remains throughout life as a warm undercoat. A long time elapses before they are ready to leave the nest: 50-60 days in kites, 75 days in the White-tailed Eagle and 90 days in the Griffon Vulture. Smaller species such as the Sparrowhawk reach sexual maturity at the age of one year, others at two to three years, the larger species at four to six years and the Lappet-faced Vulture only at eight to ten years old.

Black Kite
Milvus migrans

A raptor of average size: body length 55-60 cm (including 20-23 cm for the tail), wing length 42-48 cm, wingspan 160-180 cm and weight approx. 1,000 g. The Black Kite is brown-grey with a rusty-brown belly. The head is small and the bill short. The Black Kite has a fairly erect stance, but its gait is horizontal and often it drags its tail on the ground. In flight it has a forked tail, but when the tail is spread to its full width this is hard to distinguish. It is also recognisable in flight by its long and slightly arched wings. Its typical cry is a high-pitched screech, resembling the cry of a gull.

The range of the Black Kite extends over Europe, Asia, Africa and Australia. In this broad range six to nine subspecies have been identified. The one seen in Israel is *M.m. migrans*, which breeds throughout Europe, in North Africa and in western Asia and winters mainly in Africa.

The Black Kite feeds to a large extent on carrion and refuse. Domestic rubbish-heaps are among its favourite haunts in winter and sometimes its feeds on scraps discharged from ships. It also hunts insects, reptiles, birds and small mammals. It spends more of its time near water than other birds of prey, to catch fish or to scavenge. In Israel it can often be seen on fish-ponds in the Hula Valley and sometimes on the Carmel coast.

In the 1940s and 1950s the Black Kite was a resident, breeding in the north of the country and spreading gradually to the south; in 1952 it was even breeding in Mikveh Israel, not far from Tel Aviv. In those years it was also a very common winterer and passage migrant. As a result of poisoning by agricultural pesticides in the 1950s, both the wintering and breeding populations were eliminated and for a period of some 20 years only passage birds were seen.

In autumn only a few migrant Black Kites are recorded, on their way to winter in tropical Africa. On the spring migration they are much more common, passing through Eilat between the end of February and mid-May. The peak of migration occurs in late March and early April. In 1977 some 26,000 migrating individuals were counted in Eilat, and in 1980 37,000. The Black Kite often migrates in the morning and evening twilight. In spring 1962 a migrating flock of about 200 young individuals stayed for several months in the western Negev. At that time the fields were swarming with small rodents, supplying the visitors with abundant food.

Since 1973 Black Kites have begun to winter again in Israel: at first only in the region of Hadera in the coastal plain, but since 1975 also in the Hula Valley. In the winter of 1981/82 they were also present in the western Negev. The wintering kites arrive during the first half of October and stay until the beginning of April. Their numbers have risen from a few score to hundreds in all areas. In January 1985 some 1,000 Black Kites were counted in the Hula Valley, about 400 in the region of Hadera and the coastal plain, and a further 170 in the western Negev. At the approach of evening they gather in groves of eucalyptus to roost. In January 1976 fields in the Hula Valley were sprayed to destroy rodents. Hundreds of birds of prey died from secondary poisoning, including 76 Black Kites; another 14 recovered, and were released after treatment.

In 1972 three nests of Black Kites were found in the country, the first since 1959. Since then four or five breeding pairs have been known, all of them in the northern Hula Valley and its fringes, on the slopes of the Golan and Mount Hermon.

The nest of the Black Kite is usually found on a tall tree: eucalyptus, casuarina, or Tabor oak. Unusually, the male is the principal nest-builder, sometimes renovating an old nest, sometimes building a new one in the same tree. Before laying begins, food is stored in the nest, to supply the female in the first days of laying and incubation. The 3 eggs are usually laid at the end of March, and incubation lasts 29-31 days. The chicks leave the nest at about 40 days old and reach independence after a further 45 days.

Red Kite
Milvus milvus

Slightly larger than the Black Kite: body length 63 cm, wing length 49 cm, wingspan 185 cm, weight of the female 1,150 g and of the male 900 g. Distinguished from Black Kite by its deeper-forked tail and more rufous plumage.

The Red Kite is restricted to Europe: it breeds in Spain and Britain, through central and southern Europe to the Caucasus. Its wintering areas are also almost exclusively European.

In Israel this is a very rare winter visitor; in the last 20 years only a few sightings have been recorded. An injured Red Kite was found near Latrun on 15 May 1955; another was found dead in Mikveh Israel, not far from Tel Aviv, in 1967. A solitary individual wintered in the western Negev in winter 1982/83, and a single Red Kite was present in the same area the following winter.

Black-shouldered Kite
Elanus caeruleus

A small raptor, similar in size to a kestrel: body length 33 cm, wing length 27 cm, wingspan 80 cm and weight 230 g. It is grey, black and white.

The Black-shouldered Kite is distributed in the tropical zones of Africa and southeast Asia, also in

North Africa and the southern Iberian peninsula. Tristram saw one in December 1863 near Tyre in southern Lebanon.

In Israel only four sightings have been recorded, all of them in the region of Eilat: on 9 April 1977, on 2 April 1978, on 28 March 1982 and on 2 April 1985.

Honey Buzzard
Pernis apivorus

A raptor of average size: body length 53-58 cm, wing length 36.5-40 cm, wingspan 145 cm and weight 460-800 g. The Honey Buzzard has several colour-phases, and is distinguished from the Buzzard by its long tail (approx. 25 cm) with two dark bars at the base and another at the tip, its long neck and its relatively long and narrow wings.

Its breeding range extends over most of Europe and only rarely penetrates central Asia. It is a monotypic species which prefers clearings in forests. The Honey Buzzard winters in tropical Africa. In Israel it is a common passage migrant.

The Honey Buzzard feeds especially on the larvae and pupae of bees and wasps, raiding their nests in the ground. It also feeds on flying insects, amphibians, reptiles, chicks and birds' eggs, and sometimes even on fruit.

Flocks numbering hundreds may be seen as early as the end of August. Their autumn migration reaches a peak in the second week of September and continues into early October. This migration is spread over the whole width of Israel, but the main route passes through the area where the western slopes of the mountains meet the coastal plain. In autumn 1981 82,000 Honey Buzzards were counted near Kafar Kasem, including 27,500 on 12 September. On 11 September 1982 some 124,000 individuals were counted in the same place, out of the total of 320,000 seen in the autumn of that year; while on 5 and 6 September 1984 212,000 were counted there, out of the total of 380,000 counted that year.

In spring the Honey Buzzards are late returning, passing through Eilat from mid-April to the end of May. At first only adult birds are seen, and the younger ones begin to arrive only in the second week of May, continuing into June. The peak of the spring migration occurs in mid-May. In 1977 between 16 April and 17 May, about a quarter of a million Honey Buzzards were counted in Eilat; and on 6 May 1983 some 220,000 individuals were counted there in a single day. They begin to migrate early in the morning and usually proceed by means of dynamic, rather than gliding flight. Only a small percentage of them are seen in the area of Ein Gedi and further north; it seems that the main route veers away from Eilat in a northeasterly direction.

White-tailed Eagle
Haliaeetus albicilla

Apart from vultures, the largest raptor seen in this country: body length 70-90 cm, wing length 55-71 cm, wingspan 200-240 cm and weight 4-5.5 kg; the larger dimensions are those of the female, the smaller those of the male. The overall colour is brown-grey, and the head is large, solid and light-coloured. The yellow bill is large and strong. The wings are long and broad, the tail short and wedge-shaped and the neck relatively long. The adult is distinguished in flight by the white tail — a clear recognition mark. The tail of the immature is brown.

This species is a representative of a cosmopolitan genus comprising eight species. The range of the White-tailed Eagle is trans-Palaearctic, extending from the shores of Greenland through Europe into Asia. It is found on sea-coasts, the shores of lakes, broad rivers and large marshes. It is a monotypic species.

This eagle's diet is mainly fish, but it also preys on Coots and other aquatic birds such as divers, ducks and gulls. Small mammals, including rabbits and young deer, are sometimes hunted, and it also consumes dead fish and other carrion.

A few populations of the White-tailed Eagle are resident, although in cold winters they roam to a considerable extent. The population from northeast Europe migrates and winters especially around the Black Sea and the Persian Gulf, and isolated vagrants from this group are occasionally seen in Israel. Since the mid-1970s a few individuals, usually not more than one or two, have wintered almost every year in this country, especially in the Hula Valley and around Lake Tiberias. Most sightings occur in December and January.

Until the mid-1950s there were two pairs breeding in Israel: one in the foothills of Mount Gilboa and the other in the Hula Valley. They became extinct through poisoning from rodenticides. Laying by these pairs took place in January. There are usually 2 eggs in the clutch, and the incubation period is about 38 days. The chicks remain in the nest for about 70 days and gain sexual maturity at five to six years of age.

There have been attempts in Israel to revive the population of the species. In the mid-1970s a breeding nucleus was established at the Center for Wildlife Research near the University of Tel Aviv, and a pair has bred successfully there since 1976, raising two or three offspring every year. In 1980 a pair reared in this environment was brought to the acclimatisation enclosure in the Hula Reserve, in the hope that they would breed and settle in the reserve when released from captivity; at the time of writing (1986), these hopes have not yet been realised.

Pallas's Fish Eagle
Haliaeetus leucoryphus

An individual of this Asiatic sea-eagle, which breeds from the region of the Caspian Sea to central China and Mongolia, was observed several times in the winter of 1980/81 in the rift valley.

Bearded Vulture or Lammergeier
Gypaetus barbatus

One of the largest and most impressive birds of prey: body length 100-115 cm, wing length 77-87 cm, wingspan 265-280 cm and weight 4.5-8 kg. The female is slightly larger than the male, but in the field it is difficult to distinguish between them. The Bearded Vulture has a long, wedge-shaped tail, rounded at the tip. Its wings are long, narrow and pointed. The back and wings are bluish-black with a silver tint, the underparts are rusty-ginger (adult) or dark brown (immature). The bill is long and powerful. In flight the Bearded Vulture has a distinctive cross-shaped silhouette.

The Bearded Vulture is restricted to mountainous areas in the southern Palaearctic region and in East Africa: from the Atlas and the Pyrenees, through the Alps and the Caucasus to the Himalayas, and from Sudan and Ethiopia to South Africa. It lives below sea-level in the Judean Desert and up to 4,500 m above sea-level in the Himalayas. Three or four subspecies have been identified. The one known in Israel is *G.b. aureus*, whose range extends from southern Europe to central Asia. In Israel this is a very rare resident.

The Bearded Vulture is a carrion-eater, specialising in eating the remnants that others leave behind, in particular bones and bone-marrow, which sometimes constitute four-fifths of its diet. It will tackle bones that exceed its swallowing capacity, dropping them from a height of 50-80 m to break them into more manageable portions. It also eats tortoises, which it drops onto rocks to break the shells, and sometimes preys on live animals such as Rock Doves, partridges, pheasants, rabbits, hares and even reptiles.

According to Tristram, in the middle of the last century Bearded Vultures were breeding in Nahal Amud near Lake Tiberias and in the cliffs of the Arbel in that region. Today they are known to inhabit only the canyons of the Judean Desert and a few other areas, including the mountains around

Eilat. (Another two or three pairs are known in southern Sinai.) The nest is built in a crevice or a short tunnel, shaded from above, and always on high and inaccessible cliff-faces. It is constructed of long, thick branches. In Israel, laying takes place as early as December. There are usually 2 eggs, and incubation lasts 55-60 days. Only rarely do two chicks actually hatch, and from observations in captive conditions it is known that, when they do, the female kills the younger offspring. There are no recorded instances of two chicks surviving in the wild. The female broods the chick for about three weeks after hatching. The chick develops slowly, and flies from the nest at the age of 100-110 days. Sexual maturity is reached at five years.

In 1982, in the whole of the State of Israel only two pairs apparently remained, both of them in the Judean Desert, and neither pair nested in that year; an isolated individual was seen on cliffs in the central Negev and another in the mountains of Eilat. This was repeated in 1983 and 1984. Recently a pair of Bearded Vultures imported from abroad has been taken to the Center for Wildlife Research near the University of Tel Aviv, to form a breeding nucleus.

Egyptian Vulture
Neophron percnopterus

A mainly black and white raptor: body length 65 cm (including about 20 cm for the tail), wing length 49 cm, wingspan 150-170 cm and weight 2.1 kg. The adult Egyptian Vulture appears as a dirty-white bird. The yellow bill is relatively slender and thin and the legs long and pink. The primaries and secondaries are black and in flight the long and wedge-shaped tail is conspicuous. The immature is dark brown.

The range of the Egyptian Vulture extends sporadically over southern Europe, southwestern Asia and central India, and also North Africa and the strip of savanna to the north and east of tropical Africa. Throughout its range, except in India, lives a single subspecies *N.p. percnopterus*. The populations in India, southern Arabia and sub-Saharan Africa are resident. Those in southern Europe and the Mediterranean countries migrate in autumn to winter in the sub-Saharan belt, from Senegal to Ethiopia. In Israel the Egyptian Vulture is a fairly common migrant and summer resident in all parts of the country, and also an occasional winterer, especially in the Negev.

The Egyptian Vulture is a carrion-eater and its thin and delicate bill is well suited to pecking among bones for the remaining scraps. It is also a prominent eater of refuse and may be seen on kitchen refuse-tips together with kites and ravens. The Egyptian Vulture is also liable to prey on slow-moving creatures such as turtles, which it kills by dropping them on the ground in a manner reminiscent of the Bearded Vulture. It is also apt to crack small eggs by dropping them to the ground, and in one case an Egyptian Vulture was observed trying to break a tennis ball in this manner.

Egyptian Vultures are gregarious outside the nesting season. Sometimes they may be seen in scores, young and adult birds together, beside a carcase or a refuse-heap. In the region of Sede Boker in the central Negev, one of the most important population centres of the Egyptian Vulture in Israel today, groups numbering up to 180 individuals were regularly seen in June-July 1982.

The autumn passage of the European populations is barely perceptible, because most individuals apparently migrate east of the Jordan; only in mid-September is it possible to see scores of individuals passing every day. The spring migration is more conspicuous, extending from early February and sometimes from late January to mid-May, especially between mid-March and the end of April. Up to mid-April almost all the birds seen are adults, and from the end of April most are immatures. During the spring of 1977 some 800 Egyptian Vultures passed through Eilat, although not more than 20 in a day. Along the coasts of the Dead Sea more migrating individuals are liable to be seen, sometimes as many as 100 in one day. Apparently most Egyptian Vultures do not cross the Gulf of Suez on their spring migration, but skirt it to the north near the town of Suez, gliding over the breadth of northern Sinai and the central Negev and reaching the cliffs of the Dead Sea coasts.

Until the widescale poisoning of agricultural fields in the mid-1950s and early 1960s the Egyptian Vulture was fairly common, breeding on every cliff worthy of the name and congregating in scores on refuse-heaps throughout the country. Since then its numbers have declined considerably, although since the early 1970s there has been a perceptible recovery in its populations. In 1982 a total of about 90 pairs were breeding in the country, and in 1984 32 active nests were identified in the Negev and in the Judean Desert.

The summering population reaches its nesting sites in the Negev as early as the second half of February, but those breeding in the Golan do not arrive there until the end of March. Egyptian Vultures do not breed in colonies, but in 1982 five pairs were breeding in Nahal Gamla in the Golan Heights on a cliff-face about 2.5 km in length, and in 1984 13 pairs were breeding within a distance of 13 km on cliffs in the central Negev. The nest is usually built in a rock-crevice and is constructed of coarse branches and lined with scraps of refuse or remnants of food. Two eggs are laid between the end of March and the end of April. Incubation, by both parents, lasts 40-42 days. In most cases recorded in Israel, only one chick developed to the fledging stage. The chick is feathered at about 40 days old, and flies from the nest at 70-80 days. Sexual maturity is reached at the age of four to five years. Between mid-September and the end of October the Egyptian Vultures abandon their nesting areas and migrate southward.

Griffon Vulture
Gyps fulvus

The genus *Gyps* comprises seven species, and is the typical representative of Old World vultures. The Griffon Vulture is one of the largest raptors: body length 100-114 cm, wing length 68-72 cm, wingspan up to 280 cm and weight 5.3-8 kg. The male is slightly larger than the female, which is atypical among raptors. A standing Griffon Vulture appears grey-brown, only the neck and head being white. In flight there is a striking contrast between the light body, undertail-coverts and wing-coverts and the dark tail and wing feathers. The juvenile is similar in size to its parents but differs from them in its chestnut-brown colouring. At two years old the collar is still brown, and its colour gradually lightens from the age of three and becomes white at about five years old, when the bird also attains sexual maturity.

The range of the Griffon Vulture extends sporadically from southern Europe through Turkey and Iran to central Asia, with some penetration into northern India and a few small and isolated pockets in North Africa. In this range two subspecies have been identified, the western one being *G.f. fulvus*. The Griffon Vulture inhabits areas of steppe and desert with mountainous landscapes and high cliffs. Most of its populations are resident, but those in the Balkans and Turkey migrate southward in autumn. There are records of Griffon Vultures wintering in Egypt and Sudan. In Israel the Griffon Vulture is a resident, although there are also small wintering and migrant populations.

The Griffon Vulture feeds exclusively on carrion. Its bill is large, strong and sharp, and its neck is long, enabling it to penetrate the interior of the carcase. Its head and neck are bare of feathers. The Griffon Vulture's relatively short and blunt claws make movement on the ground and hopping easier, and its long and broad wings are suited to gliding over wide distances in the search for food. It has a large crop capable of expanding to a considerable extent. The Griffon Vulture is a social bird, breeding and roosting in colonies on high cliffs, inaccessible to both human and other predators. The birds normally return to their colonies an hour or two before sunset. Often they do not roost in the nest, but beside it. The roosting area, which is also the nesting site, is usually retained for many years, and in Spain and South Africa colonies are known which have existed for centuries. In Israel, for reasons which have yet to become clear but perhaps because of the abundance of external parasites, Griffon Vultures change the site of their colonies from time to time.

The autumn migration takes place in September-November, when up to 40 individuals are sometimes seen together. In spring the passage migrants return, especially between the end of February and the end of March.

Populations of Griffon Vultures are in decline in almost all areas, including Israel. In the middle of the last century there was a large number of colonies in this country, each containing more than 100 pairs: in Nahal Amud and in the cliffs of the Arbel, both near Lake Tiberias, in the gorges of Mount Carmel and elsewhere. In the 1940s there were still 65 breeding pairs in three colonies in the Carmel, but of these colonies no trace remains today. Currently, a group of 10-12 pairs is reckoned a large colony. The most serious damage to Griffon Vulture populations has been caused by the use of agricultural pesticides: strychnine to poison jackals, thallium sulphate to kill rodents, and more recently alpha-chloralose to destroy wild boars. In August 1972, 13 Griffon Vultures were found dead after poisoning of wild boars in the Golan. In summer 1980, 23 were found in the Golan suffering from the effects of pesticides; only four of them recovered after treatment and were released. An additional threat is posed by high-tension cables: between 1981 and early 1985, 61 Griffon Vultures have been found killed by electrocution, most of them in the Golan and a few in Upper Galilee. In 1984 only 68 pairs were breeding in Israel, at 15 sites. There is also a non-breeding population: in December 1980 some 150 Griffons were counted in the Golan, and about 200 in the same area on 5 November 1982 (some of these may have been only winterers). Today the wadis of the Golan are the principal refuge of Griffon Vultures in Israel, with secondary refuges in the canyons of the Judean Desert and some cliffs in the northern Negev, an area in which 29 nests were counted in 1984; additional colonies are located in some wadis in Upper Galilee.

Courtship usually begins in early January. A Griffon Vulture's nest is a clumsy collection of branches and grass, which requires constant repair. The female lays only 1 egg, usually as early as the beginning of January, sometimes as late as the end of March. Incubation lasts 52-56 days, and both partners brood the eggs and young. The parents warm the chick to the age of about a month and a half, and it is not left alone in the nest until it reaches 70 days old. At the age of 80-90 days the chick is capable of flying short distances from the nest, but returns to it regularly. Its final flight from the nest and attainment of independence comes at the age of 100-125 days.

In order to encourage populations of Griffon Vultures, a number of feeding-stations have been set up in the country, and birds reared in captivity have also been released

Lappet-faced Vulture
Torgos tracheliotus

The Lappet-faced Vulture is a large and powerful bird: body length 103-118 cm, wing length 75-82 cm, wingspan 255-290 cm and weight 11-14 kg. It has dark brown plumage, appearing black at a distance. Its bald neck and head are greyish-pink, with protruding folds of pink skin resembling earlobes. Its head is large, and its bill much larger than that of the Griffon Vulture. In flight, it appears almost entirely dark. The subspecies found in Israel, *T.t. negevensis*, differs from the African race as follows: it is larger and heavier; the nape and neck have only a few folds of skin, which are greyish with only those of the nape being pink; and there is no white bar on the leading edge of the underwing.

The Lappet-faced Vulture is an African bird, breeding south of the Sahara. It ceased to breed in North Africa in the last century, and since the 1930s it has been extinct in Egypt. In early 1983 it was discovered that a population of this species numbering scores of pairs was breeding in the mountains of the Arabian peninsula, some 800 km from Eilat. The Lappet-faced Vulture reaches Israel at the northernmost point of its range, and this is a population distant and separate from the main population. On account of its geographical separation, the population found in the Negev has been classified as a distinct and endemic subspecies *T.t. negevensis*.

Unlike Bearded and Griffon Vultures, the Lappet-faced Vulture never feeds at refuse-heaps. It eats fish, small bones and pieces of skin, and from examination of pellets it is evident that goat carcasses constitute the major proportion of its diet in this country. On 2 May 1964, 22 Lappet-faced Vultures were observed around a camel carcase south of Hazeva. The Lappet-faced Vulture is also capable of killing small and weak animals, especially when other food is in short supply. In Africa it takes flamingo chicks and young deer, while in the western Negev it has been observed following the plough and catching

rodents disturbed from their burrows. In the nests of these vultures remnants of rabbits, lambs and lizards have been found, either caught by the bird or taken as road casualties.

The range of the Lappet-faced Vulture in Israel is limited mainly to the rift valley between Eilat and Hazeva. In the 1940s 25-30 pairs were breeding in this area. Even in the mid-1950s there was still an impressive number of large nests in acacia trees, and a few pairs were also breeding in the central Negev. This population used to roam after the end of nesting and in early autumn, and as a result a few individuals were sometimes seen in the western Negev, where a nesting attempt was recorded in 1966 near Shirta. The decline in the population of Lappet-faced Vultures began in the 1950s: shooting by soldiers (over the years, eight individuals have been found shot), shortage of food, and injury by high-tension cables are among the reasons for this decline. Poisoning in the fields of the western Negev is in all probability a further factor.

Until they reach maturity the young birds travel far from the region of the Arava. As early as the beginning of the century a juvenile was caught near Nebi Musa, and another was caught in Jericho in 1938. Hunting of the immature vagrants has destroyed the 'reserve force' and so, within the space of a few years, the population of Lappet-faced Vultures has withered: in 1965, ten pairs were still known; in 1975, six breeding pairs and one non-breeding pair were identified. In 1979 only four pairs were breeding and in 1981 only three, producing only one chick between them. In 1983 a single pair laid an egg which proved to be infertile, while in 1984 only two pairs attempted to nest and neither was successful.

There is no doubt that Israel's population of Lappet-faced Vultures has reached the threshold of extinction, and it may already have crossed it. In order to prevent its total extinction, a breeding nucleus has been established at the Center for Wildlife Research near the University of Tel Aviv. As early as 1975, three chicks were taken from nests in the Negev, and in 1981 and 1982 more chicks were taken. In 1982 an egg was taken and successfully hatched in an incubator, and in early 1985 another egg was taken; in both cases the female proceeded to lay another egg. It is still too early to judge whether these efforts will bear fruit.

Lappet-faced Vultures move to their nesting areas as early as September, and the building or renovation of the nest begins in November or December. The nest is sited at the top of a tree, usually an acacia. It is built of long and crude branches and lined with hair, grass and the branches of shrubs such as broom. It is not placed horizontally, but is tilted towards the southwest to absorb the rays of sunlight at dawn. One egg is laid, from early September to the end of February. The period of incubation is 52-56 days. The chick usually hatches at the end of February or in early March. For the first 10-15 days both parents feed it bill-to-bill with semi-digested food; later, the food is regurgitated into the nest. The chick flies from the nest at the age of 90-100 days, but returns to it regularly over a period of two to four weeks. At about the end of May, at 120 days old, it finally leaves the nest, but stays close to its parents for a further month or two.

Black Vulture
Aegypius monachus

The largest raptor occurring in Israel: body length up to 110 cm, wing length 74-84 cm, wingspan 295 cm and weight up to 13 kg. It is distinguished from the Griffon and Lappet-faced Vultures by its all-dark plumage, the blue-grey colour of the bare skin on the face and neck, and by its arched wings when gliding.

This is the most northerly of the Palaearctic vultures, with a range extending from Spain to Tibet and Mongolia. Its monotypic population is small and restricted, and mostly resident; only juveniles and immatures roam and migrate.

In Israel the Black Vulture is a very rare migrant in October-November and in February. In recent years it has sometimes occurred also in winter. Some sightings have been recorded in the Valley of the Arava and in hills in the Negev, but it has wintered mainly in the southern Golan: three in 1984/85 and four or five in 1985/86. According to Tristram, it was breeding in the cliffs of the Arbel near Lake Tiberias in the middle of the last century.

Short-toed Eagle
Circaetus gallicus

A large predator: body length 62-70 cm, wing length 47-53 cm, wingspan 190 cm and weight 1,100-1,600 g. The Short-toed Eagle has a large head, with large yellow eyes. Its upperparts are brown-grey, while the underparts are mainly white, lightly speckled, with the throat and upper breast darker. The wings are quite long and broad (conspicuous when gliding), the tail narrow, long (approx. 28 cm) and barred.

The range of the Short-toed Eagle extends from North Africa and southern Europe through eastern Europe and the Middle East to India and central Asia. This is a monotypic species, and all its populations, except those in India, migrate in autumn to winter in Africa in the Sahel, a broad strip south of the Sahara from Senegal to Sudan. In Israel the Short-toed Eagle is a common summer visitor and migrant, and a very rare winterer.

The Short-toed Eagle often hovers, but it also hunts from a perch. Its main prey is snakes. In the Plain of Judah it was judged that snakes normally constitute about 70% of its diet. The Short-toed Eagle supplements this fare with other reptiles such as lizards and chameleons, sometimes also toads, mice, locusts, hedgehogs and songbirds.

The autumn migration begins as early as the end of August and continues until the end of October, with the peak in the first days of October. In the autumn of 1981 some 3,750 Short-toed Eagles were counted passing through the region of Kafar Kasem about 20 km northeast of Tel Aviv, and in the following year about 7,000 individuals were counted there. The spring migration begins in early February and continues until early May, with a peak in March. The number of Short-toed Eagles migrating in spring along the cliffs of the Dead Sea is considerably larger than the number seen in Eilat, from which it is evident that the main migration route skirts the Gulf of Suez to the north (where some 500 individuals have been counted every day), and disperses over northern Sinai and the northern Negev; most of the birds travel on to the shores of the Dead Sea, although some continue northward above the western slopes of the mountain ridge. Short-toed Eagles usually migrate in small groups of three to five individuals, although sometimes 10 or as many as 30 may be seen together.

A few Short-toed Eagles winter in Israel, especially in the Negev. At the end of January 1985, a total of seven Short-toed Eagles was counted wintering in the country, three of them in the Hula Valley.

The summering Short-toed Eagles arrive in early March. Several pairs may hunt in the same area, and in the late 1970s and early 1980s it was not uncommon to observe six to eight individuals together in Nahal Dishon in Upper Galilee or on the slopes of the Judean Mountains. Short-toed Eagles prefer as their habitat an environment of hills and mountains covered with sparse vegetation. They are distributed especially in northern and central parts of the country, where they are the commonest large predators seen in the summer. A few pairs are found as far south as Negba and Nahal Ha-Besor, and even in the Judean Desert and the Negev. A nest found near the canyon not far from Eilat probably represents the southernmost breeding site in our region.

Courtship begins soon after the Short-toed Eagles return from their winter quarters. The nest is usually built on a tree and is constructed of branches and twigs and lined with thin branches and green leaves.

One egg is laid, usually at the beginning of April. The period of incubation is 45-47 days. The chick flies from the nest at 70-80 days of age, when it is best distinguished from its parents by its light brown, almost sandy-coloured plumage.

Bateleur
Terathopius ecaudatus

This is a large predator, distinguished by its unique silhouette: its tail is very short, while the wings are broad. Its style of flight is also unique, and includes very rapid wingbeats, wheeling and vertical lifts. The Bateleur has black underparts, silver-white underwing-coverts and a chestnut back and tail; the legs and bill are bright red. Immatures have dark brown plumage. It feeds on carrion and snakes.

This is the most common African predator south of the Sahara. A few individuals occur as vagrants in Asia. In Israel, a single individual was recorded in Eilat on 15 April 1982. Another was reported at Kafar Kasem on 14 September 1984, but its identification has not been confirmed.

Genus: *Circus* (harriers)
The genus *Circus* comprises ten species distributed in all continents. Four species occur in Israel, all as winter visitors or passage migrants.

Harriers hunt by gliding low above the ground, their wings held in a 'V' shape and the long and narrow tail helping them to manoeuvre. Unlike most raptor species, harriers are birds of open country, not requiring cliffs or trees. They nest on the ground, and their clutch of 8 or even 10 eggs is the largest in their family. They roost among field and marsh vegetation. The Hula Valley, the Bet She'an Valley and the western Negev are the best sites in Israel for observing wintering harriers.

Marsh Harrier
Circus aeruginosus

The largest of the harriers occurring in Israel: body length 48-56 cm, wing length 37-42 cm, wingspan 115-130 cm and weight 500-700 g. The male is mainly brown, and the female is brown with a light crown, chin and throat and inner forewing. The juvenile resembles the female, although the forewing is darker. The wings are broader than those of other harriers. A rare dark morph also exists.

Eight subspecies of Marsh Harrier have been identified, in a range extending from North Africa, Spain and the shores of the English Channel to China, northern Mongolia and Japan, and also in Madagascar and in Australasia. The populations of southern Europe and the Middle East are resident,

while all other Palaearctic populations migrate and winter in the Mediterranean countries and in the tropical areas of Asia and Africa. The subspecies *C.a. aeruginosus* is a fairly rare passage migrant but a fairly common winterer in Israel, found mainly around fish-ponds and reservoirs.

This harrier occurs mostly in marshy habitats. The female preys especially on waterfowl, including Coots and small ducks. The male preys on the songbirds found among marsh vegetation and reeds, and also on small mammals, fish, amphibians and reptiles.

The Marsh Harrier passes through this country in autumn, especially in the second half of September and in early October. In autumn 1982 some 400 individuals were counted passing over Kafar Kasem, and in autumn 1983 about 480 were counted there. The spring migration is concentrated between the end of March and early April; in spring 1977, 125 migrating individuals were counted in Eilat. This bird usually migrates singly or in small groups, sometimes separate flocks of males and females gathering together. The wintering harriers begin to arrive in the country in August, but most come in early October. The last individuals — winterers or passage migrants — are still to be seen in mid-May.

Before the poisonings of the 1950s, the Marsh Harrier was a very common winterer in marshes and fish-ponds throughout the country, but since then it has become considerably more rare. In the 1960s only a few wintered in the country, although there has subsequently been some recovery in the population and in the late 1970s and early 1980s several scores of individuals were wintering every year, especially around fish-ponds. In the winter of 1975/76, eight individuals were killed by pesticides in the fields of the Hula Valley. In the winter of 1982, at a roost in the Hula Valley, there were some 40 Marsh Harriers together with about 50 harriers of other species. In 1983, 95 individuals were counted in the whole country. Most Marsh Harriers seen in Israel are females or immatures.

Until the draining of the Hula marshes, 10-15 pairs of Marsh Harriers were breeding there. These birds were exceptional in that males and females were similar, and it is possible that they were members of a separate and unique subspecies which was exterminated before it could be identified (a similar phenomenon exists among Marsh Harriers breeding in Iraq). Even in recent years Marsh Harriers have occasionally been seen in Israel during the nesting season; courtship displays have been observed in the Hula Reserve, in the Golan, on the shores of Lake Tiberias, near the reservoir of Kishon and on the River Yarkon, but no nests have yet been found.

Hen Harrier
Circus cyaneus

Body length 44-52 cm, wing length 36 cm, wingspan 110 cm and weight 310-450 g. The male is grey above, with a white rump and black wingtips. Females and immatures are brown, with a white rump, a barred tail, and a dark line across the throat. The Hen Harrier has broader wings and a heavier build than Pallid and Montagu's Harriers.

This harrier breeds in isolated pockets in most parts of Europe, and also in northern areas of Asia and in North and South America. In this range four subspecies have been identified. The one occurring in Israel is *C.c. cyaneus*, which breeds in Eurasia. The populations of western and central Europe are resident, while northern and eastern populations winter especially in southern and western Europe and the Middle East. Israel is situated on the fringe of the wintering areas.

The Hen Harrier begins to arrive in the second half of October and stays until early April, although most individuals are present in the country between November and February. A very few winter in the Nile Delta, apparently passing through Eilat in October and April. In surveys in Kafar Kasem between 1981 and 1983, about ten individuals were recorded every autumn. Even before the pesticide poisonings of the 1950s this was not a particularly common bird. In recent years a few score individuals have wintered in plains areas and particularly in the Hula Valley — in the reserve, where they roost, and in the surrounding fields. After the Marsh Harrier, this is the harrier most often seen in northern and central Israel, but it also winters in the fields of the western Negev; in January 1985, 27 Hen Harriers were counted in this latter region, out of an estimated national total of 100.

Pallid Harrier
Circus macrourus

Body length 40-48 cm, wing length of male 33-35 cm and of female 35-39 cm, wingspan approx. 110 cm and weight 300-420 g. In flight the male appears very pale below, only a few of the primaries being black; from above, it is a uniform grey-blue with black outer primaries. Females and immatures are difficult to distinguish from those of Montagu's Harrier.

This is a monotypic species which breeds in eastern Europe and the plains of central Asia, and winters in a few places in the eastern Mediterranean basin, in India and Burma and especially in tropical Africa. In Israel it is quite a common migrant and a fairly rare winterer.

The Pallid Harrier prefers plains and open spaces

to a greater extent than do other species of harrier. It feeds on small rodents, birds such as larks and pipits, and also lizards and insects.

Passage migrants occur in September-October and in March-April. Surveys in Kafar Kasem produce between 10 and 40 individuals every year. On spring migration it is hardly seen at all in Eilat, but is observed on the shores of the Dead Sea and further north. Winterers are seen most often in the fields of the western Negev: in January 1985 22 were counted in this area, out of a national total of 39.

Montagu's Harrier
Circus pygargus

Body length 45 cm, wing length 35-39 cm, wingspan 110 cm and weight 250-420 g. In flight the male appears white below with all primaries black and narrow dark bars across the secondaries; from above, it is bluish-grey with black primaries, and a dark stripe separating the secondaries from their coverts (the best identifying mark). Females and immatures are very similar to those of Pallid Harrier.

This is a monotypic species which breeds across Europe from Spain and the Low Countries to central Asia, and winters in India and tropical Africa.

Montagu's Harrier prefers marsh and fenland habitats. It feeds on frogs, lizards and locusts.

In Israel this harrier is quite common as a passage migrant, especially in September and April, and a rare winterer. It is seen mostly in the south of the country: in the southern coastal plain and the western Negev.

Genus: *Accipiter* (hawks)

The genus *Accipiter* comprises 47 species and has a cosmopolitan distribution. Three species occur as migrants or winter visitors in Israel.

Hawks are distinguished from other raptors by their broad and rounded wings and by their long tail. Their legs are long and thin. The female is considerably larger than the male.

Sparrowhawk
Accipiter nisus

Body length 30-39 cm (of which about half is accounted for by the tail, up to 15 cm in the male and 18 cm in the female); wing length of male 20.5 cm and of female 24 cm; wingspan of male 55 cm and of female 70 cm; weight of male 150 g and of female 240 g. The male is grey above, with rusty-orange barring on the underparts. The female is brown-grey above, barred with brown-grey below. The wings of the male are more pointed, while the tail is distinctively barred in both sexes and in immatures.

The Sparrowhawk has a trans-Palaearctic range,

and is distributed throughout Europe and into central and northern Asia. Six subspecies are known. Most of its European populations, which belong to the race *A.n. nisus*, are resident, but those from northern areas migrate to winter in the countries of the Mediterranean basin, in the Middle East, on the shores of the Red Sea, and along the Nile as far as Sudan.

The Sparrowhawk is a woodland bird, preferring forests interspersed with clearings, plantations and sparse groves. It feeds almost exclusively on small birds, which it catches in the air or 'plucks' from the undergrowth with its long legs. Sometimes it catches large winged insects and is even tempted by rodents on the ground — hence the secondary poisoning of the wintering hawks in the 1950s. In the years following the temporary extermination of the wintering population, the numbers of pigeons, bulbuls and some other birds increased significantly. It is logical to suppose that there is a link between these two phenomena, although since the renewed proliferation of wintering Sparrowhawks there has so far been no sign of a corresponding decline in these species.

The Sparrowhawk passes through Israel in autumn, especially during October, and in spring, from the second half of March to the beginning of May. In Kafar Kasem several hundred individuals are counted every year (219 in 1981, 513 in 1983). The number counted in Eilat during the spring migration is smaller (155 individuals in 1977).

Until the 1950s the Sparrowhawk was a very common winter resident, and in areas of suitable terrain it was possible to see one individual for every 1-2 square kilometres; it was also quite common as a migrant. The widespread use of agricultural pesticides in the 1950s destroyed the wintering population completely, for more than ten years. Evidence that wintering individuals tend to remain loyal to the same area is shown by a specimen ringed in the Jezreel Valley in 1941, and caught nearby in Kibbutz Sha'ar Ha'Amakim in 1954.

Since the early 1970s, Sparrowhawks have again begun to winter in this country, being seen from the end of September or early October to April. Their number has gradually risen, reaching several hundreds by the early 1980s. They are usually solitary, but tend to roost communally, especially in pine groves. It appears that more females than males winter in Israel.

Goshawk
Accipiter gentilis

Similar to the Sparrowhawk but larger: body length 48-62 cm (including 20 cm for tail), wing length

31 cm in male and 35 cm in female, wingspan 140-160 cm, weight of male approx. 700 g and of female 1,200 g.

The Goshawk breeds across the Holarctic region: in Europe, Asia and North America. In this area seven to nine subspecies are known. Most of its Palaearctic populations are resident. In Israel it is a rare passage migrant and a fairly rare winter visitor.

The Goshawk sometimes hunts in more open habitats than the Sparrowhawk, but normally prefers coniferous forests with tall trees. Its prey — large songbirds and mammals — is usually caught on the ground.

Over the years only a few have been recorded in the country, between mid-October and mid-May, most between December and February. In a national survey of wintering raptors conducted at the end of January 1985, five individuals were counted.

Levant Sparrowhawk
Accipiter brevipes

Body length 32-38 cm, wing length of male 22 cm and of female 23.5 cm, wingspan 65-75 cm, weight of male 170 g and of female 240 g. Similar to a large extent to the Sparrowhawk, both in size and in coloration, with the following distinctive marks: the male's cheeks are grey rather than rufous-brown; when gliding overhead, the black wingtips contrast conspicuously with the pale underwing, and the tail bars are more in number (six to seven, as opposed to four to five on Sparrowhawk) and more narrow. The female also differs from the female Sparrowhawk in having grey rather than brown upperparts. Both

sexes differ from Sparrowhawk in having red-brown irises (yellow in Sparrowhawk).

The Levant Sparrowhawk is a monotypic species with a limited range, breeding in the Balkans, southern Russia, Turkey and Iran; its principal habitats are grasslands, steppe and mountain slopes, also plantations and broadleaved forests. All populations winter in tropical Africa. In Israel it is a common passage migrant; up to the end of the 1950s it was also an occasional winter resident.

The Levant Sparrowhawk migrates in dense flocks numbering hundreds and even thousands of individuals, but most fly so fast and at such an altitude that it is hard to identify them. In autumn this species migrates especially above the western slopes of the mountain ridge, while in spring most pass over the eastern slopes. The duration of passage is short and restricted to certain periods of the year. The autumn migration reaches a climax in the third week of September: in this week in 1981, in Kafar Kasem, between 1,000 and 3,000 individuals were counted every day, out of a total of 16,500 counted there that autumn; and in autumn 1983 25,300 were counted, 6,120 of them on 26 September. The spring passage peak usually occurs at the beginning of the third week of April; in Eilat, some 6,000 individuals have been seen to pass in the space of a few days (1977 data).

A Levant Sparrowhawk ringed in Eilat was found two years later in Romania.

Dark Chanting Goshawk
Melierax metabates

Body length 38-45 cm, wing length 31 cm, wingspan 105 cm and weight approx. 500 g. A bird which in appearance combines characteristics of a hawk and a buzzard. Its overall colour is grey, with the tips of the primaries black; the tail is long (about 21 cm) and black, barred broadly below. It is distinguished by the reddish-orange cere and legs. The juvenile is generally brown, with a pale rump.

This is a bird of Ethiopian origin, inhabiting savanna environments in tropical Africa. Small pockets, discrete from the main population, exist in the Spanish Sahara and on the shores of Yemen and Saudi Arabia.

A single individual was seen on 20 April 1979 about 20 km north of Jericho.

Genus: *Buteo* (buzzards)
The genus *Buteo* comprises 24 species, inhabiting all continents except Australasia and Antarctica. Buzzards are medium-sized raptors with broad wings and broad tails. They occur in several different colour phases.

Long-legged Buzzard
Buteo rufinus

A predator of average size: body length 48-62 cm, wing length 37-46.5 cm, wingspan 145 cm and weight 780-1,250 g. The female is up to one-fifth larger than the male. The Long-legged Buzzard is a typical representative of its genus. In appearance it resembles an eagle, being a heavy-set bird with short neck and broad wings. When standing it is distinguished by the relatively long legs, which unlike those of the typical eagle are not feathered. The most common colour phase is rusty-brown, with cream-coloured head and light and unbarred tail; less typical is the 'chocolate' phase, which is chestnut-brown and sometimes appears almost black (in Israel only one instance of nesting by this type has been recorded: a pair bred in the early 1960s in Nahal Kadesh, in eastern Upper Galilee). In flight the Long-legged Buzzard shows white patches in the centre of the wings, a feature which it shares with the Honey Buzzard and the Buzzard. A gliding Long-legged Buzzard differs from the Honey Buzzard in that its wings are raised above the level of the body (those of the Honey Buzzard tend to be tilted downwards). It differs from the Common Buzzard in its uniformly light tail which lacks the Buzzard's characteristic barring; in the dark markings on the sides of the belly; and most of all in the head, which is pale and almost white.

The Long-legged Buzzard has a southern Palaearctic range, and is the ecological counterpart in this area of the Buzzard, whose range is trans-Palaearctic and more northerly. The subspecies seen in Israel, *B.r. rufinus*, breeds in the Balkans, Turkey, Israel, northern Syria, Iraq, in Iran around the Caspian Sea and further east to central Asia, Turkestan and Tibet. A second subspecies breeds in North Africa. Most populations of the Long-legged Buzzard are resident. Only those from the region of the Caspian Sea and central Asia migrate, wintering in a broad band extending from Turkey, through Iraq and Iran to northern India, also in the Levant and along the Nile, and from Somalia and Sudan to Chad. In Israel this is a common resident, an uncommon passage migrant and an occasional winter visitor; most individuals seen in the country are resident.

The preferred habitat of the Long-legged Buzzard ranges from mountainous landscapes with sparse vegetation to steppe environments, partially exposed. It spends much of its time perched on vantage points, but often glides in search of its prey. Most individuals feed on a widely varied diet: small mammals, such as young rabbits, rodents and rats, various reptiles including lizards, and songbirds, insects and locusts.

Only a few are recorded on passage. In autumn 1981, 19 migrating Long-legged Buzzards were counted in Kafar Kasem, with similar numbers in subsequent surveys. In spring 1977, 29 individuals were counted in Eilat. In a census of wintering raptors in 1985, 21 were seen in the western Negev and 76 in the country as a whole (some of these may have been residents).

Today, the Long-legged Buzzard is one of the commonest breeding raptors in Israel, nesting from the slopes of Mount Hermon, through the canyons of the Golan, the valleys of Galilee, Carmel, Samaria and the Judean Hills to the Judean Desert, to the central Negev and the Arava. Like other raptors, it was hard hit by the pesticide poisonings of the early 1950s, although it has recovered with greater success than other species. In 1979 some 60 pairs bred in northern and central Israel, and this population has remained stable since then. In 1984 27 pairs nested in the Negev and the Judean Desert alone, with an estimated ten further pairs in the vicinity.

Long-legged Buzzards usually live in pairs, each in a territory of 6-8 km². Courtship activity usually begins in February, when the pair performs undulating display flights while emitting short and sharp mewing sounds. The nest, normally on a cliff although sometimes in a tree, is about 80 cm in diameter, built of rough twigs and branches and lined with pieces of wool and other soft materials. The 2-4 eggs are usually laid in March, but sometimes not until April. The incubation period is about 28 days, and the chicks fly from the nest about 45 days after hatching.

Buzzard
Buteo buteo

Smaller than the Long-legged Buzzard: body length 59-70 cm, wing length 36-40 cm, wingspan 120 cm and weight 480-900 g. The female is 5-10% larger than the male.

This buzzard has a trans-Palaearctic range and breeds throughout Eurasia, from Spain and Britain to Japan, north of the range of the Long-legged Buzzard. Five to eleven subspecies have been identified. After the Kestrel, it is reckoned the most common bird of prey in Europe. In Israel it is a migrant and a winterer.

Almost all the Buzzards seen in Israel belong to the eastern subspecies *B.b. vulpinus*, which breeds in northern and eastern Europe and in central Asia. The other subspecies are resident or migrate only short distances, whereas the Western Palaearctic population of *B.b. vulpinus* winters in Africa — from Ethiopia through East Africa to the Cape. This subspecies has three different colour-phases, the most common being a rusty-brown colour closely similar to the Long-legged Buzzard. It is hard to distinguish the two species in the field, except by the paler head and neck of the Long-legged Buzzard and its darker belly, visible in flight, while the Buzzard has uniform rufous underparts.

In autumn this is not a particularly common migrant. Its principal passage takes place in September, but the route passes over the eastern side of the Jordan or along the Syro-African rift. In surveys in Kafar Kasem, on the western watershed of Israel, only a few individuals have been counted. In the spring, however, this is the commonest of all the migrating raptors seen in Eilat: in 1977, between 20 February and 16 May, some 320,000 individuals were counted there, about a third of them passing within the space of three days in the first half of April; on 29 March 1980, more than 100,000 Buzzards were counted there. In spring this species is also seen in large numbers in other parts of Israel, especially on the eastern slopes of the watershed.

Before the large-scale poisonings of the 1950s, the Buzzard was considerably more common in winter in these and in other areas. In the late 1970s and early 1980s it had become a quite rare winter visitor to Israel; only in the fields of the Hula Valley and the western Negev were scores of individuals seen. Its wintering population has gradually increased in recent years, and in January 1985 some 280 individuals were counted throughout the country, about 100 of them in the Hula Valley and 100 on the central coastal plain.

To date three ringed Buzzards have been recovered in Israel: two had been ringed in Finland, and the other in the region of Kazakhstan in Soviet Asia.

Rough-legged Buzzard
Buteo lagopus

Body length 50-60 cm, wing length 40.5-45 cm, wingspan 120-150 cm and weight 700-1,300 g. The female is larger than the male. Differs from Buzzard in that the tail is white and tipped with a black band. In flight from below, it appears mostly white with black patches on the sides of the belly and at the carpals and black wingtips. The head is paler than that of most species of buzzard. Its legs are feathered, in which respect it resembles some species of eagle. The Rough-legged Buzzard is also distinguished from other buzzards by its longer wings.

The Rough-legged Buzzard has a Holarctic range — more northerly than that of the Buzzard — and breeds in areas of tundra and sparse taiga. There are four subspecies. Its Palaearctic population winters in a band extending through Europe and Asia between latitudes 43°N and 55°N.

In Israel this is an extremely rare accidental. One was recorded in December 1984 in the central coastal plain, and another, possibly the same individual, was seen on 26 January 1985 in the southern coastal plain.

Genus: *Aquila* (eagles)

Members of the genus *Aquila* are the true eagles. They are large birds, and the females are 10-20% larger than the males. Their legs are strong and feathered to the toes. Their wings are large, long and broad, and their tail is rounded. The bill is large, strong and hooked. Members of this genus have a bone projecting above the eye-socket, covering the eye like a rim — hence the typically menacing expression of the face.

This genus, comprising nine species, inhabits all parts of the world with the exception of South America and Antarctica. In Israel six species are represented, of which one is resident, three are passage migrants and sometimes winterers, and two are rare accidentals.

Golden Eagle
Aquila chrysaetos

The Golden Eagle is a very large raptor: body length 75-88 cm, wing length 59-68 cm, wingspan 204-220 cm, weight of male 3-4 kg and of female 3.8-6 kg. The female is up to 20% larger than the male. This is the most conspicuous and familiar representative of the genus *Aquila*. It is mainly dark brown, while the crown and nape feathers and the wing-coverts are a pale to rusty-golden colour. The immature is darker, with the gold-tinted crown and nape even more conspicuous, and is also distinguished by the white tail, tipped with black, and, in flight, by a white stripe along the spread wing. The feet and toes and the cere are yellow. Although the White-tailed Eagle is larger, the Golden Eagle is the most powerful raptor of the Holarctic region, owing to its body structure and musculature, and in particular its long and strong toes and claws: the rear toe is 6.5 cm long and equipped with a claw 5 cm in length; no other raptor can compare with these dimensions. In flight the long wings are distinctive. Their edges, seen from below, are usually not parallel to one another, but are curved in an 'S' shape. When gliding, they are held above the level of the body, in a very shallow 'V' shape, sometimes barely perceptible. As the neck is relatively long, the head protrudes appreciably. The tail is also long, almost as long as the width of the wing.

The Golden Eagle has a Holarctic range, and is found in most areas of Europe and Asia, and also in North America where it is the only representative of the true eagles. In the Palaearctic region its range extends from the Sahara and the shores of the Mediterranean to the tundra of northeast Asia; Israel is at the southern limits of this range. Six subspecies have been identified, the one found in Israel being *A.c. homeyeri*, which is distributed from Spain and North Africa east through Turkey to Iran. The Golden Eagle prefers semi-exposed environments: mountain slopes, rocky foothills and river valleys. Most populations are resident.

These eagles live throughout the year in pairs in home ranges (well-defined areas of habitat), which can be as much as 170 km^2 in size although 60-100 km^2 is standard; sometimes the ranges of neighbouring pairs overlap. Within the home range only a small sector — the territory proper — is defended, and this is the area of roosting and nesting. The distance between nests in neighbouring territories is 4-7 km.

The diet varies according to the area. Generally small mammals constitute the major component, but these eagles also prey on birds such as geese, partridges and Rock Doves, which are sometimes caught in flight. Carrion and reptiles are also included in their diet. In Israel, especially in the Mediterranean region, they show a marked preference for tortoises, particularly in spring when these creatures are beginning to emerge from hibernation; tortoises are lifted in the air and dropped to the ground, to break their shells. In Har-Gillo near Bethlehem, a detailed study revealed that mammals constituted 14% of the diet, reptiles (especially tortoises) 34%, with birds (partridges, poultry and doves) constituting 54% of the prey. Within the home range there are a number of feeding stations, where the prey is taken to be plucked or skinned, then either eaten on the spot or taken to the nest for the chicks. This eagle spends part of the day sunning — reclining on an exposed and dusty sun-facing slope with wings spread — probably to rid itself of the various parasites concealed among its feathers.

The pair bond is prolonged and possibly lifelong, although if one of the partners dies the surviving individual pairs again. The process of courtship is continued throughout the year, but intensifies at the approach of the nesting season; it usually takes the form of display flights, with the partners diving and soaring and sometimes linking claws in the air.

The Golden Eagle was considered a very rare accidental in Israel until 1972, when, on 28 March, the first nest, with two chicks, was found in cliffs in a wadi in the northern Judean Desert not far from Jerusalem. This was a sensational discovery, although it emerged that the nesting site was not new; in the vicinity of the occupied nest there were four or five abandoned reserve nests. In spring 1973 five active nests were found, and by 1978 14 breeding pairs were known, all of them in desert or semi-desert environments, from Gilboa and eastern Samaria to the Judean Desert and the mountains of Eilat (where lizards form the most important component of the diet). In spring 1984, 21 pairs were identified in the Negev and the Judean Desert alone.

In 1979 a pair of Golden Eagles was discovered nesting in a pine tree below the field school of Har-Gillo. This was the only tree-nesting pair known in Israel, and also the only pair breeding in the Mediterranean region of the country. It continued to breed in the same nest for three years, until the female disappeared. Most of the data on the life history of the Golden Eagle in Israel are derived from observation of this pair, which was guarded during the nesting season by volunteers acting on behalf of the Society for the Protection of Nature. Some 27,000 people visited the site.

Unlike other eagles, the Golden Eagle tends to breed on cliffs or among rocks — on a ledge or in a cleft — but it sometimes nests in trees. The building or renovation of the nest usually begins as early as November. A pair may have as many as 12 reserve nests in its territory, though usually two to four. The base is constructed of quite thick branches, surmounted by thinner twigs and lined with green shrubbery, sometimes also with scraps of paper and plastic. Replacement of the lining continues throughout nesting. The nest diameter is up to 1.5 m, and after repeated use it may attain a height of 2 m; nests built in trees are larger, 3 m, 4 m or even 5 m in diameter and up to 4 m in height. In Israel laying takes place between the end of December and early January. The clutch is usually of 2 eggs (3 have been found in 10% of nests). Incubation begins with the first egg and lasts 42-45 days. Most of the time the female incubates, the male relieving her two or three times during the day. The chicks hatch with eyes open and covered with white or light grey woolly down. In many cases the older chick kills its younger sibling (a phenomenon known as 'Cainism': after Cain, killer of his brother Abel). According to European data, only in 20% of nests do two chicks survive to fledging; in this country 12 cases are known of three chicks hatching and all of them surviving. At 65-75 days old the chicks leave the nest at intervals, spending a further three months or so with their parents until they become independent. The juveniles spend a few years roaming, forming territories only when nearing sexual maturity, at about six years of age, at which stage they also assume adult plumage.

Lesser Spotted Eagle
Aquila pomarina

The smallest species of the genus *Aquila*: body length 60-65 cm, wing length 48 cm, wingspan 135-160 cm and weight 1,000-1,500 g. The female is 10% larger than the male. When standing it appears a uniform brown colour, only the wing and tail feathers being darker. In flight, it is distinguished from the similar Spotted Eagle in that the wing-coverts are paler than the flight feathers (in the Spotted Eagle the situation is reversed).

This eagle has two subspecies: one is resident in India and northern Burma; the other, which breeds mainly in wooded plains from East Germany and Russia to the Balkans, Turkey and Iran, winters in East Africa from southern Sudan to Zimbabwe.

This bird is a common autumn migrant in Israel. In autumn 1982 some 89,000 individuals were counted in Kafar Kasem, and in the following year 142,000. It appears that the entire world population of the subspecies *A.p. pomarina* follows this migration route. The autumn passage is concentrated between mid-September and mid-October; in one day, 29 September 1983, some 46,500 individuals were counted. The Lesser Spotted Eagle is the most common of the migrating eagles seen in northern Israel in spring, when its migration is concentrated between late March and early April. In the Eilat area it is more rare, and it appears that the route by-passes the Gulf of Suez to the north. In the region of the town of Suez this is the most common of all raptors in spring, and from here the route continues through central Sinai and the central Negev towards the shores of the Dead Sea and northward along the Beqa.

This eagle is also a rare winterer in Israel.

Spotted Eagle
Aquila clanga

Similar to the Lesser Spotted Eagle, and not easily distinguished from it in the field, although appreciably larger: body length 65-71 cm, wing length 49-52 cm, wingspan 160-180 cm and weight 1.4-2.1 kg. The female can be 20% larger than the male. The most reliable distinguishing mark between the two spotted eagles is the underwing pattern: in the Spotted Eagle the coverts are usually darker than the flight feathers, while in the Lesser Spotted Eagle they are lighter. Otherwise, this is an eagle of fairly uniform brown-grey colour. The plumage of the immature is speckled with white.

The Spotted Eagle is a monotypic species which breeds in an area extending from eastern Europe through Siberia to Mongolia and Manchuria. The Western Palaearctic population winters in aquatic environments in the eastern basin of the Mediterranean: in northern Italy, the Balkans, Turkey, Iraq, Israel and the Nile Delta. Only a few individuals travel further south. Most Spotted Eagles seen in Israel today are winterers; in surveys of migratory birds in Kafar Kasem and Eilat, only a few individuals have been seen.

The winter visitors arrive in the second week of October and remain until mid-March. During this period Spotted Eagles are the most common and widely distributed of the eagles, congregating in valleys in fish-pond areas. In the late 1970s and early 1980s scores wintered throughout the country. In winter 1976/77, 25 individuals were affected by pesticide spraying in the Hula Valley; 11 recovered after treatment. In a national survey of wintering raptors conducted in January 1985, 78 Spotted Eagles were counted: 17 in the Hula Valley, 19 in the Acre Valley and 17 in the central coastal plain.

Before the poisonings of the early 1950s, several pairs of Spotted Eagles regularly nested in trees on the fringes of the Hula Valley; there were also a few breeding pairs in Carmel and Gilboa. This breeding population has been exterminated, the last active nest having been observed in Hurshat-Tal in the northern Hula Valley in 1958. In 1972 an attempt at nesting in western Galilee was begun, but soon discontinued.

Tawny or Steppe Eagle
Aquila rapax

A large and heavy-set eagle: body length 69-81 cm, wing length 51-56 cm, wingspan 180-255 cm and weight 1.9-3.2 kg. The Tawny Eagle has various colour-phases but the body and head are almost always of uniform colour, usually dark brown. In flight, the adult also appears generally uniform both above and below; the wings are narrow relative to their length. The immature has dark flight and tail feathers, while its wing-coverts are chestnut-coloured, the two colours separated by a white stripe.

The subspecies *A.r. orientalis* (known as the Steppe Eagle) breeds to the east of the Black Sea, through the high steppes of central Asia to Mongolia; most winter in tropical Africa. Three other subspecies, breeding in India, in North Africa and in tropical Africa, are resident. These populations are often considered as two separate species: *A. nipalensis* (including race *orientalis*), which nests in Eurasia and migrates in autumn, and *A. rapax* (including the other races), which is resident. The typical habitats of the Tawny Eagle are grass-covered plains and semi-deserts. In Israel this eagle is a passage migrant and a very rare winter visitor.

Unlike other eagles, the Tawny Eagle feeds to a large extent on carrion, although in the Palaearctic region it specialises in catching sousliks and rabbits. In Africa it sometimes feeds on termites.

In the north of the country this is a fairly rare migrant; in Kafar Kasem in autumn 1981, only 440 individuals were counted. On the other hand it is the most common eagle in Eilat both in autumn and in spring. In autumn 1980, some 25,000 individuals were counted there, and in spring 1977 30,000. This is the only migrating raptor seen in Eilat in approximately equal numbers in autumn and in spring. The autumn migration takes place from the end of September to the end of November, and a peak of some 7,300 individuals was recorded on 23 October 1980. It appears that immatures winter further south than adults, and for this reason they appear at an earlier stage in the autumn and at a later stage in the spring. The spring migration begins as early as the end of January, and until mid-March only adults are seen; only then do immatures and juveniles join the migrants. The migration continues until mid-May, although its peak occurs at the end of February. Since most of the spring migrants turn east from the Valley of the Arava, not far north of Eilat, only a few individuals are seen on the shores of the Dead Sea or further north.

In the past this was also a common winter resident in many parts of Israel. Today it is rarely seen in winter, with most observations in the southern Negev, not far from Eilat, but also in western Negev.

A Tawny Eagle ringed in Israel was found, four months later, in the USSR between the Black Sea and the Caspian.

Imperial Eagle
Aquila heliaca

A large eagle: body length 74-83 cm, wing length 57.5-63 cm, wingspan 190-210 cm and weight 2.3-3.6 kg. The female is 10% larger than the male. This is a dark eagle, with light, almost white, patches on the head, nape and shoulders. In gliding flight its wings form a rectangular shape, from which the head and tail protrude to a greater extent than in the case of the Tawny Eagle, which is similar in size. In flight, the adult is distinguished by its underparts and wing-coverts being darker than the flight feathers; the end of the tail is also darker than its base. The immature has pale brown underparts and wing-coverts; the four inner primaries are light grey, forming a light wing-patch, and the tail is black.

The Imperial Eagle breeds in Spain, where an endemic subspecies *A.h. adalberti* exists, and from the Balkans eastward to central Asia (the subspecies *A.h. heliaca*). This latter subspecies is a rare passage migrant and a rare winterer in Israel.

This eagle, although similar in size to the Golden Eagle, feeds primarily on small mammals. In most parts of its range sousliks constitute one of the main components of its diet.

The Imperial Eagle is a rare migrant both in autumn and in spring. In migration surveys only a few scores of individuals have been counted. Formerly a very common winter visitor, it is now rare at this season. It winters in the valleys and plains, especially in the western Negev; in a census in January 1985 20 were counted in this region, with a total of 57 throughout the country.

Past reports of nesting in Israel were in all probability due to confusion with the Golden Eagle.

Verreaux's or Black Eagle
Aquila verreauxi

A large eagle: body length 80-96 cm, wing length 60 cm, wingspan 225-245 cm and weight 3.6-5 kg. As its alternative name suggests, this is a deep black eagle. Against this, the yellow legs and cere are distinctive. In flight, there are conspicuous white patches at the base of the primaries. The back and rump are also marked with white.

This is a monotypic eagle of African origin, which specialises in hunting hyraxes. Its range extends from Namibia and the Cape region, throughout East Africa to northern Ethiopia.

In Israel this is a rare accidental. One individual was caught in 1911 in Ein Gedi. From then until 1960 not a single sighting was recorded, but in that year a pair was seen in western Galilee; three years later another pair appeared in eastern Galilee, and even nested in Nahal Dishon, although the outcome is not known. This eagle disappeared from Galilee at the end of the 1960s. Since then there have been occasional sightings of Verreaux's Eagle in the Judean Desert, and especially in the mountains of Eilat and in eastern Sinai, and it is possible that it is still breeding there.

Genus: *Hieraaetus*
This genus of five species is confined to the Old World. Differing opinions exist as to the relationship between it and the genus *Aquila*. Two species occur in Israel.

Bonelli's Eagle
Hieraaetus fasciatus

A large raptor, although smaller than most eagles of the genus *Aquila*: body length 67-72 cm, wing length 47-51 cm, wingspan 155-180 cm and weight 1.5-2.4 kg. The female is 10% larger than the male. This bird has characteristics of both the eagle and the hawk: its head and bill are like those of an eagle, though its legs are longer and the scales on the toes larger than in most eagle species, but the feathering of the legs is typically eagle-like; its long tail resembles that of a hawk. In fact, Bonelli's Eagle is endowed with the strength of an eagle and the agility of a hawk. When perched, it appears blackish-brown with brown-flecked white underparts, and the tail protrudes 5-7 cm beyond the wingtips; its claws are the longest of any raptor in relation to body size, that of the rear toe being especially long (40 mm) and powerful. In flight, there is a striking contrast between the white forewing and the dark wing-coverts; the underbody appears white from a distance. There is a conspicuous white patch in the middle of the back and a dark band at the end of the tail. Immatures are distinguished by their chestnut belly and wing-coverts, their greyish tail lacking a terminal band, and their russet-brown breast; these colours gradually change over the course of about three years, when adult plumage is assumed.

Bonelli's Eagle has three subspecies. The range of the one known in Israel, *H.f. fasciatus*, extends through North Africa, the countries of the Mediterranean basin, the Levant, India and southern China. Another subspecies inhabits tropical Africa and the third is found in the Lesser Sunda Islands. Bonelli's Eagle is resident in all its areas of distribution, and prefers mountainous habitats with high cliffs, climate and vegetation being secondary considerations. Thus it has been found, in Israel, from the slopes of Mount Hermon and the Golan in the north to the cliffs of Nahal Zin in the central Negev, and from the groves of Carmel and western Galilee to the canyons of the Judean Desert.

This is a typical territorial bird, spending its entire life within a particular habitat, which may extend over 70 km^2 in the Judean Desert and over 30-40 km^2 in the more fertile Mediterranean environments. The distance between the nests of neighbouring pairs varies between 3 km and 25 km. Both members of the pair patrol and protect the boundaries of the territory throughout the year; the boundaries are marked by a particular variety of display flight, involving a series of steep dives and climbs. This is a particularly aggressive bird: during the nesting season it is liable to attack other predators, even those larger than itself. Members of the pair sometimes return to roost on the nesting cliff even outside the nesting season.

Bonelli's Eagle feeds on a wide variety of prey, from lizards to mammals. Its long and strong claws enable it to overpower animals of greater weight than itself, such as a partridge weighing 2 kg, or a fox, which may be twice the weight of the eagle, and it is even capable of carrying them in the air. In Israel, birds, especially partridges and Rock Doves, constitute about 90% of its diet; mammals such as hares, hedgehogs and hyraxes constitute about 7%, and reptiles and carrion make up the balance. In the canyons of the Judean Desert it lives in proximity to the Golden Eagle, and their habitats often overlap, although their hunting sectors are separate: the Golden Eagle, feeding primarily on hares, hunts in the higher ground of the desert and is therefore found in the more westerly sections of the wadis, while Bonelli's Eagle tends to hunt in the lower-level, more easterly sectors.

Before the large-scale poisonings of the 1950s, Bonelli's Eagle was quite widespread throughout Israel: in Mount Carmel at least six pairs bred, with two in Nahal Amud near Lake Tiberias and two in Nahal Kaziv in western Galilee, and a total for the entire country of 50-70 pairs. Preying on partridges which had eaten corn seed contaminated with pesticides led to the extermination of this eagle in the Mediterranean region of the country. In 1962, the last pair in this area was breeding in Nahal Shorek in the Judean Hills. The only surviving pairs were those breeding in the Judean Desert (nine pairs) and in the central Negev (two or three pairs), and also those in Samaria, where agricultural pesticides were not widely used. At the end of the 1970s a recovery in the population was perceived, and today 19 pairs of Bonelli's Eagles are known throughout Israel.

The impressive courtship flights take place in December: the male rises with wings outstretched and dives with wings folded in a repetitive and undulating motion, emitting a loud cry at the top of each undulation; the display flight often ends with a long dive towards the female. In Israel, Bonelli's Eagle usually nests on cliffs and only rarely in trees; only one pair is known to have nested in a pine tree, in Mount Carmel in 1959-60 (the African subspecies regularly nests in trees). It prefers hollows which protect the nest from wind and rain and from the rays of the sun. The nest is a large structure, the base being composed of branches up to 3 cm in diameter and 1-1.5 m in length; on this base more delicate materials are piled up and fashioned into a hollow by the female's bill, legs and body movements, while the

lining is of shorter and softer green branches. In the Judean Desert the eggs are laid as early as the first week of January, while in the Golan laying is usually delayed until mid-February. Most pairs lay in the second half of January, though replacement clutches may be laid in April. The clutch is usually of 2 eggs (rarely 3). The incubation period is 40-42 days, and the female bears about 98% of the burden. Although the phenomenon of 'Cainism' is less common in this species than in other eagles, usually only one chick survives. Instances of three chicks surviving, however, have been recorded twice. The chick flies at the age of 60-65 days, and for the next three years wanders extensively.

Booted Eagle
Hieraaetus pennatus

A generic relative of Bonelli's Eagle, but considerably smaller, being of buzzard size: body length 50 cm, wing length 37 cm, wingspan 110 cm and weight 600 g. This eagle has two colour-phases: one with white underparts and wing-coverts and only the flight feathers black; the other all-dark apart from the russet-brown tail. In Europe the ratio of light to dark birds is 7:3.

The Booted Eagle breeds in a band extending from North Africa and Spain, through southern Europe, Turkey, Iraq and Iran to southern Russia and Mongolia. It is monotypic. It breeds in broadleaf forests and in mixed woodland on the slopes of mountains, and winters in sub-Saharan Africa and India, in most climatic areas with the exception of jungles. In Israel it is a relatively rare passage migrant and a very rare winterer.

The main autumn migration is concentrated in September, and usually single individuals or groups of two or three are seen, flying at low level. In autumn 1982, 1,200 individuals were counted in Kafar Kasem and the ratio of light to dark birds was 4:3. In spring it passes through the country between mid-March and mid-May. In Eilat in spring 1977, 175 individuals were counted, with light and dark birds in approximately equal numbers. At this season it is more common in the north of the country.

Family: Pandionidae (Osprey)

A family comprising one genus and a single species, the Osprey.

A few characteristics, most of them associated with the Osprey's manner of feeding on fish, distinguish it from other raptors: the outer toe is capable of turning backwards, creating a more efficient grip; the

preen gland is relatively large, permitting effective lubrication of the feathers; the structure of the body feathers differs from that of the family Accipitridae and resembles that of New World vultures, the feathers being short and stiff, forming a thick and dense covering.

Osprey
Pandion haliaetus

Body length 56-59 cm, wing length 47-49.5 cm, wingspan 145-170 cm and weight 1.5 kg. The female is 5-10% larger than the male. The Osprey has a small and narrow head, with a long, narrow and sharply hooked bill. The neck is relatively long and the nape feathers form a crest. The legs are long and partially feathered; the tarsus is short and bare. On the underside of the toes there are large protuberances covered with large scales, an arrangement which improves grip on the fish; the claws are particularly long and hooked. The feet and toes are bluish-grey. At rest the Osprey is distinguished by a dark brown eye-stripe, separating the pale crown from the white cheeks and neck. In flight, it is distinguished by the long and narrow wings, kinked at the carpals and bowed when gliding. There is also a striking contrast between the dark brown back and the light belly; the belly and wing-coverts are white, while the flight feathers are greyish and speckled with black. Juveniles have the feathers of the upperparts, including the wing-coverts, tipped whitish.

The range of the Osprey is virtually cosmopolitan and extends over North and Central America, northern and eastern Europe, the whole width of Asia, the islands of the Pacific Ocean, Australia, the shores of Arabia and a few places in Africa. In this broad range six subspecies have been identified. The one known in Israel, *P.h. haliaetus*, breeds across the Palaearctic region and on islands in the Red Sea and in Somalia. It is found in all places where fish are available: lakes, pools, reservoirs etc. The northern populations of the Osprey migrate in autumn; most of the Western Palaearctic population winters in tropical Africa. Its southern populations are resident. The Osprey is a rare passage migrant and winterer in most parts of Israel, and a fairly common breeder in southern Sinai.

Fish form the major part of the Osprey's diet. In different regions it prefers different types of fish. There are some Ospreys which specialise in catching a limited number of types, others which catch whatever is available. On the island of Tiran, 52 different species of fish have been found in the diet. In addition to fish, remains of ducks, plovers and sandpipers have been found in its nests, and it is also known to attack Coots. On the island of Tiran, an Osprey was even observed splitting open shellfish by dropping them from a height of 30-40 m onto a cement barrel. The Osprey is a territorial bird in most of its habitats, and the distance between nests can be several kilometres, but in places where fish are abundant, such as the island of Tiran, a number of pairs gather in a loose colony.

Ospreys appear on the autumn migration as early as the beginning of September, but they are more conspicuous in the spring migration, especially in the first half of April. In Eilat in spring 1977 122 passage individuals were counted, while in autumn 1982 48 Ospreys were counted in Kafar Kasem. Sometimes several (usually six to nine) may be seen together resting in a field bordering on fish-ponds.

In the first surveys of wintering birds, which began in 1964, up to three Ospreys were counted every year; between 1965 and 1971 there was no record of Ospreys wintering in the country. Only since 1975 has there been some increase and in the late 1970s and early 1980s four to nine individuals have wintered each year, while in winter 1984/85 the number rose to 15.

A large resident population of Ospreys (45 pairs) is present in southern Sinai, two-thirds of it on the island of Tiran. At least one pair has also bred in Sabkhat E-Tina in northwest Sinai. In southern Sinai courtship flights take place especially in November-December, with both partners exhibiting aerobatic antics. The nests here are usually built on cliffs, bushes, mangrove trees or rocks protruding from the water. Nests are also placed on artificial structures, on towers or on the masts of derelict ships. On Tiran they have often been built on bushes some distance from water. The construction is of driftwood — branches, planks and pieces of packing-case — and lined with scraps of fabric, strips of plastic and seaweed. In Sinai laying sometimes begins in November, sometimes in February, but normally in January. The number of eggs is 2-4. The early laying date in Sinai is intended to prevent the chicks remaining in the nest during the hot season. Incubation, mostly by the female, lasts about 37 days. The chicks remain in the nest about 55 days before flying, and usually only one offspring survives. They attain sexual maturity at three years of age.

In 1981, polyandry was observed in three out of seven nests built along the coasts of southern Sinai. In one nest four males were seen together.

In the past, the Osprey was more common as a wintering bird and could be observed on most reservoirs in the country. Its numbers were, however, hard hit by pesticides and seed-dressings (which spilled into reservoirs and accumulated in fish) in other countries. In Israel it has also suffered from collisions with high-tension cables. Another detrimental factor is egg-collecting; it seems that no other bird has suffered more than the Osprey at the hands of egg-collectors (at the beginning of this century, $140 was the going rate for three eggs). In 1977 all the Osprey eggs disappeared from Tiran; although it is assumed that egg-collectors were responsible, this has not been proved (another possibility is that the eggs were eaten by Bedouin fishermen).

The fact that Ospreys tend to nest on exposed shorelines exposes their nests to many dangers. Special towers have been established in southern Sinai by the Nature Conservation Authority, and these have been successfully adopted by Ospreys.

Four Ospreys found dead in Israel had been ringed in Finland.

Family: Falconidae (Falcons)

This is a well-defined family of diurnal raptors, comprising ten genera and 60 species; of the latter approximately half are confined to the New World. The genus *Falco*, which with 37 species is the largest genus among diurnal birds of prey, includes four distinctive types, each adapted to a certain type of habitat: hovering falcons (such as the Kestrel and the Lesser Kestrel); miniature falcons (the Merlin); long-winged falcons (such as the Hobby, Eleonora's Falcon and the Sooty Falcon); and large falcons (the Saker and the Peregrine). All 11 species represented in Israel belong to the genus *Falco*.

Falcons are raptors of small to average size, varying from 60 to 2,000 g (in Israel 160-1,300 g), and the family includes the smallest of the birds of prey. In smaller species the female is slightly larger than the male, while in large species the difference may be as much as a quarter or a third. In a few species there are also colour differences between the sexes.

Falcons tend to inhabit open environments, in various climatic conditions: from the cold tundra, through steppes to hot deserts. They are fast-flying hunters, and their body structure and feathering are well suited to chasing live prey in the air and on open ground. The feathers are hard and stiff and the legs short, exposed and strong. Bird-eaters have long and studded toes, insect-eaters short toes. The wings are long, pointed and sickle-shaped. The tail is narrow and usually of moderate length. The breast bone is broad, and in species which stoop on their prey in the air it serves as an extra weapon, buffeting the prey like a hammer. The head is relatively small, rounded and mounted on a short neck. The eyes are large and dark and surrounded by bare skin; there is no bone projecting above them, and for this reason they appear less menacing than other raptors. The bill is strong and curved, with sharp edges to the upper mandible; unlike in other raptors, it is the principle killing instrument, the legs being used only for holding and carrying the prey.

All falcons feed on live prey, ranging in size from insects to large birds such as partridges and geese, and the diet may also include small mammals. They are capable of attaining high speeds, and their diving speed is the fastest of any bird. A few species catch their prey on the ground, and these have shorter claws, and a longer tail, than those which catch their victims in the air.

Falcons lay their eggs in abandoned nests of other birds or in hollow trees, on buildings or rock-ledges, without any lining. The number of eggs is 3-6 and they are laid on alternate days. The period of incubation, often solely by the female, is 25-35 days. The female protects the chicks while the male supplies food for her and for the offspring. Only when the chicks need no further protection, and their need for food increases, does the female join the male in hunting.

Kestrel
Falco tinnunculus

A small and slender-bodied falcon, with long wings and long (16-20 cm) tail: body length 31-35 cm, wing length 23-25 cm, wingspan 71-80 cm and weight 120-200 g. The underparts are yellowish-brown with dark streaking, and the back is chestnut-brown and also speckled with dark markings; the primaries are black. The head and tail of the female are chestnut-brown; in the male these areas are grey, the tail with a black bar framed in white at the tip. Adult males have a conspicuous black moustache and white throat. Immatures are similar to the adult female, but the underparts are paler with broader streaking. The male is small with pointed wings; the female slightly larger with broader and darker wings. The bill is greyish with a dark tip; the cere, legs and toes are yellow. The claws are black.

The Kestrel lives in many varied climatic conditions, avoiding only tundra, and its range extends over most of Europe and Asia except southeast Asia, and over considerable areas of Africa with the exceptions of the Sahara and the Congo basin. In this range 11 subspecies have been identified. This is the most common raptor in many parts of the Palae-arctic region, especially in Europe and also in Israel. It inhabits areas from sea-level to altitudes of 3,500 m; it has also adapted easily to living in human settlements, and in Israel it is quite common in urban environments. It is not found in large and dense forests, treeless swamps, or expanses of sand and dune in extreme deserts. Most populations are resident, but those of northern and eastern Europe and most of the Asiatic populations migrate; these winter in southern Asia, in southern Europe and North Africa, and many individuals even cross the Sahara and winter in tropical Africa, as far as the River Zambesi. The Kestrel migrates at high altitude and in small groups, and its migration is not conspicuous. A Kestrel ringed in Hungary was found in 1966 in Kibbutz Ma'anit, in the central coastal plain. In Israel this is a widespread resident, a common winterer and a somewhat rare passage migrant; the subspecies concerned is *F.t. tinnunculus*, whose range extends over the Western Palaearctic region and reaches as far as northeastern Siberia and Mongolia.

In Israel, and especially in winter, the Kestrel feeds on rodents, but also to a large extent on locusts, crickets and beetles. An adaptable and opportunistic bird, it also feeds on reptiles and small songbirds; in urban areas it has been seen to attack wagtails, sparrows, starlings and even pigeons.

During the large-scale pesticide poisonings of the 1950s, Kestrels were almost entirely eliminated, both as breeding and as wintering birds. In the 1960s the population began to recover, and since the 1970s the species has again been seen in abundance in all parts of the country, especially in urban areas and agricultural settlements. In a few places colonies of 10-30 nests have been found: for example, in an abandoned army camp at the foot of Har Avital in the Golan, in the cliffs of the Arbel near Lake Tiberias, in the Ma'arat Yonim in western Galilee, in Nahal Michmas not far from Jerusalem, and in a palm plantation in Revivim in the northern Negev.

This is essentially a solitary bird, except in places where food is abundant. In such areas it may nest in a loose colony, with about 20 m between each nest, sometimes in combined colonies with the Lesser Kestrel. Courtship begins as early as the end of January. A variety of nest sites is used: on natural cliffs or the wall of a quarry, in the branches of a tree, among palm fronds, in the abandoned nest of a Raven, and even on houses — on a window-sill or a ledge or even in an artificial nestbox. The Kestrel does not build a nest, although sometimes it gathers together a few twigs for this purpose. Often it returns to nest in the same place over a period of many years. Laying usually begins between the end of March and the end of April. The clutch contains 3-6 eggs, usually 5. Incubation begins towards the end of laying, and the female incubates alone for about 28 days. The chicks hatch over a period of a few days, at short intervals; at about 20 days old they are feathered and capable of feeding by themselves, and they fly from the nest at about 30 days old and become independent about a month after this.

In a nest on the window-sill of a house in north Tel Aviv, in which four chicks were reared, the following food items were brought by the parents to the chicks during the nesting period: 75 songbirds of various species, 16 lizards and 12 rodents of different kinds.

Lesser Kestrel
Falco naumanni

A small and slender-bodied falcon: body length 29-32 cm, wing length 22-23.8 cm, wingspan 60-70 cm and weight 95-130 g. The female is only slightly, if at all, larger than the male. This falcon is very similar to the Kestrel in shape, coloration and behaviour, but slightly smaller. Its wings are narrow, and its tail narrow and long (13.5-15.5 cm). The male is distinguished from the male Kestrel by its unmarked chestnut-coloured back and by its grey wing-coverts; it also lacks the black moustache. Females are more difficult to distinguish, although the female Lesser Kestrel may be recognised by the pale colour of the claws and by the two central tail feathers being slightly longer than the rest. In flight from below, both sexes appear paler and less speckled than the Kestrel. The Lesser Kestrel is also noisier, and its call is lower and more hoarse than that of the Kestrel. Immatures are similar to the female.

The Lesser Kestrel breeds through the southern Palaearctic region, from Spain and the Atlas Mountains through Italy and the Balkans, around the Black Sea and as far east as central Asia. It is a monotypic species restricted mostly to areas of Mediterranean and steppe climate, with only small penetration into the temperate zone. It extends north only as far as Austria and southern Russia. It inhabits steppes, pasture meadows and even urban parks, up to an altitude of about 2,500 m. Almost all populations migrate to sub-Saharan Africa (in winter this is the most common falcon seen in South Africa, and in 1967 more than 300,000 individuals were counted in roosting colonies). In Israel the Lesser Kestrel is a breeding summer visitor and a scarce passage migrant.

The Lesser Kestrel feeds especially on insects, which it catches either on the ground or in flight, and also on lizards and small mammals. It hunts in open environments including parks and gardens in large cities, where it is often seen hovering, sometimes for a period of 15-25 minutes continuously, with faster wing movements than those of the Kestrel. It often hunts in small flocks, and indeed the Lesser Kestrel is one of the most social of the falcons, both in winter quarters and in the nesting season; it breeds in colonies of two or three to more than 500 pairs, although 15-25 is average.

During the autumn migration Lesser Kestrels are

hardly to be seen at any point along the route. It seems that they cross the Mediterranean and the Middle East in high-altitude and unbroken flight, without pausing until they reach Eritrea. They are more conspicuous in spring, and in a few places there have been reports of flocks of thousands migrating by day at low level. In Israel to date only small flocks of 20-30 have been sighted, except on a very few occasions when flocks numbering hundreds of individuals have been seen. Migrating flocks are seen from the third week of March and especially during April, when they may be observed hunting in various parts of the country.

Populations of the Lesser Kestrel were hard hit by the pesticide poisonings of the 1950s; many colonies were completely destroyed, others were greatly depleted. Colonies which had comprised hundreds of pairs, such as those in Safed in Upper Galilee and in Rosh Hanikra in western Galilee, were almost exterminated. Since the late 1970s there has been a recovery in numbers of the Lesser Kestrel, and in the early 1980s several active colonies were known, with a total national population of about 300 pairs.

The Lesser Kestrel returns to Israel between mid-February and mid-March, and nesting usually takes place during April-May. It nests in cliff-crevices or on rooftops and has also been known to nest in towers and the spires of churches. The nest is a small hollow without any lining. In the clutch there are 3-5 eggs. Incubation, mainly by the female, lasts about 28 days, and during this period the males roost in groups not far from the nesting place. When the chicks are about two weeks old, they are already feeding by themselves on the food brought to the nest by both parents. In close-packed colonies the offspring of different pairs sometimes mingle in one nest. The chicks remain in the nest for about 28 days, and attain sexual maturity at one year old.

The Lesser Kestrel sometimes abandons its colonies in Israel as early as July, and normally not later than August-early September, and migrates to its winter quarters.

Red-footed Falcon
Falco vespertinus

A small and very gregarious falcon: body length 30 cm, wing length 24-26 cm, wingspan 72 cm and weight 150 g. The male is dark grey to black, with only the thighs and undertail-coverts being chestnut-brown; the legs, bill and eye-ring are bright orange-red. The female is distinguished by its light orange-russet underparts, crown and nape, and bluish-grey back flecked with black markings; a further distinguishing feature is the nine to ten black bars across the grey tail. A similar tail is shown by juvenile and immature birds. The wings are narrow and pointed, but are quite broad at their base.

The Red-footed Falcon breeds from Hungary and Czechoslovakia, through Poland and Russia, to central Asia, although sometimes its breeding range extends further westward. It is a monotypic species. It inhabits open environments with scattered trees, plantations and wooded riverbanks. All of its populations migrate in autumn, in flocks numbering scores of individuals, to winter in southwestern Africa. It occurs in Israel as a passage migrant.

The Red-footed Falcon is a slower-flying bird than other members of the genus. When hunting it beats its wings fast and regularly, and from time to time glides and soars; it frequently hovers. It feeds particularly on insects such as locusts, beetles and dragonflies, which it catches and eats in flight or on the ground. It also consumes rodents, fledglings and lizards. It often hunts in the evening.

The southward migration of the Red-footed Falcon takes place in autumn over a wide front, and crosses the Mediterranean. Until 1967 this falcon was considered a rare passage migrant in Israel. Since then the number of sightings has increased, most being recorded from late September to early November though the first individuals are noted in mid-August. In Kafar Kasem in autumn 1980 some 900 were observed, and in 1983 1,097 individuals were counted there. This species migrates at high altitude and is not easy to identify. Among all the migrating raptors passing through this country, the Red-footed Falcon is the only one which breaks its journey in Israel, sometimes lingering for several weeks: thus, for example, an individual ringed on 28 September 1983 in the fields near Kafar Kasem was observed again in the same area on 17 October 1983, which indicates that it was present for at least 20 days. At these times flocks numbering scores of individuals may be observed feeding in fields, and the falcons present in the country during the migration period also gather in roosting colonies. The Red-footed Falcon also occurs in the course of the spring migration, in April-May, but is less conspicuous then. In this season large flocks of up to 5,000 individuals are observed in West Africa, and it appears that most of its populations migrate to the west of Israel.

Merlin
Falco columbarius

The smallest diurnal raptor of the Western Palaearctic region: body length 27 cm, wing length 20-22 cm, wingspan 56 cm and weight 160-210 g. The male is bluish-grey above, the female grey-brown; both sexes have russet-white underparts, streaked with brown. In spite of these colours, the Merlin appears from a distance uniformly dark. It is therefore easier to distinguish it in flight: very fast, with rapid wing movements alternating with soaring glides; short wings, broad at the base and pointed at the tips; and long tail, which is barred in the female and with a single broad black terminal band in the male.

The Merlin's range is Holarctic, extending over northern Europe, northern Asia and North America, and restricted to cold and temperate climates. In this range ten subspecies are known. It inhabits open environments, especially moors and marshes. It is mostly migratory, European populations wintering mainly from Britain south to the Mediterranean basin. In Israel it is a rare winter visitor, seen between the end of October and early April, and a rarer passage migrant.

Since the end of the 1970s small numbers have wintered in the Hula Valley, especially in the Hula Reserve (where in the mid-1980s some 35 individuals were seen gathering to roost), on the coastal plain, in the Judean Hills, and in the fields of the western Negev (where 19 individuals were counted in January 1983). In a census carried out in January 1985, 67 Merlins were counted throughout the country, 35 of them in the Hula Valley and 16 in the western Negev.

Hobby
Falco subbuteo

A falcon with long and sickle-shaped wings and short tail (12-14 cm): body length 30-36 cm, wing length 24-27 cm, wingspan 82-92 cm and weight 160-270 g. The female is 10% larger than the male and has broader wings. Both sexes have similar plumage: dark bluish-grey above, with cream-coloured underparts densely streaked with brown; the throat and neck are white, with a conspicuous black moustache, and the thighs and undertail-coverts are chestnut-coloured. Juveniles are brown above, with thighs the same colour as the belly. The claws are long and powerful, and the bird resembles a smaller version of the Peregrine.

The Hobby's range is trans-Palaearctic and extends over most of Europe except the far north, and across certain parts of Asia and North Africa, in very different climatic regions. A single subspecies, *F.s. subbuteo*, occurs throughout this range apart from in China, where a separate subspecies breeds. The Hobby prefers open environments: ploughed fields and pasture meadows with scattered and tall trees. It frequently penetrates agricultural settlements and even towns, and it also inhabits mountainous regions and wooded hills. All populations migrate in

autumn; those from the Western Palaearctic region winter in South Africa. This falcon apparently migrates over a broad front and does not keep to fixed routes; it crosses the Mediterranean, and for this reason is rarely seen on passage in Israel. It is, however, a fairly common summer resident.

The Hobby is a fast flier, and capable of nimble manoeuvring in pursuit of birds or insects in the air, catching its prey with its feet. Sometimes it hunts in the evening and even after sunset, when it turns its attention to roosting birds and to bats. Insects are consumed in flight, while birds are carried to a branch and eaten only after the feathers have been removed. The Hobby seldom hunts on the ground.

In summer this is a fairly common falcon in the coastal plain, including settled and urban areas; it is more rare at higher altitudes, although some ten pairs were breeding in Jerusalem in 1982. The Hobby returns to Israel from its winter quarters at a relatively late stage, arriving only at the end of March-early April. Both members of the pair usually arrive together in the nesting area. The courtship flights of the male are very impressive, and at these times both partners are extremely vocal; their rapid and high-pitched monosyllabic shrieks are heard continuously throughout the day. In Israel the Hobby usually adopts the abandoned nests of Hooded Crows, but may attempt to commandeer the occupied nests of birds such as the Grey Heron. Laying usually takes place in early June, sometimes in early May. The normal clutch is of 3 eggs. Incubation begins with the second egg and lasts 28-31 days. The nesting season of the Hobby corresponds to the period in which flying insects are most common, and when there are many recently fledged songbirds which are easily caught. The chicks leave the nest at the age of 28-34 days, usually in the second half of August, and become independent some 35 days later. In October the Hobby migrates to Africa.

The Hobby has been less severely affected by poisoning than other falcons, perhaps on account of its feeding habits.

Eleonora's Falcon
Falco eleonorae

A slender-bodied falcon, of moderate size: body length 38 cm, wing length 30-34.5 cm, wingspan 120 cm and weight 400 g. This falcon is similar to the Hobby and to the Sooty Falcon. Its tail is long (16-29 cm), and its wings very narrow, long and angled in a characteristic fashion. Eleonora's Falcon has two colour-phases: about a quarter of its population have an all-dark body; the rest have a white throat, a conspicuous moustache, and a chestnut-coloured belly with heavy dark streaking. In either case, the sexes are similar.

This falcon's range is limited to the Mediterranean: it is a monotypic species which today breeds almost exclusively on the coastal cliffs of Mediterranean islands, and in 1978 its entire world population was estimated at only 4,500 pairs. It winters along the coasts of East Africa, in particular on the islands of Mauritius and Madagascar.

Eleonora's Falcon breeds at the end of the summer, at the time of the autumn migration of European birds. According to one estimate, these falcons kill as many as a million and a quarter migrating birds to provide food for their chicks.

In Israel this is a rare passage migrant, seen occasionally in the west of the country between early August and early October, and again between the end of April and mid-May.

Sooty Falcon
Falco concolor

A falcon of moderate size: body length 33-36 cm, wing length 26.5-29.5 cm, wingspan 85-110 cm and weight 150 g. It is closely related to Eleonora's Falcon and similar to it in colouring and behaviour. Its wings are long and pointed, and its tail short (13-14 cm) with the two central feathers longer and protruding beyond the others. The Sooty Falcon has plumage of uniform colour, but two colour-phases are known: one all-black and similar to the dark phase of Eleonora's Falcon (this phase is not seen in Israel); the other dark grey in the female and bluish-grey in the male. The sexes also differ in the colour of the bare parts: the legs, cere and eye-ring are orange-yellow in the male and lemon-yellow in the female.

The Sooty Falcon is a monotypic species and is common along the shores and on the islands of the Red Sea and on the coasts of the Persian Gulf. A few of its populations have penetrated into desert areas: in Egypt (both in the Arabian and Western Deserts), and in Israel in the Negev and the Judean Desert. On the shores of the Dead Sea it reaches the northernmost limit of its range. In desert areas it is usually limited to cliff and canyon environments. All of its populations migrate southward in early November and winter on the coasts of East Africa, south of the Equator, especially on the island of Madagascar.

In flight the Sooty Falcon resembles the Hobby, and it too manoeuvres adroitly and catches its prey in the air. It is especially active in the hours of twilight, sometimes even before first light and after sunset. In the heat of the day it usually rests in a shaded nook or flies to high altitudes, where the air is cooler. The Sooty Falcon normally feeds on flying insects

such as dragonflies, and on small songbirds, although sometimes it hunts larger species such as bee-eaters and sandpipers. The pair breeding near Sodom on the Dead Sea shores feeds primarily on bats, while near the shores of the island of Tiran this falcon has been observed eating fish stranded at low tide on the coral reef.

In Israel this used to be considered a very rare breeder; in a survey concluded in 1975 only seven pairs were counted. In subsequent surveys, held between 1980 and 1984, its breeding population was estimated at 70 pairs in the hills of the Negev with a further seven pairs in the Judean Desert. Other pairs are known to breed in the mountains near Eilat, on the island of Tiran and along the shores of Sinai. The Sooty Falcon returns from winter quarters to its nesting sites at about the end of April. The months of May to July are devoted to choosing a nesting place — in a rock-crevice or a hollow in the upper part of a cliff. There is no nest lining, except when an abandoned Brown-necked Raven's nest has been adopted. In Israel the distance between nests is usually 2-5 km, although it may be no more than a few hundred metres. On the islands of the Red Sea the Sooty Falcon breeds in a loose colony. The female lays 2-3 eggs in July-August, although what are probably replacement clutches have been found as late as September. Incubation, mostly by the female, lasts 27-29 days, and the chicks fly from the nest at about 32 days old. The exceptionally late breeding date of the Sooty Falcon is explained by the feeding requirements of the chicks; in the typical habitat supplies of food are sparse, and the fledging period corresponds with the autumn migration of European birds. In the hills of the Negev this falcon feeds its offspring almost exclusively on birds, 97% of them belonging to migratory species. The southward migration begins in early November.

Lanner
Falco biarmicus

A large and strong falcon: body length 34-50 cm, wing length from 31 cm in the male to 37 cm in the female, wingspan 90-115 cm, weight of the male 550 g and of the female 800 g. Its tail is relatively short, being 15-20 cm in length. The adult Lanner is distinguished by its brown-grey back, its pale brown crown and nape, and from below by its pale, almost white appearance speckled with small brown markings. The legs and the cere are yellow. The bill is more powerful than that of the related species. Juveniles are darker brown above, with heavy dark streaking below and dark underwing-coverts.

The Lanner is the Ethiopian representative of the

group of larger falcons. Its range extends over most of Africa, except the rainforests of the Congo basin and the arid zones of the Sahara. Three subspecies inhabit the Mediterranean countries and the Middle East, and in Africa two additional subspecies have been identified. Most populations are resident. The subspecies breeding in Israel is *F.b. tanypterus*, whose range extends from Libya to Sudan, Arabia and southern Iraq. The subspecies *F.b. feldeggii*, which nests in southeast Europe and in Turkey, is also a rare winter visitor occasionally seen in the northern Negev.

The Lanner tends to inhabit mountainous environments, and prefers cliffs overlooking open sectors. Its flight is relatively clumsy, but in gliding — its normal means of motion — it is the equal of other species of falcon. It hunts both in the air and on the ground; its victims are normally birds of moderate size such as Rock Doves, Quails, Jackdaws and various species of plover, but it has also been recorded hunting Teals and even Lesser Kestrels. It also consumes locusts and crickets, and sometimes kills small mammals and reptiles.

Tristram (1888) testifies that in his time this was the most common of the larger falcons on both sides of the Jordan, from the Dead Sea to Mount Hermon. Before the pesticide poisonings of the 1950s it bred to the east of the slopes of the mountain ridge, along the Jordan Valley, as far north as Nahal Kadesh in eastern Upper Galilee. Today some ten resident pairs are known, from the cliff of Wadi Zin in the central Negev to the borders of Samaria. The Lanner nests in holes in cliff-faces, laying 3-4 eggs. The incubation period is 32-35 days, and the male plays a relatively substantial part. The chicks fly from the nest at the age of 44-46 days.

Saker
Falco cherrug

A large falcon: body length 50 cm, wing length of the male 35-37 cm and of the female 39-41 cm, wingspan 115 cm and weight from 730 g (male) to 1,300 g (female). The Saker has a brown back and its head is a paler whitish-cream colour than that of other falcons found in Israel; the moustache is barely perceptible. The underwing is also pale. The tail is 19-23 cm long, and the wings are broad.

The Saker's range extends over the steppes of eastern Europe and central Asia, from Hungary to Tibet, in the space left vacant between the ranges of the Gyrfalcon and the Lanner. It also sometimes inhabits desert environments. Two subspecies are known. The Western Palaearctic population, *F.c. cherrug*, winters especially in the Middle East and in East Africa.

The Saker is a nimble and fast-flying bird, although its wing movements are slower than those of the Peregrine. It is capable of remaining suspended in the air like the Short-toed Eagle. Its diet consists primarily of mammals such as sousliks, birds and reptiles being secondary food sources. It does not hunt mammals in a vertical dive with closed wings but in a diagonal descent, thus reducing impact on contact with the ground. Although much smaller, it is a hunter no less skilled and courageous than the mightiest of the eagles.

Until the pesticide poisonings of the 1950s this was a fairly common winter visitor to Israel, especially in the plains of the Negev. Today it is a rare passage migrant and winterer, seen occasionally in the fields of the western Negev between November and March.

In 1982, a dead Saker was found in Ofira with a ring on its leg identifying it as the property of King Khaled of Saudi Arabia.

The name 'Saker' is derived from the name of a Bedouin tribe, the Banu Saker, who used to reside in what was then Transjordan and who were experts in the art of hunting with the aid of falcons.

Peregrine
Falco peregrinus

A large falcon, and one of the most impressive flying birds: body length 36-48 cm, wing length of the male 29.5-32 cm and of the female 35-36.5 cm, wingspan 95-110 cm, weight of the male 600-700 g and of the female 920-1,300 g. The adult is bluish-grey above, with dark crown and nape; the broad moustache is black and conspicuous against the white cheek. The underparts are delicately barred on a pale background, the barring of the female being more conspicuous. The immature has streaked underparts and dark brown upperparts. The body is compact and torpedo-shaped, with broad shoulders, rounded head and short neck. Its legs are large and strong, with toes longer and more delicate than those of any other falcon and well suited to catching birds in the air. In flight the silhouette of the Peregrine is anchor-shaped: its wings are long and pointed, almost triangular, and its tail short in comparison with those of other similar-sized falcons (about 14.5 cm in the male and 17.5 cm in the female); from below, it appears pale, the wings being grey with only the tips of the primaries black, and the body and wing-coverts speckled with dark markings. The Peregrine is relatively easy to identify on account of its rapid wing movements, faster than those of the Lanner and Saker; from time to time it changes from active flight to gliding flight.

The Peregrine has a cosmopolitan, although not

continuous range. It is found in all continents except Antarctica, and in all climatic regions, although it is less common in extreme conditions such as tundra, desert or tropical rainforest. Within this broad range, according to different sources, between 14 and 22 subspecies have been identified. The Peregrine prefers sparsely wooded areas and open environments, including marshes and coasts. The northernmost Palaearctic populations winter in western and southern Europe and in tropical areas of Asia and Africa. Populations of the temperate, subtropical and tropical zones are resident, only the juveniles roaming. The species occurs in Israel on passage and in winter.

The Peregrine hunts in open environments, in fields or above stretches of water, also along rocky sea-coasts and above rivers. It dives vertically on its prey, with wings folded, and is capable of attaining a diving velocity of up to 320 kph (according to some sources, up to 475 kph!). It feeds exclusively on birds, from herons, Mallards and Pheasants to small songbirds. It often attacks Starlings and wagtails at their roosts, and it is also known to prey on Laughing Doves, swifts and hirundines.

Today the Peregrine is a fairly common passage migrant in Israel, from the end of July onward and especially near the sea-coast. It is also a rare winterer between the end of August and early April, occasionally seen in the southern Golan and the western Negev, sometimes even in towns and along the coastline. In winter 1984/85, a national total of 18 individuals was counted. Most of those seen in Israel are members of the subspecies *F.p. peregrinus*, which breeds in the western and southern Palaearctic region, although it is likely that some are from the northern subspecies *F.p. calidus*, which breeds in the

Eurasian tundra from Lapland eastward.

In the past, one or two pairs used to breed in this country, in Mount Carmel and in western Galilee. These apparently belonged to the Mediterranean subspecies *F.p. brookei*. The pesticide poisonings of the 1950s destroyed the breeding Peregrines and also caused severe damage to the wintering population, which used to be relatively large.

Barbary Falcon
Falco pelegrinoides

Body length 40 cm, wing length 26-32 cm, wingspan 90 cm and weight 400-600 g. The Barbary Falcon is sometimes considered a subspecies of the Peregrine, although today it is generally accepted that it constitutes an independent species. It resembles a smaller and paler version of the Peregrine; it is distinguished especially by the rusty-brown head and nape, while the overall colour is paler, the speckling of the underparts is less conspicuous, and the primary tips are silver-grey rather than black. Its call, resembling a low and hoarse shriek, is easily identified in the desert.

The range of this falcon extends from the Canary Islands and the Spanish Sahara, through Algeria, Egypt and Israel, to southern Iran, Afghanistan and the Gobi Desert.

In Israel this is a resident and fairly common bird, especially in the Judean Desert, from Jericho and southward, with at least one pair breeding in every canyon, and it is also known in the hills of the Negev and the region of Eilat: a national total of some 30 pairs. The Barbary Falcon breeds from early March, laying 3-4 eggs. Its behaviour patterns closely resemble those of the Peregrine. It feeds especially on partridges, Rock Doves and songbirds.

Order: Galliformes (Gamebirds — Pheasants, Partridges, Grouse, Guineafowl)

Today this order comprises some 250 species, classified according to different systems into four, six or seven families. The Galliformes are ground birds whose shape resembles that of the domestic chicken. Their bodies are round and solid, with a short neck and small head. The bill is short and strong, thick at the base and slightly downcurved; the upper mandible is longer than the lower and overlaps it. These birds vary in size from 54 g (the smallest species of quail) to 11 kg (the Turkey).

A few species are adorned with a crest or a fleshy comb on the head and wattles under the throat. Sometimes considerable areas of the head are bare of feathers, and the exposed skin is brightly coloured. The wing is short, broad and rounded. The males of many species, and sometimes also the females, have a very long tail. In many cases the longest feathers are the tail-coverts. The legs are long and strong. The three front toes are developed, while the rear toe is shorter. The claws are very strong and blunt, well suited to digging. In many species the male has a spur projecting above the rear toe.

The range of the order is cosmopolitan, but most species occur in tropical and subtropical areas while others have moved as far north as the Arctic Circle. Most inhabit woods and forests, but a few have penetrated into exposed and even arid environments. Dwellers in open environments have camouflage colours; those living in areas subject to snow have white plumage in winter, whereas those inhabiting dense woodland are distinctively and brightly coloured. Most of the Galliformes are resident or dispersive birds; only one subspecies of the Quail migrates. Most species live in flocks during the greater part of the year.

Even when fleeing from enemies the Galliformes normally prefer to run, at speeds of 28-34 kph. Only when danger is close do they fly. Their flight is rapid and vigorous, and the sound of their wingbeats is clearly audible. Usually they fly at low level and only over short distances. Many species roost in trees, and even perch on branches during the day, to avoid danger from predators. Members of this order are usually mostly vegetarians, but also feed to a large extent on insects and worms.

The nest is usually a simple one, built in a hollow in the ground. The clutch is large, and may contain as many as 15 and even 20 eggs. The offspring are precocial, and are capable of feeding by themselves from their first day. They can fly at a relatively early age, long before they reach their final size. Members of most species reach sexual maturity at about one year of age, although many young birds are taken by predators.

Only one family, the Phasianidae, is represented in Israel.

Family: Phasianidae (Pheasants, Partridges)

The largest and most important family of the order of Galliformes, comprising some 163 species, most of them ground-dwellers in woodland. The centre of distribution of the family is in the central Himalayan range and in southeast Asia; the few species outside this zone are distributed through most areas of the world, except for the polar regions and South America. Four species in four different genera occur in the wild in Israel.

This family is distinguished from others by only secondary features, such as the absence of feathering on the tarsus, the toes and the nostrils. It is subdivided into two subfamilies. In the primitive species both sexes have similar or identical plumage, as in most members of the tribe Perdicini, to which all of the four species in this country belong. Many species, especially those inhabiting open environments, are gregarious.

Chukar
Alectoris chukar

Body length 32-40 cm, wing length about 15.5 cm in the female and 17.8 cm in the male, wingspan 47-52 cm and weight 375-625 g. The male and female are virtually indistinguishable, although males have a spur and are larger by about 20%. There is also a geographical distinction: northern Chukars are larger and darker. The dominant plumage colours are brown and grey. The tail is russet-brown and particularly conspicuous in flight; the flanks are pale grey with a few black bars (the small number of bars is one of the distinctions between this species and the Rock Partridge *A. graeca*, in which the bars are considerably more numerous). The chin and throat are white, and ringed with a semicircular black border blending into the black eye-stripe. The legs are of medium length, strong, and bright red, which is also the colour of the bill.

The Chukar is resident throughout its range, which extends from Bulgaria and Turkey, through the Middle East, to the Himalayas, Mongolia and northern China. In this range 14 subspecies have been identified. The Chukar inhabits areas of Mediterranean, steppe and semi-desert climate, with penetration into the temperate zone. Its preferred habitats are rocky slopes of hills and mountains, covered with sparse vegetation.

This is a very common and widely distributed bird in Israel, occurring from Mount Hermon to the Negev and also in the heights of Sinai; it is rare in the desert and absent from the most arid places, such as the sand-hills of the southern Negev and the deserts of northern Sinai. In the north of Israel, north of the valley of Be'er Sheva, the subspecies *A.c. cypriotes* is found; in the Negev, in the Dead Sea basin, the Arava and Sinai there is a desert subspecies, smaller, paler and vocally distinctive, known as *A.c. sinaica*.

The Chukar feeds especially on the seeds of plants such as tubers and onions, but also on insects. At the end of winter and in early spring, green vegetation is also consumed, especially by the females. Usually its food contains sufficient liquid, but in the summer or after eating dry seeds it needs to drink.

Chukars spend most of the year in mixed flocks of 10-20 individuals, composed of males, females and juveniles. The centre and nucleus of the flock is made up of the adult males, which tend to stay in the same area from year to year. The territories of different flocks may overlap to a certain extent, but they do not mingle and there is liable to be rivalry between members of different flocks. Towards the end of summer these partridges congregate in large flocks, comprising 100 or more individuals, and remain in these flocks through the autumn and the winter. These concentrations are especially common near water and in open fields. In flocks feeding among clumps of vegetation, a sentry is sometimes posted on a vantage point.

In the desert and especially during the summer, Chukars are active for about two hours in the morning and two hours in the evening. During the remainder of the day they rest in the shade of a rock or a bush, or among the branches of trees. In the Mediterranean region of Israel their periods of activity are slightly longer.

The Chukar and its chicks constitute an important source of food for predators. This is also Israel's most hunted gamebird. The effects of the pesticide poisonings on raptors and other animals during the 1950s and early 1960s, and a change in hunting regulations, have enabled these birds to proliferate to a remarkable degree, with populations extending beyond the former areas of distribution. Today, Chukars may be seen throughout the country, including the western Negev, the sands of the coastal plain, the Jezreel Valley and the Jordan Valley — areas where they were not found before. In some places they have become so common as to constitute a pest, as for example in the pear orchards of Sede Boker in the northern Negev where thousands gather every year to peck at the ripening fruit. They are also a nuisance in fields of agricultural produce, especially in the Negev in autumn, when alternative sources of vegetable food are in short supply.

Pairing, which usually takes place within the flocks, normally begins in January, but sometimes not until March. Pairs leave the flock to find nesting territories, in February in the desert and in early March in the Mediterranean region. Nesting is normally restricted to areas of natural vegetation. The nest is a shallow depression in the ground, about 20 cm in diameter, among vegetation, usually thorn bushes, or in the shade of a rock; this is lined only with a little grass, sometimes also with feathers. In the desert laying begins as early as February; in the Mediterranean region it begins in March and may continue until the end of June. The clutch consists of 6-20 eggs, usually 8-15 (sometimes as many as 24 eggs are found in a nest, but this is in all probability the result of laying by two females). Incubation begins with the last egg, i.e. about two weeks after the laying of the first, and lasts about 26 days. During this time many nests, up to 50% and more, are abandoned, or raided and destroyed by predators. Often replacement clutches are laid, with incubation continuing until the end of June. The males usually abandon their mates in the early stages of nesting and return to their traditional haunts, where they form the nuclei of the post-breeding flocks. Cases are known, however, both in captivity and in the wild, in which a female laid two successive clutches and each member of the pair incubated and tended one of them. Hatching usually takes place in May, sometimes as early as April or as late as the end of July (in the case of replacement clutches). The chicks are capable of feeding by themselves from their first day.

Sand Partridge
Ammoperdix heyi

Smaller than the Chukar: body length 22-25 cm, wing length 12-12.5 cm, wingspan 39-41 cm and weight 125-215 g. Males are larger than females. The female has camouflage colours, being uniform yellow-brown on the belly and vermiculated on the back. In the male, black and chestnut bars are conspicuous against a white background on the sides of the belly, and there is a white patch behind the eye; the rest of the body is sand-brown with a certain tendency towards pink. Juveniles have similar colouring to the adult female. The Sand Partridge is a remarkably noisy and vocal bird, and is often heard before it is seen.

This is a typical desert bird, and its range is restricted to a narrow belt from the Nile eastwards: in the Arabian Desert, along the shores of Arabia and in the deserts of Israel. In this range four resident subspecies have been identified. The local subspecies *A.h. heyi* is fairly common on rocky slopes and deserts in the Negev, the Arava, the Judean Desert and on the fringes of Samaria. A few individuals have also been seen in the southern Golan. This species inhabits rocky and arid environments and avoids wide expanses of sand and sand-hills. Its flocks sometimes mingle with those of the desert subspecies of the Chukar, but its habitats are warmer and drier and usually restricted to areas with annual rainfall less than 100 mm.

Outside the nesting season Sand Partridges tend to gather in flocks of 10-20 individuals, consisting of both males and females or of males exclusively. They roost among boulders or in rockfalls on the slope. In the morning they set out for their feeding areas, running and with short bursts of rapid flight close to the ground; in flight the sound of the wingbeats is clearly audible, as the primaries are sharp, separated and stiff.

The Sand Partridge feeds on seeds, buds and leaves, and it may even climb on bushes for them. After rain it feeds almost exclusively on the buds and leaves of biennial plants, although it also consumes fruit and insects. The Sand Partridge drinks water only after eating dry seeds, or in summer, and may also drink salt water; it does not, however, require large quantities of water and can survive at considerable distance from any water source. It is especially active in the cool hours of the day, and tends to hide in the shade during the heat.

At the approach of spring the flock separates into pairs, although the date varies annually according to the amount of rainfall and consequent vegetation. The male is then particularly vocal, perching on a prominent vantage point. When he is joined by a female he displays colourful courtship rituals, and from this time on the pair is inseparable. The territory is not a delineated sector, but a certain area around the temporary abode of the pair. The female, accompanied by the ever-vocal male, may investigate dozens of potential nest sites under bushes or in the shelter of rocks. She finally digs a scrape, lines it with small quantities of grass and feathers, and lays a clutch of 8-14 eggs. (In some cases two females lay in the same nest, and nests have been known to contain as many as 21-22 eggs; the female is incapable of incubating such a large number, and many of the eggs do not hatch and are abandoned.) Incubation begins when the clutch is complete and lasts 19-21 days. The chicks hatch simultaneously, and within about an hour they leave the nest. From their first day they feed for themselves. Sometimes a female parent may drive away another and adopt her chicks in addition to her own: thus it is possible to observe flocks numbering scores of chicks of different ages, usually led by a female, sometimes by a male; at a later stage the flock divides into groups of 8-15 individuals.

In rainy years it is possible to see females with chicks as late as the end of August, and it is likely that in such years Sand Partridges complete two nesting cycles.

Black Francolin
Francolinus francolinus

Body length 33-36 cm, wing length 16.5-18 cm, wingspan 52 cm and weight 350-550 g. The Black Francolin is similar in profile to the Chukar, but is larger and more colourful. The male has a black face, neck and belly, with a white mark behind the eye and a chestnut collar; the flanks are black-brown and speckled with white; on each leg, above the rear toe, there is a strong spur. The female has camouflage colours and appears dark brown from a distance; on closer inspection the speckling of brown, yellow and black is perceptible. The juvenile is similar to the adult female.

Most of the 41 species of the genus *Francolinus* are confined to Africa, and the Black Francolin is one of only five found in south and southeast Asia. Its

origin is in Asia, in the Oriental region, and its range extends in a broad band from Assam and northern India, through Iran, Iraq and northern Syria, to Cyprus and southern Turkey. The species is divided into six subspecies. The one occurring in Israel, *F.f. francolinus*, is distributed from Cyprus to Iran.

The Black Francolin was the most sought-after gamebird in Israel in the days of the British Mandate. Following the introduction of wildlife protection laws, its populations have expanded in all areas except the Jordan Valley, where during the 1970s it was seen to be in retreat, apparently owing to competition from Chukars. Today it is quite a common resident in this country along the Jordan Valley, from north of the Dead Sea to Lake Tiberias, penetrating via the Bet She'an Valley to the eastern Jezreel Valley. A few are also found in the Hula Valley. In the past its distribution was incomparably wider (Tristram 1888). Hunting and habitat changes have reduced its range in this country, as elsewhere: it became extinct in Spain in 1840, in Sicily in 1869, and in Italy and Greece (where it was apparently introduced in the Middle Ages) at about the same time.

Most species of *Francolinus* are essentially birds of steppe and woodland. The Black Francolin is a bird of valleys, although in the foothills of the Himalayas it occurs at an altitude of some 1,600 m above sea-level. Its preferred habitats are grasslands, moist fields and cultivated sectors, especially along the banks of rivers and irrigation canals. It feeds primarily on seeds, but also consumes insects, small reptiles and snails. Unlike other members of its tribe, it does not swallow large quantities of stones to assist in digestion; it is possible that the hard seeds of some

of the plants on which it feeds are adequate for this purpose.

Black Francolins usually live in pairs, although outside the nesting season they gather in groups of 10-12 individuals. During August-December they are silent and move furtively among thickets, keeping well clear of danger and predators. From January onwards, the male proclaims his territory with constantly repeated polysyllabic cries, heard most often in the morning and the evening, and usually uttered from a perch on a rock or a mound. Territorial behaviour continues until the end of July, and during this period the male is very conspicuous.

Laying begins in March and continues until June. The female digs a small scrape, which is usually lined with a few stalks and small quantities of grass. The clutch consists of 6-15 eggs, and incubation begins when the clutch is complete. The female incubates alone for 20-21 days. The chicks hatch simultaneously. They can fly at seven or eight days old, reaching full flight capacity at 22-26 days. There may sometimes be two broods.

Quail
Coturnix coturnix

The smallest bird of the order of Galliformes: body length 18-21 cm, wing length 10.6-11.3 cm, wingspan 32-35 cm and weight during most of the year 90 g. The body of the Quail is compact, its neck is short, as is the bill (about 9 mm), and its legs are short but strong. The rear toe is considerably shorter than the other toes. The Quail has camouflage colours: the basic colour is yellow-brown, mottled with brown and black; the breast is chestnut-brown, streaked white. Male and female are similar, although the male has a varying amount of black on the throat. The juvenile resembles the adult female.

The Quail is distributed over most of Europe except the far north, and in various parts of central Asia and throughout tropical Africa. Of the five subspecies identified, the one occurring in Israel is *C.c. coturnix*, which breeds from Britain to India and to Lake Baikal in southern Siberia. It is the only member of the order of *Galliformes* which regularly migrates: its winter quarters are in the Sahel zone of Africa and in India. In Israel the Quail is primarily a passage migrant in autumn and spring. A few pairs breed, and it is possible that a small population is present throughout the year since Quails are also seen during the winter.

The basic habitats of the Quail are grasslands, steppe and scrub, but it has also adapted to agricultural areas such as fields of wheat, clover and lucerne. It feeds on seeds, grass, leaves and buds, and also on insects.

Quails leave Europe about the middle of August. They migrate at night, in flocks sometimes numbering scores of individuals. Part of the journey is made on foot, and part in short stages of flight. During the day they rest in fields. From the end of August to early September they arrive exhausted on the Mediterranean shoreline, between first light and 8-9 a.m., and hurriedly take refuge in the shade of a bush or a tree.

Quails begin to leave their winter quarters in early March and cross the Mediterranean between the end of March and mid-May. In years when Quails were still plentiful they could be seen during the spring migration over the whole width of Israel, especially along the Jordan Valley.

Individuals ringed near the Bardawil Lagoon in northern Sinai, and found in Russia (three individuals), in Bulgaria (four) and in Turkey (two), give an indication of their origin and migration route. This is also attested by a Quail ringed as a chick in Russia and found near the Bardawil.

The nesting season in Israel is in March-April. The female lays 8-13 eggs in a small scrape in the ground in a thicket of vegetation; the scrape is 10-12 cm in diameter and lined with grass and straw. Incubation, by the female alone, begins when the clutch is complete and lasts 17-19 days. The chicks hatch simultaneously. They can fly at 12-14 days and are fully fledged at about 19 days, but remain with the female parent to the age of 30-50 days before becoming independent.

Between June and the autumn migration, very few Quails are seen in Israel. In all probability, after nesting they migrate to Europe, where they apparently complete a second breeding cycle, in which the offspring of the first cycle also participate.

The hunting of Quails was developed in Ancient Egypt, as is attested by wall-paintings in several tombs. Diodorus, who lived at the end of the 2nd century AD, tells of criminals exiled to Rinocoria (El Arish) spreading nets to catch migrant Quails arriving on the shore. It seems that over the generations the technique of hunting with nets fell into disuse, and although Quails played a role in the local economy of the Middle East they were not commercially exploited to any large extent. This situation changed in 1885, with the beginning of the export of Quails from Egypt to Europe. In the very first year some 300,000 Quails were exported, in 1897 about two million, and in 1906 more than three million. Since then there has been a decrease in the number of Quails exported: in 1926-34 some 300,000-600,000 were exported every year, and after 1939 the number declined sharply. It is reasonable to suppose that hunting was a significant cause of this reduction in numbers, although not the only one. During the same years there have been substantial changes in agricultural techniques in their nesting areas, and this has had an impact on their population size; the harvesting of lucerne with mechanical reapers has exacted a heavy toll on these ground-nesting birds. Simultaneously there has been a drying-out of the Sahel, the winter refuge of the Quail, and this has possibly had the most decisive influence on its population. In northern Sinai the hunting of Quails with nets has continued into the present day. In their turn, the British Mandatory, Egyptian and Israeli authorities have attempted to impose restrictions, but these have proved impossible to enforce.

Order: Gruiformes (Rails, Crakes, Cranes, Bustards)

A heterogeneous order, including birds of very different appearance, ranging in size from the Little Crake, with a body length of 18 cm and a weight of 35 g, to the Crane, with a body length of 115 cm and a weight of 5 kg.

Members of the order all have a similar skeletal structure: the tarsus is usually long and exposed; the rear toe is absent or short and set higher than the others; the wings are short and rounded. The nest is usually built on the ground or on plants growing in or near water, and only rarely in a tree. The egg is mottled, and a similar yolk content is common to all species. The chicks are in most cases precocial. Most members of the order are marsh birds, but a few inhabit open land. They are distributed throughout the world, with the exception of the polar regions.

The systematics of this order are controversial. According to Howard and Moore (1980), the order includes 12 families; five of these comprise a single genus and a single species, and in total the order consists of 44 genera and 190 species. Three families are represented in Israel: Rallidae (rails and crakes) with eight species, Gruidae (cranes) with two species, and Otididae (bustards) with three species.

Family: Rallidae (Rails and Crakes)

The largest family in the order of Gruiformes, comprising 17 genera and 122 species. Its distribution is worldwide, except for the polar regions and deserts.

Most members of the family are marsh birds, only rarely emerging into open territory. Their bodies are compact, and their plumage soft. Their tail and wings are short. Their legs and toes are long. All members of the family are capable of swimming; some (subfamily Fulicinae) have lobed toes, while others (subfamily Rallinae) do not. The head is small, and in many species there is a colourful patch on the forehead, which is especially conspicuous during courtship. The bill is usually short, conical and laterally compressed, sometimes long and slightly hooked; the bill and the legs are also highly coloured. Most species have camouflage plumage barred with shades of brown and grey; species which live on open water have uniform and more striking plumage — usually black, like the Coot. Usually there is no difference in colour between male and female, although normally the male is larger. Flight is heavy and seldom employed; in spite of this the northern species migrate long distances, usually at low level. All species have characteristic head movements when walking or swimming.

Most members of the family seek their food on dry land among thickets of marsh vegetation. They feed on both animal and vegetable food: floating plants, fruits, seeds, worms, molluscs and insects. The larger species also consume small fish and frogs.

The Rallidae live in pairs, and most of them, with a few exceptions such as the Coot, do not form flocks even outside the nesting season. All are very vocal, especially during the breeding season. The nest is built in early summer, in a thicket close by the water, usually near a marsh, a lake or a pool. It is large and sometimes lined with delicate plant material, and hidden so effectively that to this day the eggs of some 20 species are unknown. The clutch is of 6-12 eggs: the smaller species lay 6-8 eggs, the average-sized ones 11-12 and the larger ones 7-10 (in most families the size of the clutch is in inverse proportion to the size of the bird). The smaller species of Rallidae, however, lay several clutches in the course of the year, and the larger species only once; the Moorhen and the Coot are exceptions, laying twice or even three times in a season. Incubation usually begins only when the clutch is complete, but there are variations between species, and even between different pairs of the same species. In many species the female and the male share incubation, which lasts 19-21 days, similar to the incubation period of much larger species. The Rallidae also differ from other families in that the incubation of the smaller species is of virtually the same duration as that of the larger. Hatching is simultaneous or spread over a few days; the offspring are precocial, although in some species the chicks remain for some time in the nest while the male brings them food. Both parents tend the chicks and feed them bill-to-bill. The chicks attain flying ability at a relatively late stage.

In Israel six genera and eight species are represented.

Moorhen
Gallinula chloropus

The most typical representative of the family: body length 29-34 cm, wing length 16.5-18 cm, wingspan 50-55 cm and weight 190-265 g. From a distance the Moorhen appears all-black. From closer quarters its back is seen to be olive-brown and its belly slate-grey, and it is distinguished by its red bill and forehead, by its yellowish-green legs, by the white outer undertail-coverts and by a white line along the sides of the body. Males are 10% larger than females. Juveniles have dark brown plumage and the bill and forehead are less conspicuous.

The Moorhen has a cosmopolitan range, and is common in all continents except Australasia and Antarctica, and in all climatic areas except tundra and the polar regions. There are 12 different subspecies. The one occurring in Israel is *G.c. chloropus*, which breeds from the islands of the Atlantic Ocean, through North Africa, Britain and Spain, to Sri Lanka, Indo-China and Japan. The populations in central and eastern Europe are migratory, wintering especially in the Balkans and Turkey, while Israel and Egypt are at the southernmost limit of their wintering range.

In Israel the Moorhen is a common resident, but its population is reinforced by a wintering contingent. A Moorhen ringed in Israel in autumn was found the following spring in the Ukraine. These birds are common in any aquatic environment where riparian vegetation is plentiful, including sewage-ponds. Their number in this country is estimated at hundreds of pairs.

The Moorhen lives in clumps of rushes and reeds. It eats both vegetable food, including aquatic plants, seeds and fruits, and animal food, mainly insects. In winter Moorhens often gather in loose and scattered flocks, sometimes including parents and several generations of chicks from the previous summer. The resident Moorhens tend to live in pairs throughout the year, and they defend the nucleus of the territory

even in winter.

Territorial behaviour intensifies with the approach of the nesting season, which begins at the end of March and continues until the end of August. The nest, a flat basket hidden among vegetation or floating on the surface and anchored to the reeds, is usually of dry reeds and rushes, and only the laying hollow is lined with more delicate material. Often Moorhens build two nests before laying, but only one of them is used. The clutch is of 5-8 eggs; sometimes two females lay in the same nest, and as many as 13-15 eggs may then be found. Incubation, by both sexes, lasts 20-21 days. In the first nesting cycle it begins when the clutch is complete, but in replacement and in the second and third clutches it starts half way through laying. Hatching is thus simultaneous in the first case and more erratic thereafter, and the chicks hatched first join the male parent while the female continues to incubate. The chicks are fed by the parents for about the first 40 days, although they begin to feed by themselves as early as three weeks old; sometimes the older siblings, offspring from earlier broods, assist in the feeding and tending of younger chicks. The chicks are able to fly at 16 weeks old, and become independent after about a further three weeks.

Coot
Fulica atra

Body length 39-45 cm, wing length 20-22 cm, wingspan 68-75 cm and weight 500-865 g. The Coot has a broad body, not laterally compressed like that of other members of its family. Its wings are short and broad, and its tail is particularly short. It is an all-black bird except for the white bill and forehead. It has medium-length legs with very long toes, each of the three front toes lobed. The juvenile plumage has a distinct brown tone with a paler belly and breast.

The Coot breeds across Eurasia, from the Mediterranean and India in the south to southern Scandinavia and Siberia in the north, and also on the islands of the Pacific Ocean and in Australasia. Its range extends over the Palaearctic, Oriental and Australasian regions, in areas of boreal, temperate, Mediterranean, steppe and desert climate. In this range four subspecies have been identified. It also breeds, though rarely, in Cyprus, Israel and Egypt. Since the beginning of the twentieth century there has been a perceptible northward expansion, possibly as a result of climatic amelioration. This is a bird of lakes, pools and open water, not of marsh vegetation like other members of the family. The Coots of northern and eastern Europe, which belong to the subspecies *F.a. atra*, migrate in winter to the shores of the Baltic Sea, to western Europe and the countries of the Mediterranean basin, and also to desert areas in the Sahara and Sudan. A Coot ringed as a chick in Russia has been found in Israel, and Coots ringed in Israel have been found in the USSR (11), especially around the Black Sea and the Caspian, and in Yugoslavia (one) and Turkey (one). In Israel this is a common winter visitor and a very occasional breeder.

The Coot is omnivorous, but prefers mainly vegetable food: seeds, fruits, leaves, buds and green stalks. It also consumes animal food such as worms, molluscs and insects, and even small or dead fish which it catches by diving. Its dive is shallow and of short duration; a Coot is watched by gulls, and when it returns to the surface its prey is liable to be stolen. In fish-ponds, Coots also eat food-concentrates intended for the fish; fortunately, fish are not much fed during the winter, and so the damage caused is limited. Often Coots leave the water for the bank, and even enter cultivated fields to feed on the young crops; when danger threatens they scatter and run back to the water. Coots feed by day, and at night roost on the bank.

In Israel the Coot is a very common bird in winter. Migrant and wintering Coots begin to gather around fish-ponds sometimes as early as September. In October there is a considerable rise in their numbers, reaching a peak in November or early December. After the winter rains, Coots may be observed on almost any stretch of water, ranging in size from Lake Tiberias to small sewage-ponds. Sometimes they may also be seen in dense flocks on the sea-shore. In winter censuses of waterfowl the numbers counted have ranged from 12,000 individuals (1970) to 54,000 (1983), with an annual average between 1965 and 1982 of approximately 29,000. The northward migration begins as early as the end of February, but takes place especially during March. In April Coots disappear from most of their wintering quarters, and only a few individuals or small groups remain over the summer.

On rare occasions, Coots nest in Israel. Some 15 nests have been found in various parts of the country, from the reservoirs of the Golan and the Hula to the coastal plain and the reservoir of Yeroham. In the nesting season territorial aggression develops among Coots, but this is confined to the vicinity of the nest, which is a crude structure built in shallow water and hidden among vegetation. There are 6-10 eggs in the clutch. Incubation begins when the clutch is about half complete and lasts 21-24 days, with both parents participating. After hatching, the chicks remain in the nest for three or four days, while the female continues to brood them and the male brings them food; the family then separates, with each parent tending a group of chicks. The chicks start to forage for themselves at about a month old, are capable of flying at two months old, and become independent soon after.

The Coot is a commonly hunted bird, although its flesh is not particularly appetising. In Israel, the open season for hunting Coots lasts from 1 September to 31 January.

Purple Gallinule
Porphyrio porphyrio

A large waterfowl: body length 48 cm, wing length 26.5-29.5 cm, wingspan 95 cm and weight 800 g. Its dominant colours are various shades of blue. The long legs, the forehead and the large, thick bill are bright red.

The range of the Purple Gallinule extends discontinuously through the southern Palaearctic region, across the Ethiopian region, and over the Oriental and Australasian regions. In this broad range 20 subspecies have been identified. In the Middle East the Purple Gallinule is known from the Nile Delta (subspecies *P.p. madagascariensis*); from the estuary of the Tigris and Euphrates and up to northwest India (*P.p. seistanicus*); and from the shores of the Caspian Sea, northwest Iran, north Syria and central and south Turkey (*P.p. caspius*). In the past it also bred in the marshes of Antakya in southern Turkey, where it is likely that a small population survives today. The Egyptian subspecies has an olive-green back and a green-deep blue head, while the one from the Caspian has a whitish-blue head and nape and pale blue wings. The Purple Gallinule is resident throughout its range, and only a few individuals wander.

In Israel this is a very rare accidental in marsh environments. A few sightings (about 15) were made during the 1970s and early 1980s, occurring in most months of the year and especially in the coastal plain and the Bet She'an Valley. The records are of both *P.p. caspius* and *P.p. madagascariensis*.

Water Rail
Rallus aquaticus

Body length 25 cm, wing length 12 cm, wingspan 42 cm and weight 150 g. A small and dark bird, brown above and grey-blue on the belly. In adults, the flanks are barred white and dark. The bill is long (about 4 cm) and slightly curved, red in colour; the bill is the principal distinguishing feature between this species and the crakes. The feet are of average length, while the toes are very long, enabling the bird to move easily among reeds and to grip their stalks.

The Water Rail has a sporadic Palaearctic range, extending over most of Europe, central Asia and North Africa. In this range four subspecies have been identified. The populations from eastern Europe migrate in winter to western Europe and the Mediterranean basin, including the Nile Valley. The subspecies visiting Israel is *R.a. aquaticus*, whose range is Euro-Siberian and North African.

This species' typical habitats, both in nesting areas and in winter quarters, are thickets of vegetation in stagnant or slow-moving water. It spends most of its time hidden among reeds and rushes on the shores of freshwater lakes and does not often stray into the open. It swims well and seldom flies.

The Water Rail is a fairly common winterer in Israel, although it is not easily observed because of its furtive habits; only its loud and raucous cries are likely to be heard. The birds begin to arrive in this country at the end of August, and the rearguard remains until April, but most sightings take place during December-January. The Water Rail feeds especially on insects in various stages of development, and also on molluscs, worms and even dead fish, as well as on vegetable food.

Genus: *Porzana* (crakes)

Members of the genus *Porzana* are small to medium-sized birds with short bills. The genus comprises 18 species, distributed through all areas of the world; three species are known in Israel. Males are speckled brown above, and mostly grey-blue below. Females are paler, with brown-orange on the belly. The tail is short and usually held erect. Crakes have laterally compressed bodies, long legs and very long toes, ideally suited to their marshland habitats.

It is very difficult to observe crakes, not only on account of their habitats and pale colours, but also because of their times of activity; they are active particularly in the hours of twilight and in the dark. During the nesting season they are more easily heard than seen, but for the remainder of the year they are fairly quiet and solitary. Crakes feed on a variety of food: insects, snails and similar creatures constitute their basic diet, which is supplemented by vegetable food.

Crakes are weak fliers, but in spite of this they all migrate to some extent or another.

Spotted Crake
Porzana porzana

Body length 23 cm, wing length 12 cm, wingspan 40 cm and weight 65 g. Recognisable by its brown back, speckled with black and white 'eyes', by the grey flanks which are barred with white, by the brown-yellow bill with red base, and by the pale olive-green legs; the feature best distinguishing it from other crakes seen in Israel is the sandy-yellow undertail-coverts.

The Spotted Crake is a monotypic species which breeds across Europe and penetrates to a small extent into central Asia. The European population winters especially in tropical Africa, from Sudan to South Africa, with small numbers also wintering in Israel and Egypt. In Israel, however, it is more common as a passage migrant, from the end of August to early November and again from mid-March to mid-May, when it is possible to encounter it in fields some distance from water.

Little Crake
Porzana parva

Body length 19 cm, wing length 10-11 cm, wingspan 37 cm and weight 45 g. In the field it is difficult and sometimes impossible to distinguish from Baillon's Crake; it is best told by the absence of conspicuous barring on the flanks. The back of the male is olive-brown barred with black, and its underparts greyish-blue. The female is brown on the back with sand-coloured face and underparts. The legs are pale green, and the bill green with a red base.

The Little Crake is a monotypic species breeding in Europe and wintering in Israel and Egypt, but especially in central Africa. In Israel it is a fairly common passage migrant and a rare winter visitor, between September and the end of April.

Baillon's Crake
Porzana pusilla

Body length 18 cm, wing length 9 cm, wingspan 35 cm and weight 35 g. The male's back is brown and barred with dark stripes, while the flanks are barred dark and light; its face, throat, breast and belly are bluish-grey. The female is similar although with a lighter throat. The legs are flesh-brown and the bill greenish.

Baillon's Crake has a sporadic distribution in the Palaearctic, Ethiopian, Oriental and Australasian regions. In this range six subspecies have been identified. The populations breeding in Europe and Asia migrate southward in autumn, but little is known of the winter quarters of the Western Palaearctic population. In Israel it is a common passage migrant and a quite rare winter visitor, between September and April, the subspecies concerned being *P.p. intermedia* which breeds in North Africa and in Europe east to Romania.

On two occasions evidence of nesting has been found in Israel. In summer 1954 a chick of this species was found in the Bet She'an Valley, and on 5 June 1953 a nest with six hatched eggs was discovered in the Hula marshes.

Corncrake
Crex crex

Body length 24-28 cm, wing length 13-14.7 cm, wingspan 46-53 cm and weight 85-165 g. The Corncrake resembles the Quail, both in colouring and in overall appearance: its back is greyish-brown, speckled with brown-black markings; the underparts are light reddish-brown. The wing-coverts are chestnut-coloured and are among the best distinguishing features, both at rest and in flight. The male has a greyish-blue throat and supercilium, lacking in the female. The wings are broad and short, and in flight the legs dangle.

The Corncrake is a monotypic species distributed from Ireland to Mongolia and China, but is absent from southern and northern Europe. Its winter range is restricted to a narrow belt from Kenya and Uganda to South Africa.

This species is the most land-based of its family. It is a bird of fields and meadows, and not of dense marsh vegetation; accordingly its toes are shorter. It consumes both vegetable and animal food, and especially small invertebrates. The Corncrake is usually solitary. Only at the approach of migration is it likely to gather in small groups, numbering up to 40 individuals. Sometimes a solitary individual joins a flock of migrating Quails, hence the popular belief that it leads them.

The Corncrake is a fairly common passage migrant in Israel: in autumn, between September and November, and in spring, when it is most conspicuous during April-May. In these periods many exhausted and injured individuals are found throughout the country.

Family: Gruidae (Cranes)

The family Gruidae comprises four genera and 15 species, inhabiting all parts of the world except South America, Antarctica and the islands of the Indian Ocean. The centre of distribution is in central and eastern Asia, where seven species live. Some species have a very limited nesting range. All except the southern species migrate south in autumn, sometimes over considerable distances.

These are large birds of erect stance, living mostly in marshes and wet heathland. Cranes differ from storks in a number of respects, including anatomical structure, vocal apparatus, moult and breeding cycle. Cranes have long necks with 19-20 vertebrae. The head is relatively small, sometimes with bare and coloured patches, or a tuft of feathers resembling whiskers. The bill is only slightly longer than the head, and is thick at the base and pointed at the tip. The legs are long. The toes are short, the rear toe being shorter than the others and set higher; the claw of the middle toe is long and serves as a weapon in fighting. The trachea is very long and convoluted, which accounts for the particularly deep voice of cranes, clearly audible from a distance. Cranes have long and broad wings and a short and rounded tail. The dominant colour is usually grey, but some species are brown or white; the flight feathers are black in all species. Male and female differ only in size, and there are no seasonal differences.

The flight of cranes is dynamic, with neck and legs extended. Their bodies are elongated and relatively narrow, enabling them to move easily in dense vegetation, which is their principal habitat, at least during the nesting season. At rest and when threatened they stand upright.

Most species live in marshes, on wet ground and along the shores of lakes and pools. Cranes feed on a variety of food: roots, tubers, ripe seeds, juicy stalks, leaves, fruit, and also creatures such as worms, snails, insects, frogs, lizards, mice and fledglings. Their diet varies according to season and place. They roost communally on the ground, standing on one leg with the head buried under the wing.

Cranes live in pairs, and the pair bond apparently lasts throughout life. They perform colourful and extremely attractive ritual dances; these are not only courtship displays as they are performed throughout the year, sometimes in groups of three or four — apparently parents with their offspring. These dances evidently reinforce the family bond, which is also maintained by a varied range of calls and by rattling of the mandibles, in the manner of storks.

Both sexes defend their territory with great energy against intruders. Often they return to the same place and the same nest, even if the latter has been destroyed. It is evident that cranes have difficulty adapting to new habitats, and this is one of the reasons for the decline in their populations. All cranes nest on the ground, except the Hooded Crane which nests in trees. The large nest, built by both sexes, is in an inaccessible site, usually in the centre of a marsh. There are usually only 2 eggs, small and light in relation to the size of the bird. Incubation begins with the first egg and both parents participate, although the female takes the major part. The period of incubation in 25-27 days. The chicks are precocial and within a few hours of hatching they are capable of walking and even swimming. The parents feed them bill-to-bill. They can fly at 9-10 weeks old, and they then appear more brown than the adults and without bare patches on the head. They gain adult plumage only at the age of two to three years. At the end of the nesting season, cranes gather into sometimes massive flocks and migrate. The family tie between parents and offspring is maintained during migration and in winter quarters. Cranes live to a great age; a captive individual has been known to reach the age of 55 years.

At least four species of crane are today in danger of extinction, and the breeding areas of other species have been drastically curtailed. Their most serious problem is the destruction of their habitats. Hunting and harassment, in the nesting areas and along the migration routes and in the winter quarters, have also affected them severely.

In Israel two species are represented.

Crane
Grus grus

A large bird: body length 120-140 cm (of which the body itself accounts for 50-55 cm and the rest is made up by the long neck and legs), wing length 55-61 cm, wingspan 220-245 cm and weight 5.5 kg. The bill is of moderate length (about 105 mm). Most of the plumage is grey; the forehead, nape, throat and foreneck are grey-black, with a white stripe extending from the eye down to the neck, and in adults the crown is red. The tertials are long and cover the short tail (only 20 cm in length), the whole resembling a 'horse-tail'. The sexes are similar, although the males are considerably larger. Immatures are browner and darker and lack the red crown.

The Crane breeds in northern Europe and Asia, from Norway and Sweden to the eastern USSR, mostly north of 48°N, in regions of taiga and tundra; small populations also breed in Turkey and Iran. In this range two subspecies are known; the western one, which occurs in Israel, is *G.g. grus*. Most populations, except those of Turkey, migrate, usually at high altitude, around 2,000 m (flocks have been known to reach a height of 3,200 m). In stormy weather they move at lower level. They migrate in 'V' formations, both by day and by night. They are not confined to dry-land routes but cross the Mediterranean, passing over Crete and Cyprus. Most of the journey is apparently made in continuous flight. Cranes fom the Western Palaearctic winter in the Mediterranean basin and the Middle East, including Israel, and also in East Africa, where most remain in southern Egypt and Sudan.

Cranes are sometimes seen in Israel as early as mid-July. Their main migration, however, begins in mid-September, intensifies in mid-October and continues until mid-December. They are then heard and seen in various parts of Israel, but especially over the Jordan Valley, the Arava and the region of Eilat; hundreds and thousands of individuals pass this way.

The Cranes wintering in Israel begin to arrive at the end of October, and their population reaches its height in early January. In the past Cranes were familiar winterers in Israel, especially in the Jezreel Valley, but many were poisoned by pesticides in the late 1950s, and for some years the wintering population ceased to exist. In the winter of 1965/66, 49 Cranes were again wintering in the region of Lake Kishon in the Jezreel Valley, and since then the number has risen steadily from year to year: in 1967/68, 500 individuals wintered there; ten years later the number was 800, and in 1981/82 about 1,000 individuals were counted. This population disperses during the day over considerable distances, but returns in the evening to congregate on the shores of Lake Kishon. Since the early 1970s, Cranes have also begun to winter in the western Negev and in the eastern part of the central coastal plain; here, too, the populations have increased and in these two locations, in 1983/84, 600 and 200 individuals respectively were counted. In the same year Cranes also began to winter in the southern Golan, where about 150 individuals were counted, and a year later some 30 were wintering in the Hula Valley. In January 1985, the total national wintering population was estimated at about 2,500 individuals: 1,700 in the Jezreel Valley, 300 in the Golan, 350 in the central coastal plain, and 100 in the western Negev.

In the morning Cranes fly to the pasture fields. They eat large quantities of pecan and cotton stubble, but cause considerable damage by eating the budding shoots of chickpeas. They are also liable to consume vegetables, especially on Sabbaths when the fields are unattended. They also eat various animal food when available: reptiles, amphibians, sick birds, rodents and insects.

The wintering population starts to dwindle in mid-February and disappears around mid-March; at about the same time the passage population arrives. The last of the migrants are still to be seen in April.

Demoiselle Crane
Anthropoides virgo

Body length 95 cm, wing length 44-51.5 cm, wingspan 125 cm and weight 2.5 kg. Smaller than the Crane, and distinguished from it by the white ear-tufts and black neck, at the base of which is a drooping plume of black feathers.

The Demoiselle Crane breeds in eastern Turkey, and especially in a narrow strip extending from the northern shores of the Black Sea to Manchuria, south of the breeding range of the Crane. This is a bird of steppes and more arid regions. It winters in southeast Asia, India and central Africa.

This is a rare passage migrant in the skies of Israel. Two were seen in February 1963 in fish-ponds in the Bet She'an Valley, and one on 1 November 1963 in the Acre Valley. Another was observed on 5 December 1973 in fields in the western Negev. On 21 April 1977 five individuals were seen in the Valley of the Moon in the vicinity of Eilat, and another was sighted in April 1978 in the salt-pools of Eilat. One was observed over a period of more than two weeks in spring 1979, from mid-April to the beginning of May, in fish-ponds in the coastal plain. On 21 October 1984, a Demoiselle Crane was seen passing over Tel Aviv in company with a flock of pelicans.

Family: Otididae (Bustards)

This family comprises 11 genera and 23 species. Most are confined to Africa, and only a few species have expanded north and east, to Asia (especially India), and south to Australia. Only two species have penetrated south and southeast Europe. All species prefer flat, dry and hot environments, from grassy steppes, savannas and scrubland to arid deserts. Only the northern species migrate.

A family of ground birds, with squat and solid bodies, resembling ostriches in appearance, although smaller. Their size is medium to large, and weight is between 700 g and 12 kg. The female is smaller than the male, sometimes a half of his weight or even less. The legs of bustards are long, thick and strong, with only three short and forward-pointing toes; the claws are short and broad. The neck is thick and long, and the head is large with a flat crown. The bill is straight and shorter than the head, broad at the base and laterally compressed at the tip. Bustards do not possess an oil gland, but instead have powder down, especially on the breast. The wings are broad and long; the tail is broad, of short or medium length. The upperparts of bustards are camouflaged in shades of speckled brown; the belly is light and usually whitish-grey. The spread wings are distinctively patterned in white and black. The males are more colourful, and some of them are adorned with display feathers at the approach of the breeding season, on the crown or the neck.

Bustards are suspicious and timid birds. They usually walk with dignified gait, neck held erect. When threatened they run or squat, and seldom take to flight; they fly with strong and constant wingbeats, usually at low level, and glide only when landing.

Members of this family are omnivorous and feed on grass, leaves, insects, snails and vertebrates. They are capable of adapting their feeding habits in accordance with the available food sources, and can exist without drinking water.

Bustards live in pairs for at least part of the year, but in most species family life apparently does not continue from year to year. Their courtship behaviour is colourful and very impressive, although it varies considerably from species to species. Nesting is in an unlined depression in the ground. The clutch is of 1-3 eggs in larger species and as many as 5-6 in smaller species. The female alone incubates, and the period of incubation is 20-28 days. The offspring hatch open-eyed and covered with dense down. The parents, usually the female, feed them bill-to-bill. They fly at the age of 30-35 days and reach sexual maturity at two to six years old. Until this stage their plumage resembles that of the adult female. Many species, especially those inhabiting temperate zones, gather in flocks after nesting.

Houbara Bustard
Chlamydotis undulata

Body length of the female 60-63 cm and of the male 64-73 cm, wing length of the female 32-33.5 cm and of the male 36-40 cm, wingspan 145-170 cm, weight of the female 1,000-1,130 g and of the male 1,300-2,100 g. A ground bird, resembling a small ostrich or a turkey. Houbara Bustards have long and strong legs with three toes. The neck is long, as is the tail (about 20 cm), which is chestnut-brown in colour. The upperparts are sandy-brown and speckled with grey-black; the breast is greyish and the belly white. On the side of the neck there is a frill of black feathers, and a black-white crest extends from the crown. The female is similar to the male, but her feathery frills are less developed. These frills are especially conspicuous in the male after the partial moult, which takes place before nesting; at this stage they resemble a black and white apron, particularly conspicuous on the neck. The wings are narrow compared with those of other members of the family. In flight there is striking contrast between the black and the white and sandy-brown colours of the primaries and secondaries; the contrast between black and white is more conspicuous in the male.

The Houbara Bustard's range extends sporadically from the Canary Islands and the western Sahara, through North Africa and the Middle East (including Israel, Sinai, Jordan and Syria) to central Asia (Pakistan, Kazakhstan and Mongolia). Three subspecies are known. The one found in Israel, *C.u. macqueenii*, is distributed from Israel to Mongolia.

1. White Pelicans in the Hula Reserve

2. Cormorants in the Hula Reserve

3. Night Heron

4. Cattle Egret

5. Little Egrets in fish-pond at Maagan Mikhael

6. Squacco Heron and nestlings

7. White Storks with Black-headed Gulls

8. Glossy Ibis with nestlings

9. Spoonbills at Maagan Mikhael

10. Greater Flamingo

11. Ruddy Shelduck

12. Egyptian Goose

13. Shelducks

14. Tufted Ducks with Coots and Pochards

15. Black Kite

16. Egyptian Vultures

17. Griffon Vultures

18. Short-toed Eagle feeding nestling with a snake

19. Bonelli's Eagle

20. Ospreys nesting in Tiran

21. Sooty Falcons

22. Chukars

23. Sand Partridge

24. Coots in a fish-pond

25. Houbara Bustard at nest with chick

26. Houbara Bustard chick with two eggs

27. Black-winged Stilt with three chicks

28. Stone-curlew

29. Cream-coloured Courser

Most populations of Houbara Bustards are resident, but those of central Asia winter in northwestern India, Pakistan, Iran, Iraq and Arabia.

Houbara Bustards inhabit open environments with grass and scrub, especially plains or gentle slopes; they are rare in areas of extreme desert. In Israel they are concentrated principally in the south of the Valley of Be'er Sheva, in an area where annual rainfall is approximately 200 mm. They extend northward along the Valley of Be'er Sheva to the region of Jericho, but breeding pairs have also been found in the southern Arava, some 70 km from Eilat. Outside the nesting season they roam and are then also to be seen in the southern Negev. They winter in the Arava, in numbers rising in accordance with the degree of agricultural development. The development of agriculture in the bustard's natural habitats supplies it with abundant food, and indeed its largest and most dense concentrations are in agricultural sectors, but it is vulnerable to pesticides and dead and injured specimens have been found near fields that have been sprayed. The Houbara Bustard is omnivorous: it consumes fruits, seeds, buds, leaves and flowers, and is especially partial to the young shoots of desert-wormwood (*Artemisia herba-alba*) and various garlic onions; it also feeds on beetles, grasshoppers, crickets, locusts, lizards, snakes and young rodents. The Houbara Bustard can exist without drinking water, but drinks when the occasion arises.

The Houbara Bustard is active in winter during most hours of the day; in summer only in the early morning and late afternoon. It spends the hottest hours sheltering in shade. This is a quiet and timid bird. When threatened it runs with dignified gait from bush to bush, the neck stretched forward and held parallel to the ground, pausing from time to time to look around. Sometimes it freezes or prostrates itself on the ground. In spite of its bulky appearance it flies without difficulty, usually at low level, about 10 m above the ground, with neck stretched forward.

In the days of the British Mandate the Houbara Bustard was a very rare bird in this country. After the establishment of the State of Israel (1948) there was an increase in its numbers, but unrestrained hunting in the mid-1950s caused a renewed depletion of its population. Since then there has again been an increase; in a census in the western Negev at the end of July 1984, 316 individuals were counted, out of an estimated total of 600 Houbara Bustards in the whole country.

At the approach of the breeding season, sometimes as early as the end of December but usually in mid-February, the males perform impressive court-ship displays, each in his own territory. The white feathers of the neck and breast and part of the wing-coverts are erected, as are the black feathers of the head and nape. The head is tilted back on to the body, so that the bird resembles a white ball of feathers. In this posture it runs over distances of scores of metres, stops, and repeats the process.

The nest is a shallow scrape dug by the female, sometimes in the shade of a bush, sometimes in open territory. Laying takes place between March and May. There are usually 2 eggs, sometimes 3, and near agricultural land with abundant food the clutch may contain as many as 4 eggs. The female incubates alone for about 24 days, during which time the male usually stays in the vicinity of the nest. The chicks hatch open-eyed and covered in dense down striped with shades of brown, yellow and black. The female feeds them bill-to-bill, sometimes assisted by the male, and continues to brood the chicks for their first few nights. At times of danger she alerts them with faint and monotonous warning cries, and they run for shelter and hide; the mother sometimes feigns injury. The chicks are capable of flying at the age of about five weeks, but stay close to the mother until autumn.

After nesting Houbara Bustards form flocks of eight to 12 individuals, sometimes more. In the western Negev larger flocks have been counted: 37 individuals on 5 August 1982, 42 on 23 June 1982 and 51 on 12 July 1983. In this period they often congregate at refuse-tips, where they apparently feed on insects.

The Houbara Bustard has been much hunted. Its eggs are also gathered and eaten, and thus it has become very rare and even extinct in some areas. Recently there have been efforts to preserve the Houbara Bustard in many areas of the world: in Israel a breeding nucleus has been established under the auspices of the Wildlife Research Center near the University of Tel Aviv, recording the first successful breeding of these birds in captivity. In Egypt, wealthy Saudi Arabian falconry enthusiasts have been refused permission to practise their sport, and in Pakistan hunting has been banned from mid-February 1984 for a period of five years.

Little Bustard
Tetrax tetrax

Similar to the Houbara Bustard but smaller: body length 42 cm, wing length 25 cm, wingspan 110 cm and weight 750 g. In breeding plumage the male has a black neck, with narrow white bars bordering the throat and the breast. This plumage is assumed after a partial moult in March. During the remainder of the year there are few differences between male and female and immature. They are sand-brown speckled with black, and only in flight is it revealed that most of the primaries and secondaries are entirely white, except for the black tips; only the four outer primaries and the primary coverts are black.

The range of the Little Bustard extends through the dry areas of the Palaearctic region, from Spain and France to eastern Kazakhstan, to the north of the range of the Houbara Bustard. This is a monotypic species. Hunting and habitat destruction have exterminated it in many areas and greatly reduced its original range. All populations except those of southern Europe migrate. The eastern USSR population winters especially in the trans-Caspian region in Iran and Pakistan.

The Little Bustard is essentially a bird of grassy steppes and pasture, feeding on vegetable food and invertebrates. It flies to a greater extent than other species in its family; in flight the wingbeats are clearly audible.

In Israel the Little Bustard is a rare winter accidental between December and February, sometimes being seen as late as early March. Most sightings are from the Bet She'an Valley and the Jezreel Valley, but some have been recorded in the Golan, the Acre Valley, the coastal plain and the western Negev. Usually only a few wintering individuals are present, but occasionally flocks of 20-30 and even as many as 60 individuals are seen. The visitors sometimes stay in the same area for a month or more.

Great Bustard
Otis tarda

A large and solid bird: body length 75-105 cm, wing length of the male 62 cm and of the female 49 cm, wingspan 190-260 cm and weight 3.6-12 kg. The male is larger than the female, sometimes by as much as 100%, and is Europe's largest flying bird. The Great Bustard has chestnut-orange plumage, speckled with black on the back and tail. The neck and head are grey and the belly white. The male has a moustache beneath the bill. In flight grey and white wing areas are revealed. The plumage of the female is less conspicuous.

The Great Bustard today has a range extending over Spain, Germany, Czechoslovakia, Hungary, Romania, Turkey, the southern USSR and China. In this range two subspecies have been identified. The western one, *O.t. tarda*, which breeds from Europe to southwest USSR, has occurred in Israel. This bustard breeds on treeless plains, grassy steppes and extensive fields. The populations of eastern Europe and western USSR are migratory. In the Middle East they winter in Turkey and on the shores of the Caspian Sea, while in the past the Great Bustard has been known to winter as far south as the Damascus-Baghdad axis.

This species feeds particularly on vegetable food, but the young and sometimes also the female consume large quantities of insects. In spite of its size, the Great Bustard is a good flier.

In Israel this is a very rare winter accidental, with only four definite records: two individuals in 1954 in the Bet She'an Valley; a single individual in 1956 in the northern Negev; one on 1 January 1976 in the central Golan; and another on 30 September 1978 on the northeast coast of Lake Tiberias.

Order: Charadriiformes (Waders, Gulls, Terns and Auks)

A very large and varied group, comprising 18 families divided among three sub-orders: Charadrii (waders), with 13 families; Lari (skuas, gulls and terns), with four; and Alcae, which is not represented in Israel and contains a single family — auks. Members of the last-named family are ocean-dwelling birds of the Northern Hemisphere, coming ashore only to breed.

The order comprises 88 genera and some 330 species, birds of small to medium size: body length varies between 13 and 79 cm. Although members of the order vary considerably, especially in the length and shape of the bill and the length of the legs, all share certain anatomical features. The plumage is dense, capable of preventing water penetration. The dominant colours are usually black and white, with various shades of grey and brown; more variegated plumage is rare. With a few exceptions, there is no difference in plumage between male and female. There are usually two moults in a year: a full one in autumn, after breeding, and a partial one in spring, at the approach of the nesting season.

The Charadriiformes are represented in open environments in all parts of the world, from the poles to deserts and tropical regions. Usually they live in aquatic habitats. All of them with the exception of one genus (*Thinocorus*, comprising two South American species) feed predominantly on live food. Many species are gregarious through the year, and separate into territorial pairs only at breeding times. Only gulls and terns breed in large and dense colonies, although among these there are some species which are solitary breeders, while on the other hand there are waders that breed in loose colonies. Most nest on the ground and have a low rate of reproduction: usually there is only one nesting cycle per year and the clutch contains 1-4 eggs. The chicks are hatched with eyes open and covered with dense down, and most feed independently immediately after hatching.

Birds of this order have a much longer lifespan than other birds of similar size, and individuals of some species have attained ages of 30 years and more.

In Israel this is the most populous order after the Passeriformes (songbirds), with 87 species and 32 genera, representing ten families.

Sub-order: Charadrii (Waders)

A clearly defined group comprising 13 families, seven of which are represented in Israel: Rostratulidae (painted snipes), Haematopodidae (oystercatchers), Recurvirostridae (avocets, stilts), Burhinidae (stone-curlews), Glareolidae (pratincoles, coursers), Charadriidae (plovers) and Scolopacidae (sandpipers, snipes); in the last-named family six subfamilies are recognised.

Members of this sub-order are of typical appearance and are easily distinguished, although they differ considerably from one another. Size varies from the Least Sandpiper *Calidris minutilla* of northern North America, with a body length of 13 cm and weight of 20 g, to the female Curlew, with a body length of 60 cm and a weight of 1,000 g. Most birds of the sub-order are about 150 g in weight, but appear larger and heavier because of the long neck and legs. The toes are separate or partially webbed. The rear toe is usually degenerate and located higher than the others; sometimes it is entirely absent, especially in species preferring movement over dry ground. The head is round; the bill is short and solid (plovers) or long (up to 15 cm in the Curlew), sometimes curved. The eyes are large and located on the sides of the head, providing a broad field of vision. In many species, especially in the painted snipes and the woodcocks, the eyes are set towards the rear of the head, so that the bird can scan its surroundings even when the bill is immersed in mud or water. These birds are also endowed with strong auditory senses, enabling them to detect prey moving beneath the surface of the ground. The wings are long and pointed, except in some species of lapwing, and also in the woodcocks, which live in enclosed habitats. In flight the wings are not fully extended, but are sharply angled at the carpal joints between the secondaries and primaries. The coverts are long. The tail is short or of average length.

Breeding plumage differs from winter plumage; normally the moult takes place in the nesting areas, although the Dunlin changes at least part of its breeding plumage in winter quarters. Sometimes it is difficult to distinguish between different species of one genus, except by the wing pattern or call. The sexes are usually almost identical, but the female is normally larger; the case of the Ruff, where the male is considerably larger, is exceptional. Members of this sub-order have no 'song' as such, but many species emit territorial calls. There is also a variety of contact and alarm calls, some of them quite melodic.

Waders are distributed in all parts of the world, except Antarctica. Most are birds of open aquatic environments — lake shores, sea-coasts, marshes, river estuaries and wetlands — although there are exceptions: the phalaropes are found in winter on the sea, far from land; the Stone-curlew prefers dry habitats; the Cream-coloured Courser is found in steppe and desert areas; and the Woodcock in forests. Many species breed in tundra and northern wasteland, and most perform long-distance migrations. In spite of their efficient faculty of flight, however, they are primarily terrestrial and all of them walk and run well. Waders feed mostly on small creatures such as invertebrates (worms, molluscs etc.) and small fish, but also on seeds and algae. The species with a short bill and large eyes locate their food by sight, while others probe the mud with their long bill, aided by the nerve endings concentrated in the tip of the bill. They are constantly active, day and night; those relying on tactile senses for the detection of prey are more active at night.

Most waders flock outside the nesting season, especially during migration, but are solitary breeders. Only a few species, such as stilts and avocets, breed in loose colonies. Most are monogamous, with both parents sharing incubation and the care of the young in approximately equal portions, although a wide range of social relationships is known, including polygamy and polyandry. The nest is a hollow in the ground, and only rarely is it lined with vegetation or, near water, with a little mud. Sometimes stones, shells, droppings, twigs and the like are piled up around the nest, apparently for purposes of demarcation rather than for lining. There are usually 3-4 eggs, in some species only 2. They are relatively large, and in smaller species their weight amounts to a fifth of the body weight of the female (these are the largest eggs of any bird except the Kiwi in relation to the female's weight). The egg is distinctly pointed at one end; the base colour is olive-beige with dark brown mottling, a combination providing effective camouflage. Length of incubation ranges from 20 days in the smaller species to 30 days in the larger. The chicks hatch in an advanced stage of development, covered with dense down and with eyes open. Their legs are relatively long and their bill delicate and short, although characteristics of the adult are already perceptible. The chicks leave the nest immediately after hatching and feed independently, although the parents accompany and protect them. In times of danger the parents emit alarm calls and feign injury to divert the attention of predators from the chicks; the chicks crouch motionless on the ground. At three to four weeks old, the young are capable of flight.

In Israel 50 species are represented, five of them breeders.

Family: Rostratulidae (Painted Snipes)

This family constitutes a kind of intermediate stage between rails and waders. There are two genera, each comprising a single species, one of which is represented in Israel.

Painted Snipe
Rostratula benghalensis

Body length 25 cm, wing length 13 cm, wingspan 52 cm, weight of the male 114 g and of the female 135 g. The Painted Snipe resembles snipes and sand-pipers, although its legs are longer, its wings broader and its tail shorter. This is one of the few species in which the female is more colourful than the male, being distinguished by the green-grey back and wing-coverts and chestnut-brown neck, bordered below with black. A white stripe separates the neck from the sides of the body. Similar stripes, both black and white, also appear in the male, but the rest of its plumage is drabber, lacking chestnut-brown. In both sexes a gold-coloured V-shaped stripe extends from the shoulders to the centre of the back. In flight, the legs dangle.

The Painted Snipe is distributed in tropical areas of Africa, in southeast Asia from India to Japan, on islands of the Pacific Ocean and also in Australia. It is fairly common in the Nile Delta. Throughout most of its range a single subspecies *R.b. benghalensis* is known, except in Australia, where a separate subspecies has been identified. Normally this is a resident bird. In Israel the Painted Snipe is a rare accidental and possibly a very rare breeder.

The Painted Snipe is a bird of swamps, damp pasture meadows and rice-paddies. It spends most of the day hidden in dense vegetation, emerging to feed in the twilight hours. It probes in soft mud for worms, molluscs and insects. On the surface of the ground it catches grasshoppers and locusts and also eats seeds. When it senses danger it lies flat on the ground with the head turned sideways.

The first individual in Israel was seen on 20 July 1975 in the north of the Hula Valley, and another was sighted in the Hula Reserve in June 1985. A few other sightings have been recorded, all of them on the coastal plain. On 23 May 1979 a pair was observed apparently engaged in nesting behaviour near the drainage ponds in the southern part of the Mount Carmel coast, and the same phenomenon was repeated the following year, although no nest was found.

The female chooses the territory and defends it. Appropriately, her voice is deeper and stronger than the male's. She also takes the initiative in courtship, giving visual displays. The nest is a hollow in the ground, concealed among vegetation; the clutch is of 2-4 eggs. The female abandons the territory after laying and leaves the entire burden of incubation and care of the chicks to the male. She may mate again in the same season with a different partner and lay an additional clutch.

Family: Haematopodidae (Oystercatchers)

In this family there is one genus and four to seven species, according to different systems of classification. Only one species is represented in the Palaearctic.

Oystercatcher
Haematopus ostralegus

One of the larger waders of the area: body length 43 cm, wing length 26 cm, wingspan 83 cm and weight 520 g. In appearance this is a squat and thick-set bird, with relatively short neck and legs. The legs are pink, with three partially webbed toes. The bill is long (approx. 7.2 cm), orange-red in colour and laterally compressed. The Oystercatcher is distinguished by its black and white colour pattern; both sexes have identical plumage. The throat is all-black in summer plumage, paler and with a white bar in winter plumage.

The Oystercatcher has a sporadic trans-Palaearctic range, from Iceland to the shores of China and Kamchatka. In this range three subspecies have been identified. *H.o. ostralegus* breeds in Europe and occurs in Israel. This is essentially a bird of sea-coasts — rocky or sandy beaches, river estuaries or muddy lagoons — but it is also found on the banks of marshes and rivers in various climatic regions. Most of its populations migrate and winter close to the nesting areas in western Europe, but also along the coasts of West Africa, the Mediterranean and Arabia and the Persian Gulf. The eastern population winters on the coasts of China.

The Oystercatcher feeds primarily on shellfish, and its bill is well adapted to penetrating and opening the shells. It tends to feed after high tide, when the shells are opened.

In Israel this is a fairly rare passage migrant, seen along the Mediterranean coast between July and October and between March and May, in flocks numbering up to 30 individuals. It is also seen occasionally along the Jordan Valley. A small population winters in southern Sinai.

Family: Recurvirostridae (Stilts, Avocets)

In this family there are three genera and 13 species. These waders have a slender body, a relatively small head, and long legs, neck and bill; the tail is short. The plumages are black and white. In Israel two species are represented.

Black-winged Stilt
Himantopus himantopus

Body length 34-38 cm, of which about half is accounted for by the bill (6.5 cm) and by the legs (13.5 cm), wing length 21-24 cm, wingspan 67-83 cm and weight 105-163 g. The male is 10-15% larger than the female. The Black-winged Stilt is a quite unmistakable bird: its legs are bright pink and remarkably long. It has a black back and wings, while most of the other feathers are white. The plumage of the male is glossy and the colours of the female slightly more drab, tending towards brown. In breeding plumage the male usually has a dark greyish crown and nape, but the size and intensity of the grey area varies from one individual to another and is apparently dependent on age, so that white crown and nape are not necessarily signs of the female. The moult to breeding plumage takes place at the end of January, while the change to winter plumage, which is more brown-grey, starts at the beginning of June and is completed only in November. The bill is black, delicate, strong and pointed, and 1½ times the length of the head. The wings are long and pointed. Juveniles are greyish in appearance, and are recognisable especially by the grey head and neck and the pale red legs. The species is silent for most of the year apart from the breeding season.

The Black-winged Stilt has a broad cosmopolitan range in temperate and tropical zones in southern Europe, across Africa, in the Middle East, in southeast Asia, on the American continent, in Australasia and the islands of the Pacific Ocean. In this range five subspecies have been identified. *H.h. himantopus* is distributed sporadically in southern Europe, central Asia and tropical Africa, and occurs in Israel as a passage migrant, winter visitor and breeder. It is a bird of calm and shallow aquatic habitats: marshes, small lakes, salt-pools and lagoons, usually in river valleys and along sea-coasts. Nesting areas vary considerably according to changes in the surroundings, for example falls in the water-level or the flooding of new sectors. Changes are also liable to take place in the size of populations, and Black-winged Stilts were seen in unusually high numbers in central Europe in 1958 and 1965. Most of the Palaearctic population winters in tropical Africa.

The Black-winged Stilt has a fast, dynamic and straight flight in which its feet protrude far beyond the tail. Its gait is stately and graceful, but when running it is liable to lose its balance. On rare occasions it also swims. It gathers its food from the surface and upper levels of the water with rapid bill movements. It feeds on insects, molluscs, crabs, worms, fish eggs and tadpoles, and also on seeds of aquatic plants. Its long legs enable it to penetrate deeper water than most waders without wetting its feathers. On rare occasions it catches food on the bottom, immersing head and neck as far as the wings. When feeding on the surface of the ground or among vegetation, it bends its legs and stoops forward with every pecking movement.

The Black-winged Stilt is a gregarious bird even in the nesting season, and more so outside it, when it lives in small flocks that fly and move together. Even in flocks the pair bond is retained. Its calls are short and monotonous, increasing in volume and fre-

quency when warning of an intruder in the vicinity of the nest. These calls, uttered either on the ground or in flight, may also be heard in winter at times of disturbance. Bowing of the head and neck is another characteristic response to danger.

In Israel this is a fairly common passage migrant, usually in flocks of three to ten individuals. Its main periods of migration are from early August to mid-September and from the end of March to mid-April (in autumn 1978, 206 migrating Black-winged Stilts were counted at Bardawil in northern Sinai). The Black-winged Stilt also winters and breeds in this country; it is not clear whether the breeding individuals are resident, although it is known that the population in the north of Israel migrates southward. In 1960-69 the average number of wintering Black-winged Stilts was about 110, rising to 300 in 1970-74 and to 570 in 1975-83.

In the past the Black-winged Stilt was a fairly common breeder in Israel. With the draining of the Hula at the end of the 1950s, there were no breeding pairs for several years, apart from a very small population in the Bet She'an Valley. After hydrological improvements in the Hula Reserve, and with the building of reservoirs and sewage-treatment plants, the number rose again: in 1967 some 55 pairs were breeding, and the number reached a high of some 240 breeding pairs in 1973. In 1976 165 pairs bred throughout the country, and in 1982 some 80 pairs were breeding in the Jordan Valley and a further 20-30 pairs in the drainage pools of Gush Dan.

The Black-winged Stilt breeds in northern and central areas of Israel, with a few pairs nesting as far south as the Valley of Be'er Sheva. The nesting season begins at the end of March. The Black-winged Stilt nests in small loose colonies: in 1974 some 20 pairs bred by an oxygenisation pool about 1.6 ha in size in the Jezreel Valley, and some 50 pairs bred in the cess-pools of Ashdod in 1971. Colonies are usually located in concentrations of vegetation and small islands of mud standing in shallow water, 2-3 cm deep, or on an embankment or a waterside bank. The male chooses the nest site, excavates a hollow, with occasional assistance from the female, and piles up grass and small stones around it. Sometimes several nests are built side by side, or the male may build a mud tower for a nest. Four eggs are laid, although sometimes two females lay in the same nest. Incubation, by both parents, begins when the clutch is complete and lasts 22-24 days. Changes of shift take place every hour or two, and the nest grows in size as the bird coming to relieve its incubating partner brings offerings of nesting material. In the case of prolonged absence, following an alarm, the bird returning to its post wets its breast feathers to cool the eggs that have warmed in the sun. Sometimes two or three days elapse between the appearance of the first crack and the hatching of the egg. The chicks hatch approximately simultaneously, with eyes open and covered with dense down, white on the throat and blackish-gold on other parts of the body. Their legs are short, and within a few hours after hatching they are capable of standing and running. The chicks feed independently from their first day, but the parents continue to brood and warm them from time to time. They fly for the first time at four to five weeks, and the bond between them and their parents continues for a further two to three weeks. Juvenile Black-winged Stilts gather into flocks of their own towards the end of the nesting season and join the adults only in the autumn. They assume full adult plumage only at the age of two or three years.

The Black-winged Stilt breeds once in the year, but because the rate of failure is high there are often replacement clutches and the season may continue until August. Many factors can cause nesting failure: disturbance by humans, changes in the water-level, natural predation, and competition from Spur-winged Plovers. In a few instances, when the eggs of Black-winged Stilts have been threatened by flooding or in danger of dessication, these eggs have been taken and hatched in an incubator. In 1974, 65 eggs were collected for this purpose in the drainage pools of Gush Dan; 60 of these hatched and 52 chicks survived to be released in the Hula Reserve.

Avocet
Recurvirostra avosetta

A large wader: body length 44 cm, wing length 22.5 cm, wingspan 78 cm and weight 260-350 g. It is distinguished by the contrasting black and white plumage, by its bill which is black, long (8 cm) and curved upwards in the shape of a scimitar, and by its long (10 cm) grey-blue legs. Juveniles are brown-grey on the head, back and wing-coverts. In flight the Avocet is a graceful bird; its wingbeats are rhythmic and regular but shallow, as if in a kind of hovering motion, and the legs protrude well beyond the tail.

The Avocet has a sporadic range in Europe, and extending from the shores of the Black Sea eastward over the whole breadth of Asia. This is a monotypic species, which also breeds in eastern and southern Africa. Most of its European and Asiatic populations migrate; those from western Europe winter especially in tropical Africa, but also in the Mediterranean

basin and on the shores of the Persian Gulf and the Arabian Sea. Its preferred habitats are sandy or muddy sea-coasts or inland saline marshes. Often it is found in proximity to flamingoes and diving ducks. It occurs in Israel as a passage migrant, winter visitor and occasional breeder.

When feeding, the Avocet gives the appearance of 'reaping' its food from the surface of the water with sideways movements of the head and bill. Usually it wades in search of food, but occasionally it swims. Sometimes it attempts to pluck food from the bed of the pool, and appears to be standing on its head, with rear end raised above the water. It feeds especially on invertebrates such as insects, crabs and worms. The Avocet is a gregarious bird, both during and outside the nesting season. It usually migrates in flocks of six to eight individuals; the largest flock seen in Israel numbered 23 individuals.

In Israel this is a common passage migrant, especially in autumn. Between early August and the end of September 1973, some 6,000 individuals were counted in northern Sinai. It is also quite common as a winterer, and in censuses the numbers counted range from 110 (1969) to 530 (1982), with an average of 250. It is especially common in winter in the lagoons of north and northwest Sinai, where about 15,000 were counted in January 1972.

In 1961 the first known breeding pair in Israel was discovered in the salt-pools of Atlit on the coast of Mount Carmel. Two chicks hatched but later disappeared. On 20 May 1976, in the sewage-ponds of Tel Aviv, a nest was found containing four eggs, but these too disappeared. At the end of the same month at least four pairs were seen in the area, but no further evidence of nesting was discovered. In 1978, some 20 pairs nested in a drained fish-pond in the Bet She'an Valley; when the pond was refilled the eggs were taken to an incubator and about 50 chicks hatched, but only two survived longer than a week. Scores of Avocets were seen in the same area in 1979, and it is possible that some of them bred, but no nest was found. In 1982 four pairs bred in the western Jordan Valley.

The breeding biology of the Avocet is similar to that of the Black-winged Stilt. The nest is built on islands of mud and vegetation in shallow water, and the clutch consists of 3-5 eggs. Both parents incubate for 23-25 days. The chicks begin to fly at about 40 days old.

Family: Burhinidae (Stone-curlews)

Stone-curlews are birds of average size with solid bodies and large head and eyes. They have camouflage plumage. Their legs are long and sturdy, and well adapted to running. On each foot there are three toes joined at the base by a web. This family comprises two genera and nine species, one of which is represented in Israel.

Stone-curlew
Burhinus oedicnemus

Body length 36.5 cm, wing length 22-24 cm, wing-span 80 cm and weight 260-370 g. The Stone-curlew has sandy-brown plumage streaked with black; the breast is paler and the belly white. In flight the black primaries and secondaries contrast with the two light bars on the coverts. The wings are long and pointed; the tail is wedge-shaped and long (12 cm) and, when the bird is standing, protrudes considerably beyond the folded wings (a rare phenomenon among waders). The bill is straight and strong, yellow at the base and black at the tip. The eyes are large and yellow. The calls include loud wails and shrill croaking sounds.

The range of the Stone-curlew extends from the Canary Islands, North Africa and Spain, through the Mediterranean countries, central Europe and Asia to India and Burma. Six subspecies have been identified, two of which are known in Israel: the European subspecies *B.o. oedicnemus* is a migrant in autumn (September-October) and in spring (March-April) and is also a fairly common winterer; the subspecies *B.o. saharae*, which extends from North Africa and Greece to Iraq and southern Iran, is a quite common resident in Israel although it roams outside the nesting season. Unlike most members of its order, the Stone-curlew is a dry-land bird: its habitats are open fields, sandy or stony deserts and dry and exposed plains in areas of temperate, Mediterranean, steppe and desert climate. In Europe its numbers have dwindled considerably in recent years as a result of changes in land use, and also following the decimation by myxomatosis of the rabbit population, which led to rapid growth of dense grass, rendering many areas unsuitable as habitats.

The Stone-curlew tends to rest during the hours of the day in the shade of bushes. When alarmed, it

retreats in a crouched run, flying only when there is no alternative, and then over short distances; only in cases of repeated disturbance does it fly longer distances. Its flight is relatively slow, and usually not more than 20-30 m above the ground. Activity begins in the evening, when a variety of calls is heard. The Stone-curlew takes only live food, especially invertebrates such as beetles, grasshoppers, crickets and snails, also vertebrates including amphibians and reptiles, rodents and other small mammals.

Outside the nesting season the Stone-curlew is a gregarious bird; in winter its flocks number scores of individuals, and flocks of more than 100 have been seen in Israel. These flocks congregate afresh every morning in regular sites. Towards evening the Stone-curlews disperse from these assembly points with loud and raucous cries.

Nesting territories are located in quiet places, at a safe distance from settlements and other sources of disturbance. At the approach of the nesting season, which in Israel begins in April and continues to about July, the Stone-curlews become aggressively vocal. Both partners excavate a shallow scrape in the ground, sometimes beneath a small bush. The clutch is usually of 2 eggs; on rare occasions as many as 3 or 4 may be found, but this is probably the result of laying by two females. Both parents share the task of incubation, which lasts some 26 days. At times of danger the incubating bird stretches its neck forward and presses its body to the ground, or withdraws in a crouched run and takes to the air only at some distance from the nest; similarly, on its return it does not land beside the nest but at some distance away, approaching it with cautious gait. At a few days the chicks are locating their food by themselves. They are flying at about the age of 1½ months, by which time they are independent and may join in larger flocks.

The Stone-curlew breeds once in a year, but if the nest is destroyed a replacement clutch will be laid, usually containing only 1 egg.

Family: Glareolidae (Coursers, Pratincoles)

This family comprises five genera and 16 species. Four species are found in Israel: Cream-coloured Courser and Egyptian Plover, representing the subfamily Cursoriinae; and Collared and Black-winged Pratincoles, representing the subfamily Glareolinae. A family of waders of average size, usually inhabiting semi-arid environments in the Old World. The neck is short, the wings long and pointed, and the flight rapid. The bill is quite short and curved. The plumage is usually drab camouflage, with no sexual

or seasonal variation; the sexes are also similar in size.

Cream-coloured Courser
Cursorius cursor

A wader of moderate size: body length 19-21 cm, wing length 14.8-16.5 cm, wingspan 55 cm and weight 100-120 g. From a distance it appears a uniform sandy colour. At closer range its grey nape is distinctive, as is the black eye-stripe extending from the eye to the back of the neck and bordered by a white stripe above. In flight, the black primaries are distinctive; the underwing is entirely black, except for the leading edge which is chestnut-brown. The wings are long and pointed, and the tail short and rounded. The legs are long and yellowish-white. The bill is approximately the same length as the head and curved downwards. Juveniles are brown-speckled and lack the grey, white and black head pattern. This species gives alarm calls in flight, but otherwise is a somewhat quiet bird whose voice is seldom heard.

The Cream-coloured Courser of the subspecies *C.c. cursor* is distributed from the western Sahara and the Canary Islands across the whole breadth of North Africa and further east to Arabia and Iraq, including Israel and the Syrian Desert. The range of another two subspecies extends further east from Iran to western Afghanistan. Small and isolated populations (belonging to two further subspecies) are also found in the north and east of the tropical zone in Africa. The habitat of the Cream-coloured Courser is hot regions on the fringes of deserts; sometimes it also penetrates into steppe areas.

When the Cream-coloured Courser stands motionless it is hard to observe on account of its camouflage colours. At times of danger it runs very fast, pausing from time to time and standing on tip-toe to look around, and running again. Only when the threat is very close does it fly. It feeds especially on insects in various stages of development, including beetles, grasshoppers, ants and flies, also snails and a variety of seeds. It seeks its food in typical plover fashion: standing erect and still, inspecting the surroundings, running, pecking or scratching on the ground and straightening up again. Sometimes it catches locusts in flight. Outside the breeding season the Cream-coloured Courser lives in small flocks.

In Israel this is a common breeder in areas of scrub vegetation in the northern and western Negev; a few pairs also breed in more arid parts of the Negev, areas in which it is more often seen as a migrant or a vagrant, and then usually in flocks. Occasionally this population extends further northward, especially along the Jordan Valley, and thus the Cream-coloured Courser has been known to breed on the eastern slopes of Mount Gilboa, on the heights of eastern Lower Galilee, and on the northeast coast of Lake Tiberias. It also winters in the western Negev, where during December and January flocks of a dozen individuals and more may be seen.

The nesting season sometimes begins in March, but usually not until May, and continues into June and sometimes into July (newly hatched chicks were found in the western Negev on 21 July 1962 and on 27 July 1984; and in July 1976 five nests with eggs

were found in eastern Lower Galilee). Nesting territories are in open habitats without vegetation. The nest is a shallow scrape in the ground, usually unlined. Normally the clutch contains only 2 eggs. Both parents incubate, and the changes of shift take place at long intervals, usually in the late morning; during the afternoon the eggs are left unattended for two to three hours. The period of incubation is 18-19 days. The chicks hatch with eyes open and covered in down. They are capable of walking and running from their first day, but begin to feed independently only at about a week old. Even before this time the parents do not keep them under constant supervision, as do the parents in most species of birds. The chicks begin to fly at about a month old.

The Cream-coloured Courser is apparently double-brooded.

Egyptian Plover
Pluvianus aegyptius

A wader slightly smaller than the Cream-coloured Courser and with a striking colour pattern: grey above and sand-beige below. Especially conspicuous are the green-black collar and the black eye-stripe which extends to the shoulders.

The Egyptian Plover inhabits river banks in tropical Africa from Senegal and Angola to Sudan. It feeds on insects. It often co-exists quite amicably with crocodiles and even perches on their backs, but there is no basis for the popular belief (first asserted by Herodotus) that it enters the jaws of crocodiles and cleanses them of parasites.

A solitary individual was caught in the nineteenth century in the Jordan Valley and is now preserved in the British Musuem (Natural History) in Tring. Another sighting was recorded on 15 January 1979 on the shores of the Gulf of Suez.

Collared Pratincole
Glareola pratincola

A moderate-sized wader: body length 21.5-25 cm, wing length 17.8-21.1 cm, wingspan 62 cm and weight 55-76 g. A bird with narrow, long and pointed wings and distinctively forked tail. Its flight is rapid, with aerobatic manoeuvres similar to those of terns and swallows. The folded wings reach the tip of the tail or beyond. A standing Collared Pratincole blends into the background and is not easily observed. The most distinctive feature is a large cream-coloured patch on the throat, framed in black. The back is olive-brown, the primaries and tail black; the breast is greyish and the belly white. The white rump is visible only in flight; also conspicuous in flight is the russet-chestnut colour of the underwing. The bill is short (14 mm), and black with a red base. The legs are relatively short and dark brown in colour. Male and female have identical plumage, although the male is slightly larger. Outside the breeding season the head is streaked, the throat white, the stripe framing it broken, and the bill blackish in colour. Juveniles have a shorter tail than adults, the back and breast are speckled with black and white, and they also lack the distinctive bib.

The range of the subspecies *G.p. pratincola* extends sporadically through southern Europe, North Africa, the Middle East and central Asia. Two additional subspecies inhabit tropical zones in Africa. The Collared Pratincole is a bird of fields and open plains, usually near water. The entire population of Europe and Asia winters in savannas in subtropical Africa, where flocks sometimes number thousands of individuals.

This is a gregarious bird, living in flocks at all seasons of the year. It feeds especially on flying insects. It usually hunts in the morning and evening twilight, when its high-pitched calls are often to be heard. It also catches insects and reptiles on the ground (in Africa it is especially partial to locust larvae). Sometimes it stands in water and catches insects on the surface.

This pratincole is quite common as a passage migrant in Israel, in autumn especially along the coastal plain, with the peak of migration occurring at the end of August and in early September. The spring migration takes place during April and the first half of May, and the route then passes mainly through the Valley of the Arava and the Jordan Valley.

The Collared Pratincole is also a fairly rare breeder, in the Jezreel Valley, the Bet She'an Valley and the Hula Valley, although formerly it also bred on the coastal plain. The birds return to Israel in early April. They may choose a nesting site in dry stubble, pasture meadows or open and exposed territory, but it seems that they prefer to nest in cultivated fields, and thus they often form colonies in fields of cotton in early bud. Spraying with agricultural pesticides has had a severe effect on their numbers, and is one of the main reasons for their decline in this country; according to one estimate, the population has fallen by 90% since the 1930s.

In Israel, nesting, in small and sparse colonies, begins in early May. The nest is a small scrape in the ground, apparently dug by both partners, and usually unlined. The normal distance between nests is 40-70 m, although it can be as little as 15 m or as much as 120 m. In the clutch there are 2-3 eggs. Both partners incubate in turns, after the laying of the first egg. Changes of shift take place at long intervals and are accompanied by colourful rituals: the incubating bird rises to greet its partner, and then both bow to one another, arching their backs and spreading and erecting the tail. If an intruder, human or animal, appears in the colony, the birds converge on it in flight, land some distance away and feign injury. Sometimes as many as 20 to 30 pratincoles may be seen sprawled together on the ground, with wings trembling in simulated helplessness; especially when there are chicks in the nest, they may even attack the intruder. On the other hand they are quite indifferent to tractors. The period of incubation is 17-19 days. The chicks hatch simultaneously, with eyes open and covered with down. They spend two or three days in the nest before leaving it. The parents regurgitate food for them until they reach the age of about a week, and only then do they begin to feed independently. The chicks fly at 25-30 days old.

When nesting is over the birds congregate in feeding grounds abundant in insects, and by early August they are already beginning the southward migration.

Black-winged Pratincole
Glareola nordmanni

Body length 24.4 cm, wing length 18.8 cm, wingspan 64 cm and weight 90 g. Similar to the Collared Pratincole, from which it is distinguished by the black underwing. The secondaries lack white tips, and the back is also darker.

This species' range is limited to the USSR, from north of the Black Sea to Lake Balkhash. It is a monotypic species. It winters in southwest and South Africa.

In Israel this is a fairly rare but regular passage migrant, crossing the coastal plain every autumn between early September and mid-October. On 11 September 1984, 60 were counted passing through the fields of Kafar Kasem. Autumn sightings have also been recorded in the Bet She'an Valley, the southern coastal plain, Be'er Sheva and Eilat. It is more rare in the spring: there have been only a few sightings recorded, in mid-May in Eilat.

Family: Charadriidae (Plovers)

The family is divided into two subfamilies: Charadriinae (plovers) and Vanellinae (lapwings), comprising nine genera and 64 species. In Israel four genera and 15 species are represented.

Members of this family have a compact body, a short and thick neck, and long wings. The tail is fairly short, and straight or rounded. The head is rounded and the eyes large; prey is located by eyesight. The bill is short and solid. These birds gather their food from the surface.

The family has a worldwide range, with distribution in every continent except Antarctica. The plovers inhabit mainly sea-shores and freshwater margins. They do not perch on trees, fences or other prominent features.

Genus: *Charadrius*

The largest genus in the family of plovers, comprising 30 species of agile waterside birds. Their distribution is cosmopolitan. Members of this genus have strong legs. The bill is relatively short, thick and quite strong. The wings are long and pointed and the tail is relatively short, about half the length of the wing. The feeding method is characteristic: standing and looking, running and picking up, and standing again. Eight species are known in this country.

Little Ringed Plover
Charadrius dubius

This is a small wader: body length 13.5-16.5 cm, wing length 11-12 cm, wingspan 42-48 cm and weight 22-36 g. It has a greyish-brown back and crown, separated by a white collar; the throat and belly are also white. A black eye-stripe and black forehead-stripe conspicuous against a white background, and a black breast-band are good recognition marks, as is the yellow eye-ring. In flight, the wings appear grey-brown with the primaries and secondaries black; the absence of a white bar on the wing is the best means of distinguishing it from the Ringed Plover. The legs are yellowish-pink and the bill is black. Male and female are similar, although the female's collar is narrower. In winter plumage, virtually identical in both sexes, the black on the head and breast disappear or are blurred. Juveniles have a uniform brown-grey cap and a broken brown breast-band.

The subspecies *C.d. curonicus* has a trans-Palaearctic range, from North Africa, Spain and Britain to Korea and Japan. Its range extends north to 62°N, at which point its place is taken by the Ringed Plover. Two other subspecies inhabit southeast Asia and islands of the Pacific Ocean, in the Oriental region. The Little Ringed Plover usually lives on sand or shingle beaches alongside rivers and freshwater lakes in inland plains and valleys. On the coast it is found mainly in estuaries. It is also sometimes to be found in dry riverbeds and salt-lagoons. All its Palaearctic populations apparently migrate and winter in Africa, in the north of the tropical zone, extending as far south as the Equator along the Indian Ocean and the East African lakes. In Israel it is a rare breeder and winter visitor and a fairly common passage migrant.

The Little Ringed Plover usually feeds on muddy ground, in proximity with Little Stints and Dunlins. It consumes mostly insects, but also other small invertebrates.

In the autumn migration this species may be seen from the end of July. Females precede the males by about two weeks, and passage continues until the end of September, with the peak in the third week of August. In spring it occurs from early March to mid-May, especially in early April. In both autumn and spring it precedes the Ringed Plover by about two weeks. The Little Ringed Plover is also a rare winterer in fish-ponds between August and May. In winter it is not so gregarious as the Ringed or the Kentish Plover and is usually seen individually or in small flocks, although it sometimes mingles with plovers of other species. On migration larger flocks are formed.

In the past the Little Ringed Plover bred in every estuary on the Mediterranean coast, and also on shoals of shingle and silt among the meanders of the Jordan, in the Hula Valley and in the Jordan Valley as far as the Dead Sea. Pollution from oil and tar destroyed its nesting populations on the Mediterranean coast as early as 1967. Today it is a very rare breeder, confined to reservoirs and drainage pools on the coastal plain, and especially along the Yarmuk and the Jordan.

In Israel the nesting season extends from April to August, but young chicks may also be seen in September. The male chooses a nesting site on exposed ground, among sparse vegetation, affording unimpeded all-round vision. He often digs several scrapes before the female chooses one. In the clutch there are normally 4 eggs, less frequently 3 or 5. They are placed with the 'sharp' end pointing towards the centre of the nest, or sometimes, especially on the sea-coast, they are buried in the sand with only the 'blunt' end protruding above the surface. Incubation begins with the first egg and lasts 24-25 days; both parents share the task in approximately equal portions, and in warm weather they tend to moisten the belly feathers before taking up their post. Usually the chicks hatch simultaneously. They are open-eyed and covered with dense down. They leave the nest a few days after hatching and immediately begin to feed independently, but the parents continue to brood and warm them in cold weather. The chicks begin to fly at 23-26 days old. Once they are independent the females abandon them and the males, either for a second breeding cycle or to begin migrating.

Ringed Plover
Charadrius hiaticula

Similar to Little Ringed Plover but larger: body length 17-18 cm, wing length 12.5-12.8 cm, wingspan 50-55 cm and weight 42-56 g. It is distinguished by the base of the bill, orange in summer and yellow in winter, while the tip is always black. The legs are orange-yellow. In flight, a white wingbar is conspicuous.

The Ringed Plover has an arctic range, from northeastern Canada, through Greenland and Spitsbergen to the Bering Strait, with penetration to Britain and the coasts of western Europe. Its nesting areas are usually more northerly than those of the Little Ringed Plover. In this range two subspecies have been identified. This is essentially a bird of seacoasts. All its Palaearctic populations, except those of Britain and Ireland, migrate and winter in western Europe, in the Mediterranean basin, along the coasts of the Red Sea, and along the coasts and beside inland stretches of water across tropical Africa. Sometimes it migrates in large flocks.

In Israel the subspecies *C.h. tundrae* is a common passage migrant and winterer. In the autumn migration it is seen from August to the end of November, and especially between the end of September and mid-October. In the spring migration it occurs from early March to mid-May, the peak occurring at the end of April. The Ringed Plover winters between August and May in fish-ponds, where it feeds in company with Dunlins and Little Stints; its diet consists mainly of crabs, molluscs and worms.

Kentish Plover
Charadrius alexandrinus

Body length 15-17 cm, wing length 9.5-11.5 cm, wingspan 44 cm and weight 22-38 g. The Kentish Plover has a greyish-brown back and white underparts. In summer plumage the male has a distinctive russet-grey nape and a black mark at the sides of the breast; these areas are brown in the female. In winter plumage it is brown-grey and white, with a greyish-black mark on the sides of the breast. The legs are grey-black, and the bill black. In flight a white stripe is conspicuous along the wing.

The Kentish Plover has an almost worldwide range and is found in all continents except Australasia and Antarctica. The sub-species *C.a. alexandrinus* is distributed from western Morocco and Spain through southern and western Europe and the Middle East to western India and Mongolia. It is especially common along sea-coasts, but also penetrates to inland, in particular saline, stretches of

water. This is the ecological equivalent of the Ringed Plover in warmer, drier and sandier areas. The other subspecies, five in number, breed in eastern Asia and tropical Africa. Its northern populations migrate, while those in the Mediterranean basin are mostly resident. The migrants from the Western Palaearctic winter along the shores of the Mediterranean and the Red Sea, also on the coasts of Arabia and the Horn of Africa. In Israel this is a frequent passage migrant and winterer, and a quite rare breeder.

In addition to insects, the Kentish Plover consumes various species of crab, also roundworms and molluscs. Outside the nesting season this is a more gregarious wader than the Little Ringed Plover, and is usually found in small flocks.

The autumn migration begins as early as the end of June and continues until November, with a peak between mid-September and early October. The spring migration begins at the end of March and continues until early May, with a peak in mid-April.

The breeding population of the Kentish Plover has greatly diminished along the shores of Israel. In 1968 some 25 pairs were breeding on the shore at Maagan Mikhael and on nearby coastal stretches; in 1975 only a few pairs remained there, and since 1979 the Kentish Plover has ceased to breed in this and other areas of coastline. This is the result of the pollution of coastal waters, possibly also of competition with the Spur-winged Plover, which has extended its habitat in this region. In the early 1980s there were still pairs breeding in the salt-pools of Atlit on the coast of Mount Carmel and on the northern shores of the Dead Sea, and hundreds of pairs breed under bushes on the shores and islands of the Bardawil Lagoon in northern Sinai (in Atlit they also sometimes breed in such sites).

The nesting behaviour of the Kentish Plover is similar to that of the Little Ringed Plover, but the nest scrape is lined with fragments of shell and small stones even before laying, although here too, as in other waders, a decorative border is built up around the nest during incubation. There are usually 3 eggs. Incubation lasts 23-24 days and both parents participate, although usually the female incubates by day and the male at night. The eggs are covered with sand when the nest is left, and exposed when incubation is resumed.

The Kentish Plover breeds twice and sometimes even three times in a season, between March and July. Newly hatched chicks can be seen as late as August, and it is possible that these are the result of replacement clutches.

Kittlitz's Sandplover
Charadrius pecuarius

A small wader: body length 13 cm, wing length 10.6 cm, wingspan 42 cm and weight 30 g. It is distinguished by the sandy colour of the breast. A dark eye-stripe extends to the nape, with a whitish supercilium above it. Its bill is long relative to that of other plovers occurring in Israel (15 mm compared with 13 mm in the larger Little Ringed Plover). Its legs are dark, olive-black in colour.

This plover is distributed across tropical Africa, and in the Palaearctic region is found only in the Nile Delta, where it is a common resident. In Israel it is a very rare vagrant, with only two sightings known: in 1968 in Maagan Mikhael, and on 6 April 1975 in the sewage-ponds of Tel Aviv.

Lesser Sandplover
Charadrius mongolus

Body length 20 cm, wing length 13 cm, wingspan 53 cm and weight 60 g. Distinguished in breeding plumage by the chestnut breast, white throat, and black forehead, lores and ear-coverts. It is sometimes hard to distinguish from the Greater Sandplover, especially from the western subspecies (see below); the similarity is most confusing in winter plumage, when both species are greyish-brown. The feet are usually grey, almost black.

This is an Asiatic species, which breeds in the mountains of Nepal and western China, and also in the mountains to the east of Lake Baikal. Three to five subspecies have been identified. The western subspecies *C.m. pamirensis* winters in western India, on the shores of the Arabian Sea, in the Persian Gulf, on the coasts of Arabia and of East Africa. Israel is located slightly to the northwest of its migration route, and it is a very rare accidental. Sightings have been recorded on 17 March 1976, 6 March 1979 and 23 April 1983 in the region of Eilat (all were of individuals in winter plumage, a fact which may cast some doubt on the accuracy of the identification: see above).

Greater Sandplover
Charadrius leschenaultii

Similar to Lesser Sandplover both in breeding and in winter plumage, but larger: body length 19-20 cm, wing length 13.2-14 cm, wingspan 57 cm and weight 70-84 g. It is also recognisable by its long bill, about the same length as the head. Especially similar to the Lesser Sandplover is the subspecies *C.l. columbinus*, which breeds in the Middle East and also in southern Afghanistan and Azerbaydzhan.

The Greater Sandplover is distributed mainly from the Caspian Sea to China and Mongolia and as

far as Lake Baikal. In this range three subspecies have been identified. In the 1950s and 1960s it was also discovered breeding in Turkey and Syria and east of the Jordan. It winters on the shores of Australia and the islands of Indonesia, along the coasts of south Asia from Malaya to Arabia and also on the coasts of the Sinai peninsula, in the Nile Delta and the Red Sea, and southward along the shores of East Africa. In some of these areas this is the most common coastal bird.

In Israel this is a frequent passage migrant and a rare winterer on the Mediterranean coast. In autumn migration takes place between mid-June and early September, and the spring passage is between the end of March and the end of April.

Caspian Plover
Charadrius asiaticus

Body length 19 cm, wing length 15 cm, wingspan 58 cm and weight 75 g. A wader with a reddish-brown breast, distinguished in summer plumage from other plovers of similar breast colour by the white forehead and ear-coverts, and by a thin black band separating the chestnut breast from the white belly. In winter plumage it is distinguished from the two preceding species by a light and conspicuous supercilium, and also by the more striking upward tilt of the body.

This plover's range is Irano-Turanian and extends from the Caspian Sea to the steppes of Turkestan and Lake Baikal. This is a monotypic species, which winters across East Africa from Ethiopia and Sudan

---

to the Congo, Angola and the Cape. It migrates in small flocks, and its preferred nesting and wintering habitats are plains with saline soil, usually near water.

Today this is a rare passage migrant in Israel, seen especially in the region of Eilat: in autumn during August and in spring from mid-March to early May. In April 1979 several scores of individuals landed in fish-ponds in the central coastal plain, and on 7 April in that year four were seen on the beach north of Tel Aviv.

Dotterel
Eudromias morinellus

Body length 21 cm, wing length 15.3 cm, wingspan 60 cm and weight 110 g. The Dotterel's legs are relatively slender and short. In summer plumage it is unmistakable: grey neck and upper breast terminating in a white bar, bordered above with black; chestnut-coloured lower breast and black belly. White supercilia join on its nape in a 'V' shape. In winter this is a greyish-brown bird, but it differs from other similar plovers in the yellowish-brown legs and the chestnut-golden tint of the upperparts.

The Dotterel's range is mainly arctic, from northern Scotland and Scandinavia through the northern USSR to the Bering Strait. This is a monotypic species, inhabiting tundra and exposed mountain tops, above the tree-line but south of and below the snow-line. It winters in North Africa and along the Tigris and Euphrates.

In Israel the Dotterel is a quite rare winterer, preferring semi-exposed areas and often living in flocks. It is seen between November and January in the Golan and the western Negev. It tends to return regularly to the same wintering areas, and may in fact be more common than the number of recorded sightings suggests: it is not easily observed on account of its habit of standing motionless during most of the hours of the day, not moving even when closely approached. It feeds usually at night or in the early morning, mostly on insects and spiders. On 28 January 1979, 270 individuals were seen in the western Negev, the largest flock recorded in Israel.

Genus: *Pluvialis* (larger plovers)
A genus of waders of average size, with speckled upperparts. These plovers are similar to members of the genus *Charadrius*, but larger and with the tarsus 1½ times the length of the middle toe minus the claw (in the genus *Charadrius* it is 1¼ times the length of the middle toe). The toes are long, and with a small web at the base. The bill is short (about two-thirds the length of the head), straight and quite delicate;

the tip of the upper mandible is bulbous. The wings are long and pointed, the tail short and square, less than half the length of the wing. The sexes are similar, although the female is slightly paler. In summer plumage the black belly is conspicuous, turning grey in winter. In Israel three species are represented.

Golden Plover
Pluvialis apricaria

A large wader: body length 25-28 cm, wing length 17.5-18.8 cm, wingspan 70 cm and weight 110-200 g. It is distinguished both in winter and summer by gold and black speckling on the upperparts. In summer the underparts are black; in winter their colour is greyish-brown and gold. In flight the pale underwing is visible, with obvious white axillaries; this is a useful distinction between this species and the Pacific Golden Plover (which has a uniform grey underwing) and the Grey Plover (which has black axillaries). Its bill is more slender and its legs shorter than those of the Grey Plover.

The range of the Golden Plover extends from Iceland, through northern Britain and Scandinavia to the steppes of Siberia. This is a monotypic species, whose habitat is peat bogs and wastes of tundra. It winters mainly in western and southern Europe, also in North Africa and southern Turkey. The Nile Delta is one of its southernmost wintering sites.

The Golden Plover feeds on a variety of invertebrates, especially beetles, worms and small snails, but also on vegetable food (grass, fruits and seeds).

In Israel this is a rare passage migrant and a fairly common winterer between November and the end of February. It usually winters in dense flocks, sometimes numbering as many as 300 individuals, in damp heathland in valleys and plains.

Pacific Golden Plover
Pluvialis fulva

Similar to the Golden Plover but smaller: body length 23 cm, wing length 16.5 cm, wingspan 60 cm and weight 120 g. In flight, the uniform grey underwing is distinctive.

This species breeds in westernmost Alaska and across Siberia, and winters in south and southeast Asia, in Australia and New Zealand, on islands of the southwest Pacific, and also in northeast Africa. The population breeding in Alaska is renowned for its migration: in unbroken flight lasting some 80 hours, it crosses the Pacific Ocean to the Hawaiian Islands.

In Israel this is a rare accidental on the coastal plain and in Eilat, between June and November and between April and May.

Grey Plover
Pluvialis squatarola

Similar to the Golden Plover but more thickset, with shorter neck and larger neck and bill: body length 24-28 cm, wing length 19-20.5 cm, wingspan 77 cm and weight 150-250 g. The summer plumage is white, grey and black, without any gold tint. In winter it is grey, with upperparts spotted white. In flight the Grey Plover is distinguished by the white rump, and by conspicuous black axillaries.

The range of the Grey Plover extends from the arctic regions of North America and north Asia to northeastern Russia. This is a monotypic species, breeding in tundra on rocky slopes covered with moss and lichen. It winters along the coasts of America, western and southern Europe, Africa and South Asia, and some migrants travel as far as Indonesia and the shores of Australia.

In Israel this is a fairly common passage migrant in autumn, from the beginning of August to November, and less conspicuous in the spring migration, from the end of February to the end of May. Usually it migrates singly, sometimes in small flocks. As a winterer it is quite rare, appearing in small and loose flocks on sandy beaches between November and the end of January. It consumes especially shrimps, molluscs and worms.

Subfamily: Vanellinae

Spur-winged Plover
Vanellus spinosus

A large wader: body length 23-29 cm, wing length 19-20.5 cm, wingspan 70-80 cm and weight 100-170 g. Distinguished by its contrasting colours: the crown, and the throat to the breast are black; the cheeks, the sides of the neck and breast and the belly are white; while the wing-coverts and back are greyish-brown. The crown feathers are long and form a small crest. The wings are quite long and broad, and in flight their black and white pattern is clearly visible. A spur at the angle of the wing serves for both defence and attack. The legs are black, long and strong; the bill is also black. There is no distinction between male and female and no variation in plumage between summer and winter. Juveniles are similar to adults but with less contrasting plumage.

The Spur-winged Plover is a monotypic species, distributed especially in the strip of savanna south of the Sahara, from Mauretania to Kenya, also in Sudan, Egypt, Israel, Iraq, Spain and Turkey. Since 1959 it has also bred in northeastern Greece. Its northern populations (Greece, Turkey and Syria) migrate, while in other parts of its range it is resident.

In Israel this is primarily a resident, with a tendency to roam, and also a rare winter visitor and passage migrant.

The Spur-winged Plover is a bird of marshland and water margins. It feeds especially on insects such as beetles and ants, and also on spiders, worms, shrimps and molluscs. It normally lives in pairs, and the bond between partners may last one season or many years. Members of the pair usually stay throughout the year in their territory, and defend it even in winter. In winter they sometimes flock in places with abundant stocks of food, but return towards evening to their territories. Winter flocks, sometimes numbering scores of individuals, also include winter visitors, juveniles, and adults lacking a territory.

The numbers counted in surveys of wintering aquatic birds have increased, from an average of 370 between 1966 and 1974 to 1,550 between 1975 and 1983. It is likely that the population is even larger, since many individuals winter in fields, far from water.

Until the 1960s the Spur-winged Plover was quite common as a breeder in northern valleys: the Hula Valley, the Bet She'an Valley and on the shores of Lake Tiberias. Since then it has proliferated considerably as a result of the development of agriculture, especially fields of cotton, sugar-beet and cultivated flowers, and also as a result of the removal of riparian vegetation from fish-ponds and the growing number of reservoirs and sewage oxygenisation pools. Initially its range expanded to the coastal plain: in 1963, for the first time, four pairs were seen nesting at Maagan Mikhael on the northern coastal plain; in the following year the number rose to 20 pairs, and since then the population there has been stable at around 60 pairs. During the same period the Spur-winged Plover has extended its range southward to the fringes of the Negev and its population has grown rapidly. In 1967 some 50 breeding pairs were counted throughout the country; by the late 1970s this number had risen to 300, and it is reasonable to suppose that today the total population is considerably larger, as the species is quite common in all suitable biotopes.

At the approach of the nesting season territories are defended with increasing intensity, and in territorial conflicts the wing-spur is used as a weapon. Nesting territories are often in close proximity (scores of pairs used to breed on the banks of Lake Hula before it was drained). The male digs several scrapes in exposed ground and the female chooses one of them as a nest; the base is sometimes lined with small quantities of grass and dry twigs. In the clutch there are usually 4 eggs. Incubation begins sporadically with the laying of the first egg, becoming continuous with the laying of the last. Both parents incubate for a period of 22-24 days, although the female's portion is greater. Occasionally, especially when the eggs have been exposed to the sun, the incubating bird moistens its feathers before returning to its post. During this time Spur-winged Plovers become increasingly aggressive. If a human intruder enters their territory, they fly up and emit sharp and metallic alarm calls; confronted by an animal, even one as large as a horse or a cow, they stand in its path with wings spread and call. Sometimes they dive at the intruder, attacking with the bill. From observation of certain pairs it is evident that the male is the more aggressive and the one that takes the initiative. Sometimes pairs from neighbouring territories join the fray. The violence of the defensive response increases with the hatching of chicks. The chicks normally hatch simultaneously, but sometimes two or three days elapse between the appearance of the first crack in the shell and the emergence of the chick. The chicks hatch open-eyed and covered in dense down. They feed independently from their first day, but continue to rely on their parents for warmth and protection. They fly at the age of six to seven weeks, and become independent a short time after this, roaming and forming into flocks. It is possible to see flocks of Spur-winged Plovers as early as mid-August.

Spur-winged Plovers breed twice and sometimes even three times in a year. In such cases, the male tends the chicks of the earlier brood while the female incubates almost alone. The breeding season is prolonged: clutches are found as early as the end of March, and newly hatched chicks may be seen as late as September.

Lapwing
Vanellus vanellus

A large wader: body length 28.5-32.5 cm, wing length 21.5-24 cm, wingspan 85 cm and weight 145-220 g. A bird of striking colours, distinguished especially by the long and erect black crest. The upperparts are green-bronze, appearing glossy purple in certain angles of light. The nape and cheeks are whitish-grey, the belly white and the breast black. The throat is black in breeding plumage, turning white in winter plumage. The crown is black in breeding plumage, turning grey and with sandy sides in winter. The bill is black and the legs brown-pink. The tarsus is perceptibly shorter than that of the Spur-winged Plover (47 mm as opposed to 70 mm). In flight the Lapwing is distinguished by the broad, rounded wings which are dark brown above and black and white below, and the russet colour of the

undertail-coverts is also conspicuous. The female has a shorter crest and lighter crown. Juveniles are recognisable by their shorter crest and buff-fringed upperpart feathers.

The Lapwing has a trans-Palaearctic range, from Britain and most of Europe, the northern Middle East and across the whole breadth of central Asia to China. It is a monotypic species. All its populations migrate, except those of western and central Europe and of Turkey. The Western Palaearctic population winters in western Europe, in the Mediterranean countries and the Middle East, including the Nile Valley. In Israel this is a frequent winterer between the end of October and March, and also a fairly common passage migrant, although its numbers vary considerably from year to year.

The habitats of the Lapwing, both in the nesting season and in winter quarters, are grasslands with short turf and bare patches, cultivated fields, riverbanks and shores of lakes and pools. The Lapwing usually avoids green marshland, preferring the more sparse vegetation of peat bogs.

Lapwings gather into flocks outside the nesting season. In Israel it is often possible to see flocks of scores or hundreds of individuals, either in flight or walking behind a ploughing tractor, pecking among the clods in search of earthworms and grubs. They also feed on crickets, molluscs and shrimps, and often lie in wait for rodents (Günther's voles *Microtus guentheri*) beside their burrows. They also eat seeds and vegetables. Lapwings disappear from Israel during March, but may be seen again in the Hula Reserve as early as mid-June.

There is an unconfirmed report of a family with chicks in the northern Hula Valley in 1963.

Sociable Plover
Vanellus gregarius

A wader of average size: body length 29 cm, wing length 20.5 cm, wingspan 73 cm and weight 185 g. In Israel it is seen in winter plumage, which is predominantly brown-grey. Its legs are black, in which it differs from the White-tailed Plover (legs orange-yellow), which is otherwise similar. It is more easily identified in flight, when the black wingtips, the white rump and the black centre of the tail are conspicuous. The secondaries are white, while the secondary coverts and the back are greyish.

The Sociable Plover breeds in a relatively limited area, in grassy steppes in the central and southern USSR, north of the range of the White-tailed Plover. It winters in the northwest of the Indian subcontinent, along the lower reaches of the Tigris and Euphrates and in Sudan. This is a bird of fields and grasslands and it is also found in exposed desert, although not on the sea-coast.

In Israel this is a rare passage migrant in October-November and at the end of February and in March. It is also an occasional winterer, seen mostly in the western Negev: on 25 February 1983, 51 individuals were counted there. Usually it winters in this area together with the Lapwing, sometimes in combined flocks with the Golden Plover. A few sightings have also been recorded in the Bet She'an Valley (20 individuals in November 1973) and in the Golan.

White-tailed Plover
Vanellus leucurus

A wader of average size: body length 28 cm, wing length 18 cm, wingspan 69 cm and weight 150 g. The back is uniform russet-brown and the belly is sand-coloured. The legs are orange-yellow and noticeably long. This plover is distinguished in flight by the black primaries and contrasting white secondaries and some primary coverts. The tail is white, which is unique among waders.

This is a monotypic species and a typical Irano-Turanian bird, breeding along the lower reaches of the Tigris and Euphrates, also to the east of the Caspian Sea and to the south of Lake Balkhash, south of the range of the Sociable Plover. It is resident in Iraq, but the central Asiatic population migrates and winters in north India and in Sudan. Its habitat at all seasons of the year is in valleys and plains, close to shallow water. It is a gregarious bird, especially outside the nesting season.

In Israel this is a very rare winterer between September and mid-May and a rare passage migrant, usually seen in September. Sightings have been recorded in all parts of the country, mostly of solitary individuals. On 11-12 October 1979, six were seen together in the salt-pools of Eilat.

Family: Scolopacidae (Sandpipers, Snipes)

The largest family in the sub-order of waders, comprising 83 species belonging to 23 genera, grouped under six subfamilies: Calidrinae (stint-type sandpipers), Gallinagininae (snipes), Scolopacinae (woodcocks), Tringinae (sandpipers, curlews), Arenariinae (turnstones) and Phalaropodinae (phalaropes).

Members of this family have long and pointed wings. The tail is short to medium in length. The head is small in comparison with that of other waders, and the eyes small. The bill is usually slender, with length and shape varying according to genera. Most of these birds feed by probing with the bill, which has a sensitive tip. The tip of the upper mandible is flexible, capable of moving independently so that prey may be swallowed while the remainder of the bill remains closed. The legs are medium to long. The sexes are usually similar, though sometimes the female is larger, and often with a longer bill. Plumage is normally drab, especially in winter. Summer plumage is more colourful and conspicuous.

The Scolopacidae are good and fast fliers and fast runners, most often seen wading in mud and sometimes swimming. Most breed in the far north, and all migrate in winter.

In Israel there are eight genera and 16 species, all of them winterers, passage migrants or rare accidentals.

Genus: *Calidris* (stint-type sandpipers)
A genus of small waders, comprising 18 species. The body is compact, the neck and legs short, the bill short or medium (roughly equal in length to the head or slightly longer) and slender, straight or slightly curved, with a soft and flexible tip. The wings are pointed and the tail square. The female is sometimes larger and usually has a longer bill; otherwise the sexes are similar. Plumage in winter is drab greyish. Breeding plumage is more conspicuous, some species having russet or black colour.

Members of this genus are agile: they run about on a muddy shore or in shallow water, seeking out invertebrates with repeated stabs of the bill in mud. Only rarely do they locate their prey by eyesight. They gather in large flocks outside the nesting season. Their flight is very fast, and they execute aerial manoeuvres with astonishing uniformity. Often members of different species combine in flocks.

In Israel seven species are represented — passage migrants, winterers or rare accidentals.

Dunlin
Calidris alpina

One of the commonest small waders: body length 17-19.3 cm, wing length 11.5-11.8 cm, wingspan 38-42 cm and weight 42-48 g. In winter plumage the back is greyish and the belly white, and the bird is then distinguished by the long bill (32 mm, slightly longer than the head) which is curved downwards. In summer plumage the upperparts are chestnut-coloured, speckled with black and white, and there is a distinctive black patch on the belly. The breast is whitish-grey, speckled with brown markings. It is sometimes seen in this plumage in Israel, during the autumn migration and in late spring.

The Dunlin breeds in marshes and mossy heathland in north Europe and the arctic region. In this range six subspecies have been identified, two of which occur in Israel. The Western Palaearctic population winters along the shores of western Europe, in the Mediterranean basin, on the shores of Arabia, in the Nile Delta and on the Red Sea coasts. In Israel the subspecies *C.a. alpina* is a very common passage migrant and winterer, and *C.a. schinzii* is an uncommon passage migrant and scarce winter visitor.

The species may be seen throughout the year, except at the end of May and in June. The migration peaks occur in September and in April. On the coast of northern Sinai, 8,100 individuals were counted in 1973 between the end of August and the beginning of October. Scores of Dunlins may gather on coastal fish-ponds, often mingling with Little Stints and other waders.

Three Dunlins ringed in Israel during the autumn migration have been recovered: two in Egypt in January, two and three years respectively after ringing; and the third in Azerbaydzhan in November, some 13 months after ringing.

Knot
Calidris canutus

A thickset wader: body length 24-26 cm, wing length 17 cm, wingspan 59 cm and weight 130-160 g. In winter plumage it is grey, while in summer plumage the underparts are a russet-chestnut colour (this colour is distinctive during the autumn migration).

The Knot breeds sporadically in the polar regions of Asia and North America. There are four subspecies. It winters in large and dense flocks on muddy shores and river estuaries, especially along the shores of the North Sea and the Atlantic Ocean in western Europe and West Africa, in the western Mediterranean and also in South America, South Africa and Australasia.

In Israel this is a rare accidental between July and March, usually occurring singly. One individual was collected on 25 September 1970 in the pools of Maagan Mikhael. Two were seen at the same place in November 1984, and two in May 1985 on the shore at Eilat. In autumn the Knot passes by the shores of northern Sinai, sometimes in small flocks.

Sanderling
Calidris alba

Body length 20 cm, wing length 12.5 cm, wingspan 43 cm and weight 60 g. In Israel it is seen in winter plumage: light greyish above and white below. It has a black patch on the angle of the wing and a white wingbar, conspicuous in flight.

The Sanderling breeds in the arctic tundras of Asia and North America, north of the range of the Dunlin. It is a monotypic species which winters along the shores of western Europe, in the Mediterranean, in southern Asia and on the shores of Africa and America, mostly on sandy beaches.

This is a very active bird. It runs in a characteristic crouch, following the receding tide and pecking in the sand for various invertebrates, and fleeing from the returning tide.

In Israel the Sanderling is a common passage migrant along the shores of the Mediterranean, especially in autumn from the beginning of August to October, and a rare migrant in Eilat both in autumn and spring. It also winters on the Mediterranean shore from the Gulf of Acre southward, especially south of Ashdod, between December and February.

Little Stint
Calidris minuta

The smallest wader seen in Israel and the most common member of its genus: body length 13-16 cm, wing length 9-10 cm, wingspan 35 cm and weight 16-26 g. In winter plumage it is greyish above and whitish below. The bill is straight and short, the legs black and the tail grey and black.

The Little Stint is a monotypic species, breeding in arctic tundras from Lapland to northern Siberia, and wintering in the Mediterranean basin, in the Middle East, along the shores of Arabia and India and especially in tropical Africa. A ringed specimen has been known to migrate over a distance of some 1,200 km in two days.

In Israel this is a very common passage migrant and winterer, on fish-ponds and especially on recently drained pools, but also on reservoirs along the sea-coast. Hundreds and sometimes even thousands of individuals gather on muddy stretches where there are abundant supplies of food. The vanguard of the migrants arrives as early as the end of July, while the rearguard is still to be seen in May, when summer plumage (reddish-brown back speckled with black and orange-brown) is already appearing. The peak of migration in autumn is from mid-August to the beginning of September, and that in spring is at the end of April. In autumn 1978, more than 15,000 Little Stints were counted migrating along the coast of northern Sinai between mid-August and mid-October, with a peak in the last week of August. This very active and fast-flying wader tends to flock with Dunlins.

Temminck's Stint
Calidris temminckii

A small wader: body length 14 cm, wing length 9.9 cm, wingspan 36 cm and weight 25 g. It is

usually seen in Israel in winter plumage, when it is distinguished from the Little Stint by its mottled grey-brown breast, greenish-yellow legs, and white sides of the tail. The back is darker and more uniform in colour than that of the Little Stint.

The distribution of Temminck's Stint is arctic, from Scandinavia to the Bering Strait, in regions of taiga and tundra. Its range overlaps to some extent that of the Little Stint, but extends further to the west, south and east, and its habitats are usually richer in vegetation. This is a monotypic species, whose Western Palaearctic population winters in limited areas around the Mediterranean and especially in the strip of savanna south of the Sahara and in East Africa.

In Israel this is a fairly common passage migrant and winterer between August and May, generally found on freshwater margins rather than on the seashore. It never gathers in large flocks, and is considerably less common than the Little Stint.

Curlew Sandpiper
Calidris ferruginea

A large sandpiper: body length 18.5 cm, wing length 13 cm, wingspan 44 cm and weight 35-50 g. It is distinguished by its long downcurved bill and white rump, conspicuous both in grey winter plumage and in chestnut summer plumage.

The Curlew Sandpiper is restricted to tundra in northern Siberia and to islands in the Arctic Ocean, inhabiting grassy and bushy environments on hill slopes. It winters on the shores of Australia, southern Asia, North Africa and in tropical Africa. In Israel

this is quite a rare winterer, and also quite a rare passage migrant in August-September and in April-May. The migrants put on full summer plumage at the end of May.

Pectoral Sandpiper
Calidris melanotos

Body length 21 cm, wing length 14 cm, wingspan 45 cm and weight 85 g. It is distinguished by the sharp division between the dark and streaked breast and the white belly. In flight its wings are dark, without conspicuous wingbars.

The Pectoral Sandpiper breeds in North America and northeastern Siberia, and winters mainly in South America; the Siberian population travels to its winter quarters by way of the Bering Strait. This is the most common transatlantic vagrant in western Europe. An isolated individual was observed (and photographed) over a period of ten days, from 15 May 1983, in the salt-pools of Eilat.

Genus: *Limicola*
This monotypic genus is distinguished from the genus *Calidris* by the long bill, which is broad at the base, narrow towards the tip and curved downwards; the bill is soft and flexible, and only the tip is hard. The tail is square, but the two central feathers are sometimes longer.

Broad-billed Sandpiper
Limicola falcinellus

Body length 16 cm, wing length 10.5 cm, wingspan 38 cm and weight 35 g. In winter plumage this wader is grey-backed and resembles the Dunlin, from which it is distinguished by the longer bill (up to 1½ times the length of the head), short legs, light supercilium and light stripes along the crown. These stripes are also conspicuous in summer plumage, when the back is chestnut-coloured speckled with black. The belly is white in both plumages.

The Broad-billed Sandpiper is distributed primarily in northern Scandinavia, but also in small and relatively isolated areas in Siberia. Two subspecies are described. It breeds in marshes and areas of wet heathland, in coniferous forests and in tundra. It winters in southeast and southern Asia and also on the shores of South Africa, Djibouti and Kenya.

In Israel this is a rare passage migrant from August to early October, and from March to May. It is most often seen between mid-April and the end of May in Eilat.

Ruff
Philomachus pugnax

A thickset wader of average size but with considerable size differences between the sexes: male — body length 28 cm, wing length 18.8 cm, wingspan 56 cm and weight 190 g; female — body length 22 cm, wing length 15.7 cm, wingspan 50 cm and weight 130 g. It has a thick neck and long legs. The bill is of average length, and thick in relation to that of sandpipers. In winter plumage the Ruff is mottled brown on the back and greyish-brown on the breast, with a whitish belly. Its legs may be yellow, orange or red, while the bill may be blackish, yellow, brown or red. The best fieldmark is the white oval patch on each side of the tail. The summer plumage of males is completely different from that of winter. Their colours become more vivid and long display feathers develop, forming a kind of neck-ruff and ear-tufts. These feathers vary in colour from individual to individual, and the colour of the ruff is usually different from the colour of the ear-tufts; thus there are no two individuals identical in the colour of legs, bill, ruff and tufts. In Israel individuals are occasionally seen in intermediate plumage, but full breeding plumage does not appear here at all.

The Ruff has a northern Palaearctic range, from eastern Britain and Holland through Scandinavia, Russia and Poland to northeast Siberia. This is a monotypic species. Its habitats are grassland in tundra, clearings in forest and wet meadows beside lakes and rivers, sometimes even within agricultural settlements. All of its populations migrate. Most of the Western Palaearctic population winters in tropical Africa, with a minority in western Europe and in the Mediterranean basin.

In Israel this is a very common passage migrant from the end of July to mid-October, especially in early September, and from the end of March to mid-May. It usually flies in single-sex flocks, numbering 10-40 individuals and flying at an altitude of 50-100 m. It is also a fairly common winterer, usually in small groups. It occurs on muddy stretches near fresh water, banks of lakes, fish-ponds etc; only rarely is it found on the sea-coast. Often its flocks are mingled with those of other waders, especially sandpipers. It eats insects, worms and other invertebrates which it usually catches on the surface of the ground, and also sometimes consumes seeds.

Common Snipe
Gallinago gallinago

A wader of moderate size and thickset appearance: body length 26-27 cm (including 7 cm for the bill), wing length 13.1-13.5 cm, wingspan 44-47 cm and weight 58-90 g. It is a dark brown bird, striped on the head and back. The breast is speckled and the belly white. In flight a narrow white line shows on the tips of the secondaries. In relation to its size, its

bill is the longest of any bird occurring in Israel. The legs are relatively short. The wings are broad and pointed, and the tail is rounded.

The Common Snipe has a very wide range. It breeds within the Holarctic region mostly to the north of 47°N, also in South America and in tropical Africa. In this range nine subspecies have been identified. Its habitat is dense marsh vegetation with open areas. In Europe and Asia the main subspecies is *G.g. gallinago*. Most populations migrate; those of the Western Palaearctic region winter in western Europe, the Middle East and the savanna in tropical Africa. This is the most widespread of the snipes in Israel.

Unlike the majority of waders, the Common Snipe is most active in twilight, spending much of the day resting or hiding among marsh vegetation. It is usually found singly or in small groups, standing or walking slowly and digging its long and broad-tipped bill repeatedly in the mud to catch worms and insects. When alarmed it usually lies flat and motionless; only when there is no alternative does it fly, and then it rises suddenly with rapid wingbeats, uttering an alarm call as it zigzags away.

The Common Snipe is a common passage migrant and winterer in Israel. The autumn migration takes place from mid-August to mid-November, and the spring one during March and April, with the rearguard still visible in May; the first and last months also correspond to the presence of the wintering population.

Great Snipe
Gallinago media

Similar to the Common Snipe but more thickset, with larger head and shorter (6 cm) bill: body length 28 cm, wing length 14.5 cm, wingspan 48 cm and weight 110-120 g (but can rise to 200 g, especially before migration). It is distinguished from the Common Snipe by its greyer colours and the heavier barring on the belly, and by the white sides of the tail, visible in flight; its behaviour is similar, but its flight is heavier and lower, without zigzags, and it is also quieter.

This snipe's range is in the northern Palaearctic region, in Scandinavia, Poland and the USSR east to the steppes of Siberia. It is a monotypic species, inhabiting grassland among thickets of willow and birch: a drier and more wooded habitat than that of the Common Snipe (though on migration it is sometimes found in fields and open plantations or in marshy areas). The Great Snipe winters in tropical Africa, and in Israel is a fairly rare passage migrant (October-November and April-May).

Jack Snipe
Lymnocryptes minimus

A member of a different genus from that of other snipes, the Jack Snipe is similar to the Common Snipe but smaller: body length 18-20.3 cm, wing length 10-11.2 cm, wingspan 40 cm and weight 34-55 g. It is darker in appearance than the two preceding species. The head is large and the bill short in relation to that of other snipes. The tail is wedge-shaped. When disturbed it rises quietly, without alarm calls, and its flight is short-range and hesitant.

The Jack Snipe breeds in the Palaearctic region, between latitudes 55°N and 70°N, from Scandinavia to Siberia. This is a monotypic species, wintering in western Europe, in the Mediterranean basin and in the strip of savanna north of the Equator.

In Israel this is quite a common passage migrant and winterer, between October and April, especially in November. It is usually observed singly, both on migration and in winter quarters, but is rarely seen on account of its furtive habits: it tends to feed in cover of vegetation rather than in open territory.

Long-billed Dowitcher
Limnodromus scolopaceus

A wader of moderate size, with relatively long legs and long bill, at first sight resembling a godwit: body length 25 cm (including 7 cm for the bill), wing length 14.5 cm, wingspan 49 cm and weight 100 g. In summer plumage the underparts are chestnut and barred with small and delicate brown-grey markings; the back is a darker shade of chestnut and speckled with dark grey. In winter plumage the belly is whitish, the breast light grey and the back grey. In flight a white 'V' shape, similar to that of the Greenshank, is conspicuous on its back. In flight the legs protrude only slightly beyond the end of the tail.

The Long-billed Dowitcher is a monotypic species which breeds on both sides of the Bering Strait, in northeastern Siberia and northern Alaska. A single individual, in summer plumage, was sighted between 21 July and the end of August 1984 in the sewage-ponds of Tel Aviv.

Woodcock
Scolopax rusticola

A wader of squat appearance and average size: body length 34 cm (including 8 cm for the bill), wing length 20 cm, wingspan 58 cm and weight 260-350 g. The Woodcock has camouflage colours corresponding to the colours of fallen leaves: brown, black, grey and beige. The legs are short, and grey-pink in colour. The wings are short and broad, and the flight is similar to that of an owl. The bill is flesh-coloured at the base and dark at the tip, longer than the head by about a third; the tip is soft and flexible, and rich in tactile nerve endings. The eye is especially large, and the eye sockets occupy a considerable portion of the sides of the skull. The aperture of the ear is located beneath the eye, not behind it as in most birds.

The Woodcock is a monotypic species with a continuous trans-Palaearctic range, from Britain through Europe and central Asia to Japan, and a separate population in the Caucasus and northern slopes of the Himalayas. Its distribution in Europe has extended as a result of afforestation. Most of its populations migrate, and those of the Western Palaearctic region winter in western Europe and the Mediterranean basin.

The Woodcock is one of the least gregarious of the waders, and is almost invariably found singly. When it senses danger it lies flat on the ground, and only when approached to within a few metres does it break cover with loud beating of wings and flee for its life. It probes in the ground with its bill, clearing away leaves and drawing out earthworms and other invertebrates; it also consumes insects and molluscs.

In Israel this is a common winterer in groves and forests in northern and central parts of the country, but is quite difficult to see on account of its typical habitats: the Woodcock is a bird of forests, preferring mixed forests with dense and damp deposits of fallen leaves, but is also found in coniferous forests. It is especially active during twilight and at night.

Genus: *Limosa* (godwits)
A genus of medium-sized waders with a straight or slightly upcurved long bill, up to three times the length of the head, a long neck, long and pointed wings, and long legs. Plumages contain red or cinnamon colours during the breeding season and are mostly grey-brown in winter. Godwits feed mostly on invertebrates, by probing. The genus contains four species, all of which breed in the north. Two occur in Israel.

Black-tailed Godwit
Limosa limosa

One of the larger waders: body length 42 cm (including 10 cm for the bill), wing length 21 cm, wingspan 76 cm and weight about 300 g. The female is larger than the male, especially so in bill length which is up to 10% longer. In winter plumage the feathers are a uniform pale grey-brown, and the bird is then distinguished in flight by the white wingbar, the white rump, and the white tail with a broad and conspicuous black bar at the tip. In breeding plumage the head, neck and breast take on a chestnut colour.

The Black-tailed Godwit has a Euro-Siberian range, breeding in areas of heath and meadow from Iceland through western and central Europe to eastern Siberia. In this range three subspecies have been identified. The one occurring in Israel is *L.l. limosa* of west Europe and west Asia. The western populations winter in western Europe, in the Mediterranean basin and especially in the savannas to the north of tropical Africa.

The Black-tailed Godwit sometimes wades in water up to its belly, probing the bed with its long bill. It feeds particularly on invertebrates such as worms and molluscs. In winter quarters it also eats vegetable food. Its food is sometimes located by sight. This is a cautious bird, quick to fly and escape from danger. It often flies at considerable height.

In Israel this is a fairly common passage migrant from early August to early October and during April. It also winters in this country between September and mid-February, in numbers varying considerably from year to year. It is a gregarious bird, usually seen in flocks. The largest number of individuals counted in Israel was 200 on 6 December 1975. It winters in muddy tracts on the banks of rivers and lakes, and in Israel especially on fish-ponds and in the Hula Reserve, but also on sea-coasts.

Bar-tailed Godwit
Limosa lapponica

Slightly smaller than the Black-tailed Godwit: body length 38 cm, wing length 21 cm, wingspan 75 cm and weight 260 g. The bill is about 9 cm in length and distinctly upcurved. Coloration is similar to that of the Black-tailed Godwit, both in summer and in winter, but in full summer plumage the underside, including the belly and undertail-coverts, is chestnut-brown. There is no wingbar, while the tail has a few thin black and white bars and appears grey, with the lower back and rump white.

The Bar-tailed Godwit nests in tundra in northern Europe and Siberia, in a range which is more northerly than that of the Black-tailed Godwit and extends as far as western Alaska. There are two subspecies. It winters on sea-coasts, with a clear preference for sheltered areas. The Western Palaearctic population winters especially along the shores of the Atlantic Ocean, from Britain to South Africa, also in the Mediterranean basin, in the Red Sea, in East Africa and along the shores of the Arabian Sea. In Israel this is a rare passage migrant, in September and in April.

Genus: *Numenius* (curlews)
A genus of waders of average to large size with down-curved bill. The tarsus is long. The wings are long and pointed, and the tail is rounded and less than half the length of the wing. Plumage is dark brown with barring of white-cream. Male and female have identical plumage and there is no difference in plumage between seasons of the year. Members of this genus feed especially on invertebrates but also on vegetable food. They usually feed by walking slowly and probing. There are eight species, all breeding in northern areas. On migration they are liable to occur in all parts of the world. In Israel three species are accidentals.

Whimbrel
Numenius phaeopus

A large wader: body length 41 cm (including 7-10 cm for the bill), wing length 23.5-26 cm, wingspan 76-89 cm, weight of the male 390 g and of the female 440 g. This bird is darker than other species of curlew and is distinguished by dark and light bars on the head.

The Whimbrel breeds in the northern Palaearctic region, in Iceland, northern Europe, Siberia, northern Canada and Alaska. In this range four subspecies are known. Its habitat is in semi-exposed environments, sometimes close to the sea-coast but usually in sub-arctic moorland. It winters primarily on sea-shores, migrating as far as South America, South Africa and the shores of Australia.

In Israel the subspecies *N.p. phaeopus*, which breeds in northern Europe and western Asiatic Russia, is a fairly rare passage migrant, sometimes observed in flocks of up to a dozen individuals. It is seen especially during the autumn migration, between mid-August and the end of September, when it is most conspicuous on the southern Mediterranean shores and very rare in Eilat. In the spring migration, from mid-March to the beginning of May, it is seen more often in Eilat and along the Syro-African rift. It is also a rare winterer on the Mediterranean coasts, especially on rocky shores. Every year one or two individuals winter on the Carmel coast.

Curlew
Numenius arquata

The largest of the waders: male — body length 50 cm (including 12 cm for the bill), wing length 29 cm, wingspan 80 cm and weight 800 g; female — body length 60 cm (including 14.5 cm for the bill), wing length 31 cm, wingspan 100 cm and weight 1,000 g.

The Curlew breeds across most of Europe from Ireland, Britain and Scandinavia to southern France and the shores of the Black Sea, and further east to central and eastern Asia. Its preferred breeding habitat is damp heathland and grasslands near water.

There are two subspecies. The Western Palaearctic population winters on marshy and sandy sea-shores in western Europe, in the Mediterranean basin, on the shores of Arabia and the Arabian Sea, and also along the shores of tropical Africa and on some of its lakes.

In Israel this is a fairly rare passage migrant between the beginning of August and the end of October, and in March-April. It also occasionally winters on fish-ponds, but is more often seen in fields, some distance from water. It is usually found singly.

Slender-billed Curlew
Numenius tenuirostris

A very rare monotypic species, breeding only in western Siberia. Little is known of its migration patterns. There is a report of an individual which was caught on 4 October 1917 in the estuary of Nahal Ha-Bashor, not far from Gaza, and another was reported at Eilat on 12 April 1977. There are some doubts about both records, as this species is difficult to distinguish from the eastern subspecies of the Curlew *N.a. orientalis*.

Genus: *Tringa* (shanks, sandpipers)
A genus of marshbirds 20-30 cm in body length. The females are larger than the males. Their bills are long (but shorter than those of godwits), and straight or slightly upcurved. The tarsus is long. The wings are long and pointed, and the tail is square-ended or slightly rounded. Most members of the genus are grey, white and brown. Distinguishing between them can be difficult: length and colour of bill, colour of legs and vocal characteristics are often the most reliable aids. In flight there are no white wingbars (except in the case of the Redshank.) The sexes are similar, and except in the Spotted Redshank there is no striking difference in plumage between seasons of the year.

In this genus there are ten species, distributed in Europe, especially in the north, and in Asia and North America. All of them migrate. These are primarily birds of marsh and wet heathland near water, although each species has a preferred habitat. They usually consume their food, various invertebrates and especially insects, molluscs, worms and crabs, while wading in shallow water or mud, sometimes while swimming. In Israel six species are represented.

Spotted Redshank
Tringa erythropus

A large shank, with bill twice the length of the head: body length 30 cm (including 5.5 cm for the bill), wing length 17 cm, wingspan 64 cm and weight 160 g. In summer plumage it is unmistakable: a black-grey wader with white speckling on the wing-coverts and back; the belly is darker than the back, the reverse of the norm among birds. Winter plumage is strikingly different: light grey above and whitish below. The legs and the base of the lower mandible are red.

The Spotted Redshank is distributed especially in Siberia, in areas of sub-arctic and arctic climate, but also in tundras in northern Scandinavia and northern Russia. This is a monotypic species. The Western Palaearctic population winters in the Mediterranean basin and in the strip of savanna in northern tropical Africa.

The Spotted Redshank penetrates deep water to a greater extent than other shanks, and is apt to immerse the entire head and neck. Sometimes it feeds with sideways movements of the head, like the Avocet, and it is also known to swim in fish-ponds in dense flocks, catching adult and larval insects on the surface with rapid stabs of the bill.

In Israel this is a fairly common passage migrant and winterer. It is seen during most months of the year, in fish-ponds and reservoirs and also on the sea-coast, and it is not always clear whether the individuals seen in the summer are the laggards of the spring migration or the vanguard of the autumn migration.

Redshank
Tringa totanus

Slightly smaller than the Spotted Redshank: body length 28 cm, wing length 16 cm, wingspan 63 cm and weight 120 g. The bill is also shorter (about 4 cm). The legs and bill base are reddish-orange. It is distinguished from all other shanks by the white bar at the rear edges of the wing and especially by its call, a repeated melodic whistle. This is the call most typically heard in fish-ponds in winter.

The breeding range of the Redshank extends south of that of the Spotted Redshank, over most of Europe and across central Asia to Mongolia and Manchuria. In this range four or five subspecies have been identified. The subspecies *T.t. totanus*, which breeds in Europe and western Siberia, occurs in Israel. It inhabits green marshlands near fresh or salt water. The Western Palaearctic population winters especially along the shores of the Mediterranean basin, across the Middle East and on the coasts of tropical Africa. The females migrate first, the males after them and the juveniles migrate last.

The Redshank feeds primarily on crabs, molluscs and worms. Its diet varies according to place and circumstances, as does its manner of feeding: when locating its food by sight, its flocks are sparse and scattered; in water, where it probes for food with the tip of its bill, the flocks are more dense. It also feeds at night. The Redshank tends to spend most of its time in a loose flock together with other waders. When alarmed it first bends down, then takes to the air making its voice heard (this acts as a warning signal to other species too.) Its flight is fast and straight.

In Israel this is a common passage migrant from mid-June to early November, and in spring especially in March. Between these dates it is also the most common shank in winter in fish-ponds and on rocky coasts in the Mediterranean. An individual ringed on 25 November 1968 in Maagan Mikhael was found on 30 April 1969 near Volgagrad (formerly Stalingrad) in the USSR.

Greenshank
Tringa nebularia

The largest of the shanks: body length 31 cm (including 5.5 cm for the bill), wing length 19 cm, wingspan 69 cm and weight 200 g. This is a grey bird, with long green legs. Its bill is long, approximately twice the length of the head; it can be up to 6.1 cm in length and is slightly upcurved. In flight it emits a characteristic cry of three rapid syllables, which carries over long distances.

The Greenshank has a trans-Palaearctic range south of the tundra, in regions of taiga and mixed forest, from northern Scotland through Scandinavia to Kamchatka. This is a monotypic species. The Western Palaearctic population winters especially across tropical Africa, but also around the coasts of the Mediterranean and the shores of Arabia.

In winter the Greenshank usually prefers salty lagoons and muddy sea-shores. It wades in deep water, up to the belly. It feeds especially on small invertebrates and small fish which it locates by sight. When it senses danger it bobs up and down. Its flight is fast and strong, sometimes with sharp turns.

In Israel the Greenshank is a common passage migrant between the end of July and the second half of September, and in spring especially between early April and late May. It is also a fairly common winterer between these dates, found especially in fish-ponds, but also on muddy beaches and sewage-ponds. On migration, flocks numbering 30-50 individuals may be seen; in winter it is usually solitary.

Marsh Sandpiper
Tringa stagnatilis

A medium-sized shank: body length 23 cm (including 4 cm for the bill), wing length 14 cm, wingspan 57 cm and weight 65 g. In appearance it resembles a small Greenshank. It is recognisable by

its long, slender legs. In flight it resembles the Green and Wood Sandpipers, and is distinguished from them when seen from above by the white rump extending to the back and by a paler area on the inner wing. When escaping danger it emits a high-pitched and metallic monosyllabic cry.

The Marsh Sandpiper nests in southern Russia and the central USSR. This is a monotypic species, wintering especially in tropical Africa and southeast Asia and Australia, but also in the Mediterranean basin and the Middle East. Its winter habitats are similar to those of the Greenshank, though it feeds in shallow water.

In Israel this is a fairly common passage migrant, especially from mid-August to the end of September, and in spring especially during April. It is then sometimes seen in flocks of up to a dozen individuals. It is also a winterer, ranging from rare to fairly common, seen mainly on fish-ponds but also on the coast and usually on open stretches of water. In winter the Marsh Sandpiper does not flock, but often joins groups of other waders.

Green Sandpiper
Tringa ochropus

Body length 22 cm (the bill 3.5 cm), wing length 14.5 cm, wingspan 59 cm and weight 75 g. The darkest of the sandpipers: dark olive-brown above, and mostly white below. In flight its dark wings are conspicuous against the white tail, rump and belly. When disturbed, it rises up in zigzag flight and emits an abrupt trisyllabic alarm call; it flies high, usually to a considerable distance before landing again.

This sandpiper's range is from the North Sea in Norway to the shores of the Pacific Ocean east of Siberia, between latitudes 50°N and 60°N. It is a monotypic species. It differs from most other waders in that it breeds in small swamps within woodland and forests, even coniferous forests, and usually nests in trees, in the abandoned nests of other species such as thrushes and doves. The Green Sandpiper winters in western and southern Europe, in the Mediterranean countries, in the Middle East, in tropical Africa to Angola, and in south and southeast Asia.

Among the waders it is the first to migrate, and is seen in Israel as early as mid-June. The peak of its migration is in the second half of August, and it ends in November. The spring migration continues over about three months, between the end of February and mid-May, with a peak between the end of March and mid-April. It is also a common winterer beside fish-ponds and spends much of its time in drainage canals, sewage-ponds, etc., usually near bank vegetation. It is not often seen on the sea-coast. The Green Sandpiper is usually solitary, both on migration and in winter quarters.

Wood Sandpiper
Tringa glareola

A small wader of slim profile, slightly smaller than the Green Sandpiper and more slender: body length 20 cm (bill about 3 cm), wing length 12.5 cm, wingspan 56 cm and weight 60 g. The legs are relatively long: the tarsus is 3.8 cm in length, as opposed to 3.5 cm in the Green Sandpiper. The Wood Sandpiper is speckled grey-brown above, and white below with a streaked breast. In flight it resembles the Green Sandpiper, but is paler and with more distinctive speckling. Also conspicuous is the square white rump. The legs are green-yellow. When escaping danger it emits a series of rapid syllables; its call is harsher and less melodic than the Green Sandpiper's.

The Wood Sandpiper's range is trans-Palaearctic, from Scotland to Kamchatka, from 50°N to the Arctic Ocean. Its range overlaps that of the Green Sandpiper and extends further north. In a few areas, as in Finland, it is the commonest wader. This is a monotypic species and all of its populations migrate in winter. A small section of the Western Palaearctic population winters in the Mediterranean basin and the Middle East, the greater part in tropical Africa.

In Israel this is a common passage migrant: in autumn from July to mid-November, with a peak at the end of August; in spring especially in April and the first half of May. It is also a fairly common winterer near fresh water, especially in fish-ponds, and more rare on sea-coasts. On migration scores of individuals are sometimes seen together, but normally the Wood Sandpiper is found singly or in small and sparse flocks. It tends to spend more time in open habitats than the Green Sandpiper, which it otherwise resembles in behaviour.

Terek Sandpiper
Xenus cinereus

Body length 23 cm, wing length 13.5 cm, wingspan 58 cm and weight 65 g. The bill is long (4.8 cm) and upcurved. The legs are particularly short (length of tarsus 2.8 cm) and the toes are also short. This bird is grey above and white below with a finely streaked breast. Like the Common Sandpiper, it is apt to bob its tail.

The Terek Sandpiper breeds on muddy banks of rivers in coniferous forests from northern Russia to central Siberia. This is a monotypic species. The western population winters along the coasts of Arabia and Africa, from Somalia through the Cape of Good Hope to Nigeria.

In Israel this is a rare passage migrant. Sightings have been recorded at the end of summer and in early autumn on the coastal plain, and in spring in Eilat.

Common Sandpiper
Actitis hypoleucos

This is the smallest of the sandpipers: body length 20 cm, wing length 11.2 cm, wingspan 40 cm and weight 45 g. The bill is short (2.8 cm) and the legs short (tarsus 2.5 cm). Distinguished from the genus *Tringa* (in which it is included by some authors) by its rounded tail and especially by the uniform, unspeckled colour pattern of the down of the chicks. This wader is grey-brown above, with a white belly and a white stripe on each side of the breast. In flight a white bar across the wings is conspicuous. The flight call is a characteristic series of three thin piping notes.

Its range is trans-Palaearctic and extends over most of Europe and appreciable parts of Asia. This is a monotypic species, preferring pebbled or rocky banks of freshwater lakes and fast-flowing rivers and mountain streams. The Western Palaearctic population winters in western Europe, in the Mediterranean basin and along the shores of Arabia, but about 95% winters across tropical Africa. Outside the breeding season it inhabits any kind of aquatic environment, freshwater or saline.

The Common Sandpiper picks its food from the surface. It is conspicuous for its habit of bobbing its head and tail, movements which become more intense at times of excitement. It flies low over the water in hovering and rapid dynamic flight, changing from time to time to short glides on bowed wings, frequently uttering its characteristic call.

In Israel this is a common passage migrant from the end of July to mid-September and from early March to mid-May. It is also a frequent winterer on fish-ponds, beside streams and even on the sea-coast, usually found singly.

Turnstone
Arenaria interpres

Body length 23 cm, wing length 15.5 cm, wingspan 54 cm and weight about 110 g. The only representative in Israel of the subfamily Arenariinae, characterised by a short, thick and conical bill and a short and muscular neck. The bill and neck are adapted to a particular method of seeking food: turning over stones to expose the creatures concealed beneath them. The legs are short and solid (length of tarsus 2.5 cm). The Turnstone is recognisable by its black and white colour pattern both at rest and in flight, when white wingbars and white patches on the back and tail are conspicuous. In summer plumage the chestnut colouring of the back and the wing-coverts becomes more intense.

The Turnstone breeds along the shores of Scandinavia, the northern USSR, northern Greenland, northern Canada and northern Alaska. In this range two subspecies have been identified. This is a very northern wader, breeding from the Baltic Sea to 83°N. It winters along the coasts of western Europe, the Mediterranean, Africa, Arabia, south and southeast Asia to Australia and New Zealand.

This is not a timid bird, and it may be approached to within close range. It runs fast and is constantly active, turning over stones and shells up to 100 g in weight to seek out insects and crabs. It frequently scavenges, and even eats carrion.

In Israel the subspecies *A.i. interpres* is a fairly common passage migrant from August to September and again in April and May. It also winters on rocky coasts, such as the shores of western Galilee and the Carmel coast, especially in December-January. Its flocks are usually fairly dense, numbering up to 60 individuals.

Genus: *Phalaropus* (phalaropes)
The subfamily Phalaropodinae comprises a single genus *Phalaropus* and three species, two of which are accidentals in this country. Phalaropes are slim-bodied waders, with a long neck and small head, narrow and pointed wings and rounded tail. The legs are relatively short, and the three foretoes are lobed. The female is larger than the male, with more conspicuous and variegated colours and also with denser plumage on the belly. These birds are expert swimmers and are apt to winter on the sea, even at some distance from the coast. Only the male incubates and tends the chicks.

Red-necked Phalarope
Phalaropus lobatus

A small wader, and the smallest swimming bird seen in Israel: body length 18 cm, wing length 11 cm, wingspan 41 cm and weight about 30 g. In winter plumage this bird is mottled grey above, white below, and has a dark eye patch; in breeding plumage orange-brown colours are prominent on the sides of the neck and throat, and the back is cream-gold.

The Red-necked Phalarope breeds in the arctic region, in both New and Old Worlds. This is a monotypic species, whose Western Palaearctic population winters in the Arabian Sea.

The Red-necked Phalarope rides on the waves, sometimes spinning, and feeds on invertebrates which it catches on the surface.

In Israel this is a fairly rare accidental in various areas: the Hula, the shores of the Mediterranean and fish-ponds on the coastal plain. Usually a few individuals (three to six) are found together. In Eilat it is a rare passage migrant from August to October and from March to May, usually in groups of four to seven. In May 1981 more than 20 individuals were counted there over a period of ten days, and the number rose to 34 between 16th and 19th of that month.

Grey Phalarope
Phalaropus fulicarius

Larger than the Red-necked Phalarope: body length 21 cm, wing length 13 cm, wingspan 42 cm and weight about 50 g. In winter it is a fairly uniform grey above; at this season it is also distinguished from the former species by the shorter and thicker bill, which is sometimes yellowish-orange at the base. In summer the underparts are chestnut-coloured and the cheeks white, these colours being stronger and more prominent in the female.

The Grey Phalarope breeds in an area north of the range of the Red-necked Phalarope, especially in northern Siberia and North America. This is the most marine-based of the phalaropes, and its migration routes also pass mainly over the sea. It winters on the sea, especially offshore of West Africa and Chile — areas rich in plankton.

In Israel this is a rare accidental in autumn and winter, in fish-ponds and reservoirs on the coastal plain. There has been one sighting of an individual in breeding plumage in Eilat.

Sub-order: Lari

A sub-order of the order Charadriiformes, comprising four families: Stercorariidae (skuas), Laridae (gulls), Sternidae (terns) and Rynchopidae (skimmers).

Family: Stercorariidae (Skuas)

This family contains five species, divided into one or two genera. Their range extends over arctic and subarctic regions, in the wastelands of the far north and in tundra, while some are based in the Southern Hemisphere, in the vicinity of Antarctica. The northern populations migrate south, and the southern populations north, and thus they are liable to overlap in the central Atlantic Ocean, in tropical and subtropical regions. Skuas are more marine-based than gulls: outside the nesting season they roam across the oceans and are rarely seen over dry land.

These are average to large seabirds, at first sight resembling gulls. Body length is 46-58 cm and weight 350-1,400 g. The females are usually larger. Skuas have thickset bodies and strong and thick necks. The wings are narrow, long and pointed. The two central tail feathers are longer than the others, sometimes by as much as 10-18 cm. The plumage is dense. Skuas are predominantly dark brown. Most species have a light and a dark phase. The sexes are similar. The tarsus is short. The three foretoes are strong and webbed. Despite their superficial resemblance to gulls, skuas have certain aspects in common with birds of prey: on all the toes there are strong and curved claws (the foot structure, adapted both for swimming and for predatory activity, is peculiar to skuas); the bill is strong, and the upper mandible is hooked and with a cere at the base similar to that of raptors. The flight is as strong and agile as that of falcons.

Skuas feed by chasing gulls, terns and other seabirds, even attacking them with bill or wings. The victims drop or disgorge the food and the skuas catch it, usually in the air. They also capture and eat lemmings, songbirds, and prey on eggs, etc. They occasionally take fruit and carrion.

All species of skua breed on the ground, alone or in small groups, sometimes on the fringes of colonies of other seabirds. They lay 2 eggs. The chicks hatch open-eyed and covered with long, soft and woolly down of a uniform brown colour. They depend for a relatively long time on food provided by their parents, either fed to them bill-to-bill or regurgitated before them.

In Israel there are four species. Since 1979 it has become evident that three of them are quite common passage migrants, passing through the Gulf of Eilat and continuing northward over land. They winter in all probability in the Indian Ocean, and proceed northward along the Syro-African rift to return to their breeding areas.

Pomarine Skua
Stercorarius pomarinus

A skua of average size: body length 46-51 cm, wing length 35 cm, wingspan 125 cm and weight 700 g. The dark phase is greyish-brown and uniformly dark; in the light phase the belly is paler, with yellow on the sides of the neck; the crown and the forecheeks are brown-black. The wings are broad, and the Pomarine Skua is distinguished by the broad and blunt tips of the central tail feathers extending some 8 cm beyond the end of the tail. Its flight is relatively heavy.

This is a monotypic species, whose breeding range extends through northern Russia, northern Siberia, Greenland and North America. Outside the nesting season it roams the oceans, reaching the shores of central America, Australia and South Africa. It also winters around Arabia and on the shores of East Africa, and is quite common in the western Mediterranean.

This bird feeds in typical skua fashion. It also feeds on fish offal discharged from ships, and on fish which it catches itself.

The Pomarine Skua is a very rare accidental on the Mediterranean coast of Israel: a dead specimen was found on the shore near Netanya on 16 January 1968, and another individual was sighted at Maagan Mikhael on 9 December 1981. It is more common in Eilat between January and August, especially at the end of April and during May. In spring 1979, between 11 March and 2 June, 123 Pomarine Skuas were counted in Eilat. They arrive flying low over the Gulf, spiralling upwards on approaching the coast and continuing at high altitudes above the Arava. An individual found dead in Ein Gedi in May 1970, and another which was seen in the pools of Tirat Zevi in the Bet She'an Valley before proceeding northward along the Jordan Valley, are evidence that this part of the migration route passes overland.

Arctic Skua
Stercorarius parasiticus

A skua of average size: body length 46 cm, wing length 32 cm, wingspan 110 cm and weight 400 g. The tail is long and wedge-shaped, the central

115

feathers being sharp and protruding 10 cm beyond the end of the tail. This species is similar in colour to the Pomarine Skua, but its wings are narrower; in its profile and its light flight it resembles a falcon.

The Arctic Skua is a monotypic species, breeding in northern Europe, northern Asia and North America, and wintering across the oceans from Tierra del Fuego to the Cape of Good Hope, New Zealand and Tasmania. It also winters on the coasts of Arabia, and is not uncommon in the Mediterranean.

In Israel this is a familiar sight on the shores of the Mediterranean and in Eilat. In July-August it may be seen around Dove Island on the Carmel coast, attempting to prey on the chicks of Common Terns or to steal the food of the adult birds. In autumn it appears on the shores of northern Sinai in groups numbering four to eight individuals, and preys on migratory songbirds. In Eilat in spring 1979, between 11 March and 2 June, 290 individuals were counted.

Long-tailed Skua
Stercorarius longicaudus

The smallest and most delicate of the skuas: body length 48-53 cm, wing length 31 cm, wingspan 100 cm and weight 290 g. The two central tail feathers protrude by as much as 18-24 cm beyond the end of the tail. The bill is shorter and more slender than that of the other skuas, and the wings are long, narrow and pointed, without the white wing flash characteristic of the other species. There is no dark phase.

The Long-tailed Skua, which occurs in two subspecies, breeds in northern Europe, northern Asia

and North America and winters across the oceans.

In Israel *S.l. longicaudus* is a very rare accidental. A dead individual was found on the coast at Bet Yannai on 9 February 1976, and another at Moshav Paran in the Arava on 25 June 1981. In 1979, between 20 April and 12 May, eight adults were counted on the shore of the Gulf of Eilat; in 1980, between 24 July and 8 August, seven adults were counted in the same place.

Great Skua
Stercorarius skua

The largest and heaviest of the skuas, about the size of a Herring Gull: body length 55 cm, wing length 40 cm, wingspan 135 cm and weight 1.3 kg. Its wings are broad and its tail relatively short, with the central tail feathers protruding only slightly beyond the end of the tail. It is dark brown, with conspicuous white areas at the base of the primaries.

The Great Skua breeds in northern Britain and Iceland on the one hand, and in South America, Antarctica and islands of the Southern Hemisphere on the other. In this range four subspecies have been identified. The Great Skua winters especially in the Atlantic Ocean and in the southern Pacific Ocean, but also penetrates the western Mediterranean as far as Sicily.

In Israel a single sighting has been recorded in Eilat, on 3 June 1983. An additional sighting was made on 13 September 1972 at the western inlet of the Bardawil Lagoon. According to Hardy (1946), one was seen on 21 November 1936 in the Hula swamps and one on 26 March 1943 at the Yarkon River near Tel Aviv: both records are doubtful.

Family: Laridae (Gulls)

Gulls are common along sea-coasts in all parts of the world, but also penetrate to inland lakes and large rivers. In this family there are 46 species belonging to seven genera; of these 38 are included in the genus *Larus*. Most are of average to large size: body length 25-68 cm, wingspan 80-165 cm and weight 120-2,200 g.

The family of gulls is cosmopolitan and its members are distributed in areas of extreme climate, although they are more common in cold and temperate zones, and more common in the Northern than in the Southern Hemisphere. A few species have a very wide distribution. These are birds of the coast rather than of the open sea, usually not straying far from dry land. A few species breed on lakes and some are often seen in inland environments,

although not in mountainous or arid regions. In most species only a section of the population migrates. A few species are notable migrants, while some traverse the Equator on migration. In general, juveniles and immatures migrate to a greater extent and over longer distances than adults.

The body structure is strong and solid, and the neck relatively long. The wings are long, narrow and pointed, but broad in comparison to those of terns; in flight they are held at a characteristic angle, suitable for gliding. The tail is short and square, or rounded, or forked, and only rarely graduated. The plumage is thick and dense. Adults have white, black and grey plumage; brown or pink colours are rare. The underwings, the belly and the tail are usually white, the back and the wings grey or black. Juveniles are mottled brown above, with a distinctive dark band at the tip of the tail. In general the male is larger than the female and has a longer bill. The bill is strong and pointed in the smaller species, large and strong in the larger, and laterally compressed. The tip of the upper mandible is curved downwards. The bill is usually yellow or red, sometimes black, and at the tip there is often a conspicuous mark of a different colour. The legs are short and strong, and of uniform and distinctive colour: yellow, greenish, pink, red or dark brown. The three foretoes are fully webbed.

Gulls are active by day, although the Black-headed Gull is also active on moonlit nights. All are good fliers, although their flight is heavy and their wing movements slow; they often soar and glide. They also walk well on land, with the body in a horizontal posture, but seldom perch on trees or bushes. Gulls feed on a wide variety of food, usually with no particular preference. When alternative food sources are insufficient, the larger species are liable to resort to cannibalism. Gulls are capable of drinking seawater: the excess of salt is excreted via the nostrils with the aid of special glands above the eyes.

Gulls are gregarious throughout the year. They breed in colonies, sometimes numbering thousands of pairs, with each pair maintaining a nesting territory appropriate to the size of the bird. Colonies are located in open areas, usually close to the sea: on islands, cliffs, sandbanks and sometimes waste ground. Courtship behaviour is elaborate, and each species follows a characteristic ritual. The nest is a small hollow in the ground, normally with only a haphazard collection of vegetation piled up around it. The clutch is usually of 2-3 relatively large eggs. Incubation begins with the laying of the first egg, and both parents participate; the period of incubation is 20-30 days, according to the size of the egg. The chicks hatch open-eyed and covered with sparse and soft down. They soon leave the nest and tend to hide within the limits of the colony. The parents feed them bill-to-bill or with semi-digested food regurgitated on the ground. After 21-40 days the chicks fly and become independent. Gulls usually breed only once in the year, but there are liable to be numerous replacement clutches. Even in newborn chicks, the first plumage, ugly brown in colour, is visible beneath the covering of down. Adult plumage is acquired at 1½ years in small species, 2 years in the medium-sized and 3½ in the large.

In Israel 15 species are seen, members of two genera. All of them are winterers, with the exception of the Herring Gull, a few pairs of which breed in this country.

Black-headed Gull
Larus ridibundus

One of the commonest gulls in Israel, and the only one often seen far from the coast. This is a relatively small gull: body length 34-41 cm, wing length 27-31 cm, wingspan 105 cm and weight 220-325 g. It is distinguished by the conspicuous white colour at the fore-edge of the wing. The back and wings are greyish, with the primaries black at the tips; the rest of the plumage, apart from the head, is white. In winter the head too is white, with a small brown mark in the region of the ear; towards spring (in some individuals as early as the end of January), following the moult, the head becomes chocolate-brown. The adult has red legs and bill. Immature birds, up to one year old, have a yellow bill with a black tip, brown legs and chocolate-coloured secondaries; on the back there are residual traces of brown, and there is a black bar at the tip of the tail.

The Black-headed Gull has a trans-Palaearctic range, from Iceland and Britain through Europe and northern Asia to Kamchatka. This is a monotypic species, whose habitats are pools, lakes and rivers, also coastal saltmarshes. It is resident in western Europe; the other populations migrate. The Western Palaearctic populations winter especially along the shores of western Europe and West Africa, in the Mediterranean, along the shores of East Africa and also around the Arabian pensinsula and on the coasts of the Arabian Sea.

The Black-headed Gull feeds especially on invertebrates, but diet and manner of feeding vary according to place, season and availability of food. Today they also gather around refuse-dumps.

In Israel this is a passage migrant and a very common winterer. The migrants are seen between August and October and again between March and early May. The winterers arrive at the end of October, and their population grows gradually more sparse during March and the first half of April. The number of individuals wintering in the country amounts to tens of thousands. They are concentrated in two major populations: the larger one roosts on the sea-front of Tel Aviv, usually opposite the Riding electric power-station, sometimes near the port of Jaffa; the other roosts at the northern end of Lake Tiberias. At the former locality, there is an ample supply of water warmed by the cooling system of the power-station; at the latter, warm springs rise from the bed of the lake. Smaller roosting concentrations are also known on the Carmel coast and in the Bay of Haifa. The gulls roosting in the Tel Aviv region are seen every day, morning and evening, crossing the skies of Ramat Gan and Tel Aviv in arrowhead formation. In the morning twilight they disperse and fly away in search of food, in fields, fish-ponds and refuse-dumps and along the sea-coast. The gulls roosting at Lake Tiberias travel as far as the northern Hula Valley, Birkat Ram in the Golan Heights, the Dalton Reservoir and the western Jezreel Valley.

In recent years tens of thousands of Black-headed Gulls have begun to congregate around refuse-dumps in the vicinity of Ben-Gurion Airport. Because of their habit of wheeling and circling in the air, at altitudes of up to 2 km, they constitute a hazard to aircraft and various means of discouraging them have been attempted.

Two Black-headed Gulls ringed in Russia have been found in this country.

Sooty Gull
Larus hemprichii

A gull of average size: body length 43 cm, wing length 35.5 cm, wingspan 110 cm and weight 400 g. The head and throat are dark brown, the back and wings brown, the breast and mantle greyish. In winter plumage the colours are paler and the head turns to light brown. The bill and legs are greenish-yellow; the long and thick bill with a black and red tip is distinctive. This species has a red eye-ring.

The Sooty Gull is a tropical gull breeding on coasts and islands around Arabia, in the Red Sea and along the shores of East Africa to the north of the Equator. It is a monotypic species which outside the breeding season roams in the vicinity of its nesting areas. It feeds especially on discarded fish and on refuse from ships, being quite unperturbed by human presence.

This is a very rare accidental in Eilat, with the following records: singles on 13 May 1977 and on 23 November 1980; and three individuals during 1-3 June 1983. It is more common in southern Sinai.

White-eyed Gull
Larus leucophthalmus

A gull of average size: body length 42 cm, wing length 31.5 cm, wingspan 112 cm and weight 300 g. In breeding plumage its head is black-brown, which is also the colour of the small 'bib' from the throat to the upper breast. Around each eye are two crescents of white feathers. The wings are dark. In winter plumage the head has a lighter brown colour. The bill is relatively slender, slightly curved and long (about 4.5 cm), red with a black tip. The legs are yellow. The juvenile is dark grey-brown with white speckling on the head; the white crescents around the eye are already visible, and the bill is greyish.

The White-eyed Gull is a monotypic species, with a range restricted to the Red Sea and the shores of the Horn of Africa. It is a resident bird, roaming to some extent in the vicinity of its nesting areas. It is fairly common on the shores of southern Sinai and the island of Tiran, where 30-50 pairs may be seen. On 20 August 1973 a nest with two chicks was found there; some 30 pairs bred on the island between August and October 1975. Its diet consists primarily of fish.

This gull is a fairly rare accidental in Eilat, although in recent years there has been an increase in numbers. Records are usually in May, but also at various times between April and October.

Great Black-headed Gull
Larus ichthyaetus

A large gull: body length 57-61 cm, wing length 46.5-51 cm, wingspan 160 cm and weight about 1.2 kg. It is distinguished by its large and strong 'drooping' bill, about 6 cm long, yellow-orange at the base and red at the tip with a black band in between. The legs are greenish-yellow. In breeding plumage the head is black, but in winter all that remains of the black is a few darker marks in the region of the eyes and the nape. The partial moult to summer plumage begins as early as mid-January. The back and wings are silver-grey; the primaries are white, with black only near the tips. Immatures are best distinguished by their bill shape and size.

The range of the Great Black-headed Gull extends from the northern Black Sea and the northern Caspian Sea through the Aral Sea to central Asia. This is a monotypic species, wintering relatively close to its nesting areas: on the shores of India, the Persian Gulf, the Caspian Sea, the Red Sea and the Gulf of Suez.

The Great Black-headed Gull is impressive in flight, and is capable of gliding for long periods with wings spread. It is an aggressive bird, attacking and stealing food from birds such as coots, grebes and smaller gulls in a manner reminiscent of skuas. It is omnivorous, but feeds especially on live food such as fish, mammals and insects.

Until recent years this gull had not been seen in Israel (apart from two recorded by Tristram as shot, on 11 December 1863 and 29 February 1864, and a further isolated instance in 1922). Since 1967, however, it has been a fairly common winterer on the Carmel coast, with numbers approaching 200 in some years. From the mid-1970s it has also wintered in the Hula Valley, at Lake Tiberias, in the Bet She'an Valley and on the Acre coast. In the early years, Great Black-headed Gulls appeared only in the second week of January; recently, they have begun to arrive in mid-December, staying in the country until early March.

Mediterranean Gull
Larus melanocephalus

A small gull: body length 37 cm, wing length 30.5 cm, wingspan 96 cm and weight 310 g. It resembles the Black-headed Gull but is more solidly built, with a larger head and thicker bill. The head and throat are black in summer, with the black of the head extending to the nape. In winter plumage only a dark ear-patch remains. The primaries of the adult are entirely whitish-grey. The bill is thick and curved at the tip, red in colour with a black ring close to the tip. The legs are long and red. Immatures have black, brown and pale grey wings and a black band on the tail.

The Mediterranean Gull has slower wingbeats than other small species of gull, and glides more frequently; its flight resembles that of the larger gulls.

This gull's main distribution is on the shores of the Black Sea and in the Mediterranean basin, but its range also extends to Germany, Hungary, Italy and Austria. It is a monotypic species, breeding on seacoasts, in marshes, lakes and lagoons. It winters in western Europe, in the Black Sea and the Mediterranean.

In Israel this is a rare winterer on the shores of the Mediterranean between November and the end of April, also an accidental in Eilat. Often several individuals, as many as three to nine, are seen together. Occasionally the Mediterranean Gull is seen in this country in breeding plumage (as for example on 23 March 1976), but most of the winterers are immatures.

Little Gull
Larus minutus

The smallest of the world's gulls: body length 25-28.5 cm, wing length 21.5 cm, wingspan 78 cm and weight 85-150 g. It has more of a resemblance to terns than to other gulls. It is distinguished at all seasons of the year by the dark underside of the wing, with a white trailing edge. The tail is square. The wings and back are light silver-grey and the underparts white. In breeding plumage the head is all black, including the nape, while in winter plumage all that remains of the black colour is the grey crown and a light brown patch in the region of the ear-coverts. In breeding plumage the legs and bill are red; in winter plumage the legs are red-brown and the bill dark brown. The immature is distinguished by its light brown crown, speckled brown back, and in flight by the W-shaped pattern across the wings and body and the black triangle at the tip of the white tail.

The Little Gull has a sporadic range in northern Europe and northern Asia. It is a monotypic species, wintering on shores in western Europe, the Black Sea, the Caspian Sea and the Mediterranean.

The Little Gull has a buoyant flight, similar to that of terns. It flies low over the surface of the water and catches insects in the air; it also feeds on worms.

In Israel this is a quite common winterer, usually in the immature phase, on the shores of the Mediterranean, in fish-ponds and lakes beween November and March. It seems that the number of individuals increases in February. It is also a rare passage migrant.

Sabine's Gull
Larus sabini

A small gull resembling a tern: body length 30 cm, wing length, 27 cm, wingspan 95 cm and weight about 170 g. This is the only gull of the region with a genuinely forked tail. In breeding plumage the head is grey with a black collar. The outer four or five primaries are black, except for the white tips; the remaining primaries and the secondaries are white, in both the adult and the immature. On the wing there are three triangular shapes: the outer segment (primaries and coverts) is black, the rear segment (inner primaries, secondaries and greater coverts) is white, while the segment closest to the body (secondary coverts) and the back are grey in the adult and brown-grey in the juvenile. There is a red eye-ring which is also distinctive in winter plumage. The legs are dark grey, and the bill is grey with a yellow tip. This gull's flight is as light as that of a tern or a skimmer.

Sabine's Gull is an arctic species breeding on cold shores in tundra in northern Siberia, Greenland and northern Canada. This is a monotypic species, which outside the nesting season is usually pelagic and winters along the western shores of North America and northern South America, also on the shores of the Atlantic Ocean between Greenland and the Iberian peninsula, and along the coasts of West Africa to the Cape of Good Hope.

In Israel this is a very rare migrant: a specimen was collected on 15 January 1939, and since then a few individuals, usually immatures, have been recorded in August-September and December-February.

Herring Gull
Larus argentatus

The commonest of the large gulls in Israel and in the Western Palaearctic region as a whole: body length 55-60 cm, wing length 40-43 cm, wingspan 140-155 cm and weight 650-1,100 g. The head and neck are white. The back and wings are usually silver-grey, but in a few subspecies (including *L.a. heuglini*, which is a rare winterer in Israel) they are bottle-grey. The tips of the wings are black and white. Males are on average 10% larger than females, and in a given pair the male is always larger. Juveniles have brown-grey plumage, with dark primaries and tail feathers; their feathers grow gradually lighter over two to three years, and only in the third summer do they put on almost full adult plumage. The bill is strong and curved, about 5 cm in length, and yellow with a red mark at the base of the lower mandible. The leg colour varies according to subspecies: in the subspecies most common in this country, *L.a. cachinnans*, and also in the one which breeds on the coasts of Israel, *L.a. michahellis*, it is deep yellow in the breeding season and light yellow during the remainder of the year; in the other subspecies it is pink. The immature has brown-pink legs and a brown-black bill. This gull has a vigorous flight, with strong wingbeats, sometimes soaring or gliding.

The Herring Gull has a Holarctic range, and occurs in northern and western Europe, in the Mediterranean basin and in central and northern Asia. In this range nine or ten subspecies have been identified. Most of its populations migrate, but those of western Europe and the Mediterranean basin are resident, roaming outside the breeding season only as far as the nearest source of food. The migrants from the Western Palaearctic region winter in the North Sea and the Baltic, on the shores of western Europe and in northwest Africa, in the Black Sea and also in the Caspian, the Red Sea, off the Horn of Africa and around the Arabian peninsula. The subspecies *L.a. cachinnans*, which breeds between the Black Sea and eastern Kazakhstan, is a very common winterer in Israel along the Mediterranean coasts, in fish-ponds and in Lake Tiberias, and also a fairly common passage migrant and a less common summer resident. Among the wintering Herring Gulls darker individuals are sometimes conspicuous: these are members of the subspecies *L.a. heuglini*, which breeds in northern Russia and northeastern Siberia and normally winters in the Black Sea, the southern Red Sea and river estuaries in the Persian Gulf. A few pairs of the subspecies *L.a. michahellis*, which breeds in the Mediterranean, nest on islands along the coasts of Israel.

The Herring Gull is a gregarious bird, usually found in flocks sometimes of hundreds and even thousands of individuals. It is omnivorous: it catches its own prey, feeds at refuse-heaps and steals the food of others; normally it picks out molluscs, crabs and scraps of food. Sometimes it catches fish, by diving powerfully. It has shown a considerable ability to adapt and to exploit improvised sources of food, including those associated with mankind: stealing

fish from fishing boats, subsisting on refuse discharged from ships, following the plough and consuming worms and insects, and congregating in ever-increasing numbers around refuse-heaps to eat scraps of food.

The wintering Herring Gulls arrive in Israel in August and stay until April. The passage migrants pass through in autumn from the end of July to October, and in spring during March-April. Only a few individuals, most of them immatures, spend the summer in this country.

In Israel a few pairs breed on the coastal islands. The first abandoned nest was found in 1951 on the islands of Rosh Hanikra near the Lebanon border; in 1954 a family including two juveniles was observed in flight. In the early 1980s Herring Gulls were breeding in three places: the islands of Rosh Hanikra, and on a small island near Atlit and on Dove Island (both off the Carmel coast), a total of five or six pairs.

The nesting season in Israel begins as early as February-March and ends in April-May, about two months earlier than the corresponding dates in Europe. The nest is a pile of grass and seaweed in a hollow in the ground under a bush or a rock. Both parents, between whom there is apparently a lifelong bond, build the nest. In the clutch there are usually 3 eggs. Incubation, by both parents, lasts for 28-30 days. The chicks leave the nest after two or three days, but remain hidden close beside it; if they stray into the territory of a neighbouring pair they are liable to be killed and eaten. The parents feed them with any available food; both parents feed the chicks in approximately equal shares. The chicks fly and become independent at about six weeks old. From this time they will roam for a period of three to five or as many as seven years, but on reaching sexual maturity they tend to return to the place where they hatched.

Like Black-headed Gulls, Herring Gulls today constitute a hazard to aircraft taking off and landing at Ben-Gurion Airport.

Lesser Black-backed Gull
Larus fuscus

Similar in size to the Herring Gull, of which some ornithologists see it as a subspecies: body length 51-57 cm, wing length 37-43 cm, wingspan 145 cm and weight 460-870 g. It is distinguished by its black back and wings. The legs are yellow, as is the bill, except for a red mark at the tip of the lower mandible.

The range of the Lesser Black-backed Gull is limited and more northerly than that of the Herring Gull, although their nesting areas overlap in some places, and cases are even known of hybridisation between the two species. It breeds on the shores of oceans and seas in Iceland, western and northern Europe and also in northern Asia. In this range two to five subspecies have been identified. Most of its populations migrate and winter on the shores of western Europe and West Africa, in the Mediterranean basin and the Black Sea, around Arabia and the shores of the Arabian Sea and also on the coasts and lakes of East Africa. In Israel *L.f. fuscus* is a common passage migrant and a frequent winterer on fish-ponds, along the shores of the Mediterranean and in Lake Tiberias, although the number of individuals seen is incomparably smaller than that of the Herring Gull.

The autumn migration takes place especially along the shores of the Mediterranean. Flocks, composed mainly of juveniles, pass this way from the beginning of August to the end of October. The spring migration is more conspicuous, especially along the Syro-African rift. The first migrants appear at the head of the Gulf of Eilat at the beginning of March, and passage continues until mid-May and even into June. In the second half of April, as many as 1,000 Lesser Black-backed Gulls may pass through Eilat in a single day. They proceed northward along the Arava and are seen on the shores of the Dead Sea and Lake Tiberias. Every year thousands of individuals migrate along this route.

Eleven ringed Lesser Black-backed Gulls have been recovered in Israel: eight of these had been ringed in Finland, two in Denmark and one in Sweden.

Slender-billed Gull
Larus genei

Body length 43 cm, wing length 30 cm, wingspan 100-110 cm and weight 290 g. A white-headed gull which is similar all the year round to the Black-headed Gull in winter plumage, but with a longer neck and bill, which extends in a straight line from the crown. In summer the bill is dark red, and sometimes appears black. During nesting the legs are also dark red, turning to orange outside the breeding season.

The Slender-billed Gull is a monotypic species, restricted to the shores of the Mediterranean and the Black Sea, especially on lakes and marshes, fresh or saline. In 1979, 200-400 nests were found in the salt-marshes of E-Tina in northwestern Sinai, east of Port Said. Outside the breeding season its range is limited to the Caspian Sea, the southern and eastern Mediterranean, the Black Sea, the Red Sea and the region of the Persian Gulf.

This gull's diet consists mainly of fish and invertebrates, which are normally caught and eaten fresh. It does not feed on harbour-refuse or garbage.

In Israel this is a somewhat rare passage migrant in autumn (July-September) and spring (March-April) and a fairly common winterer on the shores of the Mediterranean and in the Gulf of Eilat. Six individuals ringed in Russia, most of them on the island of Orlov in the Black Sea, have been found in Israel.

Audouin's Gull
Larus audouinii

A gull of average size: body length 50 cm, wing length 40 cm, wingspan 127 cm and weight 500 g. Its back and wings are grey, and the wingtips black. Its bill is red, yellow at the tip and with a black ring close to the tip. The head is white. In winter plumage the crown and nape are delicately streaked with brown. Immatures are pale brown above, with a grey neck and crown. At long range it is not easily distinguished from the Herring Gull.

This is an extremely rare gull; its entire world population has been estimated at 2,000-4,500 pairs. It breeds only on a few rocky islands and shores in the Mediterranean. In 1974, ten pairs bred in Cyprus; at the end of the last century there was a small breeding population on an island offshore of Beirut.

Tristram saw gulls of this species in various parts of Israel, including the marshes of Kishon and the confluence of the Jordan and the Dead Sea. Since then it has not been positively identified in Israel, apart from a juvenile observed in the Bardawil on 22 March 1976. An individual was shot in Aqaba, at the head of the Gulf of Eilat, on 21 April 1914.

Common Gull
Larus canus

Similar to the Herring Gull but smaller: body length 41 cm, wing length 38 cm, wingspan 120 cm and weight 400 g. The back and wings are grey and other parts of the body white, but in winter plumage the head is speckled with brown-grey. The tip of the wing is black with white spots. The bill and legs are yellow in summer, turning to greenish-grey in winter plumage. The immature has grey-green legs and a grey bill.

This gull is quite common in northern Europe (a few breeding colonies are also known in western Europe) and in northern Asia, where the subspecies *L.c. canus* occurs; another subspecies is found in northwestern America. The Western Palaearctic population winters in the Baltic, the North Sea, along the shores of western and southern Europe, and also in the Black Sea and the Mediterranean, along the Suez Canal and in the Nile Delta. It feeds on refuse and carrion, and is often seen inland.

In Israel this is a fairly rare winterer from the second half of December to the end of February. An individual ringed in Russia was caught on 10 January 1975 in Maagan Mikhael.

Glaucous Gull
Larus hyperboreus

According to Meinertzhagen (1954), a Glaucous Gull was seen on 18 April 1914 in Aqaba. There have been no other reports of this species in the region.

Great Black-backed Gull
Larus marinus

A very large gull, in appearance a larger version of the Lesser Black-backed Gull: body length 71 cm, wing length 49 cm, wingspan 160 cm and weight 1.7 kg. Its legs are pink, at all ages. Its bill is large, solid and strong, in the adult yellow with a red mark at the tip of the lower mandible. The immature has a brown-black bill with a white tip.

This is a monotypic species, breeding on cliffs and islands on both sides of the Atlantic Ocean, in northern and western Europe and in northeastern America. Outside the nesting season it migrates to some extent, roaming the Atlantic Ocean as far south as latitude 40°N and along the coasts of Spain.

In Israel the Great Black-backed Gull is a very rare accidental. Single individuals have been recorded as follows: on 26 December 1952, 1 January 1975, 17 March 1983 and 26 March 1983, at various places along the Mediterranean coast; and in May 1983 in the salt-pools of Eilat. This species is much more common as a passage migrant on the coasts of northern Sinai, where 14 individuals were recorded on 11 September 1973 and ten during 23-27 September 1978.

Genus: *Rissa*
The Kittiwake belongs to a genus closely akin to the genus *Larus*, from which it is distinguished by the short tarsus and a rear toe which is only residual and usually lacks a claw (hence the scientific name: = 'three-toed'). The central tail feathers are somewhat shorter than the outer, and thus the tail is slightly forked. In the genus there are two species, one of which is a rare accidental in this country.

Kittiwake
Rissa tridactyla

Body length 39 cm, wing length 31 cm, wingspan 112 cm and weight 400 g. The adult Kittiwake is similar to the Common Gull, but is more slender with a lighter flight, and lacks white markings at the tips of the black primaries. The legs are black and the bill yellow. Juveniles and immatures have similar plumage to that of adults (an exceptional phenomenon among gulls), but are distinguished in flight by a black zigzag pattern on the wings and by black bars on the nape and tail.

The Kittiwake breeds along the shores of the northern Atlantic and northern Pacific Oceans, in Europe, Asia, Greenland and America. In this range two subspecies have been identified. Outside the nesting season it extends over the oceans as far as 35°N, and also penetrates the Mediterranean.

In Israel this is a rare winter accidental, seen occasionally on the Mediterranean coasts or in Eilat in January, usually following a severe storm. Normally immature individuals are involved.

Family: Sternidae (Terns)

This family contains ten genera and 43 species, 24 of which belong to the genus *Sterna*. It is a family of small and average-sized seabirds, similar to gulls. Most are silver-grey above and grey, black or white below. The crown and nape are black in breeding plumage, with the black area diminishing in winter plumage and sometimes turning to brown. Their bodies are slim in comparison with those of gulls, the wings usually relatively long, narrow and pointed, and the tail long and cleft or forked. The bill is normally straight, thin and pointed, and the legs are short. The foretoes are webbed. Except during courtship it is impossible to distinguish between male and female. Immatures differ from adults in their speckled upperparts.

The distribution of terns is worldwide, but most species inhabit tropical and subtropical areas. The majority migrate and roam, only a minority being resident. All the species breeding in the Palaearctic region migrate, and the more northerly their range the longer their migration. The Arctic Tern holds the world record for migration: every year it travels a distance of some 18,000 km from its nesting areas around the North Pole to the vicinity of the South Pole, before returning to the North Pole to breed.

Terns live in coastal areas, islands and margins of lakes. They fly with grace and agility, and their flight is as light as that of swallows. Most species hardly swim at all, bathing by dipping in the water during flight. The diet of *Sterna* terns consists primarily of fish, but also includes crabs and other invertebrates. They fly above the surface of the water, head and bill pointed downward, and when prey is sighted they hover before descending in a vertical dive, catching the prey and swallowing it in flight.

Terns usually breed in dense colonies on the ground, often in flocks combining several species. Any intruder on the colony is attacked. The nest is usually a scrape in the ground; only rarely is there any lining. The clutch contains 1-3 speckled and camouflaged eggs. Both parents share the task of incubation, which begins with the laying of the first egg. Incubation lasts about three weeks in the species known in this country, and up to five weeks in the tropical species which nest in trees. The chicks hatch open-eyed and covered with down striped brown and black on a beige background. Initially they resemble the chicks of gulls, but there is no dark speckling on the head; their legs are short and the bill delicate. They tend to remain concealed in the vicinity of the nest, although sometimes scores of chicks gather in a kind of 'crèche'. Both parents feed their offspring bill-to-bill with small fish. The chicks begin to fly and become independent at four to five weeks old.

In Israel three genera and 13 species are represented.

Common Tern
Sterna hirundo

The most common and typical representative of the genus *Sterna* in Israel, this is a small and slim-bodied tern: body length 32-35 cm, wing length 25.5-28.8 cm, wingspan 77-85 cm and weight 130 g. The back is grey and the underparts white — colours typical of most terns. The tail is very pale grey, and long and forked: length of the outer feathers up to 17.5 cm, of the central feathers 7.5 cm. In summer

the crown and nape are black; in winter plumage the colour of the crown turns to brown and the forehead is white. The bill is slender, slightly curved and laterally compressed; in summer it is usually bright red with black tip, while in winter it is wholly black. The legs are red and short.

The Common Tern has a Holarctic distribution in various climatic zones, especially in temperate and cool regions: in northwestern North America, in northern South America, across most of Europe and the whole of Asia, in North Africa and the islands of the Atlantic Ocean. In this range three subspecies have been identified. In most of these areas of distribution it is a bird of rivers, lakes and inland freshwater pools, sometimes up to an altitude of 3,000 m, usually near shallow water and grassy shores. It also breeds in river estuaries, along sea-coasts and on rocky islands. All its populations migrate south when nesting is over. The European population winters especially on the coasts of West Africa, between latitudes 20°N and 20°S, and also in Egypt and in East Africa. In Israel the subspecies *S.h. hirundo* is a passage migrant and breeding summer visitor.

The Common Tern feeds particularly on small fish. It flies slowly above the surface of the water with bill inclined downward; when it sights a fish swimming close to the surface, it swoops on it with wings half folded, head and neck entering the water (sometimes it submerges completely). Often several terns feed in the same area. The Common Tern also catches aquatic insects, worms, small molluscs, crabs, etc.

This tern is a common passage migrant in autumn from the end of July to the beginning of October, and in spring from early April to June. In autumn 1973, 3,800 individuals were counted in the Bardawil Lagoon in northern Sinai, mainly from mid-August to the beginning of September.

Common Terns breed regularly at fixed sites — the islands of Rosh Hanikra in the Mediterranean near Lebanon and off the Carmel coast, the salt-pools of Atlit, and the Hula Reserve — and in temporary colonies established at various reservoirs. Some 450 pairs breed in Israel, 50-120 pairs in each of the major colonies: Dove Island, Dor Island and Nahalieli (= Wagtail) Island, islands in the Mediterranean near the shores of western Galilee and Carmel. Colonies are dense, and in areas (unlike Israel) where several species of tern breed they may be mixed. A breeding colony of terns is a very lively place, full of incessant noise and movement. Screeching cries are constantly heard, in particular the cries of males returning with fish and the responses of the females. Especially loud cries are heard at the approach of an intruder, such as a man or a dog; rats, cats, hedgehogs and gulls also pose a threat to the colonies. Terns are liable to be extremely aggressive, attacking any intruder, even human. From time to time, for no discernible reason, all the terns fall silent and abandon the colony in a mass exodus, before returning to their places and resuming their screeching.

In Israel, the Common Terns return to breed in the second half of April. Laying begins in the first half of May. The clutch is usually of 3 eggs, laid at intervals of one to two days. Incubation starts with the first egg and lasts 20-23 days; the female bears most of the burden, but is fed and otherwise tended by the male. The chicks hatch open-eyed and covered with yellowish-beige down, speckled with dark brown; the legs are pink and the bill orange with a brown mark at the tip. They stay in the nest for two or three days and then leave it and hide in any available secluded spot, but return at night to shelter under their parents for a few more days. Both parents feed them with small fish. At times of danger the chicks are liable to jump into the water and swim to safety. At the approach of their second summer they moult into almost full adult plumage, although they do not attain sexual maturity until the age of three years and only then return to the nesting colonies.

In Israel Common Terns apparently complete only one nesting cycle per year, although many pairs lay replacement clutches in the case of failure with the first clutch. It is possible that a few pairs complete two full cycles in the year.

Common Terns in Israel leave their colonies at the end of August or in early September, even abandoning nests that still contain eggs. A juvenile Common Tern ringed on Dove Island off the Carmel coast was found in the middle of the following year in Kenya.

The main nesting sites of Common Terns in Israel — Dove Island, Dor Island and Nahalieli Island — are closed nature reserves with prohibited access. Apart from the risk of accidental destruction of the camouflaged eggs, exposure to the hot summer sun is liable to kill the embryos, but this is not the only hazard facing them. In summer 1976, only 50 juveniles survived to fly from Dove Island, and a similar situation applied there a few years previously. The reasons for this are not clear.

Roseate Tern
Sterna dougallii

Body length 35 cm and wingspan 76 cm. This tern is paler than the Common and Arctic Terns, and its tail is very long and distinctively forked (length of outer tail feathers 14-20.5 cm, of inner ones 6.5 cm). In breeding plumage the underparts are tinged pink.

The Roseate Tern has a cosmopolitan range, breeding on both sides of the Atlantic Ocean, on islands in the Indian Ocean and in the Pacific Ocean. Its populations are partially resident, roaming the oceans in the vicinity of the nesting areas, and partially migratory (though the movements are not clear).

In Israel this species has been recorded only once: at the head of the Gulf of Eilat on 4 November 1982.

Arctic Tern
Sterna paradisaea

Similar to the Common Tern in colour and size: body length 34 cm, wing length 27.5 cm, wingspan 80 cm and weight 105 g. The legs and bill are shorter than the Common Tern's, the head more rounded, and the cheeks sometimes grey with a white bar separating them from the black crown. The bill is blood-red, without a black mark at the tip. In winter plumage the bill and legs turn black, and the forehead white. The outer tail feathers are very long, with dark grey outer edges. At rest, the tail protrudes beyond the wings (in the Common Tern they are of equal length).

The Arctic Tern is a monotypic species, with a Holarctic range in parts of nothern Europe, Asia and America. It winters in the Antarctic and is the world's farthest-flying migrant.

This is a rare accidental at the head of the Gulf of Eilat in June-August. Often a few individuals stay in the area for a considerable period of time.

White-cheeked Tern
Sterna repressa

A quite small tern: body length 33 cm, wing length 24.5 cm and wingspan 80 cm. Similar to the Common Tern but much greyer: the cheeks are white, but the upperparts and underparts are all grey.

This is a monotypic species, restricted to the Red Sea, the Persian Gulf and the Arabian Sea to western India. It is a fairly rare accidental at the head of the Gulf of Eilat during April and May and November-December. Between August and October 1975, some 125 pairs bred on the island of Tiran.

Bridled Tern
Sterna anaethetus

Body length 32 cm, wing length 26.5 cm, wingspan 79 cm and weight 130 g. The upperparts are all dark grey, except for the white hindneck and forehead and the black crown and nape; the tail is dark grey except for the white edges, and is deeply forked. The underparts are white.

The Bridled Tern is distributed in tropical oceanic areas, also penetrating into areas of subtropical climate. It breeds on the shores of the Red Sea, in the Persian Gulf and also on the coasts of India, southeast Asia, Australia and the Caribbean. In this range four subspecies have been identified. Outside the breeding season it roams about its nesting areas.

The subspecies *S. a. fuligula* occurs in small flocks, numbering up to a few score individuals, at the head of the Gulf of Eilat during the summer months, especially in August.

Sooty Tern
Sterna fuscata

A tern of medium size: body length 35 cm, wing length 29 cm, wingspan 86 cm and weight 190 g. It resembles the Bridled Tern but is larger and has darker upperparts. In the field it appears black above with white underparts. The tail is deeply forked.

This tern's range extends over tropical areas in all the oceans, with some penetration into subtropical regions. Outside the nesting season it roams across the tropical belt of the oceans. This is the most pelagic of the terns, sometimes following ships at night. Its flight is heavier than that of other terns, and it is also capable of gliding.

The Sooty Tern is a very rare accidental at the head of the Gulf of Eilat in July-August, but sometimes appears in small flocks.

Little Tern
Sterna albifrons

A rather small tern: body length 23 cm, wing length

17-18.5 cm, wingspan 51 cm and weight about 50 g. Its colours are grey, black and white like those of most terns, but its forehead is always white and a black line extends from the eye to the bill. The bill is yellow with a black tip, and the legs orange-yellow. The crown turns lighter in winter plumage and is then only speckled with dark markings.

The distribution of the Little Tern is cosmopolitan in tropical, subtropical and temperate zones. It breeds in most parts of Europe (except in the far north and in tundra), in western Asia, in south and southeast Asia, along the coasts of North and West Africa, on the shores of Australia and the southern USA. In this range nine subspecies have been identified. This is primarily a bird of the sea but also of inland water margins, preferring shallow water. All the northern populations and those breeding inland migrate and winter in tropical coastal regions. The race *S.a.albifrons* occurs in Israel.

This tern feeds especially on small fish, but also on crabs and insects taken on the surface of the water. It scours the surface, either singly or in small and loose groups, beating its wings fast and with head inclined downward, before diving headlong.

In Israel this is a common passage migrant along the Mediterranean coast from early August to the second half of September, being less conspicuous in the spring (April). In autumn 1978, about 1,800 individuals were counted in the Bardawil Lagoon.

The Little Tern is also a rare breeder in Israel. The first nests were found in 1953, on a shoal exposed during the draining of the Hula. In 1955 there was a colony there of 20 pairs. This colony disappeared as the draining continued. At a later stage, the Little Tern began to breed in the salt-pools of Atlit, and since then it has bred there almost exclusively, although occasional nests are found in other areas. Its population in Atlit has increased from five pairs in the mid-1970s to 100 pairs in the early 1980s. (Hundreds of pairs also breed in the Bardawil, although, since many of the eggs and chicks are taken by fishermen, few of the young survive.)

The nesting season in this country is between May and July. The Little Tern breeds in small colonies in sandy places. The nest is a shallow depression, usually without lining, sometimes with a little vegetation or fragments of sea-shell gathered by the female. In the clutch there are 2-3 eggs. Both parents share in incubation, which lasts 19-22 days, although the female's contribution is greater. The chicks have sand-coloured down, and begin to fly at the age of 17-19 days. They reach sexual maturity at two years old or even later.

Caspian Tern
Sterna caspia

The largest of the terns, similar in size to a gull: body length 51 cm, wing length 39-43 cm, wingspan 135 cm and weight 640 g. It is similar in coloration to other terns, grey, white and black, but is clearly distinguished from them by its size and especially by the bill, which is large (about 7 cm in length), thick and red. The tail is short (about 14 cm) and forked only for a quarter of its length. There is a slight crest on its nape. The legs are short and black.

The range of the Caspian Tern extends sporadically over all continents except South America. Its most continuous breeding range stretches between the eastern shores of the Black Sea and Lake Balkhash in central Asia. This is a monotypic species, whose northern populations migrate while the tropical ones are resident.

The Caspian Tern has a strong and graceful flight, similar to that of a gull. It also glides, and flies at higher altitudes than the other terns. It feeds on fish, small birds and their eggs, and on scraps of food. It is less gregarious than other terns, breeding in small colonies and generally not mingling with other species. Outside the nesting season it usually roams in small, loose parties.

In Israel this is a rare passage migrant (August-September and March-April). It breeds, and is apparently resident, in southern Sinai, on the island of Tiran and in the region of Sharm el-Sheikh; the population there numbers 20-50 pairs.

Crested or Swift Tern
Sterna bergii

A large tern: body length 47 cm, wing length 36 cm, wingspan 125 cm and weight 350 g. It is distinguished by the bill, which is long (6.3 cm), strong and greenish-yellow, by the black legs, and by the crest on the nape (which is held erect in visual displays).

The Crested Tern is distributed in tropical and subtropical seas, especially in southeast Asia, in Oceania and also in South Africa. It breeds in the Persian Gulf, the Red Sea and on the shores of the Horn of Africa, and is a common visitor to the Gulf of Suez, but is only a rare accidental at the head of the Gulf of Eilat (recorded on 13 August 1979, 23 December 1981 and 24 June 1984).

Lesser Crested Tern
Sterna bengalensis

A tern of average size: body length 36 cm, wing length 31 cm, wingspan 98 cm and weight 200 g. Like the Crested Tern, it has a black nape crest; its bill is orange, and its legs black.

This tern has a tropical distribution: in the Red Sea, the Persian Gulf, southeast Asia and Australia; in the past it also bred on the coasts of Libya. Two subspecies have been identified.

In Israel the subspecies *S.b. bengalensis* is a very rare accidental on the Mediterranean coast and an accidental at the head of the Gulf of Eilat. In September-October 1975, some 60 pairs bred on the island of Tiran.

Sandwich Tern
Sterna sandvicensis

An average-sized tern: body length 38 cm, wing length 31 cm, wingspan 100 cm and weight 270 g. It is distinguished by the black nape crest together with the long (5.5 cm) and delicate bill, which is black with a yellow tip. Its legs are relatively long and black.

The Sandwich Tern breeds along the shores of western Europe, in the northwestern Mediterranean, in the Black Sea and the Caspian, and also on the eastern seaboard of the USA, in the Caribbean and along the eastern coasts of South America. In these regions three subspecies have been identified. The Palaearctic population, which belongs to the race *S.s. sandvicensis*, migrates and winters in the Baltic Sea, in the Atlantic Ocean opposite the shores of western Europe, along the shores of West and South Africa and also in the Mediterranean, the Black Sea and the Caspian and around the shores of the Arabian peninsula and the Arabian Sea.

In Israel this is a fairly rare passage migrant and winter visitor. Single individuals, sometimes also small flocks, are seen along the Mediterranean coasts in most months of the year.

Genus: *Gelochelidon*
This genus is distinguished from the genus *Sterna* by the short and strong all-black bill, resembling that of a gull. The tail is shorter than in *Sterna* terns — about 13 cm (i.e. about half the length of the wing) — and only slightly forked. The wings are relatively broad.

Gull-billed Tern
Gelochelidon nilotica

A medium-sized tern: body length 37 cm, wing length 30.5 cm, wingspan 108 cm and weight 220 g. The back, wings and tail are pale grey, the underparts white, and the crown in summer plumage glossy black; in winter the head is white, with delicate black streaking on the nape and a dark area behind the eye. The legs are black, and long in comparison with those of other terns.

The range of the Gull-billed Tern extends over all

continents except Australasia and Antarctica, especially in areas of Mediterranean, steppe and temperate climate. In these regions six subspecies have been identified. The one occurring in the Palaearctic region is *G.n. nilotica*. Its habitat consists mainly of inland lakes, marshes and river estuaries. The Western Palaearctic population winters in the Persian Gulf, in the Red Sea and in East Africa.

This tern's flight is quite heavy. It feeds mostly on insects and reptiles caught on dry land, but it also dives for fish in water. It sometimes continues to feed its offspring even during migration, and this phenomenon has been recorded at least twice in Israel.

In Israel this is a fairly rare passage migrant, seen in various parts of the country from early July to early October and from early March to mid-May. In autumn 1978, 410 were counted on migration through the Bardawil Lagoon in northern Sinai.

Genus: *Chlidonias* (marsh terns)

A genus of small terns, living in silted inland lakes and pools abundant in vegetation. Their range is limited mainly to areas of temperate climate in Europe and Asia, with winter quarters in tropical regions, though the Black Tern occurs also in the New World. Marsh terns are distinguished by their short legs; the foretoes are partially webbed. The bill is short, straight, thin and pointed. The tail is short, less than half the length of the wing, and only slightly forked, and the wings are long and pointed. In summer the bodies of marsh terns are dark, tending to black; in winter the upperparts are light grey, with the forehead and underparts white, and then all species are similar to one another.

Their flight is graceful and light, and they are capable of hovering for considerable periods of time. They feed in flight on insects and also on crabs and fishes, taken from aquatic vegetation or from the surface of the water. They nest in small colonies or solitarily. The nests are large and built on clumps of floating vegetation. The clutch is of 2-3 eggs, cream-brown in colour and speckled with brown. The female takes the larger share of incubation. The chicks are covered in down, light brown in colour and speckled with black.

In the genus there are three species, all of which occur in Israel.

Black Tern
Chlidonias niger

A small tern: body length 22-23.5 cm, wing length 20.4-22 cm, wingspan 66 cm and weight 40-52 g. In summer plumage its head and body are black, the wings light grey and the tail grey; the undertail-coverts are conspicuously white, the bill is black and the legs dark red. In winter the face and underparts are white and there is a black patch on each side of the breast; the tail remains grey.

The Black Tern has a Holarctic range, inhabiting marshes in Europe and central Asia and also in North America. In this range two subspecies have been identified, the Eurasian population belonging to the subspecies *C.n. niger*. This is the most northerly of the marsh terns. In winter the species migrates south to the shores of tropical and subtropical seas in Africa and America.

In Israel this is a fairly rare passage migrant both in autumn and in spring. In autumn 1973, about 240 individuals were counted on migration on the coast of northern Sinai. Before the draining of the Hula, some 20 pairs used to breed in the belt of water-lilies and hornweed in the northern part of the lake; when draining of the lake was completed, in 1958, nesting there ceased.

Whiskered Tern
Chlidonias hybridus

A small tern: body length 23-25 cm, wing length 22-23.5 cm, wingspan 76 cm and weight 62-80 g. In summer it is distinguished by its white cheeks, separating the dark grey neck from the black crown; its belly is dark grey and the tail greyish, and in flight the white underwing is conspicuous. The legs and bill are reddish. In winter plumage the crown is delicately streaked with dark brown, the upperparts are very light grey and the belly is white.

This tern inhabits aquatic environments in southern Europe, south and east Asia, Australia and southern Africa. In this range three subspecies have been identified. The Palaearctic population belongs to the subspecies *C.h. hybridus*. Both the European and the African populations winter in the lakes of East Africa.

In Israel this is a quite common passage migrant in autumn from early August to mid-October, by which time it is already in winter plumage. In autumn 1978, about 900 individuals were counted in northern Sinai. It is more common and conspicuous during the spring migration, from mid-April to June, when it is seen in full breeding plumage. Its flocks are usually dense. It is also an occasional winterer, especially on the Carmel coast and further north.

According to Tristram, the Whiskered Tern used to breed in the Hula, although there has been no later evidence of this.

White-winged Black Tern
Chlidonias leucopterus

Body length 20-23 cm, wing length 19.8-21.3 cm,

wingspan 65 cm and weight 57-66 g. In summer plumage the body and underwing-coverts are black, while the flight feathers are whitish-grey; the tail, rump and undertail-coverts are white (this white colour is also an identification mark in winter).

This is a monotypic species, with a range extending from central and eastern Europe to eastern Asia. The European population migrates, and winters across tropical Africa.

In Israel this is the most common of the marsh terns. During the autumn migration, from the beginning of August to the end of September, most of the individuals recorded have undergone a partial moult, although the underwing-coverts are still black. During autumn surveys in 1973 and 1978 in northern Sinai, about 8,000 individuals were counted. During the spring migration, from mid-April to the end of May, the bird is seen in full summer plumage (including black head). In spring, the migrating flocks number hundreds and even thousands of individuals.

Family: Rynchopidae (Skimmers)

This family comprises one genus and three species, distributed primarily in tropical areas: one in southeast Asia, one in America and one in Africa. Its distinguishing feature is the bill, which is large and laterally compressed, with the lower mandible flexible and considerably longer than the upper one.

African Skimmer
Rynchops flavirostris

Superficially, the African Skimmer resembles a large tern: body length 39 cm, wing length 36 cm, wingspan 130 cm and weight 160 g. The upperparts are brown-black, while the forehead, cheeks and underparts are white. The wings are narrow and long, the tail short and slightly forked, and the legs short. The characteristic bill is orange-yellow.

This species inhabits rivers and lakes, and also the shores of oceans, in Africa. The closest populations to Israel are those of the Red Sea and the Upper Nile.

The African Skimmer feeds especially in the evening hours, but also on moonlit nights. In accordance with these habits, the pupil of the eye is as large as that of a cat and other nocturnal mammals, a unique phenomenon among birds. It tends to fly close to the surface of the water, with uniform wingbeats, the bill open and the lower mandible appearing to plough or skim the surface. When the sensitive bill encounters

a fish, a crab or some other creature, the upper mandible closes on it at once.

In Israel only one certain record is known. A pair of African Skimmers was caught by the Yarkon River in summer 1934. One of these specimens is preserved in the museum of the University of Tel Aviv.

Order: Columbiformes (Sandgrouse, Pigeons and Doves)

This order is divided into two sub-orders, each comprising one family: Pteroclididae (sandgrouse) and Columbidae (doves and pigeons). In these two families there is a total of 42 genera and 313 species. Members of the order are distributed in all parts of the world, except at the poles.

This is a group of birds whose links with other orders are unclear. Members of the order are similar to waders (Charadriiformes) in some respects, such as the wing structure, but differ in the structure of the skeleton, sternum and legs. Columbiformes are of average size, with elliptical bodies, small heads, and legs which are short and strong and well suited for walking. The wings are strong and pointed. The plumage is thick and dense, but the body feathers are fixed loosely to the skin and are easily shed. At the base of the feathers there is soft down. Most species, with a few exceptions, have one moult a year.

The Columbiformes eat vegetable food: seeds, fruit and vegetables. All of them have a large expansible crop, where food remains for some time before digestion. In order to soften the food, water is required. Members of this order drink in a different fashion from that of other birds: they dip their bills in water and the nostrils are closed by muscular valves, enabling them to drink continously until they have had their fill. (Other birds need to raise the head from time to time, to direct the water into the throat.) Members of this order are also distinguished from others by the considerable rate of evaporation on the skin surface: this reduces the temperature of the body, especially during nesting, and may be seen as a form of adaptation to desert conditions. Members of this order spend a lot of their time on the ground, and become airborne with loud beating of wings. They nest on trees, in bushes or on the ground and their clutches are usually of 2 eggs, sometimes 1 or 3.

In Israel four genera and 13 species are represented.

Family: Pteroclididae (Sandgrouse)

In the family there are two genera and 15 species. Sandgrouse are found especially in Africa and Madagascar, also in southern and central Asia. Two species are also found in southern Europe. In Israel five species are represented, all of them belonging to the genus *Pterocles*, which comprises a total of 14 species.

These are long-bodied birds, of average size: body length is 21-39 cm and weight 360-500 g. In shape sandgrouse are similar to doves, with a small head and short neck. The wings are long and pointed, the tail graduated and in some species with two elongated central feathers. The bill is short, pointed and hard, entirely covered with horny tissue and, unlike in doves, with no cere at the base; the nostrils are partially feathered. The legs are short and feathered to the toes; sometimes the toes too are feathered. The toes are short and broad: the rear toe is smaller than the others and in some cases absent altogether. Sandgrouse have thick and hard skin. The attachment of the feathers to the skin is loose, especially on the back. The apteria (the places on the body where plumage is absent in other species) are covered with down feathers.

Sandgrouse have plumage coloration appropriate to the desert, the dominant colours being brown, orange, grey, chestnut-brown, sometimes also black and white. The males are more colourful than the females. At times of danger sandgrouse freeze, and are then difficult to observe as their colours blend into the desert landscape. The single air-sac between the skin of the belly and the muscles enables them to lie on very hot ground. Only when danger is very close do they rise up with a loud fluttering of wings; their flight is straight and fast with short and rapid wingbeats, with speeds approaching 65 kph.

The habitats of sandgrouse are in deserts and steppes. All species are resident, although the northern populations of the central Asian species migrate. Pallas's Sandgrouse *Syrrhaptes paradoxus*, whose range is between the Caspian Sea and Mongolia, is renowned for its periodic irruptions into central and even northern and western Europe. The most spectacular irruptions were recorded in 1888 and 1908.

Sandgrouse are gregarious both during and outside the nesting season, and tend to gather in flocks of scores, hundreds and even thousands of individuals. Their diet is almost entirely vegetarian: seeds, fruits, buds, leaves and root fibres, but sometimes also insects. They seek their food on the ground while walking fast. Living in hot areas, sandgrouse need to drink water every day, and usually remain attached to the same water source for a long period of time. They are liable to fly scores of kilometres in order to drink, executing impressive aerial manoeuvres and emitting constant cries, in some species a characteristic 'kit-kat-kat' sound. These sounds are heard at long distance, and often before the bird itself is seen. In the western Negev four different species can be seen drinking together. They approach the water cautiously, and land only after inspecting the surroundings for any potential danger. They drink quickly, and without pausing or raising the bill. They are less vocal when returning to their regular haunts after drinking. Sometimes they stay about two hours before flying back.

The nesting season of sandgrouse is in the spring, but continues into the summer and even into the autumn; it is possible that a few species breed twice in the year. Sandgrouse nest on the ground in a depression which is usually unlined. In the clutch there are 2 elongated eggs, each with two rounded ends. Incubation begins with the first egg, apparently to prevent excessive heating by day and cooling at night. The male normally incubates at night and the female during the day. The period of incubation varies between 20 and 26 days according to species. The chicks hatch open-eyed, and covered with brown-yellow down divided into squares by dark transverse lines. The chicks leave the nest a short time after hatching and fend for themselves. The water that they require is supplied by the males in a

peculiar fashion: when they have finished drinking they bathe in the water and accumulate a large quantity of water in the absorbent breast feathers; they then return to the chicks, which draw out the moisture with their bills. The females also supply water in this manner, although their plumage is less absorbent. When an enemy approaches the nest or the chicks, the parents perform injury display while the chicks crouch on the ground. At about three weeks old the chicks are already capable of flying.

Spotted Sandgrouse
Pterocles senegallus

A small, pale sandgrouse with long, thin tail feathers: body length 29-38 cm, wing length 18-20 cm, wingspan 60 cm and weight 215-300 g. The male has fairly uniform brown upperparts, an orange-brown throat and cheeks, and a bluish-grey eye-stripe and neck. The breast and upper belly are sandy-brown and the lower belly black, a feature especially distinctive in flight. The female has dark-brown speckling on a sandy-brown background on most of its body, with the upper belly a light beige and the lower belly black: the female differs from the male in pattern to such an extent that in the past it was considered a separate species.

The Spotted Sandgrouse is a monotypic species, distributed in hot and arid areas in a range extending from Senegal and the western Sahara through the Sahara and the Middle East to the Thar Desert in northwest India. It inhabits all kinds of desert environments — scrub, dune and rock. It is resident throughout its range.

In Israel this is possibly the commonest of the sandgrouse. It is found in most parts of the Negev, especially in the western and northern Negev and in the region of Arad. It eats various seeds, but few crop seeds, and therefore is not often seen in fields of agricultural produce. The Spotted Sandgrouse is usually found in small parties, which sometimes gather into huge flocks, especially when flying to a water source. On their way to drink they emit a characteristic disyllabic cry, 'la-ku, la-ku'. The Spotted Sandgrouse usually drinks in the morning, on hot days also in the evening. On 5 October 1983, in the reservoirs of Nizana, more than 5,000 sandgrouse of this species were counted between 06.30 and 09.30 hours. Many hundreds also drink in Nahal Habashor and from wells in the heights of the Negev; sometimes when drinking they mingle with other species.

Nesting begins in March and continues until June. Usually a few pairs nest side by side, with a distance of 1-5 m between nests; other pairs nest solitarily. The nests are located among annual plants or under bushes, and are sometimes lined with vegetation.

The clutch is of 3 eggs, sometimes 2. The chicks are covered entirely with down, even on the feet; their skin is thick and black in colour. They are flying by the age of 16 days.

At the end of summer, after nesting, Spotted Sandgrouse gather together and roost in hundreds on the ground in regular places. Even in this context they apparently retain family ties, and within a flock it is possible to observe groups of three to five individuals, walking together after landing and seeking hollows to roost overnight.

Pin-tailed Sandgrouse
Pterocles alchata

Body length 30-37 cm, wing length 19.5-21 cm, wingspan 60 cm and weight 200-270 g. The only sandgrouse in Israel with a white belly. The belly is separated from the breast by a black band; another black band separates the breast from the neck. The male has a brown-orange breast and greenish neck; the female has a sandy-yellow breast and neck, with a pair of black bands between them. The Pin-tailed Sandgrouse has two moults, a full one after nesting and a partial one before nesting. In the latter there is also some change in colour, especially on the back of the male, which turns from the olive-yellow of winter to a lighter shade of yellow. The two central tail feathers are very long, up to 16 cm.

The Iberian peninsula is the home of one subspecies of the Pin-tailed Sandgrouse, while the range of the subspecies *P.a. caudacutus* extends over North Africa from Morocco to Libya, through the Middle East including Israel, Jordan, the Syrian Desert, Iraq and Iran, and further east to Turkestan and Afghanistan. Its habitats are the fringes of deserts and areas of sparse vegetation. In most of its range this is the commonest sandgrouse, and its flocks sometimes number thousands, although perceptible fluctuations occur according to the availability of food. Most of its populations are resident, but those of Turkestan are partial migrants, moving in winter to northwest India and Arabia.

The Pin-tailed Sandgrouse is resident in Israel in the northern and western Negev, and is especially conspicuous around Nahal Habashor and in the region of Nizana. In these areas flocks numbering thousands have been counted. Sometimes it roams, so that the population in a given place varies from year to year. In summer 1961, flocks of hundreds of individuals were seen in the Bet She'an Valley, in the Jordan Valley and on the eastern fringes of the Hula Valley. It is possible that in the last-mentioned case the birds were vagrants from the Syrian Desert. A few pairs nested that year in the Bet She'an Valley.

The Pin-tailed Sandgrouse sometimes breeds in a loose colony, but normally there is a distance of hundreds of metres between one nest and another. The nests are usually located among sparse and withered vegetation, and are sometimes lined. Laying begins as early as April, but some pairs are liable to lay as late as the end of July and even in August. Usually there are 3 eggs in the clutch. As in all species of sandgrouse, the male incubates at night and the female by day. Before returning to her post, the female flies, with other females, to drink; after the change of shift, it is the turn of the males to flock to the water. In hot weather the females drink again in the afternoon. The 'kata-kata' calls which the birds utter on their way to the water source are most characteristic, and are the basis of the scientific name of the species. Sometimes a longer and more nasal cry is heard. The chicks hatch after about three weeks of incubation, and leave the nest almost immediately. They feed by themselves some 24 hours after hatching, but the female accompanies them and apparently trains them to feed. Occasionally all three chicks in the brood survive, but normally only two, in which case each of the parents tends and protects one of them. Sometimes the female leads and trains both chicks while the male stands guard. The chicks fly at about four weeks old. Families with chicks may be seen until August.

Lichtenstein's Sandgrouse
Pterocles lichtensteinii

A short-tailed sandgrouse, and the smallest seen in this country: body length 23.5-27 cm, wing length 18-19.2 cm, wingspan 50 cm and weight 235-260 g. It appears dark owing to the dense speckling, dark brown in colour, which covers the sandy-brown background colour of the body. This speckling is more crude and sparse in the male, which also has black and white markings on the crown and forehead. The female is more uniformly speckled.

Lichtenstein's Sandgrouse is distributed in mountainous and rocky environments — from the western and eastern Sahara, through Nigeria, Chad, Sudan, southern Arabia, southern Iran and Baluchistan, to the mountains of the Thar Desert in northwest India, with southward penetration to East Africa. In this range four or five subspecies have been identified. In all parts of its range this is a resident bird.

In Israel the subspecies *P.l. lichtensteinii*, whose range is in eastern Africa, Sinai and southern Asia, is a very rare bird, found only in the region of Eilat. It is more common in eastern and southern Sinai. It feeds in wadis, especially under acacia trees, and on rocky slopes covered with scrub. It does not penetrate into the open desert, and does not gather in large flocks.

It tends to visit water sources in the hours of darkness: in the morning before sunrise, and in the evening after sunset. In Eilat it drinks at a particular wadi. Little is known of its nesting habits, and no data are available from this country.

Crowned Sandgrouse
Pterocles coronatus

Body length 27-31 cm, wing length 18-20 cm, wingspan 58 cm and weight 240-290 g. One of the short-tailed sandgrouse. The male is predominantly brown-pink, and is distinguished by the black chin and the black crown-shaped mark on the forehead. The female is barred and vermiculated with dark brown, except for the unbarred yellow-buff throat.

This sandgrouse has a Saharo-Sindian range, in which five subspecies have been described. It inhabits stony desert and scrubland, including the hottest and most arid areas. The subspecies found in Israel is *P.c. vastitas*, which occurs in Sinai and Transjordan.

The Crowned Sandgrouse is resident and quite common in the Negev, but is found mainly in the central and southern parts of the region and in the Valley of the Arava. Its flocks are usually small. It is less timid than the other sandgrouse and can be approached to within short range. It eats the seeds of desert plants. It drinks at a later time of day than other species of sandgrouse and may be seen by water until about 10 a.m.; sometimes it drinks again before sunset. It is also capable of drinking salt water.

The Crowned Sandgrouse nests in the Arava in the early months of the summer (May-June); and in the region of Sede Boker, in the heights of the Negev, between August and September. In the clutch there are usually 2 eggs and occasionally 3. The length of incubation is not known. On 8 September 1981 the hatching of the first chick was recorded in a nest near Sede Boker; the other egg hatched the following day. Both parents were observed providing the chicks with water from their breast feathers. The age at which the chicks begin to fly is not known.

Black-bellied Sandgrouse
Pterocles orientalis

The largest of the sandgrouse seen in Israel, but short-tailed: body length 33-35 cm, wing length 22-24.5 cm, wingspan 68-73 cm and weight 275-430 g. Both sexes have a distinctive black throat. The back and wings of the male are yellowish-brown speckled with grey, and the head, nape and neck are grey; the chin is yellow and there is a black breast-band. The belly is black in both male and female. Apart from the sandy lower breast and black breast-band and belly, the female is yellowish with brown-black barring and speckling. In flight from below, both sexes show conspicuous grey-black primaries and secondaries contrasting with the whitish-buff underwing-coverts.

The range of this sandgrouse is North Saharan and Irano-Turanian, extending from North Africa and the Middle East to Iran, and further east and north to southeastern Russia, between the Caspian Sea and Lake Balkhash; it has also penetrated the Iberian peninsula. In this range two or three subspecies have been described. This is a less desertic species than other sandgrouse, inhabiting plains with sparse vegetation on the fringes of deserts and cultivations. The subspecies *P.o. orientalis*, which ranges from North Africa through the Middle East to India, occurs in Israel; all its populations are resident. The subspecies *P.o. arenarius*, with an Irano-Turanian distribution, migrates in autumn and winters in the Middle East and in northwest India.

This species usually drinks in the late morning, and sometimes twice in a day. Its call when flying to water is different from that of other sandgrouse and is easily recognisable: a sound resembling 'churu-churu'.

The Black-bellied Sandgrouse is resident in Israel, in the southern coastal plain, in the northern Negev, in the heights of the Negev and in the Arava. On 5 October 1983, about 1,000 individuals were counted arriving to drink in the region of Nizana. Outside the nesting season it roams. It is also a rare passage migrant and winterer, being more common as a winterer in Sinai. The origin of the winter visitors is in the steppes of Turkestan.

The Black-bellied Sandgrouse nests in the summer and usually lays only in the second half of July, although nests have been found as early as May. The clutch contains 2-3 eggs. The period of incubation is 23-28 days, but no information is available regarding the period of development of the chick between hatching and flying.

Family: Columbidae (Doves, Pigeons)

In the family Columbidae there are 40 genera and 297 species, 51 of which belong to the genus *Columba*. Their distribution is cosmopolitan, but is concentrated mainly in areas of tropical and temperate climate. About two-thirds of the family inhabit the Oriental region — in southeast Asia — and the Australasian region.

This is a family of birds of homogeneous appearance and behaviour, but with wide variation in size — ranging from that of a songbird to that of a small turkey: body length is between 17 cm and 80 cm. All species have a short and thickset body, a short neck and a small head. The bill is short, delicate and weak, usually broadening towards the tip and narrower at the centre. At the base of the bill is a soft protuberance of skin (the cere) in which the slit-like apertures of the nostrils are located. The legs are short and sometimes partially feathered; the toes are long and the rear toe is equal in length to the others. The wings are long or short. The tail is long or short, usually shorter than the wing; it is rounded or straight at the tip, and is spread in flight like a fan. A few species have a crest.

The feathering is thick, but the attachment of the feathers to the skin is weak (possibly an aid to escaping from predators). The plumage of doves is glossy and soft with a discernible downy area at the base. The tips of some feathers crumble into powdery dust, providing a thin protective layer for the plumage. In a few species male and female have identical plumage; normally their plumage is similar, but the female is paler. In some cases there is a distinctive difference in plumage between the sexes; the male is invariably larger. Juveniles and immatures are similar to adults, but paler and lack a glossy sheen. In this family the dominant colours are grey, brown and brown-purple, but in the tropical species more striking colours are found, including green, yellow and white. All species have one moult in the year.

Doves and pigeons are essentially woodland birds, although there are also bush-, ground- and cliff-dwelling species. They subsist almost exclusively on vegetable food, and it is possible to classify them according to their manner of feeding in three basic groups: those that eat fruits and buds, flowers and young leaves only from trees and bushes; those that feed on trees and bushes but also on the ground; and those that gather their food, especially seeds, only on the ground. All these species walk well, and when necessary they rise easily and with strong wingbeats. Their flight is rapid and vigorous. Doves and pigeons have a monotone and repetitive cooing call; a few species utter sibilant or nasal cries.

Most birds of this family are gregarious, and outside the nesting season gather in huge flocks. Most species breed in colonies, and are monogamous. The nest is usually built at the top of a tree, but also on cliffs, on wooden pylons or even on the ground. It is a flimsy and rather casual structure of a few twigs. The clutch is usually of 2 eggs, sometimes 1 or 3. Both parents incubate, with a fairly regular division of labour: the female incubates at night, in the morn-

ing and the evening, while the male performs this function for a few hours during the day. The period of incubation varies between 12 days in the smaller species and 28 days in the larger. The chicks hatch blind and with a sparse covering of yellow down, resembling hair. The parents feed them with 'pigeon milk': during incubation, deposits of fat build up in the epithelium of the crop and grow steadily thicker; influenced by the stimulation of prolactin (the hormone secreted by the pituitary gland, the same hormone which is responsible for the production of milk in mammals), the epithelium cells of the crop dissolve into a thick liquid, resembling a milky broth, which has a high nutritional value. The production of the 'milk' ceases gradually, at a different rate according to species, and thereafter the chicks are fed with semi-digested regurgitated food. The chicks develop rapidly and soon fly from the nest, but remain dependent on their parents for some time longer. Most species complete two or more nesting cycles in a year.

In Israel three genera and seven species of this family are represented. Of these, four are residents, two are winter visitors and one is a rare accidental.

The dove occupies an important place in Jewish religion and folklore. The dove that returned to Noah's Ark bearing an olive-sprig in its bill (*Genesis* viii, 11), has become a universal symbol of peace. The dove is mentioned 32 times in the Old Testament, as a symbol of the beauty and innocence of the loved one, especially in the *Song of Solomon*.

Rock Dove/Feral Pigeon
Columba livia

Body length 29.5-32 cm, wing length 21-23 cm, wingspan 63-68 cm and weight 190-290 g. The ancestor of the Domestic Pigeon and similar to it in shape and size, although its pattern of colours is uniform and not so varied as that of the Domestic Pigeon. Its overall colour is bluish-grey, with a tendency towards green on the head. On the wing there are two black bars; the tip of the tail is also black. The underwing-coverts are pale, and on the neck and upperparts there are glossy shades of green and metallic grey (the glossy colours are absent in the immature). The iris is orange or reddish, and bare bluish-grey skin surrounds the eye. The bill is black and the cere whitish. The colour of the legs is flesh-red.

The Rock Dove has a cosmopolitan range and is distributed in most parts of the world, although especially in the Holarctic region. In this range 14 subspecies have been identified. Today, as a result of domestication and the feral state of many Domestic Pigeons, it is difficult to know whether this range is original and natural or is the outcome of human interference. The Rock Dove is resident in most parts of its range, but sometimes roams and possibly even migrates to a certain extent.

In Israel this species is to be found especially on the eastern slopes of the mountain ridge, from the Lebanon border near Metulla, through Nahal Amud and the cliffs of Arbel to the cliffs and canyons of the Judean Desert and the region of Eilat, but also in rocky areas of the western watershed. According to the literature, two subspecies are present in Israel, although it is difficult to distinguish between them in the field: *C.l. gaddi*, whose range extends between Turkey and Afghanistan and which is reckoned to be predominant in northern and central parts of the country; and *C.l. palestinae*, which is distributed between southern Israel and Arabia. These two subspecies have a grey rump (in contrast to the subspecies inhabiting southern Europe and central Asia, which has a white rump).

The Rock Dove inhabits rocky areas, on steep slopes and in canyons, where it breeds and roosts, although it seeks its food and water in fields and open areas. The Rock Dove is gregarious both during and outside the nesting season. In the Judean Desert it is possible to observe flocks of Rock Doves every morning flying from the cliffs and canyons in a westerly direction, crossing the whole width of the desert — a distance of some 20 km — and dispersing to feed in agricultural areas. Towards noon they return to drink from waterholes and to rest in the shade of stony ravines. In the afternoon they fly again to the fields, gathering in large flocks towards evening to return to their roosting sites.

The population of Rock Doves has dwindled considerably in Israel during the last 100 years. According to Tristram, in his day many thousands of Rock Doves were to be seen in Jericho and Karantal and further east, among the monasteries of the Jordan Valley. In the caves south of Hebron hundreds of doves were present, while in the region of Nahal Amud 'words cannot convey an impression of the multitude of Rock Doves'. Only in Eilat have Rock Doves proliferated considerably in recent years, to such an extent that they constitute a nuisance, especially in the port. Many populations today are mingled with elements of Feral Pigeons.

The nesting season begins in March. Nesting areas are usually in shaded ravines of rock, but also in caves and in wells; in Eilat the Rock Dove regularly nests on buildings. On protected offshore islands such as Dove Island on the Carmel coast, it breeds on the ground in the shade of bushes. The clutch is of 2 eggs. Incubation begins with the first egg and lasts 17-18 days. The male incubates during most of the hours of the day; the female in the evening and at night. The chicks hatch asynchronously and are blind and covered with thin and sparse down. The parents feed them for five or six days with pigeon milk and thereafter with seeds softened in the crop. They fly at 3½ weeks old, and become independent after a further ten days or so. The nesting season continues until August, a total period of five or six months. During this time the Rock Dove produces two or three broods.

Stock Dove
Columba oenas

Body length 33 cm, wing length 22 cm, wingspan 66 cm and weight 250 g. A bluish-grey dove, with two short dark bars on the wings; the breast is reddish-purple in colour. In flight it is distinguished by the grey-black wingtips and the greyish-blue underwing (in the Rock Dove the latter is a paler colour).

The Stock Dove's range covers most of Europe, except for the far north of the continent, and extends to the steppes of Kirgiz in the central USSR. The Stock Dove also breeds in North Africa, and in the northern Middle East between Turkey and northern Iran. Its principal habitats are sparse and mixed forests. The populations in western and southern Europe and those of North Africa and the Middle East are resident; those of central and eastern Europe migrate and winter in the Mediterranean basin, in North Africa and the Middle East. In this range two or three subspecies have been described, the one in the Western Palaearctic region being *C.o. oenas*.

In Israel this is a winter resident between October and mid-March, and possibly also a rare passage migrant. In certain winters it is quite rare, while in others it occurs in flocks numbering hundreds and even thousands of individuals. It winters in northern and central parts of the country, sometimes extending as far south as the northwestern Negev, especially in valleys. It feeds during the day in fields, consuming seeds, buds and leaves. Its flocks often mingle with those of Woodpigeons and Feral Pigeons, and drink water from fish-ponds, winter pools and drainage channels. It roosts in trees, especially in eucalyptus groves, often in proximity to the Woodpigeon.

Woodpigeon
Columba palumbus

The largest dove seen in Israel: body length 40-42 cm, wing length 24-26 cm, wingspan 75-80 cm and weight 390-530 g. As in other species, its dominant plumage colours are shades of grey, but it is easily distinguished by a white patch on the wings and by a white patch on each side of the neck. The breast is purple. The tail is long (about 16 cm) and has a broad black terminal band. The bill is reddish.

The Woodpigeon's range extends continuously over most of Europe except the far north, also North Africa, the northern Middle East, the trans-Caspian area and the western highlands of central Asia. In this range five or six subspecies have been described, the one occurring in Europe being *C.p. palumbus*. Over the last century it has proliferated considerably in Europe, becoming a common bird in public parks and gardens and also an agricultural pest. Most of its populations are resident, but those of eastern Europe, Scandinavia and Siberia migrate in autumn, wintering in southern Europe, in North Africa, in the Middle East, and also in Pakistan and northern India. In winter it gathers in large flocks, especially around feeding and roosting sites.

In Israel the Woodpigeon is a winter resident between November and April in northern and central parts of the country. It is common in some years, rare in others, and is usually seen in small flocks of two to ten individuals. It eats seeds, fruits and green leaves, also takes olives and occasionally feeds on various invertebrates. It is very timid, and is quick to take refuge among tree foliage. Towards evening it gathers to roost in groves, usually among eucalyptus trees; in some years scores and even hundreds of individuals have been observed at roosting sites. The Woodpigeon sometimes roosts in proximity to the Stock Dove.

Genus: *Streptopelia* (turtle doves)

In this genus there are 16 species, which are distributed primarily in tropical Africa and in southeast Asia. They are distinguished from members of the genus *Columba* by their slimmer physique and smaller size, by the long and graduated tail and by the unfeathered tarsus. The feathers lack gloss. Three species are represented in Israel. (At the end of 1984, a single specimen of another species was trapped at Eilat: the Rufous Turtle Dove *S. orientalis*.)

Turtle Dove
Streptopelia turtur

In appearance a small and slim-bodied dove: body length 26-30 cm, wing length 16.6-18 cm, wingspan 47-53 cm and weight 125-165 g. The upperwing-coverts are chestnut-brown speckled with dark grey; the breast and neck are greyish-chestnut, and on either side of the neck there is a small white patch crossed with thin black stripes. The tail is black, except for the white tip and edges and the two central feathers, which are grey (darker above and lighter below). The underwing is greyish, the bill dark grey and the cere black. The iris is deep yellow and the eye is surrounded by a ring of red skin. The legs are reddish-brown. It is almost impossible to distinguish between male and female, although the female is somewhat paler.

The range of the Turtle Dove extends over most of Europe, except northern Britain, Scandinavia and northern Russia, from the shores of the Atlantic Ocean to Mongolia. It also extends over the Middle East and North Africa and covers regions of boreal, temperate, Mediterranean, steppe and desert climate. In this range four subspecies have been identified. The Turtle Dove is a bird of open environments with scattered trees, sparse forests, urban woodland enclaves and plantations. In Israel the subspecies *S.t. arenicola*, whose range extends from the Balearic Islands and northwestern Africa to Iran, northern Afghanistan and western Mongolia, is a summer visitor, while *S.t. turtur*, which is larger and darker and has a more northerly range, is a passage migrant.

Turtle Doves are exclusively vegetarian, feeding on various seeds and seedlings, leaves and other vegetable matter gathered on the ground. Their flight is fast and usually at low level, with more rapid wingbeats than those of other doves.

This is a very common passage migrant in autumn between August and early October and in spring during April and May. Flocks of hundreds and thousands of individuals are seen, especially in stubble fields and perched on electricity and telephone cables. Three Turtle Doves ringed in Eilat, two during the autumn migration and one in spring, have been recovered in southern Russia during the southward migration in August.

Although the Turtle Dove population has diminished in this country since the late 1950s, possibly as a result of competition from Laughing Doves, this is still a common summer resident in northern and central parts of Israel and also around settlements in the Negev and the Arava. The breeding doves return from their winter quarters in early April; only rarely are occasional individuals seen as early as March. The regular date of their return is proverbial: 'the turtle dove and the crane and the swallow observe the time of their coming' (*Jeremiah* viii, 7). So, too, is their constant and repetitive purring call, which is heard throughout the summer and forms an integral part of the courtship process. Turtle Doves return in flocks, which soon separate into pairs, to breed in orchards, in sparse woodland and even within settlements. Construction of the nest begins at the end of April or in early May. The nest is invariably built in a tree or a large bush, usually 2-3 m but sometimes

4-5 m above the ground. It is flimsy and sparse and there is no lining. There are 2 eggs in the clutch. Incubation begins with the first egg; the female incubates at night and by day until late morning, when the male takes over and incubates until early evening. Turtle Doves are sensitive to disturbances in the vicinity of the nest and are easily alarmed into abandoning their clutches; often they will not return to the nest where the disturbance occurred, preferring to build a new nest. During the nesting period, the male periodically performs circuitous display flights in the vicinity of the nest. The period of incubation is about 15 days. Initially the chicks are fed with pigeon milk, after the fourth day with a 'broth' of seeds softened in the parent's crop, and ultimately with whole seeds. If an intruder approaches, the parents attempt to divert its attention from the nest by simulating injury. At 10-11 days old the chicks are already fully feathered; they leave the nest at 15-18 days old, but remain close to it and continue to be tended by the parents. They begin to fly at the age of about 20 days.

Nesting continues until the end of August. During this period the Turtle Doves produce two broods, before joining flocks and migrating.

Although the shooting of Turtle Doves is permitted, this is not a popular game-bird in Israel.

Laughing Dove
Streptopelia senegalensis

Similar to the Turtle Dove but smaller, with shorter wings and longer tail: body length 26.8-30 cm, wing length 14.3-17 cm, wingspan 40-45 cm and weight

110-135 g. The body plumage is wine-brown in colour, with dark speckling on the front of the lower neck (absent in juveniles). The wings are dark: the coverts bluish-grey and the flight feathers black. The tail is 12.5 cm in length (11.3 cm in the Turtle Dove); the central feathers are olive-brown, the remainder dark at the base and tipped with white. This is one of the few species of dove in which there are elements of sexual dimorphism: the female is somewhat paler, with pale brown rather than wine-coloured body plumage. In both sexes the bill and the cere are blackish, the iris dark brown and the legs purple-pink. The Laughing Dove has a prolonged moult which extends into the breeding season.

The origin of the Laughing Dove is in the tropical regions of Africa, and its original range also extends over southern Arabia, India, Afghanistan and Turkestan. Today it is also known in the Middle East, North Africa, the Balkans and Australia. Within this range eight subspecies have been identified. Its primary habitats are areas of thorny bushes and sparse trees, beside rivers and regular water sources. In a secondary fashion it has adapted to conditions artificially created, and is often found within settlements and towns; in such places it shows little timidity and may be approached to within close range. All its populations are resident, including in Israel, where the subspecies *S.s. senegalensis* is found in abundance. The Laughing Dove is in a state of worldwide expansion: in central Asia it has advanced hundreds of kilometres further east during the last hundred years, in parallel with the expansion of agriculture. In the opposite direction, it reached Cyprus in 1909, Tunis and Algeria in 1915, Turkey in 1962 and Salonika in 1969. It has even proliferated in Australia, as a result of escapes from the open colony at Perth Zoo.

It is reasonable to suppose that the population present in Israel today derives originally from specimens brought from Africa to the mosques of this country by Muslims. Whatever the means of its introduction, references to the Laughing Dove in this country during the last century are limited to its presence in Jericho and Jerusalem, where it nested in the olive trees on the Temple Mount, and to the salt-pools of Sodom. Reports from the beginning of this century mention the presence of this bird in the mosques of Ramallah and Jaffa, and since then its expansion has been constant and apparently inexorable. The first Laughing Dove was seen in Petah Tikva in 1938; by 1957 its range extended over most of the coastal plain between Be'er Tuvia and Acre; in the late 1950s it reached the Harod Valley, and by the end of the 1960s the Bet She'an Valley and the Jordan Valley south of Lake Tiberias had been colonised. It has also extended in a southerly direction, reaching Sede Boker in 1969 and the settlements of the Arava and Eilat in 1970. It is generally supposed that this vigorous expansion, especially noticeable during the late 1950s, is linked with the disappearance of birds of prey owing to pesticide poisoning which took place in the mid-1950s. Its distribution was at first restricted almost entirely to settled areas, but gradually it has expanded into open environments.

The Laughing Dove feeds on the ground: on the seeds of wild plants, fruits and buds, sometimes also on snails and beetles. It has also adapted to eating refuse and the seeds of cultivated plants such as rice and sorghum. It usually lives in pairs, but outside the nesting season is liable to flock, especially in places such as markets, urban squares and parks, stubble fields, farmyards and barns, roosting in large numbers in tree foliage. The flock separates into pairs at the approach of the main nesting season, although many individuals continue to congregate around food sources.

The cooing of the Laughing Dove is one of the most familiar and distinctive bird songs heard in this country, especially within settlements. The courtship song of the male, which is heard in summer throughout the hours of daylight, consists of four to six or as many as eight syllables of varying length and pitch, and is thus more varied and melodic than the monotone purring of the Turtle Dove. The voice of the Laughing Dove is also heard in different circumstances, and other functions may be distinguished: territorial calls, aggressive response to an intruder, alarm and distress calls.

The Laughing Dove nests in most months of the year, except November, but especially between February and August, with two peaks: in April and June. Primarily it nests in trees and bushes, but in this country it has also adapted to nesting on man-made buildings and structures: balconies, roofs, ledges, gutters, window-sills and air-conditioning units. Nests have even been found in the grass-boxes of lawnmowers and in boots left outside to dry. Since the early 1970s nesting on low orchard trees has been observed to an increasing extent, sometimes in the abandoned nests of Blackbirds and Yellow-vented Bulbuls. On the other hand the Laughing Dove sometimes nests on the ground. Usually each pair nests in its own territory, but, especially near abundant food sources, a few pairs may breed side by side; cases have been recorded of three pairs nesting in one tree. The base of the nest is crude, while above it is a more dense layer of thinner and more delicate materials. A wide variety of materials is used in the construction of the nest, sometimes obtained

from unexpected sources: in the premises of a factory a nest has been found built entirely of wood shavings. There are usually 2 eggs, sometimes 3 or even 4 (although normally only 2 eggs hatch). Incubation begins sporadically with the laying of the first egg, becoming continuous with the laying of the second. The female incubates at night and during most of the day, while the male takes over from late morning to early evening. The chicks hatch after about 14 days of incubation; they are blind and covered with yellow down. For the first five days they are fed exclusively with pigeon milk, although some discharge of milk continues until the twelfth day. The parents continue to brood the chicks until they are six to eight days old. The chicks leave the nest after 15-16 days, but are capable of flight only at 19 days old. Then they begin to feed independently, but continue for some time to roost near their parents.

A pair of Laughing Doves usually has three or four broods in the year, although some pairs may breed as many as six times in succession. Cases of breeding in autumn are known, but the process is then much slower.

The nesting of Laughing Doves in settlements can have detrimental effects. These birds are liable to infestation by the dove parasite *Argaz reflexus*. This is a blood-sucking parasite, tending to invade human homes and causing severe irritation.

Collared Dove
Streptopelia decaocto

The largest and palest of the turtle doves: body length 28-32.7 cm, wing length 16.8-18.5 cm, wingspan 47-55 cm and weight 160-200 g. Its overall colour is pale brown-grey; the back is light grey-brown and the underparts brown and pink. The primaries are dark grey, the underwing light grey; the underside of the tail is white with a black base. It is distinguished especially by the black half collar on the neck.

The Collared Dove's original range extends between India and the Middle East, in which range three or four subspecies have been described. From here it was introduced into China and Korea; the population in the Middle East may also be the result of artificial introduction. It inhabits dry regions with trees and bushes on the fringes of agricultural areas. It is resident in almost all its areas of distribution, including in Israel, where the western subspecies *S.d. decaocto* occurs. Since the sixteenth century, when the first specimens arrived in the European sector of Istanbul, the Collared Dove has constantly extended its range westward. In 1834 it was identified in Bulgaria, and until the beginning of this century its European population was still confined to the

Balkans, but since then it has reached as far as Scotland and southern Scandinavia. In its recent areas of proliferation the Collared Dove is found near towns and villages, often living and feeding alongside domestic chickens.

The Collared Dove feeds on the ground, consuming seeds, leaves and pulses and also, when available, the foodstuffs intended for domesticated fowl and livestock. In the vicinity of the nest it is very territorial, but it congregates around concentrations of food. In autumn it flocks, and the flocks roost together among the branches of trees.

In Israel, the Collared Dove is currently found in most parts of the country except the extreme Negev. In the 1940s it bred almost exclusively in the Bet She'an Valley and the southern coastal plain. It has extended its range to the Arava only since the mid-1970s. Its courtship call is of four syllables, with emphasis on the second and fourth. Nesting takes place between the end of March and June; the Collared Dove nests in trees, preferring conifers and especially cypresses. Nesting behaviour is similar to that of the Turtle Dove: in the clutch there are 2 eggs; both parents incubate for a period of about 14 days; and the chicks fly from the nest at 18 days old.

Namaqua Dove
Oena capensis

A small and slim-bodied dove: body length 24-27 cm (including 11-12 cm for the tail), wing length 10.6-11 cm, wingspan 30 cm and weight 41-90 g. The tail, which is long, graduated and black-grey in colour, is the most striking distinguishing feature. It is also distinguished in flight by the chestnut underwings. In this dove there is a conspicuous difference between the sexes: the male has a black forehead, cheeks, throat and 'bib', bluish-grey upperparts and a white belly; the female has a greyish face and neck, greyish-brown upperparts and a light belly. Juveniles resemble females, but their upperparts have broad buff-white feather tips.

The Namaqua Dove has an Ethiopian range and is quite common in semi-arid areas across tropical Africa between Senegal and Somalia and from Sudan to the Cape. It is also known in southern and western Arabia. Two subspecies have been described, both resident. Its habitats are in savannas, cultivated and settled areas; it is absent from jungles. The subspecies *O.c. capensis* occurs uncommonly in Israel.

This dove feeds especially on small seeds on bare ground, and drinks copious amounts of water, usually in the hottest hours of the day. It nests in bushes, usually quite close to the ground.

The first Namaqua Dove recorded in Israel was caught on 9 December 1961 in the western Negev. Since then there have been a number of observations in the Arava, especially in the fields of Kibbutz Eilot, between March and November and especially during May. Usually males and immatures are seen, but there have also been sightings of pairs coming to drink together. There are also some records from the end of the 1970s in the Bet She'an Valley, and in September 1983 in the southern Golan. Although it is probable that the species was already nesting in this country, no nests were found until spring 1986, when breeding was recorded not far from Eilat.

Order: Psittaciformes (Parrots)

Family: Psittacidae

In this family there are 79 genera and 330 species. They are distributed in tropical and subtropical areas over all continents except Europe, and especially in the Southern Hemisphere. In Israel one feral species is known.

Birds which are instantly recognisable by their special and unique appearance, parrots are also unique in some anatomical features: the neck is short, the body is compact and the wings usually rounded. The tail length varies: sometimes it is very short and sometimes very long. The body length varies from 14 cm to 1 m. The plumage of parrots is very colourful and there is hardly any difference between male and female. It is sparse and stiff and under the decorative feathers there are many down feathers; the colour of the latter varies between male and female. Parrots also have powder down.

Parrots have a short, thick and hooked bill, with the upper mandible considerably larger than the lower; at the base of the bill is a cere. They are primarily herbivores, using the strong bill to split seeds and hard fruits. The thick, muscular and very flexible tongue, present in most species, is also an asset in this diet, and the crop is well developed. Their legs are short, with two toes pointing forwards and two back. This configuration enables parrots to perch vertically on tree trunks and to grip the branches firmly; it also enables them to grip food with the feet and pass it to the bill, an arrangement existing only in parrots and owls.

Parrots are monogamous and the link between partners is usually lifelong. They nest in holes and the 3-5 eggs are white. The female incubates alone and is fed by the male. The chicks hatch naked, and both parents feed them with regurgitated food until they are capable of flight.

Ring-necked Parakeet
Psittacula krameri

A small parrot: body length 41 cm, wing length 23 cm, wingspan 45 cm and weight 140 g. Mostly green in colour, it is distinguished by its long, graduated tail. The upper mandible of the bill is red and the lower blackish. The male has a black collar between the chin and the sides of the neck, turning to pink on the nape. The juvenile has more yellowish plumage, a red lower mandible and a short tail (these features disappear at about four months old).

The range of the Ring-necked Parakeet extends through southern Asia — in Burma, across India and Iran, in the estuary of the Tigris and Euphrates, and in oases of the Arabian peninsula — and also in the Sahel belt in Africa. In this range four subspecies have been described. Its habitats are sparse groves of trees in savanna environments and in agricultural areas around human settlements.

The Ring-necked Parakeet was a cagebird even in ancient times. The armies of Alexander the Great brought specimens of the subspecies *P.k. borealis* from India to Alexandria, which became a centre for trading in these birds, and it is possible that even at this time birds escaping from captivity became feral in the region of the Delta. Today Ring-necked Parakeets are widely distributed across the Delta and along the Nile Valley. In Israel these parakeets were first seen in the wild in the early 1960s, shortly after their introduction to this country as cagebirds. Initially isolated individuals were seen, but since the end of the 1960s they have been seen more regularly and in larger numbers in valleys in northern and central parts of the country; occasional vagrants have also been sighted in Be'er Sheva, Ein Gedi and Eilat.

The Ring-necked Parakeet flies with rapid wing-beats, usually in flocks at high altitude. This is a noisy bird, emitting loud and shrill monosyllabic screeches. Outside the nesting season it is gregarious and lives in flocks. In this country it consumes the leaves of various trees and numerous types of fruit, being especially fond of oranges, mandarins, medlars and peanuts; it is liable to constitute an agricultural pest.

The largest and most stable population inhabits

the central coastal plain between Ra'anana and Rishon LeTsiyyon. In the early 1980s this population numbered some 150 individuals; on 24 November 1983, in a pre-roosting concentration near Holon, 46 Ring-necked Parakeets were counted. The population in Israel is in all probability feral in origin, but it is conceivable that they are vagrants from the Nile Delta.

Before nesting the breeding pairs separate from the flocks. In this country they nest primarily in old woodpecker holes in eucalyptus trees and in recesses among palm fronds. They enlarge the aperture of the nesting hole, and signs of gnawing around the entrance are evidence of their activity. They are liable to nest in relative density, but the minimum distance between nests is about 10 m. At times of danger several pairs are likely to join forces in defending the nest. The nesting season in this country is between the end of December and mid-June. In the clutch there are usually 3-4 eggs (sometimes as few as 2 or as many as 6). The female incubates for a period of 22-24 days. The chicks develop slowly: they fly from the nest only at the age of 40-50 days, and reach sexual maturity at about three years old.

Order: Cuculiformes (Cuckoos, Turacos)

This order contains two families: Musophagidae (turacos, 18 species) and Cuculidae (cuckoos). Only the latter is represented in Israel. Members of this order have an arrangement of toes similar to that of the parrots: two to the fore and two to the rear. The bill is short and decurved and pointed at the tip. The body is lean and the tail long.

Family: Cuculidae (Cuckoos)

The family comprises 38 genera and 118 species. These are birds of average size, with long and slender bodies and long and graduated tails, and a body length of 14.5-66 cm. The wings are pointed. The legs are short, except in a few ground-dwelling species, and the claws are strong. The predominant colours are brown, grey and chestnut; there is no difference in plumage between the sexes.

Members of this family are distributed in tropical and temperate areas in all parts of the world. Cuckoos of the tropical region are resident, while those of the temperate zones migrate. Most cuckoos are woodland birds, while a minority inhabit savannas. Their basic diet consists of insects, including noxious caterpillars. A few species consume fruit and other vegetable food, also rodents and other small vertebrates.

The name of the cuckoo has become synonymous with the phenomenon of parasitical nesting, although of the 118 species belonging to the family only 50 are parasites: the latter include all the 42 species included in the subfamily Cuculinae, whose members inhabit the Old World. Cuckoos almost invariably 'borrow' the nests of songbirds, while other parasitical nesters, such as woodpeckers and starlings, exploit species closely akin to themselves. Laying in the host nest takes place in the early afternoon, which for most birds is a time of rest from daily activity. Laying is very fast and is completed within a few seconds. The shell of the cuckoo's egg is harder and thicker than that of the host bird; the development of the embryo is rapid and the chicks usually hatch within 10-11 days after laying. The chicks hatch blind and naked.

In Israel two species of cuckoo are represented.

Great Spotted Cuckoo
Clamator glandarius

About the size of a dove: body length 35-42 cm (of which about half is accounted for by the tail, up to 21 cm), wing length of the male 21 cm and of the female 19.5 cm, wingspan 58 cm and weight 94-140 g. It is distinguished by the white spotting on

141

greyish-black upperparts. The tail is long and gradu-ated, dark brown and edged with white. A grey crest protrudes from the crown, and this is erected at times of excitement. The sides of the body are saffron-yellow and the belly yellowish-white. Around the eye is a ring of bare red-orange skin. The tarsus is black-ish in colour. Juveniles are distinguished by their black crown, smaller crest, deeper yellow underparts and chestnut-brown primaries.

The Great Spotted Cuckoo is distributed throughout southern Europe, in the Iberian penin-sula, southern France and western Italy, and also in the Middle East, in Turkey, Cyprus, Syria, Lebanon and Israel to western Iran. It also occurs in Egypt and in various parts of tropical Africa. In this range two subspecies have been described. Its Eurasian popu-lations, which belong to the subspecies *C.g. glandarius*, migrate in winter to Morocco and tropical Africa, while those from southern Africa migrate north, towards the Equator; in Nigeria, large flocks of this species have been seen. Recently the Great Spotted Cuckoo has also begun to winter in Spain. In Israel this is a fairly common summer resident in northern and central parts of the country, and also an occasional migrant in July-August and February-March.

In Israel this cuckoo inhabits sparse groves on the edges of forests, urban woodland enclaves, olive orchards, eucalyptus plantations and plains with scattered trees. In Africa it inhabits savannas among acacia trees. It has a strong and straight flight, resembling that of a hawk. During flight it is loudly vocal, emitting harsh and strident cries. It feeds on various insects, pecking and scratching on the ground in search of hairy caterpillars, grasshoppers and locusts, also ants and beetles. When not feeding, it tends to remain in seclusion in foliage, especially that of trees and thorny bushes such as the sloe and the bramble, but sometimes perches on prominent and exposed branches or on electricity and telephone cables. The Great Spotted Cuckoo lives in territorial pairs, although sometimes flocks of about a dozen individuals have been seen in Israel, especially in the southern coastal plains.

This cuckoo is a parasite on only a few species: in Europe its favoured host is the Magpie; in Africa it exploits various species of starling but also the Fan-tailed Raven. In Israel it is almost exclusively para-sitic on the Hooded Crow, a species of approxi-mately equal distribution, although there is also some evidence of exploitation of the Brown-necked Raven.

The Great Spotted Cuckoo sometimes returns from winter quarters as early as the end of January or early February, but usually not until March. The period of laying lasts from February to May, and sometimes until June — the time of replacement lay-ing by the crows. Laying itself is a process of mutual co-operation between the partners: the male flies around the nest in an ostentatious manner, in order to distract the attention of the host, while the female flies low, hiding at the base of the tree and climbing furtively up the trunk. Several freshly built nests are methodically inspected in this manner, and laying takes place only in a nest where eggs are already present. The discovery of a suitable nest is a powerful sexual stimulus: both in controlled experiments and in the wild it has been observed that copulation follows immediately. The female is liable to lay an egg every two days, a total of 16-18 eggs in a season. The colour of the egg is similar to that of the Hooded Crow, light turquoise speckled with markings of light and dark brown, but is smaller and rounder, measuring 32×24 mm and weighing 11-13 g. The shell of the cuckoo's egg is also thicker than that of the crow. In a typical nest, two or three crow eggs will be found together with one or two laid by the cuckoo, although in some cases four and even five cuckoo's eggs have been found. The Great Spotted Cuckoo does not throw the host's eggs out of the nest, but it has been claimed that it pecks at them, sometimes puncturing the shells and injuring the chick embryos.

The cuckoo chicks hatch after about 13 days of incubation, compared with the 19 days that elapse before hatching of the crow chicks. They hatch blind and naked, but their bodies are strong and very muscular. Their skin is bright pink and the gullet pink, unlike that of the crow chicks which is red. They develop rapidly, but chicks of this species do not eject the host's eggs or chicks from the nest as is the case with the European Cuckoo. Initially their plumage is black, resembling that of their adoptive parents. They climb out of the nest at eight or nine days old and fly from the nest at 20-22 days old, ten or more days before their 'siblings', although for several more weeks they return regularly to the nest and demand food from their adoptive parents (by which stage they are in normal juvenile plumage).

Great Spotted Cuckoos begin the southward migration soon after the conclusion of nesting. The adults lead the way, sometimes as early as July but normally during August, and the juveniles follow at a slightly later date, in September.

Cuckoo
Cuculus canorus

Body length 31-34 cm, wing length 21-22.5 cm, wingspan 58-62 cm and weight 90-130 g. This genus, which comprises 12 species, is distinguished from the genus *Clamator* by the absence of a crest and by the fact that about two-thirds of the foot is feathered. The Cuckoo is a grey-black bird, with a long (up to 17 cm), graduated tail rounded at the tip; from above the tail appears greyish-brown, while from below it is barred with white. The lower breast and belly are barred black and white. The bill is dark, with yellow at the base. The iris of the adult is a striking shade of yellow; in the juvenile it is grey. The juvenile is also distinguished from the adult by the white patch of feathers on the nape and by the barred throat. In flight the European Cuckoo resembles the Sparrowhawk to some extent, although its wings are pointed and its flight less fast; in flight its wings are kept low and do not rise above the level of the body.

The Cuckoo is distributed over the whole of the Eurasian continent, from Britain to Kamchatka and the Philippines, and from Scandinavia to the shores of the Mediterranean. It is also found in North Africa. It inhabits most climatic zones, except tundra, extreme desert and tropical rainforest. In this range four subspecies have been identified. The subspecies *C.c. canorus* is distributed throughout Europe, apart from the Iberian peninsula, and also in the Middle East and in Palaearctic Asia. The habitats of the Cuckoo are varied and it may be found in regions of scrubland, sparse forests, urban woodland enclaves, in cultivated areas and even in marshland; it avoids dense forests. The Palaearctic population migrates south in autumn, with migration taking place at night. The Cuckoo winters in tropical Africa (Zaire, Zambia, Mozambique, Angola) and in southeast Asia.

In Israel this is a common passage migrant in autumn, in August and September, when the adults precede the juveniles, and again in spring between the end of February and May. During migration it is a familiar sight in groves and plantations. It is also a relatively rare summer resident, especially in the region of Jerusalem between Bethlehem and Bethel, but also in the northern coastal plain and the Jezreel Valley.

The Cuckoo is renowned for its call, the familiar disyllabic and two-tone 'coo-coo' (although sometimes it contains as many as five syllables), which in Israel can be heard between the end of February and the end of May. It also has a more abrasive cry, resembling the clearing of the throat; this sound is emitted by both sexes at times of excitement, while the onomatopoeic call is largely the prerogative of the male. In areas colonised by Cuckoos, the male sings almost continuously from morning to evening, usually perched on bare rocks or on bushes. Usually males and females live in segregated territories,

although for breeding purposes a female may visit the territories of several males in turn.

The Cuckoo is the most notorious of the parasitic birds: the birds most commonly exploited in Europe are the Meadow Pipit, Dunnock, Pied Wagtail, various warblers and also the Wren and Red-backed Shrike. In Israel, very few cases of egg-laying by Cuckoos were recorded until the 1970s. Since 1974 the number of sightings has increased, although it is not clear whether this is the result of the proliferation of the species in this country, or is simply evidence of a growth in the number of birdwatchers. The principal host of the Cuckoo in Israel is apparently the Scrub Warbler. The Scrub Warbler has a domed nest, and in the region where it acts as a host it is often built in thorny bushes; laying in such a nest is a difficult and precarious process. The Cuckoo chick soon outgrows the nest, causing it to disintegrate. The feeding of Cuckoo chicks by Long-billed Pipits has been observed in two sites in the northern coastal plain, on 25 June 1983 and on 4 July 1983; on 7 July 1984, a Wren was seen feeding a Cuckoo chick in western Galilee. The late date of laying on the part of some Cuckoos in this country, suggested by the above data, may be one of the reasons for the relatively small number of breeding records so far known.

Discovery of a suitable nest induces copulation and accelerates the descent of the egg into the oviduct. Laying usually takes place in the afternoon, between 2 p.m. and 6 p.m. The egg of the Cuckoo is thick-shelled; it is considerably larger than the eggs of most host species, although small in relation to the size of the Cuckoo itself. The 'sharp' end is more rounded than that of most hosts' eggs. In most cases, however, the colour of the egg closely resembles that of the host, although in a few cases the Cuckoo's egg differs considerably from that of the host (such as the Dunnock). The Cuckoo usually lays only 1 egg; where 2 eggs are found in the nest, this is the result of laying by two females. Laying is timed to coincide with that of the host. A female Cuckoo is liable to lay some 12 eggs in the course of a season, at intervals of 48 hours.

Development of the Cuckoo embryo is rapid, and hatching takes place within 12-13 days. The chick hatches blind and naked, with pink skin and a large orange-coloured gape. Food is constantly and noisily demanded. It seems that the chick is sensitive to contact with any strange body in the nest, instinctively ejecting from the nest, using the back and wings as a lever, the eggs and chicks of the host. A rival Cuckoo chick in the nest is also likely to be ejected. This instinct subsides at the age of three or four days. The chick grows rapidly and is soon larger than its adoptive parents. When it outgrows the nest, it perches on the rim and continues its demands for food. The chick flies from the nest at about three weeks old and soon becomes independent.

Most of the Cuckoos disappear from Israel as early as May and during June. They possibly return to Europe to lay again.

Order: Strigiforms (Owls)

In the order Strigiformes there are two families: Barn Owls (Tytonidae) with two genera and 11 species; and typical owls (Strigidae) with 28 genera and 134 species, of which 36 belonging to the genus *Otus*. In Israel seven genera and ten species are known, representing both families.

Members of this order are distributed in all parts of the world except Antarctica, although most species inhabit tropical and subtropical zones, especially within the Oriental region. Their habitats are varied and include tundra and arid desert, although most prefer the edges of forests and woodland. Most species are resident, and only a few of the Palaearctic species migrate.

Owls range in size between 12 cm and 71 cm and in weight between 55 g and 4.2 kg. They are easily distinguished from other birds by their large and rounded head and by their large forward-facing eyes (not located on the sides of the head as in other birds). The feathers of the face are also arranged in a manner different from the norm, forming a kind of frame around the eyes and the bill (the facial 'disc'). The facial feathers differ from those of the rest of the body, being short and compact and giving the face a quasi-human appearance. Most owls are squat in profile, appearing neckless. The wings are long and rounded and the tail short. The tarsus is relatively long and strong and usually covered in feathers.

The feathers of owls are long and soft, with the result that the birds appear larger than their real size. The dominant colours are grey, brown, blackish and yellow, flecked with markings, stripes and bars which provide efficient camouflage. Often two tufts of feathers, resembling ears, protrude from the head, and these can be moved by muscular control. As in other birds, these tufts are used to express different moods — as well as providing a useful means of identification. Among owls there is usually no difference in colour between the sexes, although the

male is smaller. Immatures have similar plumage to that of adults, except in a few species which are not represented in this country. The tips of the primaries are usually serrated on the outer edge, ensuring silent flight. The bill is short and sharp, with the upper mandible longer and overlapping the lower; the edges are sharp and the tip hooked. At the base of the bill is a cere in which the apertures of the nostrils are located; spiky feathers cover the cere and the nostrils, and thus the bill appears even shorter than it really is. The toes are strong, and the outer (fourth) is capable of turning backwards, providing a firm grip on prey. The toes are usually feathered, the claws long, powerful, hooked and sharp.

The location of the eyes at the front of the head provides binocular vision and permits precise estimation of distances, but limits the field of vision to a range of 110°. The large eye is incapable of movement within its socket, and in order to alter its field of vision the bird is obliged to turn its head or move it up and down. Some species are capable of turning the head through 270°, a procedure which also assists in the location of sound. The eye is capable of rapid adaptation in response to varying light conditions; the pupil expands in weak light and contracts like a camera shutter in strong light. Owls are able to see in daylight, but their ability to discern different colours is somewhat limited. The eye is shielded by an upper lid, not a lower lid as in the majority of birds.

Hearing is also well developed, and this faculty permits the location of prey even in total darkness. It is evident that the facial disc is capable of standing erect under muscular control, assisting in the channelling of sound waves towards the ear. Owls are capable of hearing sounds that the human ear is incapable of perceiving at all and are especially sensitive to high-frequency sounds, such as the communication calls of rodents. Tactile senses are also developed, especially in the head, where the feathers are extremely sensitive. When feeding, owls rely primarily on the sense of touch.

Most members of the order are active in twilight and at night, and only a few also hunt by day. During the hours of daylight they tend to perch motionless, with erect stance, among tree foliage or in a dark hiding place. The flight of the larger species is slow and smooth, that of the smaller ones rapid and undulating. They usually locate their prey from a prominent vantage point, by means of eyesight and especially by hearing. When the prey is located they swoop on it. Normally prey is caught on the ground or on the branch of a tree.

Owls feed especially on small vertebrates: rodents constitute the major ingredient of their diet, which also includes songbirds, small reptiles, amphibians and even fish. Smaller species subsist primarily on insects and worms. Most species catch whatever food happens to be available, and thus the larger species, such as the Eagle Owl, even prey on other, smaller owls, but there are species which prefer a specific diet. Owls catch their prey with their feet, gripping with the four toes and the sharp claws, and sometimes transfer the prey from the feet to the bill: behaviour typical only of owls and parrots. The prey is usually swallowed whole. The bird stores in its stomach the undigested items — bones, hair, skin, feathers, scales and insect carapaces — and regurgitates them in pellet form.

At night vocal communication is of great importance, and owls have a rich vocal range. Their calls are heard throughout the year, with increased intensity at the approach of the breeding season and at the time that the chicks are leaving the nest. Their calls are monotone whistling or hooting sounds, carrying over long distances on account of their low frequency, but calls serving various functions may be distinguished, such as contact cries, advertising calls, and territorial song.

Owls do not build nests. They lay in hollows in the ground or in the abandoned nests of crows and diurnal predators, but usually in dark and secluded places such as rock-ledges, crevices, hollow trees and under the eaves of roofs. In hot and arid areas they even nest in rodents' burrows, and they quite readily adopt nestboxes. The eggs of owls are rounded and white, and their clutches are usually of 3-4 eggs; the size of the clutch, like the time of nesting and the number of broods, depends directly on the availability of food. Laying takes place every two or three days. The female incubates alone from the laying of the first egg and is supplied with food by the male, who builds up a store of food beside the nest. Hatching is asynchronous, and the chicks vary considerably in size. They hatch blind and covered in thick down, which is grey, brown or white in colour and covers the whole body, including the legs and usually also the toes. The male continues to bring food to the nest and the female feeds the chicks. When there is sufficient food all the chicks survive; when there is a shortage the smaller and weaker chicks soon die of hunger. The eyes (and ears) of the chicks open at about a week old. The growth rate of the chicks is slow: they remain in the nest for three to six weeks, and leave it before they are fully able to fly. In autumn they moult to adult plumage; thereafter every bird has one moult each year, a gradual and prolonged one lasting three to four months.

Family: Tytonidae (Barn Owls)

Members of this family are distinguished from other owls by several features. The inner toe is the same length as the middle toe; the claw of the middle toe is serrated on the inner side. The skull is narrow and small, the eyes small and the bill slender and long in comparison with those of other owls. The tail is slightly forked. The facial disc is very prominent, giving the face a heart-shaped rather than a rounded appearance.

Barn Owl
Tyto alba

Body length 31.5-36 cm, wing length of the male 28 cm and of the female 30 cm, wingspan 87-93 cm and weight 250-310 g. Its face is white and outlined with short, dark feathers, giving it a heart-shaped appearance. The upperparts are golden-brown, speckled with greyish-brown marks of varying intensity and striated with dark brown and white. The colour of the underparts varies individually and between the different subspecies, from silvery-white to sandy-beige (usually speckled with beige or brown markings). Although there are no significant differences in colour between the sexes, the female, which is larger, is more heavily speckled and streaked. The wings are long and rounded. The tarsus is long and covered with narrow feathers, of the same colour as that of the belly, but the toes are bare. The eyes are relatively small and are black; the bill is whitish-yellow. This owl is often seen as a ghostly shape in buoyant, wavering flight.

The Barn Owl is one of the most widely distributed owls. It has a semi-cosmopolitan range, extending over western and central Europe, across Africa (excluding the Sahara and the Congo basin), the Middle East, southeast Asia, Australia, the USA and South America. In this range 34-36 subspecies have been identified, all of them resident. Primarily the Barn Owl is a bird of exposed and rocky environments, with caves and crevices, also inhabiting sparse and deciduous forests, fields and urban woodland enclaves. It prefers plains and valleys and seldom ascends to high altitudes, although in this country it is found in the hills of Upper Galilee. It is evidently sensitive to cold and does not store up fat during the autumn. Today it is widely found in populated areas.

In Israel two subspecies are known: *T.a. alba*, which is distributed throughout western and central Europe and along the shores of North Africa, and is common in the Mediterranean region; and *T.a. erlangeri*, which has a range extending through Arabia, Jordan and southern Iraq. In Israel the latter subspecies is distributed south of a line from Kiryat Mal'akhi to Dorot and is quite common in the western Negev, although rare in the remainder of the Negev and in Sinai; it is larger and paler than the Mediterranean subspecies, with underparts invariably white and the tarsus either exposed or only sparsely feathered. The nocturnal activity of the Barn Owl is such that it is rarely seen, and in fact it is considerably more common in this country than the number of sightings would suggest. It is found in almost every village and agricultural settlement and even in the suburbs of towns.

The Barn Owl usually spends the hours of daylight resting in dark places such as caves, rockcrevices, hollow trees, roof gables, wells and barns, less often in dense foliage. It sets out to hunt in the evening. In flight it often utters a piercing screech. It is an active hunter, flying low over fields, marshes and desert expanses, retracing its course from time to time. Above long grass it hovers, sometimes for several minutes. Occasionally it perches on a branch or a rock and scours its surroundings.

The Barn Owl disgorges one to three pellets per day. These measure 5-6 × 2.5-3 cm, with an average weight of about 30 g, and examination of their contents is instructive as to the diet of the Barn Owl. In Israel the contents of some 8,500 pellets have been examined in various places, revealing that the Barn Owl varies its diet according to season and area. In the Mediterranean region of Israel, for example, social voles *Microtus socialis* constitute about 40-70% and sometimes even 92% of the diet, shrews about 13% and sparrows 15%. In these pellets, remains of six species of bat have also been found: five of these were unknown in Israel when found, and only later discovered in the wild. In pellets of Barn Owls from the region of the Hula marshes, the skulls of water shrews *Neomys fodiens* have been found: the only evidence of the existence of this mammal in this country. Remains of various insects and beetles are also contained in pellets — eaten in times of hunger or when vertebrates are in short supply; in the month of January, and only then, the Barn Owl also eats moles. In the western Negev, the proportion of small birds consumed is as high as 50%; in this region Tristram's jird *Meriones tristrami* takes the place of the social vole. No traces have been found in this country of reptiles or amphibians in the diet.

The Barn Owl usually lives in pairs. Sometimes the territories of several pairs overlap, so that more than one pair may be found in a given sector. The daytime roost usually becomes the nesting site, although in areas lacking suitable nesting conditions Barn Owls are liable to migrate over short distances and to congregate in areas where suitable sites exist. Nesting sites tend to be traditional, and may be occupied for many years in succession, although the occupants change.

The nesting season in this country usually begins in March and ends in June, but in years when rodents are especially abundant nesting is liable to begin in February and continue until September. During this period Barn Owls may have two broods. The Barn Owl does not build a nest, but over the course of time pellets and remnants of food gather around the laying place, and the male begins to build up a store of provisions in the vicinity even before laying takes place. In the clutch there are usually 4-7 eggs, but in years of abundant food supplies the number may rise to 12. Incubation begins with the first egg (it seems that the embryo dies within three days if not incubated). The female incubates, and is provided with food by the male. Sometimes a 'larder' of 30-40 rodents is accumulated near the nest. Hatching takes place after 31-33 days of incubation. The chicks hatch with a sparse covering of white down; their eyes open at eight days old. On the tenth day a second coat begins to develop, also downy but thicker and more compact than the first, greyish above and whitish-yellow below. When the chicks are 18 days old this coat is completely developed. Only then does adult plumage begin to grow, gradually replacing the down, the last vestiges of which are shed at about six weeks old. Both parents bring food to the chicks, initially feeding them bill-to-bill with small scraps of meat; at about two weeks old the chicks are feeding independently, from the food piled up beside them. At times of alarm they puff themselves up and pant, lying on their backs with legs in the air. The chicks fly from the nest at about 55 days old, but the parents continue to supply them with food for a few more weeks. At this stage it is difficult to distinguish between juveniles and adults.

The Barn Owl plays a very important role, perhaps more so than any other owl, in preserving the balance of nature. As previously stated, in years when there is a glut of rodents, the nesting season is longer and the size of clutches larger. An indirect hint of their capacity for hunting may be gleaned from the fact than in 1975-78 77 Barn Owls were found dead after eating poisoned rodents in the fields of the Hula Valley.

In the early 1980s, under the auspices of the Israel Raptor Information Center, artificial nestboxes for Barn Owls were set up in the Hula Valley and in the Bet She'an Valley. Lack of co-operation from the farmers of the Hula Valley led to the failure of the experiment there; more positive results were achieved in the second instance, although here, too, many difficulties were encountered.

Family: Strigidae (Typical Owls)

The inner toe is considerably shorter than the middle toe, and the claw of the latter is not serrated. The skull is round, the eyes large, the bill short and curved, and the tail rounded. The chicks have an intermediate (mesoptile) down, between first down and adult plumage.

Little Owl
Athene noctua

A small owl: body length 19.5-22 cm, wing length 15-16.5 cm, wingspan 54-58 cm and weight 110-135 g. The body is squat, and the fact flat. The feathers of the face are arranged in 'frames' around the eyes, but these are less striking than in other species of owl. The upperparts are dark brown and speckled with white; the underparts are paler with dark brown markings, especially on the breast. The chin is white. The wings are broad and rounded; the flight feathers are brown, with white markings combining to form broken wingbars and with grey tips. The tail is short, and brown with four or five whitish-yellow bars. The bill is yellowish. The eyes of the adult are lemon-yellow, while in the juvenile they are pale yellow.

The Little Owl has a southern trans-Palaearctic range from Portugal and Britain to the shores of China. It is absent from Scandinavia, from the northern USSR and from regions of tundra and taiga in Asia. It is also found in North Africa, with penetration along the shores of the Red Sea to Somalia. In this range 11 subspecies have been identified, all of them resident. The Little Owl inhabits dry open environments, from sparse forests, orchards, pasture meadows and cultivated areas to rocky landscapes, steppes, deserts and cliffs.

This is the commonest and most widely distributed owl in Israel. It is very common in most parts of the country, including agricultural settlements and the canyons of the Judean Desert. It is more rare in the southern Negev. According to the literature, three or four subspecies are found in this country, although there are considerable differences between individuals, and variations in colour may even be noted in members of the same pair. In a

general sense, the northern populations are darker and these belong to the subspecies *A.n. indigena*, which is distributed in southern Europe. In the southern coastal plain lives the subspecies *A.n. glaux*, whose range extends along the shores of North Africa from Morocco to the Nile Delta; it is dark, and heavily barred below. In the Judean Desert and the Negev lives the paler and less conspicuously barred *A.n. saharae*. It is possible that the palest individuals belong to the subspecies *A.n. lilith*, which is confined to the region between Sinai and the deserts of Syria and Jordan.

The Little Owl is a territorial bird, usually living in regular pairs. The size of territories in the Mediterranean belt is about 30-50 ha. It is more diurnal than other owls, and is often to be seen perched on a rock, an electricity cable, a pole or a roof. It is especially active in the hours between twilight and darkness. In summer it subsists mainly on large insects such as beetles and grasshoppers, but also on reptiles and frogs. In winter, small mammals such as mice and shrews, and small songbirds, constitute a larger proportion of its diet. It also consumes many scorpions, especially in the desert. Its pellets are small: 2.5-4 cm long and 1.2-2 cm wide. The Little Owl has a monotone call, consisting of one long syllable repeated every few seconds at fairly regular frequency and resembling a mournful wail. It makes its voice heard especially at the end of winter and in spring, often during the hours of daylight.

In Israel the Little Owl nests between March and May. Nesting sites are crevices in rocks, hollow trees, holes in the ground, which may be 1 m or more in depth, abandoned nests of Bee-eaters, and gaps in the walls of houses, under roofs and on the surface of the ground. In the clutch there are 3-5, sometimes 6 eggs. Unlike with other owls, incubation sometimes begins only when the clutch is complete. The female bears most of the burden, although the male may possibly relieve her for short periods; he spends long periods of time in the vicinity of the nest and also brings food to the incubating female. Incubation lasts 27-28 days. On hatching the chick is clad in thick white down, which also covers the legs. This soon changes to juvenile plumage, which is similar to that of adults but darker. The chicks are tended in the nest for about 30 days. Initially the male brings food and the female feeds the chicks bill-to-bill; when the chicks are seven to ten days old, both parents leave food for them in the nest and they take it for themselves. At this stage the parents sometimes hunt in broad daylight, and the chicks are fed with small birds, field mice and reptiles, rather than with insects. The chicks fly from the nest at 30-35 days, but return to it regularly over a period of several weeks: during this time the parents continue to feed them, and the family unit remains intact until autumn. Juveniles reach sexual maturity at about one year old.

The Little Owl is usually single-brooded, but sometimes has two broods in a year.

Scops Owl
Otus scops

The smallest of the owls found in Israel: body length 18-19.5 cm, wing length 14.7-16 cm, wingspan 53-60 cm and weight 65-90 g. It is greyish-brown delicately barred with brown and with orange markings, its plumage resembling the bark of a tree. The tarsus is covered with light feathers but the toes are bare. On the head there are two tufts of feathers, like ears, which stand erect when the bird is alarmed or excited; at other times they are not conspicuous. The bill is black. The iris is lemon-yellow in the adult and pale yellow in the juvenile. There is no difference in colour between male and female.

The range of the Scops Owl extends through southern and eastern Europe, the Middle East, central Asia and North Africa. In this range six subspecies have been described, the one occurring in Israel being *O.s. cycladum*, which breeds from south Greece, through Israel to Jordan. This species inhabits open environments with a few scattered trees, in sparse forests, plantations, olive groves and even in rural settlements. In most of its Palaearctic range it is a summer visitor, migrating in autumn and wintering in the savanna belt between the Sahara and the Equator.

In Israel this is a common passage migrant in September-October and in March-April. It is also a fairly common summer resident in valleys and plains in the Mediterranean region and especially in the Tiberias Valley, the Bet She'an Valley and the Hula Valley. It is sometimes also present in winter, especially in the south of the country.

The Scops Owl spends the day hidden in broadleafed trees such as the fig or the palm, perching close to the trunk. When disturbed it stands upright, peering through half-closed eyes; if the disturbance is persistent it takes to the air in fluttering and rapid flight, in a straight line (not undulating). At sunset it begins to emit monosyllabic sibilant calls, quite melodic and pleasant, which may be heard over a period of half an hour or more, uttered at the rate of about 24 per minute. Often, especially at the approach of the nesting season, a duet may be heard: the male calling and the female replying intermittently in a higher, shriller tone. After a prolonged series of calls the owl sets out to hunt. It locates its prey from a vantage point and usually catches it on the ground. Sometimes it knocks flying prey to the ground and only then carries it in the bill to the feeding place. Only rarely does it carry prey in its claws. The Scops Owl feeds especially on insects: grasshoppers, moths and crickets constitute about 95% of its diet, while vertebrates (songbirds, mammals, amphibians and reptiles) make up the rest. On account of the large quantities of insect fragments contained in them, its pellets are brittle and not easily collected and analysed; the pellet is 2-3 cm long and 1-1.2 cm wide.

The nesting season in Israel is concentrated between March and June, although there are exceptions — both earlier and later. The male shows the female a number of possible sites in his territory: a hollow tree, the abandoned nest of a woodpecker, crow or diurnal bird of prey, among palm fronds or in a derelict building, up to a height of about 8 m above the ground. The female chooses one of these sites and henceforward uses it as a regular daytime roost. The female usually lays 3-4 eggs, sometimes as many as 6, at intervals of two days. She incubates alone from the laying of the first egg, and is supplied with food by the male. The period of incubation is 24-25 days. The chicks hatch over a period of about three days; they are blind and covered with short, dense and soft white down, extending over the feet to the toes. At six days the intermediate plumage appears, and when it is fully developed the chick is very similar to the adult. The female alone feeds the chicks, with food supplied by the male, until they are about 18 days old; thereafter both parents attend the chicks. The owlets begin to leave the nest at 21 days old, but are fully able to fly only at 33 days. From 44 days they are capable of catching prey on their own, although the family unit remains intact until the end of summer and is even retained in the southward migration in September.

Striated Scops Owl
Otus brucei

Slightly larger than the Scops Owl: body length 21 cm, wing length 16 cm, wingspan 60 cm and weight 100 g. Similar to the Scops Owl but paler: it is greyish-buff, narrowly streaked darker.

Knowledge of this owl is fairly limited, although according to distribution maps in the literature it is found discontinuously from the Syrian Desert to the Aral Sea; the population inhabiting the region between the Aral Sea and Afghanistan migrates and winters in Arabia and Sinai. In Israel this is a rare passage migrant and winterer, with a few records between November and March in the region between Eilat and Nablus.

Eagle Owl
Bubo bubo

The largest owl seen in Israel, easily recognised by its ear-tufts, up to 7 cm in length. Size varies according to subspecies (see below). The plumage coloration of the Eagle Owl resembles that of tree bark: yellowish-brown marked and barred with dark brown; the barring is more dense on the back and sparse on the breast, which is also paler. The facial disc is conspicuous. There is no difference in plumage between the sexes, although the female is larger. The eyes are large and the iris orange or yellow. The tarsus is thickly feathered, as are the toes; the claws are very strong. The primaries are considerably longer than the secondaries.

The Eagle Owl has a trans-Palaearctic range, extending over most of Europe except in the far north and west, where it has been exterminated by man. It is also distributed across Asia, except in the far north and the southeastern corner, and in North Africa. In this range 23 subspecies have been identified, all of them resident. Its habitats are varied: from hill forests, groves and canyons to flat pasture meadows and arid deserts. Usually it avoids cultivated districts and populated areas.

In Israel two subspecies are known: *B.b. interpositus*, which is common in the Mediterranean region; and *B.b. ascalaphus*, which inhabits the Judean Desert and the Negev. (In the literature there is mention of a third subspecies, *B.b. aharonii*, which today is generally considered a hybrid between these two.) These subspecies accord with the general trend existing in relation to subspecies and species: the northern birds are larger and darker in colour, while the desert subspecies, which is distributed in North Africa, the Middle East and Arabia, is sandy-yellow. The latter is also distinguished by the iris, which is gold-yellow. Body length of the male of this subspecies is 35 cm and of the female 37 cm, wing length 32 cm and 37 cm respectively, and weight 750-910 g. The northern subspecies *B.b. interpositus* is distributed in southern Russia, western Iran, Turkey, Syria and northern Israel: body length of the male 47.5-56 cm and of the female 59-65 cm, wing

length of the male 37-42 cm and of the female 38-47 cm, weight of the male 950-1,550 g and of the female 1,175-2,950 g.

The northern subspecies is quite rare on the western slopes of the mountain ridge and more common on the eastern slopes, from Nahal Kadesh in eastern Upper Galilee, through Nahal Tabor in Lower Galilee and the Bet She'an Valley to Gilboa. It is also fairly common in the scrubland of the southern coastal plains and in the western and northern Negev. The southern subspecies is a rare bird in the desert regions of Israel.

The Eagle Owl lives in pairs in which the bond is lifelong. The size of the territory depends on the amount of food available, the average size being about 12 km^2. Usually the day is spent solitarily among rockfalls, on cliffs, in wells or among bushes. This owl is active from about sunset to sunrise. When about to leave its roost it utters its 'oo-hoo' call at regular intervals. This call, with which the bird proclaims its territory, may on quiet nights resound over an area of 2-3 km. It is usually uttered from a fixed point, and only rarely in flight; when the bird is calling a large white patch protrudes on its neck. After this initial call it sets out to hunt and is then silent until after feeding.

The Eagle Owl prefers to hunt in open territory, catching its prey from a vantage point or in low flight. In Israel its diet consists mainly of various rodents, but also includes hedgehogs, fruit bats and birds such as partridges, doves and crows. In its pellets remains of birds of prey including hawks, buzzards, Osprey and Peregrine have also been found, as well as of Coot, Moorhen, frogs and fish — evidence that the Eagle Owl also hunts in marshes and fishponds. Sometimes pellets also contain insect carapaces. Large prey are plucked or skinned and the indigestible parts removed: thus, for example, it usually removes the skin and spines of the hedgehog, although hedgehog spines are sometimes found in its pellets. Small prey are swallowed whole. The pellets are very large, up to 7.6 cm long and 3.2 cm broad.

The breeding season of the Eagle Owl is early: in Israel laying has been recorded from the fourth week of January, although it normally takes place in the second half of February-early March, sometimes also during April. At the approach of laying the male becomes increasingly vocal, such that hundreds of calls may be heard in a night; most calls are uttered from the same rock or branch. During this period any attempt at imitating its call induces it to reply. The Eagle Owl nests in rock-crevices, caves, quarry walls, abandoned nests of raptors or burrows of porcupines, although sometimes in simple hollows dug in the ground. The nest is unlined, although in the course of time many pellets accumulate around it. The clutch contains 2-3 eggs, sometimes 4, and even 5 in some recorded instances. The female incubates from the laying of the second egg; the male deposits food beside the nest in a special feeding corner, and leaves immediately. In the morning he perches 100-200 m from the nest and rests there, if undisturbed, throughout the day. The length of incubation is 34-36 days. Hatching usually takes place in early March, although it is sometimes delayed until May. The chicks hatch blind and covered with short and soft whitish-grey down, extending as far as the claws. This coat soon changes to the intermediate stage of plumage down, which is yellow-grey, and this is gradually replaced by adult plumage, a process completed when the chick is about three months old. Initially only the female feeds the chicks; at a later stage both parents share the task. Usually only two chicks survive; if more than two hatch, the younger chicks die and are eaten by their older siblings. The surviving chicks leave the nest at four to eight weeks old and learn to fly at nine to ten weeks, although the parents continue to tend them until autumn. For the first two years of their lives the immature birds roam far from their birthplace, until they find a vacant territory. They reach sexual maturity at two or three years old.

Brown Fish Owl
Ketupa zeylonensis

Body length 55 cm, wing length 41 cm, wingspan 148 cm and weight 1,100 g. Similar to the Eagle Owl in shape, colouring and size, but distinguished from it by the shorter ear-tufts, bare legs and feet, more delicate barring on the breast and the absence of any pronounced facial disc. Its wings are shorter and more rounded than those of other owls.

The Brown Fish Owl is distributed mainly in India and in southeast Asia, while the range of the sub-species *K.z. semenowi* extends as far west as Syria and southern Turkey. It is invariably found near water: rivers, lakes and swamps — places where fish is available. It is well adapted to such a diet, having large claws, a long and exposed tarsus, and a leg structure similar to that of the Osprey; the claws are strong and flat and with a sharp undersurface. As a fish-catcher, the Brown Fish Owl has less need of silent flight than other owls, and consequently there are no serrations at the tips of the primaries.

The Brown Fish Owl is a territorial bird. It feeds mainly on fish, but also on birds, amphibians and reptiles found near water, and sometimes even on carrion. It hunts only at night, swooping on its prey from a vantage point and snatching it with its claws from the surface of the water.

The first sighting of a Brown Fish Owl in Israel was recorded by Canon H.B. Tristram in 1863 in Nahal Kziv in western Galilee. Since then a few sightings have been reported in the western Golan and on the western shores of Lake Tiberias, but this species is today apparently confined to streams flowing from the Golan into Lake Tiberias, and even here it is extremely rare. During the 1970s, pellets of this owl, containing particularly fish scales and crab shells, were found at eight sites in the Golan, but in a special survey conducted in 1983/84 not a single Brown Fish Owl was observed.

Little is known of this species' breeding behaviour, and in Israel, and in the Middle East as a whole, a nest has yet to be found. The Brown Fish Owl tends to nest in caves, in rock-crevices and sometimes in dense tree foliage.

Tawny Owl
Strix aluco

An owl of medium size: body length 37-39 cm, wing length 26-27 cm, wingspan 91-100 cm and weight 430-520 g (the smaller dimensions are those of the male, the larger those of the female). There are two colour-phases: the more common is dark brown above, mottled and barred brown and with white markings on the scapulars and the wing-coverts, and paler, whitish-buff below with heavy brown streaking; the other is more greyish. The Tawny Owl has a large head lacking ear-tufts; the face is pale, conspicuously bordered with grey. The eyes are large and black. The wings are relatively short, broad and rounded, the tail rounded and short. The tarsus is feathered, the feathering extending to the base of the toes. The bill is greenish-yellow in colour, and its base is covered with bristly feathers.

The distribution of the Tawny Owl extends over most of Europe, North Africa, the Mediterranean region of the Middle East and southern parts of Palaearctic Asia. In this range 10-13 subspecies have been described, all of them resident. This owl usually inhabits deciduous forests and woods, but also plantations, urban wooded enclaves, rocky terrain and rural settlements. In Israel the subspecies found is *S.a. aluco*, whose range is in Europe, Turkey and the western Middle East.

The Tawny Owl is more easily heard than seen; the calls of the male are clearly heard at night at the end of winter and in spring. Its territorial call — a long quavering hoot (traditionally represented as 'tu-whit, tu-whoo') — is, to the human ear, the most melodious call of any owl. Other calls accompany courtship, and the bringing of food to the incubating female. The courtship flight of the male is impressive, with wing-clapping (beneath the body) audible over long distances. It is active at night: from its perch on a vantage point, it hunts mostly small mammals and birds, but also frogs, lizards and even insects and worms. It lives in fixed pairs in territories.

In Israel this is a fairly rare breeder. It is found in the maquis area of western and Upper Galilee and in populated areas to the north of Lake Tiberias, in the Golan and in Carmel. Until the 1940s it was also present in the Judean Hills, with observations recorded as far south as Hebron.

The Tawny Owl usually nests in hollow trees and among root formations, but also in rock-crevices, under roofs, in barns and in the burrows of various mammals. In this country the nesting season is between March and May. In the clutch there are 2-4 eggs. The female incubates from the laying of the first egg, and the incubation period is 28-29 days. The chicks hatch covered with white down; their 'intermediate plumage' is grey-brown with diagonal bars. They remain in the nest for 35-38 days. During the first three weeks the male brings food and the female feeds them; thereafter both parents hunt. Throughout the nesting period the Tawny Owl defends its nest aggressively, and will even attack a human intruder. The chicks leave the nest after 25-30 days, and are capable of flight at about 35 days, although the parents continue to tend them for a further three months.

Hume's Tawny Owl
Strix butleri

A small and pale owl: body length 28.5-32 cm, wing length 23-23.5 cm, wingspan 90 cm and weight 160-225 g. The back is yellowish-cream, speckled with light brown and grey markings; the underparts are sandy-white and unbarred. The feathers of the wings and tail are barred brown. The tarsus is covered with white feathers but the toes are bare. The eyes are orange-yellow.

Hume's Tawny Owl has a restricted range extending from east of the Nile through Arabia to Pakistan. It is a monotypic species and apparently resident. It tends to inhabit remote places and for this reason knowledge of it is limited (it was photographed for the first time in 1973, when it emerged that its eyes are orange-yellow and not black as was earlier supposed). Today Hume's Tawny Owl is known in scores of sites throughout Israel, from Samaria, through the Judean Desert and the Arava to the Negev and southern Sinai. It is quite common in Ein Gedi, and many individuals are killed by traffic on roads along the Dead Sea and in the Judean Desert.

Hume's Tawny Owl is a typical desert bird, inhabiting rocky wadis near water. Its stance is not erect like that of the Tawny Owl, but tends towards

the horizontal. Its flight is wavering and light during hunting expeditions, but vigorous and straight when it flies from point to point. In its pellets remains have been found of Wagner's gerbil, Tristram's jird, bushy-tailed jird and other rodents, and also birds, lizards, grasshoppers and scorpions. The call of Hume's Tawny Owl is often heard between January and April: it is clear and prolonged, accompanied by a kind of short throaty cough, and is louder than that of the Tawny Owl.

Although this owl is not so rare as is sometimes supposed, very little is known of its breeding behaviour. So far, throughout the world, only one nest of this species has been positively identified: in 1974, in a well at Nahal Sekher in the western Negev. In this case, laying took place in early May and the clutch consisted of 5 eggs. Hatching took place between 10 and 21 June, and the chicks remained in the nest about 28 days, until 17 July. The food supplied to the chicks consisted mainly of greater Egyptian gerbils (66%), but also of Tristram's jird (19%) and lesser jerboas (14%). (The male of this pair was killed by an Eagle Owl.) Chicks of Hume's Tawny Owl, probably the offspring of this brood, were observed in Nahal Arugot on 17 July 1979.

Long-eared Owl
Asio otus

A medium-sized owl: body length of the male 35-37.5 cm and of the female 37-40 cm, wing length of the male 28-30 cm and of the female 29-32 cm, wingspan 94-98 cm, weight of the male 200-300 g and of the female 280-390 g. It belongs to a genus of six species distributed in all parts of the world except Australasia and Antarctica. Its basic colour is yellowish-brown speckled with dark brown. There are striking differences in colour between individuals according to age and sex: females are usually darker. The face is long and yellowish-orange in colour, with black-grey markings around the eyes, which are orange. The ear-tufts are long, although often held flat and then not obvious. The wings are long and conspicuous in flight, when the profile appears lighter and without dark markings. The toes are thinly feathered. The bill is black.

The Long-eared Owl has a broad range extending over the whole width of the Holarctic region: over all of Europe, except for the Mediterranean countries and the far north, across Asia, in North Africa and in isolated regions of East Africa, and also in North America. In this range five subspecies have been identified. The whole of the Eurasian population belongs to the subspecies *A.o. otus*. This is a bird of coniferous and broadleaf forests, but it also inhabits urban woodland enclaves, planted avenues and open landscapes with trees. Its northern population migrates, and that from the Western Palaearctic winters in southern Europe and the Middle East, as far south as the Nile Delta.

By day the Long-eared Owl perches in dense foliage or close to the trunk of the tree and its colours blend into this background. It is active only at night. Its diet consists mainly of rodents, especially field mice, which it catches in open areas, although it also subsists to some extent on small birds. It has a varied range of calls, uttered by both sexes during the nesting season; during the rest of the year it is fairly silent. The territorial call, uttered from a vantage point, especially at the start of the nesting season, is a soft cooing sound — 'hu-huhoo-huhoo' — repeated many times in quick succession.

The Long-eared Owl is a common winterer in most parts of Israel, including the heights of the Negev and the Arava. In some areas flocks of up to 20 individuals may be seen.

The first active nest of a Long-eared Owl recorded in Israel was found in the Hula Valley on 11 April 1969. From then until the mid-1970s this species was considered a vary rare breeder, confined to the north of the country and nesting only in years when there had been a glut of rodents. Since then it has become a fairly common breeder, and has even extended its nesting range to southern parts of Israel. Since the mid-1970s the number of nests observed in various parts — in the Hula Reserve, the Golan and eastern Upper Galilee — has increased steadily, but the most unexpected development has been the establishment of a breeding nucleus at Revivim in the northern Negev. In 1981 several nests were found in the Negev, and in 1982 at least three pairs were breeding in this area, in 1983 12 pairs, and in 1984 seven pairs.

The Long-eared Owl breeds in abandoned nests or among dense foliage. In the clutch there are usually 3-5 eggs, sometimes as many as 7 or even 8. The female incubates from the laying of the first egg for a period of 27-28 days. The chicks hatch blind and covered with white down; 'intermediate plumage' is light grey, darker on the face, and this gradually changes to adult plumage between the third and tenth weeks. The chicks leave the nest at three to four weeks old, but are able to fly only at about five weeks; the parents continue to feed them for a few more weeks.

Short-eared Owl
Asio flammeus

Body length 34.2-37 cm, wing length 30-33.5 cm, wingspan 95-110 cm and weight 250-315 g. Similar to the Long-eared Owl but more squat, with shorter ear-tufts which are seldom conspicuous, rounder face and yellow (not orange) eyes. In flight a dark patch is distinctive at the angle of the wing. The primary tips are darker than those of the Long-eared Owl.

The Short-eared Owl has a Holarctic range, and is also distributed sporadically in South America and on several oceanic islands. Nine subspecies have been identified. The entire Holarctic population belongs to the subspecies *A.f. flammeus*, whose range partially overlaps that of the Long-eared Owl and also extends further north, to northern Europe and Asia and to northern Canada and Alaska. It inhabits damp environments, in saltmarshes, tundra wastes, fields and moors. The Short-eared Owl migrates in winter from most of its nesting areas; the Palaearctic population winters in southern and western Europe, the Middle East, northern and central Africa and southeast Asia, in cultivated areas, on coastal marshes and also in deserts.

The Short-eared Owl is more active in daylight than most other owls, especially in the morning and early afternoon; the remainder of the time it spends resting on the ground, concealed in long grass or among bushes. Its flight is strong and straight, although its wingbeats are slow. Sometimes it circles and dives like a harrier, wings raised in a 'V' shape; sometimes it hovers like a falcon. It feeds primarily on small mammals, and seldom hunts birds.

In Israel this owl is quite common throughout the country as a passage migrant and winter visitor. Migrants are seen in October-November and again between February and April. It winters usually in small flocks between November and March.

The Short-eared Owl is also a very rare breeder in northern and central parts of Israel. Between 1956 and the present only six nests have been found in this country, the most recent being in 1979 in the Golan Heights.

The Short-eared Owl usually nests on the ground, in undergrowth or beneath a bush, and it also gathers nesting material — an exceptional phenomenon among owls. Clutches in Israel contain 5-6 eggs, although in Europe clutches of up to 16 eggs have been recorded. The period of incubation is 24-29 days. The chicks are distinguished by their black face. They leave the nest about two weeks after hatching, but begin to fly only at 24-27 days old.

Order: Caprimulgiformes (Nightjars and Allies)

In this order there are five families, with a total of 100 species. The range of the order is cosmopolitan, although two families are found only in the Neo-tropical region and two others only in the Australasian and Oriental regions. The habitats of members of the order are many and varied, including mountains, deserts, forests and steppes.

Closely related to the owls, members of this order are small to average-sized birds which are active especially at night but also in the twilight hours. Their plumage is soft and the skin of their bodies, except in a few South American species, very thin; the skin is covered with down in the areas bare of feathers. All members of the order have brown and grey colours, with orange, gold and white markings, and are thus endowed with effective camouflage. All have long, pointed wings and a long tail. The legs are very short and used only for standing. The skull is flat and the eyes relatively large. The bill is short, flat at its base and thin at its tip; the corners of the bill reach back beyond the eyes, and thus the gape of the mouth is large, and at the base of the upper mandible there are long and stiff bristles. This combination provides an effective trap for catching aerial insects in flight.

Family: Caprimulgidae (Nightjars)

The most typical family of the order Caprimulgiformes. Its range is semi-cosmopolitan, covering all parts of the world except Antarctica and Australasia, and it is the only family in its order which is represented in the Palaearctic region. In the family there are 19 genera and 74 species, 44 of them belonging to the genus *Caprimulgus*. Three species are found in Israel, one a common passage migrant and the other two accidentals or rare breeders.

Members of this family have long and pointed wings, similar to those of swallows and swifts. They are apt to wheel and turn in the air, although their wingbeats are weak and slow. Their flight is silent. The tail is long and rounded. The neck is short and the head set firmly on the body. The tarsus is very short and feathered. The middle toe is very long and its claw is serrated, as in herons, although the function of this is not clear: it may be intended to clear morsels of food away from the bristles of the bill.

Nightjars have plumage resembling tree bark and the colours of the ground. The male is usually distinguished from the female by white patches on the underside of the primaries and at the tip of the tail. Juveniles are similar to adult females. Nightjars usually live solitarily, although in areas with good supplies of food up to a dozen individuals are liable to gather. They spend most of the hours of the day perched on branches, sitting along the branch and not across it. Sometimes they rest on the ground, relying on their camouflage to such an extent that they do not take to the air until an intruder is almost upon them.

These birds feed almost exclusively on insects, such as moths, beetles etc. Roads which have warmed during the hours of the day, thus attracting large quantities of insects, are a favoured hunting ground. Their diet determines their habitat: allowing the species inhabiting desert and tropical regions to remain resident while obliging the northern populations to migrate; they migrate singly, less frequently in pairs.

Nightjars nest on the ground. At the approach of the nesting season their strident or churring calls are often heard. The female lays 2 eggs on bare ground, without any nest structure. Incubation begins with the first egg and continues for 16-20 days, with both parents sharing the task. The chicks hatch open-eyed and covered with dense and woolly down, camouflage-coloured. They take food from the parents' bills for the first 16-25 days, before beginning to fly and to catch flying insects for themselves.

On account of their diet, nightjars perform a useful service to agriculture.

Egyptian Nightjar
Caprimulgus aegyptius

Body length 25 cm, wing length 19.3-20.8 cm, wingspan 63 cm and weight 68-93 g. A bird of fairly uniform sandy colour, with a white patch on the throat.

The range of the Egyptian Nightjar is Saharo-Sindian with penetration into the Turanian zone, and is divided into four separate areas: one in the Maghreb countries, another in Lower Egypt, a third in southern Iraq and southern Iran, and a fourth in Turkestan. In these areas two subspecies have been identified. It inhabits deserts and steppes, but never far from water. All of its populations migrate and winter in two separate areas, in Sudan on the one hand and in Mali, Nigeria and Upper Volta on the other. The race *C.a. aegyptius* is a passage migrant in Israel.

The Egyptian Nightjar spends much of its time resting on the ground in the shadow of a bush or among furrows and folds. Unlike other nightjars, it also uses its legs for motion. It flies low above the ground, rising higher from time to time to catch an insect. Occasionally it hunts above or near water, and also drinks during flight. It is normally silent, making its voice heard only during the nesting season.

In Israel this is a fairly common passage migrant in the southern Arava: it is seen in the fields of Kibbutz Eilot in October and from mid-March to early May. Until the early 1940s the Egyptian Nightjar was probably a fairly common breeder on the coastal plain. At that time it was possible to hear its courtship call, a prolonged and metallic 'tur-tur', like the sound of a boat motor, and also the sound of its wing-claps in display flight; it nested in overgrown fields of love-grass. Since then only twice have juveniles been found in this country: in June 1947 near Pardes Hanna and on 8 July 1961 near Avihail, both in the northern coastal plain.

Nightjar
Caprimulgus europaeus

Body length 25.5-27.5 cm, wing length 18.5-20 cm, wingspan 57-64 cm and weight 45-60 g. At a superficial glance, in flight it resembles a hawk; its wings are long and sickle-shaped and its tail long. Its plumage is silvery-grey flecked with orange and beige, resembling tree bark or fallen leaves. The male is distinguished by white marks on the underwing and by the white corners of the tail.

The Nightjar's range is Palaearctic and extends over most of Europe, North Africa and the northern Middle East to Lake Baikal in central Asia. In this range six subspecies have been identified. All of its populations migrate, and winter across tropical Africa.

The Nightjar spends much of the daytime resting, with eyes half closed, among branches or in shade. It is especially active during the hours of twilight, pursuing and catching flying insects with great speed and agility.

In Israel the Nightjar is a fairly common passage migrant from the end of August to the beginning of November, and from April to the end of May. These birds belong to the subspecies *C.e. europaeus* and *C.e. meridionalis*. It is possible that the subspecies *C.e. unwini*, which is paler and is also often seen on migration, also winters in southern parts of the country. Sometimes in autumn, especially in the south of the country, Nightjars may be seen arriving from the sea during daylight, although usually they stay close to the shoreline and come onto dry land only at night; in the twilight they appear reddish-brown among the waves of the sea. At this season the bird is rather more gregarious, and several individuals may be seen together.

Nubian Nightjar
Caprimulgus nubicus

Similar to the Egyptian Nightjar, but lighter and more greyish in colour. It is also smaller: body length 21 cm, wing length 15 cm, wingspan 50 cm and weight 50 g.

The Nubian Nightjar is distributed in East Africa, Arabia and Israel. It is a bird of oases and desert fringes, rocky landscapes and plains with trees and bushes. In this country it is apparently resident between Jericho and Eilat, where sightings have been recorded in most months of the year. On 7 June 1980, a large number of Nubian Nightjars, including a newly hatched chick, were observed near Ein Yahav.

Order: Apodiformes (Swifts and Allies)

An order comprising three families and including the most proficient fliers of all birds. The families are Apodidae (swifts), Hemiprocnidae (tree swifts) and Trochilidae (hummingbirds). In the first family there are 18 genera and 85 species; in the second, which is restricted to southeast Asia, there is one genus and four species; in the third, which is restricted to the American continents, to South America in particular, there are 123 genera and 417 species.

In spite of the considerable differences between the families in appearance, colour, shape of bill and behaviour, they are alike in several respects. The wings are well developed, while the legs are to a great extent degenerate. The claws are curved and sharp. Characteristic of all members of the order is the shape of the wing and its bone structure: the humerus is very short and broad, the radius and ulna are also short, while the bones of the carpals are long. The secondaries are short and few in number while the primaries are very long, the longest of any bird in relation to body size. The first or second primaries are the longest, an arrangement giving greater motive power to the muscles.

The breeding biology of members of the order is also similar. The eggs are long with both ends rounded, and white in colour. Clutches are small, usually containing only 2 eggs. The chicks hatch naked and blind and spend a relatively long time in the nest, leaving it only when they are fully capable of flight.

Family: Apodidae (Swifts)

This family consists of 18 genera and 85 species. Their range is cosmopolitan, covering all parts of the world except New Zealand, southern South America and Antarctica, but they are distributed mainly in tropical and subtropical zones. Their habitats are varied and include plains and mountains, forests and deserts, although in general they prefer open environments. In the Palaearctic region there are six species, all of them migratory. In Israel one genus and four species are represented.

A family of small birds superficially resembling swallows, with body length varying from 12 cm to 33 cm. Members of this family are fast and skilful fliers, several of them capable of speeds of up to 150 kph, while one eastern Asian species is the fastest of all birds, flying at 300 kph. Their bodies are solid and spindle-shaped, the neck short and the skull flat. The wings are long and sickle-shaped with very long primaries and a few short secondaries. The tail is short with stiff feathers, and rounded, straight or forked. The body feathers are firm and smooth, and down covers the unfeathered areas.

The bill is short, triangular and curved downward at the tip. The aperture of the mouth is very large and extends beyond the eye, but has no surrounding bristles. The eyes are protected by short and dense tufts of feathers; eyesight is superb. The tarsus is very short but solid, and usually feathered, especially at the front. The leg muscles are very weak, the claws sharp and curved. The leg assists in clinging to walls and to branches of trees, but is of no use for standing or walking.

Swifts are usually uniform grey or brown in colour, with a metallic tint, and with paler marks on the rump and the belly; there is no difference in plumage between the sexes. There is one moult in the year, and this is a prolonged and gradual process, not impairing the faculty of flight.

Swifts have a fast and straight flight, with alternating stages of rapid wingbeats and gliding; they are capable of moving the wings at different rates and thus turning in the air. They fly most hours of the day and also at night, and even copulate in the air. They are gregarious birds, flying in flocks and breeding in colonies. Their colonies are located in a variety of places: woods, caves, rock-fissures, sea-coasts and roofs of buildings. The nests are constructed of various materials collected in flight and held together with saliva.

Swift
Apus apus

Body length 16.5-19 cm, wing length 16.5-18 cm, wingspan 42-48 cm and weight (varying considerably individually and in the same individual from day to day) between 25 g and 50 g.

The Swift has a characteristic flight silhouette: its wings are narrow, long and sickle-shaped, its tail is long and forked. The body is short, spindle-shaped and well suited to flight; the head is broad, flat and compact. It has dark grey plumage and in flight appears deep brown. Only its throat is whitish, this white being more conspicuous in juveniles, which also have paler wing feathers. At the end of summer Swifts appear paler and drabber.

The Swift is distributed over most of Europe, North Africa, the Middle East and central Asia. In this range two subspecies have been described, both of which occur in Israel. It is found in a variety of habitats, from rocky sea-coasts to cliff-faces and around various types of man-made constructions and buildings. Both the subspecies migrate, wintering in tropical Africa south of the Equator, and usually south of latitude 10°S (the moult starts shortly before arrival in winter quarters). This is a summer visitor and passage migrant in Israel.

The Swift feeds on flying insects, especially flies and mosquitoes, which are usually caught at high level; in Europe, where damp conditions predominate, they tend to hunt closer to the ground, like swallows. Swifts are sensitive to rain, and are sometimes forced to retreat to their nests and fast for several days. In fact, a cold and wet climate, and the resulting dearth of insects, are their only real enemies, since in normal conditions no predator other than the Hobby is capable of catching them.

In August and September the birds that have bred in Europe pass through Israel on migration; these belong to the subspecies *A.a. apus* and are slightly darker. They are seen again between the beginning of March and mid-May, especially in mid-March. A few individuals winter in Samaria and the Judean Desert.

In Israel this is a common summer resident in towns and large settlements in northern and central parts of the country. The breeding population, belonging to the subspecies *A.a. pekinensis*, which is

distributed throughout southern Asia from Israel to China, begins to return to this country in mid-February. In the streets of Tel Aviv the first Swifts are usually to be seen between 20 and 25 February, in Jerusalem in early March. The males precede the females by several days. They fly straight to the nesting colonies and roost in the previous year's nest for the first few nights. Females also return to their former nests to roost, and thus the bond between partners is renewed.

Sometimes a pair nests in isolation, but usually Swifts nest in small colonies, in secure places several metres above the ground; in each colony there are 10-30 pairs. In Israel nests are usually built under the eaves of roofs, in gaps between shutters and in holes in walls, and rarely on cliff-faces, in hollow trees or among palm-fronds. Both members of the pair gather nesting materials floating in the air: feathers, hairs, husks of seeds, scraps of paper and dried grass; these materials are stuck together with saliva. The nest itself is round and shallow. Laying takes place in early March and the clutch is usually of 2 eggs, sometimes 3. Incubation begins when the clutch is complete; both parents incubate in turns, the non-incubating partner roosting alongside the nest, and the period of incubation is 18-20 days. The chicks hatch blind and naked. Both parents feed them, with insects 'glued' together in ball-shaped masses, carried in the throat. They stay in the nest for five to eight weeks, according to the availability of food. On leaving the nest they are completely independent, spending all their time in the air, and soon migrating. They attain sexual maturity at the age of three or four years.

The summer population of Swifts remains in the country until the end of June to mid-July.

Pallid Swift
Apus pallidus

Body length 16.5 cm, wing length 17 cm, wingspan 44 cm and weight 40 g. Similar to the Swift but paler, with predominantly brown-greyish plumage and a more prominent white patch on the throat; in active flight the wing movements are slower.

The range of the Pallid Swift extends along the shores of the Mediterranean Sea — in southern Europe, North Africa and the Middle East, also in northern Syria and Iraq and on the shores of the Persian Gulf and the Gulf of Oman. In this range three subspecies have been described. Most of its populations migrate, and winter in the belt of savanna south of the Sahara, between Senegal and Sudan.

In Israel *A.p. pallidus* is a summer resident and a passage migrant. In the autumn migration it is not conspicuous; it is more common in the spring migration, being seen in the region of Eilat from early March to the end of April.

The breeding population arrives in March and stays until July. The Pallid Swift nests only in caves and rock-crevices, sometimes in proximity to the Swift (as in El-Hammah in southern Golan) or alongside the Alpine Swift (as in Ein Avdat in the central Negev). It also breeds in the hills of Sodom in the Dead Sea basin and at Zavitan in the southern Golan. Nesting behaviour is similar to that of the Swift.

Alpine Swift
Apus melba

The largest of the swifts seen in Israel: body length 19-22 cm, wing length 21-23 cm, wingspan 54 cm and weight 66-92 g (the weight may exceed this during the nesting season). The body plumage is brown-greyish in colour and the wing and tail feathers dark brown; the throat and belly are white and separated by a greyish-brown throat-stripe. The tail is forked.

The range of the Alpine Swift extends across the Old World: in southern Europe, the Middle East, the Turanian region, India and also in North, East and southern Africa. In this range eight to ten subspecies have been identified, two of which occur in Israel. All the Western Palaearctic populations winter in tropical Africa.

The Alpine Swift is a gregarious bird, similar in behaviour patterns to the Swift. On its return from winter quarters it flies in dense flocks in canyons, uttering high-pitched trilling cries (sometimes likened to the calls of falcons). Its wing movements are powerful but it is more often seen gliding, with wings swept backwards.

The subspecies *A.m. melba*, which is distributed from southern Europe to the Himalayas, passes through this country on migration between September and November and between March and May. A few individuals of the Alpine Swift also winter in Israel, especially in Samaria and the southern Jordan Valley (recorded in December and January) but occasionally in other regions (for example, five individuals seen in Rosh Hanikra on 16 December 1978).

The paler subspecies *A.m. tuneti*, which ranges from North Africa to Iran, is a fairly common summer resident in Israel between the end of February and July. Nesting colonies are known in Rosh Hanikra and Nahal Nemer in western Galilee, Nahal Dishon and Nahal Amud in eastern Galilee, Nahal Daliot in the Golan Heights, Nahal Mukhmas in the Judean Desert and Ein Avdat in the Negev.

In Israel the Alpine Swift nests only in clefts, rock-crevices and inaccessible ravines. Nesting begins in March and continues until May. The nest is attached to a vertical rock-wall and resembles a flat-topped quarter-sphere, about 7 cm in diameter and 3-5 cm in depth. It is constructed of grass, leaves, feathers and other airborne materials, compressed and stuck together in the form of cone-shaped 'bricks'. In the clutch there are usually 2 eggs, not 3 as in Europe. Both parents incubate for about 20 days. The chick hatches blind and naked. At about four weeks old it is fully feathered, and it flies from the nest at five to six weeks old.

Little Swift
Apus affinis

The smallest swift seen in Israel: body length 12-12.8 cm, wing length 13.5 cm, wingspan 34 cm and weight 22-28 g. It is distinguished by the white rump. The front part of the body is greyish-brown, with the throat whitish; the predominant colours otherwise are grey-black above and blackish-brown with a green tint below. The wings and tail are brown. The tail is short and square, and only slightly forked. The Little Swift has broader wings than those of other swifts. Because of its white rump it can be mistaken for the House Martin, although its body shape and wing movements are different.

The subspecies *A.a. galilejensis* is distributed in North Africa, and in southern Asia from Israel and Lebanon through Arabia to western Pakistan. Seven to ten other subspecies are found in India, southeast Asia and across tropical Africa. Since the beginning of the twentieth century it has extended its range considerably, reaching Spain in 1966. It breeds on cliff-faces, but also on large buildings. A few populations migrate, but most tend to roam rather than migrate as such.

The Little Swift is a very gregarious bird. It flies in flocks, with speed and agility, uttering sharp and sibilant cries, sometimes gliding with wings raised almost vertically and tail fully spread, then regaining height with rapid wingbeats. It nests in colonies numbering scores and even hundreds of pairs, although cases are known of solitary breeding. During the day the swifts disperse over considerable distances, but in the morning and towards evening they congregate in the vicinity of the colony, manoeuvring noisily and at great speed in dense flocks.

In Israel the Little Swift is apparently mainly a summer visitor, although it is resident in a few colonies. In Ayyelet HaShahar in the Hula Valley, where a systematic study of a colony has been conducted, it has emerged that between the months of

October and February the swifts leave their nests at around sunrise and return to them after sunset. Other colonies are found in the valleys of Galilee, the Judean Desert and the Negev; in these it is apparently only a summering bird.

Little Swifts become increasingly active during February; at this time they are also present in the vicinity of the colony during the hours of the day, inspecting and repairing nests and, when necessary, gathering airborne materials for the construction of new ones. The primary nesting sites are in caves and on rock-walls, although man-made constructions, including bridges and houses with broad roof-ledges, are used to an increasing extent for this purpose. The nest is bowl-shaped, with the entrance at the side, and is usually attached to vertical walls or to a ceiling; sometimes, a kind of entrance tunnel is joined to it. In some cases, nests are sited independently; in others, they are constructed in such close proximity that they appear to constitute a single housing unit. The first clutch, usually of 3 eggs, is laid in March. Incubation begins with the first egg and both parents share the task in turn; at night both stay in the nest. The period of incubation is 18-20 days. The Little Swift is double-brooded, and clutches are found as late as June: these are usually of 2 eggs, which are smaller, and the period of incubation is longer (20-22 days), apparently because of the reduction in the numbers of insects at this time and the consequent need for longer absences from the nest. The hatching of the chicks is asynchronous. They hatch blind and naked. Both parents share in the task of feeding. The chicks fly from the nest at six to seven weeks old.

Sometimes, and especially in colonies on man-made buildings, House Sparrows take over the nest, ousting the rightful occupiers. Often the nest is destroyed in the process.

Order: Coraciiformes
(Kingfishers, Bee-eaters, Rollers, Hoopoes)

According to Howard and Moore (1980), this order comprises ten families, 42 genera and 201 species, differing greatly from one another in external appearance. Their body length varies from 9 cm to 165 cm. In spite of these differences, members of the order are united by several characteristics. The three front toes are partially joined, this feature being especially conspicuous in kingfishers and bee-eaters in which the second and third toes are joined for most of their length. The foot is usually very small, bare of feathers and normally covered with large scales. Sometimes there are small feathers on the front of the leg. The claws are sharp but weak. The leg serves only for perching, and movement is limited to flight. The bill is large, sometimes very large, and normally straight. The plumage is stiff and dense.

Coraciiformes are essentially tropical and sub-tropical birds: most are confined to eastern parts of the Old World, although two families are endemic in the New World and representatives of the kingfisher family are found in both Old and New Worlds. Most inhabit woodlands near water; a few species inhabit steppe and even desert. The majority are resident,

and only those which have penetrated temperate zones migrate.

Most species have bright and striking colours. The sexes are similar, or distinguished by only minor differences; juveniles resemble adults. There are two moults in the year, a full one in autumn and a partial one in spring, but coloration varies little between seasons.

These are characteristically noisy birds, often seen perched on branches or other vantage points. They are gregarious to varying degrees. Most feed on prey such as fish, reptiles, amphibians, small mammals and insects, which are swallowed whole; a minority feed on fruit. Members of this order are monogamous birds. They all breed in holes in secluded places, many species in colonies, although laying is not simultaneous; most are single-brooded. All species, except the Hoopoe, have elliptical, white and glossy eggs. The chicks hatch blind and naked, except, again, in the case of the Hoopoe. The development of the chicks is gradual.

In Israel, four families, six genera and eight species are represented.

Family: Alcedinidae (Kingfishers)

Kingfishers are divided into three subfamilies: Daceloninae (tree kingfishers), Cerylinae (small to very large kingfishers with mottled plumage) and Alcedininae (small-bodied kingfishers generally found near water). Members of the last two subfamilies have a narrow pointed bill, while members of the first have a broader and flatter bill, sometimes curved at the tip. The bill is usually red or yellow in colour. They have a cosmopolitan range and the family is absent only from the polar regions and a few oceanic islands. In the family there are 14 genera and 91 species, 40 of them belonging to the genus

Halcyon. Most species live in central and eastern Asia, on islands of the Pacific Ocean and further south to Australia, a few also in tropical Africa; habitats are woodland or water margins. In Israel three species are known, two of them residents and one a passage migrant and winterer; each represents one of the three subfamilies.

These birds are recognisable by the solid and compact body, short neck and large head sometimes with a crest. The wings are rounded, and short or medium in length. The tail is relatively short. Their feathers are glossy, coloured green or bright blue, often with patches and bands of red or white. The sexes are identical or very similar. The legs are very short, and the tarsus small and weak. The front toes are linked together: the outer and the middle for most of their length, the middle and the inner only to the first joint.

Kingfishers are characterised by their low flight over water, strident calls and upright stance. They feed only on live food: those living near water catch fish and aquatic insects, others consume various invertebrates, also amphibians, reptiles and even birds and mammals. They swallow their prey whole; larger creatures are taken to a branch or a rock and there beaten to death.

Kingfishers generally live in territorial pairs. They breed in holes excavated in vertical walls, also in hollow trees. The laying chamber is unlined. In the clutch there are 5-8 eggs. Incubation begins with the first egg and lasts 18-24 days, with both parents participating. The chicks stay in the nest for a relatively long time, three to four weeks; even outside the nest the parents continue to feed them for an appreciable period of time.

Smyrna or White-breasted Kingfisher
Halcyon smyrnensis

Body length 27-30 cm, wing length 12-13 cm, wingspan 40-43 cm and weight 68-100 g. The most common of the kingfishers found in Israel, and the most conspicuous, both in colours and in vocal expression. The head, neck, belly and lesser wing-coverts are chocolate-brown in colour; the throat and breast are white. The back, wings and tail are blue with a turquoise tint; the colour of the wings is especially conspicuous in flight, when a white flash and the black primary tips are revealed. The bill is long and pointed and red in colour; the short legs are also red. Juveniles have crescentic mottling on the white breast, blackish legs and a yellow-tipped blackish bill.

The range of the Smyrna Kingfisher extends across the whole of south Asia, from southern and western Turkey to India, Thailand and the Philippines. In this range three to six subspecies have been identified. All populations are resident, although a few individuals are liable to roam in winter. Its habitats are near water, including marshes and fish-ponds, canals and irrigated fields; it is also often seen in sparse woodland and in landscape gardens. The subspecies known in Israel, *H.s. smyrnensis*, is distributed from Turkey to India.

The Smyrna Kingfisher spends much of its time perched on a high and fixed vantage point in its territory, uttering high-pitched and trilling calls resembling laughter. The call, which lasts about two

seconds and is repeated at short intervals, is one of the loudest calls of any bird in this country. The kingfisher becomes even more vocal in spring, and the rhythm of the call intensifies when partners meet or when an intruder appears. A different call, rapid and strident single or double notes, is heard when the bird flies from one vantage point to another or is suddenly alarmed. This species eats large quantities of mole-crickets, also grasshoppers, crabs, beetles, tadpoles, frogs and other amphibians, reptiles including lizards and snakes, various small birds and partridge chicks. Birds are caught mainly to provide food for the chicks in the nest, which are also fed with small rodents such as house mice and field mice. The Smyrna Kingfisher swoops on its prey from a perch.

Until the 1930s this kingfisher bred in Israel only on the shores of Lake Tiberias and the banks of the Jordan, and visited the coastal plain only in winter. Since then it has broadened its range, probably as a result of the expansion of agriculture and irrigation, and has become a resident in all the valleys of the Mediterranean region of the country. In 1972 it reached the mountain area of western Galilee; in 1976 it summered in Ein Gedi, where previously it had been known only in winter; and by the end of the 1970s it had reached the settlements of the Arava.

The nesting season begins at the end of March. Both partners excavate a horizontal hole in an earth-wall — on the bank of a fish-pond, on a 'kurkar' cliff, in a roadside ditch or the wall of an earth quarry. Usually the aperture is 1.5-2 m from the ground. When completed, the hole is about 7 cm in diameter and 60-120 cm in depth; the nesting chamber is a space about 15 cm in diameter at the end of the hole, and is unlined. Usually each pair nests solitarily, although sometimes nests of neighbouring pairs may be found only a few metres apart. A nest in use can be identified by the remnants of food and the footprints near the entrance of the hole. In the clutch there are 4-6 eggs. Both parents incubate in turn for 18-20 days. The chicks hatch blind and naked and stay in the nest for 26-27 days. During this time remnants of food and pellets accumulate in the nest, creating pungent smells perceptible at considerable distances. Towards the end of their time in the nest the chicks stand at the entrance and wait for their parents to feed them (at this stage they are already in juvenile plumage). They fly from the nest at about 26-27 days old; the parents continue to feed them for a few more weeks.

The Smyrna Kingfisher apparently is double-brooded, the nesting season ending in August.

Pied Kingfisher
Ceryle rudis

Body length 26-29.5 cm, wing length 13.5-14.9 cm, wingspan 46 cm and weight 70-95 g. An all-black-and-white kingfisher with a short crest. The breast, throat and belly are white, the ear-coverts black, and the upperparts black with white feather edges. There is a prominent white supercilium. The male has two black breast-bands, the upper broader and the lower narrower. The female has one broad breast-band, broken in the middle. In juveniles the colour of the band is grey and the throat and cheeks are mottled. The bill and legs are black. In flight, the wings are strikingly black and white.

The range of the Pied Kingfisher extends from Turkey to southeast Asia and from the Nile Delta southward into tropical Africa. In its range three or four subspecies have been identified. The subspecies *C.r. rudis* is common in the Middle East and in Africa; other subspecies are found in south and southeast Asia. All its populations are resident. Its habitats are near running or stagnant water, usually fresh water, but also on the sea-coast.

The Pied Kingfisher is a most efficient fish-catcher, feeding primarily on fish but also on aquatic insects and crabs. It hovers, usually 8-10 m above the water, the body horizontal, head tilted downwards and bill slightly open. When it sights a fish it closes its wings and dives vertically, sometimes submerging completely. Generally, only one in 10 or 15 dives is successful, although sometimes the success rate is higher. The fish is usually carried to the bank and swallowed there, head-first. During the day these kingfishers remain in their territories, but outside the breeding season they tend to roost communally.

In Israel this is a common bird near fish-ponds in all valleys, to about as far south as the line of the Yarkon, around Lake Tiberias and along the Jordan Valley to the Dead Sea, although in winter it may occur also in other places. Up to the 1950s it occurred only along the Jordan system, and in winter along the coast. Its wider distribution today is probably a result of the proliferation of fish-ponds.

The family unit is sometimes retained after the nesting season, and it is then possible to see as many as six birds attempting to fish side by side. Since winter 1980, about 100 Pied Kingfishers from the ponds on the Carmel coast have gathered regularly in the tamarisk grove on the banks of Nahal HaTaninim, to the east of the Roman bridge. They begin to congregate about an hour before sunset, arriving singly or in pairs, with high-pitched chirps and whistles. They roost on the tamarisk branches about 20-30 cm apart. At first light they disperse and return to their territories.

The nesting season begins in May and continues until the end of July. Pied Kingfishers sometimes nest in colonies: in 1979 scores of pairs nested a few score metres apart in Betiha on the northeast shore of Lake Tiberias, and similar behaviour has been observed near the estuary of Nahal HaTaninim on the Carmel coast. The nest is almost invariably in a bank above the water-line, although nests have been found some distance from water. The process of excavation can last as long as two or three weeks. When completed, the nesting hole is 7.5 cm in diameter and 90-200 cm in depth; at the end of the hole is a chamber 15-25 cm in diameter. In the clutch there are usually 4 eggs, sometimes 3 or 5. Incubation begins with the first egg and both parents participate, although the female's contribution is greater. The period of incubation is 18-21 days, and hatching is asynchronous. It appears that the ratio of male to female chicks is about 2:1. The chicks remain in the nest 23-26 days.

This species may sometimes be double-brooded.

In Africa it has been observed that the parents are sometimes helped during the process of nesting, and even in the feeding of the chicks, by 'assistants' — unattached males about one year old, usually the offspring of one or both of the nesting partners; sometimes there are as many as four such assistants. This behaviour, apparently the result of the surplus of males over females, has not yet been observed in Israel.

Kingfisher
Alcedo atthis

The smallest kingfisher in Israel: body length 16.5-18 cm (including 4 cm and more for the bill), wing length 7.2-7.8 cm, wingspan 24-26 cm and weight 20-37 g. It is a very colourful bird, with turquoise above and chestnut below; the throat is white, and the chestnut eye-stripe terminates in a white patch. The male has an all-black bill; the lower mandible of the female's bill is reddish-brown. The legs are red. The tail is very short.

The Kingfisher has a Palaearctic and Oriental range covering most of Europe, North Africa, central, eastern and southern Asia and islands in the Pacific Ocean. It also breeds in Turkey, northern Syria and possibly in northern Lebanon. In this range eight subspecies have been identified. Its habitats are beside lakes and slow-flowing rivers in valleys. Most of its populations are resident. Only those of eastern Europe and of central and eastern Asia, which belong to the subspecies *A.a. atthis*, migrate, wintering in the Mediterranean countries and the Middle East, especially in the Nile Delta, and along the shores of the Persian Gulf and the Arabian

Sea. It always winters near water, sometimes along sea-coasts.

Kingfishers are territorial in their winter quarters and are often to be seen competing over living space. Small fish constitute the major part of their diet, but the Kingfisher also catches various aquatic insects and crabs, including the blind crab *Typhlocaris galilaea* which is found only on the northern shore of Lake Tiberias and nowhere else in the world.

In Israel this is a common passage migrant, especially on the coastal plain, from the end of July. Between 14 August 1978 and 7 October 1978, 1,195 migrating individuals were counted on the shores of northern Sinai, most of them between 29 August and 7 September. The spring migration takes place in March and April, and sometimes continues into May. Between these extreme dates, especially between November and March, scores, possibly hundreds of individuals winter beside fish-ponds, in the Hula Reserve, along the shores of Lake Tiberias and on the Mediterranean coast.

In summer 1983, a nest of this species was reported to have been found in Israel, near Haifa, but details of this discovery are not known.

Family: Meropidae (Bee-eaters)

In this family of small to medium-sized birds weighing up to 60 g, there are three genera and 24 species, 21 of them belonging to the genus *Merops*. In Israel three species are represented, all members of this genus. Bee-eaters are distributed especially in tropical areas of the Eastern Hemisphere, more than half of them across Africa. A few species have also penetrated subtropical and temperate zones. They are absent from the New World. Species inhabiting tropical rainforests are resident; the remainder are migratory.

These are very colourful birds, predominantly green. The cheeks and throat are of striking colour, different from the colour of the breast; this difference is sometimes accentuated by an intermediate black bar. All species have a black eye-stripe, extending from the bill to the nape. The sexes are usually similar in plumage, although juveniles are paler. The plumage is soft and dense. Bee-eaters are long-bodied birds: the wings are triangular in shape, long and pointed in the migratory species and relatively short in the resident species. The tail is long, and in many species the two central feathers are very elongated and pointed at the tips (these are longer in the males and absent in juveniles). The bill is thin, long, delicate and laterally compressed. It is slightly downcurved, and at the base there are short bristles. The legs are short and serve mainly for perching; the tarsus is very short and the sole weak.

The species which are resident in rainforests usually live in solitary pairs, while those inhabiting open environments tend to be gregarious throughout the year. They feed on various kinds of insects, especially wasps and bees. The prey is carried to a rock or a branch, where it is held between the mandibles in a vice-like grip; the insect's head is beaten on the 'anvil' and its abdomen crushed, sometimes the whole of the sting is detached. The bird then tosses its prey in the air and swallows it. Bee-eaters also feed on locusts, grasshoppers and dragonflies. The undigested parts of the insect shells are discharged several times a day in the form of black and odourless pellets, 1-3 cm in length; when fresh the pellet is crystalline, but it rapidly disintegrates.

All bee-eaters nest in long burrows excavated by both partners. In some species the nesting pair has outside help in excavating the hole and in feeding the chicks; the 'assistants' are often the male offspring of the same pair from the previous year.

Bee-eater
Merops apiaster

Body length 25-29 cm, wing length 14-15.3 cm, wingspan 44-49 cm and weight 55-60 g. The bill is about 3 cm long, slightly curved and black. The iris of the adult is red. The body is compact and the wings long and pointed. A bird of very colourful plumage: the underparts are bluish-green, the crown, mantle, upper back, secondaries and coverts chestnut-brown. The underwing is chestnut and edged with black. The lower back is golden, showing as a conspicuous 'V' shape in flight. The throat is yellow, the eye-stripe and narrow breast-band are black. The tail is long, bluish-grey above and greyish below: in the male the two central feathers are up to 2.5 cm longer than the rest; they are less conspicuous in the female, whose overall colours are slightly paler (neither of these features, however, is adequate for distinguishing between the sexes in the field). Juveniles lack the elongated tail feathers and are paler, with green replacing the chestnut and gold; the iris is black, changing gradually to brown, and turning red at about one year of age.

The Bee-eater has the most northerly range of its family and is the only one to penetrate Europe. It is a monotypic species, extending from North Africa and the Iberian peninsula, through the Mediterranean countries and the Middle East, over southern and central Europe to Lake Balkhash in central Asia. All of its populations migrate and winter across tropical

Africa, from the Equator to South Africa (where a few nesting colonies have been found in which Bee-eaters have bred between September and January and then disappeared, supposedly migrating to Europe to breed again). One individual found in South Africa had been ringed in the Ukraine, a distance of 8,000 km. A few individuals also winter in the Arabian peninsula. The Bee-eater inhabits open areas with scattered trees, often near water. In Israel it is a common summer visitor and passage migrant.

During the day Bee-eaters spend much of their time perched on electricity and telephone cables, periodically launching themselves off to hunt their prey. They consume large numbers of worker honeybees. This species is thus, justifiably, considered a pest, but it also eats wasps, including the eastern wasp *Vespa orientalis* which preys on bees, and to this extent is beneficial. It also eats tree-bees, flying ants, termites, flies, beetles, butterflies and moths, usually caught in rapid and aerobatic flight. Smaller items, such as ants, are swallowed in flight. It is a gregarious bird, usually found in flocks ranging in size from a few to scores of individuals; during migration and in winter quarters flocks of hundreds of individuals may be seen congregating to roost in trees.

The passage migrants are seen in all parts of Israel between mid-August and mid-October, especially during September. The spring migration begins in mid-March, reaches a peak during April and continues until mid-May. They fly straight, and usually at high level, but their contact calls — constant piping cries — are clearly heard both day and night. Alarm calls, agitation calls and others are also distinguishable.

In Israel this is a common summer resident, arriving at the end of March-April and departing in the second half of August. In the past the Bee-eater bred in most areas of the Mediterranean region of the country, especially in valleys and on high ground. Since the end of the 1950s its population has diminished, probably owing to pesticides, and it became confined mainly to the eastern slopes of the mountain ridge: along the Jordan and in the river valleys draining eastward from the slopes — Nahal Dishon, Nahal Amud, Nahal Tabor and others. From the early 1980s it has again been found as a breeder on the coastal plain. Large colonies are also known in the region between Erez and Be'er Sheva, at the southernmost limit of its range.

Preparations for nesting begin about two weeks after the return from winter quarters. The species breeds in colonies, each comprising scores of pairs. The nest is a horizontal tunnel in a vertical bank of a river or a wadi, on a steep slope or in an embankment thrown up by bulldozers during road con-

struction. Both partners share the task of excavating the hole. Initially two or three holes are started, only one of which will be developed, so that of the scores of holes in a colony only about a third will be occupied. The process of excavation usually takes place during April, sometimes in late March or early May, and the work is normally done in the morning and the early evening; the rate of progress may be as high as 30 cm a day, although work is sporadic and the excavation process takes about two weeks to complete. The width of the hole is about 12.5 cm, its height 10.5 cm, and the length of the tunnel 180 cm or more. The nesting chamber at the end of the tunnel is 15 cm in height and 20 cm in diameter. The distance between active nests, which are recognisable by the footprints near the entrances, is 2-3 m.

Laying begins when the nest hole is completed. The clutch is usually of 6 eggs, although the number can vary between 4 and 7. Incubation begins sporadically with the first egg; both parents participate, although it seems that the female's contribution is greater. At night both adults roost in the nest, the female incubating. The period of incubation is 19-20 days. The chicks hatch blind and naked. As they grow larger, they advance to the nest entrance and wait to be fed. Both parents feed them, and in some cases it has been observed that this task is also shared by non-breeding male 'assistants', a phenomenon recorded in Israel but yet to be studied in detail. The chicks fly from the nest at about 30 days old, but return to it to roost for the first few days, and the parents continue to feed them outside the nest for a few more weeks.

The Bee-eater is single-brooded, although sometimes replacement clutches are laid. From some areas, including the coastal plain, the species disappears immediately after nesting is completed; in other regions it stays for a few more weeks, congregating in trees for communal roosting.

Blue-cheeked Bee-eater
Merops superciliosus

Slightly larger than the Bee-eater: body length 27-31 cm, wing length 14.5-16 cm, wingspan 46-49 cm and weight 32-45 g. A bird of almost all-green plumage. The cheeks and forehead are blue, the throat chestnut-orange, and it lacks a black breast-band. The underwings are chestnut. The central tail feathers are considerably longer than those of the Bee-eater and extend up to 8 cm beyond the end of the tail; all the tail feathers are greyish on the undersides.

The Blue-cheeked Bee-eater is distributed in North Africa south of the Atlas Mountains, from the Levant to Pakistan and further north along the

rest of the tail (this figure included in the overall body length). Its plumage is mostly green, but the throat, forehead and cheeks are a metallic blue. It has a black eye-stripe and a black stripe at the base of the throat. The tail feathers are greyish-khaki. The legs are black and the iris red.

The Little Green Bee-eater has a wider range than all other species of bee-eater, extending across tropical Africa from the shores of the Atlantic Ocean in Senegal to Lake Nyasa and the Sudanese coast, through western and southern Arabia and eastward along the shores of the Persian Gulf and southern Afghanistan to India, southeast Asia and Vietnam. In this range seven or eight largely resident subspecies have been identified, differing from one another in colour of throat, cheeks and crown and in the length of the central tail feathers. These extend about 8 cm beyond the rest of the tail in the African subspecies and 5 cm in the Asiatic subspecies; they are thus distinguished from the subspecies found in Israel, *M.o. cyanophrys*, which is distributed mainly in western and southern Arabia.

This bee-eater is not gregarious; normally it lives in separate pairs and is only rarely seen in small flocks. It tends to hunt from a vantage point, swooping on its prey and usually returning to the same perch. Occasionally it hunts insects on the ground. It consumes insects of various kinds, including large quantities of flying ants. It is not so timid as other species of bee-eater, and it can be approached to within close range. Its call, usually heard in flight, is a chattering sound, more melodious than those of the other species.

Only in 1955 was it discovered that the Little Green Bee-eater breeds in Israel, when a small population was identified in an oasis in the southern Arava (Yotveta). At the end of the 1950s several pairs were also breeding in the fields of Kibbutz Eilot. Since then, and apparently in parallel with increased agricultural development of the Arava and the consequent proliferation of insects, its range has extended and broadened. On 14 October 1976 at least five individuals were seen in Neot HaKikar on the south side of the Dead Sea, and in Spring 1977 nests were found there; on 29 December 1983, eight to ten individuals were seen on the northern shores of the Dead Sea. Today the Little Green Bee-eater also breeds on the outskirts of Eilat. In Israel its distribution is now limited to the Arava.

Nesting takes place in May-June, in a tunnel in sand-hills or damp earth. The length of the tunnel is 50-160 cm and its diameter 5-6 cm. The clutch is of 3-5 eggs, but little is known of the breeding biology. Outside the nesting season, parents and offspring tend to roost together in the nest.

shores of the Caspian Sea to the Aral Sea and Lake Balkhash in central Asia. It is also found in various parts of tropical Africa. In this range four subspecies have been identified. (According to some authorities, the southern Palaearctic population is classified as a separate species *Merops persicus*, and the name *Merops superciliosus* attached to the tropical populations in East Africa.) The Blue-cheeked Bee-eater inhabits hotter and drier areas than the Bee-eater: open environments with scattered trees, river valleys, oases and lake margins. All of the Palaearctic populations migrate, and most winter in tropical Africa, especially between Tanzania and South Africa. Its behaviour is similar to that of the Bee-eater.

In Israel this is a fairly rare passage migrant between the end of July and October with occasional sightings in November, and again in March and April. In the past it was quite a common breeder along the Jordan from the Bet She'an Valley to the Dead Sea, estimated at several hundred pairs (about a third of the population of Bee-eaters); no trace remains of this population. During the past 20 years only one nest of the Blue-cheeked Bee-eater has been found: near Rafa in northern Sinai on 30 June 1979.

Little Green Bee-eater
Merops orientalis

The smallest bee-eater found in Israel: body length 20-22 cm (including 2.5 cm for the bill), wing length 9.5 cm, wingspan 30 cm and weight 18-20 g. The central tail feathers protrude 3-3.5 cm beyond the

Family: Coraciidae (Rollers)

The distribution of this family is confined to the Old World. There are two genera and 11 species, of which seven inhabit sub-Saharan Africa and only four inhabit the warmer sectors of Eurasia, and also Australasia and the Solomon Islands. In Israel one species is represented.

This is a family of dove-sized and brightly coloured birds in which shades of blue are dominant. The sexes are similar. In shape they resemble crows: the body is compact, the head large and the neck short. The bill is thick and strong, broad at the base and hooked at the tip. At the corners of the bill are stiff bristles. The legs are short, and the front of the tarsus is covered with large scales. The tail is long, the wings long and broad. Rollers are good fliers and in the courtship season they perform impressive antics, including spins and aerobatic rolls. By contrast, the legs are so weak that motion on the ground is restricted to clumsy hopping.

Rollers are usually solitary or found in pairs. They spend much of their time perched on vantage points from which they swoop to catch various invertebrates and small vertebrates. They are hole-nesters, but a few species nest in artificial holes or in hollow trees. In the clutch there are 2-4 white eggs; both parents incubate. The chicks hatch naked, stay three to four weeks in the nest, and are fed by both parents.

Roller
Coracias garrulus

A blue bird similar in shape to a small crow: body length 30-32 cm, wing length 18.8-20 cm, wingspan 66-73 cm and weight 105-146 g. The head, neck and underparts are blue; the wing-coverts are turquoise in colour and especially conspicuous in flight, when they are framed and accentuated by the blue-black primaries and secondaries. The back and scapulars are chestnut-brown. The tail is mostly bluish-green; the outer feathers are longer than the others and tipped blue-black. Between July and November the Roller undergoes a full moult and takes on winter plumage: its colours tend more towards green-blue and the chestnut areas turn a darker shade of brown (it is seen in this plumage in Israel during the autumn migration). In both plumages there is virtually no distinction between male and female. Juveniles are darker than adults, more grey-brown in colour.

The Roller has a Palaearctic range, extending over North Africa, southern, central and eastern Europe, and through the Middle East to central Asia. Two subspecies have been described. It inhabits open environments, pasture meadows and grasslands dotted with trees, hill slopes and sparse woodland. All its populations migrate in autumn, wintering in savanna regions in eastern and southern Africa. The subspecies *C.g. garrulus*, which is found in the Western Palaearctic part of the range except Iraq and southern Iran, occurs in Israel.

The Roller usually lives alone or in pairs and is not so gregarious as other members of its order. Its flight is straight: it beats its wings rapidly and often glides. Its call is loud and harsh, similar to that of a crow. It feeds on beetles, centipedes, crickets, frogs and lizards, also bird chicks and young mammals. During the autumn migration it may also consume various fruits that are ripening at that time.

In Israel the Roller is a frequent passage migrant across the country, in autumn between early September and October. It is much more conspicuous in the spring migration, especially in the region of the eastern watershed, between the end of March and the end of May, with a peak in the second half of April. At this time it migrates in loose flocks, by day and apparently also at night. At this season scores of Rollers are seen strung out on telephone and electricity cables, a few tens of metres apart, in places such as the Jordan Valley, the slopes of Upper Galilee and the Hula Valley.

In the past the Roller was also a common summer resident between April and September in valleys of the Mediterranean regions of Israel, but since the end of the 1950s this population has decreased considerably, and today the bird is a rare breeder.

A short time after return from winter quarters the courtship display flights begin: the male performs impressive aerobatics, soaring in the air and then diving, rolling and spinning while cawing loudly. In this country nesting usually takes place in the months of May-June. Rollers nest in various holes, including hollow trees: thus they have nested in old Tabor oaks on the coastal plain, and in the eucalyptus groves near the Hula Reserve. In Israel they tend especially to nest in embankments, usually in the abandoned nests of kingfishers and bee-eaters, which they enlarge. Often a pair nests in proximity to an active colony of bee-eaters. In the clutch there are 4-5 eggs. Incubation begins before the clutch is complete, and both parents participate; the period of incubation is 18-19 days. The chicks hatch naked and blind and develop gradually. They leave the nest at 26-28 days old, and the parents continue to feed them for some time longer.

Chicks are sometimes found in nests as late as the end of June, but these are probably the offspring of replacement clutches, since the Roller has only one brood per year.

Family: Upupidae (Hoopoes)

A family in which there is one genus and a single species, the Hoopoe. In anatomical structure the Hoopoe is similar to other members of the order Coraciiformes, but differs in a few features such as the elliptical shape and the colours of the egg, and the fact that the chicks are covered with down. The structure of the leg is more similar to that of the Passeriformes than to that of members of the Coraciiformes: the tarsus is relatively long and covered with scales both at the front and at the rear; the claw of the rear toe is longer than that of the foretoes.

Hoopoe
Upupa epops

Body length 26-30 cm, wing length 14.2-15.3 cm, wingspan 42-46 cm and weight 46-70 g. A bird of striking colours and appearance: its overall colour is brown-pink while the wings and tail are barred black and white. From the base of the bill to the nape there is a crest of long feathers, also brown-pink in colour but with black tips (the crest-feathers are up to 7 cm in length); this is sometimes folded flat, sometimes spread like a fan. The wing is broad and rounded, the tail is straight-tipped. The bill is dark brown, and slender and curved, 4.7-5.5 cm in length and longer than the diameter of the head. The legs are greyish and the iris light brown. The sexes are similar, although the black and white colours of the female are less conspicuous; the male is also larger than the female. Juveniles are similar to adults, although their colours tend to be pink rather than brown and the bars on the wings and tail are more greyish-white.

The Hoopoe has a trans-Palaearctic range extending over the whole breadth of Europe and Asia except the northern regions, and from North Africa and the Iberian peninsula to Korea and eastern China. It is also distributed in southeast Asia and in all parts of tropical Africa, except the evergreen forests of the Congo basin. In this range ten sub-species have been identified. In all parts of the Palae-arctic region the subspecies is *U.e. epops*, of which most populations migrate in autumn and winter in the belt of savanna in central Africa. The Hoopoe inhabits open environments: plains, pasture meadows, cultivated fields, landscape gardens, plant-ations and urban woodland enclaves.

The Hoopoe is usually found alone or in pairs. Its flight is hesitant and fluttering, like that of a huge butterfly, on an undulating course, at relatively low level. It is often seen on the ground. The vigour with which it pecks is astonishing in view of the delicacy of the bill, which has no tactile nerve endings (unlike bills of waders) but is purely a digging instrument,

designed for the exposure of prey: caterpillars of various insects (especially of moths), worms and sometimes even small reptiles. The Hoopoe does not drink, but sometimes dips its food in water. While searching for food it has no fear of man and can be approached to within close range.

In circumstances of agitation, curiosity or suspicion, the Hoopoe erects the feathers of its crest; on seeing a Barn Owl, a snake or some other threat, it emits panting sounds. The territorial call of the male, often heard in the spring and uttered from some prominent natural feature, is a clipped and far-carrying 'hoo-hoo-hoo' sound, less melodious than that of the Cuckoo, repeated at short intervals. The female has a rapid and metallic rasping call.

In Israel this is a common migrant in autumn, between the beginning of August and early November. In the spring it is sometimes seen as early as the end of January, but usually migration takes place between mid-February and mid-May and especially during April.

The Hoopoe is also a resident bird in suitable habitats in the Mediterranean region, especially in landscape gardens within settlements, and in settle-ments throughout the Negev. Until the 1940s it was a rare breeder in Israel. Since then the breeding population has expanded and proliferated consider-ably from the original nucleus on the coastal plain, apparently as a result of the development of culti-vated land and pasture meadows; in the mid-1950s it even reached Jerusalem. At about the same time, the individuals breeding on the coastal plain began to remain in the country in winter. This trend gradually spread to other areas, and today the Hoopoe has apparently become a resident bird in all its areas of distribution in Israel.

Courtship sometimes begins as early as the end of February, but normally not until the end of March/early April. Nesting sites in Israel are in hollow trees, in hollow stone walls, in discarded packing cases and domestic furniture, and especially in spaces under roof tiles. Hoopoes do not build a nest as such, but pile up the nesting materials — feathers, stalks, dried grass etc. — around the eggs. In the clutch there are 5-6 eggs. The female incubates alone from the laying of the first egg for a period of 17-19 days. The chicks hatch blind, but with long greyish down on the upper parts of the body; their bill is short. Both parents feed them from the moment of hatching. If one parent senses that it is being watched or that there is an enemy close by, it is liable to stand motionless, waiting with great patience for the threat to pass. The chicks, when danger threatens them, hiss and exude a malodorous liquid from the preen glands; at the same time they disgorge semi-digested food which contributes further to the stench. During nesting the oil gland of the female is also converted to a smell-producing gland, and the droppings of the chicks are not removed from the nest. Together, these factors create such a pungent odour that cats and other predators are dissuaded from attacking Hoopoes and their nests. The chicks leave the nest at 22-24 days old.

It is possible that the Hoopoe sometimes has two broods.

Order: Piciformes (Woodpeckers and Allies)

An order comprising six families and 381 species, including woodpeckers, toucans and honeyguides. Their size varies between 7.5 cm and 60 cm. Members of the different families differ considerably in appearance and behaviour, but are united in one order on account of similarities in skull and skeletal structure, musculature and the anatomy of the leg, with two front and two rear toes: the first and fourth toes (inner and outer) are approximately parallel and point backwards. The wing is broad and rounded.

The distribution of the order is cosmopolitan, being absent only from the polar regions and Australasia and a few oceanic islands. Most species are resident. All members of the order inhabit woodlands, and most tend to be solitary. Their flight is undulating and short-range. Most feed exclusively on insects. All Piciformes breed in holes: on the ground, in trees or in termite nests. The nest is either unlined or lined only to a minor extent. The eggs are white and rounded and both parents incubate; the chicks hatch blind and almost invariably naked.

Family: Picidae (Woodpeckers)

In this family there are 26 genera and 204 species, distributed in most parts of the world; in Israel two species are represented. Body length varies between 9 cm and 55 cm. These birds are well adapted to climbing on the trunks of trees: in addition to the arrangement of the toes, the claws are sharp and curved; the stiff tail is also an aid, having 12 pinions, strong and pointed at the tips, the two outer ones very short and hidden by the tail-coverts. The two central tail feathers are the last to be moulted, not the first as in other birds, and thus their supportive function is maintained. Woodpeckers have a straight, hard and pointed bill, shaped like a chisel. It is used both to excavate nesting holes in tree trunks and to seek out food under the bark. In order to facilitate the digging process the muscles of the neck are very strong; to protect the brain from jarring there is a considerable degree of ossification between the eye sockets, and strong muscles attached to the bill absorb the counter-shocks. The bodies of woodpeckers are strong and compact; the tarsus is short.

All species feed on insects in various stages of development. To this end they have a long sticky tongue, with barbs at the sides; this is inserted beneath the bark and insects become stuck to it. The structure of the tongue is also unique: it is capable of wrapping around and enveloping the bodies of larger insects, and can protrude to a considerable distance — to the same length as that of the bill.

All members of the family nest in tree holes, roosting in them even outside the nesting season. The period of incubation is very short: 8-13 days. The chicks stay in the nest for 24-28 days.

Woodpeckers are generally beneficial birds, destroying large quantities of tree pests and wood-boring insects. They also supply refuge and nesting sites for other species of birds.

Syrian Woodpecker
Dendrocopos syriacus

The only true woodpecker found in Israel: body length 21.5-24 cm (including 2.6-3 cm for the bill), wing length 11.8-13.5 cm, wingspan 34-39 cm and weight 66-79 g. This bird is very representative of its family. Its plumage is black and white and the undertail-coverts and vent are pinky-red. The male has a red patch on the nape, while the juvenile is distinguished by its red crown and a pinky-red mark on the breast.

In origin this is an eastern Mediterranean species, with distribution ranging from Turkey, Syria, Lebanon and Israel to Iraq and Iran. During the last century the Syrian Woodpecker has broadened and extended its range, probably as a result of agricultural developments, and is today also found in Bulgaria, Hungary and Austria. It is resident throughout its range. Its habitats are in woodlands and groves, plantations and urban parks.

The Syrian Woodpecker has an undulating flight — rapid wingbeats alternating with glides; usually it flies over short distances and only rarely does it emerge into open spaces without trees. It is not often seen on the ground, landing only to hunt for ants, or to drink. It is known to peck at irrigation sprinklers, causing considerable damage and annoyance. Like most woodpeckers, this species subsists primarily on the insects found beneath the bark of trees. The Syrian Woodpecker also consumes various fruits, especially almonds in spring and pecans in autumn. It is especially partial to the latter, plucking them from the tree or hanging upside down and using the feet to extract them from the pod. The nut is taken to a feeding station — a branch, a ledge or a hole dug specifically for the purpose — where the shell is cracked open with the bill and the kernel eaten. The Syrian Woodpecker also eats the pips of citrus fruits (*Melia azedarach*) and even seeds from pine cones. It rarely needs to drink.

This species lives in pairs, in territories varying in size according to the availability of food. Woodpeckers are very secretive outside the breeding season, and even the partners in a pair are rarely seen together; sometimes they even show signs of hostility towards each other. During this period each roosts in its own roosting hole, which is jealously guarded.

In Israel the Syrian Woodpecker was formerly confined to hilly areas in the Mediterranean region, especially the groves of Upper Galilee and the forests of Tabor oaks in western Lower Galilee, Carmel, Samaria and the hills of Hebron. Its range has extended considerably since the 1930s, and at about the time of the Second World War it was seen in large numbers on the coastal plain, apparently as a result of the proliferation there of a species of small beetle inhabiting eucalyptus trees. Since the end of the 1950s its population has received a further boost, probably associated with the development of the cultivation of pecan groves, and today it is found in most parts of the Mediterranean region of the country.

Courtship begins as early as the end of December or early January and continues until shortly before laying (in the second half of April). Territory is claimed and the pair bond consolidated by loud drumming by both sexes. During this period fighting is liable to erupt between two males or two females. The bird is also very vocal at this time of the year, with a prolonged and guttural territorial cry, usually uttered in flight, and a variety of sharp and high-pitched chirping calls, expressing alarm or agitation. The pair often adopts an existing nest, which is usually the roosting hole of the male, but sometimes a new nest is excavated. Nests are usually in trees such as casuarina, carob, eucalyptus and mulberry, at a height of 1.5-6 m above the ground. Holes are normally made in the central trunk, although branches of sufficient diameter may also be used. The excavation of a new nest begins in mid-March and continues for 10-28 days, with the male performing most of the task. The diameter of the entrance hole is 4-5 cm. Once the nest site — old or new — has been chosen, both partners stay in its vicinity for most hours of the day. Syrian Woodpeckers have been known to adopt nestboxes.

Laying normally takes place in the second half of April, although sometimes it is delayed until the end of June. The clutch is usually of 4 eggs, sometimes 5, seldom 3. Incubation begins when the clutch is complete; the task is shared equally during the hours of the day, but only the male incubates at night. The incubation period is very short in relation to the size of the egg: no more than 11 days. The chicks hatch blind and naked, and are fed by both parents, with various insects. They remain in the nest for a relatively long period, beginning to leave it only at 25-26 days old; sometimes they return to the nest to roost. Even after they have learned to fly, the parents continue to feed them for a further three or four weeks. They take on adult plumage with the first autumn moult.

Wryneck
Jynx torquilla

Body length 16-17 cm, wing length 8.6-9.3 cm, wingspan 26 cm and weight 25-38 g. A bird differing considerably from the true woodpeckers: its body is long, its bill short (1.3 cm) but strong, the upperparts are brown-grey and resemble tree bark, while the underparts are paler and narrowly and delicately barred dark-brown. Its colours provide excellent camouflage. Its feathers are soft, including the feathers of the slightly rounded tail; the wings are short and rounded. The sexes are similar. In spite of differences in appearance from true woodpeckers, the arrangement of the foot is the same — with two front and two rear toes. The tongue is also long and extensible, but is not barbed.

The Wryneck has a trans-Palaearctic range from

the Iberian peninsula and southern Scandinavia to eastern China and northern Japan. In this range seven to nine subspecies have been identified. Its habitats are in broadleaf and mixed forests, in woodland clearings and on riverbanks, but it is also found in urban woodland enclaves. Generally this is a timid bird which is not easily observed. Most of its populations migrate, and those of the Western Palaearctic region winter in savannas across Africa north of the Equator.

This species' staple food is ants, termites, grasshoppers and beetles. It also seeks insects among leaves and branches. Its flight is undulating.

In Israel the subspecies *J.t. torquilla* is a fairly common passage migrant in autumn between September and October, although the vanguard is seen as early as August and the rearguard as late as November. Usually it migrates singly but there have been records of a dozen or more individuals gathering on a tree and uttering clear and high-pitched contact calls similar to those of a falcon. During migration they are less timid and more easily observed. Apparently the Wryneck is also a rare winterer in Israel (a few have been recorded during December and January). In the spring migration it is seen from early February to April. At this season it is easily observed in settlements in the Arava, where it has nowhere to hide; here it gathers its food on the lawns.

The Wryneck owes its name to the peculiar manner in which it twists its head around at times of alarm or in courtship displays.

Order: Passeriformes (Songbirds/Passerines)

The largest order in the class Aves, including more than 5,200 out of the world's total of approximately 8,900 bird species. In the order there are some 75 families grouped into four sub-orders. In Israel only the sub-order Oscines, comprising 41-53 families with about 4,000 species throughout the world, is represented. In this country 22 families containing 190 species are found.

Songbirds are distributed in all parts of the world, including the remotest of islands, and in all continents except Antarctica. They are landbirds, found in all dry-land environments.

Most passerines are small birds, a minority being of moderate size: their body length is 7.5-64 cm and their weight varies between 5 g and 110 g. Also known as perching birds, all members of the order have four toes which have evolved for gripping branches; this grip is powerful even when the bird is asleep. The wings are well developed. All species found in this country have ten primaries, although the first is small and usually difficult to locate, and nine secondaries. In the tail there are usually ten, sometimes 12 and occasionally as many as 14 feathers. In all songbirds the primary and tail feathers are moulted from the centre outwards, the secondaries in the reverse direction. Most songbirds have rather drab colours. Plumage often differs between the sexes, the male being brighter and more conspicuous.

The diet of songbirds is usually composed of insects, fruits and seeds, although some species, such as shrikes and crows, also feed on reptiles and even small birds. Sunbirds consume nectar of plants. All songbirds are efficient fliers. On the ground most species hop, but some walk. The voice constitutes a vital means of contact, and is also useful in distinguishing between similar species.

The nest is usually among vegetation, in bushes or trees, sometimes on the ground, among rocks and even in man-made buildings. The norm is a new nest for every breeding cycle, although a few species, including swallows, crows and sunbirds, use the same nest repeatedly. The usual nesting materials are thin branches, twigs, delicate roots, leafy stems and straw, and the nest is normally lined with hair, feathers and husks of seeds. Laying takes place in the early morning, and one egg is laid every day. The size of the clutch varies from 1 egg (in a few Australian species) and 2 (most species inhabiting tropical regions) to 15 eggs (tits in northern Europe); the norm is 3-6. The species breeding in Israel lay smaller clutches than their European counterparts. The period of incubation is short, usually 12-14 days. The chicks hatch blind and either naked or covered with sparse down. They remain in the nest throughout their development and the parents continue to brood them in the initial stages. They have a colourful mouth, sometimes with dark markings, designed to stimulate the feeding instinct of the parents. The chicks usually stay in the nest for about the same length of time as the period of incubation. (This rule does not apply to larger species such as crows nor to hole-nesters, which are slow to leave the nest, while ground-breeders, such as larks, stay in the nest a shorter time than the period of incubation and usually leave it before they are capable of flight). The parents continue to feed them for a few days after leaving the nest.

In many cases there is more than one brood in a year. Most songbirds reach sexual maturity at about one year old, although some species breed at three or four months of age.

Family: Alaudidae (Larks)

In this family there are 19 genera and 80 species. The largest number of species is found in Africa, which is the origin of the family. Today members of the family are distributed throughout the Old World and one species has even penetrated North America. A family of terrestrial songbirds of open environments. Their colours are usually grey-brown, and the sexes are normally similar. Larks are small to average-sized birds: body length 11-21 cm. The rear toe is long and its claw long, sharp and usually straight. The bill is usually short, straight and pointed, as in the Skylark or the Shore Lark; sometimes it is thick and solid or long, thin and curved. Larks have one moult in the year, after breeding.

Larks are ground birds: they roost in hollows in the ground. They walk and run on the ground, and do not hop as do most songbirds. They seldom perch on branches, usually doing so only to sing. Larks are birds of deserts, steppes and meadows, and only the Woodlark inhabits edges of groves and forests. Felling of forests in Europe has extended the habitats of some species.

The flight is clumsy and somewhat heavy. Sometimes larks sing from high in the air; in cold weather and in the cooler hours of the day they sing on the ground. They are capable of imitating the calls of other birds. Most species eat both insects and seeds; insects form the major ingredient of their diet in summer, and in winter more seeds tend to be eaten. Even in the most arid areas larks do not require a water source and can subsist on drops of dew, although they do not hesitate to drink when water is available. They do not bathe in water, but wallow in sand.

Larks nest on the ground, although the Hoopoe Lark sometimes nests in a bush. The nest is usually partially concealed in the shade of a bush or a rock, often with small stones piled on one side of it. The eggs are well camouflaged against the ground. There are 3-6 eggs in the clutch, usually 5. The female incubates alone for a period of 12-14 days. The chicks hatch blind and covered with sparse yellowish down which is especially long on the head and the back, providing effective camouflage. The chicks leave the nest at 9-11 days old. At this stage they are incapable of flight, and spend their first few days hiding in foliage. Juveniles have mottled feathers, changing to adult plumage in the course of the first year.

In Israel 12 genera and 15 species are known.

Desert Lark
Ammomanes deserti

Body length 16-16.8 cm, wing length 9.6-11 cm, wingspan 32.5 cm and weight 19-26 g. The Desert Lark has no striking characteristics, and it is easier to describe it in negative terms: it has no crest; it is uniform in coloration, without streaking or speckling; there is no black or white in the tail. In Israel its colouring is sandy-brown above and whitish-brown below. In the tail there are a few dark, but not black, feathers. The bill is quite thick and the first primary is relatively long, about a third of the length of the second. Juveniles resemble adults and are not speckled as are the juveniles of most lark species.

The Desert Lark has a typical Saharo-Sindian range: from Algeria, through Sinai and Arabia to the Sind Desert in northwest India, with penetration into the deserts of the Horn of Africa. In this range 25 subspecies have been identified, differing in coloration: in Arabia, a light phase living on sand has been observed alongside a dark phase living on basalt, in separate habitats. (This phenomenon is apparently the result of natural selection, developed as a response to predation, especially on the part of falcons; in areas where predators are few, in Chad for example, dark individuals may be observed seeking food in valleys of sand.) The habitats of the Desert Lark are in rocky desert, dune and scrub, ravines and wadis; it avoids areas of shifting sand. This bird is resident in all parts of its range. According to the literature three different subspecies are found in Israel: *A.d. deserti*, *A.d. isabellinus* (in the Negev) and *A.d. fraterculus*, which occurs mainly in the Judean Desert and the Dead Sea basin.

Although well camouflaged, the Desert Lark does not rely on its colours as a defence mechanism; when threatened, it does not stand motionless or crouch on the ground but escapes by running or flying. It feeds on seeds, leaves, buds and insects. It also eats scraps of food, bread crumbs and refuse. When feeding, it is not timid and may approach humans at close quarters, as often happens in Bedouin encampments and among groups of tourists. In areas where there are water holes or wells and in irrigated sectors, scores of individuals may be seen, especially in the morning, although, being wary of one another, they tend to approach the water singly and not to linger. The Desert Lark usually lives in pairs, in territories ranging in area from less than one to several square kilometres; rarely, it is seen in small flocks. During most of the year this is a quiet bird and its song is seldom heard.

The Desert Lark is the commonest and most widely distributed of the larks living in the deserts of Israel, both in the Negev and the Judean Desert, including the most arid areas. Its range extends northward along the Jordan Valley to the eastern slopes of Gilboa. Sightings have also been recorded in the heights of eastern Lower Galilee, in the southern Golan, Hermon, on the western slopes of Samaria and even on the sands of the coastal plain.

The nesting season begins in February, is concentrated mainly in March and ends in May. At the approach of the nesting period the male circles in undulating flight, uttering his melodious song, a plaintive 'tweet'. The nest is in a hollow in the shade of a bush or a large rock; it is constructed of grass, thin stalks, roots, hair and wool, but the centre is rarely lined. At the rim a 'rampart' of small and flat stones is sometimes built. In the clutch there are 2-4 eggs, usually 4, whitish in colour and speckled with khaki-brown or lilac-brown markings, covering the whole of the egg or just the blunt end. Incubation lasts 13-14 days, and is performed by the female alone. The nest is usually sited on a northeast-facing slope, enabling the mother to leave her post early in the morning to feed while the sun warms the eggs, and ensuring that in the hottest hours of the day the incubating bird will be in the shade. Both parents feed the young until they leave the nest at 10-11 days old.

The Desert Lark is apparently single-brooded.

Bar-tailed Desert Lark
Ammomanes cincturus

Smaller than the Desert Lark: body length 13-13.8 cm, wing length 8.3-9.8 cm and weight 17-20 g. It is distinguished by its reddish-brown back, a dark bar at the tip of the tail and its small and thin bill. Its song is also an aid to identification: a flutish sound repeated at short intervals in the course of very undulating flight.

This lark's range extends from the western Sahara to Pakistan, especially in areas of sand and scrub but sometimes also on rocky slopes or among dunes, in more arid habitats than those of the Desert Lark. In all parts of its range this is a resident. In this range four subspecies have been described, the one found in Israel being *A.c. arenicolor*, which occurs from North Africa to Arabia.

In Israel the Bar-tailed Desert Lark is a fairly common breeder in the western Negev, in the region of Nizana, in the sands of the valley of the Arava, and in the valley of Timna not far from Eilat. Its nesting season is March-April and its breeding biology is similar to that of the Desert Lark. Outside the nesting season it sometimes roams in quite large flocks, numbering scores of individuals. It is distributed more widely in Sinai.

Dunn's Lark
Eremalauda dunni

Body length about 14 cm. Distinguished from the pre-

vious two species by its thick bill and its tail, which appears all-black but for the two central feathers, which are a sandy-brown, the same colour as the back.

This is a resident bird of Saharo-Arabian distribution: southern Sahara, southern Sudan and across the Arabian deserts, in the most arid of habitats.

Dunn's Lark is a very rare accidental in Israel, seen on only three occasions before 1982, all in spring: near Nizana in the northern Negev; on the sea-shore at Maagan Mikhael; and near Ein Gev on the eastern coast of Lake Tiberias. An additional sighting, of three individuals, was recorded near Tel Nizana on 22 October 1983.

Black-crowned Finch-lark
Eremopterix nigriceps

A small lark: body length about 11.5 cm. It differs from most larks in its striking sexual dimorphism: the male is distinguished by the contrast between the greyish-brown back and the coal-black crown, neck-stripe and underparts; in flight, the black underwing is conspicuous. The female is similar to other desert larks, and is distinguished by the black outer tail feathers.

The range of the Black-crowned Finch-lark is in the south of the Saharo-Sindian region, and it is resident in most of its habitats. In this range four subspecies have been described.

This bird resembles a finch more than a lark, although it runs like a lark and does not hop; when it stops running it crouches, behaviour atypical of larks.

In Israel the subspecies *E.n. melanauchen* is a very rare accidental in the region of Eilat. More sightings have been recorded in Sinai and on the island of Tiran.

Hoopoe Lark
Alaemon alaudipes

A large lark: body length 21.5-24 cm, wing length 11.3-13.5 cm and weight 36-46 g. It has a long and downcurved bill and in flight shows a vivid contrast between black and white flight feathers. The upperparts are greyish sand-brown in colour; the underparts are white, the breast spotted with dark brown. The male is slightly larger. The Hoopoe Lark is a typical ground bird, with long and strong legs. The rear toe is shorter and thicker than in other species of lark, and the claws short and curved. The tail is long, with black outer feathers. Juveniles are similar to adults, but with more speckling on the upperparts and without dark spotting on the breast.

The range of the Hoopoe Lark extends from southwest Africa to northwest India. In this range four subspecies have been described. This is a typical desert bird, resident in arid areas, especially in sands, even shifting sands, but also among dunes and in scrubland. The subspecies *A.a. alaudipes*, which ranges from the Sahara to northern Arabia, occurs in Israel.

It is hard to locate a Hoopoe Lark when it stands motionless: it blends invisibly into the landscape. When threatened it escapes by running, and does not crouch on the ground; from time to time it stops, stands erect and scans its surroundings. Only when danger is imminent or when a disturbance is repeated does it fly, showing the conspicuous black and white bars on the wings; on landing these colours disappear at once and the bird blends once more into its surroundings. The Hoopoe Lark feeds especially on the larvae of beetles; in order to catch them it scrapes the sand with sideways movements of the bill. It is possible that prey is located with the aid of hearing, although the Hoopoe Lark does not tilt its head in the manner of thrushes. In some areas snails form the major ingredient in its diet, which sometimes also includes seeds.

The Hoopoe Lark is a territorial bird, living in very sparse populations in territories which can measure scores of square kilometres. Its song, heard especially at the end of winter and in early spring, is peculiar, pleasant to the ear and resembling a human whistle: it starts with sporadic and low syllables, changing to more rapid and higher notes. The song is begun from a perch on a mound or a bush, and continued in flight; the bird flies high, sometimes turning and wheeling in typical undulating flight or gliding with spread wings.

This lark is a fairly rare resident in Israel, found especially in the sands of the western Negev, but also in the valley of the Arava. In the sands of northern Sinai it is more common and more widely distributed. The Hoopoe Lark usually nests in March-April. The nest is normally at the base of a bush, often with small stones arranged at the rim; it may also be placed on small desert bushes. It is a fairly casual construction, built of small branches and twigs and lined with spiderwebs, hair, wool, threads and scraps of fabric. The clutch is of 2-4 eggs, and the more arid the region, the smaller the clutch. The egg is white with brown markings. The female incubates alone for 13-14 days, occasionally leaving the nest to seek food. On returning, she does not land at the nest but at some distance from it, and approaches the nest hesitantly and cautiously, looking all around. The chicks hatch blind and covered with sparse down, and are easily recognised by their long bill. Both parents feed them for a period of 10-12 days before they leave the nest, and continue to feed them outside the nest for a further two weeks.

Calandra Lark
Melanocorypha calandra

The largest of the larks seen in Israel, with solid and somewhat squat body: body length 18.8-20 cm, wing length 12.6-13.5 cm, wingspan 38 cm and weight 50-58 g. The upperparts are fairly uniform grey-brown, and the underparts are white with a dark patch on the side of the neck. In flight the white rear edge of the wing and the dark, white-edged tail are conspicuous. The wings are triangular, broad at the base and pointed at the tip; the underwing is dark. The tail is short to medium length (about 6 cm). The bill is deep and thick like that of a finch (although it is laterally compressed and not so broad), and yellowish-cream in colour. Juveniles are yellowish-brown with pale feather fringes, and thus appear mottled above.

The Calandra Lark has a range extending from southern Europe and North Africa to central Asia, and its distribution is Mediterranean-Irano-Turanian. This is a resident bird in cultivated fields and pasture meadows, on slopes and in valleys, not at high altitude above sea-level. In this range four subspecies have been described, two of them known in Israel: *M.c. calandra* and *M.c. gaza*.

Like other larks, the Calandra Lark is usually seen on the ground, although it sometimes rests on low branches. Usually it flies with undulating flight, at low level. Outside the nesting season it flocks, sometimes in large flocks which often mingle with those of buntings, starlings and other species of lark. During the summer it feeds almost exclusively on seeds, especially the seeds of cereals; in autumn and winter it also eats buds, leaves and insects. It regularly drinks water.

The song of the Calandra Lark is heard with greatest intensity in February. Strong and melodious and including imitations of other birds, it begins before dawn and is uttered in undulating flight, high above the ground, sometimes for long periods of time. It may also sing from a perch on a low mound.

In Israel this lark may be seen in the central and southern Golan, in northern valleys, in the heights of eastern Lower Galilee, and in valleys and along mountain slopes and in the northern and western Negev. Its population has diminished considerably in recent years. In winter the resident nucleus is reinforced by migrating and wintering individuals, whose origin is in the Caucasus and the Ukraine.

Nesting is late, between April and June, and the nest is on the ground, in long grass or under a bush. The nesting materials are dry grass and corn stalks and the nest is usually unlined; it resembles a flat basket. In the clutch there are 3-5, usually 4 eggs, sandy-brown in colour and densely speckled with lilac-brown markings. The female incubates alone for about 14 days. At about ten days old the chicks leave the nest, but remain close to it for about another week before flying, and the parents continue to feed them.

The Calandra Lark breeds twice in the year, and it is possible to find clutches as late as early June.

Bimaculated Lark
Melanocorypha bimaculata

Similar to the Calandra Lark although more russet in colour and slightly smaller: body length 19 cm and weight 50 g. The neck patches are much smaller and narrower, the tips of the secondaries lack white and the tip of the tail (not the edges) is white.

The range of the Bimaculated Lark is typically Irano-Turanian: from Turkey and Syria through Iran and Iraq to Lake Balkhash in Soviet Asia. In most of its range it breeds at a higher altitude than the Calandra Lark, usually in waste and rocky environments between 1,200 and 2,700 m above sea-level. In this range three subspecies have been described; it is not clear which of these occur in Israel. Most of its populations migrate in winter to Arabia, Egypt, Sudan and Ethiopia. In behaviour it is similar to the Calandra Lark, although its song is less trilling and has greater clarity.

In Israel this is a rare migrant, occasionally seen in small groups, and a rare winterer in the Arava. It also breeds in a few sites in the northern Golan, close to the slopes of Mount Hermon. The breeding population arrives at the end of March or in early April, and migrates as early as July.

Thick-billed Lark
Rhamphocoris clotbey

Body length about 17 cm. This bird has the thickest bill of all larks. The feathers are sandy-brown above, white with black blotches below; the cheeks are black, and a white frame surrounds the eye.

The Thick-billed Lark is distributed in the Sahara, south of the Atlas range, also in northwestern Arabia and in eastern Jordan. Israel Aharoni discovered the species breeding in the Sinai desert in 1930. This is a monotypic species, resident though liable to roam outside the breeding season.

In Israel this is a very rare accidental. On 24 May 1978, 15 individuals were seen on the mountains west of the Gulf of Eilat.

Short-toed Lark
Calandrella brachydactyla

A small lark, with short and conical bill like that of all members of its genus. The secondaries are very long, and the hindclaw is about the same length as the toe and slightly curved, both features typical of the genus. Body length 13.5-15.4 cm, wing length 8.5-9.7 cm, wingspan 28-29.5 cm and weight 19-25 g. The upperparts are streaked sandy-brown, the underparts pale cream-white in colour. The breast lacks speckling, which is one of the distinguishing features. At the sides of the breast there are two small dark patches, but these are not easily observed from a distance. The slightly forked tail is dark brown and conspicuous in flight, and the edges of the outer feathers are white.

The Short-toed Lark is distributed in southern Europe, in North Africa, in the Middle East and further east through Iraq and Iran to China and Mongolia. In this range some 20 subspecies have been identified. It lives in grassy steppes in flat and open environments, and sometimes in arid regions — semi-deserts and expanses of sand. Its wintering areas include Africa, Arabia, India, Burma and eastern China. In Israel this is a resident and passage migrant.

When threatened, the Short-toed Lark tends to crouch. Its flight is undulating and low, close to the surface of the ground and usually over short distances. It feeds on the ground, walking or running, sometimes hopping, and may dig at the surface with its legs and bill. It feeds on seeds, buds and leaves, but also on insects, especially in summer. It drinks when the opportunity arises. Outside the nesting season this is a gregarious bird, and flocks manoeuvre low above the ground, resembling flocks of waders in the uniformity of their movement. During flight, contact calls are uttered.

In Israel the subspecies *C.b. hermonensis* is a fairly common resident, and the species is also fairly common as a passage migrant (possibly two or three other subspecies), in the northern Golan, in eastern Upper Galilee, in the Jezreel Valley and in Gilboa, in the southern coastal plain and in the northern Negev.

The Short-toed Lark returns to its nesting territory in March-April; this is relatively small, 0.2-0.4 ha. The male's song flight is performed most hours of the day. Sometimes the male flies so high as to be almost invisible, although his song — a series of notes constantly repeated — is widely heard. Each 'phrase' of the song accompanies an undulation in flight. When singing the male often appears to be suspended in the air, although he also sings from a bush, fence or rock.

The Short-toed Lark nests between April and July. The nest, in a small hollow near a rock or a bush, is built of dry grass and lined with wool and feathers; sometimes it is surrounded by a rampart of small stones or gravel. In the clutch there are 2-5 eggs, so densely mottled with brown and grey markings that they appear greyish in colour. The female incubates for 12-13 days, and both parents tend the chicks in the nest for 10-11 days. The chicks fly at about two weeks old.

The Short-toed Lark usually raises two broods in the year.

Lesser Short-toed Lark
Calandrella rufescens

Similar to the Short-toed Lark, but more grey and with a darker crown. It is also distinguished by its streaked breast, and by its display flight, which is not undulating but hovering, like that of the Crested Lark.

The Lesser Short-toed Lark has a distribution of Mediterranean/Irano-Turanian pattern. In its range 14 subspecies have been described. It prefers more arid environments than those of the Short-toed Lark. Its southern populations are resident while those of the north migrate and winter in the Middle East, in Egypt and Sudan.

In Israel this is a common resident, passage migrant and winter visitor. The subspecies *C.r. minor*, whose range is from Morocco to Arabia, is especially common in the Revivim-Nizana region in the northern Negev and also in the Arava. It usually inhabits low hills and plains covered with shallow sand. Its breeding biology is similar to that of the Short-toed Lark. Outside the nesting season it roams, sometimes in large but loose flocks, flying low over the expanses of the Negev.

Crested Lark
Galerida cristata

A somewhat solid and squat-bodied lark: body length 16.8-18.5 cm, wing length 9.9-11.4 cm, wingspan 34-37 cm and weight 40-45 g. The commonest of the larks found in Israel, it is distinguished from all other larks in this country by the erect crest of feathers on the head. It is streaked greyish-brown, but the intensity of colouring varies in different areas, according to background colour and the degree of moisture in the air: from sandy-brown in the desert to honey-grey in regions of basalt. The breast is streaked and the belly is white. The outer tail feathers are russet, not white as in most other species of lark. The female has a slightly shorter crest. The bill is narrow and slightly elongated, and the hindclaw is long and straight. Juveniles have mottled plumage and a smaller crest; they attain sexual maturity at about one year old.

The range of the Crested Lark extends from North Africa to the region of the Equator except the Sahara, across most of Europe excepting the far north, and into central Asia. In this range 28 subspecies have been identified (38 according to some authorities), all of them resident. The Crested Lark is distributed throughout Israel, from the slopes of Hermon to the Gulf of Eilat. According to some sources, three (and even five) subspecies have been identified in this country, the commonest among them probably being *G.c. zion*, which occurs from Turkey, through Syria to Israel.

The Crested Lark is a ground-dwelling bird inhabiting open environments: sown fields, pasture meadows, rocky terrain, wasteland, sand, dry steppes and expanses of desert and semi-desert. It is also drawn to refuse-heaps on the edges of towns and villages, and thus its range has broadened as a result of urban and rural development. It spends most of its time on the ground, but is also liable to perch on bushes. It is capable of fast running, but tends to stand motionless when threatened, becoming suddenly airborne when danger is imminent. Its flight is undulating.

Outside the nesting season it roams and sometimes gathers in flocks of up to a dozen individuals. In this period it is fairly quiet, but as early as the end of February the Crested Lark begins to sing. Its song is a trisyllabic tune rising from the first to the second note and falling on the third. It may also imitate the call of the Kestrel, human whistling or a flute, and cases have been known of sheep dogs obeying its instructions. The Crested Lark usually sings in the course of display flight: it rises high, hovering and singing, then flies in an undulating circle and starts a fresh cycle of hovering and song, finally descending in acrobatic spirals or in a vertical dive. It also sings on moonlit nights. It is one of the first birds to wake, bursting into song about an hour before first light.

The nesting season lasts from March to June, occurring earlier in the Negev and later in Galilee. The nest, in a hollow in the shade of a bush, under a rock or in a fold of the ground, is constructed of grass, thin twigs, paper, fabric etc., and is usually unlined. The 3-5 eggs, sometimes 6, are whitish-grey in colour, speckled with delicate lilac-brown markings. The female incubates alone for 11-13 days. Only about two-thirds of the eggs hatch; the remainder are taken by predators such as crows, hedgehogs and foxes. Both parents tend the chicks, which leave the nest at eight to ten days old, although they are capable of flying only at 15 days old. When the chicks leave the nest they are tended mainly by the male, while the female prepares for a second nesting cycle.

The Crested Lark is capable of causing such damage to cultivated fields that it has been declared a pest, and is afforded no protection under Israel's wildlife conservation regulations.

Woodlark
Lullula arborea

A small lark, brown-grey and narrowly streaked. This monotypic genus is close to *Galerida*, but differs in the lack of prominent crest, in the shorter tail and more slender bill; the claw of the rear toe is long and slightly curved. Body length 14-15.5 cm, wing length 8.8-10 cm, wingspan 28-32.5 cm and weight 22-30 g. The Woodlark is distinguished by the pale supercilium, the black and white pattern at the angle of the wing, and the short and blackish tail which is white at the tip but not at the edges. It has a small crest, but this is not easily perceived.

The Woodlark breeds across Europe, excepting most of Britain, northern Scandinavia and eastern Russia. It is also a common breeder in North Africa, Turkey, northern Iran and Lebanon. Its range extends as far as Hermon, where a few pairs breed at an altitude of more than 1,500 m. In the past the Woodlark also bred in the Jerusalem area. In this range two subspecies have been described. The northern populations migrate, wintering especially in the countries of the Mediterranean basin, in southern Europe, North Africa and the Middle East.

The Woodlark feeds on seeds, leaves, blossoms and insects. When threatened it tends to freeze; only when danger is very close does it emit an alarm call, and then one bird will fly and the others follow.

In Israel this is a common winterer (both subspecies), seen in small flocks in northern and central parts of the country: in wasteland, plantations and edges of woodland and forests. It arrives at the end of September, during October and in early November and begins to leave as early as the end of February. The laggards may still be seen in April.

Woodlarks, probably of the subspecies *L.a. pallida*, return to their nesting sites on Hermon at the beginning of March. Their soft and flutish song, usually given while hovering, starts with high notes on a descending scale, and increases in volume and rapidity. The breeding biology is similar to that of other larks.

The Woodlark is double-brooded, and nesting on Hermon lasts from April to the end of June and sometimes into July. The Woodlark stays on Hermon until early August and then migrates.

Skylark
Alauda arvensis

Body length 18 cm, wing length 10.2-11.6 cm, wingspan 30-35 cm and weight 22-38 g. The Skylark resembles the Crested Lark, although its crest is small and not conspicuous. The tail is fairly long (about 6.8 cm), with white outer feathers. The bill is stouter than that of the Woodlark, but more slender than that of the Short-toed Lark. The hindclaw is long and straight.

The Skylark has a trans-Palaearctic range, extending from North Africa, Spain and Britain to Japan and Kamchatka, excluding areas of taiga and tundra in the far north, and including Turkey, northern Iraq and northern Iran. In this range ten subspecies have been identified. The northern populations migrate, and those of the Western Palaearctic winter in the Mediterranean countries and the Middle East.

In Israel this is a very common winter visitor in the Mediterranean region, especially in valleys and on hills. The birds concerned are mainly of the subspecies *A.a. cantarella* from southeast Europe to Iran, but the European subspecies *A.a. arvensis* is also involved. The Skylark is also seen migrating throughout the country. It arrives at the end of October and stays until March. Its flocks number scores, hundreds and even thousands of individuals, sometimes mingling with flocks of the Short-toed Lark.

The Skylark eats more green food than other larks, especially in winter, and is thus liable to cause severe damage in budding fields of lucerne and wheat and in plant nurseries. Like the Crested Lark, it is officially classified as a pest.

Oriental Skylark
Alauda gulgula

Very similar to the Skylark, but with shorter wings and tail: body length approx. 16 cm, wing length 8.6-10 cm, wingspan 27-30 cm and weight approx. 19.5-26 g. The plumage pattern is like that of the Skylark, but it has a clear rusty tinge to the ear-coverts, wings and rump and a noticeable pale supercilium; the crest is less prominent. The wings are short and rounded with a narrow sandy-coloured trailing edge, and the tail has sandy outer feathers. In flight, the short rounded wings and the short tail are good distinctions from Skylark. Perhaps the best distinguishing character is the call: a short buzz, often repeated once or twice.

The Oriental Skylark's range extends from southeast Iran eastward over a large area of central and southern Asia, in subtropical, tropical and temperate climatic zones. Within this range 11 subspecies have been described. It inhabits arid areas over most of its range, but also breeds on valley slopes and at river mouths, at altitudes from 1,500 m to over 3,500 m. Most populations are resident, but some northern ones move short distances and the westernmost subspecies *A.g. inconspicua*, which breeds from Iran to northwest India, is apparently partly migratory, though its winter quarters are not known.

The first record of this species in Israel occurred on 28 September 1984, when two individuals were seen in fields of Kibbutz Eilot near Eilat. From then up to 5 April 1985, a total of 16 Oriental Skylarks was identified there, of which ten were trapped and ringed; nine of these 16 were in September-November, with a further seven in December-January, and up to eight wintered in the area. The first group, presumably migrants, fed in ploughed fields, irrigated fields and an area of desert, while the winterers stayed in a field of melons. In autumn 1985, this species reappeared at Eilat on 1 October, and up to ten had been recorded by the end of the year (one ringed individual was presumably one of the 1984 birds). These were the first records of this species for the Western Palaearctic.

Shore or Horned Lark
Eremophila alpestris

A large lark: body length 17.2-19.5 cm, wing length 10-11.2 cm, wingspan 32-36 cm and weight 35-45 g. From a distance it appears a typical lark in all respects. At close quarters the black of the breast, cheeks and forecrown is conspicuous, and two tufts of black feathers are distinctive at the sides of the crown (these 'horns' are larger and more prominent in the male). The black areas are accentuated by the yellow-white background of the chin and forehead. The overall colour is uniform greyish-brown above and whitish below; the outer tail feathers are edged white. At the approach of the breeding season the colours of the facial feathers become more vivid and striking. The wings are long and pointed, the tail slightly forked. The bill is short, conical and long; the hindclaw is long and straight. The female is similar to the male, but paler and with less conspicuous black tones. Juveniles appear mottled yellowish-brown, with a blackish tail.

The Shore Lark has the broadest range of any member of its family, although its distribution is sporadic: in Eurasia it breeds north of the Arctic Circle, but also in the Balkans, Turkey, the Caucasus, Iran, the Himalayas and Tibet; in America, from northern Alaska to California and Mexico. In this fragmented range 41 subspecies have been identified, most of them resident. The subspecies occurring in Israel is *E.a. bicornis*, whose distribution ranges from Turkey to Mount Hermon. The origin of the Shore Lark is in mountain ranges, above the tree-line. It apparently extended during the Pleistocene period to the Eurasian tundra and from there to North America, where, in the absence of other larks, it proliferated in a wide variety of habitats, including desert regions. The Shore Lark is a bird of rocky slopes and alpine wastes. In the Himalayas it reaches altitudes of some 5,500 m, and on Hermon breeds at an altitude of 1,850 m and more. Part of its Israeli populations, numbering a total of some 50 pairs, winters on Hermon; other parts of this population migrate over short range.

This lark usually walks or runs, and seldom hops. In spring it tends to linger around drifts of melting snow, feeding on the flies and beetles frozen in during the winter. In later spring and in summer, it feeds on the green parts of plants and to a lesser extent on seeds. Outside the nesting season, from early August, the Shore Lark flocks and migrates, usually at low level, in parties of 10-15 individuals. This flocking is especially conspicuous in the morning, near water sources. In autumn, flocks are larger, numbering up to 25 individuals.

The Shore Lark returns to its nesting areas in the second half of March. Courtship usually begins in early April, with the male rising high in the air, singing, and descending vertically, although the song is normally uttered from a perch on rocks or boulders. The song, a bell-like sound, is heard even at night during the nesting season. The nest is usually built under a bush, sometimes under a boulder or in rockfalls, with a surrounding rim of small stones. The nesting season is April-June. The clutch is of 3-4 eggs, pale bluish- or greenish-white in colour and speckled with light grey markings. Breeding biology is similar to that of other larks.

Temminck's Horned Lark
Eremophila bilopha

Body length 15.9-16.7 cm, wing length 9.3-10.2 cm and weight 22-28 g. Smaller and paler than the Shore Lark, but so similar to it that some ornithologists see it as only a subspecies of the Shore Lark. Its overall colour is sandy-brown, with white throat, upper forehead and rear ear-coverts. The black crescent on the upper breast is smaller than in the Shore Lark, and does not join the black eye-stripe.

This is a desert bird, with a range extending from the Spanish Sahara to Arabia, the Syrian Desert and western Iraq. It is a monotypic species. In Israel it is resident in the region of Nizana in the northern Negev and also in the southern Negev, although its populations are usually sparse. Outside the nesting season it flocks in small groups and roams across the Negev. In behaviour and breeding biology it is similar to the Shore Lark.

Family: Hirundinidae (Swallows, Martins)

This family contains 16 genera and 75 species. Its origins are within the Ethiopian and Oriental regions, and most species are distributed in Africa although a few are cosmopolitan. The northern species migrate. In Israel four genera and six species are represented.

Hirundines have a slender body, 10-23 cm in length, with a structure well suited to flying. The wing is long, pointed and sickle-shaped. The tail is long and usually forked. The bill is short, broad at the base, and triangular in shape. The aperture of the mouth is large and extends back to the line of the eye. The legs are short and weak, suited only for standing and perching. The claws are strong and curved, providing effective grip on rocky protuberances; the hindclaw is shorter than those of the foretoes, an exceptional phenomenon among songbirds. The body feathers are usually metallic black or reddish-brown. Both sexes have similar plumage, identical throughout the year. Juveniles are similar to adults, although the tail is sometimes shorter.

Swallows and martins have no song as such, but utter throaty chirps and shrill squeaks. All spend much of their time in the air, flying at great speed and manoeuvring adroitly. They usually land on reeds or on electricity and telephone cables and descend only infrequently to the ground, doing so primarily to gather nest-building materials. Hirundines feed almost exclusively on small insects, caught in flight in the mouth which is held open. Most species also drink in flight. Members of the family gather in large flocks outside the nesting season, often mingling with flocks of other species. They usually roost in reeds, sometimes in concentrations of tens of thousands of individuals. A few species breed in colonies.

The siting of the nest varies according to species. The nest is normally built of mud, collected in the bill and moistened with saliva. It is constructed by both partners, and lined with feathers and soft grass. Most species nest in dark and protected places: rock-crevices, holes and in man-made buildings. The nest is either a basket-shaped quarter-sphere, as in the case of the Swallow and Pale Crag Martin, or a more elaborate structure, spherical and domed and sometimes fitted with a kind of 'lobby' (as in the case of the Red-rumped Swallow). In the clutch there are 3-6 elongated eggs, tending to be white in species nesting in darker places and mottled in other species. The incubation period is 13-15 days, and most of the task is performed by the female. The chicks hatch blind, with down on the head and the back and with a yellow gape. Both parents feed the chicks, which stay three to four weeks in the nest, twice the time spent in the nest by other songbirds of similar size.

Swallow
Hirundo rustica

Body length 15.6-20.4 cm, wing length 12-12.7 cm, wingspan 32-36 cm and weight 13-20 g. The outer tail feathers of the Swallow are longer than those of other hirundines, and the deeply forked tail constitutes a clear recognition mark. Another distinguishing feature is the blue-black sheen of the upperparts from head to tail, with a few white marks at the cleft of the tail. It is also distinguished by the russet-chestnut throat and forehead. The wings are long, sickle-shaped and very pointed. Juveniles lack the gloss of the adults; their outer tail feathers are shorter and the fork of the tail more shallow.

The Swallow has a very broad Holarctic distribution, extending over most of Eurasia and North America, except the far north, and over North Africa and southern Asia. In this range eight subspecies have been identified, two of them known in Israel. *H.r. transitiva*, which is distinguished by the reddish-cream colour of its belly, breeds in southern Turkey, Syria, Lebanon, western Jordan and Israel; most of its populations are resident, and apparently only juveniles migrate south. The subspecies *H.r. rustica*, recognised by its paler underparts, breeds throughout Europe, in western Asia and North Africa, and winters across sub-Saharan Africa; this subspecies is a common passage migrant in all parts of Israel.

The Swallow is a bird of fields and wide open expanses, usually seen in valleys and in plains up to an altitude of 1,000 m, sometimes 1,800 m above sea-level. It prefers fields near lakes, pools and marshes. It is a gregarious bird, usually breeding in sparse colonies with a few pairs nesting side by side. After nesting, the resident population gathers in traditional roosting areas, where tens of thousands of individuals may be seen arriving at dusk. In cold weather some individuals roost in their nests.

This species is common on passage in Israel, in autumn from the end of July to November, especially in September-October, and in spring (when it is more conspicuous) between March and May and sometimes into June. A Swallow ringed in Hungary was found during the spring migration in 1984 in the Arava. The migrating Swallows usually gather in dense flocks numbering 60-80 individuals. Towards evening they assemble to roost communally in reedbeds, usually near water, and thousands of individuals are liable to congregate at such sites. In Israel three such sites were known during the 1970s and the beginning of the 1980s: in the Hula Reserve; near Gonen in the eastern part of the Hula Valley;

and near Barakat, not far from Ben-Gurion Airport. The Swallows wintering south of the Sahara begin the northward migration as early as the first week of January, but migration reaches a peak in early March.

The principal breeding areas of the Swallow in Israel today are in the Jordan Valley and further north to Rosh Pinna. In the past, until the 1950s, it was a common breeder on the coastal plain, as far south as Jaffa, but disappeared from these areas with the widespread use of DDT as a pesticide. Since the beginning of the 1980s there has been a gradual but perceptible trend towards renewed breeding on the shores of western Galilee. A few pairs have also been observed breeding in Ramat Aviv.

In Israel the nesting season begins as early as March, and two broods are raised. The second brood leaves the nest in June or even in July, and in a warm and dry autumn Swallows may attempt to raise a third brood in November, although clutches laid at such late dates rarely hatch successfully. The first clutch is usually of 5 eggs, the second of 4 (in Europe the clutch may contain 6,7 or even 8 eggs). The period of incubation is 13-14 days; in Europe it can last 16 and even 18 days. The chicks do not leave the nest until they are 19-21 days old.

Red-rumped Swallow
Hirundo daurica

Body length 16.3-19.5 cm, wing length 11.5-12.4 cm, wingspan 32.5 cm and weight 15-21 g. Similar in size, shape and plumage to the Swallow. It is best distinguished by the russet colour of the rump and nape; seen from below, it lacks the dark breast-band. Juveniles have duller plumage.

The Red-rumped Swallow is distributed especially in southern Asia, from Turkey and Israel to India and the Philippines and further east, and in tropical Africa from south of the Sahara to the region of the Equator. In Europe it is restricted mainly to the Iberian peninsula and the Balkan states; small populations are found in Italy, southern France and North Africa. In this range 12 subspecies have been described. All the populations from the temperate zones migrate, and winter in India and in tropical Africa. The Red-rumped Swallow prefers hilly areas, where it reaches higher altitudes than the Swallow. It is usually found among rocks and crags rich in clefts and holes for nesting. In 1925 it was stated by Aharoni that only in isolated cases does the Red-rumped Swallow exchange its natural nesting sites for man-made buildings. Since that date it has adapted to an increasing extent to artificial structures — balconies, bridges etc. — and today it regularly nests on buildings, especially in the eastern basin of

the Mediterranean, including Israel. The Red-rumped Swallow has also penetrated plains and valleys — moving first to the Sharon and reaching the Jordan Valley in 1958. Today it may be seen hunting flying prey over cultivated fields.

This species' flight is slower and less graceful than that of the Swallow. Unlike the Swallow, which drinks during flight, the Red-rumped Swallow tends to descend to the ground for this purpose. Outside the breeding season this is a gregarious bird, and scores of individuals gather together for migration.

In Israel the Red-rumped Swallow of the sub-species *H.d. rufula*, which ranges from southern Europe, through the Middle East to northwest India, is a common passage migrant: in autumn from the end of July to early November, especially between the end of September and early October; and in spring from Mid-February to the end of May, especially between mid-March and mid-April.

This is also a common summer resident in northern and central parts of the country between April and October, some arriving at the end of March. Pairs usually breed at distances of scores and even hundreds of metres apart; only rarely do a few pairs nest side by side. The nest is fastened to the ceiling of a room, a balcony, a bridge or the like, often near a lamp. It is bottle-shaped: a nesting chamber with a long and narrow entrance tunnel. It is built by both partners, using lumps of wet mud but no straw (in which respect it differs from the nest of the Swallow). The completed nest is a large structure: 20-25 cm long, up to 20 cm in diameter and weighing 1 kg or more; it is lined mainly with soft and downy feathers. In the second half of April and during May the female lays 3-5 eggs, which she incubates for a period of 13-14 days. Sometimes a House Sparrow commandeers the nest, ejecting the eggs of the swallow and laying its own in their place. Care of the young is shared between both parents and lasts about three weeks.

Sometimes a second brood is started in July, being completed in October, when migration takes place.

Sand Martin or Bank Swallow
Riparia riparia

The smallest of the hirundines seen in Israel: body length 12.4-14.5 cm, wing length 9.9-11.3 cm, wingspan 28-29.5 cm and weight 13-15 g. This is a member of a genus of four species, which have softer plumage than other hirundines. The upperparts are grey-brown, without a metallic sheen, and a brown breast-band is conspicuous against the white back-ground of the underparts; the tail is relatively short and only slightly forked. The legs are short and weak and not feathered.

The range of this species is Holarctic and extends over most of Europe, Asia and North America. In this range seven subspecies have been described. In the Middle East, *R.r. riparia* breeds in Lebanon, and another subspecies *R.r. shellei* breeds along the Nile Valley in Egypt. The habitats of the Sand Martin are near water, where it hunts small insects above the surface. It breeds in holes which it excavates in river-banks, in gravel quarries and other types of earth-wall; usually it nests in colonies of a few to thousands of pairs. All its populations migrate, wintering in south Arabia, eastern and southern Africa.

In Israel the subspecies *R.r. riparia*, which breeds in Europe and in the northern Middle East, is a very common passage migrant: in autumn from the end of July to the end of November, with a peak in mid-September, and in spring from the end of February to mid-May; it is more conspicuous in the latter season. Two individuals ringed in Eilat have been found in Russia and Finland respectively.

Tristram reported the species breeding in Israel in the last century, but there has been no later evidence of this, although it is possible that a few pairs nest in the Golan.

Pale Crag Martin
Ptyonoprogne obsoleta

A small and pale hirundine: body length 13.4 cm, wing length 11.8 cm and weight 13-16 g. It is grey-brown above and pale below; the cheeks and throat are white. The tail is short and only slightly forked, with white markings at the tip.

This species' range extends from the Sahara

through the Middle East to India, with penetration into the Horn of Africa. In these regions seven sub-species have been identified. Its habitats are cliffs and canyons, also rocky plains. It is absent from areas of continuous dune in the Sahara and Arabia.

The Pale Crag Martin is an accomplished aerobat, gliding with impressive skill and appearing to float across cliff-faces as it seeks small flying insects. It lives in pairs for most of the year, and does not flock as do other species.

In Israel, the subspecies *P.o. obsoleta*, which is distributed from Sudan and Egypt, through Israel and Jordan to Iran, is resident in the Negev and the Judean Desert. It is especially common along the cliffs of the Syro-African rift, and extends as far north as the region of Jericho. In winter it roams, and is liable then to reach the fringes of the Mediterranean region.

This species nests in caves and rock-clefts, often near water sources. In settlements in the Arava and the Negev it is found breeding on balconies and on sides of wells. The nest is built only of mud, without grass or straw, and is shaped like a bowl or a quarter-sphere fastened to a wall. In the clutch there are 2-5 eggs, usually 3; the egg is slightly mottled. The process of incubation, hatching and fledging is similar to that of other hirundines.

Crag Martin
Ptyonoprogne rupestris

Similar to and closely related to the Pale Crag Martin, but slightly larger: body length 15 cm, wing length 12.8 cm, wingspan 34.5 cm and weight 20 g. It is also separated by its brown belly and streaked throat. In the Pale Crag Martin the underwing-coverts are paler than the flight feathers, while in the Crag Martin the situation is reversed; the forewing is also darker.

Its distribution is southern Palaearctic and extends from North Africa and Spain, through southern Europe, Turkey and Lebanon to Mongolia and China. In this range two subspecies have been described. Its habitats are canyons and rocky hill slopes, sometimes also coastal cliffs. Most of its populations migrate and winter in North Africa and also south of the Sahara, in the Sahel and in Ethiopia.

In Israel the subspecies *P.r. rupestris* is a fairly common passage migrant and a rare winter visitor in Nahal Amud and the cliffs of the Arbel in the southeast of Upper Galilee and in Nahal Shorek in the Judean Hills. In these areas scores of individuals are seen congregating before roosting. Most observations are between November and March.

Tristram recorded the Crag Martin as breeding in

Israel. Apart from a few pairs which have bred on the flanks of Mount Hermon, at an altitude of some 2,100 m, there are no other nesting records from Israel. In spring 1985, a pair or two were seen nesting on the lower slopes of Hermon.

House Martin
Delichon urbica

The House Martin differs from all other genera of hirundines in that the tarsus and the toes are feathered. It is of moderate size: body length 14.5-16.5 cm, wing length 10.7-11.5 cm, wingspan 30.5-32 cm and weight 20 g. It is also distinguished from other hirundines by its all-white underparts and by the white rump, conspicuous in contrast to the glossy blue-grey of the back. The tail is slightly forked.

The range of the House Martin extends from North Africa and over most of Palaearctic Eurasia to the Arctic Circle; in this range it is absent only from central Asia and the Saharo-Arabian zone. Three subspecies have been described. All of its populations migrate, wintering in India and southeast Asia, also across sub-Saharan Africa. Its habitats are usually rocky mountain slopes, but also cultivated land and pasture meadows. It breeds on cliff-faces, in rock-clefts and especially on buildings and under bridges, and often penetrates large European cities.

In Israel the House Martin (probably of the sub-species *D.u. urbica*) is known primarily as a passage migrant: it passes in the autumn migration between August and November and especially in mid-September; and in spring from the end of February to the end of May, with a peak in mid-March. The House Martin also breeds in the northern Golan, and since the late 1960s has begun to breed in Jerusalem and neighbourhood, as well as in the canyons of the Judean Desert; since the mid-1970s its breeding range has extended to Upper Galilee (Mount Meron and Pki'in).

The nesting season in Jerusalem and the northern Golan is between April and the end of July; during this period House Martins have time to raise two broods. The House Martin normally breeds in colonies, sometimes containing hundreds of contiguous nests. The nest is usually built in the angle between a wall and a ceiling or a ledge. It is bowl-shaped, with only a small aperture close to the ceiling. In the clutch there are 3-5 eggs. Unlike other hirundines, both parents share the task of incubation, and both spend the night in the nest. The period of incubation is 14-15 days, and the chicks remain 19-22 days in the nest before leaving it. Sometimes the offspring of the first brood return to the nest to roost with the parents, and they then help in tending their younger siblings, so that 10-12 House Martins may be present in the nest. It appears that even migrating House Martins tend to roost communally in nests along the migration route.

The House Martins migrate from the nesting areas at the end of July, and chicks which have not been reared to the flying stage at this time are abandoned. In the canyons of the Judean Desert nesting activity has been observed at the end of January, and it is possible that after breeding in Israel these pairs go on to breed in Europe. House Martins are also known to nest in their winter quarters in Africa.

Family: Motacillidae (Pipits, Wagtails)

This family comprises five genera and 54 species; in Israel two genera and 12 species are represented. Members of this family are distributed in all parts of the world, excepting islands in the Pacific Ocean, and they are among the northernmost of songbirds. Usually they inhabit open environments, especially fields, heath and wetland, and most tend to avoid perching on trees. All the northern species migrate in winter.

These are small songbirds, with narrow bodies and slender in structure. Body length 12.5-23 cm. The legs are narrow and long. The toes are long and the hindclaw long and straight, except in species living in trees. The bill is slender and straight but not long. The wing is fairly long and pointed. The tail is of moderate length or very long, the outermost feathers having pale-coloured edges. Motacillidae have two moults in the year: a full one in autumn, after nesting, and a partial change, involving the body feathers but not the wing and tail feathers, at the end of winter. The plumage of juveniles is slightly different, and they acquire full adult plumage only during their second autumn.

These birds are primarily insect-eaters, although their diet also includes spiders, molluscs and soft seeds. They tend to feed on the ground, like larks. Their movement on the ground consists mainly of walking, but they may also hop. When walking, the body is held in a horizontal posture. Food is also hunted in hovering and pursuit flight.

Most species breed in basket-shaped nests, well camouflaged on the ground, a minority in holes. In the clutch there are 5-8 eggs, flecked and mottled with brown and grey. Incubation is normally by the

30. Collared Pratincole

31. Little Ringed Plover at nest

32. Kentish Plover at nest

33. Spur-winged Plovers

34. Turnstones

35. White-eyed Gull nesting in Tiran

36. Black-headed Gulls in a fish-pond

37. Great Black-headed Gull

38. Lesser Crested Terns nesting in Tiran

39. Common Terns

40. White-cheeked Terns in Tiran

41. Little Terns

42. Caspian Terns in Tiran

43. Crowned Sandgrouse

44. Lichtenstein's Sandgrouse

45. Black-bellied Sandgrouse: male at nest

46. Turtle Dove

47. Little Owl

48. Eagle Owl

49. Smyrna (White-breasted) Kingfisher

50. Pied Kingfisher

51. Red-throated Pipit

52. Yellow Wagtail of black-headed race *feldegg*

53. Yellow-vented Bulbul

54. Blackstart

55. Mourning Wheatear

56. Brown Babbler

57. Cetti's Warbler

58. Hooded Crow

59. Orange-tufted Sunbird

60. Brown-necked Raven

female alone, and lasts 13-16 days. The chicks hatch blind and covered with sparse down. They abandon the nest at 11-15 days old, usually before they are capable of flight.

Genus: *Anthus* (pipits)

A genus comprising 34 species, distributed in all parts of the world, excepting islands in the Pacific Ocean, and especially conspicuous in the Palaearctic region. The northern species migrate. Pipits resemble larks in their grey-brown, ash-coloured and streaked upperparts, and wagtails in their delicate body structure. The underparts are pale, and the breast usually speckled with dark markings. The tails of pipits are slightly shorter than those of wagtails, and usually shorter than the length of the wing; generally the outer feathers are white. Male and female have similar plumage and in most species there is no seasonal variation. Juveniles usually resemble adults. The voice is the best aid to identification.

These are essentially ground birds, inhabiting open and treeless environments, although a few species are regularly tree-based. Their flight is undulating and more graceful than that of larks and accompanied by song, typically a monosyllabic call. Most perform characteristic display flights in the breeding season.

In Israel eight species of pipit are known, six of them passage migrants, winter visitors or rare accidentals, with only two breeding.

Tawny Pipit
Anthus campestris

Body length 16-19 cm, wing length 8-9.5 cm, wingspan 16.5-19.5 cm and weight 22-30 g. A light-coloured, slim-bodied and slender-billed pipit, similar in shape and stance to a wagtail. The upperparts are a fairly uniform sandy-brown with little streaking; the underparts are light yellowish and unstreaked. There is a prominent creamy supercilium. The tail and legs are long. Juveniles are streaked above and spotted on the breast.

The Tawny Pipit breeds over most of Europe (except Britain, Scandinavia and the northern USSR) and over appreciable portions of the Middle East and central Asia. In this range three subspecies have been described. All of its populations migrate, wintering in India, Pakistan, the southern Middle East, North Africa and the Horn of Africa. The Tawny Pipit is a bird of open and dry environments: wasteland, rocky hills, expanses of sand and sometimes fields and orchards. In Israel the subspecies *A.c. campestris* is a passage migrant, a winter visitor and a breeding summer visitor.

The passage and wintering Tawny Pipits usually stay in small flocks on the ground, a few metres apart, and hidden by low vegetation. When threatened, they escape by running; when repeatedly disturbed, they will fly to the branch of a tree, a wire fence or an electricity cable.

During migration tens of thousands of individuals are seen throughout the country: in autumn between September and November, and in spring from early March to mid-May. They usually migrate in small flocks. This species may be seen in autumn in transitional plumage, the moult being completed in the winter quarters. It also winters in the northern Negev, and less frequently in the Arava Valley.

The Tawny Pipit is a summer resident and breeder in various hill districts of Israel. Nesting areas in this country are limited to soft rock environments (chalk or chalky marl) with sparse bushes, near the watershed or to the east of it: near Gush Etzion, in the southern Judean Hills, in the Jerusalem area, on Mount Canaan in Upper Galilee, near Safad and the foothills of Hermon. The birds breeding in this country claim their territory at the end of March, when Tawny Pipits migrating northward are still present in large numbers. The male flies high in dynamic flight and then circles in long and deep undulations while uttering his monotone song — a short first syllable and a longer second, 'chivee', repeated with each undulation.

The nesting season is April-May. The nest is constructed in a hollow under a bush or rock. It is built of rough grasses and is a fairly loose structure, thinly lined with hairs and delicate materials. In the clutch there are 4-5 eggs. The period of incubation is 13-14 days, and most of the task is performed by the female. The chicks stay in the nest about two weeks and leave it before they are fully capable of flight.

Long-billed Pipit
Anthus similis

Similar to the Tawny Pipit but larger: body length 17-18.8 cm, wing length 8.9-9.7 cm and weight 27-33 g. Its bill is also longer (about 16 mm compared with 13 mm in the Tawny Pipit) and is an aid to identification. The upperparts are pale greyish-brown and fairly uniform; the wing and its coverts are darker. The breast is lightly streaked, and the belly cream-coloured. The tail is dark brown with sandy, not white, edges. The hindclaw is short and curved.

This pipit's range extends through southern Asia and across tropical Africa. It breeds in Syria and Israel, in the mountains of Yemen and Aden, in eastern Iran and Pakistan, in south India and Kashmir and also in Eritrea, Ethiopia and across tropical Africa. In this range 22 subspecies have been described. The subspecies A.s. *captus*, whose distribution is limited to the Levant, is resident in the Mediterranean region of Israel, in dry and rocky environments with scrub vegetation.

The Long-billed Pipit is a terrestrial bird, spending much of its time in pairs in exposed terrain, standing erect and not hiding in vegetation. Sometimes is also perches on bushes. It feeds especially on insects such as grasshoppers, locusts, beetles and ants, also seeds, but not green food. In winter it roams in small flocks, and is also seen in valleys.

At the approach of spring the male stands on a rock and utters his monotone song, even before dawn. This song may be heard for hours on end. The flight of the Long-billed Pipit is usually undulating, but sometimes it hovers at high altitude and sings from this position. Nesting begins in the first half of April. The female excavates a hollow with her feet under a rock, although in a relatively open location. In the clutch there are 3-5 eggs. The female incubates for 13-14 days, during which time the male sings constantly. The chicks stay in the nest for about two weeks and are fed by both parents. At times of danger, the female simulates injury in the manner typical of ground-nesting birds.

In June 1983 a pair of Long-billed Pipits was observed feeding a Cuckoo chick in Nahal Shiloh on the western slopes of the Samaria hills, and a similar phenomenon was seen about a month later not far from this site. Until these records, the Cuckoo had been known in this country as a parasite only on nests of the Scrub Warbler.

Richard's Pipit
Anthus novaeseelandiae

One of the large and long-legged pipits: body length 18.7-20.2 cm, wing length 8.5-9.9 cm, wingspan 29.5-32 cm and weight 26-38 g. In the field it is hard to distinguish it from the Long-billed Pipit and the Tawny Pipit, especially in autumn. It is recognised by its solid bill and pale supercilium, more prominent than in other pipits, and by the outer tail feathers which are entirely white. Its harsh call is also distinctive.

Richard's Pipit is distributed in east and southeast Asia, the Ukraine, Australia, New Zealand and tropical Africa. In this range 29 subspecies have been identified. The Palaearctic Asian subspecies, A.n. *richardi*, winters in India and southeast Asia.

In Israel this subspecies is a rare accidental between mid-September and early May, especially in the southern Arava — in the fields of Kibbutz Eilot — but also in desert regions and even on the sands of the coastal plain. At times, ten or more individuals are seen in the fields of Kibbutz Eilot.

Olive-backed Pipit
Anthus hodgsoni

A pipit of medium size: body length 16.7 cm, wing length 8.3 cm, wingspan 26.6 cm and weight 22 g. It is distinguished by its olive-green back, pale supercilium, and white rectangular patch above a dark spot on the rear ear-coverts; the breast is spotted and not streaked. The legs are pink. It is also distinguished by its long and sibilant call.

This species is distributed from northern Soviet Asia to the shores of the Pacific Ocean (Kamchatka and Japan), and south to the slopes of the Himalayas. This is one of the tree-dwelling pipits, breeding especially in taiga and coniferous forest. Accordingly, the hindclaw is short and curved. The Indian Tree Pipit normally winters in India and southeast Asia.

This is a rare visitor to Israel, seen for the first time in the southern Arava on 20 March 1981. Since then there have been a few more sightings in the same area, and even in Tel Aviv: in December 1984 a few individuals, in a mixed flock with Tree Pipits, stayed for about two weeks in the Yarkon Park in Tel Aviv.

Tree Pipit
Anthus trivialis

A small pipit: body length 15.3-17.2 cm, wing length 8.3-9.3 cm, wingspan 26-30 cm and weight 19-27 g. It is distinguished especially by its song flights in the breeding season. The hindclaw is shorter and more curved than in any pipit other than the Olive-backed Pipit. The streaks on the breast are more sparse but larger than in the otherwise similar Meadow Pipit; the legs are also more pink. The colour of the upperparts is fairly uniform. Its call is loud and hoarse.

The Tree Pipit breeds in all parts of Europe and penetrates central Asia. In this range two subspecies have been described. All its populations migrate, wintering in India and in tropical Africa. The subspecies A.t. *trivialis*, which is distributed in Europe and western Asia, is a common passage migrant in Israel, especially in maquis and wooded areas.

The autumn migration begins as early as the end of August, and this species is conspicuous among the migrating pipits until early October, continuing to migrate until the end of that month. The spring migration begins in the second half of March and continues until the end of May. The Tree Pipit usually migrates in small groups. Apparently it is also a rare winterer in the southern Arava.

Meadow Pipit
Anthus pratensis

Similar to the Tree Pipit but smaller: body length 13.7-15.5 cm, wing length 7.8-8.3 cm, wingspan 24-

27 cm and weight 13-19 g. It differs from the Tree Pipit in its call: a few rapidly repeated syllables. Its upperpart feathers are dark brown with whitish edges (so that the back appears streaked). The tail is black-brown with white edges and the legs are brown. The toes are relatively thick and the hindclaw longer than that of the Tree Pipit.

The Meadow Pipit is distributed over most of Europe, except in the Mediterranean countries, the Balkans, Romania and southern Russia, and its range extends into western Siberia. It also breeds in Iceland and western Greenland. The northern and eastern populations migrate south and winter in southern Europe, the countries of the Mediterranean basin and western Asia. In this range two subspecies have been described.

In Israel the subspecies *A.p. pratensis* is a fairly common winterer and passage migrant in all parts of the country, except deserts. In autumn it is the last of the pipits to arrive, in November, and in spring the last to leave, disappearing at the end of March/early April.

Red-throated Pipit
Anthus cervinus

Body length 14.3-15.5 cm, wing length 8-8.7 cm, wingspan 27 cm and weight 19-23 g. A pipit conspicuous in breeding plumage on account of the russet-brown colour of the throat (and sometimes also breast). In winter it resembles the Tree and Meadow Pipits, and is distinguished principally by the greater intensity of the streaking of the breast. Its back is also more streaked.

The Red-throated Pipit has an arctic range, from northern Scandinavia, through the tundras of northern Europe and Asia to the Bering Strait. This is a monotypic species. It begins to migrate from its nesting areas as early as the beginning of August.

In Israel this is a common passage migrant in small groups, and a frequent winterer. The groups of migrants pass during October and November, smaller numbers in September and December. The spring migration takes place between the end of March and the end of April. The Red-throated Pipit winters, especially in wet fields and pools in the Mediterranean region of the country, between October and April. Usually single individuals are seen, but they are hard to observe because they tend to hide in vegetation. This species' conspicuous breeding plumage is seen in Israel in spring.

Water Pipit
Anthus spinoletta

Body length 15.8-17.2 cm, wing length 8.2-8.8 cm and weight 18-24 g. This is the greyest of the pipits and the only one with dark legs.

Its distribution is Holarctic: in the Old World it breeds in southern Europe, across central Asia to the northeastern USSR. Six subspecies have been described. It inhabits wet meadowland in hilly inland areas. Parts of its population migrate south in autumn.

In Israel the subspecies *A.s. coutellii*, which breeds between the Caucasus and Turkestan, is a common winter visitor and passage migrant. The autumn migration takes place between the end of October and the end of November, the spring migration between the end of March and the end of April. The wintering element is also present in the country between these dates.

The Water Pipit usually winters in wet regions, and is more tied to water sources than other species. It is also seen near fish-ponds, marshes and even refuse-dumps. It is normally solitary, but scores of individuals are liable to congregate to roost in reedbeds. It feeds on small insects, molluscs, spiders and also on seeds.

Genus: *Motacilla* (wagtails)
The most familiar and conspicuous genus in the family Motacillidae, widely distributed in the Old World. All members of the genus, ten in number, tend to wag the long tail up and down in characteristic fashion when walking. The tail is usually as long as the wing or longer: it is rounded at the end and its feathers narrow. The bodies of wagtails are slender and their movements graceful. The legs are long and the hindclaw is relatively short and curved. The plumages of wagtails are not streaked or spotted, and the back is of uniform colour. The predominant colours are black, white, grey and golden-yellow. Plumage differs between the sexes and between seasons of the year. Juveniles are paler.

Wagtails prefer damp environments, banks of rivers and cultivated fields. Their gait is rapid with sudden stops; their flight is very undulating, and they utter a monosyllabic or disyllabic call. Most species flock outside the nesting season.

Pied Wagtail
Motacilla alba

Body length 17.2-20.5 cm, wing length of the male 8.7-9.6 cm and of the female 8.1-8.9 cm, wingspan 27-29.5 cm, tail length 8.5-9.3 cm and weight 18-28 g. One of the most familiar of the songbirds. A small long-tailed bird, black, grey and white: the upperparts are grey, the cheeks and throat white, the crown and breast-crescent black. Males usually have a glossy black crown and broad and glossy white forehead; females tend to have a grey crown and sometimes white forehead, but narrower than that of the male. The body feathers of the female are more brown. The juvenile male is similar to the adult female. Following the winter moult, between January and March, the nape, the throat and the breast turn black, especially in the male. The Pied Wagtail has a characteristic undulating flight, uttering monosyllabic calls with each undulation.

The Pied Wagtail is distributed over the whole of the Palaearctic region, except for the Saharo-Sindian desert strip, with penetration into the Oriental region. In this range 11 subspecies have been identified. The northern populations of the Pied Wagtail migrate, especially the subspecies *M.a. alba* which is known in Israel. The Western Palaearctic population winters in Arabia, in the countries of the Mediterranean basin, and in Africa from the north of the continent to the Congo and Tanzania. This is a bird of open environments, fields and marshes, cultivated land and even private and public gardens, both in breeding and in wintering areas, and is not at all timid in contact with humans; it feeds on the ground.

A few pairs of Pied Wagtails breed in Israel. There is also a passage element (an individual ringed in this country was found later in Eritrea), while the Egyptian subspecies *M. a. vidua* (black back in breeding plumage) is a very rare accidental.

The Pied Wagtail is a very common winterer in all parts of the country, especially in plains and valleys. In the Negev and the Judean Desert, Pied Wagtails are found in populated areas and in oases. On the basis of ringing data it is evident that most of the birds wintering in this country originate from Sweden, Norway, Finland, northern Russia and Poland. They arrive between late September and November and stay until April, when the wintering population gradually dwindles.

With their arrival in the winter quarters the flocks disperse, and most individuals seek territories. Usually a pair of Pied Wagtails (a male and a female) is found in each territory, but these pairs are not breeding partners. Of all the winter visitors to this country, only the Pied Wagtail and the Stonechat winter in territorial pairs. The same territory may be used year after year. The wagtails do not roost in these territories, but occupy them from before sunrise to early evening. In early winter they eat small insects; as numbers of insects dwindle during the winter they are drawn to any available food — worms, snails, seeds, bread crumbs, etc. — and during March the hunting of insects is resumed. Not all of the wintering Pied Wagtails colonise territories: a proportion remains in flocks, feeding at refuse-dumps or in farmyards, or following ploughs and

herds of livestock to eat the insects exposed.

Roosting colonies accommodate anything from a few score to thousands of individuals, and the birds fly 15 km and more to reach them, setting out in the evening singly or in small groups, and pausing on the way in traditional 'mustering' sites. They return to their territories and feeding areas about half an hour before sunrise. Scores and possibly hundreds of such roosting colonies (usually evergreen and thick-leaved trees, with a preference for figs, sometimes thatched farm buildings, heating systems and factories) are scattered throughout Israel. In Jerusalem in the winter of 1980/81, at least seven colonies were located, with a similar number in Tel Aviv.

Tristram recorded the Pied Wagtail as breeding in this country. From his time until 1951 no evidence of this was found, but in that year a nest was found on an island off the coast of Rosh Hanikra and another near Kibbutz Hulata in the Hula Valley. Today 10-15 breeding pairs are known, most of them in the Hula Valley and the Jordan Valley.

In Israel this species prefers to nest on sluice dams in fish-ponds, and in the Hula Reserve special nest-boxes have been provided for them. The nesting season lasts from early April to July. In the clutch there are 4-7 eggs, usually 6. The female incubates almost alone for a period of 12-13 days. The chicks leave the nest at 13-15 days old. The Pied Wagtail raises two broods in the year.

Yellow Wagtail
Motacilla flava

Smaller than the Pied Wagtail, and with a shorter tail: body length 16.6-18 cm, wing length 7.4-8.7 cm, wingspan 24-28 cm, tail length 6.5-7.2 cm and weight 16-23 g. The Yellow Wagtail has yellow underparts and mostly greenish-olive upperparts (except the head and nape).

Its distribution is trans-Palaearctic, with some penetration into northwestern America. It breeds in all parts of Europe and over appreciable sectors of Asia, including Israel, and also in North Africa and Egypt. Its habitats are mainly wet grasslands in plains. In its range 14 subspecies have been identified, differing considerably in the colours of the head, cheeks and throat of males in breeding plumage. It is more difficult to distinguish between males of the different subspecies in winter plumage, and virtually impossible to distinguish between the females and juveniles of the subspecies. Most populations of the Yellow Wagtail migrate, except the most southerly which include the Egyptian subspecies *M.f. pygmaea*. The Yellow Wagtail winters in southern Asia and in Africa, from the Sahel and East Africa to the south of the continent. In Israel this is a common passage migrant, migrating in flocks containing various subspecies.

The autumn migration begins about a month earlier than that of the Pied Wagtail: individuals are seen from the end of August and especially from mid-September to early October. The southern subspecies form the vanguard, the northern the rearguard: the black-headed subspecies M.f. *feldegg*, which breeds in the Balkans and Turkey, is the first to migrate; followed by the blue-headed M.f. *flava*, which breeds in most parts of Europe; followed in turn by the grey-headed M.f. *thunbergi*, which breeds in northern Scandinavia and in Russia; the last to migrate is the light grey-headed M.f. *beema*, which breeds in southeast Russia.

The spring migration begins in March and continues until early May, with a peak at the end of March. Again the black-headed subspecies leads the way. The blue-headed is the most common, the grey-headed fairly common. In the spring migration it is also possible to see the yellow-headed subspecies M.f. *lutea*, which breeds in Turkestan.

Before the draining of the Hula swamps, a few pairs of the black-headed subspecies (M.f. *feldegg*) nested in the fields surrounding the swamps. With the draining of the swamps, completed in 1956, this population disappeared, but following renovation work in the Hula Reserve in 1970-73 six to eight pairs of this distinctive subspecies have returned to nest in the reserve, and this is apparently the only place in Israel where Yellow Wagtails breed.

The Yellow Wagtails return from their winter quarters at the end of March, and by the end of April breeding is already in progress. The nest, in a hollow among vegetation, is built of delicate grasses and twigs and is unlined. In the clutch there are 4-6 eggs. The female incubates almost alone for 12-13 days; both parents feed the chicks in the nest for a period of 10-13 days. The chicks are capable of flight at about 17 days old. The Yellow Wagtail breeds twice in the course of the summer, in April and in July.

In northern Sinai, in Sabkhat e-Sheikh between Gaza and El Arish, the Egyptian subspecies M. f.

pygmaea breeds. This subspecies also breeds in Ghar es Safi, near the Jordanian shore of the Dead Sea.

Grey Wagtail
Motacilla cinerea

Body length 18-19.5 cm, wing length 7.9-8.8 cm and weight 14-21 g. This wagtail has a yellow breast, vent and rump, a blue-grey back and the longest tail of any wagtail: 8.9-10.5 cm. In winter it is difficult to distinguish between male and female. In summer the male's throat turns black and the yellow of the underparts becomes more intense.

The Grey Wagtail has a sporadic trans-Palaearctic range, but is absent from eastern and northern Europe. Its habitats are near running water among rocks in hilly districts. Part of the European population migrates, wintering in the Middle East and in oases of the Sahara. In Israel this is a fairly common winterer, near fast-flowing streams, from early September to early April. It usually winters singly, rarely in pairs.

Citrine Wagtail
Motacilla citreola

In the Citrine Wagtail there are considerable differences in size between the sexes: body length of the male 18.8 cm and of the female 16.5 cm, wing length of the male 8.6 cm and of the female 7.9 cm, wingspan 24.2-29.6 cm, tail length of the male 7.5-8.5 cm and of the female 7.3-7.7 cm and weight 17-22 g. It resembles the Yellow Wagtail but is distinguished from it in winter by its yellow forehead and supercilia. In breeding plumage the head and underparts are lemon-yellow, the nape black and the back dark grey. In behaviour it resembles the Grey Wagtail but is distinguished from it by its voice: a disyllabic 'tit tit' as opposed to the single 'tit' of the Grey Wagtail.

This is a rare accidental from the tundras of Siberia, Mongolia and Tibet. Most sightings are in the region of Eilat, a few in the coastal plain. In winter 1983/84 several individuals wintered in the ponds of Maagan Mikhael between the end of September and April.

Family: Pycnonotidae (Bulbuls)

In the family there are 15 genera and 121 species, distributed in the tropical zones of Asia and Africa. The origin of the family is apparently in the Oriental region. The genus *Pycnonotus* is the largest in the family and comprises 48 species, 31 of them confined to tropical Asia. In Israel one species of this genus is represented.

Songbirds of medium size, from sparrow to thrush size, with body length varying from 14 cm to 18 cm. Their wings are quite short and rounded, the tail long and square-ended or shallowly forked. The neck is short with sparse feathers, and when it is extended a bald patch is noticeable between the nape and the scapulars. A few species have a conspicuous crest. The dominant plumage colours of bulbuls are olive-green or yellow-brown, but a few have more striking colours. The legs are short and weak, the bill short and weak with stiff bristles at the corners. The sexes are similar (although sometimes the male is larger). Juveniles are similar to adults, sometimes paler.

Bulbuls are tree- and bush-dwellers, feeding on fruits and berries in addition to insects. They are noisy birds. Most species are resident, although outside the breeding season they live in nomadic flocks. The nest is basket-shaped and appears casual and disordered. The eggs are mottled in various patterns; the chicks hatch blind and naked.

Yellow-vented Bulbul
Pycnonotus xanthopygos

A bird of moderate size and distinctive behaviour: body length 19.5-22 cm, wing length 9.1-9.8 cm and weight 31-43 g. The head, cheeks, throat and tail are black. The undertail-coverts are bright yellow. Other parts of the body are brown-grey. The eye is black in the male and rather more red in the female. The male is slightly larger. Juveniles are paler.

This monotypic species is the most northerly of its genus: its range extends from southern and eastern Turkey, through Lebanon, Syria and Israel to Aden and Oman in the south of the Arabian peninsula. The Yellow-vented Bulbul is a bird of gardens, plantations and oases — any environment where trees and bushes are found. It is common within villages and towns but almost absent from cultivated fields and open terrain. In Israel this is a resident bird, very common in most parts of the country, including the more fertile areas of the Negev and the Arava.

The Yellow-vented Bulbul feeds primarily on fruits and insects. Small fruits, such as mulberries, margosa and nitraria it swallows whole, ejecting the seeds in its droppings; larger fruits, such as pears, dates and tomatoes, it nibbles, thus causing severe damage in orchards and nurseries. Insects are caught in active pursuit, or located from a vantage point. The Yellow-vented Bulbul also feeds on leaves and petals of flowers such as *Erythrina* and iris. In winter, when other food is in short supply, it also eats snails and ants and has even been observed feeding on carrion.

This species has a very varied vocal range. Especially distinctive is the territorial song, heard between March and April and beginning before sunrise. This consists of a series of fluty but staccato notes, arranged in phrases of four to six syllables and constantly repeated. Other variations on the territorial song includes imitations of Blackbirds, woodpeckers and Greenfinches; a hoarse cawing sound is uttered before roosting. Other calls, resembling the territorial song but of different rate and intensity, are heard when a cat, a snake or a Barn Owl is being mobbed or when partners meet after a temporary

separation. The approach of a human to the vicinity of the nest also provokes a noisy reaction.

The Yellow-vented Bulbul usually lives in pairs, but the pair does not necessarily comprise a male and a female, and even where this is the case it is not a breeding pair. Partners in such a pair remain in close proximity for most hours of the day, and, unlike most of the songbirds of this country, they do not maintain individual distance but regularly touch one another, preen one another's feathers and roost together on branches. Territories are jealously guarded and vigorously defended. The territory is relatively small for a bird of this size, no more than a few hundred square metres, and usually does not provide sufficient food to last the whole year. From time to time, hundreds of Yellow-vented Bulbuls, especially juveniles, gather for a noisy communal banquet in a plantation or an orchard, causing severe damage.

The nesting season begins in mid-March, reaches a peak during May and June and ends with the departure from the nest of the last brood of chicks in mid-August. During this period Yellow-vented Bulbuls often rear three broods. The nest is built by the female, in a secluded place among thin branches, 1-2.5 m above the ground. The base is constructed or broad leaves, sometimes newspaper, strips of plastic or cotton wool; on this base thin twigs are laid, held together with spiderwebs and cotton threads. The nest is basket-shaped and the interior is strewn with grasses and soft roots, although there is no lining as such. The diameter of the nest is 8-10 cm, internal diameter 6.5 cm and depth 4-5 cm. The clutch is of 2-4 eggs, whitish-lilac in colour and speckled with brown-purple markings. The last egg laid is lighter and longer. Incubation begins with the last egg, and is performed solely by the female. Every few minutes she leaves her post to hunt for food; when intruders approach the nest she simulates injury.

The chicks hatch after 13-14 days of incubation. At first only the female feeds them, but with time the male's contribution increases until it equals that of the female. Initially the chicks are fed on insects only, but the proportion of fruit in the diet gradually increases. For the first week of life, the chicks are brooded by the female at night. They leave the nest at 13-14 days old, and fly about ten days later, although at this stage they still depend on their parents for food. At four weeks old they feed for themselves, becoming independent at six weeks. Only about 15% of all eggs laid produce chicks which survive to fly from the nest.

As an agricultural pest, the Yellow-vented Bulbul enjoys no protection under the law.

Family: Bombycillidae (Waxwings)

This family contains five genera and eight species inhabiting coniferous woods and forests in subarctic regions of the Old and New Worlds. One species has been recorded in Israel.

These are songbirds of moderate size (body length 16-23 cm) possessing a crest. Their wings are long and pointed. The tail is short, and square-ended. The bill is broad at the base, short and strong, with the upper mandible slightly curved. The legs are very short. Members of the family feed on fruit, and tend to flock outside the nesting season.

Waxwing
Bombycilla garrulus

Male and female differ to some extent in size: body length 19-23 cm, wing length 10.4-12.4 cm, wingspan 30-37 cm and weight 40-64 g. A mainly brown bird, with black chin and eye-mask, yellow-tipped tail, grey rump, and red and yellow on the wings. It is distinguished especially by its large crest.

The Waxwing breeds in the northern forests of Europe, Asia and North America. At the beginning of winter it migrates south. Once every ten years or so its population increases dramatically and migrates further south, invading western Europe in massed flocks. In Israel, one individual is known to have occurred, at Sede Boker in December 1967.

Family: Troglodytidae (Wrens)

In this family there are 14 genera and 60 species. Most inhabit the tropical regions of South America, while ten species are found in North America and only one has penetrated the Palaearctic region via the Bering Strait and proliferated there.

These are small songbirds, chestnut-brown in colour with dark streaks, especially on the wings and the tail; the underparts are pale. Juveniles differ slightly from adults. The wings are short and rounded, the tail short and uptilted. The bill is thin, quite long and slightly curved. The legs are long and strong, and the toes long.

Wren
Troglodytes troglodytes

A small songbird: body length 9.5-11.1 cm, wing length 4.4-5 cm, wingspan 15.5-16.7 cm and weight 8-10 g. It is barred brown in colour. Its tail is short, usually uptilted, and is a clear identification mark.

The range of the Wren extends across North America, over most of Europe, North Africa, the Middle East and Palaearctic and eastern Asia, in areas of cool, temperate and Mediterranean climate. In this range 37 subspecies have been described. This is a bird of woodland and dense undergrowth, usually near mountain streams and moss-covered rocks, but in many areas it is also found in lowland and urban areas. Most of its populations are resident, but those of the north migrate.

The Wren of the subspecies *T.t. cypriotes*, which is distributed in Crete, Cyprus and the Near East, is a resident in Israel, in maquis of the northern Carmel, Upper Galilee and western Galilee. It has been known in Carmel only since the early 1970s and in Tabor only since the end of that decade; apparently this is the southernmost limit of its range. Outside the breeding season it roams, and it is then seen also in Samaria, the Judean Hills, in Gush Dan and even in Eilat.

This is a very active bird, but it tends to move about in undergrowth, close to the ground. It seeks its food — insects, spiders, worms and small crustaceans — in clefts, crevices and other concealed places. The Wren has a trilling and very melodious song, of surprising volume for such a small bird, heard during most months of the year and especially conspicuous during the nesting season, between February and June. In cold weather, even outside the breeding season, the Wren tends to roost in its nest, sometimes together with its offspring.

The nesting season begins in February, when the male builds several nests; in Israel, five nests have been found on one oak tree in Carmel. The nest is usually built in a secluded place, under a ledge of rock, in a cleft or a hollow tree, and when there is no alternative among the foliage of a tree or a bush. The nest is ball-shaped and domed, with an opening at the side. It is built of moss, leaves and grass; when moss is not available, catkins are used as the principal building material. In the clutch there are 4-5 eggs, and the female incubates alone for 14-15 days. The chicks stay in the nest for 15-17 days.

In Israel the Wren apparently rears two broods in a season: the first from February to the end of March, and the second, in a nearby nest, from April to the end of May.

Family: Prunellidae (Accentors)

In this family there is a single genus and 12 species, inhabiting Europe and Asia, in temperate and northern climatic regions. Seven of them are confined to the Himalayas and Tibet, while two species have penetrated North Africa. The northern populations migrate. In Israel four species are winterers and accidentals.

These small songbirds resemble sparrows in appearance, except that the bill is narrow and pointed at the tip. Accentors have grey-brown coloration, and the flanks are usually streaked. The wings are rounded, the tail slightly forked. The leg is short and strong. The bill is broad at the base and the upper mandible slightly flattened.

Accentors live mainly in mountainous areas. They are furtive in their habits, spending much of their time in dense undergrowth. They feed on insects and vegetable food. Accentors nest on the ground or in bushes; their eggs are bluish-grey.

Dunnock
Prunella modularis

Body length 14.4-16.7 cm, wing length 6.4-7 cm, wingspan 21-23 cm and weight 18 g. Resembles a female House Sparrow, except that the head and breast are grey and the bill thin. The back is brown with black streaks.

The Dunnock breeds over most of Europe, except in the far north and on the shores of the Mediterranean. In this range six subspecies have been described. It usually inhabits coniferous groves and forests, in mountainous and subalpine regions, but is also found in mixed forests and, in western Europe, in hedgerows, parks and agricultural environments. The northern populations migrate and winter in western Europe, in the Mediterranean basin and the Middle East.

The Dunnock tends to hide in undergrowth and is not easily observed. It seeks its food on the ground, especially among fallen leaves. Normally individuals are found singly. During the winter it feeds almost exclusively on seeds.

In Israel this is a fairly common winter visitor (probably two subspecies involved: *P.m. modularis* and *P.m. obscura*) in northern and central parts of the country, between November and March. It is also an accidental in Eilat.

Radde's Accentor
Prunella ocularis

Body length 15 cm and wing length 7.5 cm. This accentor has a dark brown head, a pale throat, and an almost white supercilium contrasting with the dark crown and cheeks. The belly is sandy in colour and the breast buff. The tail is long and slightly forked.

This accentor's distribution is restricted to high mountains in the Irano-Turanian belt: from eastern Turkey and Armenia, through northern Iran to the Zagros Mountains in southwestern Iran and in Yemen. In winter it migrates to lower mountain ranges across Iran, and reaches the Persian Gulf.

In Israel Radde's Accentor is a very rare accidental. It has been recorded on the heights of Hermon, in the Golan, in the Judean Hills and in Ein Gedi. A few individuals have been known to winter in these areas.

Alpine Accentor
Prunella collaris

The largest of the accentors: body length 18.5 cm, wing length 9.2-10.6 cm, wingspan 31 cm and weight up to 40 g. In colour it resembles the Dunnock, but is distinguished by black and white spotting on the chin and throat and chestnut streaks on the flanks. In flight, two pale wingbars and the white tip of the tail are conspicuous.

The Alpine Accentor has a fragmented distribution limited to high mountain ranges in the Palaearctic region: the Atlas, Pyrenees, Alps, Apennines, Taurus, Zagros, Himalayas and mountains of Tibet; it also occurs in Korea, Japan and Taiwan. In this range nine subspecies have been described. This is a mainly resident bird, moving down in winter to below the snow-line. A few individuals, mainly juveniles, migrate.

In Israel this is a very rare winterer between November and February. Most observations are of solitary juveniles (which are grey-brown and drabber than adults) in the Arbel (up to six individuals in one day), in Nahal Amud, on the slopes of Hermon and in the Judean Hills.

Black-throated Accentor
Prunella atrogularis

Similar to Radde's Accentor, but smaller and has a black throat: body length 14 cm and wing length 7.2 cm.

This accentor breeds in two widely separated regions: in the northern Ural Mountains and in Turkestan. It inhabits subalpine coniferous forests. It usually winters in Iran, Afghanistan and the western Himalayas.

In Israel one individual occurred in Jerusalem on 12 January 1982, staying in the area until March.

Family: Turdidae (Thrushes, Chats and Allies)

This family contains 47 genera and 310 species. Its members are distributed in all parts of the world, except remote islands in the Pacific Ocean and at the Poles. This is a family of Old World origin, extending to the New World only at a relatively late stage; the majority of species live in Eurasia, especially in northern and cold areas. These birds are resident in hot countries, while the northern species roam or migrate. In Israel nine genera and 33 species are represented, including 11 species of wheatear and nine species of thrush.

This is one of the largest families in the order of songbirds. According to some systems of classification it is a subfamily of a larger family in which it is combined with Muscicapidae (flycatchers); according to others it is linked in similar fashion with Sylviidae (warblers). The family is divided into two groups: wheatears/chats, which are more primitive, comprise a large number of species and are akin to warblers; and the true thrushes.

These are small to average-sized songbirds: body length 11.5-34 cm and weight 13-200 g. The wing is rounded and generally short, longer in species living in open environments and in migratory species. The tail is short or average. Colours tend to be vivid, and usually there is a striking sexual dimorphism, although in some cases the sexes are similar. Juveniles differ in plumage from adults: they are usually mottled on the throat and breast. Normally there is one moult in the year, except in a few species which have an additional partial moult in spring. Most species spend much of their time on the ground, and accordingly the legs and feet are strong. The bill varies: slender and weak in wheatears and chats, strong and even slightly curved in rock thrushes and redstarts.

Most Turdidae are ground-dwellers; a minority inhabit tree foliage. Breeding areas vary: from tundra and coniferous forest, through steppes and maquis to deserts and tropical rainforest. Many species prefer mixed terrain, grasslands with scattered trees and bushes or woodland with clearings. Insects constitute their main diet. The family contains some of the finest vocalists, including nocturnal singers.

The nests are built in a wide variety of places: in a hole in the ground, in a crevice, under or between boulders, on a tree or a bush. The construction is mainly or solely by the female: the nest is basket-shaped, built of grass and other plant material and lined with hairs and feathers. Many species have eggs of a uniform bluish colour; in others the eggs are speckled with reddish markings. In the clutch there are 3-6 eggs; incubation lasts 13-14 days and is performed mainly by the female. The chicks hatch blind, usually covered with sparse and long down, light brown or grey in colour. Both parents feed them bill-to-bill, and they leave the nest at 13-18 days old. At the juvenile stage they are mottled, especially on the underparts, and usually acquire adult plumage only during the first autumn. They attain sexual maturity at about one year old.

Genus: *Cercotrichas*
Cercotrichas is considered the most primitive genus in the family Turdidae, and in the past was included in the family of Sylviidae (warblers).

Rufous Bush Robin
Cercotrichas galactotes

Body length 16.8-17.5 cm, wing length 8.2-8.8 cm and weight 20-24 g. Distinguished by its long, graduated and rufous tail. The back is the same colour as the tail, and the underparts are pale buff. The outer tail feathers are 5-7mm shorter than the central ones (hence the graduated shape of the tail) and tipped white with black subterminal markings (this pattern is absent in the two central feathers and is hidden when the tail is folded). The bill is long and pointed. Juveniles are paler in colour and have a shorter tail.

The Rufous Bush Robin has a Mediterranean/Irano-Turanian range, and one subspecies breeds in the belt of savanna between northern Somalia and Senegal. The four Palaearctic subspecies migrate, wintering in West and East Africa, south Arabia and northwest India. This is a bird of sparse scrub, maquis, cultivated land, gardens, orchards and even coniferous plantations. In Israel two subspecies occur, one a summer visitor and the other a passage migrant.

This is an outstanding territorial bird, even attacking birds of other species in defence of its territory, which ranges in size from 0.4 ha to 1 ha. It is usually seen flying low from bush to bush, or hopping on the ground with tail held erect. It also tends to perch on bushes, short trees, posts and other exposed places. On landing it erects its tail and spreads it like a fan, exposing the black and white pattern at the tip. These tail movements are accompanied by musical chirping. This species is noted for its attractive and varied, somewhat lark-like song, uttered from a vantage point or in the course of butterfly-like courtship flight, wings raised high and tail spread. Sometimes it also sings at night. The Rufous Bush Robin feeds primarily on insects.

In Israel the subspecies *C.g. syriacus*, which breeds in southern Europe from Albania to northern Syria, is a passage migrant; it is distinguished by its dark back and greyish-tinged underparts. This subspecies migrates from early August through September, and also in April-May. It usually migrates singly or in small flocks.

The subspecies *C.g. galactotes*, which is distinguished by its more rufous back, is distributed from Portugal and Spain, through North Africa to Israel and southern Syria; it is a summer resident in Israel between April and September. Males usually arrive at the beginning of April, females a few days later. Until the 1950s, the Rufous Bush Robin was quite common throughout the Mediterranean region of Israel, and also in oases and especially along the banks of the Jordan. Apparently as a result of the intensified use of pesticides, populations of Rufous Bush Robins were depleted, disappearing almost entirely from the coastal plain and other areas. Only since the mid-1970s has there been some recovery of population on the coastal plain.

Construction of the nest begins at the end of April. The Rufous Bush Robin builds its nest in a wide variety of places, but prefers dim and secluded sites: in tree foliage, especially eucalyptus, in thick grass, also boxes and even disused agricultural machinery. In orchards and pine groves the nest is built on low branches, close to the ground. The base of the nest is a large, casual and rather shapeless structure, of crude materials such as straw, grass, leaves and rags and very often including snake skin,

which can help in its identification; usually the nest disintegrates before the end of the season. In the clutch there are 3-5 eggs. Incubation begins when the clutch is complete and lasts 13-14 days; the incubating bird may be approached at close range without causing alarm. The chicks leave the nest at about 13 days old.

The Rufous Bush Robin breeds twice during the summer, and nests with eggs may be found as late as August.

Black Bush Robin
Cercotrichas podobe

Body length 23 cm. A quite unmistakable bird: jet-black, this colour being especially striking after the moult. The bases of the feathers are grey, and a few of the secondaries are partly chestnut-brown. The tail is long and graduated, black with a white tip.

The Black Bush Robin is a bird of savanna and desert edges, distributed between Senegal and the shores of the Red Sea. A single individual was recorded on 12 April 1981 at Yotvata 40 km north of Eilat. Since then there have been several more records in the vicinity of Eilat.

Robin
Erithacus rubecula

A small bird with a rounded body: body length 13-14.7 cm, wing length 6.9-7.7 cm, wingspan 21-25 cm and weight 14-22 g. The back is olive-brown and the belly whitish. A distinctive reddish-orange area covers the forehead, cheeks, throat and breast, and is bordered laterally by a greyish-blue stripe. The tail is of moderate length and slightly forked.

The Robin breeds in all parts of Europe (except the arctic region) and also in North Africa and the northern Middle East to northern Syria, in northern, temperate and Mediterranean climatic areas. In this range eight subspecies have been described. Its populations in western, central and southern Europe, also those in North Africa and the Middle East, are resident; the northern and eastern populations migrate and winter in the Mediterranean basin, in Iraq and Iran. The subspecies *E.r. rubecula* is the one which occurs in Israel.

This is a common and conspicuous winter resident in the Mediterranean region of Israel, and is also a rare passage migrant. It may be seen in this country from the second half of October to early March. One individual found in Israel had been ringed as a chick in Russia.

The Robin feeds on insects in various stages of development. During the winter it stores up fat and its weight rises from 15g to 20g and more; these fat reserves are required for the return journey to its nesting areas.

In this country the Robin lives in maquis, forests, orchards, plantations and gardens. On arrival, each individual finds a territory of its own and guards it jealously through the winter; the size of the territory is 0.6-1 ha, depending on the amount of food and the quality of thicket cover. To proclaim ownership, the Robin utters frequent metallic calls from tall bushes, especially in the morning and the evening, although it is by nature a secretive bird. These winter calls differ from the spring song of the male, a musical warbling. The female, too, claims a winter territory of her own and sings, and therefore it is impossible to tell if the wintering individual is male or female.

Genus: *Luscinia* (nightingales and allies)

The genus *Luscinia* comprises nine species of average size. It is distributed in Europe, North Africa and Asia, in areas of temperate climate. Most species migrate in winter to Africa or tropical Asia. The body is slender and elongated, the legs long and thin, pointed and slender. The tail is of moderate length and coloured rufous-brown at the base. Body colours are various shades of brown. These birds live usually in woodland near water. They seek food such as insects and worms on the ground, usually among fallen leaves. The nest is normally located on the ground or close to it. In Israel three species are known.

Nightingale
Luscinia megarhynchos

A songbird of average size: body length 16.5 cm, wing length 7.5-9.1 cm and weight 20-29 g. The upperparts are chestnut-brown, the breast and flanks light greyish-brown and the belly whitish. The tail is long (6.7-8 cm), and chestnut-brown in colour. The bill is slender but strong.

The Nightingale is distributed across Europe, except the north and east of the continent, with extension into the Irano-Turanian zone. In this range three subspecies have been described. It inhabits sparse forests of broadleaf trees, with dense undergrowth and waterlogged ground, or riparian woodland along rivers in valleys. All of its populations migrate, wintering in East Africa and in the region between the Sahara and the Equator. In Israel this is a summer visitor and a passage migrant.

This species tends to seek its food on the ground, in fallen leaves among thickets and also in open terrain. It moves in a series of long hops, stopping from time to time and tilting its head. It is furtive and not easily located. The best indication of its presence, especially in spring, is its song, extremely rich in variety and volume. The Nightingale sometimes sings during the spring migration and so can be heard in different regions in the country and even in winter quarters.

In Israel what is apparently the subspecies *L.m. megarhynchos* is a passage migrant in autumn between September and October, and in spring, when it is more common, from mid-March to mid-May, especially in early April. Evidence from ringing suggests that the bulk of the autumn migration takes place over the Mediterranean, while in spring the migration route passes through Israel.

The Nightingale is also a fairly common breeder in the Bet She'an Valley and on the banks of the Jordan as far south as the Dead Sea. The nesting season is in May-June. The nest is located on the ground, in a pile of fallen leaves, or in the lower branches of a thick bush. It is a loose and ungainly basket shape, built of leaves and dry grasses and lined with delicate plants and hair. In the clutch there are usually 4-5 eggs, sometimes 3 or 6. The female incubates alone for a period of about 13 days. The chicks are fed by both parents in the nest for 11-12 days. The population breeding in this country migrates south in September.

Thrush Nightingale
Luscinia luscinia

Body length 16-19.3 cm, wing length 8.4-9.3 cm, wingspan 25.5-28 cm and weight 21-31 g. Very similar to the Nightingale, both in behaviour and appearance, although its overall colour is darker brown, the tail less rufous and the breast and flanks lightly mottled.

The Thrush Nightingale replaces the Nightingale in northern and eastern Europe and its range extends as far as Siberia, although there is some overlap between the two species. This is a monotypic species which inhabits wetter areas than those of the Nightingale, including marsh-woodland and waterlogged scrub terrain. The Thrush Nightingale winters in eastern tropical Africa, south of the wintering regions of the Nightingale, from Tanzania to Mozambique.

In Israel this is a common passage migrant from the end of August to October (when it is very difficult to distinguish from the Nightingale); and from the end of March to mid-May, especially at the end of April, after the migration peak of the Nightingale.

Bluethroat
Luscinia svecica

A slender-bodied bird: body length 13-14.5 cm, wing length 6.9-7.7 cm, wingspan 21-24 cm and weight 13-19 g. The Bluethroat differs from other members of its genus in the blue 'bib' on the chin and breast, larger and more colourful in the male and especially evident in breeding plumage. This bib is surrounded by a black border, which in turn is fringed with a white and a chestnut band. Sometimes there is a conspicuous red or white patch in the centre of the bib; the colour and size of this patch are among the signs distinguishing between the seven subspecies. The female usually has a bluish-grey bib, fringed with a black ring which broadens on the breast into a dark brown patch. The Bluethroat is also distinguished by its tail, rufous-brown at the base and dark brown at the tip. The upperparts are grey-brown with a prominent whitish supercilium, and the belly pale sandy-grey in colour.

This species is distributed throughout the Palae-arctic region, except in the Mediterranean and Saharo-Arabian belts. Its habitats are riparian forests along rivers and wooded areas in swampland: wetter habitats than those of the Thrush Nightingale. In autumn it migrates south and winters in North and East Africa, the Middle East, southern Iran, Afghanistan, India and southeast Asia.

In Israel the Bluethroat is a common winterer and passage migrant. It is more conspicuous during the autumn migration, from the second half of September to the end of November, less so in the spring migration, which takes place from the end of March to the second half of April. Males precede females by about ten days. From data acquired through netting in Eilat, it is evident that about 60% of the migrants there belong to the subspecies *L.s. svecica*, which is distinguished by a red patch in the centre of the blue bib and which is distributed in Scandinavia and northern Russia; 40% belong to the subspecies *L.s. cyanecula*, in which the patch is white and which is distributed in central and western Europe.

The wintering population arrives in this country in the first half of October and leaves during March. The Bluethroat winters in dense vegetation near water: marshes, rivers, banks of fish-ponds and other water sources, and also in damp agricultural fields and near irrigation canals.

White-throated Robin
Irania gutturalis

Body length 16-18.3 cm, wing length 8.4-9.5 cm and weight 21-30 g. A member of a monotypic genus closely resembling the African genus *Cossypha* (13 species) but separated from it as the only species breeding outside Africa and by its larger clutch size; it resembles *Luscinia*, but has a longer and broader tail. The male is a colourful bird with rufous-red

underparts, grey upperparts and a black tail, and is distinguished especially by the conspicuous head pattern: white throat and supercilia, black cheeks and lores, and grey crown. The female is grey-brown overall, with grey cheeks, and the juvenile is mottled.

The White-throated Robin is a monotypic species with a fairly limited range, from Turkey through northern Iraq and Iran to Afghanistan. This is a typical mountain bird, usually confined to the coniferous belt and found especially among tamarisks. It is a very rare breeder on Mount Hermon. It winters in southwestern Arabia and in Africa from Ethiopia to central Kenya.

A few isolated individuals of this species have been seen during migration periods (September and the end of April) in Jaffa, Jerusalem, the northern Arava, Ein Gedi and the heights of the Golan.

On Hermon the White-throated Robin breeds in a limited area between altitudes of 1,400 m and 1,900 m. Collection of eggs for scientific purposes apparently led to the cessation of nesting in this area in the mid-1970s; since the beginning of the 1980s it has been resumed by only one or two pairs. It returns to Hermon at the end of April. Its habitat here is rocky terrain, with scattered birch and crab-apple trees. It tends to perch on rocks, and is also seen hopping on the ground and pecking for food: insects, grubs, seeds and fruits. It flies low with tail spread like a fan, and its song is melodious and strong. In May, the female builds the nest on a tree or a shrub, 50-100 cm above the ground. The nest is constructed of cereal stalks and lined with feathers, resembling a flat cup. In the clutch there are 4-5 eggs. The female incubates alone for about two weeks, and both parents feed the chicks in the nest for a further two weeks.

The White-throated Robin migrates from Hermon as early as July.

Genus: *Phoenicurus* (redstarts)

The genus *Phoenicurus* comprises 13 species, distinguished by their elongated body and by the thin and pointed bill with clearly visible bristles. The tail and rump is bright reddish-brown in all species, in both sexes and even in juveniles. The two central tail feathers are grey-brown in colour, concealing the colour of the remaining tail feathers when the bird is standing at rest. The tail is rounded. All species tend to bob the tail up and down in a characteristic fashion.

Black Redstart
Phoenicurus ochruros

Body length 13.5-15.7 cm, wing length 7.3-8.6 cm and weight 14-18 g. The upperparts (apart from rump and tail) of the male are grey in autumn and early winter, becoming pitch-black in spring; the throat and breast are black, while the crown remains grey even in summer plumage. The colour of the belly varies according to subspecies, from grey-black to rufous-brown. In a few subspecies there is a white patch on the wing of the adult male. The female is grey-brown, including the belly.

The Black Redstart is distributed from western, central and southern Europe, through the Levant to central Asia. In this range five subspecies have been identified. This is a bird of stony terrain and slopes with rockfalls. In the Alps it lives at an altitude of some 3,000 m above sea-level, in the Himalayas up to 6,000 m; in other regions it descends to sea-level. In many areas it is found near settlements and buildings. Southern populations of the Black Redstart are resident, while those of the north migrate and winter in North and East Africa, in the Middle East and in India. In Israel this is a summer visitor, winter visitor and passage migrant.

This is a typical ground bird. It tends to perch on exposed vantage points — a stone, a boulder, a fence or a roof. It gathers its food on the ground or in rock-crevices, with a preference for ants and small beetles.

In Israel the Black Redstart winters in hills, especially in northern and central parts of the country, also within settlements in all areas, including Eilat. Most of the wintering birds belong to the subspecies *P.o. gibraltariensis*, which is distributed in North Africa and Europe and distinguished by its grey-black belly. These arrive in November and stay until the end of March; males usually precede

females by a few days. Each individual winters alone in a territory, and tends to return in successive winters to the same territory. Even in winter quarters, Black Redstarts often forsake rocky terrain in preference for ruins and abandoned buildings. This subspecies is also a rare passage migrant in Israel.

The subspecies *P.o. semirufus*, distinguished by its rufous-brown belly (the same colour as the tail), is a rare passage migrant and a very rare winterer in this country. Its breeding range is confined to the mountains of Lebanon and Syria (including Hermon). It is seen on migration almost exclusively in the Jordan Valley and the Arava.

This latter subspecies is a common summer resident and breeder on the flank of Mount Hermon, from an altitude of 1,400 m and upward. It returns to Hermon from its winter quarters in the last week of March or in early April, when the males claim their territories with prolonged strong and melodious song. The natural nesting places are clefts and rock-crevices, but the Black Redstart is capable of adapting to a variety of artificial receptacles. The nest, built in the second half of April or early May, is a flat, loose basket-shaped structure of dry grasses and pine needles and lined with hair, wool and feathers. In the clutch there are 4-6 eggs. The female incubates for 12-15 days. Both parents feed the chicks in the nest for a period of 12-16 days. The chicks sometimes leave the nest before they are able to fly, and outside the nest the male continues to tend them for a further two weeks, while the female prepares for a second, in some cases a third brood. Feeding of chicks in the nest continues until the end of July; the family unit is retained until the end of August.

Black Redstarts migrate southward from Hermon during October.

Redstart
Phoenicurus phoenicurus

Body length 13.2-14.5 cm, wing length 7.8-8.5 cm, wingspan 22-27 cm and weight 14-19 g. A colourful bird, with its full range of colours seen only in the spring. The back and crown of the male are grey, the forehead white, the cheeks and throat black, the breast, rump and tail reddish-chestnut and the belly white. The female is olive-brown overall, with underparts pale buff in autumn, and more drab in winter.

The Redstart breeds in all parts of Europe to Siberia, and also in North Africa and the Middle East, including Cyprus, Turkey and Iraq and possibly also Lebanon. In this range three subspecies have been described. Its habitats are in deciduous forests, plantations, groves and landscape gardens. It winters in Africa south of the Sahara.

The Redstart passes through Israel on migration. As early as the beginning of August individuals of the subspecies *P.p. samamisicus* are seen, distinguished by a white mark in the centre of the wing. This subspecies breeds from Turkey, through the Crimea and the Caucasus to western Afghanistan. Its migration continues until mid-September. From mid-September until November the individuals seen in the country belong to the European subspecies *P.p. phoenicurus*, which is more common.

The spring migration of the white-winged subspecies begins in the second week of March; for about two weeks there is an overlap between this and the European subspecies, which continues to migrate until the second half of May. In the course of the spring migration males precede females by a few days.

Blackstart
Cercomela melanura

Body length 14-16.6 cm, wing length 7.6-8.7 cm and weight 13-18 g. A grey songbird, slightly smaller than a sparrow, with the black colour of the rump and tail very prominent; the wings are short compared with those of wheatears. The sexes are similar; the juvenile too resembles the adult, although its overall colour is brown rather than grey. It has a habit of constantly flicking its tail.

The genus *Cercomela* is of African origin and includes nine species, the Blackstart inhabiting a narrow strip along the southern fringes of the Sahara: from Mali and Nigeria to Sudan, Ethiopia and Somalia, and thence along the shores of Arabia to Sinai, the Negev and the Judean Desert. In this range six subspecies have been described. The Asiatic population belongs to the subspecies *C.m. melanura*. This species is resident throughout its range.

The Blackstart feeds especially on insects and other small, fast-moving ground creatures, spotted from a vantage point. It also eats kitchen refuse and even fruits.

In Israel, the Blackstart has extended beyond the limits of desert and travelled north along the Jordan Valley to Gilboa, the slopes of the southern Golan, Nahal Amud and the region north of Lake Tiberias. Its habitats in this country are particularly oases and beds of wadis with an abundance of acacia trees, sometimes also quite rocky and arid slopes. In these places it is a quite common and prominent bird, showing little timidity. It maintains its territory throughout the year. It spends much of its time patrolling its territory or perching on a prominent vantage point, with wings drooping and tail spread and flicked in a characteristic and peculiar fashion.

At the approach of the nesting season, the soft and melodious warbling song of the male is widely heard. Partners begin to seek out a nesting site at about the end of February. They prefer to nest under a stone or a boulder, but have been known to choose reptile or rodent burrows. The nest is a loose, basket-shaped structure, built of grasses, roots and thin branches and lined with delicate plant material, hair and even snake skin. The area around the nest and the entrance are paved with small stones. Laying usually begins in March, the clutch consisting of 3-4 eggs. No details of incubation are known, although most of the task is apparently performed by the female. Both parents feed the chicks in the nest for a period of about two weeks.

The Blackstart apparently rears two broods in the year, since nests with young chicks are sometimes still to be found in early June.

Stonechat
Saxicola torquata

Body length 11.5-13 cm, wing length 6.2-7 cm, wingspan 21-22 cm and weight 11-19 g. The Stonechat belongs to a genus of ten species, closely related to wheatears but similar in behaviour to flycatchers. It has a short, pointed and strong bill, with well-developed bristles. The wings are relatively long and the tail short. The male has striking plumage: black head and throat, with a white patch at the sides of the neck, rufous-brown breast and sandy-white belly; its back is dark brown, and a white area on the wing is conspicuous in flight. The female is similar but paler; the head and throat are brown rather than black, and there is no white mark at the sides of the neck. After the nesting season, the Stonechat's colours are drab; they become more vivid at the approach of spring.

This species has a very broad range extending along the whole width of the southern Palaearctic region, although it does not breed in northern and central Europe and only the Asiatic subspecies are found as far north as the Arctic Circle. The Stonechat also breeds in Lebanon, in North Africa and tropical Africa. In this range 25 subspecies have been identified. This is a bird of grassy environments, agricultural fields, meadows and stretches of heathland on plains and hills, with scattered bushes or small trees. In the Himalayas and Tibet it may be found up to an altitude of 5,000 m. The populations in southern and western Europe are resident, while those of central and southeastern Europe and of Asia migrate. The Western Palaearctic population winters in the Middle East and in northeast and East Africa.

In Israel this is a common winterer in open environments: fields and wasteland in northern and central parts of the country, and also oases and cultivated fields in the desert. It begins to arrive at the end of September and during October, and stays until March. The subspecies concerned is *S.t. rubicola*, which breeds in Europe. This subspecies is also a fairly rare passage migrant, between mid-October and mid-November and during March; it is more conspicuous in the spring migration. On migration two other subspecies may be seen: *S.t. variegata*, which breeds on the steppes of Astrakhan and winters in eastern Sudan and Somalia, and in males of which the base of the tail is white and not all-black; and *S.t. maura*, which breeds in northern Russia and eastward to Mongolia, wintering in India but also along the shores of the Persian Gulf and in Arabia. This latter subspecies is smaller, with a paler breast and the base of tail less white than in *S.t. variegata*.

The Stonechat is one of the few species wintering in Israel in which a pair holds and defends a territory. The size of territory varies from 0.5 ha to 1 ha. The pairs holding territories are not necessarily breeding partners, and the bond between them lasts only through the winter.

Whinchat
Saxicola rubetra

Slightly larger than the Stonechat: body length 12.7-13.7 cm, wing length 7.4-8.1 cm, wingspan 23.5-26 cm and weight 14-21 g. It resembles the Stonechat but its colours are paler, the throat rufous-brown and the white supercilium distinctive. Its coloration is more vivid in spring, following the pre-breeding moult in winter quarters.

The Whinchat's range extends over most of Europe, reaching further north and east than that of the Stonechat and with some penetration into central Asia. It is a monotypic species. Its habitats are similar to those of the Stonechat, but usually damper and grassier, and its behaviour patterns are also similar. All of its populations winter in savanna in East Africa, south of the Sahara.

In Israel this is a common passage migrant in open habitats from the end of August to the end of October, and between the end of March and May. It is especially conspicuous in the autumn migration, when it precedes the Stonechat by two to three weeks.

Genus: *Oenanthe* (wheatears)
In this genus there are 18 species, most living in Africa and Asia, a minority in Europe and one species in North America. In Israel 11 species are seen, seven of them breeding, each in a different habitat.

These are medium-sized songbirds, most of them easily recognised by the white rump and black and white tail (only in a few species are the rump and parts of the tail rufous-brown). The wings are long, the tail is square-ended. The bill is slender and black. Wheatears are birds of open environments, often perching on rocks or on the ground. Many species have penetrated deserts. The more remote the habitat, the brighter the plumage and the more striking the contrast between black and white. The male usually differs from the female in colouring, and in six of the species known in Israel there are several colour-phases. Juveniles also differ in colour from adults, and thus some 30 plumage varieties of wheatear are to be seen in this country. Distinguishing between males of the different species is relatively easy, less so with females. Males are generally larger.

All wheatears feed on insects and are very territorial, at least during the nesting season. The song is usually short and staccato, but sometimes quite long and melodious, and is normally uttered from a vantage point or during courtship flight. Wheatears nest in secluded places: in clefts, under rocks or in rodent burrows. The eggs are greyish-blue in colour. The female bears most or all of the burden of incubation.

Black-eared Wheatear
Oenanthe hispanica

The commonest and most widely distributed of the wheatears in Israel: body length 14-16.3 cm, wing length 7.8-9.3 cm, wingspan 26-29 cm and weight 15-22 g. A very pale greyish-brown sandy colour is usually prominent in the male on the head, nape and back, breast and belly; the tips of some of the feathers in these areas become abraded during the winter and their colour becomes paler. (The Black-eared Wheatear also has a light phase, in which these feathers are white or whitish throughout the year.) The wings are black, the rump white, and on the white tail is a black inverted 'T' shape. The ear-coverts are black, and the chin and throat are also black (in about 60% of males) or light sandy-brown, like the colour of the belly (in the remaining 40%). Even in black-throated individuals there is a gap between the black of the throat and the black of the wing, and this is a useful distinguishing mark between this and other species of wheatear. The female has overall sandy-brown colouring, blackish-brown wings and a similar variety of throat types, but hardly any differences in plumage between the seasons of the year. Immatures resemble the adult female; males in their first spring are brown on the back, head and breast. Juveniles are heavily spotted and mottled.

The distribution of the Black-eared Wheatear is Mediterranean, with some penetration into the Irano-Turanian zone. In this range two subspecies have been identified. The subspecies known in Israel, in the colour-phases described above, is *O.h. melanoleuca*, which has a range extending eastward from Yugoslavia and southern Italy. This is a bird of hilly, rocky, open or semi-open environments, usually at lower altitude than the habitats of the Wheatear. (On Hermon, for example, the Black-eared Wheatear reaches an altitude of 1,600 m, while the Wheatear is found at a higher level.) The Black-eared Wheatear winters in savannas south of the Sahara and in East Africa. In Israel this is a common summer resident and a very common passage migrant.

Like other species of wheatear, this is an active bird, seen in almost perpetual motion. It hops with agility on the surface of the ground, pausing from time to time on a small hillock or a rock. Periodically it flies, at low altitude and over short range, from one resting point to another. Sometimes it also perches on terraces, fences and even bushes. Its stance is erect, but it often stoops and vibrates its tail. The Black-eared Wheatear hides and roosts in holes, in crevices and under rocks.

Passage individuals are seen throughout Israel from early August, especially in the first weeks of October. The spring migration takes place from the end of February to early May. Of the migrants passing through Eilat, 70% are of the black-throated form.

The breeding population arrives in Israel in early March, and quickly finds territories in every hilly district of the Mediterranean region, from the foothills of Hermon to Be'er Sheva. Males precede their mates by a few days. They claim large territories, 30-40 ha in area, singing loudly to proclaim their ownership. With the arrival of more males the territory size decreases to about 10 ha or less, in a process acompanied by ritual and stylised threats, and sometimes real violence. The nest is shaped like a flat basket, built of dry grasses and lined with a few delicate roots and hair. In the clutch there are 4-6 eggs. The female incubates alone, for 13-14 days. Both parents feed the chicks for about 14 days in the nest, and a further two to three weeks outside it.

The Black-eared Wheatear has one brood in the year (possibly two in the region of Hermon). Laying begins in April, but, as a result of replacement clutches following initial failure, nests with eggs may be found as late as June. In September the Black-eared Wheatears that have bred in this country return to their winter quarters.

Wheatear
Oenanthe oenanthe

Body length 15-17 cm, wing length 9.1-10 cm, wingspan 28-31.5 cm and weight 19-28 g. The male is distinguished from all other wheatears by the bluish-grey colour of the crown, nape and back; a black patch extends from the base of the bill to beyond the eye. The wing is black. These colours are more prominent in breeding plumage. Its appearance in autumn is greyish-brown. The female resembles the winter-plumage male: grey-brown above and sandy-brown below, with little difference in appearance between summer and winter. Both sexes have a white rump, and tail feathers white up to half their length with the distal half black; the two central tail feathers are black to two-thirds of their length, and the resulting inverted 'T' shape is similar to that in the tail of the Black-eared Wheatear, but with a broader cross-bar. Juveniles are mottled on the back and breast, and the tip of the tail is rufous-brown.

This species' range is the broadest of all the wheatears, extending over the whole of Europe and most of Asia, also North Africa, Greenland and northeast Canada. In this range seven subspecies have been described. All of its populations migrate at the end of the nesting season. The Western Palaearctic population winters in savannas in tropical Africa, and the number of individuals crossing the Sahara is estimated at 125 million; most other populations of this species, including those breeding in Greenland, northeast Canada and Alaska, also winter in Africa, some covering on migration a distance of 13,000 km in each direction.

The Wheatear of the subspecies *O.o. oenanthe* is a common passage migrant from mid-August to the end of November (preceding the Black-eared Wheatear by about two weeks); in spring from the end of February to mid-May. Males precede females by a few days. During migration the Wheatear is seen in open environments in most parts of the country.

The subspecies *O.o. rostrata* is a summer visitor to Israel, breeding on Mount Hermon at altitudes in excess of 1,800 m; at lower levels, between 1,400 m and 1,700 m, there is some overlap with the breeding population of the Black-eared Wheatear. The breeding Wheatears return to Hermon in early April and stay until the end of September/early October, during which period they often rear two broods. In behaviour, diet and breeding biology, the Wheatear closely resembles the Black-eared Wheatear.

White-crowned Black Wheatear
Oenanthe leucopyga

A large wheatear: body length 16.8-19 cm, wing length 10.1-11.6 cm and weight 23-26 g. It has striking plumage: body coal-black, and tail snow-white except for a small black area on the two central feathers. The adult, usually from the age of one year, sometimes two, also has a white crown and nape (until this stage the crown and the nape are as black as the remainder of the body). There is no difference in plumage between the sexes.

The White-crowned Black Wheatear is a typical Saharo-Arabian species, with penetration into Israel and Jordan. In this range three subspecies have been described. It inhabits areas of cliffs, canyons and rocky slopes in the most extreme desert conditions. It is resident in all parts of its range.

This wheatear spends most hours of the day hunting and guarding its territory. Apart from insect food it also eats scraps, and several individuals may be seen together near piles of refuse. In the hottest hours of the day the White-crowned Black Wheatear rests in sheltered places. It roosts in rock-crevices or under boulders, and each individual has a regular roosting site.

In Israel the subspecies *O.l. ernesti*, which is distributed from Egypt to Iraq, is particularly common along the cliffs of the Syro-African rift from Eilat to the Dead Sea; its northern range is limited to the region of Jericho. Sometimes, especially at the end of the nesting season, this species penetrates populated areas such as Eilat and Ein Gedi. It lives in pairs in territories 10-50 ha in size.

Nesting dates vary according to the rate of rainfall, which influences the growth of vegetation and thereby the availability of insects: in years of severe drought this species will not breed at all, while in normal years breeding takes place between the end of February and early April. At the approach of the nesting season the males are heard loudly proclaiming their ownership of territories with melodious and resonant song, although they also sing outside the breeding season. The songs of different individuals differ perceptibly, and some imitate various sounds.

The White-crowned Black Wheatear nests in rock-crevices or under boulders, sometimes in deserted buildings. The nest itself is shaped like a flat basket and is a neat structure, built of delicate twigs and grasses and lined with feathers, threads, hairs and wool. The clutch contains 2-4 eggs, sometimes 5. The female incubates alone for a period of about 14 days. Both parents feed the chicks in the nest for about two weeks, and tend them outside the nest for a further three weeks.

In the region of Santa Katarina, the chicks stay in their parents' territory until the following spring; this is not the case in the Dead Sea area, where they leave the territory as soon as they become independent.

Mourning Wheatear
Oenanthe lugens

The commonest and most widely distributed of the black and white wheatears in the deserts of Israel: body length 14.5-17.5 cm, wing length 8.7-10 cm and weight 18-26 g. The forehead, crown and nape, breast and belly are white; these areas turn rather more grey with the moult, but become white again with the crumbling of the feather tips. The cheeks, throat and neck are black, as are the wings, although the base of the flight feathers is paler, and consequently a pale patch appears in flight in the centre of the wing. The rump is white, as are the tail feathers except at the tips, which are black; the black of the two central tail feathers extends over less than half the tail length. A distinctive feature of the Mourning Wheatear is the rufous colour of the undertail-coverts, although this is not always easily observed. The sexes are similar. Juveniles have grey-brown plumage until their first moult, and appear mottled.

This wheatear is a Saharo-Sindian bird, distributed from Algeria to Pakistan and northwest India, and also found in the Horn of Africa and in East Africa. In this range eight subspecies have been identified. The subspecies familiar in Israel is *O.l. lugens*, which is distributed from east of the Nile to Damascus, northwestern Arabia and Iraq.

This is a common bird in this country in the Negev and the Judean Desert, but also penetrates eastern Samaria and extends as far north as Nahal Tirza. It is found mainly in rocky deserts, but it also inhabits grassy steppes. It lives in territorial pairs throughout the year, the territory covering an area of 10-25 ha. The female builds the nest in a rock-crevice, under a boulder or in a hole in the ground, usually on a rocky slope but sometimes in cracks in the wall of a derelict building. The entrance to the nest is lined with small stones, while the nest itself is flat, built of grass and lined with wool and feathers. Laying takes place between February and April. In the clutch there are usually 4-5 eggs, sometimes 3 or 6. The period of incubation is about 14 days, and the female incubates alone. Both parents feed the chicks, which stay in the nest for 14-15 days and usually leave it before they are able to fly. At this stage the male's share in feeding gradually comes to an end, although the female is liable to continue feeding the chicks to the age of 50 days.

The Mourning Wheatear is sometimes double-brooded.

Isabelline Wheatear
Oenanthe isabellina

A large wheatear: body length 15.3-17 cm, wing

length 9.3-10 cm, wingspan 29.3-31.5 cm and weight 27-34 g. It is sandy brown-grey in colour. The tail is black at the tip and white at the base; the rump is white. The legs are long and stance erect. The sexes are similar.

The Isabelline Wheatear, which is a monotypic species, has an Irano-Turanian distribution: from Turkey and Israel through the steppes of the Ukraine to Pakistan and Tibet. Its habitats are grassy steppes, stretches of scrub and rocky plains. Almost all its populations migrate, wintering in savannas south of the Sahara and in East Africa, and also in Arabia and northwest India.

In Israel this is a common passage migrant in all areas, in autumn from July, when it precedes all the other migrating wheatears, to November, with a peak in mid-August. It is less common in the spring migration, which takes place from the end of February to mid-April. This is also a rare winterer in the western Negev.

The Isabelline Wheatear breeds fairly commonly in the southern Golan and is a rare breeder in the plains of the northern Negev near Dimona. The nest is usually built in a rodent burrow, and the clutch contains 4-6 eggs.

Pied Wheatear
Oenanthe pleschanka

Body length 15.5 cm, wing length 9 cm and weight 18 g. A black-tailed wheatear: the male resembles the Mourning Wheatear, except that the wing is all-black; the back is also black. The edges of the outer tail feathers, and also the central feathers, are black up to half their length. The female resembles the female Black-eared Wheatear; young males have brown colours rather than white.

The Pied Wheatear is distributed from north of the Black Sea to central Asia. It winters in south Arabia and dry savannas in northeast Africa, and is also found in Cyprus. In Israel this is a rare passage migrant. It habitually perches on trees and bushes, as well as on electricity wires.

Desert Wheatear
Oenanthe deserti

Body length 14.7-16.5 cm, wing length 8.2-9.4 cm, wingspan 30 cm and weight 17-24 g. In this wheatear the male is sandy-brown, black and white, and the female sandy-brown except for the greyer wing. It is distinguished from all other wheatears by the tail, which is wholly black to two-thirds and more of its length.

This wheatear has a Saharo-Sindian and Irano-Turanian range in which three subspecies have been described. It inhabits dune-desert and grassy steppes

and is resident in desert regions, including in Israel.

Between the region of Tel Aviv and the Negev the subspecies *O.d. atrogularis* occurs as a passage migrant and winterer. It is less common than the resident subspecies and is larger, with more brown coloration on the upperparts. It is distributed from the southern Caucasus and Iran to Mongolia and the Gobi Desert, and migrates and winters in south Asia, Arabia and northeast Africa.

The subspecies *O.d. deserti* is a resident in the plains of the Negev and the Arava, being distributed from east of the Nile to southwestern Arabia. It breeds in April, nesting on the ground, especially in rodent burrows, and laying 4-5 eggs.

Finsch's Wheatear
Oenanthe finschii

Body length 14.5-16 cm, wing length 8.4-8.8 cm and weight 22-25 g. A wheatear of black and sandy-white colours: the male has sandy-white upperparts, including an almost white back. The female is slightly greyer than the females of other species.

Finsch's Wheatear has an Irano-Turanian range, from central Turkey to Afghanistan and southern Turkestan; it also breeds in northern Lebanon. In this range two subspecies have been described. Its habitats are especially steppe areas and their fringes. Most of its populations are resident; a minority migrate and winter in the Middle East.

In Israel the western subspecies *O.f. finschii* is a common winterer between mid-October and mid-March and sometimes later. At this season it takes the place of the Black-eared Wheatear in northern and central parts of the country. It also winters in semi-desert areas and in the region of the Dead Sea.

Red-rumped Wheatear
Oenanthe moesta

This wheatear is distinguished from other wheatears by the rufous rump and base of tail; the female has a rufous head. Its range is Saharo-Arabian and it is mostly a resident.

In Israel this is a rare winterer. There is a report that in the past it bred in northern Sinai (a nest was found on 12 March 1928 near El Arish) and possibly also in the Negev. In recent years no evidence of this has been found.

Red-tailed Wheatear
Oenanthe xanthoprymna

This wheatear also has a rufous rump and base of tail, although this colour is more intense than in the Red-rumped Wheatear. The back, head and nape are grey-brown. It is distributed in rocky deserts in the Irano-Turanian zone, and winters between northwest India and Sudan.

In Israel this is a rare accidental on migration and in winter in the Judean Desert and the Negev. A few observations have been recorded between December and March.

Hooded Wheatear
Oenanthe monacha

Body length 16.5-18.5 cm, wing length 9.5-10.7 cm and weight 18-20 g. A wheatear of striking sexual dimorphism: the male is black, except for the crown, nape, rump and belly which are white; the female is sandy-brown. The tail is also all-white, except for about half the length of the central feathers which is black.

The Hooded Wheatear is found in rocky environments in extreme deserts from Egypt and Sinai to western Sind in India. It is a resident bird throughout its range. In Israel it is especially common along the range of cliffs from the shores of the Dead Sea to Eilat and in canyons draining into the Syro-African rift.

The Hooded Wheatear breeds between March and May. It nests in a cleft or a hole in the wall of a wadi, not far from the ground. In the clutch there are 4-5 eggs. It appears that the female incubates alone for about two weeks and that both parents feed the chicks in the nest for a similar period of time, but there have been no detailed observations of nesting behaviour.

Genus: *Monticola* (rock thrushes)
This genus is considered an intermediate stage

between true thrushes and wheatears. It contains ten species, most of them common in tropical Africa and southeast Asia. Two species breed in the Palaearctic region and are seen in Israel. These birds resemble thrushes in their solid and compact bodies, but have a shorter tail and longer wings which, when the bird is standing, extend almost to the tip of the tail (in members of the genus *Turdus* they reach only slightly beyond the base of the tail). The bill is longer and more delicate than in the case of true thrushes.

Blue Rock Thrush
Monticola solitarius

Body length 22.4-23 cm, wing length 11.8-13 cm and weight 45-60 g. The male is outstanding in blue plumage: head, nape and underparts are bluish-grey, the wings blue-brown and the tail blue-black; the colour becomes stronger and more glossy in spring, with abrading of the brown feather tips. The female is greyish-brown with dark brown barring and mottling on the underparts. The bill is slender and long (2.5-3.2 cm), the legs long, strong and black in colour. Juveniles are brown above, with a dark orange patch on the belly.

The range of the Blue Rock Thrush extends from North Africa and Spain through southern Europe, the Middle East, Iran and Pakistan to the Himalayas, Japan and Malaysia. Five subspecies have been identified. The subspecies known in Israel, *M.s. solitarius*, is distributed in southern Europe and the Middle East. This species inhabits bare mountain slopes, usually at lower level than the Rock Thrush: in the Alps it climbs only to a height of about 1,500 m, and is replaced at higher altitudes by the Rock Thrush; in the Himalayas, where no Rock Thrushes are found, it reaches heights of 4,000 m and more. In other regions it may be found at sea-level and even below it. Some populations migrate, particularly those of eastern Asia.

The Blue Rock Thrush is a territorial bird even outside the nesting season: it tends to perch on a prominent vantage point, wings slightly drooped and head raised, watching for intruders. In spite of its adaptation to populated areas, this is a very timid bird in its natural environments. It feeds especially on insects such as locusts, grasshoppers and beetles, but also on seeds, snails and spiders, and sometimes on lizards, snakes and even mice.

In Israel this is a resident bird, quite common in mountains in northern and central parts of the country, from 1,300 m above sea-level on Hermon to 300 m below in the canyons of the northern Judean Desert. It is a familiar sight on rocky slopes and cliffs, and is even seen on the walls of Jerusalem. Outside the nesting season it is liable to roam and may be observed among low hills and even on plains. In this period, between September and April, the local population is reinforced by a few migrant and wintering individuals.

At the approach of the nesting season the song of the Blue Rock Thrush is clearly heard; a kind of fluty trill, not unlike that of the immature Blackbird, it resounds over wide distances in the canyons of the Golan and the Judean Desert. This song is usually uttered from a rock or the edge of a cliff, but sometimes in flight. The nest is located in a crevice in a cliff or a rock-wall; it is a large, flat and fairly loose structure of grass and roots, lined with fine grass and tender roots. Clutches in Israel are normally of 3-4 eggs. The female incubates alone for a period of 13-14 days. Both parents feed the chicks in the nest for about 16 days.

The Blue Rock Thrush breeds twice in the year. The first cycle is in March-April (thus chicks may be seen flying from the nest as early as the third week of April), and the second, sometimes in the same nest, during May-June.

Rock Thrush
Monticola saxatilis

Body length 19 cm, wing length 11.3-12.5 cm and weight 50 g. The male is very striking in the contrast between its chestnut-brown tail and underparts and its blue head, neck and throat; there is some white on the back and the wings are dark. The female is brown and mottled and resembles the female Blue Rock Thrush, but is paler and has a chestnut tail.

The Rock Thrush is distributed in the mountain ranges of the southern Palaearctic. It inhabits rocky and sunswept slopes from Spain, through southern Europe and the Middle East to central Asia. Two subspecies have been described. All of its populations migrate and winter in savanna environments in northern and eastern tropical Africa.

In Israel this is a rare to fairly common passage migrant: between the end of August and the beginning of October; and between the end of March and the end of April, when it is more conspicuous. In spring the males migrate first.

A few pairs of Rock Thrushes (numbers varying between two and nine in different years) breed on the flank of Hermon at altitudes in excess of 1,650 m. The species reaches Hermon in mid-April and migrates at the end of July, normally rearing only one brood. The breeding biology is similar to that of the Blue Rock Thrush.

Genus: *Turdus* (thrushes)
In this genus there are 63 species, distributed in all

parts of the world except Madagascar and Australasia. In Israel eight species are represented: one resident, one regular winterer, three other winter visitors, rare to fairly common in different years, and three accidentals.

The genus *Turdus* comprises songbirds of average size: 21-28 cm in body length. The bill is slightly shorter than the head and fairly slender, the upper mandible downcurved. The wing is long and pointed, the tail is square and relatively long. The leg is strong. The predominant colours are black, grey, brown, golden-buff, chestnut and white. Male and female are usually identical, though in some species the plumage of the female is more drab. Juveniles are mottled with pale markings.

All thrushes feed on the ground or close to it, consuming worms, snails and other invertebrates, and also fruit. Their songs are loud and melodious. They breed in a variety of environments, from dense woodland to bare mountain slopes. The nest resembles a deep and open basket, usually pasted on the outside with a reinforcing layer of mud; it is built by the female. The eggs are varying shades of turquoise-blue and mottled. Most of the incubation is performed by the female. The chicks hatch blind and covered with yellowish down, especially on the head and back. Members of this genus usually breed several times in the course of a year.

Blackbird
Turdus merula

Body length 25-28.5 cm, wing length 11.8-12.8 cm, wingspan 39-45 cm and weight 75-110 g. The Blackbird is the most prominent and common member of the thrush genus in Israel. The male is all-black, except for the bill and a ring around the eye, which are orange-yellow. Before nesting the bill turns bright orange. The female is greyish-brown on the upperparts and chestnut-brown below. Juveniles are dark brown with a mottled breast.

The Blackbird is a bird of the western and southern Palaearctic, with penetration into the Oriental region. It is common in all parts of Europe except the far north, in southern Asia from Turkey and Israel to southern China and also across India and Sri Lanka, and in maquis in North Africa. In this range 16 species have been described. The primary habitat of the Blackbird is woodland. Since the early nineteenth century it has begun to acclimatise to man-made environments. Most of its populations are resident and only those of the north migrate, wintering in the Middle East.

Wintering individuals belonging to the subspecies *T.m. aterrimus*, which is distributed from southeast Europe through Turkey and the Caucasus, arrive in

Israel in November and leave in March; a few individuals also pass through the country on migration. In winter roaming individuals may also be encountered, and small flocks, mostly of males, are sometimes seen congregating around sites abundant in food, such as olive groves.

The majority of Israel's Blackbird population, however, which belong to the subspecies *T.m. syriacus*, is resident. Today this is a very common bird in all northern and central parts of the country, as far south as Be'er Sheva. Until the 1950s the Blackbird bred only in natural woodland areas and orchards and groves in hilly areas of Upper Galilee and Carmel, especially on north-facing slopes. Since then its range has extended considerably, reaching the orchards of the coastal plain in the early 1950s. Its expansion was more gradual in the Syro-African rift, and the first attempts at nesting in the Jordan Valley were recorded as late as 1962. By the late 1960s the Blackbird was present in settlements and oases across the Negev, but its penetration of settlements in the Hula Valley was delayed until the mid-1970s.

The Blackbird usually lives in the same territory throughout its life, and outside the nesting season is tolerant of the presence of wintering individuals of the same species, especially juveniles. Blackbirds renew their territorial activity in February. Initially their song is heard in the morning and evening; as the season continues it is heard at most hours of the day, with great frequency. The song is mellow and flute-like, with a variety of notes and perceptible differences between individual voices; it is uttered from an elevated position such as a high branch or a television aerial. Laying may begin as early as the end of February, usually only in mid-March. In areas of natural woodland the usual clutch is of 3 eggs; in agricultural sectors 4 and usually 5. The female usually incubates alone for a period of 13-14 days. Both parents feed and tend the chicks for about 15 days.

In natural habitats laying continues until May, and chicks are liable to be found in nests until mid-June. In the Tabor oaks of Lower Galilee the Blackbird is usually single-brooded; in groves of common oak, where the ground is damper, it nests once in spring and again in early summer. Nesting in orchards, banana plantations and other agricultural sectors continues until August, and cases have been recorded of chicks found in nests as late as mid-September. In these areas there are pairs which apparently succeed in rearing three broods, each in a different nest.

Song Thrush
Turdus philomelos

Body length 23 cm, wing length 11 cm, wingspan 34-38.5 cm and weight 70 g. A brown-backed bird, easily recognised by the darker brown spots on the pale underparts.

The Song Thrush is very common in all areas of Europe, from Britain and northern Scandinavia to Siberia, excluding parts of the Mediterranean countries. In this range four subspecies have been described. Most of its populations, except those of western Europe, migrate and winter in southern Europe, the Mediterranean basin and southwest Asia, to eastern Iran.

In behaviour the Song Thrush resembles the Blackbird, but is more timid. In autumn and winter it is attracted to orchards and sometimes causes damage to olives. In this country its song is heard only on sunny days at the end of winter.

In Israel the subspecies *T.p. philomelos* is a common passage migrant and winterer in various environments in northern and central parts of the country, from the end of October to early April. Usually a few individuals roam together and sometimes scores gather in the same clump of bushes, but they never flock in the true sense.

Ring Ouzel
Turdus torquatus

Body length 24 cm, wing length 14 cm and weight 110 g. Similar to the Blackbird but distinguished by a white crescent on the breast and paler markings on the wing.

The Ring Ouzel has a limited and sporadic range. It tends to inhabit alpine wastes and the edges of coniferous forests in northern Europe, and in high mountain ranges in southern Europe and the Caucasus. Three subspecies have been described. Almost all populations migrate.

In Israel this is a rare winterer and a very rare passage migrant. Sometimes it winters in sparse flocks, especially in the high ground of the Negev. Observations have also been recorded in Jerusalem. It feeds on fruits, especially olives, and is noisier than other thrushes. It roosts among rocks and not in trees.

Dusky Thrush
Turdus naumanni

Body length 24 cm, wing length 12.6 cm and weight 77 g. A thrush distinguished by its rufous tail and chestnut wings. Its range extends between Siberia and Kamchatka, and it winters in southeast Asia. A vagrant individual of the subspecies *T.n. naumanni* was observed in November 1982 at the Sede Boker field study centre.

Black-throated Thrush
Turdus ruficollis

Body length 25.5 cm, wing length 13.5 cm and weight 88 g. The male is distinguished by the black throat and breast, contrasting with the white belly; the back is bottle-grey. The female is more brown, with a white throat and mottled breast.

This is an Asiatic species, distributed from the northern Urals to Mongolia, and wintering between India and Iran. In Israel it is a very rare accidental between November and February: most observations are recorded in the southern Negev, but individuals have also occurred in Jerusalem and in the woods of Umm Safa in the Samaria hills.

Fieldfare
Turdus pilaris

Body length 26.5 cm, wing length 14.3 cm and weight 100 g. Distinguished by its grey crown and nape, contrasting with the chestnut-brown back. The rump is grey, the tail black and the breast spotted and streaked as in the Song Thrush and Mistle Thrush; the belly is white. The female is slightly paler.

This is originally a taiga-dwelling bird, which has broadened its range and is today distributed in most parts of western Europe. It is more gregarious than other thrushes and tends to flock, especially towards evening, when hundreds of individuals are liable to gather for communal roosting. Its habitats are wasteland and deciduous woodland.

In Israel this is a rare to fairly common winterer and a very rare passage migrant. In some years it winters in flocks numbering scores and even hundreds of individuals, in most parts of the country, especially in deciduous plantations and vineyards; in other years it is not seen at all. Dates of arrival and departure also vary from year to year: the extreme dates are early November and early March, but the Fieldfare is most likely to be seen in December-January.

Redwing
Turdus iliacus

A small thrush: body length 22 cm, wing length 11.5 cm and weight 60 g. It is distinguished by its white supercilum, white moustachial stripe, and reddish-chestnut flanks and underwing-coverts.

The Redwing nests in Siberian taiga and in northern Europe, and winters in southern and western Europe, North Africa and uplands of western Asia. In Israel it is known mainly as a rare winterer, but is fairly common in some years. It is seen between early November and mid-March, and especially at the end of January and in February.

Mistle Thrush
Turdus viscivorus

Similar to the Song Thrush but larger and greyer: body length 27 cm, wing length 15.1 cm and weight 110 g. In flight it is also distinguished by the white underwing, in which respect it resembles the Fieldfare.

The Mistle Thrush breeds in most parts of Europe, and eastwards to Siberia and northern India. Part of the northern population from the Western Palaearctic, which belongs to the subspecies *T.v. viscivorus*, winters in southeastern Europe and the Middle East. In Israel this is a rare passage migrant in northern parts of the country in autumn and spring, and a rare winter visitor: on a few occasions scores of individuals have been seen together in November-December.

Family: Sylviidae (Warblers)

In the family Sylviidae there are 62 genera and 350 species, 134 of them living in tropical Africa, 84 in tropical Asia. There are 90 Palaearctic species, and only two are also known in the New World (in Alaska). Some ornithologists regard this as a subfamily of a larger family (Muscicapidae) made up also of flycatchers (Muscicapinae) and thrushes and allies (Turdinae).

These are small birds, with body length of 8-21 cm. Their colours are drab: usually brown, olive-green and uniform grey. The upperparts are darker than the underparts. Only the tropical and Australasian species are more colourful. The sexes are usually similar, but males are slightly larger.

Juveniles also have uniform plumage similar to that of adults. Most warblers have two moults in the year: a full one at the end of summer, after breeding, in the nesting area or close to it, and a full or partial one in winter quarters. After the autumn moult many of them acquire rather paler plumage.

The wings of most warblers are of moderate length and rounded; only species migrating from northern Eurasia have long and pointed wings. The tail is of moderate length, the tip usually straight, sometimes rounded graduated or slightly forked. Most warblers have a narrow and pointed bill. Their legs are short or of moderate length, and their stance is normally horizontal rather than upright.

Warblers feed almost exclusively on insects, which they catch in active movement. In accordance with the preferred hunting ground, they are divided into several ecological groups: reed, leaf etc. Only rarely do they leave this habitat and descend to the ground. They tend to be in continuous movement and are furtive in habits. Observation and positive identification are therefore difficult; vocal characteristics and behaviour are the most reliable aids in the field.

All warblers are territorial, and many have a characteristic display flight. Most breed in dense vegetation, often in wetland. The nest is usually a loose structure, built of dry grasses and leaves; the inner cup is deep, and there is often a covering dome. The eggs have a white, grey or pink base colour, delicately mottled with red and brown, and incubation is performed by the female or by both partners. The chicks hatch blind and naked or with sparse down on the head and back. They are tended and fed by both parents, and attain sexual maturity at ten months old or less.

In Israel ten genera and 40 species are represented.

Graceful Warbler or Prinia
Prinia gracilis

One of the smallest birds seen in Israel: body length 12.2-13.8 cm, wing length 4.1-4.5 cm and weight 6.8-7.5 g. The upperparts are greyish-brown with longitudinal streaks, the underparts greyish-white. This warbler is distinguished by its long and graduated tail (5.2-6.7 cm): it has ten feathers, each of them terminating in a black patch ringed in white. The wing is short and rounded. The male is larger, and his bill turns black towards the nesting season, while that of the female remains yellow-brown. The legs are thin and delicate, and pink in colour. The eyes are amber. Juveniles have a short tail and black eyes.

This is the only representative in Israel of the genus *Prinia*, a tropical and subtropical genus, comprising 25 species distributed from South Africa and Sri Lanka to Malaysia and Taiwan. The Graceful Warbler has the broadest and most northerly range among members of its genus: from the Horn of Africa, Sudan and Egypt, through Israel and Syria to the plains of the Ganges and the Brahmaputra in India. Eleven subspecies have been identified, all resident. The subspecies familiar in Israel, *P.g. palestinae*, is distributed between Suez and southern Turkey. The Graceful Warbler is found in gardens, cultivated areas, pasture meadows, marshes and steppe environments, but not in deserts. It also avoids woodland with tall and dense trees and little undergrowth.

The Graceful Warbler lives in territorial pairs throughout the year. In Israel the average size of territory is 0.25 ha, but this varies between seasons of the year and between different environments. The male's song reaches a peak between the end of January and mid-April. When the song itself is insufficient to deter intrusion, menacing displays are sometimes observed: the territorial male appears to dance in place, puffing out the breast, flapping the wings vigorously and uttering croaking cries. Graceful Warblers scour their territories in search of insects among leaves of trees and even on the ground, hopping with tail cocked.

This is one of the commonest birds in northern and central parts of the country and in the northern Negev. It is also found in oases, agricultural sectors of the Arava, and even in suburbs of towns and city parks. In mountainous areas such as Miron, Safed and Jerusalem, severe cold in winter is liable to deplete its populations, but these recover within a few years.

The nesting season begins in early March, earlier in urban areas. The male alone builds the skeleton of the nest, which is usually located in thickets of annual vegetation at a height of 30-50 cm above the ground, occasionally on a bush or tree. The nest is egg-shaped, with a small round entrance hole in the side. It is built of dry grasses, delicate twigs, roots and cereal leaves, and once the skeleton is completed the female adds a lining of tufts of hair and seed husks. The clutch contains 3-5 eggs. Continuous incubation begins with laying of the penultimate egg, and lasts for a period of 12-13 days. Both partners share the task of incubation and change shifts regularly; at change-over the bird returning to its post usually brings additional lining material, a fact which makes identification of nests easier for the observer, as well as adding to the nest's insulation against outside temperature changes. The female alone incubates at night. Both parents feed the chicks and clear droppings from the nest. Initially the chicks grow at a rate of 44% per day; in nine days their weight increases from 0.8 g to 7 g, the same weight as the parents. They leave the nest at 12-13 days old and the parents continue to feed them outside the nest for a further 10-15 days.

Graceful Warblers sometimes complete two or three nesting cycles in a year, starting to build a nest for a new brood while still feeding the chicks of the former brood. Their nests are vulnerable to predators and the rate of loss is very high; many pairs build five, six and even seven nests in the course of the year and the female lays four or even five clutches. Replacement clutches are usually laid within five days from the destruction of the previous nest. The nesting season continues until the end of June, and the last broods may leave the nest as late as the second half of July, and (rarely) even in the first days in August.

The young of Graceful Warblers often establish territories of their own at two months old, and some even breed at this age, an exceptional phenomenon among birds of Israel and of the Holarctic region as a whole. The intensive singing heard during July and August is usually uttered by individuals of this age. Juveniles that do not succeed in gaining a territory roam during winter in small flocks of three to 12 individuals.

Cetti's Warbler
Cettia cetti

A small and noisy songbird: body length 13.5-15.5 cm, wing length 5.9-6.7 cm and weight 14-18 g. The upperparts are dark chestnut and the underparts light brown to whitish. It is distinguished by its rounded tail, containing ten broad and soft feathers. The undertail-coverts are up to two-thirds the length of the tail. The wings are short and rounded. The bill is slender, narrow and pointed. The sexes are similar.

Cetti's Warbler has a Mediterranean/Irano-Turanian range, and is found in areas of temperate, Mediterranean, steppe and desert climate. It is distributed from Britain to Spain and North Africa, through southern Europe and the Middle East to western Pakistan and central Asia. In this range five subspecies have been described. It inhabits marsh vegetation and riverside forests. The European and Middle Eastern populations of Cetti's Warbler are resident, whereas those of areas further east migrate.

This is a furtive bird, tending to hide in undergrowth: usually only its abrupt and loud song testifies to its presence. Like many thicket-dwelling birds, it is apt to vibrate and cock its tail.

The subspecies *C.c. orientalis*, which is distributed from Turkey to Iran, is a resident in Israel in marsh and riverbank habitats in northern and central parts of the country, and is a passage migrant especially in the south.

The nest is in thick vegetation, close to the ground; it is woven from crude materials, leaves of reeds and sedge and various cereals, and is not much lined. The nest rests on stalks and shrubbery or is built among branches, but is not fixed to them as are the nests of reed warblers. It is shaped like a deep cup. The female usually lays 2-4 eggs; the egg is exceptional, being glossy brown-red in colour. The female incubates alone for about 13-14 days. The chicks are fed for about 13 days in the nest and a further four weeks outside the nest.

Nests with young chicks may be found as late as mid-June, and it is possible that Cetti's Warbler rears two broods in a season.

Fan-tailed Warbler
Cisticola juncidis

One of the smallest warblers: body length 9.9-11 cm, wing length 4.4-5.1 cm and weight 7-9 g. The back and wings are dark brown with light brown-buff feather edges, and thus the bird appears streaked. The throat is whitish, the breast and belly cream-coloured, the rump chestnut-gold. The wing is short and round. The tail is short and graduated with 12 dark brown feathers; all but the two central feathers terminate in a black patch with a white line at the tip. The tail feathers are moulted twice a year, and the tail is broader in winter plumage. The male's tail is longer than that of the female; otherwise the sexes are similar.

The genus *Cisticola* comprises 41 species (and is thus one of the most populous genera of all birds), 39 of them confined to Africa. The Fan-tailed Warbler, however, has a very broad, though sporadic range: tropical Africa, southeast Asia, islands of the Pacific Ocean to Australia, southern Europe and the Middle East. In this broad range 18 subspecies have been identified, most of them resident except for a few small populations in east Asia. This is primarily a bird of wet environments, grassland bordering on marshes, wet meadows, wasteland with cereal plants and ricefields.

The Fan-tailed Warbler is a furtive bird, and through most of the year it is not easily observed as it feeds in dense vegetation. It also moves on the ground, and is one of the few songbirds which walk rather than hop. Periodically it spreads its tail like a fan. In spring the Fan-tailed Warbler is conspicuous both to the eye and to the ear: the male flies on an undulating course, 8-15 m above the ground, and utters his song, a repeated short and high-pitched chirp. It also sings in the hot hours of the day, when most other birds are silent.

In Israel the subspecies *C.j. neurotica*, which is distributed from Syria to west Iran, is a resident bird in northern and central parts of the country, as far south as Be'er Sheva, near water but also in fields. There are considerable fluctuations in its population: it is liable to appear suddenly in a certain area, stay there a few years and then disappear again.

The nest is unique both in shape and in building materials: both parents sew together leaves of green cereal plants with the aid of spiderwebs, creating a shape resembling an open-topped inverted bottle. The nest is lined with plant material, leaves, barley ears etc. The female incubates alone for about 12 days, and both parents tend the chicks in the nest for about 13 days.

The nesting season begins in March and ends in July. During this time Fan-tailed Warblers are capable of rearing three broods.

Scrub Warbler
Scotocerca inquieta

Similar to the Graceful Warbler in dimensions and plumage: body length 10.5-11.5 cm, wing length 4.3-5.3 cm and weight 6-9 g. The head and nape are light brown with dark brown streaking, the back and wings greyish-brown, and the underparts cream-white. The tail is dark brown, fairly long and slightly graduated. The wings are short and round. The bill and legs are olive-brown. The sexes are similar.

The Scrub Warbler is the only member of its genus and has a sporadic Saharo-Sindian and Irano-Turanian range, from Morocco to Arabia and from Iran and the southern USSR to northwest India. Nine subspecies have been identified, all of them resident. The subspecies occurring in Israel is *S.i. inquieta*, which is distributed from Israel and east Egypt to north Arabia. This species lives in desert wadis, oases and rocky slopes covered with sparse scrub. It is primarily a bird of plains and valleys, although in Sinai it is found at altitudes up to 1,000 m.

This is a territorial and very active bird, hopping from bush to bush on the ground with tail usually cocked. It seldom flies, and flights are usually short, low-level and straight; when in motion it utters loud chirping cries. The Scrub Warbler seeks its food among branches of bushes, sometimes digging in the ground or among fallen leaves.

In Israel this is a fairly common bird across the Negev, along the shores of the Dead Sea and the eastern fringes of Samaria, and is also known on the eastern slopes of Hermon and in wasteland around Jerusalem. Since the 1960s it has also been seen on the western slopes of the Judean Hills and in southern Samaria.

Both sexes build the nest among bush foliage, a short distance above the ground. The nest is a large, egg-shaped structure, with a dome and a side entrance, similar to the nest of the Graceful Warbler; it is built of thin branches and grass stalks and lined with wool, feathers and hairs. In the desert nest building begins as early as the end of January, but in Mediterranean areas not until the end of February. In the clutch there are 4-6 eggs, sandy-white in colour and mottled with reddish-brown. Incubation lasts about 13 days and is performed mainly by the female. The chicks are fed in the nest for about 14 days.

In the desert there is one brood; in Mediterranean areas the species is double-brooded, nesting continuing until June. Sometimes an old nest is renovated for a second brood, with repairs beginning the day that the chicks leave it. The Scrub Warbler is a favourite, possibly the principal, host of the Cuckoo in this country; this applies especially to nests in the Judean Hills and Samaria.

Genus: *Locustella* (grasshopper warblers)
This genus contains nine species, all inhabiting the Palaearctic region, and divided into western and eastern groups of species. All of them migrate in winter to tropical regions of Asia and Africa.

Members of the genus *Locustella* are grey-brown above, with fairly uniform colouring and almost without streaking, except for an indistinct supercilium. They resemble Cetti's Warbler, but the tail has 12 feathers. The bill is slender and pointed, resembling that of reed warblers. The tail is very rounded at the tip, almost graduated; the undertail-coverts are very long, approximately the same length as the outer tail feathers. The sexes are similar.

Grasshopper warblers usually inhabit reedy vegetation. They are furtive birds, tending to skulk in cover and flying little; they walk fast among dense vegetation on the surface of the ground. Their song resembles the stridulating songs of insects. They breed in dense thickets in wet habitats: the nest is on the ground or close to it, sometimes above water, and is a basket-like structure, built of dry grass and leaves. The chicks hatch with down on the head and back.

In Israel four species are represented.

Savi's Warbler
Locustella luscinioides

Body length 13.2-16 cm, wing length 6.8-7.3 cm and weight 11-14 g. The upperparts are greyish-brown, the underparts light brown with the chin conspicuously white.

Savi's Warbler has a European and Irano-Turanian range. Its distribution in Europe is sporadic on account of its marked preference for dense expanses of reeds or mixed vegetation on the fringes of marshes. Three subspecies have been identified. It winters in East Africa, and from south of the Sahara to north of the Equator. The subspecies occurring in Israel is *L.l. luscinioides*, which breeds in North Africa, the Middle East and Europe.

This warbler spends most of its time in thick undergrowth, or on the ground, rising to a relatively high point only in order to sing. The song is also sometimes uttered in winter quarters and at staging points on the migration route.

Savi's Warbler is a common passage migrant in Israel from the end of August to October and from early March to early May. It is also a fairly common winterer, especially on the coastal plain, and a rare breeder: in the Hula Reserve, the Bet She'an Valley, the Jordan Valley and the Carmel coast.

The nest is built by the female in marsh vegetation, close to the ground. It is a basket-shaped structure, built of crude materials such as leaves of reed and sedge, and lined with more delicate grass stalks. Laying begins in mid-April and continues until the beginning of July. In the clutch there are 3-4 eggs. The female incubates alone for about 12 days, and is fed in the nest by the male. The female also takes the major role in tending the chicks. The species is apparently double-brooded.

Grasshopper Warbler
Locustella naevia

Body length 14.5 cm, wing length 6.2 cm and weight 14 g. Distinguished from Savi's Warbler by dark streaking on the back, an olive tint to the feathers, delicate streaking on the breast, and by its high-toned song.

The Grasshopper Warbler's distribution extends over considerable areas of Europe and Asia; it winters in sub-Saharan Africa and in north India. In Israel it is a very rare accidental seen on a few occasions in the course of the spring and autumn migrations in the fields of Kibbutz Eilot, where two individuals have been ringed (16 April 1978 and 18 August 1985).

Pallas's Grasshopper Warbler
Locustella certhiola

Body length 15 cm and wing length 6.5 cm. The upperparts are dark-streaked, and it is distinguished from the Grasshopper Warbler by the rufous rump and uppertail-coverts and white-tipped dark end of the tail.

This is a very rare vagrant from Siberia, which normally winters in India, southern China and southeast Asia. A single individual has been recorded: in the fields of Kibbutz Eilot on 25 February 1983.

River Warbler
Locustella fluviatilis

Body length 16 cm, wing length 7.3 cm and weight 18 g. Unstreaked dark brown above, in which respect it resembles Savi's Warbler; it differs from the latter in its lightly streaked breast. This warbler is best recognised by its distinctive song: alternating rapid and slow pairs of notes.

The River Warbler is distributed from the Baltic region to the Ural Mountains. Its habitats are in woodland on the banks of rivers and lakes. In Israel this is a fairly rare passage migrant: in autumn between September and October and in spring during May.

Genus: *Acrocephalus* (reed warblers)
A genus comprising 27 species: six are seen in Israel, four of them breeding. All are small birds and it is difficult to distinguish between different species: most have uniform olive-brown upperparts; only a few are streaked above and have a conspicuous supercilium. The underparts are paler than the back, and the throat is whitish. The tail is rounded, with 12 feathers. The tarsus is long. The bill is usually broad and flat, while in the streaked species it is thin and delicate. The sexes are similar and juveniles resemble adults. Song and wing structure are the best means of distinguishing between species.

Reed warblers are birds of marshy thickets, some preferring wetter, others drier habitats. They are furtive by nature. Mosquitoes constitute a major ingredient of their diet. The nests are usually deep and basket-shaped, of crude materials such as leaves and stalks, well lined, and tied to reeds. Both parents incubate, and both feed and tend the chicks.

Reed Warbler
Acrocephalus scirpaceus

Body length 12-13.6 cm, wing length 6-6.9 cm, wingspan 21.5 cm and weight 7-11 g. A songbird with rufous-brown upperparts and pale rufous-buff belly. The legs are dark and this is a useful guide to distinguishing it from the Marsh Warbler, which is otherwise similar.

The Reed Warbler has two distinct populations. The subspecies *A.s. scirpaceus* breeds in western, southern and central Europe and is a common passage migrant in Israel. The subspecies *A.s. fuscus*, which breeds in Turkey, Israel, northern Iran and from east of the Volga to central Asia, is also common on passage as well as being a breeding summer visitor in this country. Both subspecies migrate and winter in Africa, the eastern subspecies in the east of that continent. The Reed Warbler is a bird of marsh vegetation, with a particular preference for reedbeds. It seldom flies, and then only over short distances, at low level across reedbeds or open stretches of water; in flight the tail is spread in characteristic fashion.

In Israel the autumn passage takes place from the end of July to early November. Spring migration is seen between the beginning of March and the end of May.

The summer visitors are present in this country

between March and September. In Israel the Reed Warbler is distributed in all types of waterside vegetation, in thickets of reed and sedge but also among clumps of lythrum and elecampane. It is thus to be found along rivers, drainage channels, in residual marshes and especially on the banks of fish-ponds from Dan in the north of the Hula Valley to Eilat. With the destruction of reeds on the banks of fish-ponds, elecampane has become the primary nesting plant.

The males arrive in the country a few days before the females. They sing especially in the morning and in the two hours before sunset. Although the Reed Warbler is a territorial bird, in areas where suitable nesting places are in short supply pairs sometimes breed in conditions of relative density, in a kind of loose colony. The nesting period in this country extends from early April to the end of June. The nest is usually bound to reeds above the surface of the water. In the clutch there are 2-5 eggs, normally 3-4. Both parents incubate for a period of about 12 days, although most of the task is laid upon the female, while the male feeds her. The unusually deep structure of the nest forces the incubating bird to adopt a peculiar posture, with both head and tail pointing vertically upwards. Both parents feed the chicks in the nest for about ten days, and the chicks leave the nest before their plumage is fully grown and before they are capable of flight.

Apparently the Reed Warbler rears two broods in the season.

Marsh Warbler
Acrocephalus palustris

Body length 12.4-14 cm, wing length 6.4-6.9 cm and weight 8-11 g. Similar to the Reed Warbler, but more olive-brown above and with pinker legs.

Its range is mainly European, and it lives in thickets of riverside woodland and marsh vegetation, in rather drier areas than the Reed Warbler. This is a monotypic species. It winters in East Africa, from south of the Sahara to the region of the Cape.

In Israel the Marsh Warbler is a fairly rare spring passage migrant, more common in autumn. It is less furtive than the Reed Warbler.

Moustached Warbler
Acrocephalus melanopogon

Body length 13.7-14.8 cm, wing length 5.4-6.3 cm, wingspan 17.3-19.5 cm and weight 11-14 g. This species differs from others of the genus *Acrocephalus* in its streaked back, pure white supercilium and frequently uptilted tail. The back is somewhat rufous in colour and the crown dark brown.

The range of one subspecies, *A.m. melanopogon*, is

Mediterranean; that of another, *A.m. mimica*, Irano-Turanian. Parts of its populations are resident, while others winter in southern Europe and the Middle East. The Moustached Warbler lives in reed thickets and sedge on freshwater margins. This is by nature a quiet and secretive bird.

In Israel the Moustached Warbler is a resident bird in the Hula and along the Jordan as far south as Einot Zukim on the Dead Sea shore, and also in a few places on the coastal plain. It is also a passage migrant of varying frequency, and a fairly common winterer on the coastal plain between October and March.

The Moustached Warbler nests between April and June. During this period it is noted for its melodious and varied song, not unlike that of the Nightingale. The nest is 30-40 cm above the water, usually in reedy sites. Incubation of the 3-4 eggs is apparently the exclusive preserve of the female. The periods of incubation and of tending the chicks are similar to those of the Reed Warbler.

Sedge Warbler
Acrocephalus schoenobaenus

Body length 12-15 cm, wing length 6-7.4 cm, wingspan 19-22.5 cm and weight 9-15 g. Similar to the Moustached Warbler, but distinguished from it by the broad and cream-coloured supercilium and by darker and more emphatic streaking on the back. The rump is rufous.

The Sedge Warbler's range is Euro-Siberian and Irano-Turanian. It is a monotypic species. Its habitats are in vegetation on water margins, and it winters in eastern and central Africa.

In Israel the Sedge Warbler is a common passage migrant: in autumn from the end of August to the end of October, and in spring between March and mid-May, especially from the end of April. It is also a rare winterer in this country.

Clamorous Reed Warbler
Acrocephalus stentoreus

A large reed warbler: body length 19.2-20.1 cm, wing length 7.9-8.6 cm and weight 21-27 g. Its back is rufous olive-brown and its belly pale rufous-buff. It resembles the Great Reed Warbler and is distinguished from it by its voice, its darker-toned back and belly and its more slender but longer bill (20 mm compared with 18 mm in the Great Reed Warbler).

The subspecies *A.s. stentoreus* is distributed in marsh habitats in Egypt, Jordan and Israel; 13 other subspecies are distributed from southern Pakistan, northern India, southern China and Indonesia to the islands of the Pacific Ocean and Australia.

In Israel this is a resident bird, quite common in

large concentrations of reeds in all parts of the country, from the Hula Valley to the salt-pools of Eilat. Israel is one of the few areas of overlap between this species and the Great Reed Warbler: in the Hula they live side by side, and here the Clamorous Reed Warbler prefers thickets of papyrus and leaves the reeds to the Great Reed Warbler.

The Clamorous Reed Warbler is a territorial bird, tending to live its entire life in the same habitat (as evidence from ringing has shown) and spending most of the year secluded in thickets. Only on rare occasions does it fly, with vigorous wingbeats and tail spread. A considerable portion of its diet is gathered from the surface of the water.

Clamorous Reed Warblers become much more conspicuous at the approach of the nesting season, perching on thickets of reed and papyrus and uttering their characteristic, guttural song. The breeding season begins in April and continues until the end of July. The nest is either unlined or lined only with flowering shoots, and is located in the higher parts of the reed or papyrus thicket. The clutch is usually of 4 eggs. The period of incubation is 14-15 days and most of the task is performed by the female. Both parents feed the chicks in the nest for about 12 days.

Great Reed Warbler
Acrocephalus arundinaceus

The largest of the warblers: body length 16.5-18.3 cm, wing length 8.9-9.8 cm, wingspan 28.7-29.8 cm and weight 20-23 g. In colouring it resembles the Reed Warbler: olive-brown back, pale rufous belly and white throat. It is lighter-coloured than the Clamorous Reed Warbler and has a more distinctive supercilium.

The Great Reed Warbler is distributed throughout Europe (except the north) and central Asia. In its range three subspecies have been identified. It inhabits reedbeds alongside stretches of fresh water. All its populations migrate south, and those of the Western Palaearctic winter in central Africa.

In Israel the Great Reed Warbler of the subspecies *A.a. arundinaceus* is a common passage migrant between August and November and in April-May. It is also a rare breeder, known to nest only in undrained marshes of the Hula; its status in the Hula Reserve is not entirely clear, and the breeding population may indeed have disappeared. In the nesting season it is drawn exclusively to large reedbeds, and is distinguished by its loud and raucous song, resembling the croaking of a frog.

In behaviour and breeding biology this species resembles the Clamorous Reed Warbler, although its nesting materials are more coarse and the eggs more greyish in colour and with larger markings. The size

of the clutch is also larger, as is typical of northern species: 5 and sometimes 7 eggs.

Genus: *Hippolais* (*Hippolais* warblers)
In this genus there are six species, all inhabiting the Western Palaearctic region and all migrating in winter to Africa, Arabia and the Indian subcontinent. These are small insect-eating birds, closely related to reed warblers, from which they are distinguished by their square tail and flat bill, broad at its base. From leaf warblers they differ in their flat forehead and in the bill, which extends from the forehead in a straight line; the wings and tail are also longer and the undertail-coverts shorter. When excited they have the distinctive habit of raising the feathers of the crown. *Hippolais* warblers have plumage of uniform colour; there is no sexual dimorphism and juveniles resemble adults. Their song is distinctive and varied, uttered from a prominent vantage point.

These are birds of trees and bushes, both seeking food and building nests among branches. The nest resembles a deep and carefully constructed basket; the eggs are distinctively pink in colour, with dark purple markings. The chicks hatch blind and naked.

In Israel five species are represented, two of them breeding.

Olivaceous Warbler
Hippolais pallida

A small warbler: body length 12.2-13.4 cm, wing length 6-7 cm and weight 8-12 g. The wings are short and round. The upperparts are a uniform brown-olive, the underparts pale buff. There is a whitish eye-ring. The bill is relatively long, about 9 mm, but seems even longer on account of the flat forehead, which appears as a continuation of the bill; the upper mandible is dark, the lower yellowish. The colour of the legs varies among different individuals, from light grey to brown-purple.

The Olivaceous Warbler has a Mediterranean and Irano-Turanian range, with penetration into northeastern Africa from Egypt to Lake Chad. Since the 1930s it has extended its range northward in Europe, following the river valleys. Five subspecies have been identified. It inhabits areas of bushes and sparse trees, in relatively dry habitats but also alongside water sources. It may be found by sluggish streams, among tamarisk thickets, in orchards, parks and urban gardens. It migrates in autumn and winters in savannas north of the Equator across the whole width of Africa. The subspecies occurring in Israel is *H.p. elaeica*, which breeds in southern Europe, the Middle East and south Palaearctic Asia and winters in Ethiopia and East Africa.

The Olivaceous Warbler is an active and restless bird, hopping among the branches of trees and bushes catching insects. Sometimes it rises up to chase flying insects, and easily changes direction in pursuit of them.

In Israel this is a common passage migrant: in autumn from mid-July, and especially in August-September; and in spring from early April, and especially at the end of this month and in the first half of May. It is also a common summer resident between March and September, across the whole of the Mediterranean region of the country and especially on the banks of the Jordan.

In the nesting season, from April to June, the attractive and complex song of the Olivaceous Warbler, incorporating fragments imitated from the songs of other birds, is often to be heard, especially in the hours of twilight. The nest is usually built in the outer branches of a tree or a bush, about 1 m above the ground. It is carefully constructed of thin stalks and grasses, and linked to a few branches. In shape it resembles a deep basket. The nest is sometimes coated with lichen and spiderwebs, and is lined with flowering shoots, feathers, wool, threads and plant fluff. In the clutch there are usually 3, sometimes 4 eggs. The female normally incubates alone for about 12 days; the male feeds her, and sometimes even relieves her for short periods of time. Both parents tend the chicks for about 14 days in the nest, although the female's contribution is apparently the greater.

The Olivaceous Warbler breeds twice during the spring and summer.

Booted Warbler
Hippolais caligata

The smallest of the *Hippolais* warblers: body length 13 cm, wing length 5.9 cm and weight 7-9.1 g. It is distinguished from the Olivaceous Warbler by the white outer tail feathers; its bill is also shorter.

The Booted Warbler is distributed from central and northern Russia, eastward to Siberia and northwestern Mongolia and southward to the trans-Caspian region and Iran. Most of its populations winter in the Indian subcontinent.

In Israel this is a very rare accidental, with two records: on 14 August 1982 in the woods of Umm Safa, and on 3 May 1983 in the fields of Eilot.

Upcher's Warbler
Hippolais languida

Similar to the Olivaceous Warbler but larger: body length 13.8-15 cm, wing length 7.2-7.5 cm and weight 12-13 g. Its legs are light grey.

This warbler's range is basically Irano-Turanian:

from Israel, Lebanon and Syria to Afghanistan and Turkestan. It is a monotypic species whose habitats are olive plantations and orchards and also scrub on the slopes of mountains. It winters in Sudan, Ethiopia, Somalia and Kenya, and also in southern Arabia.

In Israel Upcher's Warbler is a passage migrant in autumn, as early as July-August, and in late spring, especially at the end of April and in early May; in the latter season it is more rare.

This species is also a fairly common summer resident between the end of April and August, breeding in mountains in northern and central parts of the country, from the foothills of Hermon to the western slopes of Samaria. It nests soon after its return from winter quarters, when its loud and distinctive song is widely heard. The nest is a small and carefully woven basket-like structure, built in a bush or a tree; it is constructed from thin stalks and grasses and lined with hairs and plant fluff. The clutch is of 3-4 eggs. No information is available on incubation and care of the chicks.

Olive-tree Warbler
Hippolais olivetorum

The largest of the *Hippolais* warblers: body length 14-16.4 cm, wing length 7.7-8.8 cm and weight 19 g. Its basic colour is olive-grey, darker on the upperparts and paler below. Its legs are dark, and its bill long and deep.

This is a monotypic species, with a breeding range restricted to the region between the Balkans and Turkey and Lebanon. According to past reports, the

Olive-tree Warbler formerly bred in Israel, but there has been no recent evidence of this. It winters between Kenya and Somalia and its migration route crosses the Mediterranean. In Israel it is a fairly rare passage migrant, especially during August and in April-May.

Icterine Warbler
Hippolais icterina

Similar to a leaf warbler, but larger and with yellow underparts: body length 13-16 cm, wing length 7.2-8.2 cm and weight 11.5-15 g.

This species breeds in parkland habitat in central and southern Europe and central Asia; an isolated population is found between the trans-Caucasus and the southern Caspian Sea. In early August it migrates to tropical and southern Africa. In Israel the Icterine Warbler is a rare passage migrant in August and September, and also at the end of April and in early May.

Genus: *Sylvia* (*Sylvia* warblers)
This genus comprises 18 species, inhabiting areas of dense vegetation especially in Europe, North Africa and western Asia, and including 14-15 known in Israel. These are small songbirds: body length 11.5-17 cm and weight 9.5-30 g. The predominant colours are grey-brown and black. Most species are sexually dimorphic. The tail is graduated, and rounded at the tip. The bill is short, with the upper mandible slightly downcurved.

These warblers feed especially on insects, caught among branches and leaves in dense vegetation, and to a lesser extent on fruit. Their calls are metallic and short; a few species have a characteristic song flight. The nest is usually built low down in vegetation: it is a basket-shaped structure, resting loosely on a concentration of branches and not attached to them. Nesting materials are mostly dry and plant matter, including roots and thin stalks, and the nest is normally unlined. The eggs are usually whitish-buff in colour and speckled with brown markings. Both parents incubate and tend the offspring.

Sardinian Warbler
Sylvia melanocephala

Body length 12.4-14 cm, wing length 5.2-6 cm and weight 9-14 g. The male has a black head and nape, a conspicuous red ring around the eye, a white throat, dark grey back and light greyish underparts; the tail is blackish with white tip and edges. The female is less vivid in coloration: grey head, greyish back, pale sandy below, and with a less conspicuous red eye-ring than the male. Both sexes have reddish-brown legs. Juveniles resemble the adult female.

The Sardinian Warbler has a typical Mediterranean range, although within this range seven subspecies have been identified. Habitats are sparse maquis, scrub, hedgerows and parks, sometimes also gardens in towns and villages. Most populations are resident, but some winter in the Sahara, in northern Iraq and in Arabia. Two subspecies occur in Israel.

The Sardinian Warbler moves constantly among thickets in its quest for insects. Sometimes, especially outside the nesting season, it also feeds on fruits, and in winter seeds constitute an appreciable portion of its diet. When it senses danger, it climbs to the top of the bush, scouring its surroundings, utters an alarm call and dives back into the thicket. When perched it periodically spreads its dark tail, revealing the white outer feathers.

In Israel the subspecies *S.m. melanocephala*, which breeds in southern Europe and Turkey as well as in the Mediterranean region of North Africa, is a fairly common passage migrant, in small parties, between mid-October and the end of November, and from early March to the end of April. It is also a fairly rare winterer, especially in the Arava, from the shores of the Dead Sea to Eilat. Migrating individuals maintain contact between themselves with hoarse and strong chirping calls, uttered from within dense vegetation.

The subspecies *S.m. momus*, which is paler, is restricted to the western Middle East. It is resident in Israel, where it is the commonest of the breeding warblers. Its breeding sites are confined to mountain slopes and hillsides in the northern and central parts of the country, and areas of the coastal plain, but outside the nesting season it also roams in other areas.

The nesting season begins as early as March, and at the approach of the season the Sardinian Warbler becomes considerably more conspicuous than at other times of the year: the males utter their attractive song from vantage points and engage in characteristic dancing display flight. The nest is built among the lower branches of a tree or a bush, thorny broom bushes being preferred. The clutch consists of 3-4 eggs, sometimes 5. Incubation is for 13-14 days and both parents also tend the chicks in the nest for about the same length of time.

The nesting season continues until May and normally each pair raises two broods.

Ménétries's Warbler
Sylvia mystacea

This bird is sometimes considered a subspecies of the Sardinian Warbler, and it is indeed difficult to distinguish between them, although Ménétries's Warbler has brown-pink underparts and the eye-ring is yellow. Its range is Irano-Turanian, and it winters in south Arabia, Sudan and the Horn of Africa.

This is a very rare accidental in Israel: in Maagan Mikhael on 4 January 1968; in Jerusalem from 21 to 29 December 1979; and at Eilat, where a few individuals have been trapped (spring 1970 and spring 1982).

Cyprus Warbler
Sylvia melanothorax

Another bird regarded by some as a subspecies of the Sardinian Warbler. It is distinguished from the latter by its black-and-white mottled belly, reddish legs and absence of red eye-ring.

The distribution of this warbler is confined to Cyprus. It is a fairly common passage migrant (October and March) and a rare winterer in the Arava and the region of Jericho. Most observations are in February-March.

Orphean Warbler
Sylvia hortensis

A large warbler: body length 15.5-17 cm, wing length 7.7-8.3 cm and weight 18-26 g. It is similar to the Sardinian Warbler but has a longer bill: 12 mm as opposed to 9 mm in the Sardinian Warbler. The male has a black head, conspicuously pale eyes, black cheeks and contrasting white throat; the back is brown-grey, the underparts pink-brown and very pale, and the tail black with white edges. The female has a dark grey head. Juveniles are similar to the female, but their eyes are not so pale as those of the adult.

The Orphean Warbler has a Mediterranean and Irano-Turanian distribution, in which four subspecies have been identified. All its populations migrate in winter: most to Africa, to the belt of savanna south of the Sahara, between Senegal and Sudan, a minority to southern India. The habitats of the Orphean Warbler are sparse oak forests, scrub, pinewoods, orchards and olive groves.

In Israel the subspecies *S.h. crassirostris*, which breeds from Turkey and Arabia to Afghanistan, is a summer resident, common between March and September in Samaria, Carmel, Galilee and the slopes of Hermon. During migration, from mid-July to mid-September and from mid-March to early May, it is fairly common in all parts of the country.

The nesting season lasts from the end of April to June, but as early as the end of March the Orphean Warbler may be seen and heard singing loudly from the top of a bush. Its song is strong and trilling, lacking the harsh croaking sounds typical of other warblers of its genus. The nest is basket-shaped and unlined, usually built on the outer branches of small trees or bushes. In the clutch there are 4-5 eggs. Incubation lasts for about 14 days, and the chicks remain in the nest for roughly the same period.

The Orphean Warbler is double-brooded.

Lesser Whitethroat
Sylvia curruca

Body length 11.5-13.4 cm, wing length 6.2-7 cm and weight 8-14 g. A mostly grey warbler, with black ear-coverts and cheeks contrasting strongly with the white throat.

This warbler's distribution extends over most of Europe (except Scandinavia and the south of the continent), in the Middle East and in central Asia. In this range ten subspecies have been identified. All of its populations, estimated at a total of some 150 million individuals, migrate and winter in East Africa and the Indian subcontinent.

In Israel this is the commonest and most conspicuous of the migrant warblers: from August to the end of October and from early March to the end of May. Most of the migrants belong to the subspecies *S.c. curruca*. It usually migrates in loose flocks numbering up to 20 individuals, which tend to congregate, especially in the desert, in one tree.

To date, nine Lesser Whitethroats have been found in this country which had been ringed in various European countries, from Britain (four), through Germany (two) to Russia. An individual ringed in Eilat on 31 March 1984 was found on 10 June 1984 in East Germany.

After the spring migration, a few pairs of this species stay behind to breed in Israel: in West Galilee, Upper Galilee and the slopes of Hermon.

Some ornithologists regard the Desert Lesser Whitethroat *Sylvia (c.) minula* as a subspecies of the Lesser Whitethroat. It is rather smaller than the latter, and lacks the black cheek-patch. This bird, distributed in the steppes of Iran and the deserts of central Asia and wintering in Pakistan and northwestern India, has been recorded a few times in the region of Eilat.

Whitethroat
Sylvia communis

Body length 13.1-14.7 cm, wing length 6.6-7.4 cm and weight 14-23 g. The male has a grey head, white throat and rufous-brown wings. The subspecies *S.c. icterops*, which breeds in Israel, has a greyer back and paler underparts than the European subspecies *S.c. communis*. The female is paler, tending towards brown rather than grey.

The Whitethroat has a European and western

Asiatic distribution, in which three subspecies have been identified. Its primary habitats are wasteland, meadows, bushes on the fringes of agricultural sectors, scrub and woodland edges, and it usually seeks its food in areas of tangled thorn and grass near the surface of the ground or among the branches of bushes. All of its populations migrate in autumn; most winter in tropical Africa, a minority in Yemen and India.

In Israel this is a common passage migrant in autumn from August to mid-October. It is more conspicuous in the spring migration, from early March to mid-May. It is also a common summer resident on slopes of mountains and hills in central and northern parts of the country — and very conspicuous in the plains of the Golan Heights — usually in a range extending north from Hadera, although in some years it is to be seen further south, as far as the region of Ben Shemen.

The breeding population arrives early, and is among the first of the summering species to take its place; it may be seen in this country from the end of February to August. The males usually arrive a few days before the females. Their song is brief and staccato but of considerable strength, and is heard especially in the early hours of the morning, uttered from the top or from the interior of a bush. At a later stage the male performs characteristic display flights: rising to a height of 20-30 m and descending gradually, gliding and hovering in turn, with wings raised above the level of the body and legs extended downward.

The Whitethroat builds its basket-shaped nest in thorns or other bushes, especially in thickets of raspberry, at a height of 50-60 cm above the ground. The clutch is of 4-5 eggs. Both parents incubate for a period of about 12 days and tend the chicks in the nest for roughly the same length of time. The Whitethroat is double-brooded.

Blackcap
Sylvia atricapilla

Body length 13-15.6 cm, wing length 7-8.2 cm and weight 18-25 g. The cap of the male is black, that of the female and juvenile rufous-brown. In both sexes the back is olive-black; the belly is greyish in the male and buff in the female. The wings and tail are greyish-brown.

The Blackcap's range covers all of Europe except Scandinavia and northern Russia, and extends into central Asia. It also breeds in North Africa and the Middle East to Lebanon. Five subspecies have been identified. Its habitats are in woodland with tall undergrowth. In southern Europe and North Africa this is a resident bird; the populations from the other parts of its range migrate and winter in the belt of scrubland across Africa north of the Equator. It has been estimated that some 340 million warblers of this species migrate every year.

The Blackcap feeds on insects, and during autumn it also consumes berries and fruits. In the desert its diet includes seeds and sometimes leaves.

In Israel this is a very common passage migrant (mainly the subspecies *S.a. atricapilla*). It usually migrates in loose flocks, between the end of August and November, and between the end of February and the end of May. In both seasons males precede females by a few days.

Spectacled Warbler
Sylvia conspicillata

Similar to the Whitethroat, but with a darker and greyer head and back. It is also slightly smaller: body length 11 cm, wing length 5.2 cm and weight 9 g. The female is paler than the male, and has a lighter head.

The distribution of this warbler is Mediterranean, excepting Turkey and the Balkans, and its habitats are heathland, wasteland and fringes of deserts — relatively exposed environments compared with the habitats of most warblers. Two subspecies have been described: one is confined to the islands of the eastern Atlantic off Africa, while *S.c. conspicillata* occurs throughout the rest of the range.

In Israel this is a resident bird in the northern Negev and in wasteland east of the mountain ridge, from Samaria to eastern Galilee. A few pairs reach as far north as the eastern slopes of Mount Hermon. It is also common in wasteland in the Judean Hills and the hills of southern Shephelah, in which area it has proliferated since the 1960s. Outside the breeding season this warbler roams, wintering in the Arava and the region of Eilat between November and February.

The Spectacled Warbler breeds twice in the year, between March and June. The nest is in low and sparse shrubbery and the clutch usually contains 4 eggs. Both parents incubate for 12-14 days, and feed the chicks in the nest for 12-13 days.

Subalpine Warbler
Sylvia cantillans

Body length 13 cm, wing length 6.2 cm and weight 11 g. A small warbler with a grey back, rufous underparts and a conspicuous white moustachial stripe. It is distributed in the western and central Mediterranean region, and winters in the western Sahara and the Sahel. In Israel this is a rare passage migrant, especially in the second half of March and early April.

Rüppell's Warbler
Sylvia rueppelli

Body length 13.5-15.5 cm, wing length 6.3-7.3 cm and weight 11-17 g. The male is the only warbler with a black throat and white moustachial stripe. The female is harder to identify. Both sexes have distinctive red legs.

This species' range is Mediterranean, from the Aegean islands through Turkey to Lebanon. Rüppell's Warbler is a monotypic species inhabiting slopes covered with thorny bushes; it winters in eastern equatorial Africa. In Israel this is a fairly common passage migrant, in loose flocks, in spring between March and the end of April; and quite rare in the autumn migration.

Desert Warbler
Sylvia nana

The smallest and palest of the *Sylvia* warblers: body length 11.5 cm, wing length 6 cm and weight 10 g. Its colour is uniform light sandy. It is distributed in steppes and deserts in central Asia and the western Sahara, and winters in North and northeast Africa, Arabia and northwest India.

In Israel this is a very rare accidental, with a few records between January and April in the southern Arava and in the region of Nizana in the northern Negev. Tristram noted this bird as a breeder in the area south of the Dead Sea; there has been no later evidence of this. In southern Sinai it is a fairly common winterer.

Arabian or Red Sea Warbler
Sylvia leucomelaena

Body length 14-14.5 cm, wing length 6.6-7.1 cm and weight 11-15 g. This warbler is similar in coloration to the Orphean Warbler, but it has a distinctive habit of vibrating its tail. The head and tail of the male are glossy black and the underparts white. The head and tail of the female are dark grey.

The origin of the Arabian Warbler is Ethiopian and its distribution is limited to northeast Africa, including Somalia, and the western shores of Arabia. In this range three subspecies have been identified. It is especially attracted to acacia trees. In Israel this is a fairly common resident in the valley of the Arava, between the Dead Sea and Eilat.

The Arabian Warbler lives in pairs in territories, varying in size between 20 ha and 70 ha. Partners roost in close proximity, even cleaning and preening one another's feathers. This species feeds especially on the caterpillars of moths, which it catches on the branches and trunks of acacias, but also on flying insects and various fruits. It also hunts for food in sand, scraping with its bill.

The nesting season extends from February to July, and during this period each pair is liable to raise three broods. At this time the song of the male is heard over a range of hundreds of metres. Both partners build a new nest for each cycle, although sometimes materials are taken from an old and abandoned nest. The nest is invariably built on an acacia tree, usually at the top, at a height of 0.8-3 m above the ground. In the clutch there are 2-3 eggs, speckled with grey and brown markings. Both parents incubate for a period of about 16 days. The chicks fly from the nest at 10-17 days, but the parents continue to feed them for about a further 40 days.

Barred Warbler
Sylvia nisoria

The largest of the accidental warblers in Israel: body length 16.5-17 cm, wing length 7-8.2 cm and weight 22-30 g. Its overall colour is greyish, the underparts are barred and the tail is long. It is distinguished by its yellow eyes, resembling the eyes of a raptor.

This warbler's range is European and Irano-Turanian and two subspecies have been identified. It inhabits areas of thorny bushes, on the edges of broadleaf forests, in plantations and along hedgerows. It winters in Arabia and in East Africa from Egypt to South Africa.

In Israel the subspecies *S.n. nisoria* is a fairly rare passage migrant in autumn (September). It is more common in the spring migration, between the end of April and the end of May, especially in the second week of May.

Garden Warbler
Sylvia borin

An all-grey warbler: body length 13.9-15 cm, wing length 7-8.2 cm and weight 14-18 g. Its range is Western Palaearctic. This is primarily a bird of undergrowth in woods and woodland edges, both broadleaf and coniferous. It winters in Africa south of the Equator.

The Garden Warbler passes through Israel singly or in small flocks, and is quite rare. In autumn it occurs from the second half of October, and in spring, when it is more conspicuous, during the month of May. This is the latest of the migrant warblers seen in Israel.

Genus: *Phylloscopus* (leaf warblers)
A genus of small warblers, comprising 41 species and thus one of the largest genera among songbirds. Members of the genus are distributed throughout the Old World, excepting Madagascar. In North Africa they do not breed south of the Atlas Mountains. They inhabit woods and groves. All species and most populations migrate in autumn; many of the Palaearctic populations winter in the Indian subcontinent.

Most leaf warblers are greenish-yellowish in colour. Their body length varies from 9 to 12.5 cm. The high forehead distinguishes them from *Hippolais* warblers, which in some cases have similar plumage. The bill is shorter than the head, slender and usually pointed. The wings are pointed, the tail is square-ended. The legs are short and weak. Even the different species of leaf warbler are similar, and song is the best means of distinguishing between them.

Leaf warblers feed by climbing and hopping among branches and leaves; sometimes they leap into the air to catch flying insects. They nest on the ground or close to it. The female alone builds a domed nest with a side entrance, well concealed and well camouflaged. The eggs are usually white with reddish-brown markings. Only the female incubates. The chicks hatch with sparse grey down on the head and shoulders and are fed by both parents.

In Israel there are seven or eight passage migrants and accidental species, and only one winterer.

Chiffchaff
Phylloscopus collybita

A small bird: body length 10.7-12 cm, wing length 5.4-6.5 cm, wingspan 17.8-20.8 cm and weight 6-8 g. The upperparts are greyish-olive, the underparts pale sandy-yellow and the legs dark.

The Chiffchaff's range extends over most of Europe and appreciable parts of northern Asia, also the northern Middle East and North Africa; seven subspecies have been identified. Its habitats are in woodland, especially forests of tall trees. All its populations migrate, except those breeding in southern Europe; wintering areas are the Mediterranean countries, oases in the Sahara, Egypt, Sudan, the Sahel belt and northern India.

In Israel this is a very common passage migrant from October to the end of November and from the end of February to April. It also winters in this country. In the wintering population it is possible to distinguish two subspecies: *P.c. collybita*, which breeds from the shores of the Atlantic Ocean to the Balkans, and *P.c. abietinus*, which breeds from East Germany to Iran. The latter subspecies, which is more common in Israel, has paler, greyer upperparts and paler underparts. In winter the onomatopoeic song of the Chiffchaff is one of the sounds most typically associated with pine forests. The bird is also found in maquis, cultivated fields, gardens and open landscape with low bushes.

Chiffchaffs ringed in Hungary and Finland have been found in Israel, and individuals ringed in this country have been found in Poland, West Germany, Finland, Cyprus and Egypt.

Mountain Chiffchaff
Phylloscopus sindianus

Previously considered a subspecies of the Chiffchaff, this species is darker: grey-brown above and with hardly any green. The breast and flanks are dark orange-brown, contrasting with the white belly. The bill is flat and thick, the legs black.

The Mountain Chiffchaff has a sporadic distribution in southern Palaearctic Asia. The subspecies *P.s. lorenzii* is distributed in the Caucasus and the trans-Caspian region. This is essentially a resident bird. A single individual was observed on 5 March 1983 in the fields of Kibbutz Eilot near Eilat.

Willow Warbler
Phylloscopus trochilus

Body length 10.3-12 cm, wing length 5.3-7 cm, wingspan 17-19.5 cm and weight 7-12 g. Similar to the Chiffchaff, and distinguished from it by its yellower underparts, especially conspicuous in juveniles, its pale legs with colour sometimes tending towards pink, and its song — a succession of plaintive descending notes. The wing structure is also different.

This warbler's distribution is Euro-Siberian and it is the commonest of the warblers of northern Europe. In its range three subspecies have been described. The Western Palaearctic population winters in tropical Africa, the majority south of the Equator, to South Africa.

In Israel this is a very common passage migrant in

autumn, especially at the end of September and in early October. It is less conspicuous in the spring migration, which continues from March to the end of May, with a peak during April. Among the migrants two subspecies can be identified: *P.t. trochilus*, which is more greenish-yellow and breeds in western and central Europe; and *P.t. acredula*, which is greyer and breeds from Scandinavia to west Siberia.

An individual ringed in the Yamal peninsula in arctic Siberia was captured in northern Sinai.

Wood Warbler
Phylloscopus sibilatrix

The largest of the leaf warblers seen in Israel: body length 12-14.2 cm, wing length 6.8-8 cm, wingspan 20-23.7 cm and weight 12 g. It is distinguished by the lemon-yellow colour of the breast, the white belly and the conspicuous yellow supercilium. The legs are yellowish.

This species' distribution is European and it is especially common in beech forests. It is a monotypic species which winters in the Sahel belt in Africa.

In Israel this is a passage migrant in small and loose flocks. The size of the migratory populations varies considerably, although the Wood Warbler is usually more conspicuous during the spring migration, between the end of April and mid-May; the autumn migration takes place between August and early October.

Bonelli's Warbler
Phylloscopus bonelli

A grey warbler, with white underparts and yellow rump. It breeds around the Mediterranean basin and in central Europe, in four separate populations. In this range two subspecies have been identified. Bonelli's Warbler winters in the Sahel.

In Israel the subspecies *P.b. orientalis*, which breeds from the Balkans to Lebanon and winters in Sudan, is a fairly common passage migrant between the end of September and mid-October, and a common migrant in spring, especially between the end of March and mid-April. According to some sources, Bonelli's Warbler has also bred in Israel, in olive groves in hill districts; there is no recent evidence of this.

Yellow-browed Warbler
Phylloscopus inornatus

A small leaf warbler distinguished by its double wing-bar and pale and conspicuous supercilium: body length 10.5 cm, wing length 5.6 cm and weight 6 g. Three subspecies are distributed in northern and central Asia, wintering in India and southeast Asia.

In Israel the subspecies *P.i. inornatus* is a very rare accidental: most observations are in the fields of Eilot, a few in Sinai. Another very rare accidental in this country is the subspecies *P.i. humei*, which is regarded by some ornithologists as a separate species (Oriental Warbler): it has paler upperparts tending towards yellow, a whitish-yellowish supercilium and pale underparts, and breeds from Mongolia to the northwestern Himalayas, wintering in the Indian subcontinent. One was recorded in Sede Boker in the central Negev on 2-3 October 1981.

Radde's Warbler
Phylloscopus schwarzi

Body length 13 cm, wing length 6.2 cm and weight 11 g. This leaf warbler has grey-brown upperparts; the breast and flanks are brown-yellow, and the belly white. The cream-coloured supercilium is conspicuous, and the bill is short and thick.

Radde's Warbler breeds from southern Siberia to Manchuria and Korea and winters in southeast Asia. A single individual was caught and ringed at Maagan Mikhael on 7 October 1982.

Genus: *Regulus*
Members of the genus *Regulus* were formerly considered to belong to the family Paridae (tits), or as constituting a family in their own right. Today they are included among the family of warblers. In the genus there are five species. They are distinguished by their minute dimensions, and are the smallest birds of the Holarctic and Oriental regions. The wings are long and pointed, the tail is slightly graduated, the tarsus is long and delicate, and the bill is small and slender. Members of the genus *Regulus* are birds of forests and woods, tending to hide among branches. They feed on tiny insects and also on fruit. The nest, a well-hidden, deep and thick-walled basket-shaped structure, is usually built in coniferous trees. The eggs are yellowish-pink with delicate mottling.

Goldcrest
Regulus regulus

Body length 9 cm, wing length 5.3 cm and weight 5-6.5 g. The Goldcrest has a greenish-brown back and pale greyish underparts. The male has an orange crown edged with black, and a white supercilium; on the wing there are two white bars. The female has a similar head pattern, but a yellow crown.

The Goldcrest is common in most parts of Europe, and between Turkey and northern Iran; it is also distributed sporadically in the central USSR, on the slopes of the Himalayas, in eastern China and in

Japan. In this range 14 subspecies have been identified. This is a typical bird of coniferous forests, where it is mostly resident; an appreciable section of its populations, however, migrate short distances in autumn, most wintering south of their breeding range, some in the Mediterranean basin.

In Israel the subspecies *R.r. regulus* is a rare winterer between November and February.

Family: Muscicapidae (Flycatchers)

A family of small songbirds which some ornithologists unite with Turdidae (thrushes, etc.), Sylviidae (warblers) and Timaliidae (babblers) in a single family. On the more limited scale adopted here, this is a family comprising 60 genera and 200 species, differing considerably from one another. Flycatchers are distributed from northern Eurasia to southern Africa, also in Australia and Hawaii. Most species inhabit tropical Asia, which is evidently the origin of the family. Those breeding in Europe migrate to Africa or India.

The body length of flycatchers is 10-20 cm and their weight 8-20 g. The bill is flat and broad at the base, well suited to catching insects in the air; the rictal bristles are well developed, helping the bird direct its bill towards the prey. The wings are longer and more pointed than those of warblers. The tail, of varying length, is normally square-ended; in some cases it is graduated. The legs are short and weak compared with those of thrushes, and ability to walk and hop is limited. The plumage coloration varies considerably. In some species the feathers are vivid and variegated, in others they are paler and of uniform colour. The sexes are sometimes similar, but more often differ. Unlike in warblers, juveniles have mottled/spotted plumage.

Flycatchers are tree-dwellers, feeding primarily on flying insects which they locate and then swoop upon from high vantage points. The species breeding in tropical areas have basket-shaped nests; most of those that have penetrated Europe have adapted to building nests in sheltered sites — hollow trees, crevices, nestboxes etc.

In Israel five species are seen, one breeder and four passage migrants. They are divided into two genera: *Ficedula* (with a worldwide total of 26 species), in which the colours are strong and contrasting and the down of chicks sparse, and which breed mostly in holes; and *Muscicapa* (total of 22 species), whose colours are paler, the chicks covered more extensively with down, and which builds open nests.

Spotted Flycatcher
Muscicapa striata

Body length 14-14.7 cm, wing length 8.6-9.2 cm, wingspan 23-27.5 cm and weight 15-18 g. This flycatcher is grey-brown above and greyish-white below, with dark streaks over the head and breast; the bill and legs are black. The sexes are similar.

Its distribution extends over all of Europe, western and central Asia and parts of North Africa; Israel lies at the southernmost limit of its range. Five subspecies have been identified. Its entire population migrates and winters in Africa south of the Sahara, from 8°N to South Africa. This species inhabits broadleaf forests, mixed woodland, plantations, gardens and parks.

In autumn the Spotted Flycatcher feeds on juicy fruits as well as insects. This is an active bird, not at all furtive in habits and generally not timid; it is often seen hunting in close proximity to humans.

The subspecies *M.s. striata*, which breeds across Europe to the Balkans, is a common passage migrant in Israel: in autumn from August to the end of November and especially during September, and in spring in April and May. The subspecies *M.s. neumanni*, which has a range extending from the Levant through Iran to Siberia, breeds in Israel, in gardens, woodlands and groves in central and northern parts of the country, especially in plains and valleys. It is paler than its European counterpart, and has a greyer back.

The nesting season is late and begins in May. The clutch contains 3-4 eggs. The female incubates alone for about 13 days and is fed by the male. The female continues to brood the chicks for a few days after hatching, feeding them with insects provided by the male; subsequently both parents feed them. The chicks stay in the nest for about 13 days, but are fed by the parents outside the nest for a further 20 or so days. The Spotted Flycatcher breeds once in the year.

During the 1960s the population of Spotted Flycatchers in Israel diminished considerably as a result of the use of agricultural pesticides, especially in the coastal plain.

Pied Flycatcher
Ficedula hypoleuca

Body length 12.2-14.5 cm, wing length 7-8.5 cm, wingspan 22-26 cm and weight 12-16.5 g. Like other members of its genus, the Pied Flycatcher differs from the Spotted Flycatcher in its more vivid and variegated colours: the male in summer has a black head, back and tail, white forehead and underparts, and black wings with a white wing-patch; in winter plumage it is similar but paler, tending towards greyish-brown. The bill and legs are black. The female has greyish-brown upperparts and greyish-white underparts, and is not easily distinguished from the female Collared Flycatcher; in general she resembles the male in winter plumage, but without the white forehead.

The range of this flycatcher is Euro-Siberian and it is common over considerable areas of Europe, excepting the south of the continent, and also breeds in North Africa and central Asia. In this range four subspecies have been described. Its primary habitats are broadleaf forests with old trees, with hollows suitable for nesting. It also breeds in artificial nestboxes and has been the subject of many studies.

The Pied Flycatcher winters in Africa from the banks of the White Nile to the shores of the Atlantic Ocean south of the Sahara, between 11°N and the Equator. In autumn its migration routes veer towards the southwest, and birds ringed in Poland and Russia have been found in Spain.

This is a fairly rare passage migrant in Israel in October and November, but common in April and early May. The subspecies concerned is *F.h. hypoleuca*, which breeds from central to north Europe and east to west Siberia.

Collared Flycatcher
Ficedula albicollis

Body length 12.5-14 cm, wing length 7.7-8.3 cm, wingspan 24 cm and weight 14 g. Similar to the Pied Flycatcher, but the male is distinguished by its white collar and rump; the white wing-patch is larger and is also conspicuous in winter plumage. The female is very similar to the female Pied Flycatcher, but with more white on the wings, distinctive both at rest and in flight.

Broadly, the Collared Flycatcher takes the place of the Pied Flycatcher in southern and southeastern Europe, but there are areas of overlap between the two species, and cases of interbreeding have even been recorded. The Collared Flycatcher breeds in broadleaf forests with large and old trees. It is a monotypic species and all populations migrate, wintering especially in savanna in tropical Africa.

In Israel the Collared Flycatcher is a very rare autumn passage migrant but is common in spring, from the end of March to early May.

Semi-collared Flycatcher
Ficedula semitorquata

According to some ornithologists, a subspecies of the Collared Flycatcher: the male is distinguished from the latter by the only partial white collar, absent from the nape (in which respect it resembles the male Pied Flycatcher), the grey rump and white-tipped median coverts. The female is grey and paler than the female Collared Flycatcher.

The Semi-collared Flycatcher is distributed from Greece and the Caucasus to northern Iran. It is more apt to feed on the ground and among leaves than other species of flycatcher. In Israel this is a quite rare spring passage migrant from the end of March to early May. It is more common in Eilat, although even here it does not appear every year.

Red-breasted Flycatcher
Ficedula parva

The smallest of the flycatchers: body length 12 cm, wing length 6.7 cm, wingspan 22 cm and weight 9 g. The male has a rusty-orange throat and breast, greyish head, grey-brown back and white belly. The tail is relatively long; it is dark brown with white patches at the base (especially conspicuous when the tail is cocked or flicked). The female is greyish-brown, with a pale sandy breast, a whitish belly, and tail similar to that of the male.

This is a woodland bird, whose range extends from central Europe and the Balkans to Korea; it winters in India and southeast Asia.

In Israel this is a rare migratory accidental: it is more common in the autumn migration (October-November) than in spring (April-early May). Most observations are in the Negev and Eilat, but the species has also been recorded in Tel Aviv, the Hula Valley and the Judean hills.

Family: Timaliidae (Babblers)

This family, comprising some 250 species, is sometimes regarded as a subfamily of the flycatcher family (Muscicapidae), from which it differs in anatomical structure and behavioural characteristics. Among members of the family there is distinct variety of appearance and shape. The tail is usually long, and sometimes graduated; the wings are short and rounded. The legs are long and strong, and the bill is usually strong and curved. There is no conspicuous sexual dimorphism.

This is a tropical family, with essentially Sino-Himalayan distribution, although representatives are also found in Africa, Malagasy, the shores of Arabia, Australia and America. Only one species, the Bearded Tit, has penetrated Europe, while four species of babbler inhabit the Saharo-Sindian zone.

All species are resident.

Babblers usually live on the ground or in dense undergrowth, and are constantly active; their capacity for flight is limited, but they move fast, with a jerky hopping motion. They normally live in groups, with close physical contact maintained between members of the group.

Brown Babbler
Turdoides squamiceps

The only typical representative of the babbler family seen in Israel: body length 26.5-29.5 cm, wing length 10.8-12 cm and weight 64-83 g. It resembles a large warbler: the upperparts are greyish-brown and the underparts paler. The feathers of the crown are black-tipped, the tail long and graduated, the wings short and rounded. The sexes are distinguished only by the colour of the eye: light in the male and dark brown in the female. The adult female also has a white eye-ring.

The genus *Turdoides* contains 26 species, distributed in dry regions of Africa and southern Asia. The Brown Babbler is endemic to the Middle East. Its range is limited to the area bounded by Oman, North Yemen, central Sinai and the Valley of the Arava, as far north as the region of Jericho. In this range three subspecies have been identified, the one found in Israel being *T.s. squamiceps*. This is a resident bird, living in acacia scrub and bushes along gorges and wadis.

Brown Babblers live in groups of three to 22 individuals; each group has its own territory. The group may contain any combination of sexes and ages. In a breeding group there is a distinct social hierarchy among both males and females. Boundaries of territories are fixed in the course of aggressive rivalry between neighbouring groups; usually this is confined to vocal threats, but fights resulting in death sometimes develop. Brown Babblers are very active, tending to move on the ground in procession, in a series of jerky hops. They are capable of moving at speed, changing direction and executing sharp turns with the aid of the tail. Over open expanses, between bushes, they take to the air in slow and low-level flight. The group usually moves together, waiting for stragglers to catch up before proceeding. Brown Babblers often gather close together, touching one another, and even preen one another's feathers. In the morning, before sunrise, they sometimes assemble and perform a social dance, in a line or in a dense mass, a phenomenon yet to be observed in any other species of bird.

These babblers are omnivorous: they feed on fruits, seeds, various creatures including lizards, geckos and small snakes, scraps of food etc. They normally seek their food on the ground, digging in the soil, turning over leaves, stripping bark from branches to expose beetle grubs, and inquisitively inspecting every novelty. Adult males do not compete over food; the first bird to find the food is entitled to eat it. Juvenile males, up to the age of three years, are liable to compete. When feeding in open areas, often one individual stands on guard; normally this is the responsibility of the dominant male.

The nesting season usually lasts from February to July, although a few pairs may nest in other months. During the moult nesting activity is suspended, but sometimes breeding is resumed in October. In years of drought there is no breeding at all, except by pairs living near refuse-tips or vegetable gardens. The nest is usually built in a fork in an acacia, but also in other bushes. The dominant male and dominant female are the principal builders, often assisted by other members of the group. The nest is a large and crude structure, of dead plant material including tree bark and thin branches, and there is no distinction between main structure and lining. In this nest the dominant female lays 3-5 eggs; sometimes other females join in, each laying a further 2-3 eggs, so that as many as 13 may be found in a single nest. The egg is glossy turquoise in colour without mottling. Incubation is performed by the dominant male and the laying females in turn, and lasts for a period of some 14 days. All members of the group collaborate in feeding and protecting the offspring, but in spite of this communal concern only four or five chicks survive in each brood.

Juvenile males attempt to stay in the territory, but most of them are driven out. Females leave the territory at one to three years old or are expelled from it at an earlier stage. They live as outcasts or join another breeding group.

Bearded Tit
Panurus biarmicus

An exceptional species in its family: body length 17 cm, wing length 6 cm, wingspan 19 cm and weight 15 g. The male is distinguished by the black moustache stretching from the base of the bill and the eye to the sides of the throat, the greyish-blue head and black undertail-coverts; its basic colour is rufous. The long and graduated tail (8.3-9.9 cm) is shared by both sexes; the female is otherwise undistinguished, being a fairly uniform brown-rufous. The bill is short, pointed and yellow. The legs are black.

The Bearded Tit is the only species in its family that has extended beyond the tropical zones. It has a sporadic range, from western Britain to the eastern

USSR. In this range three subspecies have been identified. It is restricted to reedbeds. Usually this is a resident bird, sometimes roaming outside the nesting season. It roams in pairs, in which the bond is apparently lifelong, an exceptional phenomenon among sexually dimorphic birds. At such times it is a gregarious bird.

In Israel this is a rare accidental: the first record, of four individuals, was in October 1974, in the fishponds of Afek in the Acre Valley. The Bearded Tit does not occur in this country every year; when it does, several are normally seen together. On 18 December 1982, 24 individuals were sighted in the Hula Reserve.

Family: Paridae (Tits)

The tit family comprises three genera and 47 species, 45 of them belonging to the genus *Parus*. All are small songbirds, with a body length of 9-20 cm and a weight of 10-46 g. The bill is shorter than the head, pointed and strong. The legs are relatively short and strong, and well adapted to climbing. The plumage is sometimes uniform grey or brown and sometimes contrasting — yellow, blue, white or black.

The family is distributed mainly in the Northern Hemisphere, within the Holarctic region, but also in southeast Asia and tropical Africa. Most species are resident. Members of the family live among trees and bushes. There is overlap between the distributions of a few species, but each has a preference for a certain type of vegetation and a different range of diet. Tits feed on insects in all stages of development, but also on various fruits, scraps of meat, fat and oily seeds. They are territorial birds in the nesting season; at other times they are gregarious, and often roam in flocks within a limited range.

Most species nest in holes or in hollow trees and easily adapt to nestboxes. The clutch is usually large, containing up to 10 eggs and often even 15-16; these are white, speckled with red markings. Only the female incubates. The chicks hatch blind and covered in grey down, and are fed by both parents.

In Israel three species occur, two being residents and one a very rare accidental.

Great Tit
Parus major

The Great Tit is the largest species of its genus: body length 12.8-14.1 cm, wing length 6.2-7.4 cm, wingspan 22 cm and weight 14-18 g. It has a black head and white cheeks; a black bib covers the chin and throat and a black band extends downwards from it across the otherwise yellow underparts; the upperparts are greyish-olive, and the tail is greyish-black except for the white outer feathers. The female is similar to the male but paler, and the black bellystripe is narrower. Juveniles resemble adults, but the black in their plumage tends towards dark brown and the belly is paler and whitish.

The Great Tit has a trans-Palaearctic and Oriental range and is to be found in all climatic conditions except tundra. In its range 31 subspecies have been identified. The subspecies *P. m. terraesanctae* is distributed from Syria to Israel. It is a woodland bird, preferring broadleaf and especially mixed forests to coniferous forests. It is also found in plantations and parks and is common in populated areas.

This bird is conspicuous in the landscape and very common among trees, in both rural and populated areas. It is noted for its constant activity, strong and far-carrying song and vivid colours. The Great Tit sings throughout the year, except at the time of moult and during winter storms, and vocal activity intensifies considerably at the approach of the nesting season.

In Israel this is a resident in northern and central parts of the country; recently it has expanded its range eastward and southward, and breeding has been recorded from the Hula Valley to El Arish in northern Sinai. In exceptional cases eggs may be laid as early as January, but nesting usually begins in early March and continues through April. Breeding is also known as late as May and June, but the rate of failure is so high that only a few pairs succeed in raising two broods in one nesting season. In exceptionally hot and dry years, there may even be breeding in autumn. Nests are usually built in holes and hollow trees, but also in pots, pipes, piles of bricks and even postboxes. This species easily adapts to artificial nestboxes, preferring those with an entry hole of 30-32 mm diameter. On cold nights the birds roost at their nesting sites, each individual alone. Normally the female builds a new nest for each brood, or at least adds a new lining to an old one. In Europe the clutch may contain as many as 15 eggs, one of the largest clutches found among songbirds. In Israel the norm is 5-7 eggs, a clutch of 10 eggs being exceptional. Incubation continues for a period of about 14 days. Usually the female incubates alone. The chicks stay in the nest for a relatively long time — 16-19 days — and the family unit is retained for a further week or two outside the nest.

Great Tits start to line a new nest for a second brood a day or two after the chicks have flown.

Sometimes juveniles of the first brood are seen pursuing their parents and demanding the food intended for the offspring of the second nesting attempt.

Sombre Tit
Parus lugubris

Body length 13.9-14.2 cm, wing length 7.4 cm and weight 13-17 g. Similar in size and appearance to the Great Tit, from which it is distinguished by its white breast and belly lacking a black stripe, and its greyish-brown upperparts. Juveniles are more greyish and resemble juvenile Great Tits, distinguished only by the absence of a dark belly-stripe.

This species' distribution is limited to the region between the Balkans and Iran, in which six or seven subspecies have been identified. It breeds in Lebanon, and the slopes of Hermon, where *P.l. anatoliae* is found, are the southernmost limit of its range.

The Sombre Tit is resident in the maquis of western Hermon, at altitudes between 800 and 1,700 m. Sometimes there is overlap of habitat between Sombre Tits and Great Tits. Their biology is also similar. The Sombre Tit nests between April and June on Hermon, where the maximum clutch size is apparently 5 eggs.

Coal Tit
Parus ater

A small tit: body length 11 cm, wing length 5.9 cm and weight 9 g. It is distinguished by its black crown, white cheeks, and white patch on the nape. Its back and wing-coverts are greyish-olive, its underparts greyish-white.

The Coal Tit's range is very wide, covering the whole width of Eurasia, from Britain to Kamchatka and Japan and to the shores of the Mediterranean in North Africa and the northern Middle East. Twenty subspecies have been identified. In Europe this is a very common bird, preferring coniferous woodland, especially forests of fir. Its breeding rate is high, and every few years there are extensive irruptions towards the south.

In Israel this is a very rare accidental. Observations in Jerusalem, Alonim and Galilee were noted by Hardy (1946); since then only one has been recorded, on 3 March 1977 in Tel Aviv.

Family: Sittidae (Nuthatches)

In this family there are 25 species, distributed in the Holarctic, Oriental and Australasian regions, 21 of them belonging to the genus *Sitta*. These are small and compact-bodied songbirds, with a straight, pointed and strong bill. The legs are short, the toes and claws long. The wings are long and pointed, and the tail is short with rounded feather tips. The sexes are similar.

Nuthatches feed on seeds and insects and are the only birds capable of seeking food while moving on the trunk and branches of a tree or on a rock with head pointed downwards. They breed in hollow trees and rock-crevices or in nests built of mud; the nest is lined.

Rock Nuthatch
Sitta neumayer

Body length 15 cm, wing length 7.6 cm and weight 30 g. A bird of compact build, short tail, short and strong legs, and straight and pointed bill about the same length as the head. The Rock Nuthatch has blue-grey upperparts and a conspicuous black eye-stripe; the underparts are whitish-rufous. The sexes are similar, and juveniles resemble adults but are paler.

The Rock Nuthatch's range extends from the Balkans, through Turkey and Iraq to eastern Iran. In this range five subspecies have been identified. This is a resident bird on hillsides and in rocky ravines, from sea-level to an altitude of some 2,500 m. The subspecies known in Israel is *S.n. syriaca*, which is distributed from Turkey, through Syria and Lebanon to northern Israel; it is paler and smaller and has a shorter bill (23 mm as opposed to 26 mm) than *S.n. neumayer*, which occurs in the Balkans.

Adult Rock Nuthatches are solitary outside the breeding season. This is a rather timid bird and on account of its colours, providing effective camouflage in rocky environments, it is not easily observed. Its strong and sibilant call, uttered when seeking food, is usually the first indication of its presence. It is an active bird, hopping and jumping on rocks. It feeds on insects, spiders and other invertebrates, especially on sun-facing slopes. In winter it eats seeds. It also tends to store and bury food.

In Israel the Rock Nuthatch is found on Mount Hermon, where the breeding population (Israeli) is estimated at 20 pairs. It occurs particularly along Nahal Guvta and on Nahal Shion and its tributaries. In winter 1984 a pair of the same subspecies was seen on the cliff of Ramim, above Kiryat Shemona in the east of Upper Galilee. In most months of the year, except in winter, it is possible to see groups of several individuals on Hermon; these are immatures.

In the estuary of Nahal Shion, at the bottom of the mountain, the nesting season begins in March; in the region of Mizpe Shelagim, at about 2,200 m above sea-level, not until April. At this time the Rock Nuthatch's song can often be heard, uttered from high vantage points and echoing over a wide area. The nest of this species is unique in shape: when the snow thaws the bird takes scraps of mud, moistens them with saliva and adds the crushed bodies of insects and spiders, forming a glutinous mixture with which the nest is constructed. The nest is bottle-shaped: a broad base attached to a rock and a long and narrow neck. Most of the task of construction is performed by the female. The nest is attached to a large rock or a cliff face 2-5 m above the ground, usually facing north. In clutches in southern Europe there are sometimes as many as 10 eggs; on Hermon 8 is apparently the maximum. The female incubates alone for about 15 days. The chicks remain in the nest some 23-25 days, and both parents feed them; on Hermon feeding of chicks has been observed as late as June.

The family unit remains intact some time longer before the bonds between partners and between parents and offspring disintegrate. Subsequently many Rock Nuthatches ascend to the peaks of Hermon, staying there until the onset of winter. With the first snowfalls a downward retreat begins, although even at the height of winter a few Rock Nuthatches may be seen above the snow-line, on rocks and in areas bare of snow.

Family: Tichodromadidae

Wallcreeper
Tichodroma muraria

Body length 16 cm, wing length 9.9 cm and weight 20 g. The only species in its family, which is closely related to nuthatches and to treecreepers (Certhiidae), and a bird of unique appearance and very conspicuous plumage colours. It is distinguished by its long and slightly curved bill, some 2.5 cm in length. The back and belly are grey, and the wing-coverts and bases of the flight feathers are bright red, conspicuous at rest and even more so in flight; the tips of the primaries and secondaries are grey-black, the outer primaries with white spots. The tail feathers are black with grey tips. The throat is white in winter, and turns black after the spring moult. The sexes are similar. In flight the Wallcreeper appears larger than its actual size, as its wings are up to a third longer than those of birds of similar size; the wing is also exceptional in shape, being rounded, narrow at the base and broad at the tip. The tail is straight, with broad and soft feathers. The legs are quite long and strong; the claws are strong and curved, and the rear toe long.

The Wallcreeper has a sporadic distribution in mountainous areas of the southern Palaearctic region, from the mountains of southern and central Europe through Turkey to the Himalayas and east Asia. Two subspecies have been identified. Its habitats are exposed slopes, cliffs and canyons from an altitude of 300 m above sea-level in the Alps, but especially between altitudes of 2,500 m and 5,000 m in the Himalayas, at a higher level than the Rock Nuthatch. In most of its range this is a resident bird, but in winter it migrates to lower levels and descends below the snow-line. In Israel the western subspecies *T.m. muraria* is a rare winter visitor.

This species moves rapidly on walls and cliff-faces with hops and fluttering movements like a large butterfly, wings half spread and very conspicuous. In the hours of the morning it spends much of its time sunbathing, and then, too, the wings are spread and conspicuous. The Wallcreeper feeds on insects in various stages of development, sometimes catching flying insects in the air. It is generally a silent bird.

In Israel the Wallcreeper occurs rarely between January and the end of February, being more common in some years. Its wintering areas in this country are river valleys and cliffs to the east of the mountain ridge: Nahal Iyyun, Nahal Dishon, Nahal Amud, the cliffs of the Arbel and the canyons of the Judean Desert. Each individual — male or female — winters in its own territory, although sometimes in proximity; thus in winter 1962 four individuals were seen at one site on the cliffs of the Arbel.

It is possible that the Wallcreeper occasionally breeds in Lebanon.

Family: Remizidae (Penduline Tits)

This is a small family, comprising four genera and ten species. Its origin is apparently in tropical Asia; this is suggested by the form of the hanging nests, with entrance corridors, similar to the nests of weavers. In the genus *Remiz* there is a single species. Penduline tits are closely related to tits, and some ornithologists class them together in a single family, Paridae.

Penduline Tit
Remiz pendulinus

A small bird: body length 11.5 cm, wing length 5.6 cm and weight 9 g. The crown, nape and neck are greyish-white, and the forehead and eye-mask are black; the underparts are pale chestnut-brown, the back and wing-coverts rufous-brown. The primaries are greyish-black with white edges. The tail is long and grey, the bill short and pointed, and the legs black. The sexes are similar. Juveniles are duller and lack the black eye-mask.

The Penduline Tit is distributed in southern, central and eastern Europe, in Turkey, northern Iran and the southern USSR, and further east towards China and Mongolia. Seven subspecies have been identified. This is primarily a bird of reedbeds in marshes and in riverbank woodland. It is resident in most of its areas of distribution, but periodically it expands its range and invades new areas in flocks, then disappears from them. In Israel the subspecies *R.p. pendulinus*, which breeds from central and southern Europe to west Siberia and in Turkey, is a fairly common winter visitor.

This species seeks its food especially among reeds. In summer it feeds mainly on insects, spiders and other small creatures. In winter it perches on the inflorescence of reeds and on palmate flowers, and eats seeds like a finch.

The Penduline Tit was first identified in Israel only in 1958. Since then a number of sightings have been recorded in northern and central parts of the country between the end of October and April, but its frequency varies considerably from year to year. In the northern Hula Valley juveniles occur at the end of May and during June; they are easy to identify on account of their high-pitched contact calls.

Family: Nectariniidae (Sunbirds)

In the sunbird family there are five genera and 117 species. The family is distributed in tropical regions of Australia, islands of the Pacific Ocean, and especially in Africa and southern Asia. The habitats of sunbirds are many and varied: woodland, savanna and cultivated areas at various altitudes. These birds are usually resident and territorial, or migrate in stages and over short distances.

These are small songbirds, with a body length of 11-28 cm. In appearance and to some extent in behaviour they resemble the hummingbirds (Trochilidae) of the American continent. The similarity between the families is purely superficial, based on similar habits and diet (the nectar of flowers), and on shared physical attributes such as a small body, a long bill and glossy metallic colours. Sunbirds have long decurved bills. Unlike hummingbirds, sunbirds tend to sip nectar while perched on a branch; accordingly their legs are relatively long and strong. The tail is straight or graduated; in some species the two central feathers are elongated, giving some sunbirds their relatively large body length. There is striking sexual dimorphism.

All species of sunbird build an enclosed nest of grass, roots, fibres, etc., held together with spider-webs, and suspended from the end of a branch. The clutch contains 1-3 eggs.

In Israel there is one representative: the Orange-tufted Sunbird.

Orange-tufted or Palestine Sunbird
Nectarinia osea

A very small bird: body length 10-11 cm, wing length 4.6-5.4 cm and weight 6-8 g. Both sexes are clearly distinguished by their long (1.6 cm) and curved bill. The male is conspicuously coloured: black plumage with metallic shades of green and violet on the upperparts and breast; the sides of the breast are adorned with orange-red and yellow tufts, but these are conspicuous only at times of visual displays and when asleep. The tail is short and the wings short and round. The legs are quite long and thin, black in colour. The female is grey, with a black tail. Juveniles resemble females, assuming full adult plumage at two to three months.

The genus *Nectarinia* is the largest in the family, comprising 75 species, most of them living in Africa and a minority in tropical Asia. The Orange-tufted Sunbird has the most northerly range among species of sunbirds. Two subspecies are known: *N.o. decorsei*, which is distributed in central Africa, between Mali and southern Sudan; and *N.o. osea*, which is confined to the Middle East, in Israel, Lebanon, southern Syria, western Arabia and Yemen.

In natural environments this species sips the nectar of flowers such as *Moringa peregrina*, zygophyllum and *Lycium shawii* (teaplant), and is particularly attracted to *Loranthus acacial* (acacia mistletoe). It is capable of hovering near the aperture of the flower petals, like a hummingbird, but tends rather to sip the nectar while perched on an adjacent branch. It also feeds on insects hidden in the flower, and sometimes even hunts them in flight. This is an active and inquisitive bird, moving constantly in its search for food. On account of its inquisitive nature it is easily attracted to birdtables by the offer of nectar substitutes such as sugared water.

At the beginning of the twentieth century the Orange-tufted Sunbird was extremely rare in Israel and was found only in the lower Jordan Valley and oases near the shores of the Dead Sea: in Jericho and Ein Gedi. Since the 1930s it has expanded its range in this country to a considerable extent: in Petah Tikva a nest was found as early as 1935, in Hadera the first nest was found in 1941, in Ramatayim in 1944, in Jerusalem in 1953 and in the Jordan Valley in 1955. Today this is a very common bird in the gardens of settlements and may be found in almost all parts of the country. It is reasonable to suppose that this proliferation in recent years has come about as a result of the development of landscape gardening, with flowers abundant in nectar throughout the year, such as Cape honeysuckle, Chinese hibiscus and climbing jasmine.

In winter the Orange-tufted Sunbird is liable to roam. Even before its recent expansion it could be seen at this season along the whole length of the coastal plain, as far north as Sidon in Lebanon, and also in the Jezreel Valley and in other areas. During winter it is sometimes seen in small groups, segregated by sex: in northern parts of the country more males are seen; in the Arava and its neighbouring streams females predominate.

With the approach of spring the males perch on high vantage points and sing with metallic and trilling voice, sometimes imitating the calls of other birds. The female performs most of the nest-building while the male only accompanies her. The Orange-tufted Sunbird builds an enclosed nest, suspended at the tip of a hanging branch in a sheltered place, and thus nests may often be found close to the wall of a house or on the ceiling of a balcony. The nest is pear-shaped, broad below and narrow above, about 18 cm in height and 8 cm in base diameter; the entrance is circular and located at the side. Other distinguishing features are a small awning above the entrance hole, and a trailing 'beard' of leaves and twigs hanging from the base. The main building materials are thin stalks, roots, leaves, tree bark and spiderwebs, and the lining consists of feathers, scraps of paper and leaf fragments. If for any reason the nest fails to fulfil its function, the birds tend to return to it, dismantle the building materials and use them for a new nest. The clutch contains 2-3 eggs, white and mottled with tiny greyish dots, especially at the blunt end. The female alone incubates for a period of 12-13 days. The chicks hatch blind and naked, with a short and broad bill. Both parents tend and feed them with small flies, spiders, etc., although the female's contribution is approximately double that of the male. They fly from the nest at about 13 days old, but return to it to roost for a few more days — behaviour atypical of the chicks of songbirds. The female calls them and guides them to the nest, and continues to brood them.

The Orange-tufted Sunbird is liable to breed twice or three times in the year, and cases of breeding in autumn and even in winter have been recorded. Attempts at breeding outside the normal season usually end in failure. In hot and dry years the nesting season may begin as early as January, although it normally begins in March. This species often uses the same nest for successive broods, and may even return to it the following year.

Family: Oriolidae (Orioles)

This family contains two genera and 28 species, most of them inhabiting tropical and subtropical regions in Africa and Asia. Only two have penetrated the Palaearctic region, and one of these is seen in Israel.

These are average-sized songbirds, with vivid colours, predominantly yellow in most cases. The bill is long, about the same length as the head, and the tarsus is short but strong. The wings are long. All members of the family have one moult in the year. The sexes have different plumage, and juveniles resemble adult females. All orioles are good and fast fliers, hardly ever descending to the ground; they even bathe in flight, like swifts and swallows. All are tree-dwellers in woodland and feed on insects, especially their larvae, and also on fruit.

Golden Oriole
Oriolus oriolus

Body length 23.7-28 cm, wing length 13.8-16.1 cm and weight 50-72 g. A colourful and quite unmistakable bird, the male being predominantly golden-yellow and having black wings with yellow patches at the base of the primaries. The tail is also black, with yellow outer tips. The bill is long and reddish. The female is greenish in colour, with olive-brown wings and tail and streaked underparts. Juveniles resemble the adult female.

The range of the Golden Oriole covers most of Europe (except the north), and extends eastward through the Middle East to central Asia and southward towards India. In this range two subspecies are known. The subspecies *O.o. oriolus* and also the northern populations of the subspecies *O.o. kundoo* migrate; the Indian populations of the latter subspecies are resident. Golden Orioles winter in East Africa, between Kenya and South Africa, migrating in small and loose groups of two to 15 individuals. Many cross the Mediterranean at altitudes of 200-300 m, and on reaching the Sahara climb to 1,500-2,000 m. Many migrate along the Nile Valley and are caught there. This species normally frequents high treetops and is therefore not easily observed; only rarely does it descend to the ground, where it hops with clumsy movements and flees hurriedly from any sound or threat, diving into cover.

In Israel the Golden Oriole is a common passage migrant. In autumn it is seen from the end of August to early October, and particularly in mid-September; females and juveniles precede the males by about ten days. The migrating birds feed especially on fruits such as figs and dates. The spring migration is late, from the second half of April to the end of May, and then the males precede females and juveniles by about ten days. During this period it is sometimes possible to hear the flutish and distinctive song of the male.

In spring 1983, two pairs nested in the wood of HaMeyassedim near the Hula Reserve. This was the first and the only instance so far recorded of the Golden Oriole nesting in this country. The nest resembles a carefully woven and deep basket, and is located among horizontal branches or in a fork; it is built by the female. In the clutch there are 3-4 eggs. The period of incubation is 14-15 days, and most of the task is performed by the female. The chicks hatch blind, with a covering of short grey down. They fly from the nest at 14-15 days old.

Family: Laniidae (Shrikes)

This family contains four subfamilies, 12 genera and 72 species; the genus *Lanius*, the only one represented in Israel, comprises 24 species. Members of the family are distributed especially in tropical areas of Africa and Asia; they are not represented in tropical regions of the New World, nor in Australasia. The southern species are resident, while those of the north migrate.

Shrikes are average-sized (17-28 cm) songbirds, relatively easy to identify on account of their bill, which is strong, laterally compressed, and hooked at the tip like the bill of a bird of prey. Its edges are sharp, and there are sharp tooth-like projections at the edges of the upper mandible, corresponding to indentations in the lower mandible. The plumage of most shrikes of the subfamily Laniinae is relatively drab — white, grey, black and brown; more striking tones, such as red or yellow, are exceptional. Usually there is no sexual dimorphism, except in size: the males are larger. Juveniles are mottled. The wings are rounded, short in the resident species and long and pointed in migrants. The tail is long and graduated. The tarsus is strong, and the claws are strong and curved.

Shrikes are birds of open environments, tending to avoid dense woodland. Their flight is slow and undulating; sometimes they hover. They feed only on live food: perching on a high and exposed vantage point, they dart down onto insects and other invertebrates, also small birds, reptiles and mammals. They tend to impale their victims on thorns or barbed wire; sometimes the prey is left there to dry, to be consumed at a later stage. Undigested portions of food, such as shells, feathers and hair, are ejected in pellet form. Shrikes have characteristic alarm calls, and are also known to imitate the voices of other birds.

The nest is basket-shaped, carefully constructed from twigs, branches, stalks and leaves. It is built on a tree, often a thorny variety, and is placed at the end of a branch and close to foliage. The clutch contains 3-7 eggs, coloured beige and speckled with grey markings, especially at the blunt end. The female incubates almost alone and is fed by the male. The chicks hatch blind and naked, and are fed by both parents.

In Israel seven species are represented.

Woodchat Shrike
Lanius senator

A small shrike: body length 17.2-18.6 cm, wing length 9.3-9.9 cm and weight 29-37 g. Its distinguishing features are the chestnut head and nape, and white elliptical-shaped markings on the spread wing and on the black back; a black eye-mask extends from the forehead along the sides of the head, and blends into the black feathers of the shoulder. The underparts are whitish-pink, the rump white, and the tail black with white edges. The female is similar to the male, but paler. Juveniles are grey-brown with mottled upperparts and with the white wingbar already perceptible; their underparts are whitish tending towards orange, and with delicate crescentic barring.

This shrike's range is southern Palaearctic, concentrated mainly in the Mediterranean and western Irano-Turanian regions, but with periodic extension towards the north. In its range three subspecies have been identified. All populations winter in Africa, south of the Sahara and north of the Equator. This is probably the commonest of the shrikes seen in Israel.

In Israel this is a fairly common passage migrant, in autumn between August and mid-September, and in spring from mid-March to mid-April. Its spring migration precedes by about a month that of the Masked Shrike. The migrants seen in Israel are members of the subspecies *L.s. senator*, which breeds in Europe and North Africa.

The Woodchat Shrike is also a common breeder in Israel. The breeding pairs belong to the subspecies *L.s. niloticus*, which is distributed from Turkey to Iran. This is distinguished by a white patch at the base of the central tail feathers, about 3 cm in breadth; the white wing-patch is also larger than in *L.s. senator*. This shrike is present in all districts in northern and central parts of the country, as far south as a line passing from the fringes of Mount Hebron through Be'er Sheva to the northern Gaza Strip.

The breeding population returns to Israel during March. At this time the song of the male, more melodious than the song of other shrikes, is distinctive. The bird settles in park woodland, sparse groves, olive orchards and plantations where there are broad expanses of bare ground. The nesting season begins with a courtship display, in which the male pursues the female in flight, overtaking her at intervals and rising and falling in the air, with energetic bobbing of the head. The nest is built on the outer branches of a thorny tree, sometimes on a eucalyptus or a young sapling. It is usually 1-3 m above the ground, sometimes as high as 10 m, and is well hidden in foliage; it is often surrounded by a garland of wild flowers. The female incubates the 4-7 eggs virtually alone for a period of 16 days while the male feeds her. Both parents feed the chicks for 19-20 days in the nest, and about a further three weeks

outside the nest. During this period they are extremely noisy. The juveniles leave their parents' territory at the end of May, and roam during June and July.

The breeding season lasts from the end of March to the second half of June. During this period two broods are raised.

Masked Shrike
Lanius nubicus

Body length 17-18.5 cm, wing length 8.3-9.2 cm and weight 21-26 g. In flight the Masked Shrike is conspicuously black and white: the upperparts including the rump are black, except for the white forehead, wing-panels and outer tail feathers. The underparts are very pale rufous-brown. The female is paler and distinguished by the grey-brown belly, nape and back.

The Masked Shrike has an eastern Mediterranean distribution, restricted to the region between Greece and the Persian Gulf. This is a monotypic species, all of whose populations migrate, wintering in southern Egypt, Sudan and Chad. It inhabits maquis, olive groves, park environments and hedgerows.

This species is more inclined than other shrikes to perch on the outside of trees, when it moves its long tail up and down and sideways. It sometimes catches flying insects, pursuing them in flycatcher fashion.

In Israel this is a common passage migrant. In autumn it is seen from mid-August to the end of October, and especially during September. It is more common in spring, between the end of March and the end of May, and especially in the second half of April.

This shrike also breeds in Israel, in parts of the Mediterranean region, but this population diminished greatly in the late 1950s and during the 1960s, apparently as a result of the widespread use of pesticides. Most of its breeding population arrives in April. It usually nests in dense maquis, in thornless trees such as oak, terebinth and carob, but on the fringes of the Mediterranean region tall bushes such as buckthorn are also used. The nest is usually built on a broad and horizontal branch, about 2 m above the ground. In the clutch there are 4-6 eggs. The female incubates for about 15 days. The chicks stay in the nest for 18-20 days and are tended by both parents.

The Masked Shrike normally rears two broods in a season.

Great Grey Shrike
Lanius excubitor

The largest, strongest and most solidly built of the shrikes: body length 21.5-24.5 cm, wing length 9.8-11.5 cm and weight 45-70 g. The forehead, crown and back are grey, the eye-mask black, and the underparts whitish-grey. The tail is long (10.4-11.3 cm) and graduated, black with white edges. The wings, which are short and round, are black with a white bar. The sexes are similar, although the underparts of the female are more grey and streaked. Juveniles resemble adults in the black and white pattern of the wings and tail, but their back is greyish-brown, the underparts greyish-brown with dark streaking, and the eye-mask dark brown rather than black; they acquire adult plumage during their first autumn.

This shrike's range is Holarctic and Oriental, and it is the most widely distributed of all shrikes. It breeds in northern Canada, most of Europe, North Africa including the Sahara, and Asia — from Israel, Arabia and Iraq through north India to the eastern USSR. A total of 19 subspecies have been identified. Most of its populations are resident; only the most northerly ones in Canada, Scandinavia and the northern USSR migrate. Wintering areas in the Palaearctic region are the Mediterranean countries, especially Italy, the Balkans and Turkey. In Israel this is a mainly resident bird, although in autumn a few migrating or roaming individuals may also be seen.

This species is a strikingly territorial bird throughout the year. It is liable to attack even an intruding falcon or a kite. In the nesting season it is more secretive and less easily located. At other times of the year it is often seen perched on a high and relatively exposed branch. It is often liable to approach humans, perching on a parked car or a tent. On seeing a hawk it utters a hoarse and throbbing alarm call. Its vocal range is varied and includes cries and chirps, as well as imitations of other birds.

The Great Grey Shrike is distributed in Israel on the slopes of the Golan, in the northern Hula Valley, in the Harod Valley and the Bet She'an Valley, around Lake Tiberias, in Samaria and the Jordan Valley, the hills of the Shephelah, across the Negev and in the Arava. According to the literature, three subspecies may be distinguished in this range: *L.e. excubitor, L.e. aucheri* and *L.e. theresae*.

This is a bird of trees and isolated thorny bushes, such as sloe and acacia. The date of nesting varies according to area: in the Arava in February, on the edges of Lake Tiberias and the Hula Valley in March, and in the coastal plain in April. The nest is usually built on a sloe or acacia tree, but also in other bushes and shrubs and even in coils of barbed wire. It is placed 1-7 m above the ground. The clutch is of 5-7 eggs, and the female incubates virtually alone for a period of about 15 days. The chicks leave the nest at the age of 19-20 days. They attain independence at about 35 days old, when the parents expel them from the territory.

At least in the Arava, the Great Grey Shrike breeds twice in the year; it starts building a new nest while still feeding the chicks in the first.

Red-backed Shrike
Lanius collurio

A relatively small shrike: body length 16.5-19.8 cm, wing length 8.8-10.3 cm, wingspan 28-31 cm and weight 25-40 g. The male has a grey head and nape, reddish-brown back and wing-coverts, black eye-stripe, whitish cheeks and neck, and pinky-white underparts; the tail is black, edged with white at the base. The female has a brown head and back, and pinkish-buff underparts with narrow grey-brown crescent-shaped markings. The wings are relatively short and the tail long and graduated. Juveniles resemble the adult female, but are more brown and also have narrow transverse barring on the head and back.

The distribution of the Red-backed Shrike is Palaearctic, covering most climatic areas except taiga and tundra. Northern Israel is included in its breeding range. Seven subspecies have been identified. It inhabits sparse woodland with rich undergrowth and open country with bushes. All of its populations migrate south in autumn. The European populations winter in Africa from Egypt and Sudan through Kenya and Uganda to Zaire, Angola and South Africa. On the return journey, in spring, they bypass the Mediterranean to the east and cross over Arabia, Jordan and Israel.

In Israel the subspecies *L.c. collurio* is a fairly common passage migrant in autumn, from the end of August to mid-November and especially in September. It is much more common in spring, from mid-April and especially during May. Evidently, in autumn the main migration is of the eastern European population, while in spring this is joined by the populations of central and western Europe, which in the autumn cross the Mediterranean but prefer an overland route in spring.

This subspecies is also a rare breeder in Upper Galilee and the Golan, sometimes also on Carmel, and is a fairly common breeder on Hermon. The males breeding in Israel arrive a few days before the females. Their song is weak — a low warble. Incubation of the 5-6 eggs lasts about 15 days and is performed mainly by the female, while the male feeds her. The chicks remain in the nest about 15 days.

Isabelline Shrike
Lanius isabellinus

Formerly considered a subspecies of the Red-backed

Shrike, from which it is distinguished by the creamy-buff head and nape, light brown back and pale sandy-brown flanks. The tail is reddish-rufous in both sexes.

The Isabelline Shrike is distributed in Turkestan and central Asia; it winters in southern India, Iran and Iraq and also in Arabia, Kenya and Uganda. In Israel it is a rare accidental in the migration season, especially in the Arava but also on the coastal plain.

Lesser Grey Shrike
Lanius minor

Similar to the Great Grey Shrike but smaller: body length 19.6-21 cm, wing length 11-11.9 cm, wing-span 35-38 cm and weight 41-48 g. It is distinguished by its black forehead, shorter tail, pinker underparts and more erect stance. The female has a greyer forehead and is very similar to the female Great Grey Shrike.

The Lesser Grey Shrike has a distribution extending over central Europe and western Asia; its breeding range also includes Lebanon. There are two subspecies. It winters in savannas south of the Equator.

In Israel the subspecies *L.m. minor* is a fairly common passage migrant. In autumn it is quite conspicuous for a short period, especially in the second half of August and in early September; the rearguard is still to be seen in October. It is more rare in spring, when it is seen especially in the first half of May.

Long-tailed Shrike
Lanius schach

Superficially resembles the Red-backed Shrike, but similar in size to the Great Grey Shrike: body length 23 cm and wing length 9.5 cm. It is black and grey above and predominantly rufous below; its belly is white.

This species breeds in central and eastern Asia and normally winters in the western Himalayas. A single individual was observed in winter 1983 in Sede Boker.

Family: Corvidae (Crows and Allies)

This family has a cosmopolitan range, and is represented in all parts of the world except New Zealand and Antarctica; it comprises 23 genera and 103 species.

The Corvidae are an exceptional family in the order of songbirds, both in size and in vocal characteristics. The Raven is the largest of the songbirds, with a weight of up to 1.5 kg, and even the smallest members of the family weigh in excess of 85 g. Body length varies between 18 cm and 70 cm. Their voices are hoarse and most are incapable of melodious song, but they are included in the passerines on account of the structure of the syrinx. They are capable of imitating various sounds. Crows have a compact body, and a long, strong and curved bill. The legs are strong. In the plumage of the Palaearctic species the predominant colours are black, grey and brown. The sexes are similar and males are slightly larger. Juveniles resemble adults.

Crows live in a wide variety of habitats and climatic conditions, from 400 m below sea-level in the Dead Sea basin to 4,000 m and more above. They are omnivorous, with few particular preferences. They seek their food on the ground and grip it with their feet, in the manner of birds of prey. Many of them store food and hide it in holes and crevices. They often seize and devour the chicks and eggs of other birds.

Crows are generally monogamous, and the bond is sometimes lifelong. Many species are gregarious and nest in colonies, or flock after nesting. They breed in trees or in rock-hollows. The nest is built of twigs, sometimes reinforced with mud, and densely lined. The egg is usually green-buff, mottled with olive-brown-black markings. The chicks hatch blind and usually naked, and the parents feed them with food regurgitated from the crop.

In Israel four genera and 11 species are represented.

Jay
Garrulus glandarius

A relatively large and quite conspicuous bird: body length 32.5-35.4 cm, wing length 16.3-17.4 cm and weight 160-191 g. The Jay belongs to one of the more colourful genera in the family. The body is brown-pink above, and the underparts are the same colour although paler; the rump is white. The crown feathers are long and black and liable to be erected in various circumstances. The wing-coverts are especially conspicuous with their bright blue colour and black speckling, and the wing also has a white patch. The moustache, primaries and tail are black. The tail is long and straight, the wing broad and short.

The Jay has a trans-Palaearctic range, from Norway, Britain and Spain to China, Korea and Japan; it is also common in north India and in Malaysia. In this broad range there are many separate populations and a total of 36 subspecies, differing from one another in coloration, especially that of the crown and back. The Jay is a bird of parkland, woodland and sparse maquis with tall trees. It is a resident bird in all areas of its range, although it is liable to roam over short distances. The subspecies breeding in Israel is *G.g. atricapillus*, which is distributed between southern Turkey and southwestern Iran.

Like other members of its family, the Jay lives in monogamous pairs usually attached to territories. From the flight of the chicks from the nest, at the beginning of summer, to the end of autumn, when the juveniles disperse from their parents' territory, Jays live in family units. Only in winter does the surplus of population, mainly juveniles, form flocks. In spite of its retiring habits, in populated areas it is capable of adapting to the presence of humans and may be approached to within close range. The Jay has a characteristic raucous and disyllabic call, with emphasis on the first syllable. It is particularly partial to acorns, which it also hides and buries in the ground — thus assisting the propagation of oaks.

In Israel the Jay used to be confined to western Lower Galilee, Upper Galilee, Samaria and Judea, and until the 1930s it was very rare in Carmel. Since then it has gradually broadened its range, penetrating the coastal plain in the 1960s and the Jezreel Valley during the 1970s. This proliferation has apparently come about as the result of a combination of factors, including the near extermination of the resident species of hawk and the development of pecan-nut cultivation.

During the nesting season the Jay is fairly quiet. In populated areas nest-building begins at the end of February, in natural woodland not until March. Both partners construct the nest among thin branches in the upper part of the tree: 3-7 m above the ground in Tabor oaks, 6-20 m above the ground in conifers. The higher sections of pecan-nut plantations may also be adopted for this purpose, if foliage cover is adequate. The clutch contains 2-6 eggs, usually 4. Incubation continues for a period of 16-17 days, and the female incubates for most of the time. The chicks hatch at irregular intervals, and are blind and naked at birth. The female continues to brood them for 12-15 days and at this stage the male feeds both the female and the chicks. Subsequently both parents feed the chicks, which stay in the nest 19-20 days.

The Jay breeds only once in the season, but it is evident that only about a third of nests are successful; clutches are vulnerable to depredation by Hooded Crows and even by other Jays. For this reason the building of replacement nests may be observed as late as May or early June; in such cases building materials are taken from the unsuccessful nest and re-used. The nesting season ends in July.

The family unit is maintained to the winter, though during the summer and the autumn four to six Jays may be seen roaming together in the home range.

Magpie
Pica pica

Body length 48 cm (including some 22 cm for the long and graduated tail), wing length 18-24 cm and weight 200-260 g. An unmistakable bird, with contrasting black and white plumage and metallic green tail feathers.

The Magpie is distributed over the whole of Europe and appreciable portions of Asia and western North Africa; it also occurs in the westernmost Holarctic. A small population breeds in Yemen. Thirteen subspecies have been described. This is a resident bird in all areas of its range. Its habitats are maquis, woodland and plantations, also agricultural areas and suburbs.

The Magpie has been recorded only once in Israel: in the Golan in February 1970.

Alpine Chough
Pyrrhocorax graculus

Body length 40-44 cm, wing length 28-28.9 cm and weight 260-300 g. An all-black bird with a blue tint, and with red legs and curved yellow bill.

The range of the Alpine Chough is sporadic and restricted to mountainous areas in the southern Palaearctic: from the Pyrenees, Atlas and Alps, through the Apennines, the Balkans, the mountains of Lebanon and Anti-Lebanon to the Hindu Kush and the Himalayas. Two subspecies have been identified. It inhabits cliffs and rocky slopes near grassy plains and cultivated fields. It breeds among rocks, and is found at altitudes of 1,500 m in the Alps and 5,000 m in the Himalayas. Its populations are resident, but move in winter to lower levels.

The Alpine Chough has a light and graceful flight. It is an accomplished aerobat, performing aerial antics and uttering characteristic whistling cries even during storms. It feeds on insects caught among rock-crevices, and also on kitchen refuse. On the ground it advances with combined hopping and walking gait.

In Israel this is a rare winterer on the flanks of Hermon, and its appearance depends on the climate and the rate of snowfall. In years without snowfall the Alpine Chough is merely an accidental. Normally it is seen on Hermon between August and early April, in small flocks of 10-12 individuals. The largest flock observed so far numbered 26 individuals.

It is probable that a few pairs nest at the peak of Hermon.

Chough
Pyrrhocorax pyrrhocorax

Similar to the Alpine Chough, but with glossier black feathers. Its bill is longer, and red in colour; the tail is also longer, and is spread like a fan in flight.

The Chough's distribution is similar to that of the Alpine Chough, but usually at lower altitudes. In the past the Chough was a very common bird in the mountains of Lebanon; today it is a very rare accidental on the higher slopes of Hermon.

Genus: *Corvus* (crows)

The most conspicuous genus in the family Corvidae, comprising 39 species with a virtually cosmopolitan range. Members of this genus are the largest in the order of songbirds. Seven species are represented in Israel. The tail is shorter than the wing and slightly graduated or rounded at the tip. The bill is relatively long, and black in colour. The predominant colour of the plumage is black, sometimes combined with grey, and in a few tropical species with white. In some cases the black plumage has a metallic gloss.

Hooded Crow
Corvus corone

Body length 43-49 cm, wing length 29-32 cm, wingspan 87 cm and weight 43-49 g. The subspecies seen in Israel is *C.c. sardonius*, to which the following description relates. The back, belly, hindneck and underwing-coverts are grey; the rest of the plumage is black. Since the early 1970s a few albino specimens have been observed in western Galilee.

The Hooded Crow's range extends over most of Eurasia, with limited penetration along the Nile Valley as far south as Aswan. It is generally supposed that during the Ice Age the species was driven south, and divided into three isolated populations: in southwestern Europe, in southeastern Europe and the Middle East, and in southeast Asia. Six subspecies have been identified, of which two (the western and eastern) are black, the remaining four grey; the latter are distributed between the rivers Elbe and Yangtse. With the retreat of the ice-caps, the dividing line between the populations became blurred, and hybridism between the subspecies is now commonplace. The subspecies *C.c. sardonius* is distributed from Italy and the region of the Danube, south and east through Yugoslavia, Turkey and the Mediterranean islands to Upper Egypt. All its populations are resident. In Israel this is a common bird in all parts of the Mediterranean region, especially on the coastal plain and in valleys near populated areas.

The Hooded Crow is omnivorous, and its large, thick and solid bill is capable of cracking pecan nuts and breaking the shells of small tortoises. It also eats carrion, preys on chicks and eggs and consumes wounded birds and small rodents; it regularly congregates around heaps of domestic refuse and piles of litter. It is a gregarious bird, and most of its numbers spend the year in flocks, of 10-100 individuals. Only a minority of pairs are territorial throughout the year, and the remainder disperse from the group only in the nesting season. The vocal range of the Hooded Crow is quite rich and varied: a warning cry, an alarm cry (three loud syllables) and a mustering call; this latter call is uttered at the sight of an intruder, for example a man with a rifle, and in response the flock gathers together, circling and gliding in a display of aggression. Crows are also liable to chase away falcons and herons.

Tristram considered this bird the commonest species in the country, and it was indeed very common in the early and mid-twentieth century. In the early 1960s many of the Hooded Crows in Israel were destroyed by poison intended for jackals. Since, there has been a perceptible recovery in the population, with especial proliferation in the early 1980s when it reached the Jericho region; it has also been observed in Ein Gedi. The population on the coastal plain was estimated in 1983 at 3,000 individuals, and it has become a serious agricultural pest.

At the approach of the breeding season a few pairs leave the flock and each returns to its regular nesting site, often retained in successive years. (The remaining members of the flock stay together and do not breed, since suitable breeding territories are insufficient for the requirements of all). The nest is usually located in a fork at the top of a tall tree; there is apparently a definite preference for eucalyptus, but nests are also found in cypress, oak, sycamore, and mulberry, and even on dwarf trees, electricity poles or on a ledge in an earth embankment. Laying usually begins at the end of February or in March, and the clutch contains 4-6 eggs. The period of incubation is 20-21 days, the female incubating almost alone. The chicks leave the nest at about one month of age but return to it at intervals thereafter, and remain in their parents' territory a few more weeks or months. Only at the end of summer do they join a flock, usually together with their parents.

The Hooded Crow is the main, possibly the only host in this country of the Great Spotted Cuckoo.

Jackdaw
Corvus monedula

The smallest of the crows: body length 32.5-36 cm, wing length 21-24 cm, wingspan 65-74 cm and weight 190-200 g. Most of its plumage, including the body, wings and tail, is grey-black with a bluish tint;

the nape, hindneck and sides of the neck are grey, and the crown black. The tail is straight-edged and the bill relatively short. The male is usually slightly larger than the female. Juveniles are paler and browner than adults, with bluish rather than pale grey eyes.

The range of the Jackdaw extends over most of Europe, with penetration to central Asia; it is also found in North Africa. In this range four of five subspecies have been identified. Most of its populations are resident, with the northerly ones wintering to the south of their areas of distribution. The Jackdaw lives in open and exposed terrain: fields, plantations, cliff-faces and suburbs. The subspecies *C.m. soemmerringii* is a winter visitor and resident in Israel.

This compact bird is a talented aerobat, capable of agile manoeuvring in the air even during storms; from time to time it dives at high speed with wings folded. During flight it constantly utters cries, higher-pitched than those of larger crows. The Jackdaw is a gregarious bird, tending to live in flocks throughout the year. Like other members of its genus, it is omnivorous.

The Jackdaw is a fairly common winterer in Israel between October and March. In the past scores of thousands used to winter in Israel, roosting communally in trees with starlings. Their number was reduced considerably in the late 1950s as a result of poisoning. The wintering population has recovered to some extent since the mid-1970s, but has not yet reached its former level.

This is also quite a rare resident in Israel, restricted to a few nesting colonies. In this country colonies are located in caves and quarries; the largest ones, in use for many years, are in the caves of Beit Juvrin and the quarries of Har Ibel near Shechem (Nablus), each of which contains hundreds of pairs. In recent years additional small colonies have been founded: in Wadi Kelt near Jericho (1975), in the quarry near Petah Tikva, and in a large cistern near Asira el Kibliya in the region of Shechem (Nablus).

In March, 4-5 eggs are laid which the female incubates alone for a period of 17-18 days. The chicks leave the nest at about a month old. The Jackdaw is single-brooded.

Rook
Corvus frugilegus

A black crow, resembling a Hooded Crow in size: body length 46 cm, wing length 31 cm, wingspan 93 cm and weight 400 g. The adult is distinguished by a grey and unfeathered patch around the base of the bill, making the bill appear larger than its actual size. The thigh feathers resemble short, 'baggy' trousers. The juvenile lacks these features and resembles the European subspecies of the Carrion Crow, *C.c. corone*. (It is likely that some observations in this country of the 'European Crow' in fact relate to the Rook.)

The Rook's distribution extends from Ireland and Britain to China and Korea. Two subspecies have been identified. It winters at the southern limits of its range and slightly further south, including the Mediterranean countries.

In the past the subspecies *C.f. frugilegus* of the Rook was a fairly common winterer in Israel, especially in the Hula Valley. It was completely exterminated by poisoning in the 1950s. Since 1973/74 it has again begun to winter in northern and central parts of the country and its numbers have steadily grown. From a few isolated individuals, confined to the coastal plain and the Hula Valley, the wintering population had increased by the winter of 1981/82 to hundreds of individuals in the coastal plain and further scores across the country. The Rook arrives in Israel at the end of October and stays until about the end of February.

Indian House Crow
Corvus splendens

A small crow resembling a Jackdaw: body length 38.5 cm, wing length 26.2 cm and weight 240 g. Its head is dark, the nape and other parts of the body dark grey. Its bill is relatively thick.

The origin of this crow is apparently in southeast Asia. Essentially it is resident, but it tends to accompany ships, and thus has extended its range to the shores of East Africa. It has travelled by the same means from India or Ceylon to Aden and Oman, and even to Australia, acclimatising and proliferating in these countries.

At the end of 1976, seven individuals of the Indian House Crow were sighted in Eilat. The following spring, a few pairs attempted to nest there, although the outcome of these attempts is not known. Birds of this species were seen in the area on a regular basis until the summer of 1980, when they disappeared, although occasional observations have been reported since then.

Brown-necked Raven
Corvus ruficollis

Body length 51-55 cm, wing length 35-40.5 cm and weight 550-830 g. Formerly considered a subspecies of the Raven, but today accepted as constituting an independent species. This is an all-black bird, except for the dark brown nape; this latter colour is observed only in favourable light conditions, and is lacking in juveniles.

This is a typical desert bird, with a Saharo-

Sindian distribution: from the western Sahara to northeast India, with penetration towards Somalia. Two subspecies have been identified, *C.r. ruficollis* in the Saharo-Sindian region and another in Somalia. Its range in northern Israel borders on that of the Raven, with little overlap between them, although since the 1970s areas of overlap have broadened in the Judean Desert, with the Raven's expansion into desert regions. The Brown-necked Raven is found from 400 m below sea-level in the Dead Sea valley, to 1,800 m above in the Atlas Mountains.

Many Brown-necked Ravens live in territorial pairs throughout the year, while the remainder of the population, especially juveniles, live in flocks, although here too a family structure exists. The latter are normally found near refuse-dumps, settlements and army camps, and they regularly mingle with Fan-tailed Ravens. The flocking ravens tend to roost communally, in groups of scores or even hundreds, in trees or on electricity and telephone cables. In the hottest hours of the day they often shelter in the shade of walls and north-facing cliffs, or wheel at an altitude of 500-600 m above the ground, where the air is 3-4° cooler. The territorial pairs roam their domains in search of food. The eyesight of the Brown-necked Raven is very powerful, and it is quick to spot carrion in its territory. Several species of vulture exploit this faculty and follow the ravens in their hunting trips, but the ravens do not hesitate to harass competing vultures, attacking them physically in the attempt to drive them away from carrion.

Brown-necked Ravens are omnivorous: eating scraps, insects, reptiles, birds and mammals, vegetable matter and fruit. In oases they are liable to damage date palms, and when hungry will even peck camels' dung in search of undigested food, or pluck ticks from the hide of camels. The territorial ravens tend to accompany convoys and groups of hikers passing through their territories, hoping to pick up scraps. On the ground they walk, hopping only as a prelude to taking flight.

In Israel this is a common resident in the Negev and the Judean Desert, and its distribution extends as far as Jerusalem, Samaria and the Be'er Sheva Valley. In winter it is liable to move beyond the boundaries of the desert and penetrate the fringes of the Mediterranean zone.

The nesting season usually begins as early as the end of January or early February, occasionally later. At this season territorial activity increases, and any large bird approaching the nest site will be attacked; even migrating raptors such as buzzards or kites may be killed. The large nest is usually built in a cleft on a steep cliff, sometimes in a tree; in the high ground of the Negev in trees of Atlantic pistachia, in the east-

ern Negev in acacias. In northern Sinai and the southern Negev nests are often built on electricity pylons and telegraph poles. Laying normally takes place at the end of February or during March. In the clutch there are 4-5 eggs, which the female incubates almost alone for a period of 18-20 days. The chicks stay in the nest for about five weeks.

Brown-necked Ravens apparently breed once in the year, although in oases and near sources of abundant food late clutches may be found, suggesting the possibility of a second brood, or of replacement layings.

Raven
Corvus corax

The largest of the passerines: body length 57-65 cm, wing length 39-45 cm, wingspan 110 cm and weight 900-1,300 g. This is a compact-bodied bird, with all-black plumage; the back has a violet-blue tint, the underparts a green tint. At close range, pointed feathers are visible on the throat; these project like a beard in various behavioural circumstances. The bill is strong, curved and pointed, and is black in colour. The claws are strong and curved. Conspicuous in flight are the long neck, forward-projecting head, long and graduated tail and cross-shaped profile. Its deep and guttural voice, audible at long range, is the best recognition sign. Juveniles lack gloss and have lighter eyes.

The Raven's range is Holarctic, and extends over most of North Africa, the whole of Europe and most of Asia excepting parts of the Oriental region. In this range eight subspecies have been identified. The one known in Israel is *C.c. subcorax*, which is distributed from southeastern Europe, through the Middle East to Pakistan. Most populations of the Raven are resident, except the northernmost. Its habitats are many and varied: from the shores of the Arctic Ocean and regions of tundra to coniferous and broadleaf forests, Mediterranean maquis, steppes and rocky wadis. It prefers semi-exposed hill environments.

This species has a very varied diet: seeds and fruits, insects, molluscs, live or dead vertebrates, also refuse. It uncovers the bodies of dead animals, however well concealed. Ravens sometimes gather around carrion in vulture fashion. They also plunder nests, and may even kill songbirds in flight. Ravens usually live in territorial pairs. Only the juvenile population surplus, and adults in winter, are liable to flock and to roost communally, sometimes together with other species of raven.

The Raven used to be a fairly common bird in Israel. Tristram noted it as the commonest and most conspicuous bird of the Jerusalem area. It used to breed on cliffs in the river valleys of Galilee and

Carmel and in the Judean Hills, on coastal cliffs and on tall trees in the Mediterranean region. In the 1950s and 1960s its population was almost eliminated by agricultural pesticides. Since the late 1970s there has been some recovery, and it is again possible to see Ravens in some parts of the country. They have even extended to desert areas and attempts at colonisation have been recorded, in the early 1980s, in Wadi Kelt near Jericho and at Nahal Arugot in Ein Gedi.

Courtship begins at the end of December, and takes place mostly during January. At this time Ravens perform prolonged aerobatic display flights and show increased aggressiveness against intruders, including birds of prey. The nest is on a cliff-ledge, in a crevice or on a tall tree. Laying normally starts in February, and the clutch contains 3-5 eggs. The female incubates alone for a period of 18-19 days. The young leave the nest at five or six weeks old; they stay some time longer with their parents before going their separate ways, and return to the nest every evening to roost.

Fan-tailed Raven
Corvus rhipidurus

A black raven, smaller than the two preceding species: body length 44-55 cm, wing length 45 cm and weight 330-550 g. Its bill is shorter than that of the Raven. It is best distinguished in flight: its wings are broad on account of the long secondaries; the tail is very short and barely protrudes (tail length is 15.5 cm, compared with 20 cm in the Raven). Its

voice is higher and more tuneful than that of other ravens.

The Fan-tailed Raven is a bird of Ethiopian origin, living in desert and semi-desert regions. It is a monotypic species, extending from northern Kenya, through Ethiopia, Sudan and western Arabia to Israel.

This raven is an accomplished aerobat, performing many aerial antics: it catches feathers and papers in the air, and even carries stones or twigs, drops them and dives and catches them in flight as they fall. Like other ravens it is omnivorous, although it feeds less on carrion and more on insects, fruit and scraps. It also preys on small birds.

In Israel this species is usually found only along the rift of the Arava, from Eilat to the region of Jericho, but its population is concentrated mainly between Mount Sodom and Ein Gedi. In winter it is liable to roam in other areas, reaching Jerusalem and approaching the line of the mountain ridge. This is a gregarious bird, usually congregating around the refuse-dumps of settlements in the Arava. In oases Fan-tailed Ravens are seen drinking continuously; it is possible that water is the factor restricting its expansion in desert areas, in addition to competition from the Brown-necked Raven, which is larger and better adapted to arid conditions.

The Fan-tailed Raven breeds on steep and inaccessible cliffs, and as a result little is known of its nesting biology. Sometimes a few pairs nest in close proximity. In Israel nesting begins in March.

Family: Sturnidae (Starlings)

In the family Sturnidae there are 24 genera and more than 100 species. Their origin is in the Old World, but a few species have been introduced into Australia and America. Most inhabit Africa and southern Asia. In Israel three species are represented.

This family is closely related to crows, comprising birds of small to medium size: body length 17-45 cm and weight 50-150 g. The feathers usually have a metallic gloss. Starlings have one moult in the year, and where there is a difference between summer and winter plumage this is the result of abrasion of the feather tips. The sexes are similar but often differ in size, the males being larger. Juveniles have different plumage, lacking gloss, and they acquire adult plumage in their first autumn. The legs and toes are strong. The bill is strong and long, straight in insect-eaters and slightly curved in fruit-eaters. In species living in open terrain the wings are long and the tail short, providing fast and efficient flight; in species living in woodland or among cliffs the wings are

short and rounded and the tail long.

By nature these are tree-dwellers, but they are often seen on the ground. They do not hop. Their diet consists of various insects, especially at the larva stage, worms, molluscs and even fish, amphibians and reptiles. In autumn and winter they also eat fruit. After the nesting season they sometimes form enormous flocks and are liable to cause severe damage in plantations and orchards. They are noisy birds.

Starlings sometimes breed in colonies. The typical nest is a basket-shaped structure, located in a hollow tree or a rock-crevice, a nestbox or other artificial receptacle. In areas where starlings are resident the nest may also serve as a roosting site. The eggs are glossy and blue-turquoise in colour, and only in one species are they mottled. The chicks hatch with a covering of down. Both parents build the nest, incubate, and feed the young with insects and fruit.

Starling
Sturnus vulgaris

Body length 20.3-23.5 cm, wing length 12.3-13.8 cm, wingspan 38-42 cm and weight 53-93 g. A blackish bird, with white-speckled feather tips. After the moult, which begins in July and is completed at about the end of September, the Starling appears mottled. During the winter it gradually acquires uniform black plumage, iridescent with green and purple. Towards the end of winter a change of bill colour also takes place: the black turns steadily to yellow in both sexes. During their first year, immatures have upperparts tending towards brown.

The basic range of the Starling is Euro-Siberian and Irano-Turanian, extending over most of Europe, and western and central Asia as far as the Altai Mountains. In Spain and North Africa its place is taken by the Spotless Starling *S. unicolor*; in eastern Asia by the Grey Starling *S. cineraceus*. Eleven subspecies have been identified. Its habitats are scattered trees with expanses of grass, deciduous woodland, plantations and meadows, rural and urban settlements. It may be found from sea-level to altitudes of about 1,000 m. Most populations migrate south in autumn, and winter in southern Europe, North Africa and the Middle East.

In Israel the Starling is a very common winterer between the end of October and early March, although most of the wintering population leaves the country as early as mid-February. Sometimes Starlings in full breeding plumage are seen in the country as late as early April, and there are occasional sightings in August. Starlings winter especially within the bounds of the Mediterranean region, although they also penetrate the northern Negev. According to the literature it is possible to distinguish four or five subspecies among the wintering Starlings, differing from one another in the colour of the tail- and ear-coverts and in the colour of the nape. The commonest of these subspecies is *S.v. vulgaris*, which constitutes about 50% of the population; according to data obtained from ringed specimens found in this country, the origin of most of the wintering population is in the European sector of the USSR, with some individuals migrating over a distance of some 3,000 km. In Israel this species appears in huge flocks of irregular size. In some years it is estimated that the wintering population numbers as many as 15 million individuals.

During the day Starlings disperse in flocks, numbering scores or hundreds of individuals, to fields, farms and gardens. Larger concentrations gather towards evening for noisy and communal roosting in a group of dense-foliaged trees or a reedbed, having first assembled in high and conspicuous places such as electricity cables and roofs of houses. While flying to the roosting sites the birds perform dazzling aerobatic exercises. A number of mass roosting sites are known in various parts of the country, some of them located in centres of towns, and to reach them Starlings are liable to fly distances of 100 km and more.

The species is both an agricultural pest and a hazard to low-flying aircraft; nowhere does the Starling enjoy the protection of the law.

Rose-coloured Starling
Sturnus roseus

Body length 19-23 cm, wing length 12-13.5 cm, wingspan 37-41 cm and weight 52-74 g. Similar in shape, size and behaviour to the Starling, but differing in colour: it is the only bird seen in this country (except the Sinai Rosefinch) in which the dominant body colour is pink. The back, rump, lower breast and belly are bright pink, the rest of the body being black. The female is paler, and the plumage of juveniles is brown. Both sexes are browner following the moult at the end of summer; the vivid and unique colour is acquired only in spring, after abrasion of the feather tips.

The Rose-coloured Starling has an Irano-Turanian range, from Turkey and the steppes of the Ukraine to central Asia. This is a monotypic species, feeding especially on insects such as locusts, grasshoppers and beetles. There are periodic fluctuations in population, and every eight to ten years the bird erupts in central Europe and the Balkans and may be seen as far west as Spain. The Rose-coloured Starling winters particularly in dry regions in northwestern India.

In Israel this is an accidental, seen mainly during the spring migration in April and May. It sometimes occurs in large flocks numbering hundreds and thousands of individuals, and sometimes in combined flocks with the Starling.

Tristram's Grackle
Onychognathus tristramii

Tristram's Grackle resembles a Blackbird in size: body length 25-30 cm, wing length 14-15.5 cm and weight 98-140 g. The male is all-black with a blue-violet tint, except for the inner primaries which are rufous-chestnut in colour and form a patch which is especially conspicuous in flight. The female resembles the male, but has a greyish head and neck. The bill is slightly curved, the legs strong, the tail long and the wings relatively short. Juveniles have brown-black plumage, lacking gloss.

The genus *Onychognathus* comprises ten species, of which nine are confined to Africa. Only

Tristram's Grackle has moved beyond the bounds of this continent, and it has a limited distribution in Aden, Yemen, the shores of western Saudi Arabia, eastern Sinai and the high ground of the peninsula; it is also found in the valley of the Arava, as far north as Jericho. This is a monotypic species. Its basal metabolic rate is lower than that expected from its size, and hence the storing of water in its body enables it to tolerate both high and low temperatures. It inhabits rocky ravines, cliffs and canyons. It is resident throughout its range, but roams outside the breeding season.

Tristram's Grackle feeds on the fruits of various desert plants such as nitraria, *Coridia sinensis*, *Salvadora persica*, ochadrenus, and also grapes and dates. It is likely to cause damage in plantations: in Ein Gedi for example, in the early 1960s, many individuals were shot as a result. The bird also feeds on various insects, including flies and bees, and sometimes plucks ticks from the hides of ibexes, donkeys

and camels. It also consumes domestic scraps, flying considerable distances every day from its roosting sites in canyons to sources of food in agricultural sectors and settlements. Its song is plaintive and melodious.

This is a gregarious bird at most times of the year; it is usually found in small groups composed of parents and offspring. In winter it forms flocks of 100-300 individuals. The pair bond is retained throughout the year and is even perceptible within the flock; the partners feed together, drink together and preen one another's feathers. The flocks perform aerobatic manoeuvres similar to those of Starlings. In winter flocks of Tristram's Grackles roam, and may be seen near the coast in Sharon, in the hills of Shechem (Nablus), in Carmel and in western Galilee.

With the establishment of settlements in the Arava and the Negev, this species has expanded its range considerably. Its population in Ein Gedi has grown from some 20 pairs at the end of the 1930s to several hundreds in the early 1980s, and it has also reached Arad, Dimona and points further west.

Nests are built in crevices and rocky ravines, usually inside a cave; in recent years they have also been found in shutter units of tall buildings in Arad. The nest is constructed of tamarisk branches, thin stalks, various leaves and soft lining materials such as feathers, hair and paper. It is usually adapted to the space which is occupies, but its basic shape is that of a deep plate with flat edges and a deeper inner hollow. The clutch usually contains 3 eggs, sometimes 5; they are uniform turquoise-blue in colour, sometimes mottled with sparse light brown markings. The period of incubation is about 16 days, and the female incubates alone. The chicks hatch blind and naked. Both parents tend the offspring in the nest for 28-30 days, and a further ten days outside the nest.

A few pairs complete two nesting cycles in the year, the first between April and mid-May and the second during June. The second brood is reared in the same nest as the first.

Family: Passeridae (Sparrows)

This family, sometimes considered a subfamily of the weaver family (Ploceidae) and linked by other ornithologists with finches (Fringillidae), comprises ten genera and 43 species. It is distributed in all parts of the Old World, and most species are resident. In Israel two genera and seven species are represented.

Sparrows are small songbirds: body length 12-18 cm. Their plumage is generally drab, being predominantly brown, grey and chestnut, sometimes yellow, with black and white markings and streaking.

In many species the males have more vivid and conspicuous coloration. All moult once in the year, after breeding. Juveniles assume adult plumage as early as their first autumn. The wings are of medium length and rounded. The tail is relatively long, and sometimes slightly forked. The bill is short and conical. The legs and toes are of medium length, but strong; the claws are slightly curved.

Most sparrows are gregarious, living in proximity to man and benefiting from his kitchen scraps. They all gather into large flocks, especially in winter. They feed on the ground, where they hop. Their diet is mainly vegetarian: seeds, berries, buds and leaves.

Sparrows usually breed several times in the year, many in colonies. Nests in trees and bushes are spherical; those in thickets and in holes may be basket-shaped. The clutch contains 4-8 eggs, differing considerably in coloration and markings between different species. Incubation begins with the last egg, and is shared by both partners to some extent; it lasts 12-14 days. The chicks hatch blind and naked and are fed by both parents. They develop slowly, and stay in the nest for two weeks and more.

House Sparrow
Passer domesticus

The commonest and most widely distributed bird among human habitations — in this country and in many other parts of the world: body length 14-16.8 cm, wing length 7.2-8.5 cm, wingspan 23.5-25 cm and weight 21-33 g. Its plumage is drab, most feathers being brown and streaked with black; the underparts are pale and tend towards grey. The male has a white and conspicuous wingbar, grey crown, whitish cheeks and, in the nesting season, a distinctive black bib (the breeding plumage is acquired as a result of abrasion of the feather tips during winter). The female is dull brown, without any striking distinguishing marks. Juveniles, until their first autumn, are similar to the female.

The origin of the House Sparrow is apparently in western Asia and the eastern basin of the Mediterranean; in these areas it used to breed in rocks and trees. Since the Ice Age it has apparently become attached to man and his husbandry, spreading in his footsteps westward to Europe and eastward to the steppes of Asia. The natural range of the House Sparrow extends today over most of the Palaearctic region, except taiga and tundra, and sections of the Oriental and Ethiopian regions. In this range 11 subspecies have been identified. The House Sparrow has also been introduced to North and South America, South Africa, several islands of Oceania and Australia; in all these countries it has proliferated to a considerable degree. It lives in and near houses. It usually resides in villages and towns, although it may also be found in agricultural environments; it is more tolerant of human proximity than are most other birds. Most populations of the House Sparrow, excepting those of southern Asia and India, are resident. In Israel two subspecies are known: one, *P.d. biblicus*, is distributed from Turkey and Cyprus to Israel and Sinai and is common in all parts of the country; the other, found only in the region of Eilat, is *P.d. niloticus*, which is smaller and paler and is

restricted almost entirely to Egypt.

The House Sparrow is omnivorous: it prefers cereal seeds, but also consumes insects, fruit, buds, soft shoots and flower petals, as well as domestic scraps and refuse. Flocks grow in size during the breeding season as the chicks fly from the nests, and after nesting the adults also gather in parties numbering 60-80 individuals; these flocks roost communally in evergreen trees, especially *Ficus retusa*. Flocking intensifies in autumn, and then the flocks reach their maximum size. At this season the roaming range also broadens and sparrows are then liable to cause damage in fields, plantations and orchards.

Courtship, building and lining the nest begin as early as February. House Sparrows nest in a variety of places: in holes, buildings, roofs, barns, rock-crevices, abandoned nests of woodpeckers and bee-eaters, and in nestboxes. Sometimes a Red-rumped Swallow or Dead Sea Sparrow is evicted and its nest commandeered. Nests are usually about 3 m above the ground, in loose colonies in which only the nest and its immediate vicinity are defended. In Israel laying begins at the end of March/early April, sometimes as early as February; young females tend to lay later. In the clutch there are usually 5-6 eggs, sometimes 7, and the period of incubation is about 15 days. The chicks leave the nest at 14-17 days old, and feeding outside the nest continues for a further two weeks.

While the offspring of the first brood are still being tended, a new clutch is started in the same nest. The nesting season continues until mid-July and sometimes until August. Thus a pair is liable to rear three and even four broods in the season, although the size of clutch normally decreases from one cycle to the next.

Spanish Sparrow
Passer hispaniolensis

Body length 14.3-16.7 cm, wing length 7.3-8 cm, wingspan 24-25.2 cm and weight 22-32 g. The female is almost indistinguishable from the female House Sparrow; the male is distinguished by the chestnut crown, black breast and black streaking on both sides of the body (these colours become conspicuous following abrasion of the feather tips during winter). Its voice is deeper than that of the House Sparrow.

The Spanish Sparrow has a Mediterranean and Irano-Turanian range, and two subspecies have been identified. In Israel the subspecies *P.h. hispaniolensis* occurs. Its habitats are mainly areas of bush and low and thorny trees. Most populations in the Mediterranean region are resident; those of the Irano-Turanian region migrate, wintering in southern

Afghanistan, the area of the Persian Gulf, northern Arabia and the Nile Valley as far south as Sudan.

In Israel this is a resident bird in most parts of the country, especially in northern and central areas. In some years it also attempts to nest in the Negev and the Arava, sometimes successfully. During the 1960s and 1970s its population diminished perceptibly. Outside the breeding season it roams. It is also a common winterer and passage migrant, especially in the Arava, where its flocks mingle with those of the House Sparrow. The migration season lasts in autumn from September to November and in spring from the end of February to the end of April; on migration, males precede females by a few days.

The Spanish Sparrow is a gregarious bird, nesting on trees some distance from populated areas. Sometimes scores and even hundreds of nests are built on a single bush or tree, normally a sloe. Building usually begins in March: the nest is constructed of dry stalks and grasses, and lined with feathers, hairs and wool, and the clutch is of 4-6 eggs. Nesting biology is similar to that of the House Sparrow. The Spanish Sparrow breeds once or twice in the year. Towards June the nesting trees are abandoned and the flock roams in the vicinity. The following year another tree or group of trees is colonised.

Tree Sparrow
Passer montanus

Slightly smaller than the House Sparrow: body length 15 cm, wing length 6.9 cm and weight 23 g. Its crown is chestnut but the black bib is small; it is distinguished by a black patch on the ear-coverts. The sexes are similar.

The Tree Sparrow's distribution is Palaearctic; its populations are resident, except for a few which migrate from the far north and winter in the Balkans. In Israel this is a very rare accidental, seen occasionally in the Golan and in Upper Galilee.

Dead Sea Sparrow
Passer moabiticus

The smallest species of sparrow: body length 11.5-13.1 cm, wing length 5.6-6.3 cm and weight 11-17 g. It resembles the House Sparrow, but the back and wing-coverts of the male are nutty-brown, and the wing feathers black and edged with brown-grey; it is also distinguished by the grey head and yellow patches on both sides of the black throat. In breeding plumage, the breast and belly also become yellowish; at the approach of the nesting season the male's bill turns black. The female is more uniform in colour, and is paler than the female House Sparrow.

Until the end of the 1940s the distribution of the Dead Sea Sparrow was restricted to three relatively

small and widely separated areas: one in the lower Jordan Valley, between the Dead Sea and the Damiya Bridge; the second in the valleys of the Tigris and Euphrates on the Iran-Iraq border; the third in Seistan on the Iran-Afghanistan border. These are the three hottest places in the Palaearctic region. Two subspecies have been identified; the two western populations belong to the subspecies *P.m. moabiticus*. Since the early 1950s the Dead Sea Sparrow has broadened its range considerably, breeding on the banks of the Yarmuk near Sha'ar Hagolan and reaching Mahanaim and the Hula Valley in the early 1960s. By the late 1960s it was breeding in the Arava and had reached Eilat; at the same time it extended its range along the Tigris and reached Turkey, and in 1980 it was also breeding in Cyprus.

The Dead Sea Sparrow feeds on seeds, especially those of various species of the Gramineae family, and also on insects. It normally feeds on the ground, sometimes among branches of bushes and trees. This is a gregarious bird. Outside the nesting season it wanders in the nesting area and roams along the Jordan Valley and the Arava; it is then common in the region of Eilat. Sometimes it roams in company with the Spanish Sparrow. At the approach of the breeding season the Dead Sea Sparrow returns to its nesting areas: in the Arava during March and in more northerly areas only in April.

Nesting sites are usually in dry tamarisk thickets, in conditions where there is a source of water within a range of about 100 m; in places where water sources dry quickly, incubation is suspended and nests are deserted, even those containing eggs or chicks. The Dead Sea Sparrow may breed on other trees — poplar, olive, pomegranate, palm etc. — sometimes within plantations. The nest, an oval-shaped structure with a base of woven coarse twigs 1.5-2.5 m above the ground, is relatively large; the entrance is a kind of winding S-shaped tunnel, with opening at the top, leading to the laying chamber. The male builds the frame and perches on or close beside it, singing melodiously and vibrating his wings, inviting a female to join him; if the invitation is accepted, both partners line the nest with husks of palmate seeds and feathers until the inner wall becomes smooth and well covered. Laying begins during the lining process and simultaneously the male starts building a new nest at a distance of 2-3 m from the original nest. In the clutch there are 3-6 eggs, usually 4-5. Incubation begins when the clutch is complete and lasts 12-13 days, although the period varies in accordance with the surrounding temperature and is shorter towards the end of the season, when temperatures rise. The female incubates alone, and even refuses the male access to the nest. During the day the nest is warmed by the sun, and well insulated against changes in outside temperature, such that the female is able to leave her post and feed, spending up to 60% of the hours of daylight outside the nest. It is evident that the optimum outside temperature for the eggs is 35-36°C (95-97°F); when it is higher the female shades the eggs, standing at the nest entrance, or moistens them with water brought in the feathers or the bill. Only about 40% of the eggs laid hatch successfully: many nests are abandoned, others are usurped by House Sparrows and some are raided by snakes.

The Dead Sea Sparrow normally makes use of its nest more than once in the year; the interval between nesting cycles is about 40 days, and towards the end of the season clutches are smaller. Chicks may be found in nests as late as August. In the Bet She'an Valley the Dead Sea Sparrow is liable to rear three broods in the summer.

Rock Sparrow
Petronia petronia

Body length 15-15.7 cm, wing length 9.3-10 cm and weight 26-39 g. The Rock Sparrow resembles a large and pale female House Sparrow. It is distinguished by pale stripes along the head — a supercilium and a long stripe in the centre of the crown — and by white at the tips of the tail feathers, conspicuous in flight. In the centre of the upper breast is a light yellow mark, but this is sometimes hard to distinguish in the field. The back is streaked. The sexes are similar; juveniles resemble adults but lack the yellow

breast-spot. The bill is cruder and more solid than that of the House Sparrow, and the tail shorter.

The Rock Sparrow has a sporadic range in mountainous areas of the southern Palaearctic, from the Canary Islands, through the Mediterranean countries and the Near East to Mongolia. In this range six subspecies have been identified. The one occurring in Israel is *P.p. puteicola*, which breeds only in the Levant, Israel and Transjordan. This species' distribution has contracted in recent years and it has withdrawn from central Europe. It is a bird of rocky terrain and stony slopes, often preferring chalk habitats.

In Israel this is essentially a summer resident, although sometimes a few roaming individuals are seen in winter. It returns to most of its nesting areas in March-April, to Hermon only in May. The Rock Sparrow nests in various widely separated places in mountainous areas of the Mediterranean region, and is especially common on Hermon.

The Rock Sparrow breeds in rock-clefts, cliff-crevices, caves, wells, holes in walls, trees and roofs. Sometimes the pair nests alone, but more often in small and loose colonies, where the distance between nests is 10-15 m. The nest is a large and casual structure, dish-shaped and sometimes domed. In the clutch there are 5-7 eggs. Incubation lasts about 16 days and is performed mainly by the female. The chicks stay in the nest about three weeks.

This sparrow apparently completes one nesting cycle in the year, usually starting at the end of April and ending in June. After nesting, Rock Sparrows gather into flocks numbering scores of individuals; in their movements they then resemble flocks of finches or buntings. On 22 September 1978, some 240 Rock Sparrows were counted at sunset on the wires of the cablecar on Hermon, near the lower station. Usually flocks congregate to roost in maquis. At the end of October the Rock Sparrows depart; it is not known where they winter, although a few are found at that season in hilly areas in northern and central parts of the country.

Yellow-throated Sparrow
Petronia xanthocollis

Distinguished from the Rock Sparrow by a chestnut patch on the shoulder, and double white wingbars; the yellow on the throat of the male is more vivid, but this colour is absent in the female. Its origin is Irano-Turanian, and its distribution extends from southern and eastern Iraq through southern Iran and Pakistan to India. In Israel this is a very rare accidental: a lone individual was seen on 11-12 May 1982 in the region of Eilat.

Pale Rock Sparrow
Petronia brachydactyla

Body length 14-15 cm, wing length 9.1-9.7 cm and weight 21-25 g. A pale-coloured bird, resembling a female House Sparrow. The upperparts are uniform brown, without streaking; white patches at the tips of the tail feathers form a white bar across the tail in flight. The sexes are almost identical.

This species' origin is Irano-Turanian, and it is distributed in a narrow range in western Asia: from Lebanon, Syria and Armenia to Iran, Afghanistan and Pakistan. This is a monotypic species, wintering in southern Arabia, Sudan and Ethiopia. It inhabits dry environments in steppes and semi-deserts with scattered bushes.

The song of the Pale Rock Sparrow resembles that of the Greenfinch: a short whistle followed by a cicada-like chirp. It feeds on seeds and plant food, and sometimes gathers in large flocks in fields of sorghum; it also takes insects.

The Pale Rock Sparrow is a rare summer resident on Hermon, at altitudes of 1,200-1,600 m. In certain years it is fairly common, in others it hardly appears at all. In years when it is common, many scores of individuals may be counted at water sources on Hermon. It is the last of the summering birds to arrive on the mountain — at the end of April/early May, sometimes not until the second half of May — and leaves from the end of July.

The Pale Rock Sparrow usually nests on low bushes and sometimes among rocks, thus differing from other members of the genus *Petronia*. The nest is usually small and well constructed, like the nest of a finch; occasionally it is a crude and flat structure, built only of thorny shrub. In the clutch there are 4-5 eggs, and incubation lasts about two weeks.

Family: Fringillidae (Finches)

This family comprises 19 genera and 122 species; some authorities include weavers, waxbills and sometimes even buntings in the family. Finches are common in all parts of the world except Madagascar, Oceania and Australasia. They live in all climatic regions and in various habitats. Most northern species migrate, while those of the south are residents; migration is short-range, and winter quarters are in zones of temperate climate. In Israel nine genera and 15 species are represented.

Finches are distinguished by their strong and deep conical bill. From the typical bill additional shapes have evolved in accordance with the way of life: a short and thick bill as in the Desert Finch and the rosefinches, suited to feeding on the ground; a sharp and laterally compressed bill as in the Goldfinch and the Siskin, suited to shelling seeds of the palmate type; a strong and large bill for cracking nuts and fruit stones, as in the Hawfinch; a bill with crossed mandibles as in the Crossbill, for extracting conifer seeds from their cones.

Finches are songbirds of medium size: body length 11-20 cm. The sexes are usually of similar size. They have vivid colours. Males usually differ from females and their plumage normally includes some degree of red. Juveniles tend to resemble females. Finches moult once a year, at the end of the nesting season; only in a few species is there also a spring moult. Breeding plumage is normally acquired following abrasion of the feather tips. Juveniles moult only the body feathers in their first autumn, and they then resemble adults. The tail is slightly forked.

These birds live among trees and bushes or on the ground, and they feed especially on seeds but also on insects. Their flight is undulating. They are gregarious, tending to flock after nesting; often several species are mingled in one flock. They are especially common in fields with plants of the family Cruciferae.

Finches have attractive and melodious song, heard throughout the year. They usually nest in trees and bushes; only desert species nest on the ground, among rocks. They sometimes breed in loose colonies. The nest is shaped like a flat basket, and is usually well built and lined with delicate materials. The clutch is usually of 4-6 eggs, light bluish or beige in base colour and delicately mottled with violet and red, especially at the blunt end. The female incubates alone for 12-16 days. The chicks hatch blind, covered in sparse down, and are fed by both parents. According to the type of food fed to the offspring the members of the family which occur in Israel are grouped into two subfamilies: Fringillinae, which feed the chicks with insects and other invertebrates; and Carduelinae, which feed them with seeds and other plant food, partially digested and disgorged from the crop. Most finches breed several times in the year. When the young leave the nest, the male continues to feed them while the female builds a new nest.

Chaffinch
Fringilla coelebs

Body length 13.2-16.5 cm, wing length 8-9.2 cm, wingspan 24-28.7 cm and weight 16-24 g. The male has a bluish-grey crown and nape, chestnut cheeks, throat and underparts, greyish-brown back, greenish-yellow rump, brownish wings with whitish feather edges, and brown-grey tail with white outer feathers. These colours are more vivid and conspicuous at the approach of spring, when the forehead turns black, as does the bill (brown in winter). The female is grey-brown, darker on the back and paler below. Both sexes are distinguished by a white patch on the shoulder and a white bar on the wing; these features are distinctive both at rest and in flight.

The Chaffinch is distributed across the whole of Europe except the tundra region, and its range extends to western and central Asia and North Africa. It also breeds in northern and central Lebanon. Fourteen subspecies have been identified. This is a bird of forests, woodland, groves, plantations and park environments. The populations of the Chaffinch in western, central and southern Europe and in the Middle East are resident; those of northern and eastern Europe migrate and winter in western Europe, the Mediterranean countries and the Middle East. The winter habitats of the Chaffinch tend to be more open than its summer habitats. In Israel several subspecies winter, the commonest among them being *F.c. coelebs*, which breeds in Europe, central Asia and Siberia.

The sexes have different migration habits. The females are first to embark on the autumn migration, usually travel further than the males and return to the nesting areas about two weeks later than males (hence the scientific name *coelebs* = bachelor). In spite of this time difference, they normally winter in Israel side by side, although the number of females is greater. It seems that some of the males winter further north.

Chaffinches arrive in Israel at the end of October. The males usually leave as early as mid-February, while the females stay until the end of March; a few individuals are still present in early April. They evidently tend to return and winter in the same areas, as data from ringed specimens show. Sometimes they winter in large flocks numbering hundreds of individuals, often mingling with flocks of other species. They roost in groves. A few Chaffinches are also passage migrants in Israel, especially in autumn.

Brambling
Fringilla montifringilla

Body length 14.5-17 cm, wing length 8.5-9.6 cm, wingspan 23-29 cm and weight 22-27 g. Distinguished from the Chaffinch by its head and mantle, which are black in summer (mottled grey-brown in winter), and white rump, especially conspicuous in flight. The breast is orange rather than brown-chestnut, and this is also distinctive in the female.

The Brambling replaces the Chaffinch in northern Europe, and its range extends eastward over the whole width of Asia, in taiga and on the northern limits of the temperate zone; there are a few areas of overlap between the two species. This is a monotypic species, wintering in western Europe and the Middle East. There are periodic extreme fluctuations in population size, and then millions of individuals erupt from their traditional habitats and roam over wide distances. In such years hundreds are liable to winter in Israel, as happened in the winters of 1937/38, 1974/75 and 1976/77.

Apart from these abnormalities, until 1977/78 the Brambling was considered a rare winterer in Israel, occasionally seen in the northern Golan and on Hermon between the end of October and mid-March. Since then it has become known as a fairly common winterer, especially in the Judean Hills, Galilee and the Golan, almost invariably mingled with flocks of Chaffinches.

Genus: *Serinus*
The genus *Serinus* comprises 32 species, 27 of them confined to Africa. These are small finches, usually green-yellow in colour. The bill is very short and thick. The tail is short and more obviously forked than in other finches, and the wings are long.

Serin
Serinus serinus

The Serin is the smallest of the finches in Israel: body length 11-13 cm, wing length 6.6-7.3 cm and weight 8-11 g. It is a greenish-grey bird, distinguished by its bright yellow rump. The male has a yellow head and breast, olive-yellowish streaked back, and the flanks delicately streaked with brown; these colours become more vivid after abrasion of the feather tips during winter. The female is brown-yellow and streaked below.

The origin of the Serin is north Mediterranean. Since about 1800 it has broadened its limits, and by 1960 it was also breeding in southern Sweden and in Russia. The original populations are resident, while those that have spread to central, western and eastern Europe migrate and winter in the eastern Mediterranean basin: in Lebanon, Israel, northern Egypt and Libya.

The Serin inhabits forest edges, avenues, plantations, urban parks and agricultural settlements. It is usually found in open spaces near trees. This is a gregarious bird; in winter flocks mingle with other species such as the Linnet, Goldfinch and Greenfinch. Normally it feeds on the ground, consuming oily seeds of wild plants including Cruciferae and Compositae, also seeds of pine and cypress and fruits of thorny poterium.

In Israel this is a common winterer in northern and central parts of the country, usually in flocks numbering several hundreds of individuals. In the past the wintering flocks arrived only in the second half of October; since the 1970s it has been possible to see Serins as early as the end of July and during August (these may be from the population breeding nearby). Towards evening they gather in woodland and utter their monotone chirping from amid the foliage. In midwinter the males begin to sing, a mechanical jangling sound. The wintering population disappears during March.

Since 1977 the Serin has been included among the species breeding in Israel: in that year a few pairs were found breeding in Beit Berl in the central coastal plain and Giv'at Brenner in the southern coastal plain. In the nesting season the Serin has a conspicuous display flight. Sometimes pairs breed solitarily, sometimes in small and loose colonies. In Israel the nest is usually located in a cypress tree, about 5 m above the ground. The clutch contains 3-5 eggs, usually 4. The chicks leave the nest at 14-15 days old. The Serin breeds twice in the summer, between March and the end of May.

Tristram's Serin
Serinus syriacus

Slightly larger than the Serin: body length 12-14 cm, wing length 7-7.7 cm and weight 10-14 g. It is also paler. The forehead is vivid yellow, sometimes tending towards orange, and the throat yellow; the underparts are unstreaked, and the edges of the wing and tail feathers are yellow.

The distribution of Tristram's Serin, which is a monotypic species, is restricted to the mountains of Lebanon and Anti-Lebanon. It is a common breeder on Hermon, where it reaches the southernmost limit of its range.

Tristram's Serin returns to Hermon from winter quarters at the end of March-early April. Its song, then widely heard, is more melodious than that of the Serin and resembles that of the domestic Canary. It breeds in trees and bushes at altitudes of 1,000-1,750 m, between Neve Ativ and the ski slopes. Its breeding biology resembles that of the Serin.

This species breeds twice and sometimes three times in the summer, and the nesting season lasts until July. Evidently pairs climb to higher levels for the second breeding cycle: in April and May most nests are at altitudes of 1,500 m, rising to 1,750 m in subsequent months. With the end of nesting the birds gather in nomadic and noisy flocks, numbering hundreds of individuals, and roam about the shoulder of Hermon.

Tristram's Serin migrates from Hermon between the end of September and October, wintering mainly in Iraq and also in Egypt; in the course of migration it is seen in Ein Gedi and in Yotvata (Yatveta) along the rift valley. This is also a rare winter resident in Israel, sometimes in company with the Serin.

Red-fronted Serin
Serinus pusillus

Body length 10.5-12 cm, wing length 7-7.5 cm and weight 8-10 g. Distinctive and conspicuous with its bright red forehead. The face, nape and breast are black; the rest of the body is mostly rufous with dark streaking.

This monotypic species' origin is Irano-Turanian and its distribution extends from Turkey through Iran and Afghanistan to western Mongolia. It inhabits small woods on mountain slopes, and most of its populations are resident. It winters in Lebanon, Syria, Iraq and southern Iran, close to its nesting areas. It feeds on seeds, especially those of fir and cypress.

In Israel the Red-fronted Serin is a fairly rare winter accidental, sometimes seen in small flocks mingled with those of the Serin. It is also a rare winterer.

Greenfinch
Carduelis chloris

The largest of the yellow-green finches seen in Israel, being about the size of a sparrow: body length 13-15.2 cm, wing length 7.8-8.7 cm, wingspan 26-29.5 cm and weight 20-26 g. It has a yellow-greyish rump. Most of the primaries (except their tips) and the base of the outer tail feathers are bright yellow, forming conspicuous yellow patches in flight. The tail is appreciably forked. The female is paler, brown-greyish and with a slightly streaked back. Juveniles are browner and streaked both above and below. The bill is thick, pale pink in colour.

The Greenfinch has a European, Mediterranean and Irano-Turanian range, in which four subspecies have been identified. Most of its populations are resident; only those of northern Europe migrate, wintering in southern Russia, the Mediterranean basin and the Middle East. Its habitats are woodland edges, sparse groves, plantations, olive orchards, parks and gardens.

The subspecies *C.c. chlorotica* is restricted to the Near East and is a common resident in northern and central parts of Israel. In winter, between October and March, winter visitors are also present in the country; these belong to several other subspecies, mainly *C.c. chloris* from Europe, which is darker.

The Greenfinch is a social bird. From the end of the nesting season until spring it flocks with other finches, as well as with sparrows and buntings. It feeds on various seeds on the ground, especially seeds of Cruciferae and Compositae species; it also feeds in trees and bushes, consuming seeds of cypress and pine, fruits, leaf buds and insects. The Greenfinch has a characteristic undulating flight: a few rapid dynamic movements followed by gliding with wings closed.

In early March the flocks disperse. The male engages in circuitous and undulating display flight and sings or, more typically, perches on a treetop or high wire and utters a hoarse and prolonged call. The nest is in a tree, usually a cypress, among thick and shaded branches, 2-5 m above the ground. Laying usually begins in early April. The clutch contains 4-5 eggs, which the female incubates alone for 12-13 days. The chicks stay in the nest for a period of 13-16 days.

The Greenfinch rears two and possibly three broods in the year: nests containing chicks are still to be found in July, and the feeding of juveniles outside the nest continues until the second week of August.

Goldfinch
Carduelis carduelis

Body length 11.8-14.2 cm, wing length 7.3-8.2 cm, wingspan 24-28 cm and weight 11-17 g. One of the most colourful birds seen in Israel: the face and chin are bright red, the crown and nape black, the cheeks white and bordered with a black collar; a yellow bar extends along the black wing; the rump is white, the tail black, the back and wing-coverts chestnut-brown and the belly whitish-brown. As a result of abrasion of the feather tips during winter, the back turns a richer shade of brown at the approach of spring. Juveniles are distinguished by the absence of red, white and black on the face and are streaked above and below. At 1.3 cm, the bill is long compared with that of other finches.

The Goldfinch is distributed in all parts of Europe except Scandinavia and northern Russia; its range extends to central Asia and the Irano-Turanian region, and also includes North Africa. Twelve subspecies have been identified. It inhabits woodland edges, plantations, parks and other sparsely wooded areas. It is a resident bird in most of its range. The Goldfinches occurring in Israel belong mostly to the subspecies *C.c. niediecki*, whose range is from Rhodes and Turkey to northern Arabia.

This finch prefers seeds of composites such as (in Israel) *Senecio vernalis* and *Calendula* (marigold), and especially the seeds of thorny plants such as *Silybum marianum*, *Notobasis syriaca* and *Scolymus*. In winter and early spring it may also consume conifer seeds, blossom, leaf buds, flowers and insects. The Gold-

finch tends to spend the winter in mixed flocks with other finches; these roost communally in maquis and plantations.

In Israel this is a common and widespread bird throughout the Mediterranean region; it has also penetrated to settlements in the northern Negev and the Arava. Outside the breeding season it flocks and roams, and is then liable to occur in the more barren sectors of the Negev (it is possible that the flocks seen in these areas are winter visitors of east European and central Asiatic origin).

The nesting season normally begins in mid-March. The nest is in a tree, usually in the outer branches and normally at about eye-level. The clutch contains 3-6 eggs. The female incubates for about 13 days, beginning with the laying of the third or fourth egg. The chicks stay in the nest for 13-15 days, but remain dependent on their parents for a further three weeks or so. After this they begin to flock while the adults breed for a second or even a third time; nest-building may be observed as late as July, often with the use of materials taken from the original nest. Flocks of Goldfinches increase in size at the end of summer and in autumn.

Siskin
Carduelis spinus

A greenish-yellow finch: body length 11-13.5 cm, wing length 7-7.5 cm, wingspan 19.8-23 cm and weight 10-13 g. The male is distinguished from other greenish-yellow finches by the black crown and chin and lemon-yellow cheeks. The female is browner and streaked. The tail is perceptibly forked; in flight two black bars are conspicuous along the yellowish-grey wings.

The Siskin's range is sporadic and Palaearctic, extending over most of Europe with penetration into central Asia; a few isolated populations are found in eastern Asia. This is a monotypic species, whose habitats are mainly forests of fir and other conifers. The Siskin does not migrate in the normal sense of the term, but roams in flocks in search of food. Sometimes there are widespread migratory movements, apparently in response to food shortages, and the bird is liable then to reach North Africa. In areas abundant in food it may even stay and breed outside its regular limits.

The Siskin winters irregularly in Israel: in some years it does not appear at all; in other winters it is quite common in flocks numbering hundreds of individuals between the end of October and the end of March. In this country it feeds on seeds of pine and cypress trees. A Siskin ringed in Russia was recovered on Hermon.

Linnet
Carduelis cannabina

Body length 12.5-14 cm, wing length 7.8-8.3 cm, wingspan 22-26 cm and weight 13-21 g. The male Linnet is conspicuous in spring with reddish-pink forehead and breast; at other times of the year it is distinguished by the chestnut-brown back and wing-coverts, a white wing-patch conspicuous both in flight and at rest, and by the white of the rump and tail sides. The female resembles the male but lacks reddish-pink on the forehead and breast, and is more greyish-brown with streaking below. Juveniles resemble the female but are more streaked. The bill is dark brown and is short and thick.

The distribution of the Linnet is Euro-Siberian, Mediterranean and Irano-Turanian, and its range is similar to those of the Greenfinch and the Gold-finch. Six subspecies have been identified, the one occurring in the Middle East being *C.c. bella*. Its habitats are particularly maquis, woodland edges and scrub terrain and wastelands in mountainous areas. Outside the breeding season it roams; the popu-lations of northern and eastern Europe and of western Asia migrate, wintering in the Mediter-ranean basin and the Middle East.

The Linnet feeds especially on seeds, but also on buds and fruits. In Israel it causes damage to the garden mulberry, which ripens in winter. It also con-sumes insects. Outside the nesting season it roosts communally in maquis areas and woodland.

In Israel this is a resident and common bird in the Golan, Galilee, Carmel and the hills of Judah. In autumn it flocks and roams in the Shephelah and the coastal plain and also in the Negev, sometimes in company with other finches. It is possible that its population is then reinforced by wintering indi-viduals.

With the approach of spring the Linnet returns to mountainous regions and the flock disperses, although sometimes pairs breed in loose colonies, with only a few metres between nests. In this period the melodious and twittering song of the male is often heard. The nest is built in a fork in a tree or a bush, usually in dense clumps of pine. There are 4-5 eggs, which the female incubates alone for 12-13 days, and the chicks are tended in the nest for about 13 days. Between April and July the Linnet rears two and possibly three broods.

Crossbill
Loxia curvirostra

A large finch belonging to a genus distinguished by the unique phenomenon of crossed mandible tips: body length 16.9-18 cm, wing length 9-10.1 cm, wingspan 27.9-28.8 cm and weight 30-46 g. The male has reddish-pink plumage, varying in intensity between different individuals; the wings and tail are dark brown. The female is greenish-yellow, with brown-grey wings and tail. The tail is short and per-ceptibly forked; the legs are short. Juveniles have streaked pale brown plumage and, initially, uncrossed mandibles.

The Crossbill's distribution is Holarctic, but dis-continuous. It breeds in northern and central America, across most of Europe, in northern Asia and in Turkey; an isolated population also exists in central Asia. Twenty subspecies have been described. The one occurring in Israel is *L.c. curvirostra*, which is distributed from northern and western Europe to Siberia and the Transcaspian region. This is essentially a bird of spruce forests, but it is also partial to other conifers such as firs and larches, and in the southern parts of its range it populates various types of pine woodland. The Crossbill is a resident bird, but periodically there are population eruptions; then, as also happens in cold winters or when food is short, it extends beyond its normal limits.

This species feeds especially on conifer seeds. While feeding the bird hovers from one perch to another, or moves sideways along branches; some-times it hangs from the branch by its bill, parrot fashion. In summer it also feeds on insects. It spends most of its time in trees and rarely descends to the ground, doing so only to drink; on the ground it hops. Its flight is fast and undulating. It utters its metallic song both when perched and in flight.

The Crossbill is a rare winterer in Israel, occurring at irregular dates between November and February. The first sighting of a Crossbill in this country was recorded on 12 November 1926 in Mikve Israel near Tel Aviv. Since then it has occurred on a number of occasions, in groups numbering up to 30 individuals. Quite unexpectedly, nests were found in Carmel in 1972 and 1973. In 1981 the Crossbill bred again in Carmel, and nests have subsequently been found in Ramot Menashe, Safed, Jerusalem and even in Be'er Sheva on the northern border of the Negev.

Towards March the groups disperse into pairs, which are liable to breed a few metres apart. In this country the Crossbill nests on trees of pine and cypress on the edges of forests. The nest is built at an altitude of 2-10 m, usually close to the treetop, and the clutch contains 3-5 eggs. The female incubates for 12-13 days, and during this time may be approached fairly closely. The chicks hatch with a straight and delicate bill, which only gradually lengthens and becomes crossed. They stay in the nest for 22-24 days, a relatively long period for songbirds of this size (possibly determined by the slow development of the bill). The breeding season in Israel, as so far recorded, lasts from March to May (elsewhere breeding often occurs in autumn and/or winter).

Desert Finch
Rhodospiza obsoleta

A compact finch with thick bill equal in length and depth: body length 14-16 cm, wing length 8-8.6 cm and weight 18-26 g. It has brown-pink plumage, and a vivid pink patch is conspicuous on the wings, especially when these are spread; the feathers of the wings and tail are black (male) or brown (female) with white edges. The bill is black, the legs dark brown. Juveniles resemble females.

This finch's range is restricted to the Irano-Turanian region, and extends from the Middle East and especially from eastern Iran through Afghanistan and northern Pakistan to central Mongolia. This is a monotypic species. In northern and eastern parts of its range it migrates in autumn; in southern and western areas it is resident, but roams. On migration and when roaming it is seen in Iraq, Syria and Sinai. Its habitats are in semi-arid plains with scattered bushes and trees.

The Desert Finch feeds on small seeds usually gathered on the ground, and also on leaves, buds and insects. Unlike the Trumpeter Finch, which spends much of its time on the ground, it tends to rest on the branches of trees. This is a gregarious bird, living in flocks during the winter and normally breeding in loose colonies with 1.5-4 m between nests.

In Israel the Desert Finch is an intermittent visitor. According to Aharoni, in the 1920s it was breeding in flocks in orchards and vineyards in the region of Jaffa; subsequently, breeding in this region ceased. It was a common winterer between 1935 and 1940, but then disappeared until 1958, when roaming flocks were seen in the Arava and the Negev. In the same year a breeding colony — of 100-150 nests — was identified in the northwestern Negev; in subsequent years its numbers there have dwindled. In 1965 Desert Finches nested in Revivim, and in 1971 in Kfar Rufin. Since then breeding has been reported in Be'er Sheva, in Sede Boker and especially in the Bet She'an Valley.

The nest, in a fork 1.5-3 m above the ground, is constructed of coarse twigs and well lined with wool, cotton threads, cottonwool etc. The clutch is usually of 4-5 eggs, sometimes as many as 7, and the female incubates alone for 13-14 days. During incubation she is not easily alarmed and may be approached to almost touching distance; when she does flee her post, especially when there are young chicks in the nest, she simulates injury. The chicks leave the nest at about two weeks old, and their plumage then resembles that of the female. The Desert Finch breeds twice in the year: in March-April and in May-June.

Crimson-winged Finch
Rhodopechys sanguinea

Slightly larger than the Desert Finch: body length 13.5-16.5 cm, wing length 9.5-10.7 cm and weight 30-33 g. A bird distinguished by its pink wings and cheeks; the rump and base of the tail are also pink. The male has a blackish-brown crown, and the local subspecies has a whitish nape. The female resembles the male but is paler. The legs are long.

This species has a sporadic range. Of the two subspecies, one (*R.s. aliena*) breeds in the Atlas Mountains. The other, *R.s. sanguinea*, is found on peaks and rocky slopes with sparse vegetation in the Irano-Turanian region, from central Turkey and the Caucasus through Iran to Afghanistan; on Hermon it reaches the southwestern limit of its range, and is one of the 16 species of bird which breed in Israel only on this mountain. In winter it migrates from the peaks to fields and valleys. It returns to the heights of Hermon, to altitudes in excess of 1,900 m, as early as April, but begins nesting only in May. This breeding population is small, numbering some 20 pairs.

The Crimson-winged Finch nests primarily on low bushes, but also among rocks and on cliff-ledges. The clutch contains 4-5 eggs. With the end of nesting on Hermon, these finches gather in small flocks, descend to lower levels to drink and migrate as early as the end of July. Sometimes small flocks are also seen in winter.

Trumpeter Finch
Bucanetes githagineus

Body length 13.1-15.5 cm, wing length 7.9-9 cm and weight 16-22 g. The male Trumpeter Finch is conspicuous in summer with pink forehead and underparts; the nape and back are brown with a pink tint. These colours, varying in intensity between individuals, are acquired following abrasion of the feather tips during winter. The male's bill is also striking in summer, being orange-red. In winter the male is brown-grey in appearance, with a yellow bill. The female resembles the winter male.

The Trumpeter Finch is a common and resident bird throughout the Saharo-Sindian zone, and also in parts of the Irano-Turanian zone and in central Asia. Four subspecies have been identified. The one occurring in Israel is *B.g. crassirostris*, which is distributed from the Middle East to north India. This is a desert bird, inhabiting mountainous areas, rocky slopes and cliffs, but absent from regions of dune and scrub. In Israel it is resident and fairly common in most parts of the Negev, the Dead Sea basin and the Judean Desert, and a rare accidental in the Golan and on the slopes of Hermon.

The Trumpeter Finch spends most of its time on the ground, where it feeds on seeds and seedlings, green leaves and buds and also insects, especially the larvae of grasshoppers. Although a desert bird, it needs to drink regularly, and apparently flies to water sources every day. Its flight is undulating and low. Except during the nesting season this is a gregarious bird, usually seen in combined flocks of males and females, adults and juveniles, numbering scores of individuals, roaming back and forth. It is sometimes seen in the most arid of places.

At the approach of the nesting season the flock separates into pairs, and males proclaim their territories with trumpeting calls. The nest is on the ground, under a rock or a desert plant, or in a narrow rock-cleft. Often the entrance is paved with small stones, a phenomenon familiar among desert birds. The clutch contains 4-6 eggs, which the female incubates alone for 13-14 days. The chicks fly from the nest at about 14 days old. The Trumpeter Finch is single-brooded.

Genus: Carpodacus
In the genus *Carpodacus* there are 21 species, most of them inhabiting central, southern and northeastern Asia; only one species is regularly found in Europe and three in central and northern America. These are finches with a thick bill, although less so than among members of the previous two genera. The males are predominantly pink and red; the females are streaked. Most species breed in bush, scrub and wooded habitats in high mountainous areas. The Sinai Rosefinch is an exception, both in distribution and in habitat.

Sinai Rosefinch
Carpodacus synoicus

Body length 15.5-16.2 cm, wing length 8-8.1 cm and weight 17-24 g. The male has a dark pink head and a pink body; the wings are brown, sometimes with a pink tint, and the tail is brown. These colours become more vivid in spring, following abrasion of the tips of the feathers. The female has light brown plumage and is less easily identified. Juveniles resemble the female, and the males among them assume adult plumage only at about a year old, and not during their first autumn as is the case with most finches.

The origin of this species is in southern Palaearctic Asia, and four subspecies have been identified;

three of these are found in Afghanistan and China, while the local subspecies *C.s. synoicus* is confined to the Negev, Sinai and Jordan. This is a resident bird in steep mountain regions and rocky deserts, roaming outside the nesting season. In Israel it is quite rare and is found mainly in the region of Eilat; it is more common in southern Sinai.

The Sinai Rosefinch feeds on seeds which it gathers on the ground, and on leaves, buds, flowers and fruit; it is often attracted to scraps of food discarded by hikers, and is liable to be seen around refuse-heaps. It needs regular supplies of water, and is therefore easily observed near water sources, including garden sprinklers.

The Sinai Rosefinch is a gregarious bird, and outside the nesting season it may be seen in flocks numbering scores of individuals, descending in winter from the heights of Sinai to the shores of bays around the peninsula and the estuaries of wadis. At this season it is also seen in Makhtesh Ramon in the central Negev and along the cliff of Hatsinim in the northern Negev. Towards evening the flock gathers for communal roosting in regular places — in rock-clefts and cliff-crevices.

Nesting in the Negev takes place in April-May. The nest is hidden in rock-clefts and fissures in a steep wall or cliff. The clutch contains 4-5 eggs. Little is known of the breeding biology of the Sinai Rosefinch; since the male has a brood-patch it is possible that both parents incubate. The period of incubation is about two weeks and the chicks stay in the nest for a further two weeks. The juveniles leave the nest in female-type plumage, and even breed in this plumage during their first year. Males acquire the pink coloration in their second year.

Scarlet Rosefinch
Carpodacus erythrinus

Body length 14 cm, wing length 8.3 cm and weight 20 g. The male is distinguished by its bright red head, breast and rump; its belly, unlike that of the Sinai Rosefinch, is pale greyish. The female is not easily identified in the field.

This is the only rosefinch found in Europe, and its distribution is the widest of any Old World finch, from Finland and Sweden to Japan; it is still extending gradually westward. It inhabits scrub, thickets and woodland edges in taiga, and winters in southern Asia, from northwestern and southern India to Indonesia and southern China.

In Israel the Scarlet Rosefinch is a very rare winter accidental, with a few sightings recorded on the coastal plain, in the Bet She'an Valley and the Jerusalem area. It is also a very rare passage migrant in the region of Eilat.

Hawfinch
Coccothraustes coccothraustes

A large finch, about the size of a starling: body length 16-17.6 cm, wing length 9.5-10.5 cm, wingspan 31.5-32.7 cm and weight 39-64 g. It is distinguished by its powerful and conical bill, blue-grey in summer and brown-yellow in winter. The overall colour of the Hawfinch is brown, with a black throat and blue-black wing feathers; the white wingbar is especially conspicuous in flight. The female resembles the male, but is paler.

The Hawfinch has a broad distribution, from England to Japan; in this range five subspecies have been identified. Its habitats are broadleaf forests, mixed forests, plantations and rows of fieldside trees. Part of its population is resident; northern and eastern breeders migrate, wintering in the Balkans, Turkey, northern Iraq, Pakistan and southeast Asia. This species usually winters in woodland and conifer groves, often within villages and towns. In Israel the European subspecies *C.c. coccothraustes* occurs in winter.

This species feeds especially in trees, and consumes various fruits; it is capable of cracking the stones of fruits such as cherries and splitting pine cones to eat their seeds. Only rarely does it gather its food on the ground, where it hops clumsily.

The Hawfinch was reckoned a rare winterer in Israel until the 1970s. Since then it has become fairly common in certain years between November and April, especially in Galilee, in Carmel and Jerusalem, but also on the coastal plain. In some years it does not appear in the country at all; in other years as many as 30-50 individuals may be seen together.

In the winter of 1977/78 a large number of Hawfinches wintered in Israel. In the following spring males were heard singing loudly and individuals were seen carrying nesting materials, but without palpable results.

Family: Emberizidae (Buntings)

In the family Emberizidae there are 71 genera and 283 species, most of them inhabiting North and South America. Only five genera and 42 species are found in the Old World; of the latter 38 belong to the genus *Emberiza*. This family is closely related to finches and weavers, and some ornithologists regard the genus *Emberiza* as belonging to the finch family (Fringillidae).

Buntings are small or medium-sized birds, with a body length of 9.5-21 cm and a weight of 15-60 g. They are distinguished by the short and conical bill, pointed at the tip; the edges of the upper mandible are curved, and in Old World buntings they cover the lower mandible when the bill is closed. The legs are of medium length or long; the claws are short and curved, the hindclaw being shorter than the toe itself. The tail is medium to long, and forked. Most buntings have red-brown, grey or olive plumage; only rarely does it include more vivid colours. The male is generally more colourful than the female, and juveniles resemble the adult female. Most species moult twice in the year and in many the juveniles moult only the body feathers in their first autumn.

These are essentially ground-dwelling birds, sometimes even roosting on the ground. They live in open environments and avoid populated areas. Their flight is fast and efficient. Their main diet is vegetarian, including in particular cereal seeds, but they also consume small insects. Buntings are loudly vocal birds, especially at the beginning of the nesting season; the song is usually a repeated chirp followed by a longer trill.

The nest is in open terrain, and usually concealed in a hole in the ground, sometimes among low bushes. In the clutch there are 3-6 eggs, lightly coloured, usually pale brown, with dark brown markings. The female incubates alone for about two weeks. The chicks hatch blind and covered with sparse down and are fed by both parents. They leave the nest at an early age, before they are capable of flight.

In Israel 14 species are known, all except one belonging to the genus *Emberiza*; two of these are residents, two summer visitors, and the remainder are passage migrants, winterers or rare accidentals.

Cretzschmar's Bunting
Emberiza caesia

Body length 15-16.3 cm, wing length 7.6-8.5 cm and weight 20-25 g. From a distance Cretzschmar's Bunting resembles a sparrow, but at close range the male is distinctive, with a rufous-chestnut chin, throat and belly, rufous-brown back, bluish-grey crown, nape and breast, and white outer tail. The female is paler, with a streaked breast, but is also predominantly chestnut in colour and has a little grey on the breast and nape. In both sexes the bill is pinkish in colour. Juveniles resemble the adult female, but have more streaking below and lack grey on the breast.

Cretzschmar's Bunting is restricted to the eastern Mediterranean basin, from the western Balkans through Turkey and Syria to Israel. This is a monotypic species, inhabiting areas of wasteland and sparse vegetation on rocky slopes. All of its populations migrate, wintering in Eritrea, Sudan and Arabia (between Mecca and Jeddah). In Israel this is a very common passage migrant and a common summer visitor.

This bunting spends more time on the ground than other buntings, although it may seek shelter among tree branches. It feeds on rocky slopes and sometimes in cultivated fields bordering on desert.

Flocks of migrants pass through the country between the end of August and the end of September, and between early March and early May. They are more conspicuous in spring, when flocks numbering scores of individuals may be seen. Males precede females by about ten days. In the migration season they may be seen in any field and garden, even in the desert. They rest by day and move by night, when their contact calls are clearly heard.

The breeding population arrives in March-April, and disperses to breed in hills and mountains in the Mediterranean region, from the Shephelah and the Judean Hills northward. At the approach of the nesting season the males sing their characteristic, somewhat mournful song from a tree or a bush. The nest is under a bush or a stone. The clutch contains 4-6 eggs, which the female incubates for about 19 days. The chicks stay in the nest about 12 days and leave it before they are capable of flight.

Cretzschmar's Bunting breeds twice during the summer, and migrates in October.

Ortolan Bunting
Emberiza hortulana

Similar to Cretzschmar's Bunting in plumage and size: body length 15-17.7 cm, wing length 8.5-9 cm, wingspan 24-28 cm and weight 19-26 g. It is distinguished from it mainly by its yellow throat and cheeks.

This bunting's range extends over most of Europe and into central Asia. This is a monotypic species, breeding in the eastern Mediterranean region in similar habitat to Cretzschmar's Bunting, often at higher altitudes. It breeds in Lebanon and is a rare breeder on Hermon. It winters in plains and savannas south of the Sahara, from West Africa to Somalia and Arabia.

In Israel this is a regular passage migrant in autumn between mid-August and early October. In spring, when it is more common, it passes through the country from the end of March to mid-May, and especially between the end of March and the end of April (thus at a later date than Cretzschmar's). Its flocks number scores of individuals.

The Ortolan Bunting arrives in April on Hermon, where it breeds from an altitude of 1,500 m to the shoulder of the mountain. It is very similar to Cretzschmar's Bunting in behaviour, ecological requirements and nesting biology. It migrates from Hermon in early September.

Pine Bunting
Emberiza leucocephalos

Body length 17.5 cm, wing length 8.9 cm, wingspan 29 cm and weight 28.5 g. The male is distinguished in the nesting season by its white crown, cheeks and upper breast, conspicuous against the background of chestnut-brown plumage. In winter it is paler, but full breeding plumage is assumed as early as February. The female is brown-grey and not easily identified in the field.

The Pine Bunting breeds in eastern European Russia, especially in Siberia, and also in northern China and Mongolia. Two subspecies have been described. Its winter quarters are from eastern Iran through Afghanistan and Pakistan to southern China, but it also roams westward and is known to winter in Turkey, Syria and Lebanon. In its breeding areas it inhabits coniferous woodland; in winter it is found in open terrain, but roosts among pines and cypresses.

In Israel the western subspecies *E.l. leucocephalos* is a rare accidental in winter, from November to March. Most sightings are in the Jerusalem region, a minority in Safed and on Hermon. Sometimes as many as 30 individuals winter together, usually flocking with other buntings.

Yellowhammer
Emberiza citrinella

Body length 16.5 cm, wing length 9 cm and weight 29 g. The only bunting with a yellow head, this marked with chestnut stripes; the belly is also yellow, but slightly streaked with brown. The female and juvenile are paler.

The Yellowhammer has a Euro-Siberian range, in which three subspecies have been identified. Most of its populations are resident, but the more northerly of them winter to the south of their breeding areas, particularly in the countries of the Mediterranean basin, in southern Russia and the Middle East. In Europe this is the commonest of the buntings found in open environments, grassland with scattered bushes. After breeding it gathers in itinerant flocks.

The Yellowhammer (subspecies *E.c. erythrogenys*) used to be considered a rare winterer in northern and central parts of Israel, especially on wooded slopes of Mount Hermon. Since the 1970s it has become a fairly common winterer in Jerusalem and the surrounding area, and is apparently continuing to proliferate. From early November to mid-March scores and sometimes hundreds of individuals mingle with flocks of Pine Buntings and Corn Buntings in plantations, parks and open areas with scattered trees. It roosts in pine groves in the Jerusalem area. Additional sightings have been recorded on the western slopes of the Judean Hills and in Safed.

Rock Bunting
Emberiza cia

Body length 15 cm, wing length 8.1 cm and weight 25 g. The male in breeding plumage has a grey head with black stripes, a pale grey throat, light chestnut underparts and a rufous rump; the tail is greyish-brown with white edges. Winter plumage is paler. The female is dull brown and streaked, and not easily identified.

This species' distribution extends along a narrow strip in the southern Palaearctic region: from North Africa and Spain, through Italy, the Balkans and Turkey to Tibet and central China. Eleven subspecies have been identified. The local subspecies *E.c. cia* is distributed in southern Europe and in the Levant. Its habitats are sunswept rocky slopes, including scrub areas above the conifer belt; it is sometimes found in orchards and plantations. The Rock Bunting is generally a resident bird, but outside the nesting season it roams to some extent, and usually descends from its nesting areas to winter at lower altitudes.

This bunting is a fairly rare winterer in northern and central parts of Israel from November to March, usually in flocks numbering a few individuals.

The Rock Bunting is a common breeder in the hills of Lebanon; a few pairs are apparently resident on Hermon, although no clear positive evidence of breeding has yet been found (except one juvenile).

House or Striped Bunting
Emberiza striolata

Resembles the Rock Bunting but is smaller: body length 14 cm, wing length 7.5 cm and weight 12 g. A brown bunting, its head, neck and upper breast grey and densely streaked with brown-black. It lacks the white wingbar of the Rock Bunting.

The House Bunting's range is typically Saharo-Sindian, its habitats cliffs and canyons. This is a resident bird in all parts of its range. In Israel it is quite common in the Judean Desert and on watercourses draining into the Valley of the Arava, but except in the nesting season, when the males sing from prominent rocks, it is not easily observed.

Outside the breeding season the House Bunting roams in small groups, sometimes accompanying flocks of sheep. It feeds on seeds of desert plants, and is also partial to domestic scraps. In oases such as Ein Gedi it often feeds on the seeds of reeds and reed-grass.

Breeding takes place in March-April. The nest is located under a stone or in a rock-cleft, and the clutch usually contains only 3 eggs.

Cinereous Bunting
Emberiza cineracea

Body length about 16.5 cm. A brown-greyish bunting, with yellow belly, throat and cheeks.

Its range is restricted and divided. Of the two subspecies, one (*E.c. cineracea*) breeds on islands in the Aegean and in southwestern Anatolia; this is distinguished by its grey belly and neck. The other, *E.c. semenowi*, which has a yellower belly, breeds in southwestern Iran and in Yemen. Both subspecies winter in Eritrea and northeastern Ethiopia.

In Israel the latter subspecies is more often seen. The Cinereous Bunting is a fairly rare passage migrant, occurring singly or in small groups from August to October and from March to mid-April. It is usually found in rocky terrain and on cliffs.

Rustic Bunting
Emberiza rustica

Body length 14.5 cm, wing length 7.5 cm and weight 18 g. Similar to the Reed Bunting, and distinguished from it by its white throat and white eye-stripe.

This is a bird of Siberian origin, with distribution limited to northern Europe and northern Asia; it migrates southeast and winters in Turkestan, Manchuria, China and Japan. A few individuals roam and occur across Europe and Asia.

In Israel the subspecies *E.r. rustica* is a rare accidental, seen on a few occasions in Eilat in October-
November and in March. A single observation has
been recorded in Sede Boker, in November 1982.

Little Bunting
Emberiza pusilla

The smallest of the buntings: body length 13.5 cm,
wing length 7.3 cm and weight 15 g. It is distinguished by its rufous cheeks and crown.

This bunting's origin is Siberian. It is distributed
in northern Europe and in northern Asia, and
winters in China and southeast Asia. In Israel the
Little Bunting is a very rare passage migrant,
observed occasionally in Jerusalem and Eilat, usually
during October and November; in autumn 1980, six
individuals were seen in Eilat.

Yellow-breasted Bunting
Emberiza aureola

A small bunting: body length 15.4 cm, wing length
7.5 cm and weight 21 g. The male is distinguished by
its dark head, lemon-yellow collar and belly and
chestnut back. This species has two yellow-white
wingbars.

This bunting's distribution extends from Finland
to northern Russia and across the whole width of
Asia to Kamchatka, Korea and Japan; there are two
subspecies. It winters in India and tropical Asia.

In Israel the subspecies *E.a. aureola* is a very rare
accidental, with a few observations recorded in Eilat
in the month of September.

Reed Bunting
Emberiza schoeniclus

Body length 14.5-16 cm, wing length 7.4-8.7 cm
and weight 18-24 g. The male is distinguished by its
black head and throat, and white moustache, nape
and belly. In winter the black of the head and throat
becomes grey, and the underparts are streaked.
Sometimes it may be seen in full breeding plumage as
early as the end of January. The female is brown and
streaked and not easily distinguished in the field from
females of other species of bunting. The best distinguishing sign for both sexes is behavioural: constant
flicking and spreading of the tail.

The Reed Bunting has a trans-Palaearctic range,
covering all parts of Europe and appreciable sections
of Asia; 15 subspecies have been identified, three to
five of which may occur in Israel. The southern
populations are resident. The northern populations
winter to the south of their nesting areas, those of
the Western Palaearctic in North Africa, the
Balkans, the Middle East and from Iraq to north-

western India. The Reed Bunting inhabits reeds and
rushbeds in both its breeding and its wintering areas.

In Israel this is a rare winterer, especially in areas
of waterside vegetation, between October and
February. It is also seen on migration between
February and April, sometimes in flocks numbering
scores of individuals.

Red-headed Bunting
Emberiza bruniceps

Body length 17 cm, wing length 8.3 cm and weight
25 g. A bunting of striking colours: the head, throat
and upper breast of the male are chestnut, and the
back olive-brown. It breeds in the eastern Turanian
region, from the shores of the Caspian Sea to Lake
Balkhash and Pakistan, and winters in India.

In Israel there is only one certain record of this
species: in Eilat on 22 May 1979. The Red-headed
Bunting is a popular cagebird, and it is possible that
this individual was feral.

Black-headed Bunting
Emberiza melanocephala

Body length 16.8-19 cm, wing length 8-9.6 cm,
wingspan 29 cm and weight 28-33 g. The most conspicuous and attractive of the buntings found in
Israel: the male has a black head, vivid lemon-yellow
underparts, chestnut-brown back and rump, and
dark brown wings and tail. The female is paler:
yellowish-brown on the back and yellowish-buff
below.

This bunting has an eastern Mediterranean and
Irano-Turanian range, extending from southern Italy
eastward through the Balkans and Turkey to the
estuary of the Volga, and southward to Israel. It is a
monotypic species. It migrates east, with a tendency
towards the south, and winters in northwestern
India. Its habitats are in valleys and mountain slopes
with sparse vegetation, wasteland, scrub, plantations
and hedgerows; sometimes it is seen in flocks in cultivated fields.

In Israel this is a common passage migrant, in
autumn from August to September, and in spring
from April to May. It is also a summer resident in
central and northern parts of the country. In the past
the Black-headed Bunting was a widespread breeding
bird, but its population diminished considerably in
the late 1950s and early 1960s. In the mid-1980s it is
particularly common in the heights of Galilee and on
the slopes of Hermon.

Breeding territories are established in April.
Although repetitive, the song of the Black-headed
Bunting is stronger and more melodious than that of
other members of its family, and may be uttered continually for more than an hour. This is one of the few

species of bunting which breed above the ground; in mid-May the female builds a nest on a bush or in the lower branches of a tree, up to 1.5 m above the ground. In the clutch there are usually 4-5 eggs. Breeding biology is similar to that of other buntings.

The Black-headed Bunting breeds once in the year, and begins its migration as early as the end of July.

Corn Bunting
Miliaria calandra

The largest of the Old World buntings: body length 17.2-18.3 cm, wing length 9.3-10 cm, wingspan 29.2-32.8 cm and weight 40-48 g. This is a squat-bodied bird, its plumage ash-brown and delicately streaked with black; the breast and flanks are paler and similarly streaked, and the throat and belly are white. The sexes are similar. The Corn Bunting is distinguished by its short and conical bill, pale brown-pink in colour.

The distribution of the Corn Bunting is European and Irano-Turanian, extending from Britain, Spain and North Africa through eastern and central Europe to Iran and Turkestan. This is a monotypic species. It inhabits dry open terrain, including meadows and cultivated fields. The Corn Bunting is primarily a resident bird, but outside the nesting season it roams in large flocks, sometimes in company with larks and pipits. Only the more northerly populations migrate, wintering in north Arabia, Israel, northern Sinai and northern Egypt.

In Israel this is a resident bird in northern and central parts of the country, a common winterer between October and the end of March, and a passage migrant between September and the end of November and during the spring months.

The breeding limits in Israel normally extend as far south as the Dorot-NirAm axis in the southern coastal plain, although in years when rain is plentiful they may reach the Dimona-Revivim axis in the northern Negev. Males are territorially vocal between the months of March and May, although their typical song — a high-pitched mechanical jangling sound — may be heard as early as the end of February, before the flock separates into pairs. The nest is usually built on the ground, behind a bush or in long grass, sometimes on a low bush. The clutch contains 3-5 eggs, which the female incubates alone for 12-14 days. The chicks leave the nest before they are capable of flight.

In Israel the Corn Bunting apparently breeds once in the season, and by June flocking is resumed.

Birdwatching Sites in Israel

This list has been kindly supplied by David Fisher of the Ornithological Society of the Middle East (OSME). It has been drawn up primarily with the West European birdwatcher in mind, and therefore features those species likely to be of most interest to such a visitor. The emphasis is on bird species seen in the spring, which is presumably the season in which the European birdwatcher would be most likely to visit Israel. Further information on birdwatching in Israel can be obtained from the Society for the Protection of Nature in Israel, 4 Hashfela Street, Tel Aviv 66183, Israel. For general information on birdwatching in the Middle East, contact the Ornithological Society of the Middle East, c/o The Lodge, Sandy, Bedfordshire SG19 2DL, England.

Mount Hermon

Mount Hermon lies in Israel's northeasternmost corner and is the highest mountain in the country (2,224 m). Consequently a number of species that are rare or absent in the rest of Israel can be found there. As there is a ski resort high on the mountain, a good road exists allowing visitors to drive up to about 2,000 m. Owing to the location there is heavy military activity in the area, but birdwatching from this road is normally allowed. The main road from Qiryat Shemona runs through a cross-section of habitats and bird faunas, via the ski village of Newe Ativ and the Druze village of Majdal Shams, where a checkpoint has to be passed through to gain access to the road to the ski slopes. The mountain's breeding specialities include Woodlark, White-throated Robin, Black Redstart, Blue Rock Thrush, Sombre Tit, Rock Nuthatch, Pale Rock Sparrow, Rock Sparrow, Tristram's Serin, Crimson-winged Finch and Rock Bunting.

The Golan Heights

The Golan Heights lie to the south of Mount Hermon and are typified by open rolling grassland, much of which is cultivated. Military activity is considerable on the Heights and some roads are closed to the public, but these are always well marked. The Heights contain a healthy raptor population, including in particular Griffon Vulture and Long-legged Buzzard, both of which should be seen during a visit. The small pools and lakes on the Golan often hold wintering duck flocks which remain until quite late in the spring, with Wigeon, Tufted Duck and Pochard all present in good numbers. The grassland habitats are good for larks, Calandra Lark being particularly common, and in the southern parts the Isabelline Wheatear is quite a common breeding bird. A local very rare wintering speciality is Radde's Accentor, which can sometimes be seen near habitation such as around the kibbutz at Merom Golan. In winter, large flocks of finches which feed in the fields are comprised mainly of Chaffinches, Serins, Greenfinches, Goldfinches and Linnets, but scarcer species such as Brambling also occur and should be looked for.

The Hula Nature Reserve

The area contained in the Hula Nature Reserve is all that is left of the once extensive marshes that filled the Hula Valley. The rest was drained for agriculture and to rid the area of malaria during the middle of the twentieth century. The reserve is run by the Nature Reserves Authority and is open to the public from 09.00 to 16.00 hours. The entrance is at the end of a side road which leaves the east side of the main road from Rosh Pinna to Qiryat Shemona, approximately 10 km north of Rosh Pinna. There is a sign to the reserve on the main road at the turning. The nature trail inside the reserve leads to viewing platforms and a tower hide, and leaflets about the reserve are available at the entrance. Large numbers of waterbirds breed and winter at and pass through the Hula, but it is particularly famous for its large flocks of migrant White Pelicans. Birds of special interest include wintering Spotted Eagles, Hen Harriers and Merlins, and breeding Marbled Teals and Cetti's, Moustached and Clamorous Reed Warblers. Large numbers of herons, egrets, ducks and waders are often present. The adjacent fish-ponds on the west side of the reserve also hold good numbers of waterbirds and, though private, bird-watchers are allowed to walk around the banks.

Lake Tiberias (The Sea of Galilee)

Rather surprisingly, the Sea of Galilee does not attract very many waterbirds and, apart from small numbers of grebes, ducks (mainly Tufted Ducks), gulls and the occasional Pied Kingfisher, little is to be seen from its shores. The hills around the lake, however, hold good numbers of landbirds, and the northern end seems particularly rich. Nahal (Wadi) Amud to the northwest of the lake and Nahal (Wadi) Yehudiyya (from Gamla) to the northeast are well worth visiting, and are scenically impressive as well as rich in birds. Of special interest here are Egyptian and Griffon Vultures, Bonelli's Eagle, Black Francolin, Little Swift, Long-billed Pipit, Blue Rock Thrush and Great Grey Shrike.

Maagan Mikhael & Ma'yan Zevi

At Maagan Mikhael and Ma'yan Zevi is a large complex of fish-ponds which lie along the Mediterranean coast some 25 km north of Netanya. Most of the pools at Maagan Mikhael have been turned into a waterfowl refuge, though the area is closed to the public during the breeding season in the spring. An area alongside the stream immediately south of the ponds is, however, open to the public all year, as are the more northerly pools of Ma'yan Zevi. Access to both areas is from the inland road which runs parallel to the new coastal motorway a kilometre or so to the east. Waterbirds are abundant throughout the year, and most of the species occurring regularly in Israel can be found here. Of particular interest are the wintering flocks of Great Black-headed Gulls, wintering and migrant Temminck's Stints, all three species of kingfisher, and small numbers of Citrine Wagtails that seem to be increasingly regular.

Bet She'an

Bet She'an lies some 25 km south of the Sea of Galilee and is surrounded by fish-ponds and pools. Many of the birds migrating up the rift valley in spring stop off to rest and feed in this area, and large flocks of White Storks can often be seen here. Depending on water-levels any of the ponds can hold waders, and so it is necessary to explore a little to find the most productive ones. In spring up to ten Ospreys may be seen together standing in the fields, from time to time visiting the ponds to fish. The area has been largely ignored by most birdwatchers in the past and would probably produce some interesting results if visited more frequently.

Jerusalem

Anyone planning to spend time in Jerusalem might think that the prospects for birdwatching are rather poor. This is far from the case. All of the wooded hills around the city hold Syrian Woodpeckers, Sardinian Warblers and Jays, while the wider wadis contain fruit orchards which hold many migrants as well as large numbers of wintering finches and buntings. Of particular interest in these orchards are the wintering flocks of Yellowhammers, which often include small numbers of Pine Buntings. The bare rocky hillsides around the wadis are home to Long-billed Pipits, and many migrant passerines drop in to rest during spring and autumn. Not far from the edge of the city Short-toed Eagles can often be found, while Lesser Kestrels nest in some numbers in the city itself.

The Dead Sea and Ein Gedi

The Dead Sea depression has a different climate from the surrounding area and consequently a number of interesting birds can be found there. It is the main stronghold of the Fan-tailed Raven in Israel and these birds can usually be seen from the main road along the west side of the sea, the historic hill fort at Massada being a particularly good site. Tristram's Grackle is another frequently encountered species, and although it is also scattered throughout the Arava Valley further south it is usually easier to find around Ein Gedi and at Massada. Ein Gedi is famous among birdwatchers as the best place to see Hume's Tawny Owl, a Middle Eastern speciality hard to find elsewhere. For several years one or two of these owls have had a habit of feeding from the perimeter fence of the field school, atttracted by the moths that collect around the spotlights. Other typical birds of the area include Sand Partridge, Blackstart, Mourning and White-crowned Black Wheatears and Scrub Warbler. In the spring the cliffs above the west side of the sea are used by migrating raptors searching for thermals, and many hundreds of birds can often be seen passing north each morning. Of particular interest here is the number of Lesser Spotted Eagles present in these flocks as this species is much scarcer at Eilat; these eagles have probably migrated via Suez and across the Negev Desert. There is a nature reserve in Ein Gedi at Nahal (Wadi) David, run by the Nature Reserves Authority, which is open from 09.00 to 16.00 hours.

The Negev Desert

The Negev lies to the south and southwest of Be'er Sheva and consists of stone and sand desert normally with little vegetation. After winters of heavier rainfall, however, the desert can be carpeted in a mass of shrubs and flowers which create a beautiful scene. The main access point is along the Be'er Sheva to Nizana road, which runs through a cross-section of desert habitats containing most of the area's more interesting bird species. Military activity here is considerable and some tracts beside the road are closed to the public. It is best to birdwatch from the road. The army have a number of firing ranges in this area and if you prefer quietness when birding try to visit on the weekend. Species of particular interest here include Houbara Bustard, Cream-coloured Courser, Spotted, Black-bellied and Pin-tailed Sandgrouse, Hoopoe and Temminck's Horned Larks, Desert and Mourning Wheatears and Spectacled Warbler.

The Arava Valley

The Arava Valley runs from the Dead Sea to Eilat and is the northern extension of the Syro-African Great Rift Valley. A number of African species reach their northern limit here and the area is of considerable interest to birdwatchers. Anyone visiting Eilat by road will almost certainly drive the length of the valley, and will consequently see a number of the more interesting species from the car. These may include Lappet-faced Vulture (now very rare), Little Green Bee-eater and Brown-necked Raven. A few stops are required, however, to search for some of the smaller birds and favourite areas for this are at Hazeva and Yotvata. A lengthy walk in the acacia scrub at either site should produce Arabian Warbler and Arabian Brown Babbler, as well as many migrant species in spring and autumn. Cyprus Warblers winter in the valley and also frequent the acacia trees; most leave by the middle of March.

Eilat

Eilat is undoubtedly the highlight of any spring or autumn birdwatching trip to Israel. Lying on the migration route of many African-Palaearctic migrant species, it forms the first green patch that most birds see after crossing northeast Africa and the Sinai. Many birds stop to rest and feed and the fields can often be full of migrants. Raptors pass over in vast numbers, with 1.1 million being counted in the spring of 1985. The habitats around the town include sea, beach, salt-pans, date palms, fields, deserts and wadis, all of which are attractive to different groups of birds. There are many areas to visit around Eilat, and any visiting birdwatcher should go to the Tourist Information Office or the Nature Reserves Authority. Regular species of special interest here include Brown Booby, Western Reef

Heron, Sooty Falcon (summer), Greater Sand-plover, Slender-billed Gull, Lichtenstein's Sand-grouse, Hooded Wheatear, Dead Sea Sparrow, Desert Finch and Sinai Rosefinch (winter).

Hundreds of species pass through Eilat each year, including many rarities, and the keen birdwatcher should try to spend as much time here as is possible.

Bibliography

Afik, D. and Pinshow, B. (In press) Notes on the breeding biology of the Arabian Warbler (*Sylvia leucomelaena*) in the Arava.

Aharoni, J. 1942. Change of dwelling place of some birds in Palestine and an experiment in the reasoning power of *Cinnyris osea* Bonaparte. *Bull. Zool. Soc. Egypt* 4: 13-19.

Alkon, P.U. 1974. Social behaviour of a population of Chukar Partridge in Israel. PhD thesis, Cornell University.

—— 1979. Social behaviour and short-term population fluctuation in Chukar Partridge. *Proc. 10th Sci. Conf. Israel Ecol. Soc.*

Argyle, F. and Gal, B. 1978. Birds in Eilat, Spring 1978. SPNI.

Arnold, P. 1962. *Birds of Israel*. Massada, Tel Aviv.

Atkinson-Willes, G.L. 1969. The mid-winter distribution of wildfowl in Europe, northern Africa and southwest Asia 1967 and 1968. *Wildfowl* 20: 98-111.

Austin, O.L. *et al.* 1961. *Birds of the World*. Hamlyn, Feltham.

Baker, N. 1982. Diurnal migration of Golden Oriole over the Mediterranean Sea. *OSME Bull.* 9: 3.

Bangs, O. 1911. A new swift from Palestine. *Proc. Biol. Soc. Washington* 24: 195-6.

Bannerman, D.A. and Bannerman, W.M. 1958. *Birds of Cyprus*. Oliver and Boyd, Edinburgh.

—— and —— 1971. *Handbook of the Birds of Cyprus and Migrants of the Middle East*. Oliver and Boyd, Edinburgh.

Bates, G.L. 1939. Races of *Ammomanes deserti* in Arabia. *Ibis* ser. 14, 3: 743-6.

Beidermann, E. and Robertson, I. 1981. The occurrence of the Pine Bunting in Israel. *Sandgrouse* 2: 96.

Bigger, W.K. 1921. Migrations of *Cynnyris* and *Onychognathus* in Palestine. *Ibis* ser. 11, 3: 584-5.

—— 1925. The breeding of the Common Tern in Palestine. *Ibis* ser. 12, 1: 294-6.

Bijlsma, R.G. 1983. The migration of raptors near Suez, Egypt, Autumn 1981. *Sandgrouse* 5: 19-44.

Bodenheimer, F.S. 1935. *Animal Life in Palestine*. Jerusalem.

—— 1937. Prodomus fauna Palestinae. *Men. Inst. d'Egypte* 31: 52-69.

—— 1937. Problems of animal distribution in Arabia. *Proc. Linn. Soc. Lond.* 150: 47-9.

Bourne, W.R.P. 1959. Notes on autumn migration in the Middle East. *Ibis* 101 (2): 170-6.

—— 1960. Status of grey shrikes in East Mediterranean. *Ibis* 102 (3): 476.

Boyd, A.W. 1917. Birds of the Suez Canal Zone and Sinai Peninsula. *Ibis* ser. 10, 5: 539-57.

Bruun, B. 1981. The Lappet-faced Vulture in the Middle East. *Sandgrouse* 2: 91-5.

—— and Singer, A. 1969. *British and European Birds*. Hamlyn, Feltham.

—— and —— 1978. *Birds of Britain and Europe*. Hamlyn, Feltham.

—— *et al.* 1981. A new subspecies of Lappet-faced Vulture *Torgos tracheliotus* from the Negev Desert, Israel. *Bull. BOC* 101: 244-7.

Burton, J.A. (ed.) 1973. *Owls of the World*. Peter Lowe, London.

Cameron, R.A.D., and Cornwallis, L. 1966. Autumn notes from Azraq, Jordan. *Ibis* 108: 284-7.

—— *et al.* 1967. The migration of raptors and storks through the Near East in Autumn. *Ibis* 109 (4): 489-501.

Carruthers, A.D.M. 1910. On a collection of birds from the Dead Sea and Northern Western Arabia, with contribution to the ornithological knowledge of Syria and Palestine. *Ibis* ser. 9, 4: 475-91.

—— 1922. The Arabian Ostrich. *Ibis* ser. 11, 4: 471-4.

Cheesman, R.E. 1923. Recent notes on the Arabian Ostrich. *Ibis* ser. 11, 5 (2): 208-11, 359.

Christensen, S., *et al.* 1981. The spring migration of raptors in Southern Israel and Sinai. *Sandgrouse* 3: 1-42.

Clarke, J.E. 1982. The Houbara Bustard in Jordan. *Sandgrouse* 4: 111-14.

Cramp, S., *et al.* (eds.) 1977-85. *The Birds of the Western Palearctic*. Vols. 1-4 (further vols. in prep.). Oxford University Press, Oxford.

Dement'ev, G.P., *et al.* 1966-68. *Birds of the Soviet Union*. Vols. 1-6. Israel Prog. for Sci. Translation, Jerusalem.

Dmie'l, R. and Tel-Tzur, D. 1984. Heat balance of two starling species (*Sturnus vulgaris* and *Onychognathus tristrami*) from temperate and desert habitat. *J. Comp. Physiol.* 155: 395-405.

Eshbol, Y. 1981. Plovers in peril. *Israel Land and Nature* 6: 116-21.

Etchécopar, R.D. and Hüe, F. 1967. *The Birds of North Africa*. Oliver and Boyd, Edinburgh.

Flaxman, E.W. 1982. Observations of raptor migration in Jordan, May 1982. *OSME Bull.* 9: 4-5.

Fry, C.H. 1984. *The Bee-eaters*. Poyser, Calton.

Gooders, J. (ed.) 1969-71. *Birds of the World*. Vols. 1-9. IPC, London.

Goodwin, D. 1949. Notes on the migration of birds of prey over Suez. *Ibis* 91 (1): 59-63.

—— 1970. *Pigeons and Doves of the World*. Brit. Museum (Nat. Hist.), London.

—— 1976. *Crows of the World*. Brit. Museum (Nat. Hist.), London.

Grant, P.J. 1982. *Gulls: a guide to identification*. Poyser, Calton.

Grzimek, K.C. (ed.) 1972-75. *Animal Life Encyclopedia*. Vols. 7-9. Van Nostrand Reinhold.

Hardy, E. 1946. *A Handbook of Birds of Palestine*.

—— 1947. Occurrence of Northern Lappet-faced Vulture in Palestine. *Ibis* 89: 355-6.

Harrison, C. 1975. *A Field Guide to the Nests, Eggs and Nestlings of British and European Birds*. Collins, London.

—— 1982. *An Atlas of the Birds of the Western Palaearctic*. Collins, London.

Harrison, J.M. and Hovel, H. 1964. On the taxonomy of *Athene noctua* in Israel. *Bull. BOC* 84: 91-4.

Hartley, P.H.T. 1946. The food of the Kestrel in Palestine. *Ibis* 88: 241-2.

Hollom, P.A.D. 1959. Notes from Jordan, Lebanon, Syria and Antioch. *Ibis* 101 (2): 183-200.

Hovel, H. 1958. Ornithological observations from the surroundings of Haifa. *Aquila* 65: 367-8.

—— 1960. Some notes on breeding of Desert Bullfinch (*Rhodospiza sharpii*) in Israel. *Bull. BOC* 80: 75-6.

—— 1964. The Chestnut-banded Sand Plover in Israel. *Bull. BOC* 84: 105.

—— (In press) *Checklist of the Birds of Israel*. SPNI.

Howard, R. and Moore, A. 1980. *A Complete Checklist of the Birds of the World*. Oxford University Press, Oxford.

Hutson, H.P.W. 1944. Some notes from Syria and Palestine. *Bull. Zool. Soc. Egypt, Syria/Palestine Suppl.*: 6-7.

—— 1947. On the migrations of *Merops apiaster* and *Merops superciliosus* in the Middle East and India. *Ibis* 89: 291-300.

Inbar, R. 1982. Sandgrouse in quest of water. *Israel Land and Nature* 7: 138-41.

Jennings, M.C. 1982. A breeding record of Lappet-faced Vulture from Arabia. *Sandgrouse* 4: 114-15.

—— *et al.* 1982. First breeding record of Pink-backed Pelican (*Pelecanus rufescens*) from Arabia. *Birds of Saudi Arabia*: 478-82.

Karmali, J. 1980. *Birds of Africa*. Collins, London.

Kemp, A. 1982. *The Birds of Southern Africa*. Winchester Press.

Lambert, F.R. and Grimmett, R.F. 1983. Bald Ibis (*Geronticus eremita*) in Israel. *OSME Bull.* 10: 12.

Leshem, Y. 1979. Golden Eagles in our back yard. *Israel Land and Nature* 5: 70-5.

—— 1980. The Negev and Judean Desert: last chance for Israel's raptors. *Israel Land and Nature* 6: 28-33.

—— 1981. The occurrence of Hume's Tawny Owl in Israel and Sinai. *Sandgrouse* 2: 100-2.

Macfarlane, A.M. 1978. Field notes of the birds of Lebanon and Syria 1974-1977. *Army Bird Watching Soc.* No. 3.

Mackintosh, D.R. 1944. A short note on some birds in Lebanon. *Bull. Zool. Soc. Egypt, Syria/Palestine Suppl.* 6: 10-14.

Madge, S. 1981. The subspecies identity of Little Green Bee-eater in southern Israel. *Sandgrouse* 2: 107.

Man, S. 1980. Jay notes. *Israel Land and Nature* 5: 117-22.

—— and Hochberg, O. 1982. Pecan plantation change habitats of forest birds. *Israel Land and Nature* 8: 10-14.

Mendelssohn, H. 1975. The White Stork (*Ciconia ciconia*) in Israel. *Die Vogelwarte* 28: 123-31.

—— and Paz, U. 1977. Mass mortality of birds of prey caused by Agodrin, an organophosphorous insecticide. *Biol. Conserv.* 11: 163-70.

Meinertzhagen, R. 1954. Some aspects of spring migration in Palestine. *Ibis* 96 (2): 293-8.

—— 1954. *The Birds of Arabia*. Oliver and Boyd, Edinburgh.

Merom, C. 1960. *Birds of Israel*. Hakibbutz Hameuchad, Tel Aviv. (In Hebrew)

Mienis, H.K. 1980. Two additional cases of predation on land snails by the Song Thrush in Israel. *Levantina* 29: 341-3.

Mikkola, H. 1983. *Owls of Europe*. Poyser, Calton.

Moreau, R.E. 1972. *The Palaearctic-African Bird Migration System*. Academic Press, London and New York.

Nelson, B. 1973. *Azraq Desert Oasis*. Allen Lane, London.

Nielsen, B.P. and Christensen, S. 1969. On the autumn migration of Spotted Eagles and Buzzards in the Middle East. *Ibis* 111(4): 620-1.

Paran, Y. 1980. Some notes on waterbirds observed in Egypt and North Sinai. *OSME Bull.* 4: 2-5.

—— and Paz, U. 1978. Autumn migration of waterbirds on the north coast of Sinai. *Abstr. Post. Pres. 17th Int. Orn. Congr.*: 43-4.

—— and Shluter, P. 1981. The diurnal mass migration of the Little Bittern. *Sandgrouse* 2: 108-9.

Paz, U. 1976. *The Rehabilitation of the Huleh Reserve*. Nature Res. Authority Publ.

—— 1978. Population dynamics of Graceful Warbler (*Prinia gracilis palaestinae* Zedlitz) and the significance of clutch-size in song birds (Passeriformes). PhD thesis, Tel Aviv University. (In Hebrew)

—— 1982. The fauna of the Holy Land at the end of the Ottoman period. *Israel Land and Nature* 7: 104-10.

—— 1983. Portrait of Palestine Sunbird. *Israel Land and Nature* 8: 7-10.

Pihl, S. and Gal, B. 1978. Birds in Eilat, Spring 1977. SPNI.

Porter, R.F., *et al.* 1981. *Flight Identification of European Raptors*. Poyser, Calton.

Pyman, G.A. 1953. Autumn raptor migration in Eastern Mediterranean. *Ibis* 95(3): 550-1.

Rothschild, W. 1919. Description of a new subspecies of Ostrich from Syria. *Bull. BOC* 39: 81-3.

Round, P.D. and Walsh, T.A. 1981. The field identification and status of Dunn's Lark. *Sandgrouse* 3: 78-83.

Safriel, U. 1968. Bird migration at Eilat, Israel. *Ibis* 110: 283-320.

—— 1980. Notes on the extinct population of the Bald Ibis in the Syrian Desert. *Ibis* 122: 82-8.

Shirihai, H. 1982. The autumn migration of Steppe Eagles at Eilat, Israel, 1980. *Sandgrouse* 4: 108-10.

—— 1986. Identification of Oriental Skylark. *Brit. Birds* 79: 186-97.

—— 1986. The Small Skylark, a species new to Israel and the Middle East. *Sandgrouse* 7: 47-54.

Sheppard, R.W. 1933. Notes on the birds of Jerusalem. *Auk* 50: 179-86.

Simmons, K.E.L. 1951. Raptor migration in the Suez area. Autumn 1949-Spring 1950. *Ibis* 93: 402-6.

—— 1954. Behaviour and general biology of Graceful Warbler. *Ibis* 96: 262-92.

Sultana, J., *et al.* 1975. *A Guide to the Birds of Malta*. Malta Orn. Soc.

Summers-Smith, D. 1963. *The House Sparrow*. Collins, London.

Sutherland, W.J. and Brooks, D.J. 1981. Autumn migration of raptors, storks, pelicans and spoonbills at Bellen Pass, Southern Turkey. *Sandgrouse* 2: 1-21.

Tchernov, E. 1961. Outlines of the Palaeolithic avifauna in Palestine. *Bull. Res. Coun. Israel*: 205-7.

—— 1962. Palaeolithic avifauna in Palestine. *Bull. Res. Coun. Israel*: 95-131.

Tristram, H.B. 1865. *The Land of Israel*. London.

—— 1884. *Fauna and Flora of Palestine*. PEF.

Undeland, R.E. 1964. Verreaux's Eagle *Aquila verreauxi* in Sinai. *Ibis* 106: 258.

Vaughan, R. 1964. *Falco eleonorae*. *Ibis* 103a: 114-28.

Vaurie, C. 1959-65. *The Birds of the Palearctic Fauna*. Vols. 1-2. Witherby, London.

Voous, K.H. 1960. *Atlas of European Birds*. Nelson, London.

—— 1973. List of recent Holarctic bird species. Non-passerines. *Ibis* 115: 612-38.

—— 1977. List of recent Holarctic bird species. Passerines. *Ibis* 119: 223-50, 376-406.

Welty, J.C. 1982. *The Life of Birds*. Saunders Coll. Publ., New York.

Witherby, H.F., *et al.* 1937-41. *The Handbook of British Birds*. Vols. 1-5. Witherby, London.

Woldhek, S. 1979. Bird killing in the Mediterranean. Eur. Comm. Prev. of Mass Destruction of Migratory Birds, Zeist.

Yom-Tov, Y. 1974. The effect of food and predation on breeding density and success, clutch-size and laying date of Crow (*Corvus corone*). *J. Anim. Ecol.* 43: 479-98.

—— 1980. Interspecific nest parasitism in birds. *Biol. Rev.* 55: 93-108.

Zahavi, A. 1957. The breeding birds of Huleh swamp and lake. *Ibis* 99: 600-7.

—— and Dudai, R. 1974. First breeding record of Blandford's Warbler (*Sylvia leucomelaena*). *Israel J. Zool.* 23: 55-6.

Zuckerbrot, Y., *et al.* 1980. Autumn migration of Quail in the north coast of Sinai Peninsula. *Ibis* 122: 1-14.

Index

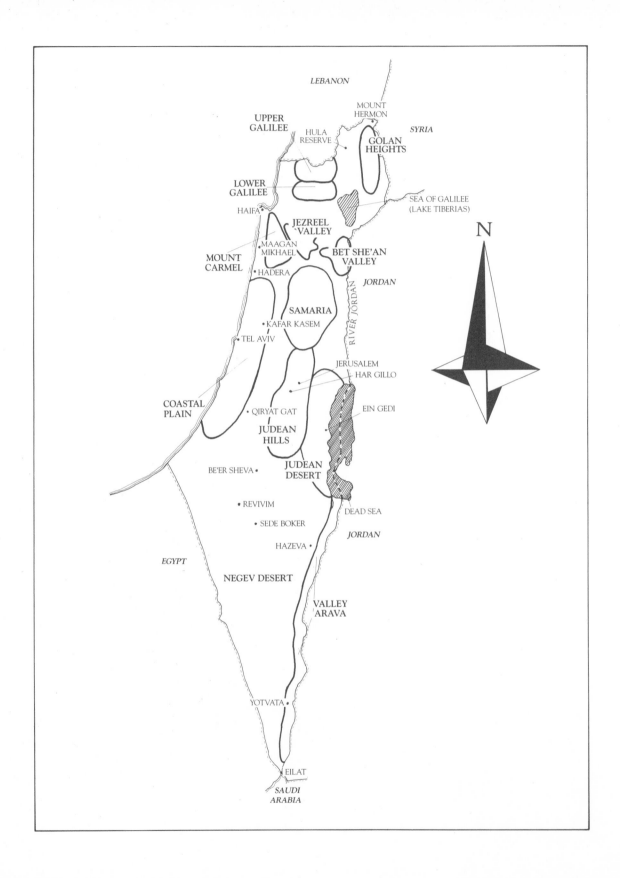